A Superior State of Affairs

By

Tom Maringer

© 2004 by Tom Maringer. All rights reserved.

No part of this book may be reproduced, stored in a retrieval system, or transmitted by any means, electronic, mechanical, photocopying, recording, or otherwise, without written permission from the author.

First published by AuthorHouse 04/30/04

ISBN: 1-4184-2762-4 (Paperback)

Printed in the United States of America
Bloomington, IN

This book is printed on acid free paper.

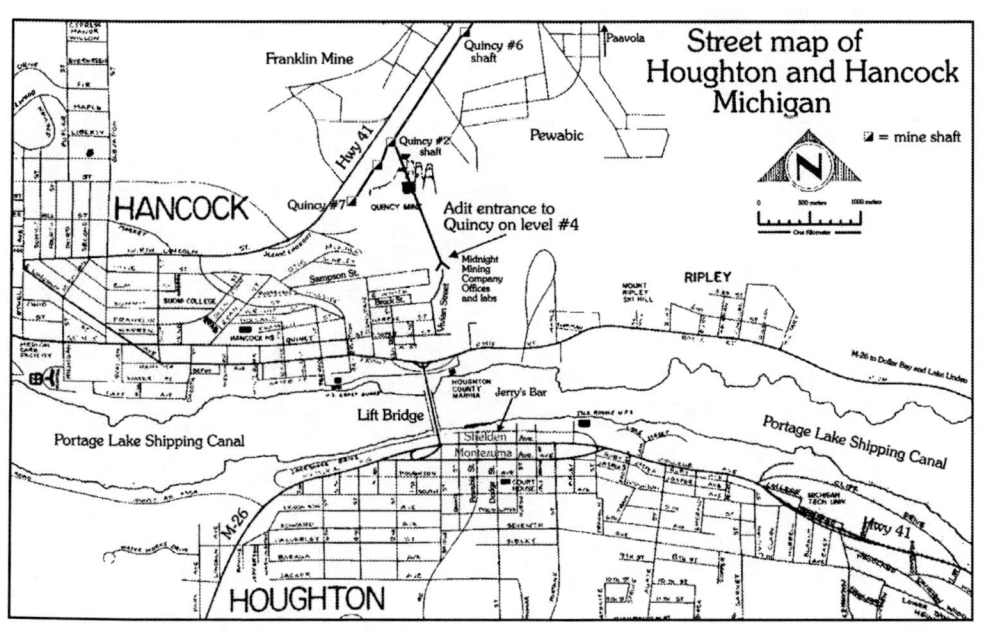

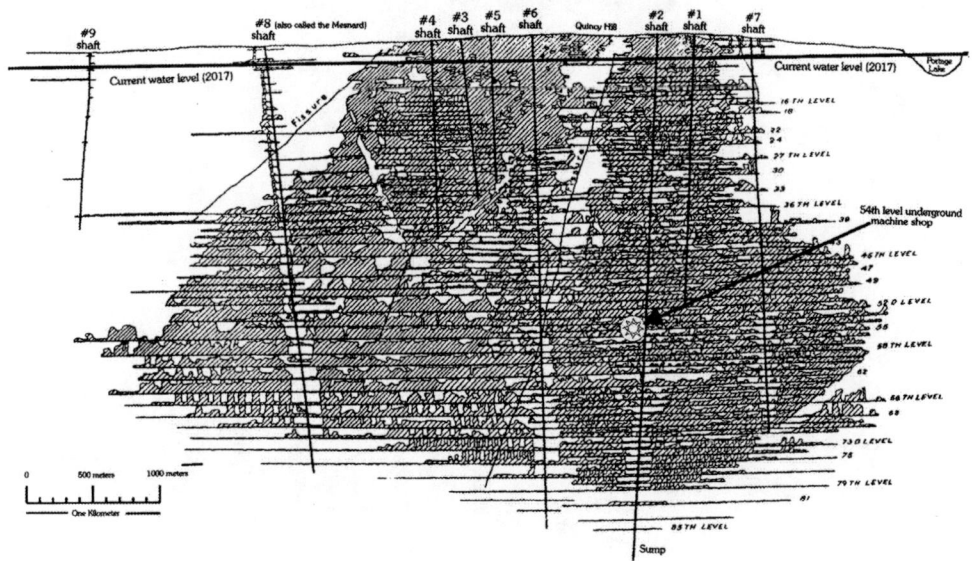

Arne Harjaala and Toivo Hautamaki operating a hydraulic drill on the 54th level of the Quincy Mine, circa 1906

CHAPTER 1

Tiny bubbles streamed upward from a minuscule point on the side of the glass, an endless column of spherical soldiers marching upwards in perfect cadence through the amber fluid. Digger Puttonen sat staring at them, captivated by the precision of their motion, brows furrowed as if his mind probed the phenomenon for some deep cosmic significance. He tried to use the concentration to brush off the heavy melancholy that had settled over him like a mantle of new-fallen snow, then shook his head slowly... it was no good, the stuff clung to him. Familiar scenes danced at the edges of his mind, clamoring for attention. With his elbows on the bar, Digger cupped his face in his hands and gave up his resistance, letting the demons within have their way.

Just two years earlier his life had been very different, everything had seemed so exciting, he had felt so confident and full of purpose! But now, even though all those plans had come to fruition more spectacularly than he'd ever dared to dream, he was locked out, separated from everything he'd ever cared about.

"Digger they call me," he whispered to himself, recalling the origin of the nickname he'd been given as a freshman geology student at Michigan Tech. "Ha, if they only knew. I'm a fake... a phony... a fraud." He looked at his image reflected in the mirror between the half empty bottles of tequila and vodka. His light brown hair was conservatively long, framing the round face and falling over his ears onto his shirt collar. A curly full beard and mustache hid the self-deprecating curl of his lip. He had steadfastly refused to trim his beard in the current foppish style. His sky blue eyes peered blearily past the wire framed glasses into their likeness in the dim light of the tavern. "Everybody thought I had some kind of amazing talent for finding things." His voice rose to a mumble."SHIT! I can't even find my own nose half the time anymore, not unless it's stuck in a beer glass. We were the ones that got the whole damned project started in the first place, it was our idea... Joshua, James, and I. It was our baby! And now... Josh... what did they do to you man? Did you even see it coming? Those other assholes barely even understood the concepts much less the implementation. And did they help us then, at the beginning? They wouldn't even lift a goddamn finger! It was like pulling teeth just to get permission to do it on our own!" Digger lifted his head to the right, took another sip, and gazed fixedly through the paneled wall of Jerry's Bar towards the labs under Quincy Hill, across the frozen Portage Lake shipping canal. "But now... oh yes... NOW they swoop in, like vultures on a rotting carcass, claiming they supported the project all along. And now they say..." Digger snorted with frustration. "Now they're saying I'm no longer an asset. NO LONGER AN ASSET! I can't believe that idiot Farley stood there and said that shit to my face! I ought to go over there and kick some of their pompous assets!"

Digger felt the heat of anger rising in his abdomen, and rather than push it back down, he went ahead and let it rise, he helped it up, felt his face flush, his temples throbbed... "No!" he decided suddenly, not now. He knew how to let his anger work for him, he knew how to control it, but in a fleeting crystalline moment of sober clarity he realized that this was neither the time nor the place. He experienced a roaring sound in his ears as the delayed adrenaline rush hit him, he let it pass, then took another sip and sighed heavily. "Ah, the blessed amber nectar, so soothing, so............"

He stared into his beer glass and tried to think about what to do next. That was always the big question wasn't it? Getting himself sloshed had seemed to be an answer to the short term variant of the question, as well as a way to avoid dealing with the long term aspect. "I shouldn't feel this way!" He said to himself under his breath. "I should be happy." But the mere thought of the abstraction called "happiness" seemed to make him sink ever deeper into despair, as if the contemplation of the very concept was driving away the reality. Digger noticed suddenly that there were no more bubbles in his glass. He squinted and examined it more carefully. Fact: the glass appeared to be quite empty except for some bits of foam slowly sliding down into the interior from the rim. The descriptor "empty" seemed to indicate a condition that might possibly be correctable. He looked up then and caught the knowing eye of the barkeeper, who silently walked over, refilled the glass from a tap, and withdrew the necessary amount from the pile of money lying on the counter. Digger raised his glass in thanks and took a sip. Ahhh... fresh and cold, the water of life it seemed. How many had he drunk since he came in here? When was it? It had been light out at the time, he remembered that! He looked out the window and saw the falling snow swirling in the light of the mercury vapor lamps. He shrugged... okay, so it was dark out now, so what else is new. In Houghton Michigan it was dark most of the time in the winter. This far north the sun rises late and sets early, people knew that and expected it. How many glasses of beer had there been? The question was undoubtedly profound and, for the moment, grabbed Digger's full attention and concentration. Wait a minute! If he could simply apply the powers of reason to the problem, treat it as if it were a college examination, he might be able to deduce the answer. Digger had always been good at tests. Let's see now... he'd started with a handful of paper money on the bar. Pawing at the dwindling pile left, he tried to count it. The numbers on the crumpled wad of bills swirled in his vision. Well, there was a smaller pile than there had been earlier, and now there were some plastic coins as well.

He heard a dry rasping sound and looked to his right. The guy next to him was trying to spin one of the coins on the bar. It would quickly slow down and fall flat with a hollow click. "Hey Digger, lookit dis here. Da sumbitch don' spin worth a shit. Dey don't spin so good like dose old metal ones used ta." Digger nodded silently, mechanically, trying to remember what he had been thinking about before the old coot had interrupted him. "I mean, lookit dis crap!" The weathered face of Arne Harjaala grinned at him, the hand clutched a few of the plastic chips off the bar and held them in a gnarled fist. "Why, I remember when we got paid wit' real money boy... I'm talkin' about gold an' silver, da real goddamn ting! At least back den ya could punch a hole in a dime and use it for a washer if ya needed one bad enough."

Digger pulled his eyes away and examined his own pile more closely. The molding of the coins was not even particularly well done, the parting line could easily be seen on the edges of the quarters. "Money" they called the stuff. People seemed to think it was important for some reason. He repeated the word to himself over and over until it lost all meaning... "money, money, munny, munny, muhny, muhnee, muh-nee, muh-nee-muh-nee-muh-nee..." It became a sort of hypnotic mantra. "Money": some pieces of thin plastic textured to imitate paper, with pictures of dead guys on them... pieces just about the right size for wiping your butt. That's it, "dead-guy butt-wipes" that's what they are! But hell, they're not even made of paper anymore, it's some kind of damn petroleum product nowadays, some kind of poly something-or-other... not even absorbent enough to use them in the toilet. What about the round things though, "chips" they call those, though some old-timers sometimes still used the word "coin". Dead guy's pictures appeared on them as well. About all they're good for is to spin on the bar and see how long they keep going. But like ol' Arne said, they just don't spin so good anymore. And what's the deal with all these dead guys anyway? Money... it's just this stuff you leave on the bar; if there's enough of it a guy comes around and fills your glass. Hmmm. Well, maybe that's not such a bad deal after all! Somehow it seemed to matter how much of it you had. If you had the right number you could do anything, so they said. Sixty million was a big number. Sixty million dollars would buy a lot of beers, more than..........

Suddenly Digger remembered that he'd been trying to figure out how many beers he'd had. Since he didn't know how many of the butt wipes he'd left on the bar to begin with, there was no logical way to deduce the number of beers he'd consumed. Digger felt a profound sense of failure at being unable to solve the problem he had set for himself. He shook his head gravely and gave himself a resounding "F" on the impromptu exam. "SHIT!" he said out loud, to nobody in particular. It was just as well, none of the people in the bar paid him any attention, not even Arne. He gave a short laugh, which came burbling out as a snort.

Digger looked over at his companion on the adjacent barstool. The grizzled old miner was a fixture in Jerry's Bar, telling tall tales and droning on endlessly about fictitious events from his supposed youth. They were goofy, impossible stories. His cheeks were sunken and the wrinkles in his face were deep and coarse. He looked to be at least eighty, but still had a full head of short hair, almost snow white, and a growth of beard that looked like about five days worth. He moved slowly these days, but with a compact grace that told a careful observer that he had been a powerful man in his youth. Almost nobody paid any attention to old Arne anymore though. Digger was the only one who still sat with Arne at the bar, and even Digger tuned him out some of the time. Something had happened to old Arne Harjaala years and years ago, nobody seemed to know just exactly what it was, but he was definitely "out of it" they said. He was friendly and well liked though, if you didn't have to listen to him for too long at a stretch. He lived in a dingy little apartment on the next street above the bar on some kind of government pension, just enough to keep him out of the snow. Arne could be found in Jerry's most any time of the day. Sometimes he was just sitting quietly sipping his beer, but most often he would be found staring off into the distance and talking endlessly in a monotone voice about weird stuff. People tended to find it disconcerting. Once in a while some new bar patron would sit down and try to talk to him, but they would invariably get bored or annoyed and drift quietly away. A couple college boys came down once, Digger remembered... said they were working on a psychology paper and recorded some of Arne's ramblings, but they lost interest after the course was over and they got their grade. About once a year some guy in a suit would blow in from out-of-town and would come to talk privately with Arne for a few minutes, leave an envelope with the barkeeper, and then disappear again. Digger had tried asking questions of the barkeeper, but never could get any further than to find out that Arne had once been a miner... as if he couldn't tell...

Digger had been sitting next to Arne all afternoon... or was it night now? He looked around, there was no clock above the bar. Wasn't there usually a clock above the bar? He had essentially tuned Arne's monologue out for a while... except for that little bit about the money... hearing it but not really listening to it, as if it were the constant droning of a construction crew's jackhammer. But something had penetrated his self-imposed isolation, something Arne had said. What was it? The words floated through his mind like tangled ticker-tape in a stiff breeze. He tried to focus his attention on Arne's words. It was a difficult task. A combination of the beer he'd consumed and the habit of tuning Arne out conspired against him.

He closed his eyes and tried harder. Arne's musical Yooper accent was familiar, but his words seemed to be strung together far more coherently than usual.

"So dere we was see, down on da fifty fourth level of da number two at da underground machine chop dere. We start feeling da ground moving den see, just real gentle, like a rowboat rocking a little on a calm lake. But den dere's all dis noise see, like a roaring noise, like it's a big waterfall or someting. I'm jus' sittin' on a stool by da lathe in da shop dere, off da side of da drift, and den dese two guys come running down. 'Hey...' says one of 'em, and den dere's dis big like a 'whoosh' and dose guys are just gone, smeared on da wall like so much ketchup. Den ore cars and twisted rails come shootin' down da tunnel from da direction of da number six, along wit ragged pieces of flesh I just guessed were some udder guys, and then everyting went all dark. Dere's still all dis noise dere in da dark, slowly dyin' out, but it never touched me, never touched me at all."

Digger blinked his eyes repeatedly and tried to focus on his companion. "Arne!" he said in a harsh whisper, but Arne took no notice and kept talking.

"So den, after a few minutes everyting seemed ta like settle down and I got my carbide lamp goin' again an' I seen what happened ta Toivo, an' den I go on over to da shaft, an' it's all just a shambles, like it was a war or sometin."

"Arne!" Digger said again, louder this time.

"Oh yeah, hi dere Digger. Ya want ta buy me a beer eh?"

"Uh... yeah, sure Arne." Digger waved to the barkeeper, pointed to Arne's empty glass and the pile of money still on the bartop. "Listen Arne, what are you talking about? Something about a mine disaster?"

"Oh yeah, da big one ya know, back in nineteen ought and six it was, da big air blast dey called it. I was working in da number two shaft when da whole ceiling of da big stope of da number six come down all at once. Dat's what dey tol' me later was da cause of it. Laumontite dey blamed it on, said dere was a vein of it in da hanging wall dere an' it just cut loose all at once I guess. It pushed all dat air down da shaft and out da drifts where all us guys was workin' den, down deeper in da mine. Nobody ever tought it could happen like dat see? 'Course we dint know what was happenin' at da time, just seemed like da world was comin' to an end. God it was awful! You young folks just don't know, it was bad den. Dere was no such ting as da "good old days" I tell ya. Times were tough, really really tough back den. You know, I oughta tell ya, dere was dis udder time......."

Digger was wide awake now. He felt as if a bucket of cold water had been thrown into his face. He felt a tingling on the back of his scalp, just like that time when he'd found a big chunk of native copper buried six inches below the surface. He'd just had that funny feeling and he'd dug there and found a solid 100 kilo mass of float copper. The professor of the summer Field Geophysics course and the whole class, more than twenty people, had seen him do it. That was when they'd given him his nickname, Digger, and it had stuck ever since. He looked at the calendar on the wall behind the bar, a glossy photograph of a scantily clad young lady holding an air impact wrench graced the top... she looked very friendly. Below her feet the lettering said "January, 2017" The little squares with numbers in them were crossed out up to the one with the number 18, in the column marked "Wed". Digger squinted hard, trying to make the numbers come out right, then he interrupted Arne's continuing monologue...

"Arne, hold on a second, you're saying that you were there during the 1906 Quincy mine disaster?"

"Yep, dat's right boy. I was dere." Arne leaned close and breathed yeastily in Digger's face. "I tell ya, I seen da whole ting, it was terrible I tell ya, just awful. Everyting was all tore up, and the smell, Jesus, it was worse dan anyting you can imagine. Dere was dust and blood and puke and guts and pieces of guys all over da place. I trew my lunch up right dere. God you just can't believe it, it was worse than............"

Digger shook his head sadly. "Arne, that's impossible, there is no way......"

"...worse dan when we was fightin' dose damn Spanish bastards on San Juan Hill. You know, dat Ol' Teddy done us proud dat day I tell ya, why I said to da guy next to me, I sez 'yep, dat guy is goin' places in dis world.' Yep, dat's what I said, but dat was nuttin' like da mine disaster. Dat was bad, God it was jus' really really bad." Arne started to sob a little, his eyes getting wet with tears. Digger had never seen Arne display any emotion before. "And da worst ting was... Digger I got ta tell ya, I got ta tell somebody! Da worst ting... was being alone down dere. God dat was spooky... everybody... everybody was dead but me, an' it was as dark as da pit o' hell. Da telegraph didn't work, hell I couldn't even find it. Da power was out, an' water was hissin' and sprayin' all over da place from da broken hydraulic lines. Even da ladder in da shaft was all broke up, I was too scared to try to climb it, I was more'n half a mile down, so I had ta just stay where I was and' hope somebody would come. I stayed right dere Digger, musta been eight or ten hours, I don't know, 'til I got so scared I had ta try to go somewhere, I didn't know what ta do! Everyting's soakin' wet 'cause of the water sprayin' around. I tried ta make it over to da number six, it was da only way I could go. I managed to get my carbide light goin' but I dint have any fresh carbide so it dint last long. When it starts ta go out, I lit some little candles I always carried, but dey weren't much... and finally I'm all alone in da dark. I don't know how long... a long time. I remember dat I started gettin' really hungry. And den... dat's when da blue light come." Arne sat up straight and looked around, taking a deep breath. He stared dreamily at Digger with a quizzical look in his eyes. "Yeah... I can remember it now. All of a sudden I can remember it..."

"Arne, listen to me, that was more than a hundred years ago! Do you understand? There is no way you could have been there, you're just daydreaming!"

"But I was Digger! I was dere, I remember da whole ting, right up until da blue light come. Yeah, it's like I can remember da whole ting now. I couldn't remember it before! How come I couldn't remember? What's happenin' ta me? Dere was dis blue light see? I thought, "Tank God dey come to rescue me!" But it wasn't no rescue party. It was something else...dis blue light come and den... and den..." Arne got real quiet, seemed to sober up a little. He looked around the room from the corner of his eye, and turned slightly to face Digger. He was shaking a little and his hand went out and gripped Digger's forearm in a surprisingly strong clasp. "Listen Digger," he said conspiratorially. "Don't you tell nobody what I'm tellin' ya now, okay? Please?" Digger looked at him. Arne's mouth was twitching slightly, and his eyes... his eyes were filled with terror, there was no faking that. "Please Digger, ya got ta promise me, you tell nobody okay? NOBODY! I mean it. I been shootin' off my moutt where I shouldn't ha' been."

"What do you mean Arne? What's this about a blue light?" Digger asked.

The bartender was walking over towards them, wiping down the bar with his cloth and looking at them. "Say, youse guys okay down here, you look a little pale Arne?"

Arne managed to stammer out, "No, s'okay Jack, just talkin' is all, just talkin'... could sure use anudder beer though," he laughed nervously.

Jack pursed his lips and looked thoughtfully at Arne for a moment, then at Digger, who nodded and pushed another dead guy butt wipe towards him. Digger pretended to drunkenly examine another crumpled bill while Jack filled Arne's glass, giving the pair a suspicious glare.

"Hey Jack, did you ever take a good look at this stuff? It's not even made of paper anymore, did you know that? They try to make it look like paper, but it's just a damn piece of plastic trash. Can't even use the things for buttwipes anymore. Ha!" Digger tried to slur his words a little more than necessary.

Jack looked up disappointedly. "Yeah Digger I know, they've been like that for ten years now, what do you think I am, stupid or somethin?" He moved off down the bar to handle a drink request at the other end.

Digger's sixth sense was working overtime. He was trying to think. It was not an easy task considering the amount of alcohol flooding his brain cells. Why should his "finder" sense be activating like this? He tried to tell himself that there was certainly nothing to the story. Arne's tales were legendary for their ridiculousness, everybody said that he was just a crazy old man. Digger checked himself... "But wait a minute," he thought." Just who is this `everybody?' And why does what `they' say have to be accepted as any kind of truth?" Digger had seen enough impossible things happen in his 34 years to be severely skeptical of the so-called "popular wisdom". And why was he suddenly so suspicious of Jack? Arne sat there with a worried expression looking at him. Digger tried to think...

He remembered the time he'd been working on his master's thesis. He'd needed some information on a certain drill core log in the Jacobsville sandstone. The card catalog at the Michigan Technological University library had listed the exact reference he needed, but it wasn't there on the shelves where it was supposed to be. He checked with the librarians, but it hadn't been checked out. "Probably shelved in the wrong place," they had told him resignedly. In frustration he had spent the better part of the day in the library then, looking up alternative references... and then it happened. Walking down the stacks, he'd felt this same feeling... he'd stopped, looked up, and there it was. The book he needed for his thesis was right there, in a completely different section of the library, misfiled, just like they had said. The sensation he had now was the same. He had come to accept it as the "finding what I'm looking for" feeling, without really understanding or caring enough to pursue its nature.

Digger made a sudden decision and turned to face his companion."Okay Arne, I tell nobody."

Arne breathed a sigh of relief. "God tanks kid. Jesus you had me worried dere for a minute. Hey, did I ever tell ya about da time..."

Digger stared hard at Arne and interrupted his tale. "But I have a price," he said.

Arne stopped talking and looked at him again with a worried expression. He smiled and laughed abruptly as if it were a joke, but Digger's expression did not change, his eyes were steady and one eyebrow was raised in question. "Hey Digger, don't do dis ta me, I... I got no money, you know dat, dey give me just enough ta live on, please I......"

"Who gives you the money Arne?"

"I don' know, some guy from da government or sometin'. I don' know who it is, he never tells me, he jus' asks some questions an' goes away. Look Digger, it's not much, barely enough ta live on ya know. Please... I..."

"What sort of questions do they ask? What are they trying to find out?"

"Just stuff about da mine, like exactly where I was, an what da blue light looked like an' stuff. But I dint used ta be able ta remember so good den. But dey said not ta tell anybody else about it, an' I should tell Jack if I remember anyting new. So maybe I should tell Jack I remembered some new stuff hey? Maybe I should do dat now."

"Relax Arne, don't worry, look, it's not money I want, I just want to hear your story, all of it. You don't need to tell Jack about it yet. We've been drinking buddies a long time haven't we? I'm probably the only guy that still listens to your stories. All of a sudden you start making sense, you start remembering some things, and I just want to hear about it. You know I've always been interested in stories about the old copper mines. I promise I'll never tell anyone, if that's what you want, but I can see that you're in some kind of trouble, and it seems to be related to these stories somehow. I'm interested, and maybe I can help you. But, Arne... I have to know what the problem is. Fair enough?"

"So, youse guys want one last beer then? Last call." Jack startled them by looming up suddenly.

"No, no thanks Jack." Digger tried to keep the excitement out of his voice. "I think we've about had it for tonight."

He looked around the room, it was virtually empty now. A couple of college kids from da Tech were over in the adjoining room still playing pool. Jack left the bar and went over to give them last call. The clock over the bar said 12:50. Had that clock been there before? How could it be last call already? Had he been here that long? He looked over at Arne who was struggling to get into his heavy gray winter coat.

Digger climbed into his own heavy blue parka and they shuffled to the door together, Digger called out, "G'night Jack!"

"Yeah, see youse."

Digger thought he saw Jack give them a strange sidelong look from under his bushy eyebrows. "Get a hold of yourself Digger," he thought to himself. "You're getting paranoid now." He tried to relax, calm down a bit, but that old feeling was burning at the base of his scalp, and the adrenaline seemed to be pumping through his bloodstream at a furious pace. As soon as they opened the door they were hit by a ferocious blast of icy wind. He glanced at the big round thermometer mounted next to the door. The needle hovered just below minus twenty Celsius mark. Shit, it was like a damned blizzard or something! They turned left out of the door, and hurried into the force of the wind. Digger glanced back through the door just as it swung closed and saw Jack pick up a cordless phone and begin punching buttons. The snow was blowing so hard out of the west that visibility was down to just a few hundred feet, there were no cars or people within sight on Shelden Avenue. As they passed the alcove in front of a sporting goods shop Digger stepped into it out of the wind, and pulled Arne by the sleeve in after him.

"I'll walk you up to your place okay?" he shouted at Arne to be heard over the roaring wind. Arne looked at him and shivered slightly, then nodded. Digger just couldn't shake a weird feeling of wrongness coming over him. Over the years he'd learned to trust these feelings, and now was no time to quit, even if they didn't make any sense. He hesitated. "Listen Arne, I want to check something out okay? You stay right here, hunker down out of the wind behind this sign here, okay? Try to stay out of sight if any cars come by." Arne looked quizzically at Digger, caught the serious look in his eyes and nodded. Responding to a whim, Digger quickly took off his coat and turned it inside out before putting it back on. It had been blue when they left the bar, and was now a bright red. Digger then continued walking at a normal pace, and turned left up the next street towards Arne's house. He tried to keep his eyes open and looking around despite the bitter cold and the stinging sharp particles of snow driven by the wind. Christ, where had this weather come from? He carefully walked up the steep street towards the block above, the hard packed snow making a croaking sound with each step, barely audible over the wind. He kept on until he reached the cross street on the level above, even with the entrance to Arne's upstairs apartment. Everything looked normal... except for a black Hummer parked on the hill facing him one block above. That was strange! The street department started plowing about 3 A.M. every morning, all cars had to be off the streets by then to avoid being towed, or sometimes simply plowed off the street. You almost never saw cars parked on the street that late, not more than a few meters from an open bar anyway. That must mean... what did that mean? Digger was still having trouble thinking. Let's see... okay, either they're from out of town and they don't know about the parking rules, or they're visiting somebody and plan to move it soon... or... what?

He kept walking forward towards the Hummer. Who drove those damn things anyway? The price had come down in recent years but they were still pretty expensive as four by fours went, and real fuel hogs too. Digger tried to examine the car as he approached without appearing to do so. The squat four door wagon was mostly covered with snow, but not very deeply he noticed... not as deeply as, for instance, the other cars parked nearby, safely tucked into their carefully dug-out parking spots. So it hadn't been there very long. He tried to slow his walk a bit, to give himself time to think. He purposely slipped and fell, playing up the drunk act a bit, letting the alcohol loosen him up. Making a show of looking both ways down the one way street, he crossed Montezuma, away from Arne's apartment towards the car. He was less than fifty feet from the Hummer now, and could see that the passenger side window had been rolled down a little bit, wisps of vapor or smoke rose from the opening and were whisked away by the driving wind. "Holy Shit!" He thought to himself, "Somebody's in there!" Digger redoubled his drunken act with ease and made an exaggerated effort to peer up at the street sign, and then walked east on Houghton Avenue as if he were lost. He thought now only of how to get out of sight of the mysterious black Hummer and back to Arne without arousing suspicion. He felt sure that these people were looking for Arne. He still didn't know why, but he was convinced by the prickling sensation at the back of his neck that it was something important, something real, something that he, Digger Puttonen, desperately wanted and needed to find out more about. Out of sight of the Hummer he took a deep breath, shed his drunken gait, and hurried back downhill towards where Arne was hidden. There was no explaining it rationally, but he suddenly felt more alive than he had for years. It was almost like the old days as a bad-boy geology student, breaking into the abandoned mines and going down the old shafts looking for mineral specimens and firsthand experiential knowledge. The potential of danger stimulated his senses to a razor's edge. He thought again about Arne then, cold and scared and all alone, and quickened his pace, hurrying into the swirling snow.

Tom Maringer

Miners preparing to descend in the Quincy #2 mancar, circa 1906

CHAPTER 2

Frank Giacoletti leaned back in his chair with his feet up on his desk and stared out the window at the driving snow. A cold cup of coffee and a stale, half eaten glazed donut mocked him from the windowsill. He looked down at his gut, starting to swell slightly over his belt now. When the hell had that started? He'd always been in excellent shape in the old days. He was not unaware that comments had been made within his hearing about how he was "letting himself go". He shook his head in self deprecation, then refocused his eyes to look at his reflection in the window. His hair formed a speckled salt-and-pepper horseshoe around the bald top of his head. The cheeks were sagging he thought, like the extra chin, and the brown eyes looked tired.

Except for that E-mail message that had come through over the computer network an hour ago it had been a quiet night. It was almost always quiet around the Marquette Michigan office of the F.B.I., at least since the Federation of North America back in '09. Nothing but small time stuff ever happened in this neck of the woods. Frank had been transferred up from the Detroit office four years earlier. There had been an "incident", and Frank had gotten sent to the "North Pole", as the Detroit agents lovingly referred to duty in the Upper Peninsula. Frank had been the logical choice of course; he was a native. They'd explained the assignment to him by saying that he would have a "rapport" with the locals. Yeah, right!

The inhabitants of the Upper Peninsula were notoriously uncooperative with Federation agents as a rule, not even trusting the Michigan State Police, who were usually regarded as an occupying foreign police force from "down below". There was still a simmering separatist movement, a group of "Yoopers" who were lobbying in the legislature that the U.P. should separate itself from the state of Michigan and form its own state, to be called Superior. They called themselves "Soopers". A few even suggested seceding from the Federation itself, but these were a decided minority. Nobody in the federation government or the FBI really understood the Sooper movement at all, which had gained momentum after the Quebecois had achieved independence from the Dominion of Canada back in '06. Frank Giacoletti, they had said, was the perfect guy to be in the forefront of the F.B.I. presence in the U.P.

The Giacoletti family immigrated from Italy and had settled in the Copper Country and the Iron Range back in the 1800s, they'd been miners and lumberjacks during the boom times for the area. By the time Frank was born however, the copper was mostly gone or too deep to get at, and the really high grade iron ore was already used up... most of it sent to the bottom of the ocean during World War II. Even as a child Frank had known that he would have to get out of the U.P. or go nuts. He had applied himself assiduously at school, getting outstanding grades, starring on the school hockey team, and then when the chance had come to apply to the F.B.I. Academy he'd jumped at it. He had been one of the few who survived the change of government in '09 when English-speaking Canada had joined the former United States and all of Central America in the new North American Federal Union. He had risen steadily through the ranks during a series of choice assignments, Philly, D.C., Orlando, Moosejaw, Vancouver, Acapulco, Detroit... and then there had been the incident, and here he was in this damned snowbound hell-hole. Even Calgary would have been better than this! When he left this place he'd thought it was for good. Frank knew that some people liked it here... the long winters, the big lakes, the history and the culture. For Frank Giacoletti though, the Upper Peninsula of Michigan had always been a place of misery and despair, of mind numbing boredom and limb numbing cold. He knew without a doubt that his career was as good as over. There would be little that he could ever do here to distinguish himself. He'd been banished to this wasteland, and that was that, end of story. Sometimes he even toyed with the idea of quitting the Bureau and joining up with the Soopers. A lot of their ideas were sincerely valid, and could potentially help the local economy emerge from the stagnation imposed by the apathy of a state government five hundred miles away in Lansing. The lack of a tax base made the option difficult however. The mineral wealth of the region had been carted away long ago. Five hundred miles from Lansing he mused. Ha! More like five hundred light years.

Oh... sometimes there was a little excitement up here. Sometimes the college kids at Northern or Tech would bring up some kind of drugs to share with their friends, and things would get out of hand. And then there were the locals with their clandestine methamphetamines, and their "ice" and "cat" labs scattered here and there. Occasionally a domestic dispute would erupt in gunfire, usually during the coldest part of the winter, when cabin fever made everyone just a little crazy. The Soopers had thus far limited themselves to peaceful acts of civil disobedience and tax protest. For a hard-bitten professional federation agent of Frank's style though, it was all kid stuff.

There was a knock on the frame of the open door, and Frank looked up. Jimmy Canaris looked at him with eyebrows raised. "So, what should we do then? It's almost two o'clock. You want me to warm up the Hummer?"

"Are you kidding? In this weather? Hell Jimmy, E-mail or no, I'm not driving a hundred and seventy klicks up to Houghton in this blizzard. We could end up stuck out there on the road somewhere and freeze to death for Christ's sake! If anything it's probably even worse up there than it is here."

Jimmy frowned. "I don't know captain, that message from Washington sounded pretty urgent. We could throw some emergency gear and our cross-country skis in the back just in case."

Frank looked over at Jimmy. He could see the light of excitement in Jimmy's powder blue eyes. His tall lanky frame and shock of stiff blond hair that stuck out at all angles made him look like the scarecrow from The Wizard Of Oz. Frank remembered the excitement of his own first big case. Hell, the poor kid probably wouldn't get a wink of sleep if he had to wait 'til morning. He just didn't understand these "urgent" messages from headquarters yet. Ninety nine times out of a hundred you had to hurry your ass someplace on the double, then stand around and wait for days or even weeks for something to happen. Of course... there was always that one other time... he hesitated.

Jimmy spoke again.

"Uh captain, I uh... I took the liberty of getting all the stuff together already, just in case. We could be ready to roll in about ten minutes if you give the word."

Frank smiled and shook his head with amused tolerance. Jimmy was a good kid, bright and resourceful, fresh out of the Academy. Jimmy had been with the office less than six months, but he had done his homework. He was a native of Thunder Bay, Ontario, had spent two years in the Unified Command Special Forces, was an expert in winter orienteering and marksmanship, and participated competitively in the local cross country ski races. On his own time he had driven around on the back roads and had familiarized himself with the complex geography of the region. It was time to get him onto a real case, if that's what this was. "Okay Jimmy, let's do it!"

Jimmy's face lit up. "Aye aye Cap'n, we'll be ready to shove off at four bells."

"Make it five after okay? I want to brew up a fresh pot of coffee and fill a thermos, and cut that navy crap."

"Yes sir!"

Jimmy hurried off towards the storeroom with a spring in his step. Frank called out after him.

"And don't forget to bring the printout of that message from H.Q., I want to study it a bit more on the way."

"Yes sir!"

Frank got up out of his chair and stretched, "Yep," he thought to himself, smiling, "that Jimmy is okay, but now it's time to get this old butt in gear." First he went to the break room off the hall and started a fresh pot of coffee, dumping out his cold cup and tossing the stale donut in the trash. He then took a duffel bag down off a shelf and started stuffing things in... a thermal suit, some heavy gloves and other important pieces of winter clothing, sleeping bag, radio gear... He checked the pistol he kept in a shoulder holster and started walking out the door. Almost as an afterthought he reached up on a shelf and threw an extra box of 10mm cartridges in the bag. He filled the thermos and shed his shiny dress shoes for an old pair of swampers by the door to the garage, before switching on the telephone answering machine and heading down the hall towards Jimmy and the waiting vehicle. He paused a moment at the door. Bureau policy held that an agent should be on duty at the office at all times. He tended to run his office a little loosely though, as so little ever happened around here. The next shift was to start at 6:00 A.M., just four hours away. For a few moments Frank considered calling to get them in early, but rejected the idea as being overly paranoid. He left a note telling them what was up, along with a copy of the message transcript from H.Q. Why had they put it in priority "one" encryption mode? It didn't make sense, it was a simple assignment. The phrase "most urgent" was common in messages from headquarters, but of course those guys could not appreciate the difficulties of U.P. winter storms. Oh well, Sammy had the mobile phone number if they needed him... still.........

He reached for the phone, then heard two quick honks from the Hummer's horn in the garage, Jimmy was anxious to get going. He chuckled a little, and waved at the phone dismissively.

"Get some sleep you guys," he said to it, then turned towards the door. The Hummer's powerful engine could be heard warming up, a deep throaty rumble that sounded reassuringly confident against the howling of the wind beyond the garage door. Jimmy stood by the squat black vehicle as Frank entered.

"All set? You want to drive, or you want me..?"

"Go ahead Jimmy, you take the first shift, best soften up the tires a bit right off though," Frank said as he heaved his duffel into the back.

"Yes sir!"

Frank surveyed with satisfaction the equipment that Jimmy had stowed, raising his eyebrows as he recognized a large molded thermoplastic rifle case. Jesus, the kid thought of everything! He hated to imagine how much stuff Jimmy would put in a backpack. They got into the four-door wagon, chugging smoothly now, and warm as toast inside. "Say Jimmy, you really think we need all that stuff? You've got enough equipment back there to get us to the north pole!"

"Well, not quite captain, but I just believe in being prepared for any contingency, who knows what we're getting into here. Besides, the extra weight will just give us better traction."

"Okay, but what about the Barrett? Why bring the big gun out on this one? It sounds like a simple pimple investigation to me."

"I don't know, I just, well, I felt that it would be prudent, you just never know."

Frank shrugged as Jimmy used the dashboard control to lower the tire pressure to 20 p.s.i. all the way around for better traction in the deep snow. Frank then punched the garage door remote control button as Jimmy revved the motor a couple of times before dropping the transfer case into four high and the gear shift into low. He stepped on the accelerator and charged out through the four foot drift that had blown up against the door, turning right out of the short driveway and heading out towards Highway 41. The door closed quickly behind them, and within moments they disappeared into the night, the low purring of the Hummer's engine quickly swallowed up by the heavy veil of falling snow.

CHAPTER 3

George Frederick Sherman sat with his back to his guest and gazed north out of the huge picture window of his office. His gaze strayed to the Chicago skyline dominating the horizon and the cluster of high tech assembly plants in the foreground. He smiled as he contemplated the fact that he personally owned them all. Behind him an employee waited to speak with him. He mused on the situation and recalled the axiom he had once heard from another great industrialist to the effect that one did not rise to such a position of power and authority by being kind and polite to subordinates. He allowed his hireling a few moments to fully appreciate their lowly position in the power structure of the corporation. When he heard the telltale signs of nervousness: a shuffling of the feet, an attempt to clear a dry throat, he whirled about and barked, "Report!"

"Yes sir! The results of our investigations into the Midnight Mining Company suggest that it would be an excellent candidate for acquisition sir. The real assets are fairly low, but several significant patents and other publicly undisclosed intellectual properties position the company to gain considerable market share in several high growth fields in the five to ten year time frame."

"What fields?"

"Uh, let's see," papers were shuffled, "that would be: undersea mining, ore recovery, resource management, oil exploration, pollution control... sir, the list goes on for quite a while."

"I see. What do you mean by "considerable" market share?"

"Sir, our computer projections show them to be capable of dominating those industries within ten years."

George Sherman jumped up out of his chair to face his subordinate. His chiseled face and shock of bristly red hair contrasted sharply with his underling's thin sallow face and ponytail of brown hair. Steve Sanders pushed his wire framed glasses up on his nose and tried not to flinch at his boss' icy gaze.

"What? You're telling me that this little upstart company is going to claim more than fifty percent of my market share in ten years?"

"Well, that's how the projections look sir, and we've refigured them every way possible."

"So, what are we doing about it?"

"Sir, as per standing orders, a generous offer was made to try to buy the company."

"And...?"

"They refused to sell sir."

"So? Double the offer!"

"No sir," said Steve with some hesitation. "You don't quite understand. We tried that already. It wasn't the offer that was the problem. They simply refused to even consider selling, under any circumstances, for any price."

"Hmmm, that's rather unusual."

"Yes sir, we thought so too. Rather than bother you with this we brought in Mr. Jameson on the project. As you know he has had some previous successes in similar situations."

"Okay, good thinking." Sherman grudgingly had to compliment Steve's procedure. "But if Jameson is on the case, why are you here?"

"Well sir, you see, there have been some complications. Mr Jameson has encountered an unusual situation and has requested your authorization to, ahem, um, apply "sanctions"... as he puts it... to some of the more recalcitrant individuals involved. Also, there seems to be another factor in that we have information indicating that federation officials are involved in investigating certain aspects of the Midnight Mining Company operations. The problem is growing sufficiently complex and troublesome that it was felt that perhaps your personal direction of the project would be advisable. Mr Jameson has suggested also that perhaps a board meeting is in order."

"I see." said Sherman as he leaned back in his chair and for several minutes he gazed through Steve's chest into the distance in a very disturbing way. Looking up finally he said, "So, Jameson has requested a board meeting eh?"

"Yes sir. His latest communication, on a secure channel, indicated that he had left two associates, uh... Scott and Jeff, to monitor the situation. They are under orders to observe only, to take no action until further notice. Jameson himself is due to arrive here sometime this evening."

George Sherman sat in his chair again and leaned back, closing his eyes and steepling his hands in contemplation for several minutes, until Steve began to wonder if he'd fallen asleep. At last he spoke. "I agree, this is too important to be dealt with by ordinary means. I want a full report, all details on my desk before midnight tonight. Be ready to brief me on more recent developments by seven o'clock tomorrow morning. Relay this message to Jameson over his secure channel with his personal encryption algorithm: 'Code 9, 8:00 A.M. tomorrow.' You've done well to bring this matter to my attention. That will be all, Dismissed!" Sherman turned away and began poking keys on his computer.

"Yes sir... Uh sir?"

"What is it now?"

"Sir, I've taken the liberty to prepare the report already, I have it here. This folder contains a written overview of the situation, and here is a 16 gig optical disk containing detailed files on all the principals of the Midnight Mining Company, as well as everything we could dig up about their operations and resources. I've integrated the data with a search and association program to assist you in finding the information you need."

"Well all right! That's what I like to see, a little hustle around here! Which search program did you say this was?" George inserted the disk into his computer's floppy port and started punching a few buttons.

"Oh, just a little something of mine."

"I see. Okay, dismissed, but I still want that briefing at seven."

"Yes sir!"

Sherman watched Steve leave the office out of the corner of his eye. Not bad! He'd have to watch this kid, he was a real self starter. People who could think ahead and anticipate the company's needs could either be very good... or very bad for an organization, depending on where their loyalties lay. He made a mental note to himself to find out more about Steve Sanders. Then returned to the study of Steve's report on Midnight Mining Company. Oh yes... very good... yes... Oh! This is big alright. George Frederick Sherman would certainly want to handle this project himself. He thought his ancestor, William Tecumseh Sherman, the Union general of Civil War fame would certainly have approved entirely of the plan that began to form in George's mind. It would be a bit messy of course, the Shermans were famous for that, but when it was over.....

He punched a button on the desk intercom. "Marsha?"

"Yes sir?", a woman's voice answered.

"I want a full meeting of the board in my office, tomorrow morning at eight A.M. sharp."

"Yes sir. I'll inform them immediately."

"Oh and Marsha, and this is very important, tell each of them that this meeting is "code 9". If anybody misses this one.... well, let's just be sure they're all here, alright?"

"Yes sir. I'll tell them."

Sherman sat back in his chair and gazed out of his fourteenth floor window again. Steam rose from the square heating units clustered on the flat roofs below, falling horizontally into a layer of shimmering haze which gleamed in the light of the waning crescent moon. To the north there were the lowering clouds of a winter storm moving in. He smiled again, though if anyone had been there to see it, they would not have been particularly comforted by that smile. Once the Midnight Mining Company belonged to him, there would be very few people with the power to stop him from doing virtually anything he wanted. If it was as big as they said, and he had every confidence in his computer people, then this was the biggest thing since the microchip. He rubbed his hands together and chuckled. Oh this was going to be great! He turned back to the computer and started doing his homework. He'd be at it all night, and by 8:00 A.M. tomorrow his knowledge of the situation would be encyclopedic. Then there would be the "board" meeting, though of course, a board meeting at Sherman Industries meant something quite different than it did at most other companies. Sherman would present the data to the board, and the members, in their own so delightfully direct and visceral way would offer suggestions as to how to "sanction" the "problems" that Sherman had defined. Sherman would then select from among their plans, or propose one of his own, and make the final selection of personnel and method for dealing with the problem. Jameson was usually the person who kept the minutes of these board meetings, in especially encrypted files. Chris Jameson was the only member of the board who worked for Sherman full time, his most trusted lieutenant. Jameson had been with him for years and his loyalty had never been in question. George smiled again in anticipation and turned back to his computer. Outside the window, the gloom deepened as the cloud bank obscured the moon and a heavy snow began to fall.

CHAPTER 4

Digger Puttonen hurried down Dodge street back to Shelden, sliding on the hard packed snow half the way down the hill on the soles of his boots. He turned left at the corner after checking to see that nobody was around, and scurried along the snowy sidewalk as fast as he could manage against the stiff wind. When he had to pass Jerry's Bar he stooped low under the window in case somebody was inside watching. His paranoia was now thoroughly aroused and he wanted to take no chances on being seen. He recalled one of his college buddies once proclaiming the axiom that "total paranoia is total awareness." He chuckled to himself a little. Right now that was sure how it felt.

He ducked in behind the sign in the alcove in front of Weber's Sporting goods, and found Arne sitting there shivering, a light dusting of snow effectively concealing him from sight. Arne looked up with a worried expression as Digger sat down next to him.

"Okay Arne, here's the deal. There were some guys up there by your apartment waiting around in a black hummer. I have the feeling they're looking for you, or maybe for both of us. We need to get someplace safe and figure out what to do." Arne nodded wearily.

"How you doing? Can you walk for a while?"

"Ya sure, I feel pretty good, a little cold now, but if we get moving I'll warm up fast eh?"

"Okay, let's go then." said Digger as he started to help Arne up. At that moment Digger heard the low rumble of a car engine and pushed Arne back down. "Hang on a second Arne, let's see who this is first."

The wind had died down a little, but the snow was falling even harder than before as Digger peered through the crack between the sign and the stone of the building through a little hole in the plastering of snow. He could now see a black humvee approaching slowly with its lights off, possibly the same one he'd seen parked above. He quickly lay back down by Arne and shoveled a few armloads of the dry powdery snow over his legs and boots, which stuck out far enough beyond the sign to be seen from the road if the vehicle pulled up even with them. Digger signaled Arne with a raised hand to lay very still. Arne seemed to understand and froze as a trick of the wind induced a momentary calm.

The car slowed as it approached, then stopped in front of Jerry's Bar. Two doors opened, then shut again. The creaking of boots in the snow could be heard approaching. Terror filled Arne's eyes as they listened to the eerie squeaking of the snow; such a common everyday sound, now suddenly fraught with apprehension.

Digger began to formulate a desperate plan of escape when he heard a voice:

"Where'd they go?"

"Hell if I know, Jack said they came out and turned down this way, one guy with a dark blue coat, and the other guy's was gray."

"Well they didn't come by us, and I can't see any footprints with all this snow falling, so they must be heading for the lift bridge."

"Yeah, I guess so." The wind picked up again and swirled in the streetlights.

"I'm getting cold, let's get back in."

The croaking footsteps receded, followed by the slamming of the vehicle doors. The hummer rumbled slowly past them, heading off west towards the lift bridge over the Portage Lake shipping canal, connecting Houghton with Hancock. It was the only bridge across, the only way onto the Keweenaw Peninsula.

Arne and Digger got up and shook themselves off. "Shit Arne, what the hell is going on? Man this is weird!"

"Digger, listen, der's some 'tings I ought ta tell ya about dis deal."

"Listen Arne," Digger interrupted. "I want to hear them, but right now we've got to get out of here. Okay, look, I think they've gone off to try to catch us on the bridge. They probably think we're trying to get over to my place in Paavola, so that's obviously the last place we should go, and they may have set up some sort of surveillance device at your place. Let's head on up the hill towards Dodgeville. I know somebody up there, we might be able to crash for the night and get something to eat. Then we can talk."

Arne hesitated, then nodded resignedly. "Okay, dat's a long walk from here, I guess we better get going den."

"Come on Arne, we'll make it." They walked slowly up the hill on Pewabic Street, and Digger noted with satisfaction that the black humvee was no longer parked at the corner above. Arne seemed to be having trouble walking, losing his balance and leaning heavily on Digger's arm for support. By the time they reached Montezuma, just one block up, Arne was swaying.

"Sorry Digger, dint know I was so tired. I don't know if I can make it. I feel really cold."

"It's okay Arne, we'll just take it slow, don't worry." But Digger was very worried, he knew how fast hypothermia and frostbite could strike. If their situation didn't improve soon he thought they'd have to make for Arne's place after all, surveillance or no. They crossed the street and started up the next block, even steeper than the first. Digger was constantly looking around through the heavy veil of falling snow for any possible threat, when he noticed a glow in the west, obviously a vehicle coming down the road towards them, though they could neither hear it nor make out any details yet.

"Come on Arne, let's get behind this snowbank just in case okay?"

"Ya sure" said Arne wearily, as they lay down behind a four foot pile of snow that had been thrown up along the edge of the road by the city snowplows.

Digger peered over the edge of the crusty, dirty snow as the car approached. The first detail he could make out was that there was only one headlight. Then he heard the sound of it penetrating the deadening veil of falling snow, a clanking noise accompanied by the coughing, wheezing sound of an engine that desperately needed a tuneup. Finally it came close enough to view, creeping along at barely twenty klicks per hour.

"It's a Nova," shouted Digger exultantly.

"What?" said Arne.

But Digger had already jumped up and was standing in the full light of the street lamp with his thumb out in the traditional gesture of the hitchhiker soliciting a ride. The Nova locked its brakes and slid to a stop on bald tires twenty meters further down the road. Digger ran over to the driver's side as the lone occupant rolled down the window. A woman of indeterminate age, peered from the window and eyed him. She was wearing a blue stocking cap with close cropped brown hair poking out from beneath it, there seemed to be no other occupants of the vehicle. She smiled tentatively.

"Hey, youse guys okay out here? What's with your friend there eh?" she asked, jerking her head towards where Arne still lay in the snowbank, struggling to get up. "You guys drunk or something?"

Digger smiled back, "Well, yeah, a little... right now we're just really cold, can we get in?"

"Well, where ya going?"

"I don't know yet." Said Digger with a worried expression that he could not quite hide. "Where are you going?"

She seemed to perceive more from his words than perhaps he intended, took a hard look at him, then reached over and pushed open the passenger side door.

Digger ran over to help Arne get in, pushed him towards the middle, then got in himself and pulled the door shut. It didn't seem to latch properly, so he pushed it open to try slamming it again.

"Here, hook this on the handle there," the woman said, handing him the hooked end of a rubber bungee cord.

"Oh, yeah, okay." Digger hooked the bungee onto the door handle, and let it pull the door shut.

"Try not ta lean on it okay?"

"Yeah, sure."

With a loud grinding of gears she got the car moving again. "Hey that's a lot better now, that's all I needed was a little ballast. You guys are giving me better traction now. Hey now, I'm Joan, and I'm heading out toward Chassell. How far youse goin'? Ya goin' to da Tech?"

"Hi Joan, this is my friend Arne, Arne Harjaala, and I'm Digger Puttonen."

"Hi Arne, Hi Digger, a couple o' local boys eh? Where was it you were goin' then?"

"Well, we really don't exactly know where we're going. We can't go home right now, and we just need a place to sleep, and something to eat, and a little time to think about things."

"Okay boys, now I can tell you're in some kind of trouble. You just tell Joan about it and we'll see about settin' it right okay? What is it? You had an argument wit da wife and she throwed you out right? Am I right?"

"No, nothing like that I'm afraid. Neither of us is even married you see." He looked at Arne, who turned to look at him and shrugged. "Something really weird is happening, there's some guys chasing us around, we don't know why yet, but I'm really worried about it. I think they're watching my house, and we spotted them watching Arne's apartment. We just came out of Jerry's bar after a long night, and still can't seem to think straight."

Joan looked at him with a more serious gaze. She could tell this was no prank, these guys were worried. "Okay," she said. "Tell me about it. Did you see 'em? What did they look like?"

"No, we never actually got a good look at the guys, just white guys in heavy black nylon jackets was all I saw, driving a black humvee."

"A black humvee? Are you sure about dat, a black hummer?"

"Yeah, why?"

"Well, dere's not many of those things around ya know, and even fewer that are black. The only ones in the county that I know of belong to da feds, those F.B.I. guys that are always nosing around poking into stuff. If they're tryin' ta pick you up it could be a serious problem."

"The F.B.I.? What would they want with us? How do you know it's them?"

"I don't know why they're after you, you haven't told me anything, yet. As ta how I know it's them, trust me, I keep track of things like that okay? So here's the deal guys, I'll take you over to my place and put you up for the night. In the morning we'll talk, and then you can decide what you need ta do, and I'll decide whether I want ta help ya."

"Gosh, thanks Joan..." began Digger. "I... I don't know what to..."

"Don't thank me yet, I got ta find out some things still."

They drove on past the Michigan Tech campus and out of town along U.S. Highway 41 towards Chassell, about five miles away. The ride was cold, as the car heater blasting at full power was incapable of overcoming the invasion of cold air through the unsealed door and the rusty floorboards. Still, it was better than being outside! They rode for the most part in silence, simply huddling together to try to stay warm. Joan took a right turn in the tiny village, then several more turns on smaller lanes until finally they turned down a long plowed driveway and pulled up to a low ramshackle house tucked in at the edge of a pine forest. Except for the snow shoveled away from the front door and one window, it seemed to be almost completely covered with the white stuff. Several pairs of cross country skis could be seen standing in the snowbank by the door, along with two snowmobiles. Joan drove a few meters past the house and into the open door of a large barn building close by.

"Come on guys, let's get you warmed up eh?" Said Joan, getting out of the car. She pulled four large plastic grocery bags out of the back seat and set them down in the snow outside the big door. Digger unhooked the bungee cord and tumbled out the passenger side, lending a hand to Arne following him. Digger noticed that the lower level of the barn was nearly full of stacked firewood, there must have been at least twenty full cords in there.

They went out the large door behind the aging maroon 1974 Nova. Joan began swinging one side of the door shut, pushing hard against the resistance of the snow that had fallen since the last time the door had been dug out. Digger noticed and grabbed a snow shovel that was stuck in the snowbank, clearing away the accumulation so that the doors could be closed. Then he went over and picked up two of the Red Owl grocery bags to help carry them to the house. Joan smiled at him and said "thanks".

They walked the short distance to the house. A warm glow was emanating from the window, lighting up the falling snow and creating a fluffy halo around the house. The smell of wood smoke was in the air, and the sound of music could be heard through the door as they approached. They entered the first door into a sort of outer vestibule, where they stomped the snow off of their boots. The music and the sound of conversation could be heard even louder from here, and when they entered the second door, Digger was amazed. There were at least a dozen people in the room, about equal numbers of men and women. Three guitars were being busily played, along with a fiddle, a flute, and a mandolin. There were calls of "Hey Joan" as they entered, a few waves and raised eyebrows at the newcomers. The three then took off their coats and boots and sweaters, went over to the wood stove that was practically glowing with heat, and started to warm themselves up. Without even being asked, one of the people fetched them some bowls of the venison stew that was simmering on the stovetop.

"Here ya go. Youse looked like ya needed it eh?"

"Hey, thanks a lot."

"No problem! In dis place ya got ta help each udder ya know."

Digger looked at Arne and took a deep relaxing breath. Arne smiled in return. It seemed that it might be okay after all. "Let's just try not to think about tomorrow," said Digger to himself. "We'll deal with that when the time comes."

He looked around the room surveying the faces of the people. These seemed like really good folks, friendly, intelligent, and talented from the sound of the music. Halfway through his second bowl of stew he started relaxing a bit, and began to feel the music seeping down into his bones. Arne had already stretched out on a mattress in a loft above the kitchen, and seemed to be fast asleep. Digger looked around the room for Joan. He found her leaning against the wall by a bookshelf across the room, looking straight at him. He hadn't gotten a very good look at her until now. In the car everyone had been so bundled up. She had dark hair, kept short in a page boy, flanking rosy cheeks and full lips that had no need of makeup. She stood upon sturdy thick legs and had wide rounded hips. When their eyes met she did not look away, but just smiled at him in a friendly way and waved her hand, gesturing him over to her side. He looked around the room a little nervously, but nobody seemed to be paying any attention to him at all, except Joan of course. He went on over, still spooning stew into his mouth as he went.

"Hey guy, you feeling better?" she asked.

"Yeah, thanks, this is great. Are these all friends of yours?"

"Ya sure, mostly neighbors. All these folks live within a couple o' miles. Most of them came on skis, some on snowmobiles."

"Cool! You guys get together like this often?"

"Oh yeah, you bet, once a week at least. Makes the winter not seem so long ya know. Hey, you want go sauna?"

"You have a sauna?"

"Ya sure eh?. Got to have a sauna! I just checked it a minute ago, nice an' hot, about a hunnert eighty degrees."

"Wow, sounds great!"

Digger blushed momentarily as he thought of being alone in the sauna with Joan. He wondered about the dress code... some people wore bathing suits to sauna he knew, though nudity was more traditional. It looked as though he would find out soon. Joan grabbed a couple of towels from a shelf and smiled at him, gesturing for him to follow. His hopes of being alone with her began to soar, but were dashed when she suddenly stuck her head back into the room and shouted "Sauna's Hot!" before closing the door behind her. They were in another outer vestibule on the back of the house. Joan opened the outer door and they ran less than ten meters on a shoveled path to the smaller sauna building. It was of the two room type. The outer room had rows of pegs for hanging clothes, an iron door to load wood into the heater, and a cedar door with wooden handle opening into the heated part. Two small windows looked into the inner chamber, an oil lamp sat on the ledge of each, the only light for both rooms. While Digger had been examining the room with his back to Joan, she had been taking her clothes off.

"So, you coming in or not?"

He turned around and she stood there unashamedly naked with an impish smile on her face, then she turned and slipped quickly through the inner door to the sauna proper. God but she was beautiful! He'd had no idea that the concept of woman had ever found expression in so perfect a form! Not that she was likely to ever be asked to model for a magazine... she was far from the emaciated, top heavy type those editors always seemed to prefer... but she exuded a sense of animal power that he had never experienced before except once, when he had been fortunate enough to get a close look at a herd of wild horses before they got his scent.

Digger hurried then to get his clothes off. By the time he was halfway there several more people filed into the changing room and began doing the same. He pulled on the wooden handle of the inner door and slid through the opening so as to let as little of the heat out as possible. He was hit immediately by a fierce blast of hot air, and gasped: "Hot!"

"Here, sit down on da lower bench for a while ta get used to it."

"Yeah, okay." he stammered out, trying not to breathe.

Others began filing in and filling the wooden benches until the place was pretty well packed wall to wall with naked human flesh. A bucket of cold water was passed around and people would drink from the wooden ladle, or douse a little over their heads. It was just getting to the point where Digger felt he could stand it no longer when somebody yelled. "SNOW ANGELS!"

Immediately everybody ran outside, Digger included, jumped into the fresh soft powder snow stark naked, waving their arms and legs to form the classic snow angels. Digger was no amateur at it either, and Digger's snow angel was unanimously judged to be the best. After about twenty or thirty seconds of this, people started feeling cold again, and they filed quickly back into the hot sauna.

The second round in the sauna was not quite as hot as the first, and a bit more relaxed. Conversation tapered off, and after a while people started dousing off with buckets of cold water and drifted out with expressions such as "thanks for the great evening Joan", and "see youse next time at our place". As the last group went out to the vestibule to dry off, Joan went with them and continued the conversation while they were dressing. Digger went along too, thinking the sauna session was over, but Joan had simply wrapped herself in a towel rather than getting dressed, so he did likewise. After the last guests had left she turned to him and said:

"I want to go in for one more, join me?"

"Sure." He replied. Before going back in he checked the thermometer, it was an older one, in Fahrenheit, and was down to 155 degrees now. They sat together on the top ledge for a while before Joan spoke again.

"You said your name was Digger, not a very common name. Seems like I heard it before, but I can't remember when. What do you do?"

"Well, I used to be a principal partner in the Midnight Mining Company, you know, up on Quincy Hill."

"Oh yeah, that was you?"

"Yeah, 'WAS' is the right word, they've kicked me out."

Joan looked over at him. "Is that what this chasing around is all about?"

"I don't know, could be I guess."

They were silent for several minutes until Joan began again. "You know Digger, I've always found that the sauna is the best place to talk when you want to get to the truth. Sitting in the buff next to another person, with your sweat dripping off and mingling on the floor... well, makes it easy to get things off your chest. I want you to tell me what's going on. I want to hear all of it, and then I'll tell you some things about myself."

Digger looked at her with a worried expression. "Y... You probably wouldn't believe it," he stammered.

She turned her face back to the front, brought her knees up to sit cross legged, closed her eyes, and said: "Try me. Come on, spill it."

So Digger sighed and began telling her the story as he knew it. He told her about how he and some other Michigan Tech graduates had started the company based on some inventions and concepts they'd come up with while at the university. Things had been tough at first of course, the university was unwilling to even let them use equipment. Still, they persevered and there were a couple of real successes. That was when the university had sent in a controller, saying they had supported the research and deserved a share of the pie. Then other "money" people had come in and had eventually bought out all the other younger inventors except for Digger and the two other principal partners. One of the partners, Josh Freeman, had died in mysterious circumstances, the death ruled accidental by the coroner. He told her about the big fight at the company, four of the other board members had wanted to accept a seemingly attractive offer from Sherman Industries to buy the entire company. Digger and his other partner, James Dolittle had refused to go along with it. As board members they had a right of veto if they voted together. He had tried to explain... he had tried to tell them that the company had too much potential to sell now. The profits in the long run would make any proceeds from the sale look puny by comparison, but they would hear none of it. They had filed a grievance with the court declaring him medically unfit to continue on the board. Illegal as hell of course, and groundless as well, simply a nuisance to put pressure on him. They still couldn't sell without his signature, which he was not about to give them. Their latest offer had been sixty million dollars for his share alone, more than the entire company was worth on paper, but a mere fraction of the value of contracts that could be signed within months if all went well. The whole situation had sent him into a severe depression and he had turned to beer to salve his wounds.

Then Digger detailed, as best he could, the events at Jerry's Bar that very evening, of how Arne had remembered something... exactly what, he could not reveal because of his promise to Arne... and of the bartender's suspicious actions on overhearing part of their conversation. He digressed into a little of his own past to explain a little about his talent for "finding" things, how he could know when the sense was functioning, and how he had acquired his nickname. When he came to the part in the story where he approached the black hummer and noticed the wisps of vapor blown by the wind from the open window, she looked at him appreciatively with eyebrows raised, and when he reached the part where they overheard the two men talking she almost choked.

"You mean this all happened tonight?"

"Yeah, just before you picked us up. Pretty weird eh?"

"And you have this sixth sense or something that helps you find things you're looking for, even if you don't know you're looking, and alerts you to trouble even if you can't see anything wrong?"

"Yeah, well... works part of the time anyway. Yep, that's about it."

After a long pause Joan nodded and spoke. "Okay, good story. I would have a hard time believing it at all, except that I have something of a talent too. I can tell when people are lying. I can tell a little lie from a big lie, and I can tell a subtle twisting of the truth from the whole truth. I know for a fact that you're not lying, so now I'm going to tell you something about myself. The downside of my talent is that it is almost impossible for me to lie. I don't know why, but believe me, that's how it is, it hurts my brain to even contemplate the idea. So when I tell you about myself I want you to believe me when I say it's the truth. Will you trust me that far?"

Digger stared at her with big eyes, and simply nodded.

"I am one of the leaders of a group of political activists who are working to promote the secession of the Upper Peninsula from the state of Michigan. While you may have heard jokes about this group, I assure you, this movement is absolutely serious. We have been working quietly for years to get people who are sympathetic with us into positions of power in the state and federation government so that they can help us when the time comes."

Digger continued staring at her as Joan paused for a moment and took a deep breath, then she continued.

"The new state will be called 'Superior', and we think the capital city should probably be in Marquette or Calumet, we haven't decided which. For this effort to be successful we need to have the cooperation of the Michigan Governor, both state senators, and all the congressmen from the U.P districts. As of this week we have that support, we are almost ready to move. Lower Michigan is willing to let us go because we have been, for many years, a "drain" on the tax base as they say. We cost them more than they can tax us.

"For the new state to be successful we will have to come up with an economic resource base to sustain us and make Superior a productive member of the North American Federal Union. If it looks to congress as though we will have a hard time making ends meet financially, they will not approve our secession from Michigan."

"Why are you telling me all this?" asked Digger.

"I want you with us for three reasons. First, we understand that your company is poised to capture a significant share of the world market in high tech goods. This could be the economic and industrial base we so desperately need. I had planned to talk to you about this anyway, but fate has dropped you into my lap.

"Second, you have a psi talent that would be extremely useful to us in the critical takeover phase that will be coming up very soon. I don't need to take your word for it, I can feel it in you. We would like to make this a peaceful shift in power structure, but we just don't know if there may be armed resistance from some quarters. You may be able to help us find and defuse those trouble spots before someone gets hurt. So, what do you say? If you join us I may be able to help you out of your predicament more easily than you imagine. We have a fiercely loyal following already in place in many parts of the U.P. and elsewhere."

"But I'm booted out of the company, I can't help you. Sherman will probably move the whole thing elsewhere if he gets hold of it."

"That's why you need me."

"You mentioned a third reason."

"Oh yes. Digger, I'm sorry if I seem too direct in this, but as I said, it is very difficult for me to lie, and certain common sorts of personal interaction, such as conventional courting behaviors, well, they involve a lot of shaded truth and sometimes deliberate falsehoods. My romantic life has always been difficult because I just can't play those games."

"What are you saying?"

"I'm saying Digger, that I am strongly attracted to you. I think I am safe in assuming that the feeling is mutual?" She looked down at his lap.

Digger suddenly noticed that his turgid soldier was standing to attention. "Oh God!" he stammered out, covering himself with his hands. "How embarrassing!"

"No", said Joan smiling. "I think it's sweet. Come on, you don't have to give me your answer now. Let's dry off and go inside. I want you in my bed tonight!"

She slipped out the door, grabbed one of the lighted oil lamps, and then he heard the outer door slam. "My God!" he thought. "She must have run to the house stark naked!" He thought about that for a few moments and his face flushed, then he got up, toweled off, and followed in like fashion taking the other lamp and nothing else.

From the outside, the glow of two oil lamps could be seen shining out of the bedroom window, making a shimmering halo of light in the still falling snow for over an hour before they winked out. The cold dark stillness reigned once again over the isolated little house on the outskirts of Chassell Michigan. It would be many hours yet until the dawn.

CHAPTER 5

The vehicle skidded slightly as Jimmy Canaris pulled the humvee out onto U.S. Highway 41 and headed west towards Houghton. There were few cars on the road due to the severity of the winter storm, but the squat four wheel drive vehicle seemed to be having no trouble. Frank Giacoletti looked over at Jimmy, who seemed relaxed and confident. Leaving the driving to the younger agent's capable hands he turned to the transcript of the message from headquarters that had sent them scurrying out into the snow on a night like this. He reached up and turned on the map light. "Okay", he thought to himself, "may as well be thorough, we've got plenty of time to think about things before we get to Houghton."

He unfolded the single sheet of computer paper, and noted the decryption headings. It had been sent through under priority one encryption, meaning that the necessary decryption code was sent along as a separate item, encrypted normally with the special algorithm set for that particular day and office. It was an unusual system, usually used only with items that were particularly sensitive politically. The paper was headed "F.B.I. Special Investigations Branch, Washington D.C." Frank had never heard of the "S.I.B." as he supposed they called it, but new branches came and went with some regularity in the bureau, at least, since the reorganization eight years back. It did not particularly surprise him that he didn't know of it.

"Say Jimmy, you ever hear of a branch of the bureau called "Special Investigations?"

Jimmy hesitated a moment as he veered towards the side of the road to avoid an oncoming truck taking up most of the road. The truck whizzed past with a rumble of chains and a cloud of blowing snow. "Uh, no... doesn't ring a bell. We could check it out with our Info-com system though if you want."

"Yeah, let's do that," Frank said with a thoughtful pause. "If we're going up here on a wild goose chase I want to know who sent us. Okay, let's see, how does this thing work again?"

Jimmy smiled a bit. The computer part of his job was his favorite. He found it amusing that some of the older guys still had a hard time figuring it all out. "Well first, go ahead and hit the power button to boot the system up."

"Yeah, I know that much." Frank poked a button on the wide console between the front seats. A small screen lit up a dark blue color in front of him, angled so that it could be seen by either occupant. A few moments passed as a series of cryptic computerese messages flashed briefly on the screen, then the screen turned a pale sky blue and the message appeared in large white letters "READY".

Frank may have been ignorant of many of the fine points of the system, but he'd had occasion to use a similar onboard computer before. He pulled the folding keyboard holder to himself and hit the "escape" button. Of course, the newer FBI computer systems were all state-of-the-art voice activated, but here, as at other backwater offices, they made use of surplus equipment from the big outfits. At least it worked... most of the time.

Jimmy smiled and said "Yeah!" as the screen lit up with a series of choices. Frank started pondering the options as Jimmy tried to watch both the road and the screen. Frank noticed, looked over and said, "You want I should drive for a while?"

"Okay, sure," Jimmy replied.

"Let's pull into this Busy Bodies store up here, they've usually got fresh donuts by this time."

Jimmy giggled. "Okay boss. Whatever you say."

They pulled into the plowed parking lot of a convenience store on the edge of town and went inside. The elderly woman behind the counter recognized the older man.

"Hiya Frank," she said. "Whatcha doin' out this time o' night eh?"

"Hi Martha," he answered. "We're just taking a little drive, thought maybe you'd have some of your special donuts done by now maybe?"

"You bet, took a batch out about ten minutes ago, how many you want?"

Frank looked over at his companion. "Hey Jimmy, how many you think you'll want?"

"Oh, I don't know, three or four maybe."

"Okay Martha, better make it two dozen, I know this kid, once he gets going there's no stopping him."

Martha put the steaming gooey glazed donuts in an old fashioned waxed paper bag (the only place in town that still used them), Frank paid for them at the counter. As they went out the door Martha called after them. "You boys be careful out there, it's going to get worse before it gets better ya know, blizzard warning they're saying now."

"Thanks mom," said Frank with a smiling wink as they left. They got back into the still running hummer and got back out onto 41, heading out past the last lights of town.

Now with Frank driving he said to Jimmy, "Okay computer boy, tell me what you can find out about the Special Investigations Branch."

Jimmy started punching keys, and while Frank couldn't tell exactly what was going on, he really didn't care, he had the right man on the job, and Frank Giacoletti was never one for micromanaging his people. He let the silence hang as Jimmy pursued his work. Occasionally Jimmy would exhale long "Hmmmm", or a "What?", until after about 30 minutes Frank could stand it no longer.

"Jimmy," he said in a tone of utmost strained patience, "got anything for me?"

"I gotta tell ya captain, this is kinda strange. Okay, first I check out S.I.B. in the standard bureau register. No listing. Then I went into the telephone and E-mail directories, still nothing. Finally I tried the encryption key notebook and I do find a mention of S.I.B. special encryption codes, but when I try to pull them up I get a message that just says 'access denied'. Strange!"

"Strange that access is denied?"

"No, strange that I could find the notebook in the first place."

"Is that it?" Frank said with concern.

"No, then I went ahead and established a satellite uplink to the big mainframe computers at H.Q."

"You can do that even in this weather?"

"Yeah sure, it seems to be a little noisy though. I'm having it do a double back-check to be sure we get it all straight. Anyway, I did a gopher on the return E-mail address from the posting we got, and guess what?"

"Just tell me please."

"I got into a file that we're probably not supposed to access, but apparently somebody forgot to restrict it. It describes the organizational structure of the Special Investigations Branch, and, get this, it gives their statement of purpose, as well as the path to their home directory on the UNIX mainframe.

"Okay, I'm all ears."

"Here goes: The members of the S.I.B. are directed to keep the detailed workings of the branch a top secret. Information regarding the investigation of psychic phenomena and other paranormal activities that have national security implications is too sensitive for the general public, or even bureau officers not specifically indoctrinated into the S.I.B. Every effort shall be made to use only S.I.B. personnel in an operation. If outside agents are called in they must be told as little as possible about the purposes of the operations they are assisting in. Extremely limited explanations of S.I.B. purposes will be given to outside agents."

Both occupants of the vehicle were silent for a while, Jimmy punched a few more keys, then suddenly gave out a "Whoa!"

"What's wrong? You're not kidding around about that stuff are you?"

"No sir, I just read the screen aloud, but that's not all, I lost my uplink connection suddenly just a few seconds ago."

"Is that unusual?"

"Well, not really, but I was just trying to access the S.I.B. home directory, and pulled up a list of names of members of the S.I.B. when it seems the system crashed. It could be a coincidence of course, but it seemed the timing was awfully good. Personally, I think somebody caught me snooping and pulled the plug."

Frank gave a long tired sigh. It looked like this one might be more 'interesting' than he had really bargained for. "Did you get any names before it crashed?"

"Just, the first one on the list."

"Well?"

"S.I.B. Chief of Operations: Leonard G. Howarth."

"Howarth?, are you sure?"

"Yeah, just got the one, but I'm pretty sure about it. Why, you know him?"

"Yeah, I know him," was all Frank said, but Jimmy could tell by the tone of his voice and the set of his mouth that now was not the time to press for further details.

"Okay Jimmy, now we have some idea who called us out, maybe that will help us make sense of the assignment, read that out to me again will you please?"

Jimmy unfolded the thin sheet and read out loud:

****

18 Jan. 2017   24:47:09 EST
From: F.B.I. Regional Headquarters, Washington D.C.
Special Investigations Branch
To: Office Agent in Charge, Marquette Michigan.
Code 1, most urgent.

Proceed at once to Houghton station. Link with Houghton area agent Samuels if possible.

PRIMARY OBJECTIVE: Acquire individuals for questioning:
1----   Anthony (Digger) Puttonen, 34
2----   Arne Harjaala, 95 (?)

SECONDARY OBJECTIVE: Keep primary objectives and all activities Top Secret. All communications to be encrypted code 1. No open telecommunications will be used except in life-and-death emergencies.

Two agents from S.I.B. central will arrive A.S.A.P. to take over investigation. Hold individuals in safe custody until arrival.

Recognition code: 'Wednesday morning, 3 A.M.'

****

Jimmy stopped reading.

"That's it huh?" asked Frank.

"'fraid so."

"Okay Jimmy, let your magic fingers do their stuff and tell me everything you can find out about the two individuals we're supposed to pick up. Two Finns by the sound of their names, Puttonen and Harjaala."

"Yes sir."

For some time the only sounds were the muffled rumble of the engine, the swish of the wipers every few seconds brushing the dry snow from the windshield, and the click-clack of the keys as Jimmy Canaris worked to find out more about the subjects of the investigation. They moved steadily Northwest at 35 to 45 kilometers per hour through heavily falling snow. The reading of outside temperature held steady at just below minus twenty degrees Celsius. Frank kept the headlights on low to keep from blinding himself by lighting up the swirling haze of airborne flakes. For some time they encountered no other vehicles on the road.

If Frank and Jimmy had bothered to tune in to a local weather channel, they might have discovered that the biggest winter storm of the century was churning towards them from Canada, picking up moisture as it moved across the comparatively warm waters of Lake Superior. Accumulations by morning in the Keweenaw area were expected to be in the meter-or-more range, with fifty kilometer per hour winds and drifts to three meters or more in places. Still, in blissful unawareness, the hummer moved confidently north, disappearing quickly into the night.

CHAPTER 6

Back in the computer lab at Sherman industries Steve Sanders walked in and slumped into his swivel chair in front of a large and complex computer terminal. A face peeped over the sound insulating panel separating his cubicle from the one next door. A shock of curly red hair drooped over the green eyes and freckled face of Eileen Donovan.

"So how'd it go Steve? What kind of mood is he in today?"

"Oh, not too bad I'd say. He seemed to think I'd done the right thing by bringing this Midnight Mining Company affair to his attention, says he'll take care of it personally from here on."

"Oh really?"

"Yeah, except he wants a briefing at 7:00 A.M. on anything new that comes up." Steve logged into the E-mail program, and began typing the coded message to Jameson as Sherman had directed.

"What's that mean, another all-nighter?" asked Eileen when he paused.

"Well, depends on what comes up I guess."

"Anything coming up now?"

Steve looked at her with an amused grin. "Ah, and what do you mean, Eileen my dear?" Steve checked over the message a second time, then hit the "send" key.

Eileen wiggled her eyebrows at him. "Well, if you're not too busy," she said, "there are certain advantages to having a high security computer room and being able to lock it."

"Oh, I see."

"Just what the blind man said... but he didn't see at all."

Steve left his cubicle and went around the corner to Eileen's work station. She gave him an impish smile, took his hand and led him into a storage room that they used every once in a while for "conjugal visits" when the work load got too tough for them to make it home for the evening.

Steve and Eileen had met here in the computer lab two years earlier, fallen deeply in love, and had moved in together just six months later. The work at Sherman industries was really quite exciting, they had all the best and latest equipment and software to work with, and were given a great deal of freedom in accomplishing their set goals. Mostly they juggled figures in the stock market, always seeking companies who were overextended and vulnerable to hostile takeover or buyout. The programs Steve and Eileen had written to project future performance of firms based on numerous input variables had been instrumental in allowing Sherman to identify these companies in a timely manner.

Both Steve and Eileen were among the best in their fields, combination software programmers and hardware technicians that could make any conceivable computer system sing. The unusual fact about them as a couple was that there was no personal conflict about work. Unlike many couples who share a job description, they were able to function productively together without friction, and still maintain a stable romantic relationship.

Lately they had begun to have discussions about the work they were doing. Neither had ever been particularly politically motivated or astute, being more inclined to pursue their studies and interests to distraction. Still, there had been nagging hints dropped from time to time in the company, and they had both begun to suspect that perhaps Sherman Industries was not the nice, respectable, socially conscious firm they had been led to believe in. Recently they had been forced to accept the possibility that people were even intentionally hurt from time to time. Still... a bird in the hand, as they say... it was a pretty good job, and they could scarcely complain about the pay.

As the door closed to the storeroom, the words "message sent" flashed briefly at the bottom of Steve's monitor. The computer lab became very quiet, the newer optical CPUs did not require cooling fans as the old electronic devices had. The "big" mainframe sat in a cabinet mounted on one wall, about the size of a small microwave oven, silently displaying its operations on a small screen. Once in a while a soft "whoosh" would signal that the room's ventilation system had activated. After a while some soft moans could have been heard... had anyone been present to hear them... coming from behind the storeroom door. A soft beeping sound came from Steve's terminal, unheard by Steve and Eileen, lost in each other's arms. The beeping stopped after a while and words began to slide across the screen.

"Incoming coded message, urgent, urgent, urgent, urgent." In the upper right corner a time code changed from 01:59:59 to 02:00:00.

The sounds from the storeroom began to increase in intensity as the words continued to silently glide across the screen:

A Superior State of Affairs

"Urgent, urgent, urgent, urgent............................"

CHAPTER 7

The office of the FBI's Special Investigations Branch in Washington D.C. was just a little chilly, budget austerity measures instituted after the big shakeup required keeping the thermostat just below the comfort zone in winter. A thin coating of dry snow could be seen covering the ledge outside the fourth floor window. Leonard Howarth bunched his bushy eyebrows and glared at his secretary. "What do you mean I can't get a flight into Houghton OR Marquette? This is an emergency Sandy, I HAVE to get there tonight!"

"Sorry sir, the airports are closed due to a severe winter storm, I could try to find a flight to another airport in the region and arrange ground transport if you like?"

"SHIT!" Leonard exploded with legendary temper. He made a theatrical attempt to calm himself by wiping his dry forehead with a handkerchief. "Yes, okay, go ahead, dammit!" He stomped off to his glass walled office, then stuck his head back out and said, "And get Halbrook in here on the double will you please Sandy?"

For a moment Leonard Howarth hung his head wearily. He no longer felt like an important Federation agent in charge of a critical investigation. He was just "Lenny" again, with things going wrong as usual. He rubbed his eyes and thought about the phone call. This could be the big one, it could make or break his career, he HAD to get up there to handle it himself.

"Yeah chief?" Said another agent poking his head in the door. Harry Halbrook was pushing 40 himself, with a bit of a gut to show for it and a bald spot to match, but he still moved like a youngster.

"Get in here Harry, we got problems."

"What's up?"

"The airports are closed up in U.P. Michigan due to a severe winter storm. We can't get there tonight, no way. Sandy is working on getting us up there by another route, but that will take more time, which we haven't got."

Harry came in and sat in a faux leather covered armchair in the corner of the immaculate office, but said nothing. He knew his boss well enough that he didn't need to prompt his thoughts. Leonard rubbed his temples and glanced at the clock on the wall. It was just 3:00 A.M. and they were getting nowhere.

"Okay Harry, you sent the E-mail to the Marquette station right?"

"Yes sir, and the Houghton station guys are still out looking for the subjects, they're saying they can't understand how they could have slipped away."

"Well, they're not used to dealing with these kind of people either. Okay, who have we got up there? We may have to work more closely with them than I'd hoped."

Harry poked some keys on an electronic notebook he was carrying. "Okay boss, looks like the Station Chief up in Houghton is a newer guy, Bob Samuels, never heard of him. Looks like they brought him in from Montana and North Dakota. The Marquette chief is an older guy named Frank Giacoletti, seems like I've heard the name somewhere before."

"What?"

"Something wrong?"

"Did you say Frank Giacoletti?"

"Yeah, what's the matter?"

"SHIT! Oh lord please, anybody but Frank!" Leonard hung his head again wearily and slammed his fist down on the desk.

"What's wrong sir?"

"It's a long story, suffice it to say that the last time I worked with Frank it was a disaster. He was my best friend for years, and then there was this thing over in Detroit when we were both stationed there. Damn, I never thought I'd see him again after I landed this S.I.B. gig."

"Are you saying we'll have trouble getting cooperation?"

"Cooperation? If that's our only problem then we're on easy street boy. No, I'm afraid it's much worse than that, it's personal."

"Personal?"

"Look, I don't want to go into it right now okay? We've got the two most important subjects this branch has ever followed. Both have just gone into critical phase, and they've apparently linked up. Can this be a coincidence? I don't think so! I think this is the big break we've been looking for, this is the one that will put Special Investigations, on the map and make those fools upstairs in Mexico City sit up and take notice!" Leonard slammed his fist on the desk for emphasis.

"Sir, I guess I don't quite understand why you think it's so important. We've got one guy who seems to remember stuff from before he was born, and another guy who has a sixth sense about finding things. So they get together.. so what?"

"Look Harry, trust me okay? You're pretty new here and this is an unusual branch of the bureau. We do things a little different here. The director has been trying to get us shut down for over a year, but somebody high up is plugging for us, I don't know who. We've had just enough moderate successes to keep our doors open, but it's been tough. You're the first new guy we've had in five years. I've got a feeling about this one, when two of these psi talents team up, there's no telling what might happen. We need to get our butts up there A.S.A.P. before those other idiots muck it up. We don't want the subjects to completely disappear off the face of the earth, believe me, it's happened before."

Sandy poked her head in the door.

"Sir, I have some travel information for you."

"Shoot."

"Bang!"

Leonard looked up at her incredulously. She just beamed a big smile at him.

"What?" he asked with a perplexed expression.

"You said "shoot", so I said "Bang", just thought the situation could use a little humor."

Leonard laughed and shook his head. "Okay, touch, Sandy. What's the scoop on flights to the U.P?"

"Well, looks like Green Bay and Duluth are both snowed in too, but if you hurry you can catch the redeye for Minneapolis, then borrow a four by four from our station there and drive on up."

"How long a drive is that?"

"Oh, about five hundred kilometers."

"Okay, not bad, puts us a day behind, but it's better than nothing. Let's do it. When's the plane leave?"

"3:55 A.M. today sir. If you get out the door in ten minutes we can get you on it with no problem."

"Okay Harry, grab your stuff, let's roll." Leonard got up from his chair and with a spring in his step picked up two black nylon duffel bags and headed for the door. Harry disappeared for a few moments, then appeared with two more.

"How's that Sandy, fast enough?"

Sandy looked surprised at the quickness with which they'd gotten ready to leave, but just shrugged and called downstairs for a car to be brought around to the front door. It was only a fifteen minute drive to Dulles intercontinental airport, they'd have plenty of time to get there. Sandy shook her head with amusement as she watched them go. They were almost like children the way they'd chase around after butterflies. She made sure the car had left, then went back to her desk and calmly picked up the phone, dialed a number, and spoke for about twenty seconds before hanging up.

She leaned back in her chair for a few moments and let out a deep sigh. A passing thought made her stop and give a prayer that she'd done the right thing. She hoped the phone call had not put them in any danger. Still, you've got to go with your roots sometimes. She clutched a rosary to her breast and sent out another prayer for Harry and Leonard's safety, then picked up her purse and walked to the door. She turned and looked around a little wistfully before locking it and turning away.. If they ever found out what she'd done, she'd probably never see the place again.

CHAPTER 8

Frank Giacoletti and Jimmy Canaris had been on the road for over an hour now, making slow but steady progress in the deepening snow. They had passed the towns of Negaunee and Ishpeming, and U.S. Highway 41 had reverted to a two lane road. The snow continued to fall heavily, Frank was steering mostly by the metal poles along the side of the road. He glanced over at Jimmy who had been pounding the computer keyboard furiously for some time, and had finally paused, staring at the monitor screen.

"Okay cap'n, I've got some information for you on the subjects."

"Alright! Tell me about this Digger guy."

"Anthony Michael Puttonen, nickname Digger. Born in Hancock Michigan, September first, 1982. No criminal record. Let's see, there's a couple of moving violations, and his name is mentioned in some investigations of breaking and entering on mining company property while he was a teenager. His family has lived here for decades, his father is of Finnish descent and his mother from an Italian family."

"Haven't you got anything else? I want to get a feel for the guy. What's he do for a living, any hobbies?"

"Okay, hang on a second. He's listed in 'WHO'S WHO IN AMERICAN HIGH SCHOOLS' for his senior year back in two thousand. He was a four point student, Science Club president, National Merit scholar, and got a full ride academic scholarship to Michigan Tech on a fellowship. Seems to have no interest in sports at all... no wait... he was a member of the cross country ski team for a year."

"So he's something of a nerd eh?" said Frank. "What else? You got anything more current?"

"Yeah, I did a search of the business sections of a couple of local papers and came up with some stuff, including an in depth interview a couple years ago."

"Good, what's the gist of it?"

"Well, looks like he was a star student at Tech, majoring in Geology with an minor in Mining Engineering. He got his B.S. in '05, M.S. at the University of Colorado in '07, and started work on a Ph.D. at Vancouver right away. His dissertation research focused on techniques of resource recovery from old abandoned mines. In '09 he came back to Michigan Tech for post-doc work, then formed a small company in conjunction with three other graduate students, and called it Midnight Mining Company."

"Okay, I've heard of that, they're using some kind of robots to work the old mines or something?"

"Right, together with these other guys he invented some semiautonomous robots that could seek out and excavate copper from flooded and abandoned mines. Between them they've got fourteen patents, with seven more pending. In this article he talks about one in particular, a device they're calling a Spelioscope. It's a contraption that you can use on the surface or underground to investigate the structure and nature of the nearby rock. You take this acoustic clay and stick two sensors on the rock at least two feet apart, then put a pair of special goggles on. The sensors pump various frequencies of ultrasonic sound into the rock, then pick up the echoes, and with a powerful minicomputer the result is displayed in the goggles as a full perspective view, as if you're looking right into the rock. Let's see, there's a geophysics professor making a statement that this is one of the most powerful geophysics tools ever developed. Digger says that it could never have happened without the cooperation of all these people from different technical disciplines, and they wind it up saying that orders for the things are coming in already, even though it's still in the development phase. Negotiations are underway with manufacturers to build and market them."

"Is that all? The guy's an inventor. What's that got to do with us? Can you find out anything else?"

"Okay here we go, here's an article in the Wall Street Journal about it. It says that this little company is one hot property on the stock market, but that this Digger guy and his partner James Dolittle personally own the majority block. There have been rumors of a power struggle within the company, and several hostile takeover attempts."

"I still don't get it. What does any of this have to do with the S.I.B.? They're supposedly involved in paranormal activities. This sounds like business as usual."

"Well cap'n, there is one little mention in this other article quoting Puttonen as saying that he got his nickname because of a "talent" for finding things. He goes on to admit, under questioning, that he's had E.S.P. researchers do tests on him, then he won't say anything about the results."

"Hmmm, okay what about this older guy?"

"Arne Harjaala, no middle name listed, claims his birthday is April 17, 1882. Age, 95, with a "question" mark"

"What?"

"Yeah, this is really weird. We've got an agency file on him from the forties, and I also pulled up a local paper from 1944 that mentions his name. It's an uncommon name, so I also ran a search of military records and telephone subscriber listings."

"So.... what's the deal?"

"Well, I don't know what to tell ya. There definitely was an "Arne Harjaala" born in Calumet in 1882, we've got a military record during the Spanish American War, and a photograph. Then he comes back to the U.P., gets married, and works in the Quincy mine until 1906, when he's listed as 'missing, presumed dead' in a mine accident."

"So... it can't be the same guy then."

"But check this out, from the January 20th, 1944 local paper. 'MAN FOUND ALIVE IN QUINCY MINE AFTER 38 YEARS'. Apparently he just showed up at the elevator on the 54th level of the number two shaft, half starved with a big gash on his leg. They took him up and handed him over to the Sheriff, charging him with trespassing. The Sheriff makes a statement that the guy is very disoriented and telling some kind of a wild story. Here's a photo of the guy in the paper, and... whoa... it's got to be the same guy cap'n! Here's the picture of him in military uniform in 1898, and here's the one from the paper in '44. It's the same guy."

"How can that be? Did he just fall asleep all that time or what?"

"I don't know, but it might be the reason that the S.I.B. is interested."

After a pause Frank nodded. "Yeah, I think you're right. Okay, what have you got on him since then?"

"Not much, the agency opened a file after some local threatened to kill him. He apparently had a mild stroke when he approached this lady who he said was his wife. She took one look at him, said he was the devil and came after him with a knife. According to this file he's been in and out of several mental health clinics, diagnosed as borderline schizophrenic and sporadically catatonic, and now lives in an apartment in Houghton on a stipend from the S.I.B. There's nothing in this file more recent than five years old, which happens to correspond with the formation of the S.I.B."

"Special Investigations is supporting him?"

"Apparently so."

Frank mused a while. "So... ol' Lenny Howarth is involved in this eh? Something weird is going on here. I don't like it when one branch of the agency tries to keep stuff secret from everybody else, and I especially don't like the fact that Lenny is in charge of it. We may have a more interesting ride ahead of us than I thought!"

They passed the Lake Michigamme State Park sign. While the frozen surface of the lake could not be seen in the darkness, the steep hills around it could be sensed by a deeper looming darkness and the way the wind shifted, making the snow seem to swirl and eddy in the headlights. They drove for the most part in silence, drinking coffee, eating donuts, exchanging occasional small talk, and trying to keep each other awake as they moved forward through the hypnotically illuminated veil of falling snow.

Finally they reached the intersection of Michigan State highway 28, the traditional halfway point between the two major cities of the Upper Peninsula. Now the highway turned almost due north, directly into the wind, which increasingly seemed to buffet the car. The snow drifts seemed to grow larger as they continued, and Frank was forced on several occasions to gun the motor to make it through.

"Hey Jimmy, how about finding us a radio station eh? Maybe a little music, and hopefully a weather forecast. Seems like it's getting rougher out here, I barely made it through that last drift."

"Sure thing, let's see what we can get."

Jimmy clicked on the F.M. radio set, and set it to "seek" a station powerful enough to give a clear signal. He skipped over a couple of stations loudly blaring the currently popular "techno-flap" music, then let it settle on one playing some cool jazz.

"That sound okay?" Jimmy asked.

"Yeah sure. Miles Davis isn't it?"

"Sounds like it to me."

They listened to the song for a while, a jazzy brass rendition of "Love Me Do", and then the D.J. came on the air. "Okay all you listeners out there in radioland! This is Johnny Thomas coming to you with a little Miles Davis on WGGL F.M. It's tomorrow already, The time is 3:45 A.M. Thursday January 19, and for those of you who have trouble remembering when you write a check, the year is 2017. I hope that anybody out there listening is snug at home in bed, 'cause I'm here to tell ya man, it's NASTY out there. The Federational Weather service has issued a severe winter storm warning for the areas surrounding Lake Superior from Thunder Bay to Saint Ignace. High winds, cold temperatures, and heavy snow are combining to make an extremely dangerous situation. All schools are closed in the entire U.P., and even Michigan Tech, which has only closed school for weather six times since 1956, has called off classes for both today and tomorrow. Houghton County snow removal crews are having trouble getting to their equipment, so don't expect the plows to get out by their usual times. We suggest that everybody just stay home and stay warm today, unless it's an absolute emergency. Have some hot cocoa, cuddle up with a friend, and stay tuned for further updates. Some hot news... The Michigan State Police has issued an emergency measure allowing anyone saying 'Cold enough for ya?' to be legally pummeled to death with a frozen spaghetti noodle. Also... and this is for real... astronomers in Australia have reported unusual and intense solar activity. If it continues they predict some spectacular auroral displays and possible disruption of communications. And now, how about a number from the classical period, Herbie Mann playing "Theme from Cries and Whispers" from his 1972 Turtle Bay album. This is the morning Jazz show on WGGL F.M. from Michigan Technological University in Houghton Michigan. Tomorrow is today at M.T.U.!"

The gentle tones of the flute began to filter through the vehicle as the two sat in silence for several minutes. They were still making headway, but more slowly now, in a lower gear, churning through the snow rather than gliding over it. There were several drifts that Frank was able to force the hummer through only with fairly desperate measures. Finally Frank broke the quiet. "Man, I hope we didn't make a big mistake coming out here tonight!"

"Yeah." Jimmy answered seriously.

"I'm starting to think about calling the guys in Houghton to let them know where we are in case we get stuck."

"The orders said..."

"Look, I KNOW what the orders said Jimmy. They said no open telecommunications except in an emergency. If we get stuck out here in this blizzard it will damn well be an emergency don't you think?"

"Yes sir, but we still don't know how sensitive an investigation this is. The way the orders were coded is an indication that the situation is perhaps more critical than we suspect. If continental security concerns are involved..."

"Okay look, we'll just let them know we're on the road. We won't say anything about the investigation on the air okay? It's just a routine check-in if anybody's listening, all right?"

"Well, H.Q. might see it differently. It's your call of course captain, but we could wait a while yet, see how it goes out here, and still make the call later."

Frank sighed. "Yeah, okay. Let's see if we make it to L'Anse, then we can decide. I'm afraid now that if we even stop we'll never get going again. The snow out here looks like it's well over half a meter deep. Look at that, we're kicking snow up with the bumper almost constantly now, not just in the drifts like before."

Jimmy stared out the windshield in wonder, the wipers now barely able to keep it clear. "Man I've never seen it snow like this, does this happen often around here?"

"Are you kidding? No, this is a big one, even for this area. I remember one big blizzard when I was a kid, but it was nothing like this. If there hadn't been plows down this road a few hours ago we would be getting nowhere. This is probably a fifty or hundred year storm, something like that.... SHIT!" There was a loud thud. Frank slammed on the brakes and skidded a short distance, then the hummer tilted sharply to the right and came to a stop.

"What the hell was that?" Frank cursed. "SHIT! This is all we need."

Jimmy tried to push his door open, but found it blocked by deep snow. He rolled down the window leaned out for a look. Blowing snow and freezing air flooded in through the open window.

"There's something out there, I can hear something, sounds like an animal."

"What?"

"Yeah, a deer maybe, I think we hit a deer and then slid off the road into the ditch, how is it on your side?"

Frank tried his door, and found that it could be opened without too much trouble. He closed it again.

"Okay, close your window, let's get into our boots and snowsuits and see if we can get out of this mess."

The WGGL diskjockey was just coming back on. Frank clicked off the radio before he could start talking about the snow again, and then turned off the motor. A sudden eerie silence seemed to fill the vehicle, followed by the whistling of the snow-laden wind through the open window. Jimmy rolled the window back up, then asked sheepishly, "Want to make that call now captain?"

Frank gave a long sigh, then nodded. "Yeah, I guess we'd better. Who's supposed to be on duty, that Samuels guy?"

"He's the station chief, yeah."

"Okay, try to raise him on the phone, let me do the talking."

Jimmy picked up the handset of the cellular telephone, punched in a digital code that supposedly encoded for a secure channel, though everyone knew that there was virtually no such thing anymore. He punched in another number to ring the Houghton FBI station. A squawking noise emanated from the speaker, followed by, "Yeah? Who is this?"

"Giacoletti, Marquette office, calling Samuels."

"You got him, what you up to?"

"We're on our way up 41 to your district."

(a pause) "Tonight? Are you crazy? What the hell for?"

"Let's just say we got a code 1 okay?"

"Oh, yeah, okay... you got one of those too eh? I thought we were the only ones. Hmmm. So, where are you now?"

A Superior State of Affairs

"We're just a few miles south of L'Anse, looks like we hit a deer and are off the road in a snowbank. We're going to try to dig our way out, but thought we'd check in with you, let you know we're on the way."

"You hit a deer? What the hell was a deer doing out in this blizzard? They usually bed down in foul weather."

"Christ Samuels! How the hell do I know? I'm no expert on the sleeping habits of wild ruminants. All I know is we hit it and now we're stuck with two wheels off the roadbed until we dig out of this."

"Well don't you dare waste it."

"What?"

"You just gut out that deer and bring it with you, that'll be some pretty good eating later."

Frank was astonished. "Look Samuels, we're stuck out here in a goddamn blizzard in the middle of fucking nowhere and you want me to bring you a road kill deer? And you're asking me if I'm insane?"

"I, just don't like to waste food is all, save me the liver. Say, is there anything else I can do for you?"

"Yeah, have some hot coffee ready for us, we hope to be up there in a couple of hours, say, 6:30."

Frank looked over at Jimmy, who raised his eyebrows and shrugged.

"Well, maybe more like seven o'clock. Make a reservation at the Copper Crown would you? We're going to be bushed by the time we get there."

"Will do. Stay warm guys, see you soon. Out."

"Yeah, 'bye."

Frank sighed heavily again then, looked over at Jimmy and said, "Well, let's see what we can do."

"Okay cap'n. I'm coming out your side." Frank got the door open and climbed out onto the road, Jimmy scrambled across the hump and followed him, switching on the headlights as he came. They walked around to the front and saw the deer, a young buck, probably two years old, lying in the snow, struggling feebly to get up, eyes wide with terror. Jimmy got close enough for a good look. "Broken femur sir, probably the hip too by the look of it. No way he'll make it. Shall I.......?"

"Yeah, I guess so, go ahead."

Jimmy drew a compact automatic handgun from a shoulder holster inside his coat, and walked around behind the deer. He drew back the slide to load a 10mm round into the chamber, then released it with a sharp "snick" sound. Holding the weapon pointing straight up, he thumbed off the safety and crouched in the snow as close as he dared to the struggling animal, out of reach of the flailing hooves, then took careful aim. He waited there for over a minute, until the young buck ceased it's struggle for a moment, then there was a loud "pop" sound, amazingly muffled by the falling snow. The animal jerked momentarily, and then lay still, mercifully killed by a single bullet in the back of the neck. Frank was impressed.

"Cleanly done." He told Jimmy.

"Thanks. You want me to clean it?"

"You've got to be kidding, can't we just leave it?"

"And waste all that meat? What about what Samuels said? There must be at least thirty kilos of prime venison here."

"To hell with Samuels! Look Jimmy, we haven't got time, we've got to get dug out of here."

"Five minutes tops, I promise. If you'll get those collapsible snow shovels out of the back and put them together, I'll have this done by the time we're ready to start digging."

Frank shook his head and looked out into the gloom and wind. He chuckled to himself, then said to Jimmy.

"Okay son, whatever you want, just don't get your fingers frostbitten though."

With a cheerful "Yes sir captain!" and an exaggerated French style, palm outward salute. Jimmy got to work on the deer in front of the car while Frank went to the back to get out the shovels Jimmy had packed. Pulling a four inch blade handmade knife from a pouch sheath on his belt, Jimmy expertly opened the carcass and removed the entrails, throwing all but the heart and liver to the side of the road. The two saved organs he placed back inside the body cavity. True to his word, by the time Frank came around to the front with the two shovels, Jimmy had the deer ready to throw up onto the roof of the hummer. Frank helped him heave it up, the body still limp but stiffening quickly in the cold. It seemed to lay so securely in the bed of snow that had accumulated on the roof that they didn't even bother to tie it down. The tie down rails would probably keep it from sliding off. Jimmy used a splash from the coffee thermos to clean his hands, and wiped the knife off with a rag. He then resheathed his knife, dried his hands on his shirt, and put his gloves back on.

They set to the task of digging out the front of the vehicle first, where it had plowed deeply into the heavy snowbank. They worked silently and steadily at an easy pace, with the front part of their snowsuits zipped partly open in front to avoid becoming overheated and sweaty. The left hand tires were still on the road level, while the ones on the right side had apparently slumped off into the ditch beneath the snowbank. The trickiest part of the operation would be getting the right hand tires out of the ditch and back up onto the roadbed. The winch was virtually useless to them, there were no trees or usable anchors within range that would give an appropriate vector of pull. Jimmy took a handsaw and headlamp and disappeared into the woods for a few minutes, returning with an armload of cedar branches and twigs. After several more trips back he had a sufficient quantity to line the crude ramp they had excavated so that the knobby tires of the hummer would have some traction up the steep side of the ditch. Both men were familiar with getting out of such predicaments, and both knew that it was better to take a little extra time and be certain of success rather than do a mediocre job and risk getting stuck even worse. They meticulously cleared the path in front of the right rear wheel, trying to force it to stay in line with the front, forward about ten feet, then up the bank at a gentle angle and back onto the road.

Finally they were both satisfied with the preparations. Frank started up the motor again, got the heater cranking, and loaded the snow shovels into the back, without bothering to dismantle them. The effort had kept them warm, though fingers and toes had inevitably gotten chilled. He had Jimmy brush the snow off before he got back into the now warming vehicle.

"Time check," said Frank, through the open driver's side window.

Jimmy pulled up his sleeve and looked at his watch. "Looks like it's about quarter to six captain. We spent almost two hours out there."

"Could be worse, let's just hope this works!" Frank pulled out the thermos of coffee, offering it to Jimmy standing outside.

"No thanks, go ahead, finish her off."

With a nod of thanks Frank tipped up the thermos and drained the last few tepid sips of grainy coffee. He gunned up the motor just to be sure he had the power available, waited for the speed to drop back to idle, then eased the transmission lever into first gear. Jimmy took up a position in back of the vehicle to help push. The automatic transmission gave a little start as it engaged, then the car started moving forward slowly. Frank gave it more gas and urged it gently up the ramp. The right front wheel came up onto the road, then the back fishtailed out, sliding off the carefully built ramp. Jimmy fell on his knees, then scrambled up and pushed with all his strength. Frank fiercely resisted the urge to step on the gas, he knew better than that. He turned the wheel to the left and hoped the front wheels could pull her on out. At the last moment, when it seemed they'd lost all headway, the back popped up with a lurch and they had all four wheels on the road again.

Jimmy ran up and jumped in on the passenger side, zipping his suit open as he closed the door. They gave each other the "high five" and breathed a big sigh of relief. They were still miles from their goal, but at least they were back on the road, even if they were sideways. Frank did some careful back and fill and got pointing back in the right direction again. He carefully eased the gearshift into second and allowed the powerful motor to do the work of chugging through the heavy resistance of the snow.

As they had been digging, the wind had lessened somewhat, the cold seemed slightly less intense, but the snow continued to fall relentlessly. The darkness around them seemed to press tightly against the window, the snow flakes pelting the windshield constantly forming themselves into the shapes of ghostly faces peering jealously into their warm refuge. Both men were much more comfortable now with the steady throbbing of the motor keeping the whispering of the wind at bay. They proceeded north, and after a few klicks they came to an area where the lights along the road became more frequent, and finally they pulled into the village of L'Anse nestled at the foot of Keweenaw Bay. With great relief they saw ahead the familiar red and blue sign of an open HOLIDAY gas station. This chain of convenience stores is ubiquitous throughout the North Country. Filling the niche of the old general stores, they have become the late night hangouts for generations of teenagers in remote snowbound towns, and tonight was no different.

Frank pulled the hummer into the parking lot, alongside three other cars that looked, from the accumulated snow, as though they'd been there awhile. To the other side were parked nine snowmobiles in a neat row. They weren't particularly low on fuel, but after their excitement they just wanted to get out of the wind and cold for a while. About a dozen teens were hanging around the tables inside sipping soft drinks or hot cocoa, playing video games, and listening to music on the juke box. Everybody in the place looked up in surprise as they came in. One young man wearing a black leather jacket, of Native American blood by the look of him, came up to Jimmy.

"Hey man, you're not from around here."
"Nope." Replied Jimmy.
"You just came up the highway then?"
"Yep."
He turned to the others and said in a loud voice.
"Holy shit youse guys, they just come up the highway."

Turning back to Jimmy he was about to ask more questions when the proprietor of the store, an older fellow, came around from behind the counter and said to the young Indian, "That's enough for now mister Yellow Knife, let these poor guys warm up a bit okay?" Jamey shrugged and went back to sit with his friends, who continued to be most interested in the newcomers. "Sorry about that fellas, these kids don't have much to do even on the best days, and you're the first people up the highway since about six o'clock last night, so naturally we wonder how it is out there. Must be something pretty important to get you out traveling on a night like this eh?"

Frank had a bad feeling about this. Perhaps it would have been better not to have stopped. He had not anticipated the very action of driving up tonight as drawing so much attention. "Oh, not really, we're just stupid I guess, started heading up without checking the weather report, just figured it would have to stop snowing sometime you know."

A Superior State of Affairs

The proprietor gave him a curious look, and glanced back and forth from Frank to Jimmy. Then shrugged his shoulders. "Well then, what can I do for youse?"

Suddenly Jamey shouted out, "Hey mister Dobbs look, they got a deer on the top o' da car out dere."

All the kids peered out the window, steaming up the glass worse than before, and Dobbs, the proprietor, craned his neck to see. Jamey dashed out for a few seconds to examine it, then came back in and said, "Looks like a spike buck, smashed hip. What'd you do, hit it on the road?"

Jimmy fielded the question this time. "Yeah, it was an accident. We hit it and swerved into the ditch, took us about two hours to dig out of it. Thought we'd go ahead and bring the deer with us."

"Where was that?"

"Oh, twelve or fifteen klicks back down the road I guess."

"Was it dead when you hit it?" Asked Jamey curiously.

"No, like you said, broken leg and hip. There was no way it could have survived, so I shot it in the neck."

"Oh yeah? What'd you shoot it with?"

Jimmy hesitated. Frank walked over to them from the counter. "Why so curious son?"

"Oh no big deal, just that you probably hit it while crossing the Ojibway reservation. My tribe has exclusive hunting rights on that land, and my old man is one of the tribal elders. So, I think I got a right to ask what you shot it with."

Jimmy looked at Frank, who nodded. Jimmy pulled open the front of his snowsuit to reveal the butt of the handgun nestled in its shoulder rig, then he took a thin flat wallet out of his shirt pocket and flipped it open. It was a badge, complete with the now-famous holographic flying eagle, impossible to counterfeit.

"Feds eh?" said Jamey, "carrying a concealed Smith and Wesson compact 10mm automatic. Kinda makes ya wonder doesn't it?"

"You seem very knowledgeable," said Frank grudgingly.

"Well, I know my way around I guess. The thing is, what do I tell my dad? 'Hey dad, by the way, two feds came in the middle of the night in the snowstorm and poached a deer off the reservation.'? Boy he wouldn't like that! That kinda stuff drives him berserk. He'd probably have his congressman pounding the door of the F.B.I. director down in Mexico City by this afternoon."

Dobbs broke in then. "Look, Yellow Knife, there's no reason to stir up trouble with the tribe, not now, not with everything that's been going on."

"Don't worry mister Dobbs, there's no trouble. This is just something that I have to report to the elders about. I'm just trying to figure out what to tell 'em."

Frank looked like he was getting a little angry and was about to speak, when Jimmy put up his hand and cut him off. "Look, Mister Yellow Knife, it was just an accident. We didn't intend to kill the deer, it just happened that way. Rather than leave the meat to the coyotes, we threw it on top of the car. We really had no particular idea in mind except that we didn't want to see it wasted. Now how about this? What if we give it to you, as a representative of the Ojibway tribe. You can bring it to your elders to do with as they see fit, and please extend our apologies for the loss to the herd."

Jamey Yellow Knife broke into a huge grin and stuck out his hand to exchange a "low five" with Jimmy. "Deal. Hey, you're okay for a white guy. You sure it's alright with him?" He said, gesturing with his thumb towards Frank, who still looked a little bewildered.

"Yeah don't worry, it's okay."

"Cool, hey, can I buy you guys something, hot coffee or somethin'?"

"Yeah sure," said Jimmy. "What're you having Captain?"

"Oh, coffee I guess."

Jimmy nodded in agreement and The young Ojibway called out, "Three coffees mister Dobbs, larges, it's going to be a long night."

"It already has been," muttered the proprietor as he turned to fill the order. The three sat together at the table nearest the door. The other kids made no pretense of returning to their earlier conversations, all attention was on the booth. Frank decided to open the conversation to try to steer it away from themselves. He was already feeling very unsure about whether they had already compromised the security of the operation, whatever it was.

"So, your dad's a tribal elder you said?"

"Yep, named me Yellow Knife of all things, but most people just call me Jamey. Supposedly I'm being groomed to be a tribal leader, that's what they say anyway. I don't know about that, but I do like to keep my eyes open, and I see things that are going on, sometimes things that others don't see."

Frank put one elbow on the table and looked at Jamey. "So, what are you kids doing out at this time of the night, shouldn't you be at home?"

The kids all laughed at this. Jamey just pointed outside, "Snow day man, no school for the rest of this week. Actually we just ended up here. A couple of my friends came in to town earlier, then worried they might not make it home, so we came in with the snowmobiles to pick 'em up. But heck, it's a lot more fun hanging out here than back at home, and besides, old Dobbs would have been lonely."

Jamey said that as Mr. Dobbs approached with a tray of coffees, and three donuts as well. He smiled. "They're good kids sir, really they are. I mean, they look rather rough and all, but there's no trouble around here like they have in some places. When they're here I don't worry about tending the place alone."

"Thanks mister Dobbs, said Jamey pulling the tray to himself and passing out the coffees. Yeah see? We're Straight Edge." He pulled out a chain from beneath his shirt and showed it to Frank, it was quite plain with a simple "X" symbol.

Frank looked perplexed. "What's that?"

Before Jamey could answer Jimmy interrupted him.

"They're Straight Edge captain, that means that they've taken a vow to live an honest life without drugs or alcohol. It's a movement that started back in the nineties as a protest against the drug culture of the baby boomers. It's low key, but very positive in outlook."

Jamey looked at Jimmy again, with increased respect. "Yeah." he said, "You're okay."

Frank sipped his coffee and watched the two younger men. He could see it now in Jamey Yellow Knife as he had seen it earlier in Jimmy Canaris... the potential staring back out at him. At first all he had seen was the tough looking clothing and the wild hair style, but looking into his eyes Frank could see the sharpness. There was none of the dullness there that he was used to seeing in the kids they brought in on drug charges. These kids were on the right track and he had no doubt that this young man would one day be chief of his tribe. For one thing he was extremely good looking, and in this tribe it was the women who held the strongest voting bloc. After a while the other kids became bored with the trio and turned back to other pursuits. Jamey noticed Frank looking at him and queried by raising his eyebrow.

Frank spoke over the rim of his cup, in a low voice. "So, what kinds of things do you see? What's going on around here?"

"Well, I can tell you this, when two Feds come up from Marquette in the middle of a blizzard, something's got to be going on! But besides that... oh, I don't know what I should tell you. There's always something going on with the tribal council, petty political stuff, my old man gets bogged down in that crap pretty heavy sometimes. But then there's the independence movement, the Soopers, you've heard of them I suppose?"

Frank laughed, "Yep, ever since I was a kid they've been talking about that. A pipe dream is all it is, the U.P. could never make it on its own." He spoke the standard line, as he had heard it shoved down his throat a thousand times until he believed it himself.

"Well, if you say so, but I overheard some of the elders talking in the sweatlodge last week, and it seems that some of the Soopers were here asking whether we'd support them if they made the move to secede... like... soon. These guys seem to be taking it pretty seriously. There was also some mention of weird things happening around Houghton and Hancock, I didn't find out what, but the word has been quietly passed around that we should stick pretty close to home for the next couple of weeks."

Frank was dumbfounded, and sat at the table with his jaw dropped half open. Here they were, Federation law officers, with electronic gizmos up the wazoo, a chain of command, and all the advantages of a modern law enforcement organization, coming up the peninsula in response to a top secret coded message from Washington, and they run into some teenagers in a convenience store that seemed to know more about what was going on than they did! He glanced over at Jimmy who raised his eyebrows and shrugged. Jamey just sat there looking at them. His eyes were a deep chocolate brown glinting merrily out from between the strands of his long dark hair. "So, I told you what I know, you gonna play the game and let me in on what's going on?" said Jamey.

"Sorry son, we can't do that, you know, ongoing investigation and all that. I can tell you that your elders have given you some good advice though, it would probably be best to stick pretty close to home for a while."

"You take the deer now." Said Jimmy pulling back his sleeve to look a his watch, "It's after six o'clock already, dawn will be coming in a couple of hours. Maybe you should be getting on home eh? Look, the storm seems to be dying down now."

They looked out through the windows and sure enough, the snow was coming down at about a forty five degree angle now, instead of blowing almost horizontally, and the intensity of the snowfall seemed to be decreasing. Jamey nodded his head, looking at them both, but mostly at Jimmy. He fished a pencil stub out of his jacket pocket and began writing on a paper napkin. "Look guy, I don't know what's going on here, but I can see it's something. If it turns big and it might affect my people, I want you to call me, leave a message. Okay?"

Jimmy was about to laugh at the suddenly serious tone in Jamey's voice, but something held him back, he nodded solemnly and took the napkin, carefully folding it up and zipping it into his front breast jacket pocket. "Will do."

Jamey jumped up suddenly and turned from the two agents. "Let's roll guys," he shouted, and the other kids started getting their cold weather gear on and heading out the door. Jamey and one other grabbed the deer by the legs and slung it over the back of one of the snowmobiles, cinching it down with bungee cords. With a rumble and roar the herd of unmuffled snow machines took off in a cloud of blowing snow and headed back east up the highway towards the Ojibway Reservation.

"You guys want anything else?" Dobbs asked.

"Yeah, how about a place to sleep? Somehow I just don't think we're going to make it to Houghton tonight." Frank answered.

"Well, it's a little rough, but I have a guest room in the house right next door that you could use, there's a shower there, we rent it out in the summer tourist season a lot. You'll have to turn the heater up, we keep it down low while we're not using it, but it warms up quick."

"Sounds great! We'll take it."

"It's seventy five a night."

"No problem."

"Okay, I'll show you the way. You can leave your car right there if you want."

Frank and Jimmy went out and grabbed their bags of personal items, locked up the hummer, then followed Dobbs around the side of the Holiday store up a short shoveled pathway to a cozy looking bungalow, where they were shown their room. It wasn't exactly the Waldorf Astoria, but it was snug and well insulated. Dobbs turned up the heater and left the room with a "Good night" to go back over to his store. Frank and Jimmy, with hardly a word, shucked off their outer clothes, climbed under the thick quilts on the two twin sized beds, and were sound asleep almost instantly. Out side the falling snow seemed to be a little less heavy to Dobbs as he headed back along the path. The wind was a trifle less bitterly cold. He looked out to the road now, and could see that the drifts were still there across the roadway. There would probably be no more business this night, but soon the snow plows might get out, and then he would see a sudden increase in his traffic. He got back to the store and flipped on the TV again, starting the old pirate movie he'd been watching when all the action had started hours ago. He laughed at the characters on the screen, stripped to the waist and dripping with sweat, complaining about the heat. Hard to even imagine with snow swirling at the door! As he settled back into his chair he reached for the phone. He knew somebody that would be very interested to hear about the events of this evening. Very interested indeed!

CHAPTER 9

Steve Sanders groggily awoke on the floor of a large storage closet piled with boxes of computer storage disks and spare hardware, with the corner of a shelving unit digging irritatingly into his back. Eileen lay next to him on the piece of foam rubber sound insulation in a disheveled pile of clothing. He sat upright with a start.

"Holy shit, what time is it?"

"Steve, what's the matter?"

"We fell asleep, what time is it?" Eileen sleepily looked at the watch on her wrist. "Just after six."

"SHIT! I can't believe this, I've got to give Sherman a briefing at 7:00 sharp. Come on, we'd better check out the status board." The pair got up hurriedly and pulled on a few pieces of clothing that had been scattered around on the floor and lower shelves in the storage area. As Steve turned to open the door to the computer lab Eileen grabbed him by the hand and pulled him to her. He smiled and embraced her warmly and indulged in one more long tender kiss. "I love you," he murmured softly, as she nuzzled her head of red hair under his chin and purred, then released him and pushed him gently towards the door.

When he got back to the computer terminals the message was still sliding across the screen. "URGENT, URGENT URGENT...."

"Oh great! "He said. There's an urgent incoming message waiting, I wonder how long that's been there. Crap!"

Eileen went over to her terminal and called out, "That's not all either, there's a large volume of traffic on the regular intelligence channels. Something big must be going on."

Meanwhile Steve had sat down and was furiously pounding the keyboard with one hand and clicking the mouse with the other, playing the computer as a virtuoso musician would play a violin. He worked through the encryption codes on the incoming urgent message, then displayed it.

"Oh great, it's from Jameson. He's stuck in the blizzard up there and won't make it to the meeting this morning. Sherman will be furious! Jameson was the one who called the meeting, and by now it's too late to cancel it!"

"Steve, it's not your problem. Let Sherman deal with that. We're just 'puter monkeys, let's just gather the info and put it together for your briefing, that's all we can do."

"Yeah, yeah, I know. Just do your job."

"It'll be okay, you'll see."

"I hope so!"

For a while they just worked to collect and organize the incoming data for the seven o'clock briefing before George Sherman in his office. There were messages from the other board members, all saying they'd be there by eight A.M. sharp, all except Jameson of course. There were several scrambled phone calls from people identified only by code names, with cryptic messages that presumably Sherman would understand.

Steve and Eileen had been told relatively little about the real nature of the business of Sherman Industries. They knew that Sherman was energetic and predatory in his pursuit of companies which he thought he could use to boost his market share. They were aware of a number of somewhat shady deals that had been made, and which ultimately made a great deal of money for their employer. They tended to be pragmatic about such things, after all, they were paid well, and though their home life was virtually nonexistent, at least they did get to spend most of their time together. One of Steve's duties as a software engineer was to try to devise decryption programs that could read intercepted files from their competitors; it was a frustrating way to spend his days, as encryption methods generally stay ahead of the abilities of interceptors to decode them. As a matter of routine, Steve had begun to run his programs on incoming encryptions that would ordinarily go straight to George Sherman. Presumably they contained confidential information, but Steve considered himself enough of a "company man" after two years here that he felt justified in using the messages as "test runs" for his decryption programs. It had been relatively seldom that he had been successful, though such files, when read, generally tended to contain sensitive... yet to his mind, dull... financial information.

As Steve and Eileen worked to compile the information Steve would bring to the briefing with Sherman in less than an hour, the encrypted files ran through the decoder as a matter of course, Steve had set up his machine that way. The light next to the optical drive bay would flash repeatedly as files were loaded to it from both computers. In a small box in the upper left corner of Steve's screen there was displayed a series of messages, scrolling downward as the encrypted files were loaded. The messages were all the same: "ACCESS DENIED". It was one of Steve's greatest disappointments in life that he had thus far been unable to develop decryption programs that worked reliably on the newest code types. He scarcely even noticed the repeated failure messages scrolling by. He was working along steadily, with the work about eighty percent finished and a half-hour still to go when something unusual in the periphery of the screen caught his attention. He stared at the message for a few moments. "ACCESS GAINED, FILE MIL11817.CRP, SIZE 45,846 DECODE NOW?"

Steve called out in a tense hoarse voice: "GOT ONE!"

Eileen poked her head over the divider. "Are you kidding? You got a decode?" Steve nodded vigorously. "What is it?" She said.

"It's a file sent from Julius Miller, one of the board members who's coming in tonight. It's about forty five "K", and is associated with an noncoded text file, sent together."

"What do you think we should do?"

Steve looked at his watch. "Well, right now I think I'd better get this disk filled up and get my butt up to Sherman's office. I don't want to be late, you know how he is. I think I'll just copy it off onto another disk and check it out later. I don't think it would be a good idea to leave it lying around on the harddrive."

He hit the "N" key, then inserted another diskette into one of the optical ports on the front of the CPU and hit a few keys, then pulled it out and threw it unlabeled onto the desk. "Okay, help me now, I got to get rolling here. They worked together for another five minutes and had the optical disk ready to go for the briefing. He slipped it in his front shirt pocket and stood to go.

"Hang on a minute." Eileen called out

"Huh? Whadaya need?" She came around the partition and stood on his toes facing him.

"You can't go until I get one more kiss!"

"Oh, is that so?" He said teasingly.

"Yes, so you may as well just give in gracefully."

"Oh well, if it's inevitable I guess I'll just have to suffer thr............"

Eileen shut his mouth with hers. They shared a long and delicious moment, then parted reluctantly.

"Now you'd better go."

"I guess."

"I love you."

As Steve walked out the door, he turned and said. "I love you too. Wish me luck."

Eileen mused that she was glad that Steve was the one who had to talk to George Sherman, the guy always gave her the creeps. He would smile at her in a way that made her feel naked and dirty. She shivered and walked back towards her cubicle, passing Steve's desk along the way. Her gaze fell upon the insignificant looking unmarked diskette lying there on top of some papers. Such a common looking sight on a 'puter jockey's desk, still it was contraband if Sherman ever found out. She stood there a while trying to decide what to do. She had never felt comfortable with Steve's little game of trying to decipher the internal encryptions. They both knew it could mean their jobs if it was discovered, which never seemed to bother Steve that much. She guessed it was some kind of male testosterone risk-taking behavior. She looked at the disk. She should probably just erase the thing, that would be the safest thing to do, still.....

On a whim she sat quickly at Steve's terminal, poked the disk into the drive and entered Steve's password. The message flashed on the screen, "ACCESS GAINED, FILE MIL11817.CRP, SIZE 45,846 DECODE NOW?"

Eileen hit the "Y" key, and then a message flashed briefly, "DECODING MIL11817.CRP NEWFILE MIL11817.TXT"

She hit the "Q" key to invoke a simple text reading program, chose the "B" floppy drive when prompted, and was rewarded by a pale green screen filled with text. She tried to scan the text quickly, hitting "Page Down" every few seconds to get the sense of it. It seemed to be the report of a field operative giving details of assignments recently completed, and those in a planning phase. She furrowed her brow for a moment. Hadn't Steve said that this was a board member? This seemed rather odd. She checked the disk to be sure that the decoded file was on it, then cleared the screen and retrieved the disk. She felt rather uneasy sitting at Steve's desk, mostly because her back was to the door. It gave her a queasy feeling in her spine, as if someone were watching over her shoulder.   Back at her own terminal she felt more comfortable, put the disk in a drive port and viewed it again, this time taking her time and bringing in the noncoded letter file also. Yes, it was from Julius Miller, who said he was coming in to the board meeting. She paged quickly to the end of the decoded file to check the sign off. It ended:

".... Respectfully: J.M.

P.S. Please consider using my professional services if you decide to pursue the Sanders sanction recommended above. Suggest immediate action. DELETE THIS FILE NOW!"

What did this mean, Sanders Sanction? She paged back up to the beginning, okay, it was only about eight pages, she decided to read it all. Feeling nervous and looking apprehensively towards the door as if someone was about to burst in, Eileen started reading.

The first two pages of the text described preparations that had been made in the pursuit of a previous assignment. As she read through it Eileen was caught up in the detail and thoroughness of the planning. Stakeouts and electronic surveillance of a subject named "D. Johns" were minutely described, and the subject's movement patterns were tabulated. After a row of asterisks there was a line that simply read, "SUBJECT SANCTIONED. CONFIRM, PAGE 2, 1/17 CHI. TRIB. ART. 3"

Subject sanctioned, what could that mean? The confirm line seemed to indicate the January 17th edition of the Chicago Tribune, the third article on page two. She flicked the "Alt, Enter" keys to blank the screen while keeping her place, and opened her newspaper account, keying in the appropriate details to bring up the article in question. On her screen there appeared a short article with a grainy, but nonetheless graphic photograph of a human figure lying sprawled and shattered on a city street. The article read: "   Wealthy financier David Matthew Johns apparently committed suicide this morning by jumping out of his 47th floor office window. Officials are unsure about the motive, but items found at the scene suggest that he was distraught over recent financial reversals....."

Eileen sat back as if she'd been slapped in the face. The guy was murdered! Sherman had put out a contract on him, and Miller killed him! A rushing sound filled her ears as the adrenaline rush hit. She took a deep breath, swallowed, hit "alt. enter" again to get the text file back and kept reading. The next two pages contained a similar description of another "sanction". This time Eileen did not bother to follow up the confirmation, she felt reasonably sure that she had stumbled onto the real thing here, action reports of contract killings... positive proof of George Sherman's criminal activities. No wonder his business was so successful!

After the second sanction report there was a progress report on a current surveillance operation. The tightness in her stomach only increased now, she started to feel almost nauseous. The report began:

****

Internal security surveillance report. After several failed attempts to insert data line pickups in the computing services section, a visual and audio surveillance was successfully installed one month ago. Automatic recording and editing equipment has delivered to us very disturbing information concerning the activities of subject Sanders S. Subject has been observed attempting to decode internal encrypted files. Frequent conjugal visitations with female coworker seem to negatively influence job performance and system security. Personality profiles would indicate extreme individualism coupled with high loyalty and morality factors. Intelligence quotient extremely high (not measurable on standard tests).

The decoding programs that subject has written and subsequently turned over to supervisors do not seem to be the same as the ones subject uses on his own machine. Independent projections indicate that a breakthrough on decoding is imminent.

Conclusion:

Subject highly productive, but unpredictable. Suggest possibility that decoding program work can be completed from work already done without subject's participation. Unless subject can be turned to us (doubtful considering personality profile) recommend immediate sanction: subject Sanders S.

Surveillance subject Donovan E. Subject coworker of above. Personality profile stable, high group cooperation index, leadership capable. Morality factor medium, loyalty high, extreme development of vengeance potential. Intelligence quotient extremely high (not measurable on standard tests). Subject has been an accomplice to many offenses of aforementioned subject.

Conclusion:

Of the two subjects, the female is considered by far the more dangerous. Recommend immediate sanction: subject Donovan E.

Suggested action:

1. Terminate subjects
2. Seize computer files
3. Bring in company people to complete the work

Respectfully: J.M.

P.S. Please consider using my clean and reliable professional services if you decide to pursue the Sanders sanction recommended above. Suggest immediate action.

DELETE THIS FILE NOW

****

"So this was it eh? The bastards are going to kill us!" She said under her breath. Eileen felt a rising panic begin to swell within her, then noticed it subside and fall away, replaced by a grim determination. She smiled as she thought about how they had assessed her vengeance potential. Well, they'd gotten that much right anyway! Her mind kicked into overdrive as she tried to figure out what to do next. Steve had gone up to Sherman's office to deliver the disk and a briefing on what it contained, but it was unlikely that he would actually read the file for some increment of time, say, fifteen or twenty minutes perhaps? She thought again about the callous way in which their deaths were being proposed, and smiled to herself at the thought that they considered her dangerous. She thought briefly about trashing the place, then realized that there was still a surveillance camera somewhere in the room. She consciously suppressed the desire to look for it, knowing full well that with apertures as small as 1/16 of an inch possible, she would never find it, and the search would only alert anyone monitoring the room that something was wrong.

They would have to escape from the building and disappear, that much was sure, but she wondered about whether they could do much damage on the way out. A smirk crossed her face as a plan of action crystallized, with a part of her mind she was a frightened little girl, but that part now watched with fascination as a very cool and collected Eileen Donovan set about to wreak vengeance upon the corporate entity known as Sherman Industries.

First she went over to Steve's computer and activated the optical tape drive backup system, to dub all the programs and data stored on his 684 gigabyte harddrive to a crystal disk cartridge the size of a cigarette pack. Since Steve's machine held all the same programs as her own, as well as his experimental decryption program, she copied off her personal files to a floptical diskette, and began to destroy the computer.

To someone uninitiated to the world of the computer viewing the scene, it would have looked quite normal. Eileen sat at the keyboard and typed at various keys. But internally, the results were disaster. She rebooted the computer with "ctrl-alt-del" then hit "delete" to enter the CMOS basic setup program. With fingers barely able to execute the commands her brain sent to them, she ran the disk utility that reformatted the entire harddrive, completely wiping out all the information there. She put the backup tape into her purse and sighed with a sense of regret as she looked at the now dead screen that had been her companion for over two years.

She walked as casually as possible over to Steve's machine, where the tape backup had just finished, put that tape into her purse and performed the same virtual decapitation on his machine as she had done to her own. Finally she walked over to the mainframe. This was a little trickier, but she knew that Steve had created what he called a time-bug and had loaded it into the machine some months before. He had told her it was their insurance policy, and while she had disagreed with him at the time about loading it, she was glad it was there now. It was a nondestructive sort of virus, resistant to being found by virus detection programs since it worked in a fundamentally different way. With the entering of a certain key word, the program could be activated, which would allow an interval of time to be set before the big machine would turn itself off. At the Sherman Industries main offices, all the door locks, elevators, telephones and lighting systems were controlled by the central computer. Steve had thought of it as more of a joke, a prank he might pull someday, but Eileen now saw it as a way to buy them time to get away.

She typed the key code sequence, careful to add the capitals and punctuation marks correctly. "One Two! One Two! And through and through The VORPAL blade went snicker snack!" The humming machine responded with a simple: Enter Time (min) blissfully ignorant of the fact that it was about to commit cybersuicide.

She jumped as the door opened and Steve walked in. "Hey babe, what's up?" Then his brow furrowed as he looked at the dead screen of his computer. "Whoa, what happened?"

Eileen called to him. "C'mere honey, I want to show you something."

He walked around the room dividers and over to where she stood by the mainframe. Her finger was gently on her lips in a signal not to speak, he was obviously confused, but could see from the screen that she had activated the time bug. Eileen reached out and drew Steve to her in a hug. In this position she could whisper into his ear discreetly.

"Steve, I opened that encrypted file and read it. Sherman is heavily into some serious criminal activity, including murder. We are under surveillance here. He knows about your playing around with the encryptions and they think they can complete your work without you. We're now considered dangerous and expendable. That file from Miller recommends that we be killed immediately, and he's offered to do it." She felt him tense, but held on tighter. "I've got all the backup cartridges in my purse, I reformatted the drives on the two desktops, and keyed the time bug." He nodded silently. "How long do you think it will take us to get out of the building?"

Steve was breathing heavily now. "Uh, not less than five minutes, possibly as long as ten, if nothing goes wrong."

"What do you think then? How long should we set it for?"

Steve reached over and typed the number "15", then looked over at Eileen. "You ready?"

She shrugged. "As I'll ever be, I guess."

"Well, okay then, here goes."

Steve pushed the F3, F6, and F9 keys simultaneously, then hit "enter". The number "15" then changed to "14:59" and started counting downward by seconds.

Eileen punched a button on the telephone answering machine, then spoke aloud. "Hi, this is Sherman Industries computing services department. We've gone out for breakfast right now, but your call is important to us. Please leave a message at the tone and we'll get back with you just as soon as we can."

"Okay, let's go." Steve said, and put his hand on the doorknob.

"Just one more thing." said Eileen.

"What is it?"

"Just this." She kissed him quickly, "I love you. Let's not die now okay?"

Steve smiled. "The feeling is mutual, now come on, let's blow this popstand!"

He opened the door, looked both ways out in the corridor, and headed down the hall at a normal walking pace, Eileen just behind. As the door closed behind the phone began to ring, but they had already turned the corner of the hallway and didn't even hear it. If someone had been in the room listening, they would have heard four rings, a click, the message Eileen recorded, then the voice of George Sherman speaking in a jovial and friendly tone. "Hi Steve and Eileen, hey, good work on the briefing materials, very useful and interesting. The reason I'm calling is that I'd like you both in my office at nine o'clock sharp, I've got a big surprise for you! See you then."

The monitor screen by the mainframe blindly continued to display the timer; "13:23--13:22--13:21...................."

CHAPTER 10

Leonard Howarth and Harry Halbrook stood by the baggage carousel in the airport in Minneapolis, Minnesota. The bags had not even started coming into view on the conveyor belt, but already people were jockeying for position in the front row adjacent to the carousel. Frank and Harry stood back and waited. Their suits were rumpled and their eyes looked bloodshot as they stood there. Through the large windows the first light of day could be seen shining in the heavily overcast sky. Leonard was shaking his head. "I can't believe they do that," he said.

"Sir?" Harry looked confused.

"Look at them, herding around the baggage carousel like a bunch of cattle to the feed trough. It's stupid! They're not making the bags come out any more quickly."

Harry smiled. He had traveled with Leonard before and knew that this was one of his boss' big pet peeves. It would take every bit of his considerable store of patience, tact and diplomacy to keep this trip running smoothly. Leonard tended to cut a pretty short fuse on his patience when it came to these "field trips" as he liked to call them. Up to this point things had not been going well. They had been diverted from their destination of choice by a severe winter storm in Michigan's Upper Peninsula. Only as a last resort had Leonard agreed to fly in to Minneapolis and drive up the rest of the way, but things seemed to be getting worse as they went along.

The flight in had not gone well. First, there had been delays at Dulles before takeoff, then the pilot announced icing problems and had had to land the plane in Columbus, Ohio for deicing before continuing on in to the Twin Cities. Since they had been late in arriving, the gate schedules were all thrown off, and the plane had been forced to sit on the taxiway for over an hour waiting for a gate. Now they were here, and the agent from the local office that was supposed to meet them with a car was not.

Harry looked at his boss, who was obviously fuming and impatient, then over Leonard's head to the large digital clock on the wall. 7:46 A.M. It had been a long night. Leonard would almost certainly want to start driving immediately, but Harry had been studying the maps and had a pretty good idea of the distance involved... just over five hundred kilometers. He had also been paying attention to the weather channel, snowfall reports, and forecasts. He was in his old stomping grounds now, having been born in Rhinelander and gone to college in Bemidji. Harry desperately wanted to suggest to his boss that they get a room somewhere and some sleep before tackling the drive, but he could anticipate Leonard's answer.

Finally the baggage started to trundle slowly along the conveyor belt, out of the floppy plastic doors, and onto the curved metal carousels. The crowd surged even tighter around it so that Leonard and Harry could no longer even see whether their bags were there. Harry walked up closer to get a better look. The minutes passed slowly as bag after bag slowly moved past the crowd. People lunged forward to grab one, then struggled to get out of the press, like dogs running off to eat a choice morsel. The crowd started to thin, then finally their two bags emerged, and Harry picked them up and brought them back.

"Okay, that's everything I think. what do you want to do now?"

Leonard thought, "Since nobody's here to pick us up I guess we'll have to get a cab and get downtown. God what a pain in the ass!"

"Listen Boss, we got a long way to go, if we want to be in any kind of shape when we get there we're going to need some food, and some rest. I suggest that we call in to the local office, let them know we're here, and arrange to get picked up later on after we get some shuteye."

"What? No way! We've got to get up there. Those other guys up there have no idea of the importance of this, they'll geek the whole investigation!"

"Agent Howarth?"

Leonard and Harry turned to stare at a smiling young man who had approached them. He had shoulder length brown hair tumbling out from under a black and white knitted stocking cap, with a ridiculous looking fuzzball on the top. Leonard looked him up and down, he wore a disgustingly dirty red down jacket, torn jeans with the knees of his long underwear showing through, and olive drab combat boots so worn that they looked as if they were about to fall apart. He stuck out a hand partially covered with a fingerless black leather glove.

"Hi, agent Jason Desnick at your service." His left hand held out the holographic ID card that confirmed he was the genuine article.

"Captain Howarth." Said Leonard with trepidation. "You look like shit."

Jason laughed. "I generally work undercover operations in the neighborhood, they pulled me off of an unproductive stakeout assignment and sent me over to pick you guys up. The other guy couldn't wait around after he found out that you were delayed. Rough flight huh?"

"You could say that."

"Well here, lemme grab your bags, we're parked right outside."

Without waiting for assent, Jason picked up the suitcases and started heading for the door, Leonard and Harry had to hustle to keep up. Outside the door in the blowing snow sat an ancient Ford Bronco four by four, a skycap stood by and looked relieved to see Jason, smiling as Jason slipped him some cash. The vehicle had probably been a pale blue color at one time, but a front right fender of olive green, patchy Bondo work and some scattered primer made it look like a junk heap.

"We're not riding in that, are we?" Said Leonard with a smirk as Jason and Harry loaded the luggage in the back."

"Hey captain, don't let looks deceive you. This is what we here call "urban camouflage." I can park this baby in the worst parts of town and nobody will give it a second look, but under the hood we've got a freshly rebuilt 386 cubic inch engine, all the running gear is in top condition and the heaviest duty that can be shoehorned into this frame, and we've got brand new snowtires. This sled can boogie I'm tellin' ya.

Leonard just stood there looking at Jason with an inscrutable gaze. Who was this guy kidding, he sure didn't look or act like any agent Leonard had ever met.

"Like I said captain, don't let looks deceive you. Come on, get in. let's roll."

Harry climbed into the back seat while Leonard got into the passenger seat up front. Jason hopped in, gunned the motor and took off in a cloud of blowing snow. He guided the vehicle out of the airport parking lot and got onto the freeway, running at a speed which was quickly passing all the other cars on the road. Harry tapped Leonard on the shoulder and pointed to the back of the vehicle. Leonard now saw that the back was piled with gear aside from their own. Duffel bags of indeterminate contents, snowshoes, and camping equipment.

Leonard looked over at Jason who was driving with focused intensity. "So, where we goin?"

Jason handed him a crumpled map. "Well, I figured the quickest way was to head up 35 and pick up 8 over to Rhinelander, then head up into the U.P. on 45. That sound okay?"

Leonard glanced back at Harry who shrugged and nodded.

"What makes you think you're going with us, I thought the arrangement was for us to pick up a vehicle and drive up ourselves."

"Well, you're certainly free to rent a car if you want, but all I was told that your mission, whatever it is, was time sensitive and important. This is the best car we've got for the job, and where this car goes, I go. I'm also the best snow driver, and I know those roads, I drive up there pretty frequently to visit friends. If you want to get stuck out there in the snow on your own, be my guest. I'd be happy to drop you off at a rental agency."

"We're going to need some food, and some rest." Harry said, leaning on the front seat.

"Here, grab the wheel a second." Jason took Leonard's left hand and unceremoniously slapped it on the steering wheel, then turned around without letting off the accelerator at all, and dug around in the back seat to find a bag. "Here we go, bacon and egg biscuits, coffees and some donuts, that suit you?" Leonard gulped slightly as Jason took the wheel back and casually said, "Thanks, there are some blankets and sleeping bags in the back, feel free to make yourselves comfortable and catch some zees. I'm fresh from eight hours sleep." Leonard opened the top of one of the coffees and sipped; it was still hot. "Listen, if anyone can get you up there fast it's me. You don't have to tell me what it's all about if you don't want to. My captain said it was some kind of hush-hush deal. Just relax and enjoy the scenery for a while, this is God's country up here we like to say."

"Okay, thanks." Leonard heard a rustling sound from the back and turned to see that Harry had drawn a blanket over himself and was already settling down to catch some sleep. The coffee tasted good and the biscuit and donut seemed to revive him some. He looked over at Jason without speaking. This guy was not a run-of-the-mill agent! He wondered whether he might be recruitable to SIB. At that moment Jason looked over at him and smiled briefly before turning his attention back to the road. A chill ran up Leonard's back, but he was not apprehensive. He unaccountably felt safe here in this beat up Bronco careening up Interstate 35. The slapping of the windshield wipers clearing the falling snow was hypnotic. Leonard grabbed a pillow from the back and happily fell asleep leaning against the window as the Bronco chugged inexorably north towards the Upper Peninsula. As Leonard Howarth drifted off to slumber he briefly wondered what he would find there. His thoughts turned to his childhood, and those wonderful two weeks he'd spend at his grandparent's farm outside Iron River every summer... fishing in the lake with his grandfather and uncles... the rope swing over the pond... lemonade on the screened in back porch on hot days, or hot chocolate on cool mornings... the dogs begging for attention and fetching sticks from the pond......

Jason glanced at the two sleeping figures and smiled as he chewed a donut, then licked his sticky fingers and wiped his hands on his pants. He had a good feeling about Harry, but Leonard was a whirlwind of frustration, anxiety, and suppressed anger. He hoped this city boy knew what he was doing up in the north country. Yep he decided... something big was definitely coming down, he could smell it. He took a deep breath and composed his mind, paying scant attention to the road. Energies were focalizing in the area toward which they so speedily rushed.

Jason couldn't quite see it all yet, nor could he tell what part he would play, but he knew he had to be there... there was no ambiguity in the orders he'd been given. In his mind shadowy images swirled, connected to each other by thin tendrils of light. The images of these two men and his own were deeply entangled in this web of connections, and the center of the web was on the Keweenaw Peninsula.

The Bronco shuddered slightly as he passed a snowplow and headed into the somewhat deeper snow ahead. The roaring of the big diesel engine and the clanking of the plow's tire chains receded into the distance behind. His passengers were sound asleep and did not even stir. He turned off the windshield wipers to see if the falling snow was dry enough to just blow off on its own, decided it was and left the wipers off. He stretched a little, took another sip of coffee, and settled in for the long drive.

CHAPTER 11

When Digger awoke, the bedroom was dark and quiet; the air smelled of woodsmoke and feather pillows. Joan lay snuggled on her right side with her back up against him. He took a deep slow breath and reminisced about the night. He was tantalizingly aware of the smoothness of her buttocks as they rested against his thigh. What had he ever done to deserve this? He breathed deeply again and silently prayed that she felt the same way; being with Joan last night had been different than with any woman he'd ever known. Digger had been around the block a few times... he had even been engaged once... but the intensity of feeling he had for Joan startled him. He desperately hoped it was not just the lingering effects of the alcohol. He recalled a number of "next mornings", but none had been accompanied by the sense of inner rightness he felt now. Digger rolled to his right and allowed his body to spoon with hers, his left hand resting in the saddle of her waist while he nuzzled her hair with his face. God, but she smelled good! He could not recall ever being so entranced by a woman's odor before. It wasn't a perfume, though if such an aroma could be bottled he was sure it would become a best seller, but just the soapy clean and sexy musk of woman... the woman he loved. Loved? There was that word again! Could it be, after knowing her only a few hours? He had avoided that word all his life. This didn't feel like what he had imagined "love at first sight" would be like, but rather it seemed like the feeling shared by lovers long apart, finally reunited. He felt the tingling sensation in the back of his head again, and this time there was no doubt, he had found what he was looking for.

She woke slowly, yawned, and stretched like a cat, allowing him to feel the steel spring muscles ripple under her smooth skin, then she rolled over to face him.

"Good morning." She murmured sleepily.

Digger began to feel a panic, What if she didn't feel the same way about him? What if this was just a one nighter to her? He stammered... "Joan, I, uh..."

"Shhh. I know. I feel it in you, you've fallen in love with me, you're scared at the suddenness of it, and you want to know if I feel the same."

"Oh Joan, yes, that's it exactly... how do you..."

"I do Digger, I do. I love you with all my soul. I think I knew it from the moment I picked you up on the road, but in the sauna I was sure. There was just something about you, we were meant for each other. I don't claim to understand how such things can be, but I know what I know."

"Oh Joan, last night was unbelievable, I... I never even imagined it could be like that."

"For me too."

They shared a long slow kiss. "Good morning," she said again.

"Good morning darling," he answered. They embraced passionately. "Uh, Joan, before we go too far there's something I feel I have to tell you."

"Oh, what is that?"

"I need to pee."

Joan giggled, "Well, I do too. Come on."

They got up, Joan put on a robe and Digger wrapped a large towel around himself as they went through the kitchen to the bathroom. With the bathroom light on Digger finally got a good look at Joan's face in full light, her eyes sparkled beneath a disarray of disheveled hair. He gasped from the sheer intensity of her beauty. She wiggled her hips for him before sitting on the potty. "Do you like?" she asked.

He just nodded. "Uh, Joan... can I ask you something?" He said.

"Sure."

"I still don't know your last name. It just seemed that, well, after we, uh... I mean... if we're going to... uh..."

"Niemi," she said simply.

"What?"

"Joan Margaret Niemi is my full name."

"Oh okay, thanks. A good Finnish name."

"Well, my folks always thought so anyway."

They took turns at the toilet and after finishing in the bathroom they went out into the kitchen again. It was still dark outside, the wind had died down for the most part, snowflakes could still be seen drifting near the windowpanes, clouded and frosty with condensation. It was 7:47 A.M. by the digital clock on the stove. Arne seemed to be still fast asleep in the loft and breathing deeply. Joan picked up a small plastic box attached to a long cord and brought it into the bedroom; it had a small light flashing on it.

"I turned off the phone ringer last night before we..." she smiled, "Looks like there are some calls, I'd better check them. Anybody calling at that time of night could mean it's important. They sat on the bed and she punched the button. The machine started talking....

"Hello, you have three messages: BEEEEP. 'Hey Joan, J.B. here. I've got a couple of relays for you, one is from Mister Dobbs over in L'Anse, says there's a couple of Feds from Marquette trying to make it up to Houghton in the snowstorm, he's putting them up for the night in his cabin, and will call again when they leave. They're close mouthed on why they're going up, but apparently they hit a deer on the road on the reservation, and Yellow Knife Junior got on their case and confiscated it. Then there's a message from a person named "Sandy" in D.C., said you'd know who she was. She says that a couple of S.I.B. agents are also on their way up, rerouted through Twin Cities and coming up tomorrow by car. Their targets are a couple of fellows by the names of Harjaala and Puttonen. Sandy says watch out, these guys sometimes play dirty. Okay then, check ya later.' BEEEEP

'Hi Joan, it's Ruth. Something strange is going on up here in Paavola, there is a strange black car cruising around watching the ways in and out. Thought you'd want to know.' BEEEEP

'Joan, hey this is Freddie. Uh, there's a guy with Illinois tags nosing around Hancock asking about Midnight Mining Company. One of our fellas checked him out with a hidden metal detector and it looks like he's carrying some heavy heat. Big scary looking guy too, scar across his face, says his name is Jameson... I talked with the secretary up at the M.M.C. office, name of Miriam, but she clammed up and looked pale when I mentioned the guy. My guess is he's trying to pull some kind of strong-arm trick, don't know what it's all about though. Later'. BEEEEP

That was your last message."

Digger sat frozen on the bed. "Then it's not my imagination!"

"I'd guess not."

"What kind of information network do you have going on here?" he asked, surprised that she could find out such things on such short notice.

"Well, I told you that we were working towards statehood for the U.P., There are lots of things to arrange before that can happen. One of the main things is to have a reliable source of information. This was just the tip of the iceberg, just the stuff they felt was important enough to call with in the middle of the night. These people are collecting all sorts of information on economic, social, and criminal activities in the area. We have sources placed in a lot of offices in the County, State and Federation governments. Some stuff we give anonymously to the local police and let them deal with. Often we just collect the information and wait. We have to know who we can trust when the time of crisis comes, and we have to know when outside players come in and threaten our interests."

"And you're right in the middle of it?"

"Yep, stick with me and you're in for one heck of a ride!"

"What if something happens to you?"

"With you here? I'm not worried, but I'm not the only one you know; this movement is highly decentralized. I could disappear and the work would still go on."

"I'm confused though, what do the Feds want with me and Arne, and what are we going to do?"

"Well lover, I think that we should have a nice big breakfast and a large jug of coffee, and then you and Arne will sit down and tell Joan all about it. I still don't understand what they want with you, although it's clear that there must be something. I don't like the sound of that guy from Illinois that Freddy was talking about. Maybe we can sit down and figure it out together." Digger took the answering machine back to the kitchen and moved to flip the light switch on the wall, but Joan gently stopped his hand. "But for now," she said, "there's at least an hour before dawn, and Arne's still asleep. I think maybe we should go back to bed for a while."

"Oh, sorry, are you still sleepy? I guess we did get to bed rather late."

"Who said anything about sleep?" She tugged at the corner of the towel he had wrapped around himself and pulled him into the bedroom, then closed the door. The house grew dark and quiet again, except for some small comfortable sounds, hardly noticeable at all.

CHAPTER 12

Steve Sanders and Eileen Donovan walked quickly down the hallway on the third floor of Sherman Industries corporate headquarters. They took the same route they always used when heading towards the parking lot at the end of the day, or taking a meal break during a long shift. They had to walk down a long "S" shaped corridor with first a right-angled turn to the right, then another to the left before emerging at the north end of the building where there were three elevators and a stairwell. The carpeted hallway had more of the air of a luxury hotel than an office building. Tasteful pieces of art hung at irregular intervals between the doors leading to various offices. Aside from occasionally meeting people in the hallway and exchanging pleasantries, neither of them really knew anybody else on the floor. Sherman kept his people compartmentalized with respect to their work, the two computer techs scarcely even knew what else was being done on their floor. Visitors were rare, and were always escorted by security personnel.

Right now the carpet muffled their footsteps, yet heightened their fears of meeting someone just around the next corner. Unconsciously they joined hands, which seemed to calm them both down somewhat, relaxing their gait to a more normal pace. Steve resisted the temptation to peer furtively around the corner of the right hand turn, and was relieved to find nobody in sight when they rounded it.

"What's the time?" Eileen asked in a low whisper.

"About thirteen and a half minutes, plenty of time, don't worry." Steve answered in the same voice.

"Okay. Can't we hurry a little more?"

"We want to look like everything is absolutely normal if we meet anyone."

"Yeah... normal." She said.

Steve smiled. "Right."

Just as they were about to turn the corner to the left a door opened as they passed it. A younger, slightly heavy woman with thick glasses and an armload of boxes came out and seemed startled to see them.

"Hello," Eileen ventured in a convincing and uninterestedly casual tone.

"Hi." The woman answered noncommittally as they passed. Then she averted her gaze and fell in behind them as they continued down the hall.

Arriving at the elevators Steve poked the "down" button, and they settled in to wait. The middle elevator passed them by going up, and Eileen noticed that it went all the way up to fourteen, George Sherman's exclusive floor. Steve seemed to notice also. Almost immediately it started back down again.

"Hey, why don't' we just walk down? I could use the exercise." said Eileen, perhaps just a little too loudly.

"Yeah sure, okay," answered Steve.

With a glance and smile at the unknown woman, the pair walked to the stairwell and slipped quietly through the door before they knew whether the elevator from fourteen had actually stopped on three or not. They skipped quickly down the stairwell to the first floor and looked around the corner into the spacious lobby. There were two large men wearing suits loitering around the reception desk bearing that inescapable look that seemed to characterize plainclothes security men. Eileen pulled Steve back into the alcove before they could be spotted and pointed silently to the indicator above the middle elevator door. The lift had stopped on the third floor and then headed back up. Steve nodded, then motioned to Eileen to follow. They headed back into the stairwell, then down another flight to the service level, emerging into a dimly lit corridor filled with all the ducting, wiring and piping that such large buildings need. A gentle thrumming of machinery filled the air, accompanied by a somewhat oily smell.

"I didn't like the looks of those two guys up front," said Steve.

"Me neither, how's our time?"

"Just over ten minutes left. We could go for the service entrance at the south end, though there's no reason to think they're not watching that too, if they're onto us."

"What choice have we got?"

"Not much, come on, we'd better hurry."

They started jogging along the corridor, heading deeper into the bowels of the complex, making for the lower level entrance on the far side of the building. Fortunately Steve was somewhat familiar with the labyrinthine passageways on this level, as he had installed a substantial portion of the computerized building controls network. The pair trotted along, turning this way and that, along narrow passages between banks of electrical conduits and piping, then finally they emerged into a large machine shop room near the center of the building. Several workers could be seen, minding their own business. One guy looked up from his work at a big milling machine and waved hello.

"Hey Steve!"

"Oh, hi Carl." The man sauntered towards them wiping his hands on a dirty blue shop towel. "You know my partner Eileen?"

Carl stuck out a meaty hand in greeting. "Don't think I've had the pleasure," he said, then smiled at Steve. "Hey guy, hadn't seen ya down this way for a while, they keepin' ya busy up there?"

"Yeah, pretty much. Hey Carl, I really appreciate that time when you broke my fall off that ladder."

"Hey kid, don't mention it. Say, you okay? You look like something's eatin' you." Steve smiled, Carl was one of the good guys around this place... he made a sudden decision.

"Listen Carl, I told you before that I owed you one, and now I'm paying off."

Carl's eyebrows furrowed, he glanced at the worried expression on Eileen's face, her shifting feet, obviously impatient. "Whatcha talkin' about?"

"Can't explain it all, there's no time, just this: Get yourself and anybody you consider a friend out of the building within the next..." he looked at his watch, "eight minutes. Got it?"

"Okay... but, uh... hey, what's up?"

"The computer's going down for the big sleep."

Carl's eyes grew large and round. "You mean... all the doors? All the lights? The elevators? Everything?"

"You got it, eight minutes. We're heading for the service entrance, you coming?"

"Yeah, go ahead, I'll be along in a minute," Carl said and turned hurriedly away, "there's a couple other guys I gotta tell."

"Okay, go... and be careful, some of Sherman's goons may be around, and they're playing hardball."

"Okay, thanks."

It was obvious that Carl took Steve completely seriously because he hustled across the room with amazing speed for his bulk as Steve and Eileen headed down a wider and well lit corridor towards the lower door. They went at full run now, and at last came around a corner and could see the open cargo bay of a truck that had been backed up to the loading dock; just to the left of it was the regular sized exterior door below a lighted "EXIT" sign. The air felt decidedly cool here, only now did they both realize that they'd left their office in such a hurry that they'd forgotten their coats... too late now for such worries.

As they skidded into the loading dock area the door of the service elevator hissed open and two men emerged. One was white and the other black; both wore bulky suits which made them look out of place in this part of the building. Steve berated himself for not thinking of that before, they could have been here three minutes earlier if they'd gone for the service elevator in the first place. Too late now.

The darker skinned of the two men said to the other, "Hey Adam, isn't that them?"

"Yeah, I think so... Hey you! Yeah... you two," he called out.

Eileen tried to be charming. "Hey fellas, what's goin' on?"

"Sanders and Donovan right? Mister Sherman wants you in his office on the double."

Steve countered: "Yeah, we'll be there in a few minutes, our appointment is at nine. He's got a board meeting starting in just a couple minutes, we were just going to dash out to the Denny's around the corner, catch a bite, and be back about quarter 'til.."

"Our orders are to bring you up there now," said Adam.

"Listen guys," tried Eileen, "we've been up all night..." Her face reddened slightly. "...working, there's no point in keeping us sitting in Sherman's waiting room until the meeting is over. We'll be back, I promise."

"Listen you dumbshit wirehead," said Adam. "I'm tellin' ya to get your ass into that elevator NOW." His manner had taken a decidedly aggressive turn. Steve took a deep breath, if there was any doubt before, this put it to rest. Sherman's thugs had always been very polite to them in the past. Now these men had a cold look in their eyes, as if they no longer considered Steve and Eileen to be living breathing human beings, as if they were already, already......... Steve looked at Eileen, who pleaded with her eyes, then measured the distance to the door. The black guy looked alert and had his right hand inserted into his left jacket front, NOT a good sign. Steve checked his watch... just under two minutes left. He tensed to make a lunge at the nearest man, knowing he had little chance of success.

"Hey Steve! How ya doin'?" Carl trotted into the room with two other fellows in mechanic's dungarees right behind him, all of them carrying heavy crowbars or wrenches.

The black guy with his hand in his jacket took no notice, but simply stared icily at Steve, the other guy yelled out, "What're you guys doing here, get back to work, this is none of your business."

Carl smiled and kept walking up to the white guy. "Sure it is Adam. This here is my friend Steve. Steve, meet Adam. Adam's one of the rottenest sons of bitches dirtying the face of God's green earth. I don't know whose asshole he had to tongue to get this job but..." Adam growled and reached into his jacket to pull out his weapon, but Carl's crowbar came down with a crunch on his right arm before he had brought it on line. The firearm went skittering across the floor towards the outside door as Adam screamed with pain and sagged to his knees clutching his arm.

In the meantime the black guy had drawn his gun and rather than defend his partner, was holding it steady, aimed at Steve's chest. Three other guys that had been unloading the truck with front end loaders now stopped what they were doing and watched curiously. "Everybody freeze!" he yelled. The firearm was still pointed at Steve.

Adam got to his feet, clutching his broken right arm and glaring with rage. Carl stood watching Adam with amusement. "So friend, what are you going to do now?"

Through clenched teeth Adam answered him. "I'm going to take these computer nerds up to Sherman's office as ordered, and then I'm going to come back down here and kill you."

"Carl, it's me they want, take Eileen and get out of here," said Steve.

Adam turned and answered. "No! We want her too, and all the rest of you now that you've made up your minds to stick your noses in where you shouldn't have."

"And then what?" said Eileen. "We go upstairs and then you shoot us where there are no witnesses? We already know that Sherman is a murdering son of a bitch. Did you know that Sherman was the one that had David Johns murdered a couple days ago? Huh? Did you? He was one of the wealthiest and most concerned black businessmen in the state, Sherman had him killed because he wouldn't play ball."

Adam started to speak, but his partner lowered his gun and spoke up instead. "Sherman did that? Hey man, I was at his funeral... he's my Aunt May's brother in law. That guy was cool, he helped a lot of people."

"You shut up Robbie." Said Adam. "Don't you believe anything they say, they're lying, just trying to confuse the issue."

"It's true Robbie." Said Eileen with sympathy. An assassin named Miller did it on Sherman's orders." Robbie sighed heavily, he put two and two together and inevitably came up with four. He made up his mind and put the gun back into its holster.

"Don't you dare walk out on me Robbie!" Shouted Adam, still clutching his arm. Robbie walked past him with infinite disdain. "Fuck you, asshole."

"Robbie you goddamned nigger you better get your ass back over here and do your job or I'll tell Sherman, that's an order!"

Robbie walked past Steve and Eileen towards the door, picked up Adam's gun where it lay on the floor and walked back. Everyone else in the room stood stock still watching. Adam smiled and said, "That's better! Okay, now......"

Adam's words were cut short as Robbie handed the gun to a surprised Steve, then looked at Adam and sadly shook his head. "You'll never get it Adam.

Some things just aren't worth the price." Then he turned and quietly walked out the door. Steve stood there holding the gun in his hand.

Adam's face showed his horror. "No, please.. I...." He sank to his knees blubbering uncontrollably.

"Steve, how's our time?" Eileen cut in.

"Uh, about fifteen seconds. Okay everybody out now, move!"

Carl motioned his guys out the door, the three who were unloading the truck decided to go with the flow and clear out even though they had no idea what was going on. Steve was the last to leave, he turned and looked back at Adam who still knelt on the floor cradling his wounded arm.

"Do me a favor, would you please? Tell Sherman we quit." Suddenly the lights all went out and a series of sharp clicking sounds echoed through the building as every door reverted to the default "locked" condition. The big firedoor came sliding down over the loading dock with an echoing boom. Steve took one last look at the frightened form of Adam, barely visible by the cold gray light leaking in through the door, then closed it behind him and left. Out of curiosity he tried the handle and found it locked. He turned and saw Eileen standing there, hugging herself in the cold wind. The others were all running away, heading for the parking lot already. Not knowing what else to do with the pistol in his hand, he stuck it in his belt and started trotting around the building towards the lot where Eileen's car was parked.

As they jogged Eileen panted, "Steve, what're we going to do about the gate?"

"I don't know, we'll have to just play it as we go."

As they came around to the front of the building there were a few people milling around in confusion. They were probably morning shift people, trying to get in and finding their keycards to be ineffectual at the door. Eileen got out her keys as they ran to her small red Chrysler Neptune. Steve hopped in on the passenger side and they were moving almost immediately as the electric motor spun up the flywheel. The gate turned out to be no problem. They sped past the gatehouse and right over the chainlink barrier that had already been run down moments earlier, by Carl and his buddies driving a heavy truck. The gatekeeper could be seen though the window of his cubicle, struggling to unlock the door, his face a twisted mask of fear and confusion.

They took a right on 119th and headed west towards the apartment they shared on the 12,000 block of Emerald. "How long do you think we've got until they get it together?" asked Eileen as they slid dangerously around a corner.

"Not less than twenty minutes, maybe as long as an hour, I wouldn't bet on more. We won't get far in this thing though, it doesn't have the range. We'll have to take my truck."

"Steve, what are we going to do? I mean, all I was thinking about was getting out of there, but where do we go now? If those guys can off a guy like Johns, what chance do we have?"

"Relax honey, let's grab some stuff and try to work it out." They reached their place, parked in the handicapped spot by the door and ran in. Eileen went to the kitchen and threw some food into a bag, then scooped up all their warm clothing into a pair of large trash bags, ran back outside and tossed them into the back of Steve's ancient 1992 Chevy S-10 pickup. In the meantime Steve had gone down to the storage locker in the basement and brought out all their camping gear and dumped it in the truck. Total elapsed time at the apartment... just seventeen minutes. They ran up to the apartment together one last time, snatching a few oddments... a camera... Eileen's notebook computer... Steve's flute, and some food from the fridge, then they careened back down the stairs towards the street.

On the ground floor they were met by a middle aged woman in robe and slippers, with her hair done up in rollers and carrying a newspaper. "Hi Eileen. Going somewhere with your friend?" she said.

"Oh, Hi Mrs. Donitz. Yeah, we decided to take off early for the weekend you know, maybe head over to my grandma's place in Ann Arbor."

"Oh won't that be nice!"

"Yeah, well, bye now."

"Okay then, have fun you too, and tell your grandma hello from me will you?"

"Sure, you bet, oh, and Mrs. Donitz, if anybody from work asks where we went, please don't tell them alright? It's kind of a honeymoon thing."

"Oh? Did you get married honey?"

"No, not yet."

"Well, okay, whatever you say," said Mrs. Donitz.

The pair skipped down the stairs towards the truck. "Hang on a second", said Steve. "If we leave your car here they'll know we're in the truck. If we take both cars and then ditch yours somewhere, then they'll have to look for both, it might throw them off for a few hours."

"That sounds good. If Mrs. Donitz keeps true to form they'll think we're heading for Ann Arbor even before they ask her. Let's start out in that direction, then drop the car, maybe with a flat tire. Then we cut out some other way."

"Good thinking," said Steve. "I'll follow you."

Eileen drove the electric car a few miles east on I-94 towards the intersection with I-90, then pulled it to the side of the road. She picked up the pistol that had belonged to Adam from the front seat next to her, got out of the passenger side door. While squatting down alongside the car, she thumbed the safety off and pulled the trigger hard in double action mode, putting a bullet into the tread of the little car's front tire. It hissed flat in about two seconds. She then flipped the safety lever up, dropping the hammer safely back into carrying mode, and picked up the spent brass cartridge case from the snow, slipping it into her pants pocket. Eileen climbed into the waiting truck and was looking carefully around as Steve put it in gear and pulled back onto the highway.

"Which way should we go?" asked Eileen, squirming to make herself comfortable in the cramped cab. She looked back into the truck bed and could see that, to someone watching them go by, it would look as though they were just driving a load of trash to the dump; the back was piled with black plastic garbage bags full of lumpy things.

"Do you think anybody saw us, or heard the shot?" Eileen asked.

"Well, there have been people going by the whole time, but you know Chicago, nobody even so much as gave us a second look."

"Yeah, I figured as much."

"So, where should we go Steve?"

"Well, which way would they expect us to go?"

"We can't go east since that's what we told Mrs. Donitz."

"Right."

"West or South would be the logical choices if we want to try to get lost. The country is more open that way."

"North then."

"You think?"

"Sure, don't you remember your Uncle's cabin up on the Keweenaw. Heck, we could hole up there and nobody'd ever find us. Maybe we can get our bearings and see if we can't get some help. We have the data cartridges, we could put Sherman behind bars for good just with what we've got on his shady business dealings, much less with the new stuff."

"Steve, have you ever been up there in the winter?"

"Not to the cabin, but I was at Michigan Tech for a year remember? I know the area a bit."

"Steve, living in a college dormitory doesn't count, that cabin is way up by Eagle River. That's pretty rough country this time of year. It's right by the lakeshore."

"Look, we've gotta do something okay? You got any better ideas?"

Eileen furrowed her brows and thought for several minutes as they continued to drive east on the freeway. "Well, they probably won't expect us to head that way."

"Right, come on, scoot over here next to me, yeah, that's better. Don't worry, we'll be okay. We got lots of food, a pile of cash, nice warm sleeping bags, a tent, snowshoes, hey, we even got us a gun." He picked the pistol up off the floor where Eileen had laid it and blew across the barrel, like the cowboys in the old western movies used to do.

"Steve, would you please put that thing down."

"Okay, here, stick it in the glove compartment."

"Can't we just throw it out the window or something, I hate even having it in here."

"What are you talking about, you did pretty good with it back there, and we may need it yet," said Steve seriously. "Hey, there's a Stop and Shop, let's cash out our accounts at the automated teller."

"I guess we'd better, " Eileen answered, "now we know what he was doing when he had us track people's withdrawals. We've probably got just one chance to get at our money before they start tracking us and shutting down our access."

"Well, we're even further east now, hopefully that will reinforce the idea we're heading towards Michigan."

"Hopefully."

The rickety old truck stopped at the convenience store, they gassed up and withdrew as much cash from their bank accounts as the automated machines would allow. Steve got back on I-94 and headed in the opposite direction... up the Lake Michigan shoreline north. The snow was not too bad... not here... not yet, but as they headed north out of the city it slowly grew deeper, falling heavily as they went. They talked about times they had shared together, other road trips and winter ski outings, and Eileen's summertime visits to her uncle's cabin up on Lake Superior. For the moment, they just enjoyed the vacation feeling of being on the open road with a pocket full of money and no place special to go. It was a good feeling, a happy adventurous feeling. Both of them knew in the backs of their minds that it might not last, that there might be professional killers on their trail... perhaps even already... but that thought was suppressed for the time being. Eileen leaned against Steve's shoulder as they moved slowly and steadily northward past Waukegan and eventually they passed the sign saying "Welcome to Wisconsin".

Steve put his arm around her and said softly; "You did good honey, thanks." He kissed her hair.

"You did too." She said. "Somebody really must be looking out for us."

"Yeah, lucky thing we ran into Carl."

"Yeah. I wonder how he's doing."

"Oh, I wouldn't worry about Carl and his friends, they know their way around pretty good." He paused in thought... "Look... Eileen, I don't know what's going to happen from here out."

"Me neither."

"What I mean is... well, up until today I thought we had our lives pretty well planned out. You know, we'd make some money... buy a house in the suburbs... get married someday... all that. But now, babe, I don't know what to say. I can't see much past that road sign up ahead."

"It's okay Steve..."

"No, it's not okay!" Steve said with conviction. "I need to have at least one thing I'm sure of."

"What are you saying?" asked Eileen. There was a long pause before Steve answered.

" I guess Mrs. Donitz gave me the idea, but... well.... Eileen, would you marry me? now... today?"

Eileen sat up and looked at Steve as he drove. "Are you kidding?"

"I've never been more serious in my life."

"Okay then."

Steve looked over and met Eileen's eyes for a moment, then looked back at the road and smiled. Eileen snuggled back up against his side and closed her eyes. Life with Steve was always filled with surprises. She never knew what to expect next, and she liked it that way. She breathed in the smell of his flannel shirt as the little pickup truck chugged steadily on northward through the deepening snow.

CHAPTER 13

The harsh light from the flashlight lying on his desk gave an eerie look to George Sherman's face. Behind him the wan gray light of morning peeped in through the heavy closed curtains. Julius Miller had never seen him in such a state. Even in ordinary circumstances Sherman exuded an oily aura of tension and fear, but now it crashed upon the others in waves of malevolent force.

"I WANT those two! Do you understand? Nobody does this to me, NOBODY!"

The door opened awkwardly on broken hinges, and a man in a black suit carrying a flashlight entered. "Report!" barked Sherman.

"Sir, power is still down, and the doors are still all locked."

"I can tell that you damned fool, what's being done about it?"

"Well sir, we've got some men in mechanical working on firing up the old backup generator by hand. It's been years since anybody's had to do this, the computer always started it as necessary."

"Make a note for the future; manual backup training to be mandatory for all mechanical personnel."

"Yes sir."

"What about the computer?"

"Well, that's a little trickier sir. Our best people, at least, the best ones we have left, are down there now. I hate to bother them as they're working as fast as they can to try to figure out what the problem is. Best I can make out, the, um, ...the others, the ah....."

"Traitors!"

"Yes sir. The traitors have apparently placed some type of automatic self shutdown program into the mainframe. It won't reboot normally, we think there may be a virus interfering with the boot sequence. We'll have to reload the operating system from scratch to get a clean boot, it could take several hours.

They're working with their own power supply now and have called for emergency support from the software vendor."

"Why can't you just restore from backup? Those things are supposed to be backed up every day aren't they?"

"Sir, the backup cartridges are missing too, we're having to get all new stuff from the vendor. We should be thankful it didn't happen on a weekend or we wouldn't have been able to get hold of anybody."

"I'll try to remember that," Sherman said sardonically. "Is that all?"

"Uh, yes I think so."

"Then get out."

"Yes sir."

The man reflexively tried to close the door, then gave up quickly and walked off down the dark hallway. Sherman glared around at the six men in the room. "Well, what do you think?" He seemed calmer now, his rage having subsided to a quiet seething."

Julius Miller looked at the other men in Sherman's office, men of his own breed, professional assassins. When he looked at Sherman he saw George's eyes boring into him like cobalt steel drill bits. George Sherman was the only man in the world that frightened him. The others looked at him also, expecting him to speak. He was the senior member of the board now, with Jameson missing. It was his right to speak first after Sherman.

"We'll have to bring them in, at least one of them alive, and find out what they know and who they told about it, in order to minimize the damage."

"Very good Julius," said Sherman mockingly, his face reddening. "OF COURSE, we need to bring them in, you pigeon-puke eating moron! The question is WHO is going to do it, HOW, and most importantly, WHEN?"

There were eyebrows raised around the room, George Sherman had never been so insulting to one of their group, much less to one in so senior a position. Julius Miller had a long and stellar record of clean missions for Sherman. Julius calmed the rising blood lust rising in his gut, there would be time for that later, he cleared his throat for attention and spoke calmly. "I'll get them myself sir," he said evenly. "They'll probably head south. As soon as the computer is up again we can track any financial transactions they make; we know their vehicles, their family, and their friends. In the meantime I'll go to their apartment and see what I can find, I might even catch them there though I doubt it. Still, they can't know very much, can they? They can't possibly know what our capabilities are, or what our policies are for dealing with such situations. They won't get far."

"That's just it Miller. We don't know how much they know... But something tipped them off to make a run for it just before they were to be dealt with, and they have the computer data storage tapes with everything on them.

EVERYTHING do you understand? Not just about me, but you and everyone else in this room as well."

"But sir, those are all in top security encrypted files aren't they? Surely he can't have broken all of those codes."

"Of course Julius, he hasn't broken them all... yet... but our friend Steve is one of the top encryption men in the world, even though we've been extremely careful to be sure that he doesn't realize that. All this time he's thought that his encryption schemes were just a hobby on the side, when that's been the real focus of his employment here. At the moment of breakthrough he decrypts one of our own files, one of YOUR files I should mention, then he spooks, and absconds with everything, him and that damned bitch of his."

Miller regained his composure. "Sir, my recommendation is..."

"I don't give a flaming rat's ass about your recommendation, just get out there and get them."

"Yes sir, just as soon as....."

Suddenly the lights in the room came on and a series of clicking noises echoed down the hallway as all the doors in the building returned to their ordinary settings. Sherman steepled his hands together, cocked his head to one side and looked at Miller with raised eyebrows. No words were necessary.

Julius Miller accepted the data cartridge Sherman handed to him without thanks, turned and left the room. He was angry with Sherman for humiliating him in front of the board, but determined to do a good job on this mission and regain his superior's favor. This would be no simple pop job though, he needed at least one of the two alive for questioning. They were smart too, he knew that. Well, this was his game, his turf. Julius was a hunter, one of the best in the business. He had their files out and had already briefed himself on the location of their apartment. As he passed the front desk and headed to his car he relaxed himself by imagining all the various ways that he might accomplish his task, each imaginary scenario accompanied by vivid memories of successful past sanctions. He smiled to himself as he always did before a job. Ah it was good, a clear goal, no decisions to make but tactical ones... make it good, make it clean, and if at all possible, make it look like an accident.

CHAPTER 14

A cool gray glow filtered in through the window over the bed as Digger awoke a second time. He rolled over and looked at the digital clock on the nightstand, it read 9:37 A.M. The events of the night before were a little hazy in his mind, but the smell of the bed and the feel of the sheets confirmed to him that it had all been quite real. He heard a rustle behind him and turned to see Joan standing there looking at him. She had already gotten dressed in jeans and flannel shirt, with her heavy boots showing a few sticking snowflakes, melting to a dewy wetness.

"Well, sleepy head, how you feeling this morning?"

Digger stretched and yawned. "Don't really know yet, give me a minute." He got his feet placed on the floor and stood up, just a little shakily. His head ached dully, but not too bad, he'd had much worse hangovers from less alcohol. He suspected that the adrenaline pumping of the previous night had burned it off. He moved to get his clothes from the chair where he'd tossed them the night before, and found them missing.

"They're in the wash, smelled like beer and cigarettes... disgusting. So, how's the head then?"

"Good. I feel good," he said, taking a deep breath. "How about you?"

"Happy." She answered and smiled. He went over to her and enveloped her in his arms for a moment, and shared a gentle but brief kiss. "Here's something you can put on until your clothes are done." Joan held out a worn pair of brown coveralls with a red flannel lining. "I usually wear them over my clothes for working outside, but they ought to fit you okay with nothing underneath."

He chuckled a bit and climbed into them, they were a bit snug on him, but he was able to zip them up all the way. She stood back and eyed him approvingly. "Yes, that will do nicely, but just one minor adjustment is necessary."

"Oh? and what is that?" he asked. She reached up and pulled the zipper down about four inches to his mid-chest.

"Yes, just right." She smiled. "I might have to get you to wear those for me sometime, you look delicious in them. But for now, what do you say to some breakfast?"

"Sounds good," Digger answered, while Joan walked to the door and opened it. Shuffling feet and the sounds of cookware and utensils banging around could be heard just around the corner from the kitchen. Joan disappeared and Digger sat down on the edge of the bed to pull his shoes on. A heavy wave of wholesome kitchen smells hit him as he sat there. He detected coffee, pancakes (or perhaps waffles, hard to tell from the smell) and the unmistakable aroma of bacon frying. Since he didn't have his socks on he decided not to bother lacing the boots up, but walked out to the kitchen with his laces dragging. He tuned the corner just in time to see Arne flipping a pancake nearly to the ceiling, then deftly catching it in the pan.

"Good catch Arne!"

"Oh dere you are Digger. Hey, and a good morning to ya. How's about a cup o' coffee then?" Joan had disappeared somewhere.

"Oh man, sounds great!"

"This is da real stuff Joan's got here, not dat plasticky stuff dey sell at da Red Owl." Arne poured Digger a tall flagon of the brown fluid and Digger put his face down close and breathed in deeply.

"You have no idea how good that smells! Gosh, where'd you learn to flip cakers like that Arne?"

"Oh heck, used ta cook for da lumberjacks in da winter up da peninsula back when. Seems like it's all comin' back ta me now."

A dark look passed quickly over Arne's face for a moment, then he brightened again. "Hey, look here Digger, bacon, da real 'ting too, not dat pressed turkey crap."

Digger leaned over the pan, not too close for fear of getting spattered by the sizzling grease, and took a deep breath through his nose. "Wow, smells like it's maple sugar cured or something."

Joan walked in with an armload of stovewood and stomped snow off of her boots. "There's a guy that smuggles some of that across the lake from Thunder Bay once in a while for me. That's one of the things we're going to do if we become a state, repeal the prohibition on pork products. Every since the poultry lobby got in back in the 1990s there's been no pleasing them. Ha, enough politics, let's eat!"

There was quite a stack of pancakes already on the table, and Arne was just putting the bacon on a plate. Joan went into the pantry and brought out a fancy cut-glass bottle with a ground glass stopper. She held it as though it were something precious, and Digger gasped. She nodded, smiled, and turned the bottle so that he could read the label. It said: "Real Maple Syrup, product of the free Dominion of Quebec".

At last they sat down to eat. Arne dug in with a gusto that Digger had never seen in him. Come to think of it, Digger had hardly ever seen Arne when he wasn't drinking. Arne seemed unimpressed by the sumptuous fare, but Digger was as awed as if he were dining with Prime Minister Hernandez herself. It had been years since such foods had been available to folk of ordinary means in these parts, and Digger wondered how Joan could have afforded such luxury.

The meal was everything Digger imagined and more. he experienced a feeling of being transported to his childhood, of staying over at his grandparents cottage in Eagle River back in the old days. He felt like a kid again. For Arne the sense of comfort was more subtle. The taste and smell, the activity of cooking had brought him to his past as well, but rather than recalling his childhood, he remembered himself as a young adult, cooking for the lumbermen in the woods, and for the other soldiers during his stint in the army. Those were the "good old days" for Arne, back before his job at Quincy Mine, before his life had gone horribly awry.

Joan savored the fare as much as the two men. She didn't mention it, but this was as special a breakfast for her as it was for them. She had made some friends in high places who had offered her these precious luxuries of a bygone era. She smiled and looked at her guests. There was very little conversation aside from the severely practical matters of "pass the butter please", and "is there any more coffee?" She lifted her coffee cup and breathed deeply the heady aroma of the Irish Creme blend. She looked over the rim of her cup at Digger, and met his eyes. He gave her a big smile, then dug back into the quickly dwindling pile of pancakes on his plate. She continued to watch him. There was no doubt in her mind that he was "the one". She had felt the possibility the moment he had gotten into her car... indeed... she had felt something even before that, when she had merely seen the shadowy figure on the side of the road, wreathed in swirling snow. She and Digger were almost the exact same age, both had grown up in the Copper Country, but they had never met, she was sure of that. Why? She looked at Arne and felt a tug of affection for him as well, not in the same way, not as she would a husband or lover but more as she would feel for a grandfather, or a favorite uncle. Arne glanced over and smiled, giving her the thumbs up before plowing back into his plate. It would do him good she thought, he's so skinny and frail looking. Joan wrestled within herself with conflicting thoughts. On the one hand her psychic talent told her that these men were being straightforward and honest with her. Her intuition told her that they were somehow important to her mission, to the political movement which had become the central focus of her life for the last six years. On the other hand she loved them, especially Digger. She flushed a little when she realized how forward she had been the night before, but he was so shy, and she had to make sure he knew where he stood with her.

Both men finished their plates at about the same time, using the last pieces of pancake to soak up the last precious traces of the maple syrup. Digger got up and took his plate to the sink, and ran some hot water into the basin as he leaned forward and looked out the window that faced the south.

"Still snowing like crazy, but the wind has died down some at least." He stretched and yawned before turning off the hot water that quickly fogged the cold window over the sink. Joan watched him stretch and secretly reveled in the way the tight overalls pulled up tight around his buttocks and revealed a bulging in the front.

Arne got up, "I'll help ya," he offered, but Digger waved him back.

"No way dude, you cooked it, Joan's the hostess, I'll clean up."

"Thanks guys." said Joan between bites. "I'll give ya a hand when I'm finished."

"Take your time. No hurry, I have a feeling we won't be going anywhere soon."

Digger took the dishes from Arne's place, and put away some of condiments as Joan finished her plate. He quickly washed up the dishes and pans in the sink, and set them in a rack to dry. Joan brought hers over just as he was finishing and gave him a hug with one arm as she dropped the dishes into the steaming basin of hot water. Digger kissed her on the forehead, then she turned her face up and kissed him on the lips. They heard a chuckle and turned. Arne was leaning his chair back and sipping at his coffee cup.

"Oh, don't mind me." Said Arne, smiling broadly. "You two look good together."

Joan and Digger came hand in hand back over to the table, Joan brought the pot of coffee from the stove and they sat down. They sat down and refilled their cups, sitting quietly for several minutes, then Joan put a serious look on her face and broached the subject they had been studiously avoiding. "Look fellas, we gotta talk about some things. Digger already knows... but Arne, we had a phone call last night from a friend of mine. It turns out that the FBI is looking for you, looking for both of you. We need to find out why. I told Digger before, and I'm telling you now Arne, that I'm part of a group that is working to help the U.P. secede from Michigan and become a state on its own. Lots of people are working, in lots of places to try to make that happen. I have a feeling that you guys are somehow tied up in it all, but I still don't understand how."

Arne got a haunted look in his eyes. "Digger, I told ya ta tell nobody."

"I didn't Arne, she figured out some on her own, but I didn't say anything about what you told me last night."

Joan raised one eyebrow in surprise, but said nothing. Arne looked back and forth between them. They both looked at him, and Arne could see that he was loved. He could trust these two.

"What is it ya want ta know?" Said Arne.

"Well, I don't understand what the FBI wants with you, what it is that you consider so secret, or why I get this strange feeling from you."

Arne got a faraway look in his eyes. "I forgot ya see, for a long time I just forgot everyting. Oh sometimes I'd remember a little, but it always made me sad, made me want ta drink more, made me want ta drown da memory because I couldn't stand the thought."

"Forget what Arne? Were you in a war?"

"Oh yeah, I was in a war, but dose were really pretty good times for me, no, it wasn't dat I was trying ta forget."

"Would you tell us Arne? Please, I think it's important." Said Joan.

Arne looked pained: Digger spoke up. "Arne, it's okay, you're with friends now. We'll do everything we can to make sure you're safe."

Arne took a long deep breath, closed his eyes for a moment, then looked at them both, sighed, and began....... "I was born in Laurium on August 21, 1882." Digger heard Joan's breath draw in with a gasp, but Arne kept right on...

"I remember growing up dere, my dad was a miner at da Calumet and Hecla mines. He came with his family from da old country as a kid. My mom was from the Welsh people who moved dere about da same time. It was a hard life I guess, my dad worked long hours, but he became a shift captain and was doing pretty good. I had two younger brudders, and one older sister. I remember we used ta have a breakfast like this on special days, like Christmas morning. I always helped mom in the kitchen, especially after she broke her hip one time, so I learned ta cook pretty good.

"I went ta school all da way through da 8th grade, did pretty good too. and then one winter, I remember I was fourteen den, it was a bad time... and my dad died in da mine. My sister had got married da year before and moved ta Hancock wit her man, but they weren't too flush with dough, he was a miner too, and couldn't help us much. I got a job with the lumberjacks dat would cut timber up da Keweenaw in da winter. Well, I was always kinda small even in dose days, and dose guys figured I couldn't do much, 'til they tasted my cooking! So dat's what I did the winter of '96-'97, I cooked for forty guys at a lumber camp and sent home my pay to my ma. My younger brudders was helpin' her out around da house, and things was okay.

"I got a reputation for cooking good, and you know, Calumet was a pretty wild place in dose days. Dat summer I got a job cookin' at a fancy eatin' place in town. That was real different of course, I had ta learn a whole other way of cooking, it was more like cooking at home. It was while I was there dat she come in. I can't describe how I felt... well... maybe you know. Dis beautiful young girl comes in with her ma and pa for dinner one night. I seen her as I was workin' and just couldn't believe my eyes. I set my hopes on winning her right den and dere. It was stupid I know, her folks was rich, but Maggie was really someting.

"Anyway, dat first time I seen her I listened when dey ordered, and I took a rose off one of the tables and trimmed it and put it on her plate like a garnish. When she got it she looked right up at me, where I was staring at her over the counter and she smiled. Well, I found out who she was and started courting her. Her dad din't like me much because I was young and just a cook and he wanted more for her. Besides, he was an old Army man, a veteran of the Civil War, and didn't think a fella was a man unless he's been in da Army."

"Dat winter dey asked me back to da lumber camp, but I was doin' so good in town I said 'no'. And besides, I wanted to be near Maggie. My ma was doin better too, and my brudder Willie was workin' wit da horses for da city. Well, it was dat winter if you remember, I'll never forget it... February 15, 1898, dose Spaniard sons of bitches sunk da battleship Maine down in Cuba. All da guys was signin' up for da army, and I seen my chance ta get in good wit Maggie's pa, so I joined up too."

"So, I said good-bye to Maggie and my ma and went off to da army. Well, it wasn't long before dey figured out I knew how ta cook for a big bunch of guys, so I become da cook aside from regular soldier stuff. I fought down dere wit Teddy Roosevelt himself, an' I got letters from Maggie almost every week. Well, when it was over I went home and Maggie was still there waitin' for me. I asked her to marry, and she said she would, so we hooked up in June of ought one, when I was eighteen and she was seventeen. Da only person mad about it was Eino Maki, who I guess was her boyfriend before I come along. He never quite gave up on her, and he hated my guts for stealing her away, as he thought of it."

Arne stopped, picked up his coffee cup, and took a sip. He looked at Joan and Digger who were staring at him in rapt attention. "You sure I'm not borin' ya?"

"No please, Arne." Said Digger. "I've known you from the bar for a long time, but I never heard any of this, I never knew you were married."

"Yes, please go on." Said Joan.

"Well," Arne rubbed his chin. "I guess I sorta put it all in the back of my mind for a long time." He took another sip from his coffee cup, then continued. "Ya see, those were good times for me. Maggie and me, I can't even tell ya, we was the happiest couple I can imagine. We lived at my ma's house in Laurium for a while, then the diner closed down and we moved down ta Hancock where I went ta work at the Quincy. My ma wasn't too happy about it, seein' that dad had died in a rockfall, but the money was decent so I took it." We had Reuben in '03, and then little Annabelle in '04. God they was such sweet kids. I loved 'em, and they loved their pa. I remember comin' home, just before...... comin' home that last time, little

Reuben came running up and threw his arms around my neck as I bent down, and Anna comin up too."

Arne's chin started to quiver, Joan reached out and put her hand over his. "Arne, I know it's hard, but I want you to tell us as exactly as you can what happened at the mine that day, I think it might have something to do with all of this other stuff that's going on."

"Okay Joan, just give me a minute."

Joan squeezed Arne's hand tighter, and Digger got up to check the woodstove. He opened the damper with a metallic squeak, then the door. After poking the remnants around a bit He put two more logs in, closed it up and turned the flue damper down again. When he returned to the table, Arne looked up at him, his eyes wet with tears. Digger smiled and squeezed Arne's shoulder.

"Ya see," began Arne. "Losing a child is da worst ting dat could ever happen to a person, but it was worse than if they had died, because I was the one that died, not them."

Joan furrowed her brow. "I don't understand Arne, what do you mean you died?"

"You'd better start from the beginning." Added Digger.

"Okay, well, it was like any udder day, around Easter it was, maybe da seventeenth of April I think. It was nice out that night, the sky was clear and beautiful. I was workin' da graveyard shift den, going down at midnight and comin' back up about nine da next mornin'. I kissed Maggie good-bye, and looked in on the kids sleeping before I left. I walked over to da adit on Vivian street, lit my carbide lamp, and walked up to da number two shaft. A bunch of udder guys was there, and I rode da mancar down with 'em and got off at da fifty fourth level. That's da machine shop where I was workin' on sharpening some rock drills for da guys down furder in da mine, fifty four was only about halfway down... deepest mine in da world dey used ta say it was. I remember it was me and Toivo Hautamaki was dere, we had some four inch pipe to cut and tread on da lathe, and all dese rock bits ta sharpen. A few years back dey had set up dis shop down dere in da mine so as not to have to cart da stuff up and down da shaft so far. So me and Toivo was workin dere most all da day. Machinist was pretty good work, better pay and not so dangerous as drifting or stope work or powderman, though I done all those too. We broke off for pasties about four, and some guys come up from below wit some more bits to sharpen and dey ate wit us. It was pretty close ta quittin' time, I guess about seven or maybe a little later, that everyting went crazy.

"So, I'm sittin' on dis stool see, takin' a minute, while Toivo's leanin' against the side of the lathe dere about five feet away, havin' a smoke. We start ta feel da ground move den see, real gentle like, so ya wouldn't even notice if ya weren't sittin' still. I look over at Toivo and he looks at me; we both been underground a while ya know; feelin' da ground move is not somethin' that you ever expect ta happen. And den dere was dis noise. I can't tell ya what it was like really, cause I never heard nuttin' like it before nor since. It was like roaring noise, like a waterfall or someting, but mixed wit da croaking of metal bein' torn up, and da screams of men scared shitless. I was just sittin' on da stool dere in da machine shop. It was open to da tunnel on one side see? Toivo takes a couple steps towards da drift, and den dese udder two guys come running down. One guy looks over and sees us and says "Hey...", dat's all he said, dat's all he had time ta say. Den dat roaring noise is getting louder and dere's dis big like a "whoosh" and dose two guys are just gone, nothing but a bloody mark on the wall. All dis stuff comes crashin' down da drift, ore cars and twisted rails come shootin' down da tunnel from da north, from da direction of da number six. Da air got all choked wit dust, and I saw stuff bangin off da walls in da shop. I just dropped to da ground and covered my head while da noise was so loud I thought I was dyin. After a little bit da noise starts dyin' out, it's still dere like, but not so loud. I look up, and all da lights are out. I called out for Toivo, but he dint answer. Da air is full of da smell of rock dust, mixed wit' hydraulic oil and human shit, a horrible smell. Da high pressure water lines was busted, sprayin' water all over everyting. I always keep a candle and a couple matches in an oilskin pouch in my pocket. I got it out and lit it, tryin' ta protect it from da spray that was drenchin' me. I called out for Toivo again, no answer, I crawled over towards where I thought he was, then I saw him. A big chunk of iron rail had wrapped around the corner of the room and cut him right in two. God it was awful, I puked my pasty up right dere. I dug in my bag and got out my carbide lamp, got it lit and looked around more wit da better light. It was unbelievable. Da whole place was just torn to shreds; only da stool where I was sittin was left in one piece. I figger da blast of air sorta made an eddy in da room, it swirled around and around and I was just lucky enough ta be in da eye of it. Da noise of da blast had died away, and except for da hissin' and drippin of da water, dere was no sound. I went out to da shaft and looked around, I yelled and dere was no answer, just pieces of bodies and a bad smell everywhere. God, how can I even tell ya, dere's no way, no way ta tell ya. I dint know what was happenin'. I never heard nor seen anyting like it. It was like da hand of Satan reached up out of da pit of hell and ripped da place to pieces. And I was left, just me, out of all dose guys I'm da only one what lived. But den... den is when da blue light come."

    Arne looked up, he had been staring fixedly at the table while he was talking. Digger an Joan were silent as Arne looked from one to the other.

    "I... I don't know if I can talk about da rest. It's so... you'll tink I'm nuts like everybody else. It just don't make no sense!"

    Joan looked at Arne solemnly. "I believe you Arne. I may not understand how some of these things could be, but I truly believe that your story is real and that it's what you experienced."

Digger nodded agreement. "You talked a little about the blue light before. I think it's important, it may be the key to understanding what happened to you."

"Yeah, okay, I'll try. My throat's gettin' dry. Ya got anything?" Said Arne.

"You bet, how about some apple juice?" Joan said, on her way to the refrigerator.

"Ya sure, dat'd be great."

She brought the glass of juice back and set it in front of Arne, who sipped at it. Digger had found a piece of paper and was busy making a sketch of the mine, trying to portray the location of Arne's experience. He was quite familiar with the Quincy, so it was a fairly accurate sketch showing the number two shaft, the adit on the second level that led out to the Vivian Street entrance in Hancock, and the underground machine shop. Arne looked at it and nodded, pointing to the spot on the map.

"Okay, so what's this about a blue light?" Asked Digger after Arne had refreshed himself and seemed to calm down a bit. "Was it a rescue party?"

"Nope, not yet. No rescue party ever used a light like dat. Sometimes I see it again in nightmares, a deep dark blue, almost black, but so bright it hurts your eyes just ta look at it. Ya see, dere was no point in tryin' da shaft, it was too tore up ta be safe, so I decide ta try to make it over to da number six, if it's okay, or even da number eight if I had ta. I figgered I could catch a ride up from dere, I didn't feel like I could make it so far up da ladder anyway. So I'm walkin' along da drift dere, headin' north past all dis wreckage and stuff. And den I seen it, slowly movin' down da tunnel towards me. It was... well... da only ting I can tink of is a fish net. I was like a scoop net dat filled da whole tunnel, kinda bowed in da middle, but it wasn't made of no string. The look of it was like the way a soap bubble looks, all shiny like that, with little ripples, but it was glowing wit dis deep blue light dat made it look like someting out of da night sky. When I seen dat I was scared shitless! I tried ta run back da udder way, but dere was so much crap all over I couldn't make no time. As it got closer I could hear dis sound too, it was like a bee buzzing maybe, but that just made it worse. I got so scared I tried ta run, and finally I tripped over a piece of iron and hurt my leg, I rolled over, and den it was on me. I could see it comin towards me, I could sorta see through it some, like lookin' into a clear lake and you can see the bottom. It passed over all da junk on da floor, but when it got ta me, when it touched my foot da buzzing got louder and dere was dis yellow glow like fire all around my foot. I screamed, and when I looked, I could see through it and my foot was gone. I tried ta move and couldn't. I just screamed as it moved up my body and finally over my head."

Digger was sketching frantically on the mine map. "Was it about here Arne?" He said.

"Uh, maybe a little further down, yeah, about there."

"What happened?" Asked Joan. "What was it?"

Tom Maringer

"I don't know what it was, but someting happened there. I was lyin' on da floor, just like before, and I looked back and I could see da thing moving away from me. Da bulging side was towards me now, and I could see through a little, I could see da wreckage all over da tunnel floor through it, but where I was, dere wasn't any! Da floor was like regular, da rails was all in good shape. Anyway, after it went a few more feet past me it just vanished wit a sound like pullin' a cork out of a bottle. My leg was hurt pretty bad, a big open cut above my right ankle, bleedin pretty good, still got da scar. So hell, I don't know what to do anymore. None of it makes any sense at all. Anyway, I tried ta tie my leg up, but it's still bleedin a lot. I headed on back towards da number two shaft, kinda limping along, and I get to da machine shop, and it's all lit up with fancy lights, and there's all these brand new tools, and there's four guys in dere. Dey looks over at me and one guy says, "Hey, who da hell are you?" and I says, "I'm Arne Harjaala" and da guy says, "Well what are you doin here?", and I says, "I work here." So dis guy says, "like hell you do!" just like that. My head is spinning and I'm feeling dizzy and I musta passed out I guess, because da next ting I can remember I'm strapped in a stretcher on da mancar goin' up da shaft. We got to da shaft collar and deres all dese folks around, in funny lookin' clothes, and dey put me in an ambulance like nothin' I ever seen."

Digger sat with his mouth open in awe, Arne noticed him and thought that Digger didn't believe him. "I'm tellin' ya Digger, it's God's honest truth. I went down in the mine in April of 1906, and when I came back up later da same day they told me it was 1944. I know it sounds crazy, but that's what happened."

"No Arne, it's okay, I believe you, I really do. I'm just thinking, I may be able to shed some light on this after all, I need to think about it for a while, but please, go on with the story if you can."

"Well, dis is da worst part. First dey think I'm just some nut wanderin' around in da mine an' dey got da Sheriff down dere and he's gonna charge me wit' trespassin. I'm tryin' ta tell 'em who I am. Da mine manager comes over and sez dey got no Arne Harjaala on da payroll. I'm gettin' mad now an' I sez to send for my wife, Maggie Harjaala, on Sampson Street in Hancock. Dey says dere's no such name on Sampson Street. I'm gettin' real shook up now, dey got me in dat bed at da hospital and I tell 'em ta try again, Maggie Harjaala, 113 Sampson Street. After a while dey come back, with dis older woman in her sixties, with gray hair. I look at her, and it's her, it's my Maggie, but she's old, and she's holdin' on some guy's arm and it's Eino Maki, that slimy son of a bitch that wanted her back in school days. She took one look at me and looked at the Sheriff and said. 'That's not Arne Harjaala, Arne died thirty eight years ago.' And then she turned to Eino and says 'It must be a demon who's stolen his soul.' She pulled out a knife and comes at me with it. 'Come out foul demon, release him,' she yells. Dey had ta pull her off and drag her away. Den Eino comes and says if I ever try ta talk to her again he'll kill me. I got ta tell ya guys, I went crazy. Da whole day was just more dan I could stand, I started screaming and yelling. I was tryin' ta get outa da bed dey had me strapped down on. I got one arm free and was gonna get out and run after Maggie when dese four big guys all in white came and held me down, and a doctor did someting to me, gave me a shot or someting."

"After that dey put me in a place where dey keep crazy people. There was a big war goin on then too, and they'd bring in guys dat were so shot up dey were like raving all da time about bombs and war stuff. I had ta wear a straitjacket sometimes when it got bad, and dey would give me pills dat made it so I couldn't think, and sometimes dey put electric shocks in my head. Sometimes some people would come and ask questions about what happened, but I couldn't remember anything. I could never seem to remember anything until just last night. After a while dey let me go out, and I had some jobs, like sweeping floors at the Douglas House Hotel and like that. Dey told me I could drink all da beer I want, so I said 'sure, why not'. Den a few years ago some new guy comes around and starts asking questions. He said he believed my story and dat if I ever remembered anyting else about what happened I should just tell Jack da bartender at Jerry's, Jack knew how ta get hold of him. He gave Jack some money, and set me up wit a place just up from da bar. I never liked him much though, kinda slippery sorta character, name of Howard or something like dat, and he never said where he was from, or why he wanted ta know about it. Does it make any sense to youse guys?" Arne looked up at them with pleading eyes.

Digger and Joan looked at each other and Arne and both nodded. Digger had been scribbling furiously on his sketch of the mine. "This is incredible! This is the first known instance of time travel! Look, over at Midnight Mining Company we've been working with a lot of wild mathematics doing the high speed modeling for the exploration machines. There's a theory of knowledge which states that anything that has ever been known, can be known again. There's a formal mathematical expression of it, but the gist is that there is no law preventing us from looking into the past to retrieve lost knowledge, we call it 'The Law of Conservation of Information.' We've used the theory to construct a device that we're calling a 'tempiloscope'. You focus the device on a place and time with a set of coordinates using the computer, and then you can see what was there at that time. We figure the archaeologists would just love it. It has other uses too."

Arne looked confused, but Joan chimed in.

"This is for real? You've done this?"

"Well, we've got a crude prototype, and have had some success with it, though it's terribly hard to control. But here's the thing! We've been assuming that objects can not be moved in time. Our math seemed to indicate that they could be, at least in the forward direction, but all our attempts to do so have failed. We concluded that there must be a prohibiting factor involved, but I think I see something here, a clue. And here's the other thing..." Digger looked at Arne. "Our equipment is set up deep in the mine. Not only do we have a lease on a convenient and private space, but it's the only place where surface turbulence in the earth's gravity field will not disturb our results. We figured it was a safe spot to try to move some things around in time. There's nobody around, it's been stable for many years..."

"You mean, you can do that?" Arne said, incredulous.

"No... well... I don't know... The experiments never got so advanced, we gave up long before we could have done what happened to you. But your description of the appearance of the field threshold, the color, the bulging, even the yellow flashes, they all fit."

"Do you think that your research is the most advanced in this area?" Asked Joan. I mean, what if someone else..."

"That possibility is almost inconceivable." replied Digger.

"Well, if you didn't... then who... what?" Arne was looking at Digger trying to understand.

"I didn't... at least... not yet! I'm not saying that we don't... the language of temporal displacement is awkward. I need to look at some of these equations again in a new light after your story. I'm seeing a possibility here that we overlooked before, a possible special case solution in which we might actually be able to move objects in time. There's still the energy problem though."

"The energy problem?" asked Joan.

"Yes. Time is like a current that flows in one direction. Moving forward in time would result in a release of energy, while moving backward in time would require an input of energy. The amounts are really very large, we don't know yet how we could deal with it.

"You mean, I can't go back?" asked Arne.

"Oh, Arne, I'm sorry. If we had the energy of five atomic bombs available we might be able to send you back, but..."

"I'd still be old wouldn't I?"

"Yeah, there's no turning back that clock. The math is quite clear, time travel has a lot of problems associated with it, temporal friction for one." Both Joan and Arne looked at him with consternation, and he realized that the concept was difficult to explain, he slowed down and tried again. "Okay look, in ordinary time we all move forward at the same rate through the time dimension. There's a kind of friction that keeps us from going faster than normal, like driving a car down a steep hill in low gear. What we figured out how to do is take the brakes off, but like that car that starts going too fast, we need a way to slow back down... we need something to absorb all that energy, the way your brake linings do.

"So... I kind of fell down a hill?" asked Arne, confused.

"Yeah, that's one way of looking at it. I don't know where all the energy went though, or when, in our current objective time, the operation took place, there may be no way to know. The key point is that since we have the evidence of your experience, it did happen, it must therefore be possible, maybe not now, but soon.

"But... you didn't do it?"

"No..." Digger held his chin in his hand with his eyes clamped shut. "Say, with that figure of 38 years, I should be able to calculate a rough idea of the temporal friction constant! Listen Joan, have you got a computer I can use?"

"Yeah sure, there's a notebook in the drawer over there."

"Great, I had a data cartridge in my pocket last night..."

"Over on the table by the washer, looks like the same kind I use."

"Yeah, oh hey, nice unit! I'll download this program and see if I can figure out what's going on here."

Arne was still trying to make sense of it all. "Hey Digger, I still don't get it. If you don't know how it works yet, then how did you do it?"

"Well Arne," Digger said as he poked at the keys of Joan's computer. "I think I probably did do it actually, or at least, my equipment did. It just hasn't happened yet!"

Arne sat back down at the table shaking his head. Joan took his hand and just held it for a long time. Digger inserted the data cartridge to download and came back over to the table where Joan and Arne were sitting. Things were starting to click into place in his mind. He put a hand on Arne's shoulder and said: "It's okay Arne, relax. We're safe now."

CHAPTER 15

Looking out the window of the Sky-Light Diner in Rhinelander Wisconsin, Chris Jameson could see the pale gray light of early morning glowing drearily in the eastern sky. Traffic was light on the highway, even though it was a workday. The snow was deep and still falling. Even though the snowplows had come through once already in the early morning, the only cars not struggling had four wheel drive and good snowtires. Jameson casually leaned back, looking out of the blue metal telephone enclosure back towards his seat at the counter. The waitress was just in the process of refilling his coffee cup. She looked up at him and smiled, he waved and returned the gesture as best he could. A smile however, was an expression that did not sit well on the face of mister Christopher Jameson. A keen observer might have deduced from his lined and scarred face, coarse gray hair and sallow skin that he was perhaps in his mid sixties, possibly a fisherman or hunter who'd spent a lot of time outdoors. Such an observation would have been rather far from the mark. Had they looked close enough to gaze into his pale blue eyes they would probably have turned away with an unexplainable, yet visceral sensation of dread. He was a hunter of men, he looked at all people as potential prey. His was not the skill of urbane speech and delicate persuasion. Jameson dealt in fear, dwelt in fear, traded fear as a commodity. In most cases all he had to do was look into someone's eyes and make a suggestion in that deep throaty rasp of his; it was as good as done. If this method did not suffice, then he could be astonishingly direct and brutal in his response. Chris Jameson was very very good at his job.

If more ordinary methods of persuasion did not suffice, it was to Jameson that George Sherman inevitably turned, and with good reason. Many a lucrative deal had taken place to Sherman's benefit because of Jameson's whispered suggestions. Contrary to appearances however, he was only 32 years old, one of the few surviving veterans of the disastrous first wave of the U.N.'s invasion of Cyprus in 2009. The experiences he had endured in those hellish few hours had changed him horribly, entirely aside from the deep scar that ran from his right temple to the center of his upper lip. Today he chose to wear the scar openly, for it had suited his purposes. Tomorrow he might appear as a very different person, for he had learned in his youth that disguises were a great help in getting things done. This natural skill was enhanced by army intelligence instructors in school, and had saved his life on several missions before Cyprus, and on many occasions since. As he stood in the phone booth he wore only the simplest of disguises, a hairpiece, some latex to increase his facial wrinkles, and some padding to make him look much heavier than his actual 75 kilos. The key to a good disguise was always the posture. Speech however, had always been Chris Jameson's weakest point, and he knew it.

Finally he heard the phone ring at the other end. Jameson had been trying intermittently for over an hour to call Sherman's office from this pay phone. His cellular phone line was not working because of the storm, and he didn't trust the banks of credit card phones. This seemed to be the only phone in town that still took coins, or 'chips' as most people now called the plastic discs that passed as small change.

After two rings a woman's voice answered. "Sherman Enterprises. How may I help you?"

"It's Jameson." He rasped out. "I need to talk to Mister Sherman, code 9." He glanced at his watch, it was almost 9:00 A.M.

"Yes sir Mister Jameson, please hold." Marsha's voice had turned cold. Talking with Jameson seemed to have that effect on people.

As he waited he took a small device out of his coat pocket and clipped it over the telephone handset. It would allow him to speak with Sherman privately by encrypting the signal. His mention of "code 9" would assure that Sherman would engage a similar device at his end as well.

"Yes?" said a brusque recognizable voice at the other end.

"Jameson here, I was unavoidably detained from the board meeting, and have been unable to get a line in until just now."

"Looks like there are difficulties all around, everything was down here due to computer sabotage."

"What happened at the board meeting?"

"We put the Midnight Mining Company project on hold for the moment while we deal with the sabotage problem."

"Who did it?"

"It was Sanders and Donovan, those two nerds in computing. They crashed the whole mainframe and made off with all our compressed and encrypted data files."

"Well, they won't be able to do anything with those, right?" Jameson ventured.

"They also took the decryption programs."

"Oh, I see. So what's being done about it?"

"It was Miller's fuck-up that spooked them, so I put him on their tail. He should run them to ground soon, and then he can clean up the mess he made so that we can get on with business as usual."

Jameson curled his lip in disgust. He hated that slimy little toad Julius Miller. The guy looked like a librarian or a tailor. Such a weasel! He allowed himself a momentary fantasy involving his hands wrapped around Julius Miller's throat.... "What about the rest of the Board?"

"They're still here, we've been waiting for your report on the Upper Michigan situation."

"I have it right here, I'll transmit in a moment. In a nutshell, the principals are being difficult, we may have to get rough. I've got Scott and Jeff keeping an eye on things up there right now, while I tried to get down to talk with you. But maybe it's better this way. You can send the rest of the board home, my boys and I can take care of this if you just give the word."

Sherman thought a moment. "Go on back up, but take no direct action, repeat, no action! Something funny is going on, and I'm not laughing. I have every confidence in your abilities Jameson, but I have a feeling that there's more to this situation than meets the eye. Midnight Mining Company is an absolutely critical acquisition for us. Nothing must happen that will squelch the deal! If you can't get them to sign without busting any heads, then I'll have to come up myself and give it a try before turning the situation over to the board."

Jameson's eyebrows shot up. He had never known Sherman to actually "take the field" personally... an interesting development! "Yes sir," he said. "I'll head back up, you can make contact at the Downtowner Motel."

"Understood, transmit now."

Jameson took a cord from the miniature notebook computer under his arm and inserted it into the "data" socket on the phone, tapped a few keys, waited several seconds while several gigabytes of data flashed across the fiberoptic lines, then hung up the phone.

He walked back to his place at the counter, took a sip of coffee, and mused over the irritating fact that he would now have to reverse his tracks back up highway 45 into Michigan's Upper Peninsula. He looked outside, the snowfall seemed a little less intense, but still coming down. There was still no sign of his vehicle, an '11 Dodge Furlow. He had run into a ditch in the heavy snow late last night trying to hurry down for the board meeting and had lost the oilpan on a hidden concrete culvert. He had convinced the mechanic that it would be wisest to work on it immediately. It was supposed to be delivered at the diner by 9:30 A.M. at the latest.

He mused at the snowfall outside, allowing himself for a moment to be transfixed by the mesmeric beauty of the swirling patterns that sparkled in the light of the outdoor floods. Fleeting images from his youth flashed through his mind, never staying long enough to really get a grip on them. He could almost remembered sledding as a child, but then the momentary thought of children triggered those other familiar mental images from Cyprus, those scenes that he would never forget if he lived ten thousand years, though he had tried every imaginable method. His eyes took on a hard, distant look as they narrowed, his stomach bunched up in knots, and his jaw took a square clenched set. The waitress came back around with the coffeepot, but took one look at his brooding visage, and saw something strangely frightening in his face. She turned away. Whatever it was that he was thinking about, she didn't want anything to do with it.

After a while Jameson went back to the phone and called the repair shop. The guy who answered sounded frightened as he told Jameson that he was waiting for parts. The flywheel had been damaged as well as the oilpan, he'd have it done by 2:30, maybe 3:00 at the very latest. Chris Jameson began to get angry, then realized that it would do no good. The car would be done when it was done. "Okay" he said, and hung up. He settled into the booth and tried again not to think of those children's faces. His guts churned for the millionth time as his efforts to banish those scenes failed. He stared into his coffee cup, poured a little cream into it and watched as the light brown storm swirled in the dark seas of his cup. He hated it when he got into one of these moods. It seemed that only when he was "working" could he focus this rage outside himself. The rest of the time his self-hate was so powerful it threatened to consume him from within. He dropped his head to the table so that no one would see the the anguish in his face, though no tears fell. "Why?" he cried out silently. "Why did I have to live to see that? Why didn't you take me too? "

And then the old familiar voice came back, a shrill tinny voice from some dark shadowy crawlspace of his mind, mocking any pretense towards goodness that ever threatened to erupt from his fevered psyche. "Because you're scum, you deserve it everything you get. How DARE you ask for better! You lived and they died, so pain and torment is all you can expect for the rest of your life. You had the chance once and you blew it, you saved yourself. You're a filthy pus-sucking COWARD. You have no right to even THINK of getting out of this hole you dug for yourself. You're nothing but a ...."

Chris Jameson fell asleep in the booth hearing the familiar voice going on and on with the litany of his many sins, his unfinished coffee rapidly cooling next to him.

CHAPTER 16

Eileen slept for the better part of an hour as Steve drove the aging Chevy truck north on I-94 through the driving snow. Road conditions in the Milwaukee metropolitan area were improving due to exceptional devotion on the part of the road crews. Eileen stirred and yawned, opening her eyes.

"Hmmm, where are we?"

"Hey sleepyhead, just coming into Menominee Falls. I figured we'd take 41 over to Oshkosh."

"Yeah okay. Are you getting hungry?"

"Yeah, you?"

"Starving. If you see anyplace that sounds good, let's get something okay?"

"Whatcha hungry for? Burgers? Tacos? Chinese?"

Eileen closed her eyes dreamily and murmured "Pancakes".

"That sounds good to me!"

"Yeah, but not those doughy masses of fluff they serve at IHOP, I want some real homemade buttermilk pancakes, with sunflower seeds cooked in, and with peanut butter and yogurt on top, and maybe some real maple syrup."

"You've gotta be kidding. There's no restaurant in the world that makes them the way your mom did, and you can hardly get maple syrup any more. This is a hopeless quest!"

"Maybe not, we've got some groceries with us, if they're not totally frozen, some crunchy peanut butter and vanilla yogurt I think... no syrup though. "

"What? You're going to go into a restaurant with a bag of groceries and just bring your own condiments?"

"Sure, why not?"

Steve laughed. "Okay, pancakes you want, pancakes you got! I'm setting my radar beacon on "PANCAKE" and giving it a 30 degree sweep forward. If any pancakes come within range we'll know about it."

They moved steadily north through snowbound farming country towards the southern tip of Lake Winnebago. They passed a number of restaurants and fast food joints that just didn't appeal, then a small weathered sign poking out of the snow caught Steve's attention.... "Peg's Pancake Palace, exit 1 mile on right." He pointed it out to Eileen. "What do you think? Want to try it?"

She smiled, "Sure, let's be adventurous."

They left the freeway at the next exit, and drove east for about a mile, finally arriving at a large log cabin type structure with a sign on the roof saying "Peg's Pancake Palace," and then in smaller letters below "The Best Pancakes in the Inhabited Universe!" There were about a dozen cars and trucks parked in the lot out front. One was just pulling out and Steve got the spot near the door. The cab had been fairly warm, so they zipped up their coats, put on gloves against the cold, and hopped out of the truck. Steve stopped for a moment to check the stuff in back. The black plastic trash bags containing all their earthly belongings were covered with snow, but secure and riding well. Eileen came around the back to his side, and they held each other's gloved hands as they walked up towards the door. An elderly man was coming out just as they reached it. He smiled in a friendly way and held the outer door open for them. He picked up a snow shovel that was leaning against the vestibule wall just inside the door and headed outside, tucking in his scarf as he went. Eileen got the inner door and held it for Steve. They entered the restaurant, noted the "Please wait to be seated" sign, and stood there, shucking their coats in the cozy warmth of the establishment, hanging them on hooks near the door. The smells coming from the kitchen were delicious! Three cooks could be seen over a countertop dashing about. The interior decor was a rather eclectic mixture. The lacquered roughhewn beams glowed warmly golden brown in the light of the incandescent fixtures. A native stone fireplace at one end had a blazing log fire going, and several people were sitting near it drinking coffee. On the walls were a number of interesting items. On one wall the theme seemed to be mining, with old miner's caps, lamps, and tools displayed. Another wall held a collection of antique cross-country ski equipment, while the third seemed to be devoted to music. There were four vintage acoustic and electric guitars, a couple of saxophones and three silver flutes lovingly displayed in velvet holders, as if they were intended to be taken down and played. They did not look at all dusty.

While they were looking around, a woman came up to them and said... "Welcome to Peg's Pancake Palace, would you like a table or a booth?"

Steve looked at Eileen and shrugged, Eileen said... "How about that booth near the fire?"

The hostess nodded and led them towards it, where they seated themselves. She was a handsome woman in her early seventies, with long salty brown hair and sparkling brown eyes. She wore a dark blue dress with a white blouse, and a heart shaped pendant made from a deep red stone. "Here are your menus." She said. "Be sure to let me know if there's anything special you need. Amber will be with you in a minute. My name's Peg. Enjoy!"

Steve stuck his nose in the menu as Eileen looked around a little more. "Check out this place Steve. It's in the middle of practically nowhere, just that tiny little sign out on the highway, but look, the place is hopping!"

Steve looked around as another couple came in the door, greeted by Peg and led to a table. All around them were people eating and talking, the delicious smells of pancakes and coffee permeating the air, along with the comforting aroma of the big fireplace. "Yeah, well check out the menu and you'll see why. I bet these are mostly locals, not people coming in off the freeway."

Eileen opened her menu and was amazed. This was no ordinary pancake house! Pancakes of every description were available, custom mixed and cooked to taste, along with a variety of condiments that made her head spin. Amber the waitress came by with the coffee pot, filled their cups and took the order. Eileen was able to order exactly what she had told Steve she wanted... Sunflower seed pancakes with peanut butter, vanilla yogurt, and a side of real maple syrup. Steve ordered crepes with sour cream and cherries. When they received their food, it was even better than they had imagined, the pancakes crisp yet light, the peanut butter homemade in house, the cherries fresh, and the dairy products locally made. Peg was walking by and Eileen reached out to her as she passed.

"Peg, excuse me, but I've just got to compliment you on your superb menu and cooking. These are the best pancakes I've had since I was a little girl. You're the only one who makes them the way my mom and dad did."

"Oh thanks honey, that makes my day!"

"I've tried to order pancakes with peanut butter and yogurt in a hundred restaurants, and they always look at me like I'm crazy, but you actually have it that way on the menu!"

Peg's brows furrowed in thought. She sat down in the edge of the booth next to Eileen. "So tell me, where are you from, if you don't mind."

"Well, I was born in Hancock Michigan, lived there 'til I was about four I guess..."

Peg's face lit up. "Oh my God I thought you looked familiar! You must be Jane's little girl, Eileen!"

Eileen was stunned. "You know my mom?"

"She was my best friend for a long time, we lived together when you were just a tiny baby. I'm your Godmother! She's the one who taught me how to make these great pancakes! Oh, what a small world. You've sure grown up haven't you? I just can't believe it! Gosh, I haven't heard from Jane in years."

Just then the door opened and the older man came back in after shoveling the walk. He stomped the snow off his boots and hung up his coat and hat. Peg called to him. "Tom, come over here, you'll never guess who this is!"

Tom came over smiled, and said "Hi."

"Guess who this is." Tom looked back and forth between Steve and Eileen, then shrugged his shoulders and shook his head. "It's Janie's daughter Eileen, our Goddaughter remember? ... the duplex up in Hancock?"

Recognition dawned in his face. "You've got to be kidding!" He said, and sat down next to Steve in the booth, shaking his hand. "Wow! So, what brings you here?"

Steve spoke up now... "Oh just heading up towards Oshkosh, got hungry and saw the sign."

Tom and Peg looked at each other then, unreadable glances passing back and forth. "The sign?" said Tom, "which sign was that?"

"You know, the old one out on the freeway, out on U.S. 41." Tom swallowed hard and took a deep breath. He got up, and bent down to whisper something to Peg, then with a smile and a wave got up and walked off. Peg stayed at the booth looking intently at Eileen and Steve.

Eileen looked confused. "What was that all about?"

"He'll be back in a minute. You've just given us something of a shock... you see, because we don't have a sign out on the highway, never did. We pretty much just do a local business here."

Steve shook his head a bit and did a double take. "Say what? But we saw it, it was a small weathered sign on the right hand side, set back off the road a ways. We never would have found the place except for that."

Peg nodded slowly. "I don't doubt you in the least, but I'd better let Tom explain. Things are finally becoming clear to me that have been cloudy for a long time. Excuse me for a moment." Peg got up to check out a couple that was just leaving. While she was up Tom came back and sat down next to Steve again. He was wearing jeans and a blue plaid flannel shirt that matched his deep blue eyes. In his hand he held a weather-beaten, coffee-stained and yellowed envelope that looked as though it had sat on the dashboard of a car in the sun for a long time... actually, it had.

"I found it under some stuff in my workshop downstairs. I had to read it again to be sure I remembered it right. You must be the ones, there's no other way to look at it."

"I'm sorry mister," said Steve, "I don't understand what you're getting at." He looked at Eileen across the table. She shrugged and raised her eyebrows. Tom

Looked back and forth between them. There was a "ka-ching" of the cash register, and Peg came back and sat next to Eileen.

"Okay", Tom began, "I'll try to take it from the top. You see, it was about this time of the year, six years ago, that I had what I call a "mystical experience" up in the Nicolet National Forest along the Peshtigo River. I was cross country skiing all alone, kinda late in the afternoon, maybe two miles from the cabin me and a couple of other guys had rented for the week. It had gotten real cold, maybe thirty below, but I was feeling pretty warm and moving along steadily. Well, I came to a place where the trail took a big detour to go around an arm of the river. I figured the ice looked pretty good with a foot or so of snow on top, and what with the cold, so I'd save myself some effort and take the short cut across the ice. I made it right out to the middle, then heard this creaking noise and felt the ice under me just give way into slush. I guess the river current had thinned it out. Anyway, I threw myself out flat to try to spread the weight, but it was too late, my skis and lower body went into the water. I slapped my arms on the surface to try to haul myself out, but the current was pulling on my skis, there was nothing to get a grip on, and I was being pulled backward into the water."

Tom reached across and held Peg's hand, she was shaking a little bit.

"How did you get out?" Asked Eileen after a few seconds.

"At that moment, I had given up all hope and knew I was a goner. I called out to God and prayed for acceptance into heaven. There was little else that I could do! Then something very strange happened. I felt a strong and gentle pull under my arms, and looked up to see an ethereal glowing form of golden light. A beautiful loving face smiled at me and pulled me out of the water and set me on the shore. Of all the things I could have said, the only thing that escaped my lips was "Why?".

"The words that the 'angel of mercy' spoke to me were like bells and choirs of light and music. As soon as I got back to the cabin I wrote them down on the back of this envelope, so I would never forget them. Reading them aloud off a piece of paper they sound all dry and cracked, but listening to her speak was like listening to a great symphony. And here they are, word for word, exactly what the angel said to me after saving my life from the river."

He pushed the envelope over to Steve, who held it sideways so that both he and Eileen could read it.....

"My child, have no fears for the destiny of your soul, for you are known and loved by the Father above, yet your tasks here on earth are not yet finished. There will come to you a daughter of God and her soulmate. Seeking nourishment for body and spirit, they will see a sign and be guided to you. Great danger pursues them. Without your help they may perish, and if they are lost, many more will follow. Give them whatever assistance you are able, this is all we ask. Peace be upon you my child, go now and seek warmth."

Steve sat stock still staring at the table with a brooding look. Eilleen started sobbing softly. Peg put an arm around her and said gently... "Are you guys in any kind of trouble?" Eileen nodded.

Tom got up from the table. "Peg, why don't you take Eileen back to the house, Steve and I will move their car around back and we'll meet you there." He looked around. Both Steve and Peg nodded. Eileen took a deep breath and got the sobbing under control, she wiped her face with a cloth napkin from the table. They all got up from the table and started getting coats, Peg went over and said something quietly to Amber, who nodded, gave her a ticket from the pad in her apron pocket, and went about her business. Tom dropped a couple of bills on the table for a tip.

After getting their coats, Peg and Eileen went through the kitchen and out a back entrance, along a shoveled path to a small log house tucked in the edge of the woods behind the restaurant. As they entered the outer vestibule Steve's white S-10 came around and parked by the door, out of view from the road or the main parking lot. Steve and Tom got out and followed the women in. After shucking coats again Peg led the way into a cozy sitting room with beautifully upholstered comfortable couches and chairs. As Tom loaded a chunk of wood into the fireplace, the other three sat down. Eileen began to cry again, the feeling of safety let her release the hardness that had kept her emotions in check thus far..

"It's okay honey, you're safe now. Whatever it is that's wrong, we'll do our best to set it right. Now you just tell aunt Peg all about it okay?"

Eileen nodded and looked at Steve, who took a deep breath, closed his eyes, and started talking............

CHAPTER 17

Frank Giacoletti awoke to the smell of fresh coffee. He opened his eyes and peered over the edge of the thick down comforter, and saw Jimmy Canaris sitting in a rocking chair in the rustic log cabin, sipping from a styrofoam cup. "Hey, you gonna offer me some or hog it all yourself?" Frank said.

"Oh, good morning captain. There was a coffeemaker and a filter full of java all ready to go, so I took the liberty. Here, I'll get you a cup. Sleep well?"

Frank twisted his neck and was rewarded with a popping noise. He sat up and yawned. "Like a rock, what time is it? Is it light out already?"

Jimmy smiled as he brought Frank a cup of steaming coffee. "Yep, after noon I'm afraid. We'll get a late start, but it looks like the plows have been through, so it should be no problem driving the rest of the way up."

Frank took the cup gratefully and held it as if it were a cherished icon. "Well, I guess it's time to get moving." He sat for a few seconds more and sipped his coffee before getting out of the bed.

Once they were moving it didn't take them long to get their gear together and out to the Hummer. The snow was still falling, though not quite as heavily as the night before. Frank jumped into the driver's seat and started up the engine, slapped the heater control to "high", and they went into the Holiday station. Dobbs was still there, or perhaps back again, they couldn't tell. "Hey, good morning you guys, you sleep good?"

Jimmy answered. "Great. Even though the room was pretty cold when we got in it, those down comforters kept us toasty warm."

"Yeah, my wife and her cousins make those, got some for sale if you're interested. Here's their card."

Jimmy took the card as Frank stood by the food counter and started looking over the breakfast offerings. "Thanks, I'll keep that in mind, looks like the plow's been by, what's the weather situation this morning?"

Dobbs poked a few buttons on the computer behind the counter. "Looks like you're clear to Houghton-Hancock anyway. More snow coming tonight, but the crews are getting caught up. You're all right if you stick to the main roads."

"Thanks mister Dobbs." Said Jimmy. "Cap'n, whatcha want for breakfast? I'm buying!"

Frank chuckled. "Oh, the big spender eh? How about a couple of those waffles, an order of that fake bacon stuff, a large coffee and one of these cheese danishes."

Dobbs moved over to the hot food counter and dropped a couple of waffles in the toaster. "And for you?" he said, looking at Jimmy.

"Double it, sounds good to me too, unless you have any real bacon."

Dobbs chuckled. "Not too likely, what with the new rules and all." Jimmy nodded understandingly. As Dobbs worked behind the counter Frank and Jimmy served themselves coffee from the tap, and sat in the booth by the front window. The snow was blowing pretty hard, but the sky was bright so it looked like it was mostly just surface snow being moved around by the wind.

A white four wheel drive Dodge pickup, probably an '03 or '04 model, came in from the east, careened off the highway and skidded to a stop by the front door. Two men piled out and hurried into the store. Frank's back was towards the door, but Jimmy saw that they apparently took notice of the Hummer parked off to the side, and exchanged some comment about it. As soon as they entered They went up to the counter, and talked to Dobbs for a few moments in subdued voices. Dobbs looked a little worried, then nodded towards the two FBI men. Frank looked questioningly at Jimmy, not wanting to turn around and stare. Jimmy returned a shrug and raised eyebrows.

The two newcomers helped themselves to coffee, then came over to the booth and introduced themselves. "Hi, I'm Joe Running Bear, and this is Joshua Sharp Axe. Mind if we sit down?" he said as they shucked off their heavy coats. Their ruddy complexion, narrowed eyes and rugged features marked them as native Americans, probably from the local Ojibway tribe. They were both older men, easily in their sixties or better, with knowing eyes that had seen many troubles... and those eyes looked troubled now. Handshakes were exchanged all around, then Frank and Jimmy scooted over to make room in the booth. Joe looked at Frank, as the older man present, and said, "So you're the guys that shot the deer on the reservation last night eh?"

"Hey, we can explain, it started as an accident....."

Joe smiled, "No, don't get me wrong, Jamey's my son, he told me all about it. We understand what happened. No it's something else... we think you may be able to help us."

Frank looked puzzled. "Jamey seems like a fine young man, but I don't understand, how can we help you?"

"Well, look, this is hard to talk about with outsiders, and I'm not sure where to begin. Some disturbing things have been happening around here, and we're not getting any help from the local authorities. The Sheriff is... well... let's not get into that right now. Since you're Federation men, and you're coming up at this particular moment, we thought you may be able to do something."

"Listen Joe, I don't think that's our department, we're detectives, not administrators, I think maybe you need to call...."

"Just listen a minute Frank, that's right isn't it... Frank? Okay, we've talked to those guys, believe me, nobody will lift a finger, we think they might be bought off, by who we don't know. Then last week there was a big tribal pow-wow.... you want to tell 'em Josh?"

"Ya sure. So like he says, we're having dis meeting see? All da tribal elders from da whole U.P. coming together, must ha' been twenty of 'em."

"Twenty two." Said Joe.

"Yeah, right... So we're having a sweat lodge, kinda like a sauna, singing da old songs, talking over tribal politics, and with us is old Chokes Horses, he's like the oldest guy alive in the tribe, some people say he was in the first World War he's so old, way over a hunnert but nobody knows for sure. Usually he's real quiet, hardly ever says a word, but he's very respected in the tribe. Anyway, he starts having a spirit vision right there in the sweatlodge, he was trembling and rolling around like a youngster and calling out in the old tongue. And he describes his vision out loud, and it's like this old story that we've heard around the lodge since we were children, but with new details. He told of a time of great danger coming upon us, when our very world would balance on the knife edge of disaster. He told of how there would be a great snowstorm, and how a spike buck would give its life to bring to us the ones who could change this fate. There would be a young one, of great skill and compassion, and an older one, carrying great pain within, yet with a deep wisdom." Joe and Joshua looked back and forth between Frank and Jimmy expectantly.

Frank started... "Uh... you're kidding right?"

But Jimmy reached his hand out to touch Frank's arm and whispered. "I don't think so sir. I had a feeling something big was up, but I never dared hope for a spirit vision."

"What? You mean you believe in this stuff?"

Jimmy ignored Frank, turned to Joe and asked: "What makes you think the vision referred to us?"

"When Jamey and the kids came in last night with the spike buck, old Chokes Horses was there, he started trembling and went and looked it in the eyes. He said that it was the one, the buck he saw in the vision. That means that you two must be the ones who can help us."

Frank raised his shoulders... "Even if we are these ones you talk about, we have no idea of what your problem is, much less how to help you."

Joe shook his head. "I'm sorry, it's so hard to explain, we are not asking for favors, we want to help you. Between what Jamey saw in you last night, and the vision of Chokes Horses we believe that you are the ones, but the vision went further, and spoke of things yet to come. I cannot tell you all of these things for fear that such knowledge might steer you from your appointed path. If you are successful then we may yet live in peace and prosperity. If you fail... if you fail, Chokes Horses says he sees only fire and flames and the ridgepole of our lodge broken in many pieces. We ask only that you remember us, remember that you do not stand alone. We stand ready to help in any way we can. Jamey gave you a telephone number. Do you still have it?"

"Yes" said Jimmy, "right here in my pocket."

"Good, keep that number, memorize it. If you call it, we will come, for the destroyer is near, we hear the breathing of his horse, we shall all need all the help we can get. Tonight we fast and pray to the Great Spirit for assistance, and we will pray for you, for your strength to be great, your skill unsurpassed, your spirit indomitable, and your wisdom deep. We bring you two gifts. For you my son..." he said, speaking to Jimmy... "this totem of the spike buck for whom you showed such compassion." He gave Jimmy a leather thong on which was strung a tiny pouch woven of deer hair. Jimmy accepted it with a nod. "The spike buck is young, yet strong and full of courage. He does not yet know all the ways he might go, yet still he chooses the right path. And for you..." he said looking at Frank, "...this stone of wisdom. When the choice is hard and the way unclear, this will help you." He gave to Frank a small rounded pebble, deep red in color. Frank looked very confused, but accepted it graciously.

Joe and Joshua stood up abruptly. Joshua spoke up. "We must go, some kind of trouble up at the casino. Don't forget to call us if you have need, and beware, for there is great danger." Without a further word or glance the two donned their coats, hurried out the door, got into the truck, and took off towards the west in a cloud of blowing snow.

"Okay then, here's your breakfast." Dobbs arrived with a tray laden with steaming hot food. He seemed to notice the consternation on the faces of the two men, and looked out the window after the rapidly receding pick-up. "I couldn't hear what they were saying to you, but I've known those two since we were cubs together. Good men, I'd trust either of them with my life at the drop of a hat." Frank and Jimmy both looked up at him, Dobbs looked back and forth between them. "Just in case you're wondering." he said, turned and went back to the counter.

They dug into their food silently for a while. Finally Frank asked Jimmy: "Well, what'd you think of that?"

Jimmy sighed, "Pretty wild story alright, but I'm not ready to just write it off. It's just too weird. I mean, those guys don't just go around playing pranks like that on white boys like us. Why would they bother?" He looked Frank straight in the eye. "I think we'd better go in there eyes open, prepared for something unexpected."

Frank was having the same feeling, but was reluctant to trust in hunches. He'd built his career on solid detective work, not vague feelings of dread, or the cryptic warnings of native mystics. "Like what Jimmy? We're going up here to pick up some guys for questioning. No big deal, just routine stuff."

"Yeah, but what about this Howarth guy who wants them? It sounded like there was something weird there. And why call us? Why couldn't Samuels handle a simple pickup on his own? Then the deer, and all this weird stuff with the Ojibways... I got a feeling we need to watch out Frank. I think we should call Samuels and see what's going on up there, but no matter what he says, let's be careful okay? I'm going to check my weapon and be sure I have a full clip."

Frank Giacoletti furrowed his brows and thought hard. This was just too weird! He looked across at Jimmy mopping up the last few drops of syrup with his waffle. A good kid alright, if this was something serious he couldn't ask for a better partner, he knew Jimmy'd watch his back. Frank had checked Jimmy's military records when he'd hired him on. Jimmy's resume' had consistently understated his accomplishments. He'd been with the second drop team on Cyprus when the U.N. had gone in to try to break up that turf squabble between the Greeks and Turks. Jimmy's unit had landed in a hot zone, hated by both sides. This kid had taken over command after both officers and NCOs had been killed, and had gotten most of the rest of his men out alive, better than most of the other drop teams did. He'd gotten the bronze star for his action, and never even mentioned anything about it. Frank felt his palms sweat. Shit! Why was he so damned nervous. He remembered the "incident" down in Detroit that had gotten him sent up to this place, his disgrace in the bureau. The memory of the smell of smokeless powder and blood struck him in the face like a blow from a heavyweight boxer. He clenched his right hand, closed his eyes, and said a silent prayer... a feeling of calmness flowed over him like a warm blanket. He suddenly felt a sense of life flowing through him, as if he'd just arisen from a sickbed after years of paralysis. He opened his right hand and looked at the pebble that lay there. Okay then, if this was to be the big one, he'd meet it with both eyes open. He took a deep breath and felt the air rush through his lungs like something totally new and strange. An electric tingle coursed up his spine as he got to his feet and started putting on his coat. Jimmy got up and looked at him strangely. Frank could see the leather thong of the totem around his neck.

"You okay cap'n? You look different."

Frank nodded, "Yeah, I feel okay. I feel more okay than I have in a long time." He started to put on his gloves as Jimmy went to the cash register to pay for breakfast, then stopped for a moment and looked again at the smooth mottled red pebble that lay in his hand. Frank smiled, then he reached into his coat and put the pebble in the left pocket of his brown flannel shirt and buttoned it before putting on his glove. Then they thanked Dobbs for his help and went out the door to the Hummer, warmed up and waiting.

CHAPTER 18

Leonard Howarth woke with a dry feeling in his mouth, a crick in his neck, and his ears tingling with the sound of Harry and Jason laughing over the rumble of the Bronco's motor. He stretched and yawned and looked outside. The snow was still coming down slowly, but the road was fairly clear and they continued to move along at a high rate of speed for the conditions. He looked at his watch and noted that it was now just after 2:00 in the afternoon.

"Hey Boss." said Harry, "Jason was just telling me a story about some guys over near Iron River that took a leaky boat out on the lake, spent more time bailing than fishing, then ended up having to hitchhike home after it sank. You want to hear it? It's pretty funny."

"Some other time maybe. Where are we?"

Jason spoke up. "Well, we've been on the road about four hours, you got yourself some good zee time, and we're about a half-hour from Rhinelander. Your home town right Harry?"

"Yep, born and raised, up to high school anyway. Too bad we won't have time to hang around any, I haven't been back there in years."

Leonard looked up sternly... "Yeah, well we don't, we've got a job to do." He looked a little remorseful when he saw the hurt look on Harry's face. He diverted his gaze to study the gauges on the dashboard. "Tell you what guys, looks like we're going to need a fuel stop soon, and tank up on food and coffee. Since you know the place, how about guiding us to a good fast restaurant around there, if there is such an animal."

Harry's face lit up. "Well, my favorite was always the Sky-Light Diner. Kinda an old-fashioned place with a counter and booths, they make the best hash-browns anywhere, or used to last time I was there. In junior high we used to go there all the time after the movies."

Jason chimed in.. "Yeah, I know the place, little turquoise colored concrete block place, kinda art-deco looking?"

"Yep, that's it." Answered Harry.

"Look guys, I don't care if it's purple or pink just as long as we can get something to eat, gas up, and get out of there in minimum time okay?"

Jason put his hand to his forehead palm outward in a mock French salute. "You got it!"

Harry helped Jason with directions as they got into town and left the highway. The Bronco pulled up to the door and Jason said, "I'll drop you guys off here and go gas up. Order me a double veggie-burger and fries with a side salad, I'll be back in a minute." They jumped out and Jason drove down the street a little ways to a gas station, where he filled the gas tank, checked the oil and washer fluid levels, and washed the crud off the windows. He stepped up to a pay phone, slipped a card into the slot and punched a long-distance east-coast number. The phone was picked up after one ring, but no voice spoke. Jason looked around casually to see if anybody was watching, then spoke into the handset. "U.N.E.C. four-two-niner seven... Rhinelander heading north, subjects on board, trouble ahead." Then he hung up and returned to the Bronco, driving it back to the Sky-Light. As he pulled in to the one available parking slot near the door, two men emerged. One wore the uniform of a Standard Oil Co. service station attendant, the other wore a long coat and looked rather disheveled. After speaking for a moment the man in the coat gave something, perhaps money, to the other man, and moved towards the blue Dodge Furlow with Illinois plates in the slot next to the Bronco on the right. Jason looked at the man. He was tall, heavy, and yet powerfully built, with gray hair and a deep scar on the right side of his face. Their eyes met for the merest instant and Jason felt waves of pain and anguish rush over him. He got out of the car and went around the back and along the right side to where the fellow was just getting into his car. Jason reached out and touched his hand as he was about to close the door. The man with the scar looked up at him, there was no fear in those eyes, only a swirling vortex of shame and rage. Images flashed through Jason's mind in a way that had become only too familiar to him. He saw with crystal clarity a fleeting image of children's bodies, burned and mangled beyond recognition, he saw the agonized squirms of those not yet dead, and heard their cries. From somewhere deep within him, some inner recess where a light always shines brightly, words welled up and came to his lips like the froth on a bubbling spring... "It wasn't your fault." he said to the man. Jason looked down into the cold blue eyes of Chris Jameson, which seemed to soften with confusion at his words. With his right hand he patted Chris gently on the left shoulder as he passed by and said softly, "You have been forgiven." Jason continued to the diner and entered. He was used to strange things happening, it was part of his job, his real job, but he never really got used to feeling the force and depth of another's pain and anguish. It surprised him sometimes, the horrors that people hold in their hearts, their shame effectively shielding them from accepting the all powerful flow of celestial forgiveness. He felt a belated surge of adrenaline hit his system as he stepped through the door.

The food was just arriving as he sat down next to Harry in a booth near the front. Leonard was busy with his plate, Harry looked at Jason... "Who was that guy? You know him?"

"Nope, never seen him before, just some guy." He watched the tow truck with the address of a Standard station on the side pull out from the end of the parking lot and leave. The driver was the one he had seen the scarfaced man talking to. He blinked his eyes and memorized the address of the station, just in case it turned out to be important. Jason looked back at the scarfaced man, who sat stock still staring off into space with his hand on the ignition, then shook his head and started his car. Jason wondered for a moment whether his words would have any effect on the man, then he smiled inwardly. He had done his part, now it would be up to others. He felt an inner confidence as he felt support flowing to him from outside. Yes, whatever happens... it will be okay!

Jason turned his attention to the food. A huge veggie burger laden with toppings greeted his hungry eyes. The big question now was: should he go for the knife and fork technique, or just grab the thing and ask for extra napkins? He decided to just dive into it with both hands. Life is meant to be lived!

CHAPTER 19

Anna Sorensen stood staring out of her office window, high up in the United Nations building. Below her seethed the teeming city of New York, fog seemed to rise from the multitude of belching vehicles thronging the city's streets. Her dark brown hair was tied in a bun behind her head, her gray eyes surveyed the city with a look of sadness. She wore a simple uniform of deep blue-green, bearing a shoulder patch inscribed U.N.E.C. with a symbol emblazoned below it depicting the globe held up and protected between cupped hands. The only feature that distinguished her uniform from that of the three others in the room was the small pins attached to her collar tabs, two tiny golden seven pointed stars.

She turned to the others and sighed. "If we can't pull this off, you know what it means?" The others stood silently, signifying their assent with simple nods. "This is quite possibly the most important operation we've ever mounted, and more than ever it is of paramount importance that the agents of the national and continental governments remain unaware of our involvement. Who do we have on the scene?"

One of the others, a small wiry man stepped forward, and punching a few buttons on a hand held notebook computer he said. "Number 4297 is the best situated at the moment, he was placed in deep cover in the Twin Cities FBI office over a year ago, and is escorting the two SIB men to the area now. He just checked in less than an hour ago reporting good progress and an insight of trouble ahead."

Anna turned. "Four two nine seven? Get me his file please."

"Right here ma'am."

"Good, let's see, born in Rio, rescued at the age of five from a street gang... brought up as UNEC in a family in Ontario Canada... precognizance point two, empathos point seven, telekinesis point four. Interesting..... an unusually high empath for a male. Who else have we got?"

"Well, we have another agent in deep cover in the Upper Peninsula area, number 6606, but we've had no formal contact for over two months. We could attempt communication by non-material means if you think it wise."

Anna sighed and rubbed her forehead. "Yes, I think we should. Have one of our best resident telepaths try to impress upon 6606 that a base link should be reestablished with all speed. Okay then, if four two nine seven is all we've got for now, then we'll have to throw most of our support to him. What's the situation report?"

"On disk ma'am, a complex series of events are focalizing in the northwestern quadrant of Michigan's Upper Peninsula, an area we have never concentrated on much before. Some minor temporal anomalies have been detected in the area, the SIB has mobilized to investigate. Industrialist George Sherman has some people converging on the area, and local psionic activity has increased at least ten fold in the last thirty days."

"Sherman again? That man seems to have his fingers in just about every dirty little pie in the Northern Hemisphere!"

"Yes ma'am, and he's expanding his influence throughout the Pacific basin in heavy equipment, ocean floor mining, and major construction contracts. He's gotten wind of what those folks up in Houghton have come up with, and he thinks he sees huge profits from illegal use of their techniques."

"Alright." Anna smiled to her juniors, who smiled back. These were good people she knew, citizens of the world and not just of any one territorial nation. The members of the super-secret United Nations Environmental Command were all selected as children under the age of five from orphanages and homeless shelters the world over. Of every race and polyglot mixture imaginable, the children selected were those who tested as both highly intelligent and ethically motivated. They were raised in adoptive family units of four or five, given massive doses of parental love and support, yet encouraged to find their own individuality and core of inner strength. Finally, while attending regular public schooling for socialization skills, they were indoctrinated into UNEC through summer training camps devoted to the fostering of global scale thought and action, as well as the detection and encouragement of psionic talents. Every agent had passed stringent global loyalty tests, to be sure that the malignant virus of nationalism had been completely rooted from their souls. Anna looked at their faces with pride and confidence.

"This may be the largest challenge we've faced yet. Forces are gathering here which could shape the course of world history from our time forward. It is given to us to help direct this course." She smiled. "Leave me now, I'll look over the material and see if I can think of anything else we can do. Notify all empaths over a rating of point three, distribute the photo and rough location of four two nine seven. They'll know what to do." The three nodded curtly to acknowledge and filed out silently. Anna Sorensen looked out the window again and sighed, then softly spoke aloud. "Our hopes ride with you four two nine seven." She glanced at his dossier... "Jason Desnick.... fare well and God speed."

She sat at her desk then and closed her eyes. She had been surprised to hear the number 6606 mentioned, though she had kept her startlement pretty well concealed. Why had she done that? Was she ashamed? She thought back many years to the UNEC summer camp in Labrador, between her junior and senior years of high school. That was the year they'd been issued their numbers. She stood next to him in the line, he was #6606 and she was #6607. She remembered his face, his smile, the surging feelings of young love stirring in her heart, the warmth of a shared sleeping bag in the northwoods tamarack beneath a canopy of stars and mosquito netting. All these years and they hadn't spoken or written. And now, of all places, he turned up here. She wondered why he had never answered any of her messages, for almost a year after that summer she had tried to write or call.

Slowly she allowed her mind to slip into a stillness. Her training allowed her to quell the inner clamor much more effectively than most people could. She sought the core of light, found it, and began to flow with it. She sensed a presence, a deep communion with a higher power, as if a loving hand were on her shoulder. Her intent was to ask for help and guidance in the current crisis. Instead she found that images of 6606 kept rising unbidden into her mind. Almost she burst into tears with the frustration, but the still small voice came to her and said: "Fear not child, and be not ashamed of love. Your skill at your craft, your faith in God, and your trust in your companions will see you though. And remember, no matter where you go or what you do, I am there with you always."

And then Anna Sorenson did cry tears of joy, and though someone seeing her cry might have mistaken the tears for pain and anguish, someone who knew her well would perhaps notice a little less creasing on the forehead, some tension loosened in the shoulders, and a bit more smile than usual at the corners of the mouth. She wiped her tears with a cloth handkerchief emblazoned with the insignia of her rank, then smiled and got busy reading the report lying on her desk.

CHAPTER 20

Julius Miller drove his '14 Toyota Millenium exactly at the speed limit along the freeway through Chicago. He was always careful never to attract attention to himself. In fact, he had done quite a thorough sociological study, and carefully patterned his habits after the "average" American adult male. He smiled as he thought of the conversation he'd just had with Mrs. Donitz, the neighbor of his targets. It had been quite simple to say that he was their uncle, and she had told him that Steve Sanders and Eileen Donovan were on their way to Ann Arbor to visit Eileen's grandmother. Miller didn't really believe it, but it was his policy to check out the simplest options first. It was just possible that they were in fact stupid enough to give away their destination that easily. He tapped a few instructions on a keypad on the dashboard of his car, and Sherman's information network began to churn data. Ah good, back on line at last.... yes, oh how interesting, they had just withdrawn a rather large sum of money from two separate cash machines located... yes, right along the highway headed east out of town. All right then.

Julius was a small man, middle height, slightly overweight, with nondescript features. The very harmlessness of his appearance was his greatest asset in the business of assassination. Even paranoid underworld bosses would often, in their arrogance, allow this puny man to approach more closely than any other. The favorite weapon of this mousy assassin was not the knife, gun, or garrote favored by many of his fellow board members. No, he enjoyed the intellectual approach... the traditional aristocratic weapon of poison. His methods were many. He seldom used food or drink anymore, it was so droll and common. He most enjoyed the use of contact poisons that could be delivered by the shake of a hand, or the turn of a knob, then take effect within a few minutes. He smiled when he recalled David Johns leaping out of his window in terror just five minutes after Julius had left his office. He had even been able to see the body hit the ground himself... most satisfying. A phony business deal, a simple shake of the hand, and the transfer of a powerful dose of hallucinogen designed to induce intense claustrophobia. They almost always went out the window. He smiled. So easy, and so very lucrative.

He noticed a car parked along the side of the road ahead with a flat tire. It looked like a red Chrysler Neptune, one of the two vehicles his targets were known to have access to. He slowed, checked the license, yes, this was one of them! He pulled over and backed up to the car, parking well off the shoulder of the busy interstate. The right front tire of the car was flat, and the doors were locked. In a break between cars Julius pulled a narrow hooked strip of metal from the inside of his jacket, and deftly jimmied the lock open on the passenger side. Miller slid into the seat and began looking through the glove compartment... nothing much but the usual car information. He looked in the back seat and saw nothing, then felt under the car seat. His hand fell on something, which he pulled out... a Rand McNally road atlas. It was folded open to the Michigan page, no surprise there, but Julius noticed then that the upper half of the page, the part that should have represented the Upper Peninsula, was missing. Hmm. "So my dear Steve and Eileen, where have you gone eh?" He said out loud. "Did you go to Ann Arbor like you told your neighbor, or are you smarter than that, hmmm?" Julius replaced the atlas where he'd found it, relocked the door, and returned to his car. He ran another electronic check seeking the location of the last electronic transaction that the pair had made. The cash withdrawal was still the last one. He also ran a check, using some pretty sophisticated tricks, of any phone calls to or from their apartment or Eileen's grandmother's house. There were no results that suggested any connection.

Whatever character faults might be laid upon the tally sheet of Julius Miller, no one could say that he was impatient. He decided to run to ground the Ann Arbor connection, then decide which way the pair had gone. It had not occurred to him before that they might have gone north, until he found the torn atlas, but more and more it seemed to make sense, and it pleased him that they were running, as he saw it, up a tree. Had they gone south he felt he might have had greater trouble tracking them down, but up among the big lakes there are only so many places one can go. So much the better.

He pulled back onto the highway and settled in for the drive to Ann Arbor, his mind clear and uncluttered. He put a CD in the player on the dash, his favorite... Mozart's requiem.

CHAPTER 21

Digger stood up and stretched after a few minutes of poking at the keys on Joan's laptop computer. He went to the stove and topped up his coffee cup, then sat down at the table again. Arne sat with his head bowed, overcome by emotion. Joan sat behind him, rubbing his shoulders. She looked at Digger. "So, what can you tell us? I think we're both still confused by all this 'time travel' talk. How did you ever come to discover these things? It doesn't seem like something a geologist would come up with."

Digger looked at them both. "Well, I wasn't alone. How much time you got?"

"How much do you need?" said Joan.

Arne looked up at Digger with pleading eyes. "I lost my family and da whole life I had. If I could understand how, or why..."

Joan looked at him for a moment "We're not going anywhere."

"The whole story?" Digger asked. They nodded together.

"Okay then. I'll have to go back a ways. It all started back in graduate school. I was working on my doctorate in Geology, living at the big house up at 113 Samson Street in Hancock. Yes Arne, I recognized the address... it was the same house you and Maggie and the kids lived in way back. Several other grad students lived there too, sharing the house. Me and some other guys would do a lot of midnight mining... that's what we called it... we'd sneak into the old abandoned copper mines and explore, looking for mineral specimens, or just trying to figure out the layout of the mines. It's amazing how huge and complex they are, you'd never guess just looking at what's visible on the surface. Anyway, it was a lot of fun, dangerous of course, but very exciting, both physically and intellectually. We were able to access some parts of the Quincy mine that nobody had been to in fifty years or more."

"Well, one of the guys I lived with, Joshua Freeman, had the room next to mine. He was not particularly into mining or outdoor adventures, he was much more... uh... 'self-contained' might be the word. Josh was a physics major and a very unusual guy, sort of a functional autistic I guess. Some people considered him almost an idiot savant, but he was no idiot. He hardly ever went out or socialized at all, he could never talk to girls, but his mind was always working. He argued with his professors a lot, which got him into a great deal of trouble, because he was usually right and they didn't like that. I think he was probably a real genius when it came to the subject of electromagnetic field physics. He could work really complicated problems in his head in seconds, stuff that would take most people, even the professors, a half hour or so to work out with the aid of a computer. In his senior year he presented a well crafted paper arguing strongly against the Big Bang theory of cosmology and he wanted to pursue it as a thesis topic. His professor refused to even consider his argument, gave him a D-minus on the paper, squashing any plans of using it for his Master's research. Josh made a big stink about it, sent the paper to some world class guy at Stanford, who praised it as groundbreaking work. Of course, this put Josh in even worse hot water with the other faculty on campus."

Joan spoke up... "Digger, you keep using the past tense talking about Joshua, did something happen?"

"Hang on, I'm getting to that. So anyway, Josh was always in his room working on his computer, he had a program he wrote himself to do modeling of all these equations that he'd been working on. So one day, about three years ago, I stopped at his room just to say hi, and he was grinning like the Cheshire cat. 'I finally figured it out', he said, and I'm like... 'what?'. He told me he had finally put the final pieces into his field theory. The theory of everything."

"What?" asked Joan. "You mean the unified field theory that Einstein and everybody else have been chasing after for the last century and more?"

"Ah, you know about that. Yes, Josh said he thought he'd solved it... well, not so much that HE had solved it, as that he'd found the solution."

"There's a difference?"

"Josh explained it to me this way... he said that the entire history of scientific inquiry had been built upon the shoulders of those who had gone before. Now, this is both good and bad... not only do we have the recorded experiments and observations of scientists who came before us, but we also have their preconceived notions and unfounded assumptions unconsciously represented in the database."

"Sorry, I'm not following you," said Joan.

"For instance, scientists have long postulated a four dimensional universe, one which has three spatial dimensions and one of time. Virtually all of the discipline of physics is premised on this assumption. For ordinary everyday events this assumption gives results that are very close to measurable values, well within error limits in fact. For this reason the assumption is generally regarded as valid. Only in certain specific situations does this assumption get in the way. The problem is that, for most researchers, the assumption is seen as so fundamentally basic to everything, that any deviation from it is viewed as error. Invalid assumptions can therefore, lead conservative minded scientists AWAY from the truth."

Joan furrowed her brows. "Well then, if the universe is NOT four dimensions, what is it?"

"I'm not sure, but at the very least we need to be able to ask the question without being laughed out of the discussion. It's a good question, and we should not assume the true answer is 'four' just because a great many famous people have said that it is."

"So... how does this relate to Joshua and Midnight Mining Company?"

"I'm trying to lay out the groundwork so that you'll understand the significance of what I'm about to tell you. So anyway, Josh was concerned about this problem of assumptions in scientific inquiry, and he wondered whether there might be some method of excluding them, of 'filtering' them out of the stream of human knowledge. He came up with a plan involving a computer program that he wrote, called ALBERT. He named it after Albert Einstein, arguably one of the greatest physics geniuses of the 20th century. For all the wonderful work that he did, Einstein was guilty of making basic assumptions on philosophical grounds. For instance, he promoted, without observational support, the basic assumption of the speed of light as an absolute limit, not only for mass, but for information as well. He also assumed, for the sake of simplicity, that the universe as a whole does not rotate. These simplified the cosmological calculations conveniently, and since that time virtually every subsequent worker has continued blindly with these same assumptions, despite the fact that trans-light velocities and/or a rotating universe can very simply explain a great many observational anomalies without recourse to extreme theoretical complexities like superstring theory and all that nonsense.

"So the computer program ALBERT that Josh wrote and cobbled together from bits and pieces, was designed to deduce correlations between data variables. Josh used it to independently deduce the fundamental laws of physics from scratch, scrupulously avoiding the introduction of any philosophical assumptions about how the universe works. It was really an advanced piece of AI or 'Artificial Intelligence' software, since it encouraged the asking, rather than simply the answering, of questions."

Digger took another sip of coffee and spoke to Joan and Arne listening at the kitchen table.... "You see, I knew he'd been holed up in that room all this time, but nobody ever really knew what he was working on, he kept it pretty much to himself. The guy was a real world class genius, and a damned good programmer too. Even his physics professors couldn't understand or accept what he was trying to tell them, much less anybody else. So anyway, Josh gave ALBERT nothing but observational data, including accepted error limits, and forced the program to formulate the underlying laws capable of predicting the observed results. He was essentially recreating the entire history of scientific inquiry. It would have taken years and years of core time on the old electronic computers, but the new fast optical processors which were just getting cheap at that time could do it in a matter of a few days or weeks. ALBERT independently deduced Newton's laws of motion within the first few days, based simply on a collection of astronomical observations. Josh didn't seem to think that was any big deal. Over a period of time, with the availability of massive quantities of astronomical and particle physics data that Josh downloaded over the internet, ALBERT deduced all the known laws of physics, all of them! That was when things started getting interesting... ALBERT started coming up with new ones, stuff related to the strange behavior of subatomic particles. The computer was making no assumptions at all about the universe, it had no preconceived notions about how things work... no ego to be bruised or embarrassed. While a limited version of the big bang theory did emerge at one point, the computer program discarded it based on some contradictory deep space observations from the Hubble telescope. ALBERT told us that to explain the universe, it had to postulate a minimum of seven dimensions, and it used a complex modeling subroutine to determine the underlying physical laws which are found to hold without exception. We were totally blown away by the implications, but we could think of no observational proof that anyone would accept, it was all way out on the fringes of known technology.

"It was in this period of time that Josh tried to present some of his simpler findings that argued against the big bang theory to his professors, and he ended up in deep hot water. Conventional cosmology is very much founded on that theory, so if they had taken him seriously it would have been such a revolution of thought that modern physics would have been turned on its head. Graduate students are not supposed to do things like that. So anyway, about that point ALBERT dried up, it kept requesting more data after exhausting everything that was available in electronic form. Then Josh made the conceptual leap that ultimately opened the door to the universe. We brainstormed about the assumption problem, and Josh reasoned that the selection of data which was supplied to ALBERT could possibly be unintentionally imposing some basic assumptions that he didn't consciously recognize. To circumvent this possibility, Josh wrote a subroutine that gave ALBERT the ability and resources to search for information itself. We arranged to give it internet access to the Library of Congress archives, as well as to all the technical literature databases that are on-line through the university.

"It was incredible! ALBERT began downloading, sorting, collating, and correlating data 24 hours a day, and kept it up for four weeks! Josh wasn't been able to do a single other thing on the computer. Especially interesting was the fact that ALBERT spent a large fraction of all that connectivity time looking at entries classified under the headings: metaphysics, religion, and philosophy. ALBERT worked out its own subroutine for assigning error probabilities to the data, cross-referencing material between different cultural bases. It gave us a seventy percent correlation between physical data and all known metaphysics... and a ninety eight percent correlation after self-contradicting metaphysical sources are excluded.

"Well by this time, a couple of the other guys in the house had gotten interested in this stuff, one of them was James Dolittle, an electrical engineering grad-student. He just quietly sat down and started studying the screen of Josh's computer as we sat there talking. Equations and diagrams were flashing across the screen in real time as we watched, Josh was rerunning the program sequence to show me. ALBERT had deduced an entire new system of symbolic logic, and then went on to formalize a new and unique philosophic symbolic system of relative value. Finally a series of statements were displayed upon the screen, one at a time, eventually making quite a long list.... things like:

'Do unto others as you would have them do unto you.'
'I think, therefore I do. I feel, therefore I am.'

"There were a number of statements that were either word-for-word, or very close to classic philosophical statements from many cultural and religious backgrounds. There was lots of other stuff too, including a set of sixteen equations that appeared to describe trans-light speed reality... involving identities and wave velocities that were based on multiples or powers of V_c (the speed of light), as well as others which seemed to describe the nature of time itself. And finally there was a set of coordinates, with seven groups of numbers and symbols. As we watched, some of the numbers changed. Josh was really excited. 'So what do you think?' he asked me. And all I could think of to say was, 'Hey man, this is it!' Finally, after being quiet the whole time, James spoke up. 'Those are our coordinates, our position in space-time, right?' He caught on to the thing immediately and asked the next question, 'Why are there seven sets of numbers?'

"You see, ALBERT not only deduced that there were at least seven measurable dimensions to the space-time continuum of the known universe, but it went ahead and displayed our coordinates in that continuum. Now, this is so startling an event that I have to explain a little. We can know our position on the face of the earth in terms of our Latitude / Longitude, or Universal Transverse Mercator coordinates. We can use whatever system we want, but we must always remember that we humans invented the system. It works for us only because we designed it, defined it, and make it work. ALBERT displayed our position in space time according to some system that we did not know and could scarcely even conceive of. It is analogous to a primitive tribesman being given an advanced Global Positioning System unit that describes his position on earth, not only in terms he has never conceived, but in symbols he cannot understand. And... as in that situation, the display of those coordinates implies a greater functioning of intelligence and organization in the universe than anybody has guessed. Immediately we asked the questions: 'Where do those numbers come from?', and, 'Who defined the coordinate system that they relate to'."

"So," said Joan, "this implies the existence of God?"

"More than implies, it proves there's something bigger, more encompassing than what we see and hear and feel with our material senses, or even with our scientific instruments. But ALBERT was the ultimate skeptic, it accepted nothing as fact except observation. All deductions were accompanied by probability brackets. Before it would agree to accept the law of gravitation it went through some three hundred thousand observations of astronomical and experimental data, and even then it gave it merely a high probability. The amazing thing to us was that ALBERT correlated physics with what we usually call metaphysics, apparently finding some sound basis for comparison, and produced a number of new laws with very high probabilities. We figured there should certainly be some testable predictions we could make based on these deductions, so James and Josh and I set out to do so.

"So Josh gave James and I each a disk containing a full set of the final deductions that ALBERT had come up with, basically something to study, a primer course in seven dimensional physics. Our task was to try to come up with experiments that could either refute or confirm some of the statements... to try to find areas of disagreement with conventional physics. One of the key features seemed to be that any point in space-time could be described by a set of coordinates. This seemed to imply a "fixed" nature to space, including the concept of an absolute center. This interpretation was totally at odds with the conventional big-bang physics. So our first project was to design an experiment which could determine which of the two diametrically opposed views was correct."

"And just when was this again?" Joan broke in...

"This was in January of 2012, just about five years ago."

"The problem was that none of us were well enough versed in big telescope work to know what observations to make, much less would we be able to get access to Hubble or even a big ground-based telescope."

"And were you guys trying to do this in the context of your academic work?" Asked Joan.

"Well, none of the professors wanted to hear about it, it was too weird for them, so it was just a sort of private project. Josh tried to get somebody at the computer center to be interested, but they were still pissed off that he had "wasted" so much mainframe core time with his ALBERT project. Finally James came up with a device he hooked up to a notebook computer that would record the changes in the universe coordinates we were receiving. You see, the amazing thing was not so much that such coordinates could exist, it was that we were able to receive them in an intelligible form. The computer would display a continually changing set of seven long numbers when we asked for our coordinates. This implied that some really fundamentally strange effect was taking place. It was as though we'd been given a modem hookup straight to some universal central computer or something! The implications of that idea are so unsettling that we had to try to confirm this, it was just too unbelievable to go shouting it around without proof. I mean... computers just don't DO things like that!"

"So Digger," said Joan, "it sounds like the three of you started working together then? Was it just the three of you, or were there more people involved?"

"No, at first it was just Josh, James, and me. We seemed to have very complementary talents. Josh could come up with these wild equations to describe some heretofore unexpressed aspect of reality. I'd brainstorm some kind of thing it would be useful for, and James seemed to be able to whip together an experimental device for testing."

"What about money, didn't it cost a lot to build this equipment?"

"Well, you've got to understand that these equations are really simple. It's like high school math at most. The computers were just standard high end stuff, like most grad students have. Josh had simply made one of those once-in-a millennium conceptual breakthroughs. It was just a different way of looking at things. James made most of the stuff out of junk parts lying around at the university. That is what eventually got us into trouble as I'll explain later. At the time, nobody cared because most of it was pretty worthless old equipment, some of it dating back to the nineties. From the very beginning it seemed to me that there would be some very practical ways that these ideas could be put to use, if they worked. So the way it worked out was that Josh's interest was mainly academic, he looked at it as pure basic research. James was interested in the workings of the devices that could be built based on Josh's ideas, the beauty of a concept carried through to material completion. My interest was to have it all mean something in the end, to DO something with it. We formed Midnight Mining Company, naming it such as a sort of a joke spoofing the exploring James and I used to do, mostly at night, down in the old abandoned mines, and also because we were able to get digs underground in part of the old Quincy Mine."

"So that seeing-into-rock thing you were talking about, was that one of the uses you came up with?"

"Yeah, that was my idea, we call it the Speleoscope, actually it's based on some rather old sonar technology commonly used for remote viewing underwater. The new thing was that we were able to design and build, based on one of the new principles, a simple, cheap, digital microphone. This was important because it could encode not only a wide range of frequencies and amplitudes, but also the vector, or direction of the sound source, to a very fine degree of precision. We were able to build an experimental device and test it in our basement. It was the most uncanny thing I've ever seen, that first view on the computer screen. We placed the speleophone on the floor, stuck it down with some acoustic clay, and turned it on, just passively without a sound source turned on. We expected to be able to form an image with a focused acoustic energy source but not without. While I was fiddling with getting the sound source hooked up James tapped me on the shoulder and motioned for me to look at the computer monitor. It was like looking into a block of murky ice... we could see at most about 100 feet straight down into the ground below our feet. The detail was not at all bad, iron pipes showed up quite well, the contact between gravel and bedrock was clear, and you could even see fractures in the bedrock. I remember being so excited that I jumped up in the air. When my feet hit the floor, it was as if an electronic flash had gone off. The scene was momentarily illuminated clear as day. A few seconds later a truck went by on the street out front and looking downward it was as though somebody had walked by with a lantern. It was totally amazing! We all realized now that we were onto something big, really really big! We had confirmed just one of the predictions of the new equations, allowing the function of the special microphone we called the speleophone, and we had one very marketable device essentially designed and prototyped. We went ahead at once and formed a corporation, moved into the little lab underground in the Quincy, and decided to try to show off the speleoscope, maybe even try to sell it, in order to raise capital for further research.

"That's when the trouble started. We talked some of the geology and engineering professors into coming over to the lab for a demonstration, even offered them free coffee and donuts. So these guys come over and we put the scope on the wall, set up the monitor next to it and turned it on. By this time we had learned to use an inaudible multifrequency sweep sound source to illuminate the scene. You could see clearly into the rock at least 300 feet, all the way to another tunnel which appeared as an hazy translucent object within the vision field. The view was a full three dimensional virtual reality model of the actual rock structure. Bits of native copper the original miners had missed appeared as bright strings and dots suspended in the rock. The silence was deafening for about 20 seconds, then they all started talking at once. They insisted on a couple repositionings of the speleoscopic receptor to eliminate any chance of fraud, then they doubted us no longer! There was one kinda oily guy at the back of the room, name of Farley Grundwalder, some sort of university financial administrator who had come along uninvited. He wanted to know where the equipment had come from. So we admitted that a lot of it had come from junk storage rooms in the electrical engineering and physics departments.

"To make a long story short, the university, at the instigation of Grundwalder, ended up threatening to sue us for theft of property if we didn't cut them in for a piece of the company, so we had to issue stock, and give the university a 49% share in the company. Farley rigged it so he would get to be the overseer of the project. He somehow got us the use of all the rest of the rooms that had been quarried out in the Vivian Street adit of the Quincy Mine, and there we were.

"Well in some ways it wasn't so bad, we had a much bigger budget for equipment, surprisingly big in fact. I had no idea the University had that kind of money to throw around. The bad part was that they wanted to keep everything supersecret, which was a real blow to us, as we had planned to show off some of our stuff at the big technology trade shows. They squashed that idea flat. Then they brought in all these so-called "security consultants" who cut off our internet access, and generally made it really tough to get in and out of the place to get any work done. A whole raft of patent attorneys showed up then also, and Farley himself turned out to be a real first class asshole. He kept pushing Josh to come up with more new equations, but by this time Josh had gotten into the metaphysical end of his research, and was devouring eastern mysticism and the teachings of Jesus, correlating those with the metaphysical results of his research, much to Farley's disgust. He essentially told Farley where to stick it. Then one night, late last year, Josh was found dead on the street by Hancock police: drug overdose was the autopsy result... methcatenone.

"Now I can tell you, straight up, as one who's tried a little of just about everything that's out there and who knew Josh as well as anybody in the world... Josh never had the slightest interest in any drugs. There is absolutely no way in the world that I can believe that he ever was involved with a slimy street drug like 'cat'! The local police went to his room and said they found paraphernalia, so the death was reported as accidental overdose. And somehow, after the police were there, ALBERT disappeared from Josh's computer and backup files. I never believed it personally, and now, after the events of last night, I don't think we have to look very far to figure out what happened. At first I figured it was just some con scheme gone wrong, complete with planted "evidence", but now I think he was murdered as a security risk, and maybe the local police were in on it. Now that I remember it, they had removed all the "evidence" by the time the F.B.I. guys arrived, and there was quite a stink about it. My guess is that somebody decided that Josh had done all the productive "real" work he was going to do, and was therefore no longer needed. James and I they still needed though, for the time being." Digger shook his head sadly. "Josh was one of the nicest guys you'd ever want to meet, and probably THE smartest. Aside from being my friend, it was a terrible waste of intellectual resources to kill him"

"So Digger, was that about the time that the papers stopped doing articles about you?" asked Joan. "Seems like for a while there you were in the news every once in a while, some sort of feature story about 'local boy makes good' or whatnot. Then nothing."

"Right, well Farley and his security guys decided that the stuff was really sensitive and kept everything bottled up tight. We still went in and worked on our projects, but we could no longer take them out of the lab, or talk to anybody about them. Farley's a pretty smooth talking piece of business, and he more or less convinced us it was for the best. Once the reporters couldn't see any of the cool stuff, they soon lost interest. Seemed like a big mistake to me, giving up all the free publicity and all that. But the work went on, and we were coming up with some pretty wild stuff, some of it nobody has heard about yet, until now anyway." Digger looked at Arne. "We found out some important things about these different dimensional coordinates, especially the time coordinate, which behaved in a different way from all the others."

"We found a sort of texture or substance of time. It can be visualized by imagining that you are floating along in a strong river current. The structure of the universe you visualize as being the points along the bottom and shore that you pass by as you are swept along. You really can't change the flow. Time is sweeping us along at a more-or-less constant rate... we pass by each moment almost unseeing, focusing usually on the next one downstream. Now time exerts a great deal of friction against us as we are pushed along. It is quite difficult to try to swim against the current, to go back in time, the energy requirements would be ridiculously high. Information however, has no mass, a point I'll come back to in a minute. The equations did seem to reveal a possibility for moving a material object in time. After all, we're moving forward in time right now as we speak. One difficulty would be to specify time space coordinates with sufficient accuracy. Also, the energy requirements we calculated seemed to make the idea quite impractical. Until I heard Arne's story just a while ago I hadn't considered it seriously. From what I can tell now, moving forward in time would actually release energy, lots of it. I need to get with James to see if we can deal with that energy somehow, but I see now that it may be possible..." Digger looked at Arne. "...sorry, it MUST be possible to move something forward in time, though we have no evidence yet of anything going backward. What you need to understand though, is that this is no science fiction space opera. You can't just step into a machine and travel in time, there are serious repercussions to consider, all the classic paradoxes for instance, entirely aside from the energy problem."

Arne looked a bit confused, Joan looked thoughtful, trying to grasp it all.

"I'm sorry Arne, it's so hard to explain, the language has no vocabulary, not yet anyway. As I said, information has no mass, so there is no impediment to the transfer of information in time, at least not from the past to the present. One of the last things Josh did before his untimely death was help James and I build a device that literally opened a sort of cosmic port hole on any set of coordinates we chose to enter into it.

Our first attempts were dismal failures, it turns out that it's extraordinarily difficult to specify all seven coordinates for a specific location in time space, when we are still unable to even visualize a seven dimensional matrix. We worked more or less by trial and error, and eventually we were able to see some things. Any place and time that we could specify by the coordinates, we could look at. It was like looking through a window, or into a crystal ball, actually, it is a crystal ball. You could see, but not touch. Any break in the containment immediately crashed the machine. We couldn't take any samples of anything bigger than a photon, nor leave anything behind, but we could use all sorts of instruments to record various forms of electromagnetic radiation. Basically you can look at anything you want as long as you don't try to touch it, the image is clear as a bell, variable in magnification, and complete with full spectrum electromagnetics. The research possibilities are tremendous! Archaeology, paleontology, history, cosmology, climatology, all these and more will be completely revolutionized."

Joan looked astonished. "Digger, I never heard about anything like this before, this is amazing... just think of what you could do."

"Oh hey, we did almost nothing but brainstorm about that! Dozens of research disciplines would pay dearly for time on this machine. We were just about bursting a gut wanting to tell somebody about it. Using spectrographic analysis we could sense air and surface temperature, solar flux, magnetic field strength and direction, you name it. All the varied disciplines of earth science will be forever transformed because now you'll be able to point this thing at any past event and really see what happened, not just guess about it. The principle of conservation of information is an extremely powerful tool for the advancement of science. But Farley and those other guys continued to insist on absolute secrecy. They didn't care about just looking into the past. The main thing they kept hounding us to come up with, was a way to move objects in time. We discarded the idea due to the incredible amount of energy that we calculated would be required to overcome the temporal friction, but like I said, Arne's presence suggests that there must be a solution to that problem that we initially overlooked."

"Digger, what about the present, can you see elsewhere at this time?" asked Joan.

"Ah, you've hit upon it! Yes, they also wanted to use it for real-time remote viewing. This would be easy, if we were ever able to solve the targeting problems, but it worried us too. Such a device would then be useful for all kinds of surveillance, including the military sort, and with the tense world situation, we were afraid the Federation guys would come in and want to take it away from us."

"So it would be a very useful spying device."

"Yes, I'm afraid so. Not to brag or anything, but 'fantastic' might be a better word. I kept trying to emphasize the wonderful life-improving aspects of this thing, but unfortunately, there were some that saw it in a different light. Farley brought in some representatives of an anonymous 'investor' secretly, and showed them around the lab when none of the three of us original partners was around.

We got the word from a friendly night watchman named Aaron and hurried up there. These guys were talking about keeping everything top secret and using the technique to gain advantage in various financial and commodities markets. Farley had convinced them that we would eventually be able to actually grab objects from the past and bring them forward. They were thinking in terms of desecrating ancient tombs, and robbing gold from places where it was known to have been stored. They obviously did not understand the implications of the mathematics involved, or the paradoxical problems, not to mention the morally reprehensible aspects of their plans. Apparently however, Farley made some kind of side deal with them and started hiring "assistants" for us, people that seemed very reserved and never talked much about themselves, but wanted to know everything about the technology, far more than necessary for their jobs. It was obvious they were plants, trying to pump us for information and make us expendable. James and I have done our best to give them as little as possible, but for the last six weeks we've had the 'tempiloscope' running pretty much 24 hours a day. Farley may have decided that he knows enough now, and that we're superfluous. We've been trying to keep as much from him as possible, to protect ourselves, but I'm afraid, thinking about what happened to Josh, and the way we've been pushed out, that he... or somebody... wants us dead."

"Don't worry Digger, you're with Joanie now. I think I'm starting to get the picture. Were there any other inventions that might be involved?"

"Let's see, we had several other projects underway at the same time. One of my favorites involved some little computerized underwater mining robots that we designed. Then we set up a completely automated machine shop two years ago so that the computer could build them... self replicating machines... the dream of the so-called "space age". They're little submersibles with speleoscopic sensors that can seek out and extract high grade copper ore left behind by the miners in flooded mines. We call them "grunts", the name is not an acronym for anything, but representative of the barely audible sound that their active acoustic sensors make... almost sounds like some weird animal or something. They're semiautonomous, programmed with a full three dimensional map of the mine, and given a link to a central computer that coordinates their movements. They scoot around in the mine, using ultrasonic drills to reach ore near the surface of the rock, scan deeper into the rock to fill out the map, and return when their fuel cells are low or their load capacity is reached. All data from each grunt sortie is added to the data base, so that the digital mine map they each carry becomes updated daily. There are about two dozen grunts working the Quincy now, and more constantly in production. The system would be ideal for all sorts of abandoned mines, as well as sea floor mining, space colonization, disaster rescue, resource recovery and so forth. The potential market is huge, so we have a great opportunity to make a lot of money licensing this sort of thing. It's not as glitzy as the time travel thing, but there's a heckuva lot of cash involved in any deals we might make."

"I've heard a little about the mining robots", said Joan, "and I'm getting the drift of the kind of big money potential that you're looking at. An industry like this, based in the U.P. could be the basis of the economic revival we so sorely need if we're to become independent from Michigan. But, that potential is also the cause of your problems." Joan held her forehead in both hands with her eyes closed, concentrating hard. "Somebody smells that big money and is evidently moving in to try and take over, and it doesn't sound like the government, although the FBI may have gotten wind of it and is just now trying to get into the act. So... do you think this guy Farley is responsible for Josh's death?"

"It's very possible. I never had the impression he was quite that nasty, or had any guts, but who knows... he could be in with somebody else who does, maybe the investor he talked about."

"Okay, what about more recently, what's happened in the last few days that led up to this...." she looked back and forth between Digger and Arne a couple of times. "...this situation."

"Well, let's see... today's Thursday the 19th right? James and I took last weekend off and did some cross-country skiing up at his cabin on the lake by Eagle River. When we showed up Monday morning, Miriam, the head secretary at the office, was looking real agitated and told us Farley wanted to see us. We go into his office and he says that some big company down in Chicago had heard about us and wanted to buy us out, cash up front. They had offered three hundred million dollars! Our total capitalization to this point had been on the order of about ten million, so it was an absolutely astounding offer on the face of it. Farley wanted to sell right away, before they changed their minds. As controller of the university's share of 49% of the business, he stood to personally gain quite a lot from selling at this point. James and I however, while we were not immune to the lure of that much cash, were already convinced that it was worth very much more than that. In fact, the size of the initial offer convinced us that somebody else was seeing the potential in this that we had always seen. We talked about it a while, then told Farley that we did not want to sell, not at any price, that the future of the company was too great to sell out now. He was livid! He tried every sort of inducement, then finally resorted to threats, which we laughed off as ridiculous and walked out of his office."

"What sort of threats Digger?"

"Oh, some garbage about how he had big important friends who would not let some piss-ant graduate students stand in the way of business... sounded like complete bullshit to us. Well, the next day I came in early, a big winter storm was brewing so I rode my snowmobile down from Paavola. If you've never visited the site, you go up Vivian street in Hancock until you run into a rock wall with a steel door in it. We have our offices there, just inside a security alcove within what used to be an entrance to the Quincy Mine. Once you're checked in... if they let you in... you walk straight into the hillside a few meters and you're in a big modern office with a dozen desks and computers and whatnot. If you're cleared for the labs you go through another door into the old drift, a tunnel in the rock originally cut back in the 1800s, but widened several times. The lab spaces are chambers cut out of the rock, mostly located on the left hand side going in. The very last one is where James and I work, the temporal lab. If you continue down the tunnel you quickly get into the old part of the mine, you can walk right up to the burned out remains of the huge number two shaft, over twelve thousand feet deep.

"Well now, this was on Tuesday morning, just the day before yesterday. Farley was in earlier than usual, sitting on his desk and smiling in a particularly disturbing way as I came in. The conversation went like this:

"'Oh, here he is! Doctor Digger Puttonen himself dragging out of bed at this hour.'

"'G'morning Farley, you sure look unusually happy today.'

"'Well why not? I'm about to make a lot of money for my alma mater, as well as for myself... and you for that matter.'

"'What are you talking about? I thought James and I told you we didn't want to sell.'

"'Ah yes, well you see, Mr. and Mrs. Freeman, parents of the late Josh Freeman and executors of his estate, have decided to go along with us, which leaves you and James together controlling only 34% of the company. We can do anything we want now, and there's nothing you can do about it, as the new owners will undoubtedly want to install a new board of directors. Somehow I'm quite sure your names will be missing from the list of candidates. I suggest you take the money and count yourselves fortunate.'

"Just then James showed up. 'Hey Digger, what's up?' he says

"'Looks like Farley's gotten Josh's folks to go along with the sale, they're going to try to cut us out of the company,' I told him. James just laughed and said, 'You can't be serious?'

"So that sleazy weasel Farley Grundwalder says, 'Oh, I can assure you mister Dolittle that we are quite serious. The offer from Sherman Enterprises is much too good to turn down.'

"'Have you had a lawyer's advice on this?' asks James.

"'Of course, it's all perfectly legal.'

"'Well you must have a pretty stupid lawyer then, because as I recall in the original incorporation papers we set it up such that eighty percent of the stock must be transferred for the new owners to be able to put in new directors. We did it that way so that if any two of the three original partners agreed to stick with it, we couldn't be forced out. It's all in there.'

"Then Farley comes back with, 'Yes, well we've discussed that particular clause of the contract at some length. It's quite unusual and quite possibly will not hold up in a court of law. In fact, we know a judge who agrees with us on this. If you force the issue that's exactly where this situation will end up, in his courtroom. I assure you that Sherman is willing to spend a lot of money on the best lawyers to see this thing through. Unless you want a lengthy and expensive court battle, which you would certainly lose, I suggest we come to a settlement. We're talking sixty million dollars apiece for each of you.' Farley's eyes glittered and he spoke slowly with an almost obscenely oily voice. 'Think about it boys... sixty million dollars!'

"Well, I wasn't sure, but I figured he had us in a pretty tight bind. There was no way James and I had the cash on hand to fight it out in court, and our only assets of any consequence was our stock in the company, which we couldn't borrow against if it was involved in litigation. I looked at James, and he shrugged his shoulders.

"'And what would we have to give up?' I asked Farley.

"And he said, 'Everything, you walk out of here with your personal effects, and of course, the sixty million dollars. The computers, the software, the equipment, patents, and company name will all remain in our possession.'

"'Our possession?' says I. "You mean Sherman's don't you?'

"'Just a figure of speech.'

"'When are we supposed to be out?' I asked him.

"Then Farley grinned from ear to ear, 'cause he knew he had us. 'They're supposed to have your checks up here by Friday, we sign papers and you're out that afternoon.'

"I nodded my head with resignation, and got a quick facial signal from James. 'Listen Farley, this is a big decision, we've got to talk about it.'

"'So go ahead, talk.' he says to us.

"Farley smiled and waved as James and I walked down the tunnel towards the labs. The bare light bulbs hanging from the ceiling hung down low enough to almost touch our hair as we walked under them. It was cool but not cold in the tunnels, we carried our coats. Once we were at the grunt lab we sat down and looked at each other. 'What do you think?' I said to James.

"'I think it's bullshit. I don't think they can really do it, they're just trying to scare us out.' he said.

"'But they do have a lot of money behind them, they could buy a judge.'

"'Maybe... but we're here in the lab now... maybe we can do something to assure ourselves access to the material if we have to bail. I mean heck, okay, they've got the patents in the company name, they've got copies of all our files, but you and I are the only ones that really know how this stuff works. We could scarf all our files, and if we have to bail, we could use that cash to start up again, keep going.'

"'Hmm, sounds too easy. I've got the basic stuff backed up on crystal media which I keep up at the house. How about you?' I said.

"'I've got backups in my parent's safe-deposit box in Waukegan,' said James.

"'Okay, that's our failsafe. But I really don't want to let this go. This is our baby, for Josh's sake, I think we should try to hang on. Sure sixty million is a pile of cash, enough to start over again... maybe, but you and I both know the potential is in the billions with this.' James nodded. "And how can we be sure we can trust Sherman to let us go that easy, after what happened to Josh I'm not too sure any life insurance company would touch us with a ten meter pole.

"The noise level in the room increased as one of the grunts was hauled up the access tube on a chain for regular maintenance. It was G-27, one of the newer Mark 4 advanced models equipped for backup use in underwater rescue. We walked over to the access shaft and watched as the five meter long bronze and stainless cylinder was hoisted into a maintenance cradle and plugged itself in for systems diagnostics.

"I looked at James and he looked back. We both looked at G-27. His bushy black brows were furrowed as he thought hard. 'You know,' he said, 'we should try to set up some sort of backdoor into this place before we leave, just in case.'

"James was looking at the grunt. We knew that since the water level had stabilized in the 1980s between the eighth and ninth levels, that travel within the mine above the water table was very restricted. There was the Vivian Street adit, and the number two shaft at the southern end. The adit was strictly controlled access, and the #2, which had burned out in the 1940s, was just a gaping maw at the top end, capped with a heavy steel floor plate inside the preserved shaft house that dominated the Hancock Michigan skyline. There were no longer any rails or ladders in the number two, just a big dark hole going down into the earth at about a fifty five degree angle.

"The only other entrances to the mine were the other seven shafts, all of which were securely capped with concrete and steel, except for the number six and number eight. Those two we had sabotaged as our private back entrances to the mine. Sometimes we'd do a little underground rockhounding, looking for copper crystals, native silver, or the greatest prize of all... datolite nodules. The six was over a mile away, and the eight almost two miles. Both had access to the mine, but the connections to the offices and computers at the southern end of the mine were deeply flooded, much too deep for ordinary diving equipment. They had never been considered security risks, and besides, as far as most folks knew, they were as securely capped as the others.

"So we decided we could program G-27 to work in an area over by the number six. We figured we could probably smuggle out one of the remotes and if things seemed desperate enough we could try to use the grunt to slip inside, if necessary. It had never actually been tried of course, not with a live human in an underground setting, but we thought it was worth setting it up as a backup. We programmed the patrol path that G-27 would follow on its following sorties then loaded it to the computer. A few seconds later the door opened without a knock and Farley Grundwalder walked in. He walked over and watched as the G-27 grunt was probed by the robotic arms and sensors of the maintenance cradle.'

"'You guys have done very well, it's a beautiful thing you've created here... self replicating and self maintaining machinery. It's time to turn the operation over to people who understand business. You guys would be bored to tears by the day to day running of this thing as a real business, it's just not your style,' he says. I told him that the whole project would come to a screeching halt if we weren't there.'

"He just laughed. 'Oh really?' he says, 'It should interest you to know that all of the data has been analyzed, and the decision has been made that you two are no longer considered assets to this company, while I have worked tirelessly and supported this project from the beginning.' Farley's face was turning red with a flush of anger. 'My business sense and expertise have brought us to this jumping off point. I was the one who put on the suits, flew to the meetings, and schmoozed the bigwigs. All of your recent decisions on the other hand, have been towards public disclosure of proprietary information, and towards pure research rather than economic applications. Pushing pushing, always needling, looking for ways to poke fun at me. Now it's my turn, get it? You are no longer an asset to this company!' Farley shouted in my face, then he seemed to calm down again and adjusted his tie. 'You know, if you're just a bit careful, that money will see you through the rest of your lives, you'll never have to work again. Man, I envy you that.'

"'So what if we happen to like working?' I said.

"'So work, what do I give a shit? But remember, anything covered by the patents, or developing from that, belongs to this company. You'll be paid for the rights in full, but no royalties, and no use rights, that's the deal.'

"'You can't do that!' says James.

"'Oh yeah? Well, you'd better just take the money and get your asses out of here, because that's your only option. If you try to hang on we can, and will, have you found mentally incompetent, removed from the board, and stripped of all rights. Oh, and by the way, if you're thinking of visiting that whiny ass liberal lawyer of yours, he's suddenly found himself the beneficiary of a long lost relative, and has decided to take a long vacation... in Brazil.' and then he started laughing in our faces.

"We were devastated! It looked like they had won. Farley smirked and walked towards the door. 'So why don't you just empty your desk drawers now,' he says. "Oh and by the way, security has been instructed to strip search you on your way out. No electronic media or devices will be permitted to leave these premises. Your key card combinations have already been revoked. Have a nice day!' He walked out the door and down the hall.

"James walked to the door and leaning out shouted: 'Yeah, well chuck you Farley!'

"'Oooh, snappy comeback!' I said to him when he came back in.

"'Yeah, well I always wanted to say that.' he says back.

"'I think we'd better get busy, we may not have much time. What about the remote? You heard him, no electronic devices.'

"'Don't worry, I could probably build another simple one with the stuff I've got laying around in my garage. In fact, I think I can.' said James. So anyway, we got busy and backed up every computer file on high density optical crystals and put them in the cargo hold of G-27. We sent the grunt to do an 'ore resource distribution analysis' near the upper levels of the #6 shaft area, which we figured was the most easily accessible from outside, it was also a standard type mission for a Mark 4 and would not seem unusual if anyone checked the control panel and status boards. The analysis tasking would insure that the cargo hold would remain sealed during the mission. That done we started clearing the personal items out of our desks. A pair of cocky security guards sauntered in and stood silently watching us as we finished up. I took a good look at them, but they were both unfamiliar, apparently new employees. They escorted us down the long tunnel, and true to Farley's word, they searched us quite thoroughly before letting us out the door. I had stuck a duplicate backup crystal in my shorts just to see what they'd do. They called Farley in when they found it.

"'So... Scott and Jeff found you trying to steal company property eh? Well, I think we'll let it go this time children, no damage done, just don't let it happen again.'

"He was laughing at our backs as we walked out into the open air. It was dark gray and snowing heavily when we got out, about 1:00 P.M. I had left my snowmobile parked in the woods up above the adit covered with a plastic tarp over it. I couldn't face digging it out of the snow right then, so we decided to go over to the Finlandia in James' vehicle and have pasties for lunch. They were good, but it was tough to enjoy them. James brought in a little notebook computer that he'd left in the glove compartment of his car and worked up a schematic for the remote controller that we'd be able to use to call the grunt in from close range. He gave me a memory crystal with the schematic on it, just as a backup but neither of us really had much hope. In fact I was getting one of my "bad" feelings about the whole situation. Finally James got into his truck to drive home to his wife and kids in Lake Linden. I walked out of the Finlandia and down the street towards the bridge, stopping in every bar I passed.

A Superior State of Affairs

"Well from that point until you picked me and Arne up on Montezuma Street, I was pretty much just trying to drown myself in alcohol. I crashed at the Dog house that night, got up yesterday morning and started drinking again. I haven't talked to James since the Finlandia, in fact I'm starting to get worried about him now. I'd like to try to call him, but I'm afraid that might make matters worse." Digger took a long slow sip of his now-cooled coffee after the long story. Arne sat just nodding his head and looking rather shaky.

Joan sat stock still with eyes closed, as if meditating before she spoke. "Well Digger, it sounds pretty weird alright. I agree that you shouldn't try to contact James yet, at least not openly. We've got to figure out why the FBI is involved in this. It's possible they may be more or less on your side, but with the kind of money and influence you're talking about, they may either have been bought, or be out to grab it all for themselves. The existence of a back door into your offices and labs is comforting, though it sounds like things would have to be pretty desperate before you'd want to try to use it. Hmmm. So the rough guys are from Chicago eh? Sherman Industries? Maybe I can make some quiet inquiries about that and find out something."

Digger looked exhausted and was simply nodding to Joan's monologue with his head hung down. Joan got up and walked around so that she stood between Arne and Digger, she put her arms around both of them. "Come on guys, it's not so bad." She kissed Digger on the cheek, then Arne, then Digger again, finding his mouth this time. "Why don't you go put on some music while I make a few calls. Whoa, it's past noon already, no wonder I'm feeling hungry."

Digger got up and started flipping through the CD collection. Arne looked up at Joan, she smiled at him and winked, then she went to the bedroom and activated a rather sophisticated looking communications console. Arne got up and started poking around the kitchen looking for potatoes.

CHAPTER 22

Chris Jameson sat for a long moment in his car, the words of the stranger echoing clearly in his mind. His shoulder felt warm where the man had lightly touched him in passing. He shook it off and started his car. It probably meant nothing, maybe the guy thought he was talking to somebody else. He pulled out of the Skylight Diner parking lot onto the highway and started heading towards the middle of town, where he found the signs for U.S. Highway 41 and followed them. Within a few minutes he was outside town moving steadily north up the recently plowed road. The snow was still falling though not as heavily as before. He thought about turning on the radio, but decided against it for now.

The memory of the mysterious encounter in the diner parking lot returned to his mind. Who was that guy? Chris recalled what he was thinking about when the guy came up to him. It wasn't hard to conjure up... those images had haunted him for the last nine years. What had the guy said? You are forgiven? It wasn't your fault? How could he have known what I was thinking about? Was it my face? What did he mean by that?

Chris drove on automatically into the blowing snow, into the hypnotic pattern of flakes swirling towards the windshield, deflected moments before hitting his face. It was like flying into a sea of stars. Unwanted, yet irresistible in its insistent force, the memory came flooding back into his mind once more, like a video tape seen over and over again, unable to eject from the player......... the sounds echoed in his ears.......

Chris Jameson sat behind his 7.62 mm machine gun in the door of the helicopter as it swooped down over the dusty gray island of Cyprus in the pre-dawn light. The blade wash whipped the tips of his long hair that stuck out from under his helmet. Goggles covered his eyes, the only sounds were the voices of the pilots, radio traffic was quiet. The Turks and Greeks had recently gotten into a nasty little shooting war over the island, and the situation threatened to tear apart the NATO alliance. The U.N. decided to bring in troops to enforce a "hot" peace. Chris' job of the moment, as door gunner, was to protect the troops that would be dropping in on the LZ from attack until they were able to establish some positions. Afterwards he would have a different task, one more suited to his particular skills. The chosen landing zone was a schoolyard just on the Turkish side of the green line. Intelligence said the school had been abandoned for at least a week this close to the front lines.

It was not one of the wisest missions the U.N. had opted to try... dropping a mere 3,000 lightly armed "peacekeepers" onto a mined and fortified island bristling with several tens of thousands of troops and high tech weaponry. The secretary general thought that if he dropped a bunch of blue helmets in there, the combatants would come to their senses rather than be seen as standing defiant to the power and prestige of the United Nations. Some people never learn.

The helicopter hovered ten meters above the edge of the school yard as others swung in and dropped off their cargoes of rifle-carrying, blue-helmeted U.N. troops. Chris heard the popping of rifle fire as troops already on the ground engaged a foe off to his left, out of his field of view. The pilot yelled something over the intercom, then he felt a searing blast of heat and was knocked to the floor. The explosion tore off the whole front of the aircraft and the chopper began to spiral lazily towards the ground. As he fell in agonizingly slow motion, Chris could see before him that they had flown into a trap, the troops on the ground were being cut to pieces, all around him other helicopters were exploding in flames. A raspy voice he recognized as the Colonel erupted in his ear shouting "What's going on down there?"

Chris shouted back. "Ambush, the school..." and then the chopper hit the ground hard, he dived out the door and rolled, grabbed a rifle from a fallen comrade and was about to start running when he was immediately knocked to the ground by the explosion of the helicopter behind him. A jagged shard of metal caught him on the right side of his face and opened a huge gash from his upper lip to his right temple, tearing off his goggles and helmet in the process. The blood flowed freely and tasted salty in his mouth, but he felt almost no pain. Bullets still sang in the air as he sought cover amidst the bodies and wrecked equipment. Finally, lying still, he could hear the fire coming from a low building across the street from the school. It had a stone facade with narrow windows all along the facing wall. Perfect ambush position against a force with only light arms. It must have been faulty intelligence... that building was supposed to be empty. He kept his face to the ground and lay still, hoping that the shooters would think him dead.

He heard it coming then, a familiar sound in the sky above. An A-10 Thunderbolt, passing low and slow taking a look at the situation, then two more coming in faster. Chris knew the drill, buried his face in the hot asphalt and covered his head with his arms and opened his mouth to protect his ear drums. Two titanic explosions slammed him down against the pavement like a tennis racket wielded by the Jolly Green Giant. For about thirty seconds there was a rain of debris and then silence. When he raised his head the building across the street was gone, just.... missing. In its place was a smoldering mass of rubble and twisted metal. He looked at the LZ. Nothing moved but a few of the severely wounded. Of over 300 men and women on the landing zone, he was the only one left standing. Blood streamed down his face and neck and wetted his shirt. Dust caked on it. He stood and tried to wipe his neck with a bandanna but just managed to smear the blood around. The adrenaline that had kept his heart pumping like fury for the last several minutes finally gave out and left him shaky and light headed. He felt his face with his hand, touched the smooth hard surface of his protruding cheek bone and had a sudden queasiness in his stomach. The sun rose through the smoke and lit the scene with a ghastly glare. He turned and looked at the school. It was smashed and pulverized also, but one wall and a doorway were left standing. He guessed that his fragmentary radio message had brought the bombs there as well. Chris walked towards the school, knowing that he should lie down and conserve his strength until somebody came to help him, but drawn by the doorway. He tied the bandanna over his face, like a cowboy bandit in the movies. He checked the rifle... full mag, safety off, shit, the poor fuck hadn't even gotten a round off before he got hit. He flipped the safety on and shuffled cautiously towards the school, heading towards an area that seemed less damaged. Yes there was a door, smashed and broken now, but leading downwards, perhaps a bomb shelter. He put his head in the door and heard a soft whimpering. The darkness was almost complete as he descended the shattered steps into the cellar of the schoolhouse. Some great pressure surged in his chest that he did not understand, the air was thick and heavy, the whimpering louder and more insistent. As he reached the bottom he could see nothing, but the smell of urine, of feces, and of unwashed bodies was overpowering. He took a step forward, slipped and fell over something soft and wet. Oh God no! He felt around him, bodies, small ones, packed tightly together in the small cellar, burned and broken. Children's voices in the dark calling for their mothers, gasping for a last breath of air. Slowly his eyes grew accustomed to the dark and the scene was illuminated by the light from the entrance, and from a jagged hole in the ceiling... a hole made by a bomb, a bomb from an airplane that he had called. Chris reeled and screamed, tripping and falling again and again in his haste to climb the stairs and flee from the scene etched upon the back of his eyelids. It felt as if a nightmare had invaded the light of day and thrown it's sticky spider webs into the deepest recesses of his mind, dragging his soul into the depths of suffering and agony for all eternity.

  Chris could recall nothing clearly after that moment, until he was placed on the street in Chicago Illinois in civilian clothes some months later. If he tried he was rewarded only with fleeting, hazy images of hospital wards, of officers speaking to him of bravery in combat, and people looking at him with pity in their eyes. He had a bag of clothes over his shoulder and a purple heart medal in his front shirt pocket. His discharge papers said that he was suffering from "Post Traumatic Stress Disorder". All he understood about his ordeal was that he was dead inside. Death was all he knew, all he could think about, death had pervaded the core of his very soul, and Chris had always been very good at sharing what was within himself with others. From this time onward, Chris had hated children, or rather... he hated seeing children, because they always made the tape start over again, that damned tape, and once it started, he could never stop it until it finished all the way through to the end...

As Chris replayed the tape in his mind for the millionth time, he heard again the words of the stranger, echoing soothingly within his mind, and found himself arguing with them...

"It wasn't your fault," the stranger had said.

"What do you mean it wasn't my fault? I was there!"

"Did you kill them?"

"I was the one that called in the air strike!"

"That was a mistake. It wasn't your fault."

"They never go away, they won't leave me alone!"

"That's because you never let them. You hold on to this pain, you want this pain. You feel you deserve this pain."

"Yes, I do, I deserve it."

"Truly my son, it is not necessary, it wasn't your fault, you are forgiven, you have always been forgiven."

"But how???"

"You need not concern yourself with that, just know that as of this moment you are forgiven your sins. Go forth and sin no more."

Chris shuddered spasmodically, as if he's just been slapped in the face, and gripped the wheel tighter. He looked around himself, everything was just as before. He was still driving the car north on highway 41, the snow still swirled before him... but something was different. He looked around the interior of the car. He noticed the warm comforting air surging from the heating ducts. Was it like that before? He'd never noticed how wonderful it seemed to have that source of warm air in contrast to the outside cold. There was a tiny leak in the driver's side window, he put his nose close to it. Ah... how fresh and clean the air smelled. He remembered smelling air like that as a child. He looked out the window. The sky was still overcast and snowing, but where it had seemed simply a dreary gray before, now the sky seemed alive, a shining crystalline gray, like polished metal. Trees loomed up through the blowing snow and swept past him. Their branches looked like fingers, fingers reaching upward to the light, straining, growing... were these trees unusual? Had they always looked like that? They swayed slightly in the wind as if they were dancing to some unheard music.

Music, thought Chris, and he punched the power button on his dash board stereo. He had to look for it as it was so seldom used. He got a talk show and punched the "seek" button. Evidently the station he found specialized in golden oldies, They were playing "Blackbird" by The Beatles. The sounds that fell upon the ears of Chris Jameson could hardly have had a more profound effect. Tears welled into his eyes as he drove. Tear ducts that for nine years had been frozen were thawed in one glorious moment. He was barely able to keep the car on the road as he drove, sobbing in great gasps. Up ahead there was a roadside rest area. He pulled in and parked, then let the tears out full force until they were spent. When he opened the door of the car and stepped outside, it was as a new person. This was a whole new world to him, like taking that first 'giant leap for mankind' onto a new planet. He stepped into the snow and heard it squeak beneath his shoe. What an interesting sound! He walked to the visitor's center... there was a young couple there looking at the map board, and two children chasing each other around the lobby. He watched the children for a moment, unsure of himself. He felt a joy bubbling up within him at the sound of their happy little voices. This was when the tape would usually start. Out of habit Chris tried to shut down his emotions to be able to stand it, but the tape failed to engage. He stood, and was able to listen to their little voices, and hear them for just what they were.

The little boy, maybe five years old ran towards him, chased by the older sister. As the boy tried to make a sharp turn around Chris' legs, he slipped on the wet floor and went down with a loud "thwok" hitting the back of his head on the floor. He immediately began to cry loudly and the mother rushed over to comfort him. The father of the children, then scolded the sister harshly and turned away to continue looking at the map. The little girl looked very hurt and began to sulk in the corner of the room by the drinking fountain. The little boy was now whimpering softly in his mother's arms, not hurt badly.

Chris walked to the drinking fountain, bent over to take a drink, and said quietly to the little girl. "It wasn't your fault. It's okay."

She looked up at him, frightened at first by his hideously scarred face, then she looked into his shining eyes, smiled at him and said, "Thanks mister."

Chris walked outside again, a whole new sensation filling his heart. Once outside he took a deep breath, and felt the tiny flakes of snow melt on his tongue. He climbed up a snowbank and took a few labored steps into the knee deep snow, then turned around and fell backwards with his arms and legs outstretched stiffly. He lay for a few moments in the pillowy softness of the snow, little clumps of it falling into his face and melting. He stared at the snow drifting down below the stretched out branches of the trees overhead. The little girl he had spoken to came out of the visitor center, looked over the edge of the snowbank and said, "Hey mister, whatcha doin?"

Chris' mouth broke into a wide grin, "Just making a snow angel" he said as he waved his arms and legs in the powdery snow.

CHAPTER 23

The room was quiet for some time after Steve finished telling the tale of their escape from Sherman Enterprises, and their trip north so far. Peg looked around the room... everybody looked pretty glum and serious. "You know what we need around here?"

The others looked up expectantly. Tom shook his head "No."

"We need a wedding. We haven't had a wedding at the palace for a long time! You kids really want to get married?" Steve and Eileen looked at each other, hugged, and both nodded. "Okay then, it should be a fairly quiet thing I guess, we shouldn't do anything that will let somebody track you down, but that doesn't mean we can't have some folks over and have a nice reception party, it'll all just be on a first name basis. Tom, will you call Pizza Bob and see if he'll do the service? Let's say... about nine tonight. The license is a problem as the paperwork would locate you here, so let's set it up so that it will be filed later, say two weeks later? Maybe in a different town?"

"Yeah, I bet Morty down at the courthouse can do that for us." said Tom.

"Okay then, I'd better check the restaurant and start making some calls, we can do it in the main room right out front, no last names need to be mentioned. Our regular customers will be thrilled!" Peg got up and motioned to Eileen. "Come on honey, I'll show you a room you can use, and I've got something else I want you to see."

They went into a small bedroom, to a closet. Peg opened it and brought forth a long white gown. "I made this for a friend who changed her mind at the last minute. She was about your size I think. We can fix it if it's not quite right."

Eileen was stunned. "Oh Aunt Peg, it's beautiful, it's just what I always dreamed of. I don't know what to say! I'll try it on right now."

"Okay, but don't let Steve see you in it until later."

Peg held the dress up in front of Eileen and eyed the cut. "Yes, I think it will just about fit. I'd better go check on the restaurant, back in a bit. You get some rest okay, and don't worry," Peg put her hands on Eileen's shoulders and looked her in the eye, "you're safe here."

In the meantime Tom motioned for Steve to follow and they went down a hall to the kitchen, then through a door and down a flight of wooden steps to the basement. Steve looked around in amazement. The place was a workshop simply crammed with tools and equipment everywhere he looked. Every wall was covered with nails and hooks from which hand tools of every description hung. Every square centimeter of floor space was occupied by some piece of equipment or other, except for just enough space to move around them. It was definitely a shop built for use by only one person at a time, two would get in each other's way constantly. Tom noticed Steve's slack-jawed expression...

"Yeah, it's quite a pit at the present, needs cleaning up, I know... that's what Peg keeps telling me, but... I know where every tool is, well... most of them anyway. Let's see, what was I looking for? Oh yes!" Tom lifted a knife from the benchtop and handed it to Steve.

"I've never seen anything like it." Steve said as he turned the blade over in his hands. It was about ten inches long overall, the steel blade was a gleaming dull gray with a smooth matte finish. The handle was a dark gray, almost black, with a rough scaly texture. The blade was spear-pointed, about 5 1/2 inches in length with an odd hump on the upper edge which came back about halfway to the handle. He turned the knife this way and that in his hand, it seemed to move as part of him. Tom watched with interest.

"So, now that we can talk guy stuff for a while... I didn't want to say much in front of the women, but you two may be in for some rough stuff. I don't know anything about this Sherman guy, but I know the type. In fact, it was partly to get away from that sort of thing that we moved up here and started this place. Tell me, how do you feel about weapons?"

"How do I feel about them? Well, I've never had much use for them I guess. In school I would run from a fight if I could, but I was on the college fencing team and did pretty well. I like knives and swords but I don't care much for guns. In fact, the one we got as we escaped from Sherman is the only handgun I've ever held. This knife feels good in the hand though, where'd you get it?"

"Oh, it's something I used to make way back when, used to be in the knife business back in the seventies and eighties, before the knife laws. I want you to have it. It comes with a slim thermoplastic sheath that rides on a shoulder harness. Before you leave we'll set you up with it and you can practice the draw. It's lightning fast once you get used to it."

"Gosh, Tom, I don't know what to say."

"You don't need to say anything, just take it, you may need it. Come on, there's a stair here at the back and we can get the stuff out of your truck, out of the snow. Maybe we can make some better sense of what you've got and prepare you for the journey ahead." Tom and Steve then shuttled up and down the steps several times carrying wet black plastic bags full of all the things Steve and Eileen had taken with them when they fled. Steve also fished the pistol out of the glove compartment and handed it to Tom, who expertly dropped the magazine and cleared the chamber of a live round before examining it. He locked the slide open, sniffed it, and looked down the muzzle.

"Yep fired recently, but seems to be in pretty good shape, at least the lands are still sharp. Smith and Wesson model 6906, 9mm compact automatic. We'll clean it up a bit and see what it'll do. Let's see, what about this other stuff here, let's dry these things out over here by the wood stove and try to come up with some better stowage than these plastic bags." As they unpacked the hastily thrown together packages, Tom noticed a slim brown leather case. "What's this?" He asked.

"That's my flute" said Steve.

"May I look at it?"

"Sure."

Tom opened the case and inspected the parts carefully before putting it together, then whistled appreciatively. The flute had a warm golden color and a high polish. "Wow, do you play a lot Steve?"

"Well, no, not really. It was my uncle's you see. He recently passed away, but for some reason he felt I should have it. I haven't played for years, not since they kicked me out of marching band in high school."

"Kicked you out?"

"Yeah."

"Let me guess... unauthorized improvisation?"

Steve was slack jawed for the second time in an hour. "How'd you know?"

"Oh, I don't know, just sounds like somebody else I once knew. Mind if I try it?"

"Be my guest!"

While Steve unpacked and arranged some of the goods to dry, Tom played a few little ditties and scales on the flute.

"This is an awesome instrument Steve. Do you have any idea what it's worth?"

"No not really, it's the only thing I got from my uncle's estate, he was a professional musician out in Santa Fe for a long time, but like I said, I haven't played seriously in quite a while, but I still like to have a flute around. I don't know the brand names, but I figure it's just a plated mid-level instrument. Sometimes I just pick it up and play random little things while I meditate, but they don't mean anything."

"Oh, I wouldn't brush them off like that! Such tunes may have more power than you know, and this is no mid-level instrument! This is a solid 14k gold Haynes, one of the finest instruments made anywhere in the world. Who was your uncle anyway?"

"Herbie Mann, my grandmother's brother on my father's side, he died in 2003."

"Oh wow, this is Herbie Mann's flute?"

"Yeah, you know of him?"

"Know of him? I've got a collection of his records going back to 1964. He's my favorite, my inspiration."

"Well then you'd better keep this Tom."

"Oh no! That I could not do, no, it was a gift well given, and you may appreciate it more than you do now before all is over. Your uncle probably saw more of the musician in you than you see in yourself. Besides, if you get really hard up for cash you could sell it, but whatever you do, don't take less than about ten grand for it."

"Ten thousand? Are you kidding?"

"No, not at all, it's worth more like twenty, but at a pinch you might have to accept ten."

"Wow, okay then, it's our ace in the hole. Let's see, what else have we got that's of use?"

Tom found some sturdy duffel bags and boxes and after making sure everything was set out well to dry they went back upstairs. Eileen was just coming out of the bedroom with a smile on her face, and Peg was coming in the front door stomping snow from her shoes. The light of day was fast waning to night behind her as she shut the door.

"The restaurant's okay, Amber's taking care of things." Peg said as she hung up her coat. "What you guys been doing down there anyway?"

"Oh you know," Said Tom, "just puttering around. We got the stuff out of the back of the truck to dry out. So okay, we're going to have a wedding tonight, but then what? I'm not sure what comes next."

Eileen spoke up. "Like we said before, we had thought of going up to my uncle's cabin by the Superior lakeshore near Eagle River Michigan. I have a key, it's very remote and private."

"Does anybody at work know about the place?" Peg asked.

"I don't see how they could, Uncle Herman is my dad's brother in law. I've only met him a couple of times as a little kid, but my mom ended up with a bunch of my dad's keys when they divorced, and she gave them to me to give back, but I never got around to it, and I still have them."

"I guess that'd be a good enough place then," Peg answered, "but why don't you just stay here, we have an extra room and all, you'd be safe here."

"Gosh aunt Peg, that's no nice of you to offer, but I feel like we need to go, don't you Steve?"

"Yeah, I feel like we're being drawn north, like it's just something we have to do."

"Have you had a vision then?" asked Tom intently.

"No, just a feeling," answered Steve. Tom and Eileen nodded.

Peg looked worried. "I don't like it, some guys are trying to kill you and you're going to go tooling around the countryside in that truck that they know all about. Can't we do something?" She looked at Tom, pleading.

"Well," Tom answered, "we can certainly arrange for a different vehicle, How about the old Willys?"

"What? That piece of junk?" Peg retorted. Their debate seemed heated but Steve and Eileen noted a tone of amusement in Tom and Peg's voices.

"Hey, ol' Gertie looks a bit funky, but she runs great, and she'll plow through a pretty big snowdrift, and with the winch it can get out of a tight spot like nothing else. And anyway, Wisconsin plates won't look as out of place in the U.P. as Illinois plates would. So it's settled then... right?"

Steve and Eileen looked at each other and shrugged. Eileen looked at Peg who was smiling. "Gosh, you guys have been so kind to us, I just don't know what to say."

"There's nothing to say, you saw the letter. We've been waiting for you for years, we just didn't know who you'd be! If it wasn't for you I'd have lost Tom back then, so don't feel beholden to us. It's what we want to do, it's what we need to do."

"One other thing," said Tom, "Eileen, how do you feel about weapons?"

"I don't care for them." said Eileen firmly, "Why?"

"There is some danger ahead of you, or behind you, hired assassins apparently. It's one thing to believe in nonviolence as a political theory, but it's quite another to allow yourself to be murdered for no good reason. You'll have the beginnings of a family now, would you be willing to defend yourself, or Steve, from deadly harm?"

Eileen closed her eyes and breathed deeply. She opened them and looked again at Steve. "Yes", she said without taking her eyes off of his.

Peg looked at Tom and they both looked at the young lovers embracing. Then she signaled with her eyebrows to Tom, and they went to the kitchen, leaving Steve and Eileen alone. She put her head against Tom's broad chest and held him tight for a long time, as he stroked and kissed her hair. She looked up and asked... "Will it be okay?"

"Yeah, it'll be okay."

Tom Maringer

Finally she broke away and sighed, looking at the kitchen. "Well, I don't feel like fixing anything to eat right now, with a wedding taking place in three hours I'm too wound up, maybe we should go over to the Palace for something to eat. The kids will need their strength, and we'll only have cake at the reception." They went back to the other room. Steve and Eileen agreed, and so the foursome put on their coats and headed out the door into the darkness and swirling snow for the short walk to Peg's Pancake Palace for dinner.

CHAPTER 24

The parking lot of the L'Anse Holiday station had only a few centimeters of dry, powdery accumulation since the early morning plowing. Jimmy Canaris got into the passenger's seat of the hummer while Frank entered on the left. They took off in a blowing cloud of snow, heading west cross the bottom of Keweenaw Bay towards Baraga. A stiff cold wind was blowing in off of the lake on their right, weaving a delicate tapestry of small drifts across the freshly plowed road, but the hummer paid them no heed as it churned its way through the gray veil. The light seemed to grow steadily brighter for a while, as if the clouds were thinning overhead, but snow continued to fall, in tiny flakes that seemed insignificant individually, but oppressive in their multitude. But machines can be built to deal with almost any weather extremes, given time, and as they went along they noticed quite a bit of activity as people dug out from the previous night's deluge and got out onto the freshly plowed roads. The community of Baraga seemed particularly astir. At most of the homes along the highway shovels and snowblowers could be seen in action, clearing drives and walkways. Kids and adults were all outside, and an unusually large number of snowmobiles seemed to be in use. The turn off to the reservation's casino had been plowed with particular attention to detail, Frank noticed, and the giant billboard advertising its presence seemed already to have been brushed clear of accumulation. Frank took a sip from the mug of hot coffee he held between his legs. "So... can we get any news? Any clues as to what's going on? We ought to at least check in with station and let them know where we are."

"Can do sir," answered Jimmy enthusiastically. He pulled the keyboard to himself, booted up the computer, and then picked up a handset."

"We'd better not use an open channel Jimmy, we're still under security procedures until we hear otherwise."

"Right sir. I thought we'd try for a direct link via the Federation geostationary satellite #6K over Brazil. If we get a pretty straight stretch of road I think we can get a good lock, and I can key for scramble... is that tight enough for you?"

Frank smiled. Damn but this kid was good at this stuff! "Yeah, sounds good. Find out who's at the desk." Jimmy poked some buttons on the computer for a few seconds.

After a while a voice answered... "Yeah?"

Frank took the phone. "Hey Sammy, you get our message?"

"That you Frank? Yeah we got the message. What the hell is going on?"

"Yeah, me and Jimmy are still on the road, had a rough trip last night. We're okay though, heading north towards Houghton, just outside of Baraga now."

"Well listen guy, it's a good thing you scrambled this call, all holy hell seems to be breaking loose here."

"What do you mean?"

"I mean you guys took off without calling a replacement. There were about a dozen messages on the machine when me and D.J. got here. Some mucky muck at H.Q. has been calling requesting reports, which I don't have. There's some kind of native powwow going on down by Manistique that's got the locals all in a tizzy. I sent D.J. down there in the Blazer, so I'm here alone 'til Janice comes in, hopefully any minute now. I know she asked for a week off to go skiing, but I called her in early this morning, we're getting pretty busy."

Frank thought for a moment. "Hmm, okay, don't worry about headquarters, I'll take care of them later. Sorry about bugging out without calling, I guess I didn't take this thing too seriously, felt like you deserved some sleep."

Sam chuckled. "Yeah well, thanks for that, but clue me in okay, I've got a bunch of calls coming in, and I'm trying to get the county guys to deal with them for now. What's going on with youse guys?"

"Sammy, if I knew I'd tell ya. But I think you're right, something is going down and we'd better be ready for anything. I'd say get everybody you can in there and prepare to spend the night. We might need you. If you've read that coded email message then you know almost as much as we do. One thing though, I think you hit on something about that powwow, see what you can find out about what's going on with the Ojibways, whatever's happening, they're in the thick of it. Find out about an elder named Chokes Horses, and another guy Joe Running Bear." Frank put his hand to his left breast for just a moment and felt the smooth roundness of the red stone riding safely in his pocket, the one that Joe had given him back in L'Anse. He wondered if it really held any kind of power, then chided himself for being superstitious. What kind of stone was it anyway, he should find out...

Frank's thoughts were interrupted as Sammy answered, "Okay Captain, but check in from time to time okay? You gave us a bit of a scare when we got here and found the place deserted."

"Will do. Catch ya later."

"And good luck, you watch yourself out there."

"Thanks." Frank handed the handset back to Jimmy, who placed it back into its cradle and kept poking at the computer keys.

"I broke that connection without losing the satellite link." He said. "but there seems to be some kind of strong electromagnetic disturbance making a mess of things here, I'm having to use a triple checksum now to get a consistent signal, and still I'm losing a character every now and then."

"Jimmy, please tell me in plain English..."

"There's a lot of static on this line."

"I thought there wasn't supposed to be static on a digital hookup."

"There's not. There must be some sort of solar storm or something, some outside influence is corrupting our signal."

"Couldn't it just be the snow storm?"

"Well, no, not really. That shouldn't have much to do with it at all actually, not on this frequency. I've got a good satellite lock, we should be getting a clean signal."

"What is it you're trying to do?"

"Well, I thought we could try that S.I.B. directory again, maybe we can get a little more info on those guys, maybe some more names."

"Okay, try if you want, but I don't guess you'll have much luck."

"Oh, why's that?"

"Remember, you said you saw Leonard Howarth's name?"

"Yeah."

"Well, he and I go way back. If he's involved with it, you probably won't find out much. He was always a secretive know-it-all son-of-a-bitch, and always did his best to keep everybody guessing."

"Not a team player then?"

"Only if you're on his team." Jimmy looked quizzically at Frank after this remark. "Look, just watch out okay, Lenny doesn't like me much, I was a thorn in his side in Detroit and he probably won't like you either if you're associated with me. It's kind of a personal thing. We were good friends once, and then we had a major falling out over... over an operation that went sour."

"Too bad." Offered Jimmy.

"Yeah well, sometimes you get the bear, sometimes the bear gets you." They drove along in silence for some miles. Jimmy prodded the computer for a while with no results, then gave up. As Frank had predicted, he couldn't find any trace of the Special Investigations Branch in the FBI computer. He looked out the window. It really was incredibly beautiful when you looked at it from a vantage point of comfort. The surface of the lake was a milky white, fading into gray into the distance across Keweenaw Bay. They veered west, away from the lake, and would soon be traveling along the Portage Lake shipping canal that cut through the

Keweenaw Peninsula, towards the village of Chassell. He recalled that on a clear day you could easily see the other side of the natural canal, deepened by dredging for the use of the big ore boats, but today there was too much snow in the air to see that far. The trees were heavily laden, the cedars, tamaracks and firs looking like castles in a fairy story. Maples and poplars stretched their bony fingers towards the sky, reaching outward and upward, seeking for.....

"Six, Six, Oh, Six" Jimmy gave a start, glanced at Frank, who noticed nothing. He had heard the numbers spoken quite clearly, but not through his ears.

"Oh my God!" he thought to himself, "It's a call, after all these years it's a call." He relaxed a bit, closed his eyes, and allowed his mind to quiet in order to receive more clearly.

"Six, Six, Oh, Six. Situation Alpha Omega," Jimmy heard clearly in his mind. His eyes widened, not just A call, but THE call. The crux authorization to use any and all of his attributes, even to the point of breaking his carefully prepared cover, to render aid in a world crisis. Was it as big as that? Since early childhood Jimmy had been one of those trained for this moment, but he had no idea of what it might mean, indeed, even those who had trained him had little idea. He took a deep breath and opened his eyes. They passed a sign saying "Welcome to Chassell Michigan" as they came to a more thickly settled area. Two cars passed by going the opposite direction, each followed by a billowing cloud of blowing snow. As they came into town Jimmy noticed quite a way ahead of them an aged maroon Chevrolet Nova with a roof rack that pulled up to a stop sign from the west, and waited for them to pass. He thought to himself that the car had plenty time to pull out, and he glanced curiously at it as he and Frank drove past. Three figures were in the car, all heavily dressed for the weather, but he could tell nothing more about them. Jimmy felt a strange interest in the figures in the car, but could detect no reason why. Frank continued driving through town, obeying the general rule suggesting a slower speed within incorporated areas. The road signs suggesting this were all buried in the tall piles of snow the plows had created along each side of the road. He glanced curiously at Jimmy and noted the expression on his face.

"What?"

"Oh nothing, just checking out that car we passed, seemed like they could easily have pulled out ahead of us, they had plenty of time, I wonder why they...."

"Yeah, well I'm glad they didn't, we'll be able to make much better speed without a slowpoke in some old junker in front of us. I'm anxious to contact Samuels and find out what this whole deal is about."

"Yeah." Jimmy twisted around to see the Nova turn north on Highway 41 behind them, then shoved it out of his mind as he turned his thoughts back to the "message" he had just received. He had been in deep cover so long that he was really quite surprised to hear at last from UNEC again, and even more surprised to hear the "Alpha Omega" code. It could only mean that there was a serious crisis of global significance, and that he was called to help. But what crisis? Where? He had a rather low rating as a telepathic, it was not his area of expertise, but he tried to calm his mind and think in the tightly focused way his teachers had endeavored to help him learn...

"Six, six, oh, six, here. Query situation? Confirm Alpha Omega?" Almost immediately he heard an answer, in short clipped clear English words, resonating clearly, with a vaguely familiar feel...

"Six, six, oh, seven, here. Crisis imminent, Alpha Omega confirmed, temporal anomaly, political secession/consolidation, possible military intervention/revolution. Next 36 hours critical. four, two, nine, seven, FBI cover: Jason Desnick, will arrive shortly and take command. Will accompany S.I.B. agents. Make contact and coordinate. Love is. Good luck."

Jimmy was startled. Six, six, oh, seven? It was Anna! Scenes from that summer so many years ago raced through his mind, a surge of hormones flooded his body and suddenly his underwear felt restrictive. "Love is," she had added... she remembered him! It was what they had said to each other when they parted. But then, why had she never returned any of his calls or letters? No time for that now. It seemed now that somehow this trip in the snow was indeed part of a much bigger affair than he had guessed, though he began to appreciate that his sense of urgency to get on the road may have had more behind it than he had realized at the time. At the moment however, he was simply a passenger in a vehicle, chugging north towards the destiny that lay ahead. Whatever that destiny was, it would have to wait. That would be then, but this is always now! There was nothing he could do at the moment to prepare himself for what was to come, except to lighten the mind, and clear it for right action at a moment of decision. He took a deep breath and glanced over at Frank. It seemed to Jimmy that a great deal of time had passed since they had last spoken, so much had happened! In the world of sight and sound however, only a couple of minutes had elapsed.

"Whadda ya say to some music cap'n?" Jimmy ventured.

"Sure, go ahead." Jimmy hit a button and the thundering sound of the last part of "In the Hall of the Mountain Kings" by the Norwegian composer Grieg came over the air. As the last few lines faded away the D.J. came on.

"Good afternoon Copper Country. This is your host Big Bob Billings bringing you the noon show. It's one thirty in the P.M., Thursday, January 19th. Boy didja see the snow last night eh? Here at the WGGL station we measured sixty two centimeters. And guess what? Yep, you guessed it, more's comin', probably almost much again eh?. One good thing though, it'll be a little warmer tonight, with a low only down to about minus twenty, that's about zero Fahrenheit to you folks that haven't quite got the hang of this metric stuff yet. No more of that minus thirty stuff for a couple of days at least. The wind will be dying down some too, that'll help with the wind chill and the drifting snow anyway. Okay, the snowplows are running late today, as if you haven't noticed. Took a while to dig them out of their sheds this morning. If you're on a back road and you're still snowbound, just call your boss and tell 'em I said it's okay to stay home today. Today's high looks to be right around minus twelve degrees, practically a balmy summer's day! Last night's low was about minus thirty two, that's Celsius of course, and snow forecast for today of about another fifty centimeters.... " The D.J. went on to give a report on which roads would be cleared first on the winter storm emergency priority schedule. Jimmy switched channels to one playing some soothing music as they entered the Houghton city limits, passed the Michigan Technological University campus, and came into town proper on Shelden Avenue. Frank pulled the Hummer under the plowed awning at the front door of the Downtowner Motel and got out without speaking, leaving the engine running, Jimmy was sitting still with his eyes closed as if asleep.

Frank went to the desk and asked for a room, and then made a local call from the house phone. When the line was answered by a female voice he spoke.

"Samuels please."

"One moment, who may I say is calling?"

"Frank Giacoletti."

"Yes sir" After a few moments a male voice answered.

"Samuels here"

"Okay, we're in room 316 at the Downtowner. Can we meet for a briefing?"

"Sure. Can you come over here? You know where the office is?"

"Yeah, okay, be there in five."

"Okay, we'll have a fresh pot of coffee."

"Good man!"

Frank went back out to the hummer and pulled back out into the sparse traffic heading west on Shelden. Jimmy seemed to wake up. "Did you get enough sleep last night?"

Jimmy smiled. "Yeah, I'm okay, just resting my eyes." They turned right to cross the shipping canal lift bridge, then left across the hill on the Hancock side, and up two blocks to an old brick building in which the local Federation Bureau of Investigation office had its tiny rooms. They took one of the last remaining parking spots in the small lot, locked up the hummer and went inside. Fred Samuels met them in the vestibule where they hung up their coats and greeted them both with a shake of his big meaty hand. Fred stood almost a head taller than either of the two other men, and wore a non-regulation green plaid flannel shirt and black denim pants. The rounded shiny tips of old-style black leather combat boots could be seen poking out from beneath his cuffs. His once dark hair was graying at the temples and growing quite thin on top. His dark eyes peered from beneath salt and pepper eyebrows that bobbed energetically in a disturbing way. He ushered them through

A Superior State of Affairs

the break room for coffee and donuts, paused to ask his secretary that they be undisturbed for a while, then led them into his small office and shut the door. He offered them two wooden chairs near the side of his desk.

Frank set his coffee cup on the desk, leaned over and dipped his donut in the coffee, took a big bite dribbling a few drops on the floor, then spoke around it with a muffled voice... "So thpill it thamuels, what the hell ith going on? Why'd we have to rithk our neckth hauling our atheth up here in the middle of the night?" He sat with a mocking expression of curiosity on his face, chewing his donut loudly.

Samuels looked out the window. "The middle of the night? seems to me you guys took your sweet time getting here." He pointedly glanced at the digital clock on the wall, which chose that precise moment to click over to 2:00 PM.

Frank swallowed the bite of donut. "Okay so we had some trouble on the road, but you know what I mean. Did H.Q. tell you what it's about?" Fred leaned over closer to Frank and spoke in a lower voice, as if he was afraid of being overheard.

"Listen Frank, this is no joke. We had a call from the director's office this morning. Do you understand? The big lady herself, spinning her sticky webs down in Mexico City. Madame Hernandez is interested in this thing, whatever it is. She says to cooperate with this Howarth guy, give him everything he asks for. We were asked to pick up those two guys for questioning. That's it, that's all I know, apparently that's all we're supposed to know. But the subjects apparently copped to us and spooked, managed to give us the slip somehow, and we've lost them. The guys from Washington are supposed to be here sometime today to take over the case, but they haven't called in or anything, and I'm afraid there's going to be hell to pay for letting these guys get away. But so far, there are no crimes involved, so I don't know what we can hold them on anyway. If we pick them up on a G.Q. we'll have to let them go in 24 hours. They're both locals, we've got their places under surveillance, but nobody's showed yet, not since last night."

Frank could see that Samuels was upset about losing the two, though he was confident it would never have happened if he had been here. "Okay, so let's go over it. How'd you lose 'em."

Samuels sighed deeply. "Okay, we got a scrambled call Thursday night from this agent Howarth...."

"Lenny Howarth?"

"Yeah, that's him. He says he needs these two guys for questioning on a federation case, keep it quiet and don't ask questions. Okay, no big deal right? But that we should just sort of "pick them up" real smooth like, and hold them here on whatever we can think of until he arrives. So he gives us their 10-40... they're sitting getting drunk over in Jerry's bar, you passed right by it just a couple blocks before the motel across the canal."

"Okay, so you went in the bar?"

"No, the barkeep is in with Howarth apparently, tipped him to something, but he didn't want them taken in a public place like that. So we were supposed to wait on the street by this Harjaala's apartment and pick up him, or both of them there. The snitch bartender called as they left the bar, and then they just disappeared! They must have gone a different way or something. We chased around for a while looking, but, no good."

"Come on man, this doesn't wash! What haven't you told us? How were you supposed to recognize the guys?"

"Jack said they both had on dark coats, one was gray and one was blue, so we were looking for two guys together wearing dark coats... no big deal. But all we saw was one guy with a red coat, so it couldn't have been either one of them. And they couldn't have been spooked, it was all kept real quiet, unless Jack let something slip, but I don't see how."

Frank put his forehead in his palm and mocked sobbing while shaking his head. "Well think man, come on, how could they have gotten away from you? Where could they have gone?"

"I suppose they could have gone down under the parking deck between some cars, or hidden in the snow, but that would mean they knew somebody was looking for them. Anything else and we'd have spotted them."

"Okay, so what does that tell you?" asked Frank patiently.

"That they were spooked?" Frank nodded condescendingly. Fred Samuels protested... "But I'm tellin' ya Frank, there's no way, I don't see how..."

Jimmy broke his calm silence and spoke up. "Once the impossible has been eliminated, whatever is left, however improbable, must be the truth."

Samuels looked at him with an exasperated expression, then at Frank. "So, we're hiring philosophers now?" Frank ignored the comment.

"It's from a Sherlock Holmes story," said Jimmy.

Frank said, "Yeah, well somehow these guys got wind that something was up and got the slip on you. This Howarth guy must have anticipated a problem like this, or he would never have called to get us to come up here as backup. Now look Fred, we know something about Howarth that maybe you don't know. He's head of the Special Investigations Branch... ever heard of them?"

"Umm, no, don't believe so. Is it new?"

"Yeah, pretty new I think, but also quite secret supposedly. From what we can tell they investigate people with psychic powers. My guess is that something is going on here that's political, not criminal. Somehow these two guys are mixed up in it, and it has something to do with some alleged psychic something-or-other."

"Psychic powers huh? So you're thinking that might explain how they got onto us and gave us the slip?"

"Could be. So, you've been at this post how long now?"

"Eight years I guess."

"You like it here?"

"What, are you kidding? It's okay I guess, but I'd just love to get a post further south, out of this snow."

"Well listen, if we do good on this one you can probably write your own job description anywhere you want, but if we screw it up, they'll probably send us up to James Bay or some damned place. Look, I know this Howarth guy. I've worked with him and I know the kind of butthead he can be. I don't want to have to depend on him for information." Samuels nodded as if he understood. "I want you to dig up everything you can on both of these characters okay? I'm going over to talk with this bartender guy and see what I can get out of him. You try to figure out what's the deal with this Puttonen and Harjaala. Meet us at the Crown about one for lunch?"

"Sure, but how about we make it the Kaleva, their pasties have been great this week."

"Done deal, get your best guys on it okay? You got a good hacker?"

"You bet."

"One then." They shook hands, and Frank made a point of turning his reversible coat inside out before putting it on as they left. The fact that the coat was now red instead of blue was not lost on Fred Samuels, who turned back inside with a self deprecating scowl and a throaty rumble like a bear.

Frank and Jimmy went back out to the hummer and drove back across the Houghton-Hancock lift bridge. The wind had lessened almost to a dead calm, but the tiny flakes of snow continued to fall. It seemed to Jimmy, sitting in the passenger seat, that when they were in the middle of the bridge, they were no longer in the real world at all, but driving from a familiar yet foggy nothingness behind, into a similar but unknown misty void before them. The girders and cables began to accumulate a delicate mantle of white frosting. Jimmy sat calmly and thought again of Anna............. "Love is!"

CHAPTER 25

After finishing his double veggie-burger with everything, Jason Desnick had to make a trip to the bathroom to wash the ketchup and pickle juice off his hands. He excused himself and walked across the worn white linoleum tile floor towards the door labeled 'MEN'. As he walked past her, the waitress looked up from clearing the booth where the scarfaced man had been sitting. Her face revealed an inner pain that seeing that man had somehow caused to rise to the surface. As their eyes met for the merest moment Jason saw a vivid scene in an instantaneous flash, as through the eyes of a little girl... A large man, evidently her father, is angry and yelling at her mother. The little girl tries to stop them. The man reaches down and slaps her face, hard. She falls to the floor screaming in pain. "Dianna!" cries the mother and kneels down to cradle her. She looks up to see the angry face of her father. The face changes to that of the man who had been sitting in the booth, then changes back again to that of her father. They are very similar except for the scar. Jason glanced at her uniform, she wore an engraved brown plastic name tag that said "Dee" in gold letters.

As she broke eye contact and moved to pass by him, Jason spoke softly. "Dianna, the angels sang on the day you were born." Then he turned away to the bathroom past the telephone before he could see the astonishment on her face. As he stood at the urinal he reflected that he had touched two minds in the span of an hour, more than usual for an entire week. Briefly he wondered whether there was any significance to this, then reflected that perhaps both were part of the same "situation" he had been sent to deal with, this focalization of energies in a particular geographical area. He briefly hoped that this last contact would not endanger his cover, but rationalized that he could hardly turn his back on a brother's pain, in this case that "brother" was a woman.

When he returned to the table Leonard and Harry were just getting their coats. Leonard turned to Jason and spoke in a soft but reprimanding voice. "What are you doing hitting on that waitress? You know we're leaving right away."

"Sorry, couldn't help myself." He answered with mock sheepishness.

"Well whatever you said, she ran into the back crying."

Jason nodded, and thought that this was probably best in such a situation. The shedding of pain through tears was an old remedy, but still a good one. "Sorry, you guys ready to go?"

Harry was paying the tab at the front desk, Jason looked back, noticed that there was no tip, went back and dropped a ten on the table. They went out and got back into the Bronco, pulled out of the parking lot and headed north out of town on State Highway 17.

Jason drove them northward on a narrow two lane highway between high snowbanks, but it had been plowed recently so conditions were not bad. Still, they were forced to travel more slowly than they had gotten used to on the larger, more traveled road, and Harry began to fidget. He looked at Jason quizzically. "What was the deal with that waitress back there? What did you say to her?"

Jason kept his eyes on the road for a moment before answering, decided to tell the truth rather than evade the question. It was a foregone conclusion that he would not lie. "I told her the angels sang on the day she was born."

"What? What the hell kind of a thing is that to say?" said Leonard.

Jason smirked as if embarrassed. "She looked upset about something, I just said it, thought it might cheer her up."

"Yeah, well it obviously didn't work," Leonard commented. "From her reaction I thought you had said something obscene or suggestive."

Harry was leaning forward with his head between Jason and Leonard. "I don't know." He said. "It didn't seem to me that she was angry, upset maybe, but not mad."

Leonard looked at him somewhat disapprovingly. "Yeah, well we've got a job to do, and I don't want to get sidetracked with my driver coming on to every waitress we meet."

Jason sensed an opening. "So, just what is this job anyway?"

"We need to pick up a couple guys for questioning in the Houghton/Hancock area. No big deal." Leonard answered matter-of-factly.

"Couldn't you just get the guys up there to do it? What's the big hurry?" He swerved out to the left to pass a couple of snowmobiles traveling on the road in the same direction.

"They're not supposed to be on the road like that." Leonard said after the noisy machines were left behind. A long silence followed, Leonard looked at Jason. "So, what do you do at the Twin Cities office?"

"Well, like I said, they had me working narcotics, undercover a lot, surveillance, that sort of thing."

"You like it there?"

"Oh, I guess it's okay, I wouldn't mind traveling more often."

"Really? Hmmm."

"Why, you want to offer me a job working for you?"

"Maybe, if you're the right sort of person. You interested?"

"Maybe, if it's the right sort of job. What do you guys do, if you don't mind my asking?"

"Ever heard of the Special Investigations Branch?"

"S.I.B.? Sure, heard of it, don't know much about it though, seems like nobody will say anything."

Harry stared at Leonard as if he could not believe that the topic was even being discussed. "Boss, umm, do you think.....?" Leonard cut him off.

"The deal is, agent Desnick, the world is changing." Jason nodded as if this were completely obvious. "Ever since the turn of the century there have been an increasing number of recorded incidents of psionic ability erupting from the general population. This is no longer fairy story stuff, this is for real. Do you believe in telepathy Desnick?"

"Well, I guess I have no reason not to."

"Good, because I can prove to you, beyond any shadow of a doubt, that it's real. What Special Investigations tries to do is identify the people who have these abilities, and determine where their loyalties lie. If we can, we recruit them, if not, we try to marginalize them."

"Marginalize?" asked Jason quizzically.

"Yeah, make them look like idiots so nobody pays them any attention, make them harmless."

"What's the point of that?"

"Don't you see, Desnick? A single telepath who happens to have loyalties other than to North America could wreak havoc with our security. Why, he could pass secrets through locked doors, transmit secret codes, all sorts of things."

"And that's what this trip is about? Somebody up there has psychic powers and you want to marginalize them for political purposes?"

"Only if we can't get them on our side. What do you say, sound interesting? We can always use a good man, especially one who knows his way around the bad parts of town."

"Why the secrecy though? Why not put it out in the open? Seems like you'd get more public interest and cooperation that way."

"Sorry kid," Leonard instructed, "you don't seem to understand the global situation. Everybody seems to think that the big continental consolidations are a stabilizing influence...

"Well sure, that's what everybody been saying for years, " Jason replied.

"You're right, that's what they've been saying, and it's been a good thing as far as regional conflicts go. The larger sovereign units allow for more diversity within them, so that the Basques were able to form their own little state within the European Union, the Kurds have a semi-autonomous region within the Mid-East Confederacy, and even Pan-Africa put an end to the bloody nationalistic wars and skirmishes that used to plague that region."

Jason was interested. "And you haven't even mentioned the partitioning of Texas or the split of North and South California," he interjected.

"Precisely, local conflicts have eased, but you may not appreciate the fact that the restructuring of the United Nations has brought these continental confederacies to the very brink of nuclear war several times in recent years."

Jason looked startled. "Really? It must have been kept very quiet then."

"Oh yes. The public story is all of peace and harmony and a new age of enlightenment. The U.N. can now effectively prevent or deter small conflicts, but the growing agitation over dwindling resources, global warming, the rise of the great multinational corporations, and the shrinking global economy, has put a great deal of pressure on the leadership of the continents. They all want to try to get their share any way they can."

"And you're saying that some are thinking war?"

"That's right."

"So, you want to use individuals with psychic talents to prevent a war?" asked Jason as he drove.

Leonard looked sternly at Jason. "Prevent... or win. But that's not my job, I just identify the talent and try to get them on our team, try to get them to work for the North American Federal Union. So son, what do you think? Do you want to come work with us?"

"I'd have to check with my captain."

"Don't worry about it, I have the authority all the way from the director, to commandeer anybody I want. Your boss won't argue if he knows what's good for him."

"What about other abilities besides telepathy? Do you care about those or what?"

"Ah, so you know something about these matters?"

"Well, I've done some reading, you know, science magazines and stuff."

"Yes, we're concerned with all sorts of psionic talent, but especially telepathy, precognition, and telekinesis. These are the ones that pose the greatest security risks as well as the greatest strategic benefits."

"What about empathy."

"I have yet to see a confirmed report. Even if it's real, my opinion is that it is of no strategic significance. Empathos reportedly involves nothing but feelings and emotions. It therefore has no relevance to our investigations, as we are concerned with information and actions. So anyway, are you interested?"

"Yeah, count me in."

"Okay then, I am the captain of this outfit, and I answer only to the director herself. Consider yourself an assistant to Harry here for the duration of this operation. After that we'll figure out a permanent billet for you." Jason glanced at the digital clock on the dash as they cruised northward towards Eagle River Wisconsin, it was just after 1:00 P.M. Leonard continued to brief him on the current situation. "So we've got these two, this young fella, Digger Puttonen, and an old guy named Arne Harjaala. We've been keeping an eye on both of them for quite some time. Harjaala is an interesting case, he was found in one of the mines back in the nineteen forties, injured, disoriented, and claiming to be a man who disappeared in a mine accident in 1906. We've got a whole file on the guy. Well, back in the sixties the old FBI did an investigation on the guy, and all his claims seem to check out. But he's suffering from some kind of schizophrenia or catatonia or something, can't get more than three words out of him strung together coherently. You might say he marginalized himself. We inherited the files when I founded the SIB six years ago. We've got the old guy on support, and we have somebody that keeps an eye on him, in case he says anything interesting. His case is extremely unusual as it seems to be a genuine case of temporal dislocation... time travel, the only case of its type that we know of. If we could figure out how he did it... well, it would be a feather in our cap.

"Now this Puttonen fellow is just the opposite, a pretty typical psi case. We have both documentary and allegorical evidence that he has a sort of telepathic ability, but it appears to be very diffuse and sporadic. He has seemed harmless in the past, finding some rocks buried beneath the ground and stuff like that, but in the last couple or three years he's become involved in developing some rather startling new technology. Late last night I got a call from my informant that Harjaala and Puttonen were drinking together in the bar, and that suddenly Harjaala started talking and making sense, and he was talking about the mine."

"The mine?" asked Jason.

"Yes, the place where the temporal dislocation allegedly occurred. Now it's one of the basic facts of this business that one psychic is a problem, but get any two or more together and you have a possible recipe for disaster. There seems to be a strengthening of their abilities as you get them in close physical proximity to each other, don't ask me why... I don't know. We don't quite understand the effect yet, which is another reason we want to recruit these folks. So anyway, our computer simulation indicated there was at least a 98% probability that something of inter-continental political significance is taking place in the area. So here we are, trying to get up there to deal with it, and this damned storm is making a mess of things."

"So, what have you done so far? Are these guys in custody yet? Are they being charged with anything?"

"I wish I knew if they were in custody, but I don't want to risk calling the local station on an open line. Sometimes just the action of making a phone call seems to alert these folks, it's like they pick up the intent right out of the air. It's my experience that the best method is for me to physically travel to the place, and just walk right up to them, catches them off-guard. I asked the local boys to make the pick up, and also requested additional back-up from the Marquette station a couple hours away just in case there were problems. And no, we don't charge them, we just pick them up on a "generalized questioning" warrant for continental security."

The outlying houses of Eagle River Wisconsin started coming into view. They came into the center of town and turned left on 45 heading north. As they neared the outskirts of town they passed a big red barn on the right that had a flashing digital sign on the side saying "Tonight only: NepTune Live!!" The parking lot was already half full.

The snow continued to fall, and was building up to a considerable depth on the road, but the traffic seemed pretty normal and there were two clear tire tracks to keep the Bronco on line. Eagle River was left behind as they headed further into the northwoods. Hardwood forest, the trunks starkly dark against the white snow, contrasted with stands of pine which held the snow in white mountainous masses. The smell of woodsmoke drifted in the air from the chimneys of houses as they passed. Jason mused on the fortunate turn of events that had brought him an invitation to join S.I.B. He would have to be somewhat cautious he knew. These men would become suspicious if he showed too much knowledge of their business. "So captain?" Said Jason.

"Yeah?"

"When you get these guys in custody, then what? We can't hold them more than a day on a gen-cue. Do you just ask them about where they stand straight out or what?"

Harry spoke up. "No, we have a technique all worked out... kind of a good cop, bad cop thing. We come out with some phony accusations, accusations that have been made by some unnamed third party. That gets 'em a little disoriented, then we get them to expound a bit, protest against their being held. Then in the cell they're put in next to somebody else, who happens to be one of ours, my guess is that Leonard's thinking about you for this job. We try to get them to talk as much as possible in a stream-of-consciousness type manner, then we subject the recording of their ramblings to a computerized content analysis. You'd be surprised how revealing that is."

"Really? Is that something new?" Jason tried to keep the concern out of his voice. He was quite familiar with the technique, and knew it's capabilities.

"It's something fairly new we just recently got hold of," said Leonard. "Actually they've been doing the computer analysis part for a while, but it's never been used in quite this way before."

"So, you have to send the stuff back to H.Q. for the analysis?"

"Oh no, we've got all the equipment right here with us. In fact, if we'd been recording this conversation we could have performed such an analysis on this exchange right now. But of course, since you're an FBI man we have no concerns about where your loyalties lie."

Jason could tell that the statement was sincere, and not just by the tone of voice. He was glad for that, because he was not sure what the content analysis would reveal about his loyalties. It seemed to him quite possible that it might reveal something that he would rather not divulge at this precise moment. He would have to be very careful indeed.

They continued driving north through lightly falling snow, towards the town of Land-O-Lakes and the Michigan border.

CHAPTER 26

Julius Miller drove east on interstate 90 out of Chicago, the radio tuned to the educational station playing soothing classical music. He turned over in his mind the various possibilities that confronted him. His quarry was well known to him. He had studied their history, habits, and psychological profiles in intimate detail. He felt that he knew them perhaps better than they knew themselves, certainly their strengths and weaknesses anyway. Julius had access to surveillance data covering most of their movements for the last several months. Unfortunately he had been unable to review the material on the last three days due to the emergency situation. He recalled with considerable discomfort that Sherman had mentioned that the file the traitors had decrypted and read was one of his own. Evidently Sherman had a means of gaining this information that was unknown to him. In due time he would review the data himself and find out for certain.

The last known destination of his targets, according to their nosy apartment neighbor, was Eileen's grandmother's house in Ann Arbor. Julius had no doubt that Mrs. Donitz had been telling the truth, as far as she knew it, but he was not so trusting as to believe that such information had been hers to know. For the moment he followed that lead, but based on experience he gave it less than a 20% chance of being accurate. He noticed that he was approaching the outskirts of South Bend Indiana and glanced at his watch... it was about a quarter past noon, he drove along in a light blowing snow, the sky bright though overcast. He poked a button which booted up his car computer and activated a cellular phone. He crisply spoke aloud the word, "enigmatic", which caused the computer to autodial a special number. The customized equipment in his car automatically encrypted the data transmission, which would require similar equipment at the receiving end. It was merely one of the adaptations he had made to his personal environment in response to the demands of his profession. A simple "beep" advised him that an uplink had been established.

While many of those who loved computers still preferred the precision of the old fashioned keyboard, Julius Miller was one of those who used computers only in pursuit of his other objectives. He had grown rather fond of recent advances in voice activation. It was true that such an interface caused things to run slowly, especially if the speaker had sloppy speech habits, but Julius found the problems quite worth the benefits, especially as he spent so much time in his car.

The explosion of computer capabilities in the late 2000s and early teens, together with business deregulation in conjunction with the Federation of North America, had resulted in the birth of numerous new entrepreneurial schemes. While it was true that the computing giants of the last century had mostly crumbled during the recent depression due to their sheer size and arrogance, this had left a lot of room for smaller ventures using new techniques to build customized optical processors for special purposes in low production runs. There was also a booming data services industry fueled by millions of computer literate but jobless people seeking any way to make a living. It had proven quite cost effective for Julius to subscribe to a variety of anonymous digital surveillance service rather than try to perform surveillance activities himself. He had only to connect up to the service's computer to download data from any one of the current operations he had going at any one time. The enemies of his primary employer were numerous and he was kept quite busy.

Now he spoke out loud. "Video data transfer."

A synthetic human voice answered. "User eye dee".

Julius spoke loudly with clear precision. "Jubal Harshaw."

"Password."

"Something wicked that way strums."

"Specify camera."

"Sherman computing services."

"Specify start time."

"Zero seven hundred, one, sixteen, seventeen."

"Specify stop time"

"Twelve hundred, one, nineteen, seventeen."

"Would you like all data, or selective edited?"

"Edited"

"Specify edit out parameters"

"Zero change, one minute."

"Data requires three point seven four terrabytes. Confirm data transfer, Yes or no."

"Yes" As soon as Julius spoke this last word a data stream began to flow, he turned the sound volume down but left it loud enough to hear. Sometimes he fancied he could even understand the data stream, though he realized this was quite impossible. He continued driving east for the next five minutes as the ultra-high resolution video data file transferred to the crystal storage media installed in the ashtray of his car. It used less than one percent of the data storage capacity of his system. Finally a voice returned.

"Data transfer complete. Specify action."

"Exit."

"Do you wish to exit this system and logout? Confirm, yes or no."

"Yes"

"Thank you for using Dated Data Demand Services. Your account will be debited eight thousand four hundred and sixteen dollars for this transaction. Remember DDDS when you need customized and confidential information management services"

The line went quiet and Julius reached for a set of eyeglasses, which he put on. These particular glasses were rather a new product on the market, something he found quite useful. It was capable of showing a computer monitor screen in one eye, while the other eye was free to watch the road. The computer itself was imbedded in the temples and wire frames surrounding the lenses and video monitor. The Federation Highway Patrol had conducted a high profile campaign to discourage their use while driving, and a hefty fine could be levied against those found DWW (Driving While Wired), as such use constituted a significant and dangerous distraction for most people. Julius however, felt that he could easily scan a surveillance tape while driving the freeway.

He spoke again to his computer. "Video."

"Specify filename." It responded.

"New file." He answered, a shortcut key which triggered the most recently downloaded file of matching type. Immediately he saw a scene looking over the shoulder of Steve Sanders sitting at his computer in Sherman Industries. A time code in the upper left corner showed 0700/1/16/17. Using clipped vocal commands Julius narrowed the field of view to Steve's computer screen and caused the display to run at a very high rate of speed. He noted, as he had before, that Steve was illicitly using his decryption software to try to hack into incoming encrypted messages. Each time a decode would flash on the screen, Julius would slow down the video to real time and check the filename. Most of them were meaningless and not particularly sensitive financial data files. According to his editing instructions, any time sequence in which nothing changed for over a minute was deleted, so he quickly moved through the massive video log until one of the decodes caught his eye. Julius glanced at the time signature code which read 0652/1/18/17. As before, he slowed the video down and focused on the filename. What he saw made his blood freeze cold....

Access Gained. File MIL11817.CRP, size 45846 Decode Now? It was his own message, he recognized the file name and format. Quickly he scanned forward to see Steve download the file to disk, then Eileen activating the decoding sequence, scanning the file, and taking the disk out of view of the camera. He also observed her destruction of the harddrive and drew the only possible conclusions. He pulled the car off the road to give his full concentration to the situation. His first action was to retrieve the file from his working directory and review it, including the psychological profiles of the subjects.

In all the long and less-than-illustrious career of Julius Miller, he had never been compromised this badly. Out of ninety three successful sanctions, only three had been classified by the coroner as murders. All the others had checked out as "accidents" or "suicides." Julius Miller had never failed in a mission. Suddenly a supposedly simple payback job had become terribly personal, all because these two young fools had stumbled onto this action report file almost by accident. If it had not been for that event they would have been lying stone cold in the trunk of his car two hours ago. There could be no mercy in this sanction, no dragging out of the game of cat and mouse. He must get to them quickly, before they had an opportunity to pass on the information on that disk. The fact that he must also retrieve the disk meant that there was an added difficulty.

Obviously the marks knew that they were targeted before they left the building. Only in that case did the sequence of events begin to make sense. While one part of his mind was irritated at the setback he had been dealt, another part of him thrilled at the prospect of a real contest, and enjoyed the fact that an important puzzle piece had been correctly fitted into the picture. This time he was after someone who knew they were marked for death, who knew they were probably being stalked. This time he would prove to Sherman how great were his skills. And that filthy reprobate Jameson, never a shred of respect had Julius ever gotten from that scar-faced baboon. Now it would be different. Jameson would have to respect him!

But think now... where would they go? Not Ann Arbor certainly, that had been a feint, but if not there, then where? A really classic feint would have been in the same direction as the intended, but Julius did not think that Steve and Eileen would be capable of such subtlety. No, they had gone either West, North, or South. He thought for a moment of a way in which he might confirm the direction, discarded it as too expensive, then reconsidered. He had used the traffic control system only once before, through an associate who had access to the Federation Highway Department computers. It was risky and very expensive, but Julius reminded himself that this time, his own neck was on the block. This was no longer a simple pop job for monetary compensation. He was fighting now for his very survival. He made the call, mentioned a license plate number, then rang off and waited. In the meantime he drove to the next exit, turned around, and headed west back towards Chicago. Twenty minutes later the call came. The automatic system of speed control on Federation highways monitored the speed of every vehicle, and digitally scanned their license numbers. The information was highly controlled, but with enough palm grease and the right connections Julius had learned that even such supposedly confidential information could sometimes be accessed. A voice on the phone spoke gruffly:

"What's it worth to ya?"

Julius thought a moment. "Have you got a location?"

"Yes"

"Fifty thousand if it's within the last two hours."

"Umm, yeah, just barely. A vehicle with that plate was traveling north on I-94 through Racine at 94 kilometers per hour at ten eighteen this morning."

Julius nodded. Yes... that made sense, he was quite sure that the tip was genuine. "Thank you, check your account on Monday, you should find it to your liking." The line clicked dead.

"So, they went north eh?" thought Julius to himself. The squirrel goes up the tree where he thinks he's safe, but also where his choices are diminished. Julius smiled to himself as he felt his resolve harden and his will focus on the task ahead. So, they tried to send him on a wild goose chase, and managed to waste a couple of hours of his time eh? No matter, once he had the scent there was no escaping this bloodhound. He turned the bitter flavor of his anger over in his mind, relishing the taste, and decided to use something a little more brutal than usual with these two. He turned to the details of the sort of equipment he might use to accomplish his task. He had always tried very hard to vary his technique so as never to establish an M.O. that the police could use to identify his work. Some of his less inventive colleagues would simply find some method that accomplished the task and with which they had developed some skill, and just kept on doing it the same way every time. The fools! A true artist was much more thoughtful than that. The last time he'd used a blowgun had been over ten years ago, and in quite another part of the country. Yes, it might be just the thing for this one. He could probably take at least one of them that way. If they were together, and with a little luck he might just get them both. He thought of the joy he would have, carving the ninety fourth and ninety fifth notches into the shaft of his custom made gold handled walking stick. His thoughts turned happily to the details of how he would fashion the darts, out of.... ice, yes! Perfect! Julius turned on the radio and thrilled to the sound of La Traviata.

CHAPTER 27

Digger put on a music CD, an old copy of "Best of Hubert Laws". He watched Arne rummaging around the kitchen for a moment, then walked into the bedroom and looked over Joan's shoulder at her communications console. "Wow, some setup you've got here," he said.

"Yeah, well, when you're running a revolution, you've got to keep in touch."

"Pretty serious about this secession thing then?"

She looked at him briefly. "Oh yeah. Looks to me like things are coming to a head real soon now. I'm sending out the call. We've been ready for this moment for months now, and I'm sure this is it. On receiving this message all the units will go into action at once. We'll have people marching with signs down in Lansing, and in Marquette, as well as Saint Ignace, Houghton, Sault St. Marie, Iron Mountain and Escanaba. The Ojibways have already started a big gathering down there. Our people in congress will introduce a bill already prepared. All our plans are going into motion.... Now!" She pressed a button on the keyboard of the console, and it began autodialing telephone numbers automatically, leaving a coded message at each. "Okay, that's that, now it's our turn."

"Our turn? What do you mean?" Digger asked. He was standing in the doorway, behind him Arne was washing potatoes.

"Well, it's clear that somebody is trying to get control of Midnight Mining Company away from you, possibly more than one group. Whoever it is, I'm sure they won't care about our campaign for independence. They would probably try to make off with the goods, like they did with the copper and the iron, and leave us in poverty again. We've got to stop them."

Digger smiled. "It wouldn't work."

"What do you mean?"

"The tempiloscope just wouldn't work anywhere else. That's what Farley and these other guys just don't understand. It's true that lots of the stuff we've come up with would do okay elsewhere, but it seems obvious that it's the tempiloscope that is causing all the stir. Don't you see, it's this place, it's the Keweenaw." Joan furrowed her brows and shook her head to indicate she did not understand.

"There's no other place on earth that is geographically and geologically quite like the Keweenaw Peninsula Joan. We're right on the isogonic line, so true north and magnetic north are aligned. The thickest crust on the planet is right beneath our feet, like a great keel extending down into the earth's mantle. This serves to magnify and focalize gravimetric field lines, resulting in a matrix through which the tempiloscope can function." Joan gaped at him.

"Are you serious? The equipment will only work here?"

"Yes, and it has to be underground, at least a hundred meters, but the deeper the better if you want meaningful results."

"Isn't there anyplace else in the world? South Africa? The Andes?"

"Not really, no place even one tenth as good."

She smiled. "And nobody else knows this right?"

"Probably not. I just confirmed it a few minutes ago, though we suspected it all along. The only other person who knows enough about it to verify the deduction is James Dolittle, and he hasn't heard about Arne yet."

"This is fantastic Digger! Alright, we have our ace in the hole. Even if they get hold of the technology, they can't move it, but they don't know that yet. Hmmm. And just who is "they" I wonder. Is it Sherman alone, or are others involved too." Digger stood and watched the wheels turn in Joan's mind. He was more convinced now than he was the night before that this woman was meant to be his life partner. Their minds seemed to mesh together like finely machined gears. The communications board continued making its automatic calls. Joan jumped up, a look of deep concern on her face.

"Digger, what about your partner James?"

"What about him? I saw him the day before yesterday, before I went out drinking, he was heading home. Oh! You don't think....."

"Who knows? If they went after you, and missed, they might try for him. I think we've got to try to get in touch. And like you said, he can confirm your idea that the stuff will only work here."

Upon hearing her talk about James, Digger suddenly had a familiar tingling feeling in the scalp on the back of his head. "Yes" he said, "But we need to be careful. Damn, who are these guys anyway? Why don't they just leave us alone?"

"Too late for that." Smirked Joan. "You've gone and opened Pandora's box, and now we have to deal with it. You know, you've been looking at this new technology from the viewpoint of research tools and environmental management.

I love ya for it ya know! But take the point of view of a corporate or military mind for a moment, if you can. From their point of view these tools are way too powerful to let some academics and boy scouts have fun with them. Those guys will do anything to get hold of this stuff, and it looks like they've already made their first moves. So it's up to us now. Got any ideas?" Digger pinched his face and tried to think. Joan got up and came to Digger, putting her arms around him and squeezing tight. She looked up at his face as he thought.

"I think we can go to town." he said at last. "Nobody will be looking for your car. It's cold enough that me and Arne can bundle up in scarves and stuff so nobody will recognize us."

"Okay so far, then what?"

"Well, maybe we just see what happens I guess, go with the flow?"

"I'd rather have something a little more definite in mind. I mean, I trust your instincts, but we need a plan to work from."

"Okay, how 'bout this... James and Barbara live over towards Lake Linden. My place is up in Paavola. Right near there is the old number eight shaft. James and I have a message drop there, a hole under a rock at the shaft collar. We used to use it years ago to let each other know who was underground and when they went down, for safety purposes. We've used it a couple times since then. If he needed to contact me, and was afraid to leave a note at my house, I know he'd use the drop if he could get there.

"So, we could cruise by the Vivian Street adit and see what's happening there. Maybe we can tell by the cars whether something's going on, I'd recognize any that are usually there. Then we can go up and check the drop, and maybe cruise past my place to see if it's being watched. There are some things I'd like to pick up if possible, some equipment we can use. Then we figure out what to do from there. I don't know about going to James' house, that might not be a good idea, even if he's there."

Joan sighed and nodded. "Okay, I guess that will work." She took a look at the communications console. It had worked through only a small fraction of the numbers it was to call. "We'd better get moving."

They went into the kitchen where Arne was just finishing peeling a bunch of potatoes. He looked up. "Hey youse guys, I found some good lookin' taters here. I thought about maybe steaming them." Something in their faces caught his attention. "What is it now... something wrong then?"

Digger spoke up. "We don't have time Arne, we need to go. Something's happening out there and we need to go deal with it."

Arne put down the peeler and nodded. "Okay then, let me get my coat and I'll be along. Lemme just put these taters in da fridge though."

"I said we need to go Arne, me and Joan, but you can stay here if you want. We don't know what's going to happen."

"Nah Digger, if you go, I go. After what we been through in the last day I trust ya. Anyway, I don't know what I'd do out here by myself, prob'ly start thinkin' about drinkin', and somehow, I just don't wanna do that." Joan looked at Arne with new respect, and helped him find a plastic bag for the potatoes.

Joan left the communications console making its calls, then threw a few pieces of electronic equipment, including her computer, into a bag and set it by the door. She checked the thermometer by the door, it read minus fifteen Celsius. They put on all their winter gear, including long underwear and double socks... Joan found some extras the men could use... then went out to the barn. The snow that had fallen overnight was nearly a foot thick, and it took a bit of shoveling work to get the doors open. Joan looked at the thick snow and shook her head. "This is not a great snow car Digger. I think we should put the chains on for more traction. It'll slow us down, but we'll have a better chance of getting where we're going."

Digger nodded. "Okay, where are they?" Joan turned out to be pretty handy with a pair of pliers, and without as much trouble as Digger feared, they had the chains mounted on the rear wheels, and the engine warmed up. Joan drove the car out into the snow and backed it around facing down the driveway while Digger and Arne pushed the doors closed again and got in. Soon they were moving slowly but steadily down Joan's long driveway. Arne sat in the back with the bag of gear that Joan had packed. When they got out to the road they stopped for a moment. Joan turned to Digger and took his gloved hand in hers.

"Thanks for last night eh?" she said softly.

"Thank YOU!" he smiled.

"Just remember Digger, I love you, and we're going to get through this thing okay?"

"Yeah, I know."

Arne leaned forward for a moment. "Listen you kids, don't ever take love for granted ya got that? Never! You don't know what you got here, I mean, you t'ink it's great, ya... but you don't know yet just how great it really is." Joan turned around and gave Arne a big kiss on the cheek.

They turned right and in a mile or so came to Highway 41 in Chassel. Looking down the road to the southeast they saw what looked like a black Humvee closing on them. Digger and Joan looked thoughtfully at each other, and she hesitated to pull out in front of it, though it was still a ways off. Besides, it was moving pretty fast, faster than they would be able to go with the chains mounted. They waited, not wanting that thing behind them on the road.

The hummer breezed past them in a cloud of snow, all they could make out was that it was painted black and that there were two figures inside. Joan looked at Digger.

"Did you get anything?" she asked.

He cocked his head to one side, "Yeah, well, something I guess... not what I expected..."

"What do you mean?" She pulled out into the road behind the hummer, which quickly receded into the distance.

"Well, I expected to either get a negative feeling or a neutral one. If it was the same guys who were looking for us last night then I would expect a sense of 'nasty'. If it was someone unrelated I'd expect nothing. But what I felt was, well, a sort of mixed feeling. Hard to explain. Whoever is in that car has something to do with all this, what that may be I can't say."

"That's a lot!" Joan commented. "Do you usually get that detailed a feeling from situations?"

"Now that you mention it, no. The ability seems to be growing stronger since you picked us up."

"Yeah, I've been noticing that too."

"I just thought of something." Said Arne from the back seat.

After a pause, Digger responded. "Yeah? What?"

"I haven't even thought about drinkin' a beer 'til jus now. Usually I'd be on my stool by dis time, or sittin' in my room wit' a liter. But ya know... it's not like I'm tryin' not ta think about it, jus' that... I don't rilly want one is all."

Digger nodded, but Joan looked thoughtful. They passed the MTU campus, heading into downtown Houghton. Digger pulled the scarf up over his face in case anybody might recognize him. As they passed Wadsworth Hall a few kids emerged with signs on poles. One of them said "Superior, it's more than just a State of Mind".

"Is this your doing?" Digger asked. looking at Joan.

"Probably, but it's just starting; you aint seen nothin' yet. So, where you want to go first?" she asked.

"Well, let's cross the bridge and cruise past the adit, to see what we can see."

They turned right onto the lift bridge into Hancock. The roads here were well cleared, but the snow began falling harder again. The growling noise of the chains changed tone as they crossed the steel and concrete structure. The far side of the bridge came into view, as well as the steep hillside with its unshoveled pedestrian stairway. The road to Ripley, Dollar Bay, and Lake Linden veered off on the right, the Nova turned left with the main way across the face of the hill and up into town. Digger pointed right, and Joan turned up the steep hill onto Dunstan Street, then took a right on Cooper heading back east. At Vivian Street they turned north again. It was a tree-lined residential street, with closely spaced older homes dating from the 1920s and earlier, when the mine was in its heyday. These would have been the houses of the shift foremen and level bosses. They drove north up the street until they could see the narrow driveway heading towards the mine entrance. The looming dark mass of the hill could be sensed, though not directly seen, through the falling snow.

"Okay," said Digger, "Let's just turn left and drive past the entrance, I want to see who's here."

Joan slowed the car and began to make the left turn onto Rock Street. If they had continued straight they could have driven right into the mine entrance. Digger slumped down and peered over the dashboard. He noticed only one strange car in what he could see of the narrow, angled parking area, The security guard Aaron was there at his post, but a man stood by the front gatehouse talking to him that Digger had never seen.

"I don't like it." He said. "I was afraid there'd be a lot more people here, but there's not. I've never seen that guy before around here, and I've got a bad feeling. Let's get outa here!"

Joan drove smoothly out to Dunstan Street, and turned right, grinding slowly up the hill to Sampson. She turned left and continued after the road turned partly uphill and became Hillside. They turned right on White Street and arrived at the flashing yellow indicating the junction with U.S. 41. They turned right again and continued up to the top of Quincy hill. The big number two shaft house and the mine museum passed by on the right. As they drove, Digger got out the computer and some disks, poked a few keys, then slipped the disk into a plastic bag. At the road to Paavola, about two miles later, Digger motioned Joan to turn, then had her stop within a few dozen yards. He tore a scrap of paper from a brown paper bag on the floor and scribbled a few words, then put that in the bag as well. An unplowed road ran to the right between some old ruins of mine buildings. Steam could be seen rising into the air about a hundred yards away.

"What are we doin' here?" asked Arne. "Dis is da number eight."

"Right, this is where James and I have our message drop. I want to leave a copy of this disk there, and see if he's left anything."

"You want us to come too?" Joan asked. Digger opened the car door and bent down to look at the ground. Some foot tracks had been made some hours before, shrouded into rounded depressions, but not yet completely obliterated by the fresh snow.

"No, I don't want to be seen stopped here. Why don't you go back out to the highway, drive a couple miles, turn around and come back. Give me about five minutes, I'll be here."

"Okay then, be careful, we'll be back in exactly five minutes."

The car drove off and Digger followed the foot tracks up the old unplowed mine road until he was level with the column of steam. Sure enough, the oblong depressions in the snow turned that way. He arrived at the shaft collar, a poured concrete footing half a meter high and thick. The opening was about ten meters square, a series of railroad rails had been welded together to form a grid across the top. The grid was spaced closely enough to keep people out, but allow air and bats to pass through. He stepped up onto the wet rails and took a deep breath of the warm, moist mine air. He looked down into the darkness between the rails and tried to visualize the shaft descending at a fifty five degree angle into the ground. The old steel rails that the ore cars had ridden on could be glimpsed disappearing into the gloom. The darkness below was a great contrast to the almost blinding whiteness of the snow covered landscape. The warm wetness of the mine, the delicate sound of water running down in thin trickles called to him. The mine was so deep, over 4,000 meters on the incline, that geothermal energy kept the water warm, and kept the entrance from freezing up except in the very coldest of weather. Digger went off to one side of the cap, reached through the rails, and found the crowbar that he and James kept hidden there. He then moved to the other side, located the one rail that they'd managed to break loose, and levered it aside until he could just squeeze between the rails. He took off his heavy winter coat, and lowered himself until only his head and shoulders were above the cap, feeling with his feet until he found it, the point of a rock sticking out of the wall. Quickly he ducked under the collar and scrambled carefully to the ladder, climbing down six steps facing outward. He then stepped off the ladder onto one of the ties that held the rails, crossed the shaft on the tie, and moved to the side of a large but inconspicuous rock.

Years ago he and his buddies had entered this mine surreptitiously to search for mineral specimens, particularly datolite. They had evolved a series of such message drops to keep each other apprised of who was underground in which mines. It had been years since the other drops had been used, but he and James still kept this one active, mostly for fun. Digger used both hands to pivot the large stone. Underneath it was a hollow in the gravel and accumulated detritus of mining. Sure enough, within the hollow was a bulky plastic bag. Digger grabbed it, and shoved it into his front pants pocket without examining it, then took the one out of his other pocket and carefully placed it within the hollow. He had expected a drop from James to contain just a piece of paper, but he could feel there was something else in the bag as well, too large to be a computer disk. He glanced at his watch in the pale light which filtered through the grid above, three minutes had passed since he had left the car. He hurried back up the ladder and slipped between the rails. After repositioning the loose rail and replacing the crowbar, he hurried back down his own trail. The snow began to stick to the wet surface of his pant legs and freeze there, turning them stiff. As he reached the road Joan and Arne pulled up and he got in. They continued east towards Paavola.

"So, did you find anything?"

"Yeah!" Digger fished in his pocket for the packet. "Didn't look at it yet though." He opened the ziplock bag and removed a small plastic box with a simple switch on it. It looked quite amateurishly made. There was also a tightly folded piece of paper. "Looks like there's a note here." Digger removed it and read out loud...

> 7:10 a.m. Thurs, Jan 19, 2017
> Digger:
> I hope you find this. Things have been strange after I left you yesterday, weird calls in the middle of the night. Got to thinking about Josh and things, got kinda scared. I have Barb and the girls to think about! We got the keys to a neighbor's cabin up in Eagle Harbor. We've been there a few times before, but hopefully it will be untraceable. We're going there, now. It's right on the shore, the sign says "Johnson's Rest". I have the cel, but don't call unless it's a real emergency, you know how easy they are to trace.
> Here's the remote I promised. Just flip the switch and put it into the water and the nearest grunt will respond. Sorry about cutting out, but I can't take chances anymore like in the old days. Hope you understand.
> Good luck!
> James

Digger sighed with relief. "Thank God, at least they're safe. That's one worry off my mind. They traversed the two miles to the little village of Paavola, and started seeing the roofs of the old miner's shacks. Most of these were now restored and refurbished, much nicer now than they had ever been in the mining days. Digger motioned to Joan to turn left on the second street they came to, then he hunkered down again. There was a dark blue '05 Jeep Cherokee parked further down the road, with two young men sitting in it. He glanced at his house as they went past. Sure enough, there were fresh looking prints in the snow at the door, and branching to the front windows. Someone had been checking the place out. They cruised past the parked car, trying to look casually disinterested. Digger kept his face turned away. He could feel the suspicion of those in the car beating down upon him like prickly needles. They kept driving, and Joan pulled over by a house towards the north end of the road. At once the suspicion ended, their actions seemed normal.

"This is Ruth's place." Said Joan. "She's a friend of mine, and almost a neighbor of yours. You know her?"

"Sorry no. I don't really know many people up here."

"Too bad, I thought we'd just stop and visit, it would explain to those guys what we're doing here, and she may have noticed something herself, she left us one of those phone messages last night."

They all got out and went up to the door, the path was freshly shoveled. Joan knocked loudly on the windowless wooden door. A faint barking was immediately heard, becoming louder as an interior door was opened.

The outer door opened to reveal a middle aged woman with long graying brown hair. She brightened immediately when she saw Joan. "Joanie! Good to see you, come on in." A large black Lab sniffed at their legs as they entered, then frisked about them. "My dog's name is Oby," said Joan.

They went into the vestibule and took off their coats and boots, walking into the cozy interior in stocking feet.

"So... didn't expect to see you, today of all days." Ruth embraced Joan in a warm hug. "Got the call this morning. I was just getting ready to go downtown. I guess we're having a big rally eh?" She looked towards Joan's companions.

"Ruth, this is my friend Arne Harjaala, and my... uh... special friend, Digger Puttonen." They shook hands, Ruth raised her eyebrows at the mention of "special friend". Oby appeared to have adopted Arne, and was sitting at his side begging for attention.

"Puttonen eh? Don't you live just down the street?"

"Yeah."

"Interesting coincidence meeting you today, as there was a guy here just this morning asking if I knew you."

Digger's heart sank. "Really?" he said in a distinctly unenthusiastic tone.

Joan stood to one side, Ruth looked at her. "Joanie, is something wrong?"

"Could be. Listen Ruth, we're trying to get to Digger's house, but it seems like there's some guys out there watching it. We stopped over here to see what we could see. Are those the same guys you called about earlier?"

Ruth looked out the window. "Yeah, they've been hanging around all day. One of those guys came to the door. He was real polite and all, said he was with the FBI, and did I know an Anthony Michael Puttonen, also known as Digger. I told him 'no' of course. Gosh Joanie, don't stand in the doorway, come on in and have a seat. What's going on?" Joan, Arne, and Digger entered the cozy living room and sat down. Arne sat in a big overstuffed chair, and Oby sat next to him, leaning on his leg, and reveled in having his ears scratched. Digger and Joan sat together on a big couch.

"We're not really sure, but I'm afraid to say too much, in case they figure out we came here."

"Don't worry about me. Just tell me what you can, and let me know how I can help."

"Well, it's complicated," Joan said. "Seems like we need to just sit and think for a little while, mind if we stay for a bit?"

"Not at all, how about a nice pot of tea?" They nodded. Ruth began to bustle in the kitchen. Joan sat still on the couch, holding Digger's hand, closed her eyes in meditation, and began to seek guidance in the dilemma.

CHAPTER 28

George Frederick Sherman glowered at the man sitting across from him as the black limousine hurtled along I-90 past downtown Chicago towards O'Hare airport. "You let them take your gun? A couple of computer nerds took your gun away from you?" Sherman shook his head in mock sadness, then spoke softly. "You fucking moron! Why did I ever let your uncle talk me into hiring you? I must have been crazy!"

"But it wasn't my fault mister Sherman, it was that other guy, Carl somethin', from the machine shop, he's the one that hit me with a crowbar, and then that nigger Robbie, he picked up the gun and gave it to the guy."

Sherman's eyes narrowed and grew suddenly as cold as the howling wind outside. "You know, I guess it's really my fault, I should have realized that a person as bigoted as you would have some other serious mental deficiencies as well eh? I was the one that sent a kid to do a man's job. Well, we'll deal with Robbie and Carl in due time, don't you worry. Cases of outright betrayal receive special attention in my organization. But Adam, people who don't do their job in this company... well... we just can't keep them on the payroll if they don't carry their weight." Two other stern-faced men sat flanking Adam, who leaned forward towards Sherman, pleading in his eyes.

"But Mister Sherman, I'll do better, I swear. I'll get those two myself if you want me to."

"Oh? Do you really think you could? How would you go about it do you think?" asked Sherman, feigning polite interest.

"Uh, I guess I'd find out where they live, you know, and then pop 'em. Just give me a chance Mister Sherman, I... I'll do anything you want."

George Sherman face relaxed and he smiled in a friendly way. "Really Adam... anything?"

"Yeah, sure, you just name it."

"Alright Adam. Right now I want you to jump out of this car."

"What?" Adam gulped after a long hesitation.

"I said... I want you to open that door... and jump out of this car."

"But mister Sherman... we're doing at least ninety klicks."

George craned his neck to glance at the speedometer. "Yeah, that's about right." He pointed to one of the other men. "Tony, would you please open the door for our friend here?"

"Yes sir mister Sherman." The man reached a thick muscular arm out and opened the door, which immediately let in a blast of icy cold air and swirls of snow. Adam looked terrified, shrank back into his seat.

"Adam, I'm starting to get cold here, I think you should go ahead and jump now."

"No, please, I swear I'll do better."

"Good! Show me now. I want to see you jump. If you survive that, you can take a few days off, then come back to work next Monday and we'll forget the whole thing ever happened, okay?"

Adam could see that Sherman was quite serious. He nervously got up from his seat and crouched by the door, eyeing the situation, awkwardly zipping the collar of his jacket up high, and looking for a good landing spot. He did not like the idea at all. He glanced pleadingly at Sherman one more time. But Sherman just smiled and waved goodbye. Adam steeled himself to jump, clutching the cast on his right arm against his chest and craning his neck out the door to look for a smooth place. They were crossing the overpass over I-294, about to reach the other side... Adam focused on an opening between signs, aiming to roll down the steep embankment of soft snow on the far side of the bridge. He tensed for the jump. Just before they reached the spot however, Sherman gave a quiet signal. Together, he and one of the men put their feet up, and pushed Adam out the door forcefully. There was a muffled scream and a "thonk" as Adam hit a sign pole head first, knocking it flat into the snow. The two men glanced at each other, and shrugged. Sherman took a quick and approving look around. Only two other vehicles were visible on the bridge at that moment, one ahead of them. and the other behind. Both were extended vans with markings of wholly owned subsidiaries of Sherman Industries. Both were filled with men who would do whatever he asked them to do, without asking questions. They understood clearly the price of incompetence in Sherman's organization. Tony pulled the door closed as they slowed on the approach to the airport.

Chicago's O'Hare airport was closed due to the snowstorm, but when they pulled to a metal gate that led out onto one of the smaller runways, they were let though. A sleek corporate jet stood ready and warmed up, and snowblower crews were busy making a path for it to take off. All three vehicles pulled up near the plane. Immediately men jumped out from the vans and began loading heavy

A Superior State of Affairs

looking black leather and nylon bags into the cargo doors of the jet. Sherman's car let him off right at the stairway leading to the cabin door. The driver got out and opened the left hand door of the limousine, Sherman climbed the steps deliberately, turned left and entered the cockpit. He immediately sat in the copilot's chair and strapped himself in.

The man in the pilot's seat, turned to him with an extended hand, speaking with some trepidation. "Sir, pleased to meet you at last. I'm Crowell, Nate Crowell."

Sherman put on his smiling face and took the other's hand in a firm grip. "Glad to meet you. Good that you were able to make it today."

"Well, they said it was rather urgent."

"Oh yes, very urgent indeed."

"Well, you see sir, the weather is pretty bad, I really think that it would be better...."

"There's a bonus in it for you." interrupted Sherman.

You see, we might get off the ground, but there's no knowing what we might....

"Twenty thousand."

".... what we might encounter on the way, severe icing perhaps, and the destination....

"Oh hell, let's make it thirty thousand."

"... the airport at the destination is closed, we don't know yet if they can even ......

"Forty thousand."

"....if they can even plow a landing lane for us, and the lights, there won't be any lights."

"Look Cromwell..."

"Crowell sir."

"Whatever, look, if you can get us there alive, even if you have to put this baby down with gear up, there's a fifty thousand dollar bonus in it for you, and I'll take full responsibility for any damage. Do whatever you have to do, but get us there. I'd do it myself but I don't have anywhere near as many hours on this equipment as you do. You're the most expensive pilot I've ever hired. I want to see how good you really are, now let's get going."

Nate Crowell nodded worriedly and began going over the preflight checklist, examining gauges. He double checked one digital readout and spoke up. "I'm reading a load imbalance, too much weight in back. Can we move some of that forward?"

Sherman opened the cabin door looked back. All sixteen seats were filled, and four men sat on the aisle floor at the back of the cabin. "You four on the floor, move to the front." They scurried to comply. Sherman shut the door. "That better?"

Crowell checked the readout again sensing strain on the landing gear struts and converting to gross weight and distribution. "Yes, barely, we're right at our load limit here."

"Well, let's get moving then. I want a minimum time course, fuel consumption be damned. We'll climb as steeply as we can to forty-five thousand feet to get above the weather, then north on a mag heading of three five five, at maximum speed until we're practically right overhead, then we drop in full flaps. Got it? Just like old times right?"

"Crowell gulped, "yes sir."

The radio spoke up... someone at the tower wanted to know what the hell was going on. "Ignore that, just get us off the ground," Sherman snapped. Nate flipped on the landing lights, illuminating a narrow lane disappearing into the snow ahead. One snowblower driver looked up startled as Nate powered up the engines for take off. Men and equipment scattered from their path as the aircraft started to move. Nate didn't want to guess what it had cost Sherman to bribe some airport official to arrange for the runway clearance in this weather. Then he thought about the fifty thousand dollar bonus, that was enough to solve a lot of Nate's problems. He was worried, he had been flying long enough that he'd seen his share of close calls. There was no fear in his heart, just a deep and abiding respect for all the numerous things that could go wrong. This flight was awfully risky. He had no idea what was so important that Sherman would make such a desperate move. He centered himself with the thought that if they didn't make it, well, his problems would be solved then too, just in a different way. He glanced at the clock as he pushed the throttles forward to taxi, mentally noting the time at 3.35 CST. At least he wouldn't have to worry about other air traffic. There would be few if any craft up in this abominable weather.

Sherman proved to be an efficient copilot, and they finished the checklist together by the time they moved towards takeoff position on the freshly plowed runway, already piled with two inches of new snow. They taxied to the end and turned, Sherman got on the intercom and said simply. "Hang on boys." Nate pushed the throttles forward to ninety percent and they were soon in the air and climbing. He felt Sherman's hand on top of his, pushing forward. If it had been any other copilot he would have been angry. Sherman pushed the levers all the way to one hundred percent. Crowell had never operated these engines at more than ninety percent, it was his policy of caution, always leaving himself a little headroom. He didn't like it, but there was no gainsaying the determination in this man. Sherman motioned for him to steepen the angle of climb. He checked his airspeed and grudgingly assented. They climbed steeply through the snow into a bright afternoon sky, everything gray-white about them. The light slowly grew, and then suddenly they burst out of the clouds into a blazing blue sky. This was the part Nate Crowell lived for. Man! What a thrill to be at the controls of a powerful machine hurtling through the sky, basking in the sun. He looked down at the roiling clouds below, then ahead at the dark piles of grayness clustering on the northern horizon, and he thought with some trepidation of the descent into that mass. The pilot's paradox... there was no escaping it, no matter how much fun it is to be up in the sky, eventually, you have to land. He thought back to his navy days back before the Federation had unified the branches of the military... remembered the terror of trying to put down an F-15 on the deck of a rolling flattop. A brief flush of adrenaline ran through him as he recalled it, then he pushed the memory back down and concentrated on the present.

They leveled off at 45,000 feet, Nate went to back the throttles to eighty percent. Sherman kept them at ninety, wasting fuel profligately for a few minutes shaved off their flight time. Nate briefly wondered again what could possibly be so important, thought about the looks on the faces of the men in back, the bulky shapes of their baggage, and then decided that maybe he didn't want to know.

Sherman unbuckled his belt and went back to the cabin, closing the door behind him, leaving Nate Crowell alone with the glory of his sky. Back in the cabin, Sherman hunkered down next to the two men who had shared his limousine. "Tony, I want you to call Jameson, make sure we have transportation waiting for us when we get there okay? At least three big cars, preferably vans, at the Houghton airport. Call the airport again, make sure they understand we'll be landing in about an hour, whether they clear for us or not. Get them to clear the runway, I don't care what you have to say, I don't want this plane wrecked if we can help it."

"You got it boss" Tony said as he flipped open a cellular phone and began to punch numbers into the keypad. Sherman slapped him on the shoulder in a friendly way. Then stood up, as nearly as he could in the low passageway.

"Your attention please." He shouted, the murmur of conversation died immediately, all eyes forward. He picked up a packet and handed it to the first man, who took an envelope and handed the packet on. "Here is a map of the area we are coming into. Our objective is to take physical possession of the corporate offices of a small business. We bought it fair and square, but there has been some resistance to us taking over. If you'll notice on the map it is no ordinary situation. The offices are located in a tunnel of an old copper mine, several hundred feet underground. We have two of our own men, Scott and Jeff, inside, posing as security guards, and the director will do whatever I say, so there should be no problem getting in. There's a five thousand dollar bonus in this for each of you, so let's make sure there are no screwups alright?" The men cheered happily at the mention of the bonus. Then Sherman looked more grim and they quieted down. "You've all been on this sort of mission before. So you know things can get messy sometimes. We may face some resistance from the F.B.I., but as far as we can tell there are only three or four of them up there. The locals are already in our pocket. If you have to take out a fed, do it quick and quiet and we'll try to cover it up. We don't want a big scene here, we just want what's rightfully ours."

"There are only two possible ways into the mine," Sherman continued. "One is through a shaft house on top of the hill. Nobody uses it, it's a hundred and thirty meters almost straight down! But we don't want anybody sneaking in that way, unlikely as such an attempt might be, so we'll post a sniper and support team there. All the connections to the other shafts are flooded too deeply to use scuba gear, so we won't need to worry about those."

"The other way is a tunnel right in the middle of the city of Hancock. This is the main entrance, all fancied up and nice. That's where the rest of us will go. We'll put a team on the outside to control the parking area, establish an inner defense perimeter, and assign the rest to relief and patrol as needed, inside or out. The command post will be the first available room within the entrance, probably the front office."

"When we arrive I'll go in personally, with two men, the rest will wait for our signal. Once we're in, anybody who's not with us goes out. We talk them out, push them out, or throw them out, whatever we have to do. Don't kill anybody unless it's absolutely necessary, or on my direct orders, but don't hesitate if they draw weapons. We'll have transportation waiting for us on touchdown. Please review the operational plan, memorize it, and give it back to Tony for disposal. Keep the map sheet on your person in case we get separated. Good luck"

Sherman squatted down again. "Tony, you get Jameson on the line?"

"Yeah, he's there, said he'd have two four wheel drive station wagons and a closed van waiting for us."

"Good man, What about the airport?"

"Not so good, I got the guy's wife, she keeps saying it's closed, and her husband's not there. Sounds like a pretty "mickey mouse" outfit to me."

"Okay, try her again, don't get rough... try to sound scared, like it's an emergency. If that doesn't work, call the county Sheriff, maybe he can get the county plow up there, but make it quick, we'll be on the ground in..." He looked at his watch. "...about fifty five minutes."

Sherman went forward to the cockpit and closed the door behind him. He scanned the instruments; course 355, airspeed 515, checked the automatic location display, all quite satisfactory. He buckled himself back into the copilot's chair and settled down to about thirty five minutes of level flight.

Nate Crowell cringed at the thought of the man sitting next to him, but did a good job of maintaining his outward calm. He had been in Sherman's employ for almost five years now, though this was the first time he'd ever met the man personally. Still, stories and rumors abounded in the company, things were said about Sherman in locker-rooms in hushed voices, things that made his blood freeze, even if they were only half true. Right now however, he had more immediate concerns.

"Sir, what's our runway situation at Houghton?"

"No problem, they'll have it plowed and lit by the time we get there. When we get close I'll punch up the radar transponder and we can make a neat instrument landing. Piece of cake."

Nate breathed a sigh of relief. Now he could enjoy the view a bit. Sherman looked out the side of his eye at the pilot and smiled. He did not believe in allowing his employees to worry, that was his job. Let them enjoy themselves, and then when the real crisis situation arises they'll be in better shape to handle it. He himself however, was plenty worried, and not just about landing the plane, though neither his face nor his manner showed it.

CHAPTER 29

Chris Jameson drove north on highway 45 at the highest rate of speed his vehicle could manage. His driving skills were such that he kept it on the road and only skidded a little now and then. He had passed Bruce Crossing some half an hour earlier, when his cellular phone began to beep. He picked up without speaking. A crackling interference made hearing difficult.

"Jameson, you recognize my voice?"

"Yeah Tony, barely, your signal is weak."

"The man himself will be landing at the Houghton/Hancock airport in about forty five minutes. We need the runway plowed, and at least three large vehicles. We are thirty people with baggage. Can you do it?"

"Tell him not to worry, plows are on the way. I'll be there in twenty five minutes, waiting with two large wagons and a van."

"Great! You need me to relay a message?"

"Nothing I can't tell him in person."

"Okay, see you soon."

"Yeah, right."

The car careened north on 45, skidding slightly under expert control. Chris flipped the phone closed again and slipped it into his pocket. He was impressed... Sherman could move pretty fast when he wanted to. Chris had always been impressed by Sherman's ability to resolve himself to a task and carry it through, doing whatever it took to succeed. That was one of the things that had attracted him to Sherman when he had come home from Cyprus. The bandages had come off his face, and the doctors had wanted to perform some plastic surgery to make it look normal again, but Chris had refused the offer. The face he saw in the mirror, ugly and disfigured, matched perfectly the visage he saw within his soul. Chris recalled the morning he stepped off the plane at O'Hare. He had returned to Chicago, three years and an eternity from when he had left.......

It had been a hot day in summer then. He didn't know where else to go, so he took a cab to the only real home he had ever known; the Our Lady of Suffering Orphanage at the corner of 127th and State on the South Side. He got out of the cab and paid the driver. He stood there on the curb and looked up at the building. The brown brick exterior looked the same as ever, but the windows were all boarded up, and a hand lettered sign said: "For Sale or Rent" with a phone number. Chris wore civilian clothes, but his haircut and his government issue duffel bag marked him as a returning veteran, a common sight in those post-Cyprus days.

He had thought to just stop here and talk with the sisters, just... get his bearings before trying to find work or a place to live. In the back of his mind was the hope that they might be able to help him find a sense of closure within his tortured soul, but apparently the place had fallen on hard times and closed up since he had last been here. He reflected that there would probably never be closure for him. He lightly shouldered his heavy bag and began walking towards up State Street towards downtown... he thought he remembered a strip of cheap hotels in this direction. The sun was hot and there was scarcely a breath of breeze. His nostrils flared. The city streets gave off the familiar yet disquieting sense of decay and turmoil, yet there was less intensity here than in the cities of Asia Minor and Palestine, where he had spent the last three years. He sensed a listlessness and despair that he could not recall feeling here before.

The sidewalks and streets were sparsely populated. The neighborhood had gone downhill since he'd been a boy here. After walking about four blocks he passed three young men who were leaning casually against the wall outside a small shop that openly sold illegal tobacco products and adult magazines. His head was down, his heart confused, but he was not so disoriented as to fail to notice that they fell in behind him, and were beginning to close the gap.

At the subtle "snick" of a pocket knife being opened, he whirled around, just in time to catch one of them trying to slit open the back of his bag. Chris dropped the bag and stood, silently yet defiantly, with hands on hips, as the three spread out to surround him. They were an unusually mixed lot, one was a big redheaded white guy with small piggish eyes and a hairy barrel chest showing through his muscle shirt. A small, skinny, Hispanic looking fellow with long hair slicked back in a pompadour stood next to him, sidling casually away. Chris turned his head to look into the eyes of a shaved headed black man, older than the others by several years. It was he who had the knife, and he who seemed to be the leader of this motley crew. As Chris met his eye the black man spoke.

"Hey man, the war hero returns! Oooh baby, looks like they messed you up bad." He pointed at the scar on Chris' face and laughed. As Chris faced him, one of the others grabbed for the bag. Chris jumped back to defend it, the man retreated across the sidewalk, biding his time. The little group seemed to know what they were doing. Passersby on the sidewalk seemed to pay no attention to what was going on, as if it were a routine shakedown, a commonplace event.

"Hey now, what you got in there man? You got some dope? Brought back some of that Turkish hash I bet eh? Or maybe some money? I bet they gave you a big wad when they sent you back eh? Yeah? Am I right eh? Payment for that scar maybe?"

Chris said nothing, but bent as if to pick up his bag. The thugs chose that moment to strike. Quick as lightning, Chris' foot jutted out in a back kick that took the redhead in the solar-plexus. The man emitted a deep throated "Unnnnhh!" and went down on his back. The other two closed in, Chris feinted with a spinning heel kick at the Hispanic, who ducked. He let the spinning motion carry him around and connected the heel of his boot with the wrist of the outstretched arm of the black guy on the other side. The knife went skittering out into the street. He looked up into the face of the Hispanic as they both rushed him. He delivered a simple knockout punch with his right fist to the jaw of the little guy, then spun and lunged with his open right hand, grabbing the black guy by the throat. The man's eyes went wide and white as he gurgled and croaked, kicking feebly with his feet, hands clawing at Chris's tightening vise. Chris' face was twisted with rage, the muscles and veins stood out starkly on his forearm, his scar stood out in pale contrast to the bright red of his face. He gave one last squeeze, and with a dull wet crunch the man's windpipe collapsed. Chris dropped him, dead and twitching, to the pavement; no emotion showed on his face at all, simply exhaustion. He looked around. Several people now stood on the street and watched in fascination. The little Hispanic was still out, the redhead was getting up and looking at the carnage with disbelief.

"Jesus Henry Christ, you killed him! Lookit that, he's dead."

Chris looked at him, saw the fear in the big man's face, and just said, "Yeah," matter of factly. The man backed away from him and started running.

Other people began to gather around looking at the dead man on the sidewalk, he saw a cel phone flip open out of the corner of his eye. He picked up his bag, shoved some clothes back into it that had come out through the slashed hole and started walking slowly up the street in the same direction he had been going. An approaching police siren could now be heard in the distance. His mind was a blank, a darkness fell over him. Only dimly did he realize that the police would probably arrest him, and he would probably go to jail for a long time. The possibility seemed hazy and unreal, as if it were going to happen to someone else, his feet seemed to move in slow motion as he shuffled along, the voices of people around him formed a muffled unintelligible cacophony. The adrenaline that had energized him in a battle-frenzy now drained away and left him with a nauseous feeling in the pit of his stomach. The death did not bother him, though he briefly wondered why he had killed only the black man and let the other two go.

There was a squealing of brakes, a car pulled up next to him; the door opened. "Get in," said a gruff voice. At that moment it seemed to Chris Jameson that his choices were rather few, so he shrugged and got into the car. He was in the back of a long, steel gray limousine, with his bag on the floor between his feet. A heavily built man in a dark suit closed the door but ignored him. The limo sped off. He looked up at the man sitting across from him, and gazed into a pair of cold blue eyes that looked somehow familiar. They were rather like those he saw when he looked into a mirror.

"I saw what happened," said the man as he handed Chris a clean handkerchief. "Thought you might need a ride."

"Thanks," Chris said simply. He wiped the sweat from his brow, and then some blood and phlegm from his hand.

After a thoughtful pause the other man spoke again. "You handled yourself pretty well back there." Chris said nothing, but simply stared at the floor as the man continued. "Listen, I can drop you off anywhere you want. On the other hand, I can always use a man like you in my business. You looking for work?"

Chris nodded slowly. "Yeah, I am", he said. He looked at this man who had just taken a huge risk for a total stranger.

The other man nodded and stuck out his right hand. "Sherman, George Sherman."

"Chris Jameson," said Chris as he took the hand, and shook it firmly, his clasp met with a grip nearly as strong as his own. He sensed immediately a turning point in his life.

Chris awoke from his reverie as he realized he was moving a little too fast, going down a curving hill into Painesdale. The snow had stopped falling some time ago, and he had allowed his speed to slowly increase. As he struggled to hold it in a left turn, the car skidded silently to the right on the hardpacked snow, and careened sideways into the snowbank, grinding along with a loud crunching sound, slowing down before coming off the snowbank again. Back in control Chris realized he had let Sherman fluster him again, but it was over now. Sherman would arrive at the airport, and unless he made other arrangements, there would be no cars waiting, and no plowed runway either. He would be livid, and eventually, Jameson would probably have to face him. How do you tell a man of that sort that you've been changed, changed from the inside, that you never want to kill another living thing again? Sherman would never understand, of that Chris was quite certain. He felt that he understood Sherman as perhaps few people could, because he had been very much like him.

Only now... now that the dead part inside him had come alive again, could Chris see what the effect of that aberration of his soul had been. So much had changed, in so short of a time, that Chis had little sense of what it all meant. He felt two powerful and yet conflicting urges. One told him to stop somewhere and simply sit and think, for a long time, to try to sort it all out. The other told him to get back up to Houghton as fast as he possibly could, there would be time to think later, or perhaps along the way. It was this latter urge that Chris acted upon, not clearly knowing why. Perhaps, being a man of action, this way seemed easier than the task of facing his own self in contemplation. All he knew was that he would have to try to fix some of the damage that he had caused. He ached with guilt over the thought of some of the things he'd done for Sherman over the years... the lives he had destroyed, the hopes and dreams he had crushed, the fear that he had laid in the hearts of innocent people. He knew there was no repairing all the damage, but this time... this time he would try, no matter what it took, he would try.

Time passed swiftly for Chris as he concentrated on his driving, until he came to Atlantic Mine and looked at his watch. Sherman's plane would be landing at any moment. He had been careful in dealing with Sherman to always look the same as he had that first time, letting his scar show. Sherman surely knew that he used disguises in his work, but Jameson doubted that Sherman had ever seen a photo of any of them. He pulled in at Chippewa Motor Sales. There was a guy on a blue ford tractor with a front end loader clearing snow from the lot. He jumped down as Chris pulled in.

"Can I help you sir?" he asked.

"Looking for a four by four."

"Well, uh, most of the newer ones are gone, been selling real well just lately. I've got a couple older models here, we got a '99 Jeep Cherokee with under a hundred thousand miles on it." He walked a few paces and brushed some of the snow off of a rusting station wagon with a cracked rear window, and a paint job that had once been white.

"How much?"

"Let's see... are you wanting to trade in? That's a fourteen model you're driving right?"

"Yeah."

"Well, there's not much call for those, but I can maybe move it, in time. Tell you what, since you've got an honest face, I'll take the trade-in plus a thousand cash and call it a deal."

Chris smiled to himself as he set his poker face. He knew the deal was a bad one, he could practically see the dealer licking his lips in anticipation. His own estimate was that his car would bring at least four thousand more than the old Jeep. "Let me drive it a bit."

"Sure, let me get the key." Chris checked the tire tread, then opened the door with a loud squeak and got in. The upholstery was in terrible condition, it smelled as if whoever had owned it previously had kept a large dog kenneled in it. The dealer came back with the key, handed it to him. "Yeah, she drives like a beauty."

Chris said nothing, but was glad to hear the engine start up easily, even with the temperature still hovering around twenty below. He pulled out into the road and drove about a half mile on some of the back streets in town, taking the turns a little faster than was reasonable just to see how it handled. He was quite pleased, and drove back to the dealer's lot. In times past he might have intimidated the man into giving him a better deal. He found the situation amusing now, and relished the thought of dickering in a friendly way with the fellow. He pulled it back into the plowed space on the lot and got out, giving the Jeep a critical look, while out of the corner of his eye he saw the dealer sizing him up.

Chris turned to the guy and said, "Damn thing smells like dog shit."

"Oh, well, we haven't had time to get it detailed yet, that can be fixed up in a jiffy."

"I like the smell of dog shit."

"Oh, well, in that case we can leave it just the way it is." The man was definitely off his stride now, the remark had taken him completely by surprise and given Chris an opening.

Chris pulled out a wad of cash and slowly peeled off five one-hundred dollar bills and a folded up title. "I need a week", he said, holding the money and title out to the dealer. The man hesitated.

"I'm sorry? I don't understand."

"I need a set of plates, and a week before you register the sale, will that be a problem?"

With a grin the dealer motioned Chris into his shack. "No problem sir. Just let me get the title for you and we'll call it a deal." Chris went out to shift his luggage from the Millennium to the Cherokee. He knew he had gotten a bad deal financially, but he was in a hurry and wanted a vehicle than would not be traceable to him, at least for a little while. He also needed something that would do better in the snow than his little Millennium.

They exchanged keys and Chis said, "...and could you please keep it out of sight for a few days... don't want the wife knowing I sold her car, you know?"

The dealer agreed smilingly, assuming that the car was stolen and the title a fake. He was getting such a good deal however, he was willing to assume the risk. Only later did he learn that the title was quite genuine and that he had just made a lot of money on one deal. He never found out any more about it though, and never realized the significance of the transaction to events that would shortly make headline news worldwide.

Chris got into the car and headed down the road, near the shopping mall entering Houghton city limits he stopped at a Holiday station. The gas tank on the Jeep was nearly empty. He filled it up and went inside, paid in cash, and went into the bathroom with a small bag. After locking the door, he went to work. His face he quickly covered with a base that hid his scar, he added more gray tones to his hair, red to his nose, two large warts, some appliances that made his ears stick out, and contact lenses that changed his blue eyes to brown. He emerged four minutes later, adopting a slightly hunched posture and a completely different gait.

Chris bought a donut and cup of coffee, there was no sign of recognition in the clerk's face, even though he had paid for gas not five minutes before. As he received his change he said "Thanks, have a good day." to the clerk in a voice that was slightly higher in pitch and a little more nasal than the one he had used earlier. Beside the door was a newsie, he dropped in a quarter and scanned the current headlines. The only item he found of interest was a science report of the occurrence of a major solar storm, and predictions of resultant difficulties with communications, he recalled the garbled conversation with Tony and nodded to himself. He got into the Jeep and drove into town, planning his next moves. He knew his way around town pretty well by this time, but needed some information. He decided that his first visit should be to the Midnight Mining Company office at Vivian Street, where he had left Scott and Jeff with orders to assist that toadsucker Farley Grundwalder in evicting the computer nerds. He cringed at the thought of the pressure he had put on the secretary there to set up the meeting with Grundwalder, she had been so terrified by his subtle threats and his manner. He decided that he'd try to make it up to her somehow, but there were bigger things happening just now, things he had to try to put a stop to.

He came down the hill as the snow began to fall with renewed vigor again, and started across the Houghton/Hancock lift bridge. The phone on the seat next to him began to beep, demanding his attention. He glanced at his watch again, and decided to just let it ring. Let Sherman wonder what had happened to him. He smiled to himself and realized that, with his disguise, to all intents and purposes, the old Chris Jameson had disappeared from the face of the earth. As of this moment he was a new person, a better person. He scarcely even noticed the black hummer crossing the bridge in the opposite direction.

CHAPTER 30

When Steve Sanders awoke he was temporarily disoriented. Eileen was not in the bed next to him. They had laid down for a moment after dinner and he seemed to have dozed off. The events of the day shimmered in his mind with a gauzy flatness, seeming more like scenes from a movie he had watched than waking reality. The room was strange to him, and the insistent sound of someone knocking at the door could not be ignored. He blinked his eyes widely, trying to get them to focus on the thin ribbons of bright light streaming in from the hallway through the gaps around the wooden door. He yawned as the door opened and Tom's grizzled and unshaven face looked in.

"Hey there sleepyhead, you're getting married in a half hour and all you can think of to do is lie around lollygagging in bed?"

"What?"

Tom laughed at the confused look, guessing Steve's dilemma. "Yep, it wasn't a dream, the girls are giggling around somewhere, messing with dresses and ribbons and such. The preacher is here already. You'd better get your butt out off that bed and get cleaned up. Bathroom's down the hall on the right. Feel free to use the razor and towels and whatever else you need. Eileen picked out some suitable clothes for you, over there on the chair. Showtime is in about thirty minutes." Steve looked startled.

"What time is it?"

"Almost eight thirty"

"What day is it?"

"It's the evening of Thursday, January 19th, and in case you're wondering, the year is still 2017. You've only been asleep for about an hour. We tried to check the news, but there's some kind of solar storm or something, blocking just about all broadcast communications. We've just got a local cable TV station still on the air, they're scrambling like hell trying to find out about it. The telephones are still working, at least the ones on ground cable networks, but just about everything else is down."

"What?"

Tom walked into the room and flipped on the light. "Son, you're starting to sound like a feedback loop. Get yourself put together and come down for a cup of coffee to perk you up. Don't take too long now! If I don't see you downstairs in five minutes I'll be back with a bucket of snow." Tom walked out the door, turned and gave a big grin as he closed it behind him. Steve was not sure, but he thought the threat of a bucket of snow was quite possibly sincere. He threw back the covers and put his feet on the floor, rubbing his face and stretching. The room had a warm cozy feel to it. He had been so exhausted earlier that he had simply collapsed next to Eileen on the bed that Peg had prepared for them. He yawned again and stood up, making his way out the door to the bathroom. He found a new boxed toothbrush, a comb, and a double blade razor laid out on the sink, so he brushed his teeth, worked the tangles out of his hair, and shaved, trying to piece together the whirlwind events of the day. It was, apparently, not over yet.

Looking halfway presentable in the mirror, he hurried back to the bedroom and put on the black dress pants and pale blue shirt he found there. He skipped lightly down the stairs and arrived at the kitchen just in time to see Tom pouring two cups from a coffee pot. "Ah, just in time, I was about to go scoop up some snow..." he said smiling.

"Ah, thanks," said Steve, accepting the cup offered him with a nod. "I feel a little disoriented."

"Not to worry for now, events are taking their own course, and for the moment you might just want to go along for the ride. You won't regret getting married, trust me on this one. Eileen's a fine girl."

"Oh, I'm not anxious about that. I've loved her for a long time. No, it's everything else, the stuff at work, running for our lives, stumbling in here, just... everything. It's all happened so fast. For years every day was just like every other, then suddenly everything has changed. Now I suddenly haven't the faintest idea where I'll be and what I'll be doing at this time tomorrow, much less next week or next year. It's just kinda...."

"What? Scary? Exciting? Exhilarating? Intimidating?"

Steve laughed and took another sip. "Yeah, all of that."

"Well, first things first, you're the sacrificial victim at a tribal ritual today. Your job is just to look scared but bluster through the affair. It's not my specialty, Peg usually arranges these things, I just act as gofer and support team. Uh, I don't suppose you've got a ring do you?"

"Oh shit!"

"Don't worry, we'll figure out something." Just then they heard the front door to the outside open and close. A few moments later Peg and Eileen came in, laughing about something. Eileen looked happier than Steve ever remembered seeing her.

She came over and planted a kiss on his forehead. "Hey babe," she said and smiled.

"Hey, how's it going?"

"Just fantastic. I can't believe it. The kitchen is doing a wedding cake made of layered crepes; the minister is here. Oh Steve it's just wonderful."

"Well," interjected Tom, "now that we're all here there are a few things we need to talk about."

Peg looked disapprovingly at him. "Do you have to get serious now? We're having so much fun."

"Look, these kids are being chased by professional assassins, do you have any idea what that means?" Peg said nothing. "Well I do. This wedding is important, but what comes after that? Do you have any suggestions?"

Steve and Eileen looked at each other. Eileen spoke up. "I guess we figured to just go on up to the cabin at Eagle River Michigan and stay out of sight there. It's quite remote except for a few other cabins, and I don't think we could be followed there, not if we're driving a different vehicle."

"I'm not sure about that, but what about other traceables, credit cards and such?"

"We're not using them, we cashed out first thing, we've got enough to live on for quite a while."

Tom nodded. "Yeah, I think that will be okay. Chances are that after a few weeks this thing will blow over. If not, come back down in the spring and we'll see what else we can do. I assume that you feel it would not be appropriate to call the police."

"We've been working for Sherman for several years now. Only now are we realizing some of what he's been up to. I'm pretty sure he's got the Chicago city police in his pocket. Beyond that..." he shrugged, "maybe the FBI would be safe, but even then, I'm not sure about trusting them, and I certainly wouldn't want to just call on the phone."

"Neither would I. Okay then, I guess you kids can take care of yourselves. You plan to leave this evening right after the wedding?" They nodded assent. "Well then, we haven't much time. I need to run you through the drill on the Willys, we need a ring, and I need to fit you out for carrying weapons." Peg shook her head in frustration.

"Oh for God's sake Tom, can't you quit thinking about weapons for one minute?"

"Look Peg, I know you hate the things, but we already agreed that they need something just in case. I gave a Vorpal knife to Steve, and Eileen's agreed to carry the nine millimeter. It's the same model as the one I have, so I'll just readjust my holster and shoulder-rig to fit her." Peg looked unsure. "Come on Peg, this is your Goddaughter and her true love here, are you going to leave them defenseless against some fat-cat corporate torpedoes?"

"Okay, okay... I just don't like the whole idea of it is all," Peg replied resignedly, "and don't worry about the ring, we went through my jewelry box and found one that will work." After a pause she lamented. "I mean, why do they have to go at all? Why can't they just stay here until things cool off? All this running around and chasing and guns and knives is just stupid don't you think? You'd think you were all a bunch of school children playing war, or cops and robbers."

Tom was about to answer, but Eileen spoke up. "No Aunt Peg, he's right. We can't stay here. I can't even explain why, but we need to deal with this problem ourselves. We have information that can put a lot of people connected with Sherman Enterprises in prison for a long time, probably including George Sherman himself. We were a part of that for a couple of years, closed our eyes to what was going on around us." Steve nodded in agreement and spoke up.

"You guys have been so great, really... we never expected to find any help like this along the way. With what you're doing for us we'll be better prepared, in all ways, for whatever happens. But I'm like Eileen, I feel we have to go up there to that cabin for a while. Call it a honeymoon if you like. I think we'll be safe, I mean, who could follow us there, with a different vehicle and all?"

"All the same," Tom put in, "I want you both armed at all times. As soon as you leave here you'll be at risk. Steve, you put on that knife rig now, you can wear it under your suit. I want it to become like a second skin for you, and practice drawing it a bit in front of the mirror so you don't slash the front of your coat." Steve nodded and went upstairs to fetch the knife. "Eileen, let's get you fitted for the pistol, obviously you won't wear it with the wedding dress, but after that, I want you to wear it all the time, your down vest will conceal it nicely." He turned towards the basement door. Peg motioned in the opposite direction towards the front door.

"Okay, you children go play with your toys. I need to get back over and supervise the preparations." She glanced at her watch. "Countdown stands at twenty minutes, so don't dawdle."

Tom and Eileen went down the basement steps to the workshop. Tom led the way through the small but efficient machine-shop with many closely spaced machine tools. A compact metal lathe, milling machine, belt-grinder, rolling mill, parts tumbler, electric furnace, and three antique mechanical coining presses lined the path to a small wooden door. A cluttered workbench and other tools could be seen in the further reaches beyond. He flipped a light switch and led the way through the thick door into a narrow echoless room. Near the door was a small table, at the far end the light shone on a simple bullseye pistol target hanging from a string. "This is my practice range." He said. It's only 25 feet, but you can get the feel of how a gun shoots, and it's quite soundproof, Peg insisted that I install heavy acoustic panels all the way around." Eileen nodded but said nothing.

"Okay, here's the weapon I want you to carry." He handed her the pistol lying flat in his open palm, it was the same one she'd used to flatten the tire of her little electric car. She took it, flipped the safety lever to "safe" and thumbed the stud that dropped out the magazine. She checked it quickly, noting that it was full, all twelve rounds showing, and laid it on the table. Then she pulled back the slide, revealing an empty chamber, and locked the slide back. She then turned the gun and looked into the muzzle, using her thumbnail to reflect a little light. Tom's eyes were a little wide.

"May I?" asked Eileen.

"Be my guest," said Tom, backing off a couple of steps uprange.

She picked up two sets of ear protectors from the table, handed one to Tom and put the other on. Then she inserted the magazine, released the slide, and thumbed off the safety. She held the gun in both hands and aimed at the target, carefully squeezing off the first shot in double-action mode.

"Looks like it's about two inches below the black," Tom said. She then fired the remaining eleven rounds in quick succession. All were tightly clustered in the black center of the target.

She barely heard the explosive whoop from Tom through the hearing protection, but when she took them off and handed him the empty weapon he was laughing. "Damn girl, where'd you learn to shoot like that?"

"Oh, my uncle made me learn as a teenager, he was into the tournament circuit, I got a few low level trophies, nothing big, I always hated it though."

"Well, that's okay, you know how to do it, that's the main thing." Tom was running a swab though the barrel. Here's the shoulder rig, just slip it on under your vest and we'll adjust the straps. The gun sits here on your left, and two extra magazines on your right. Twelve rounds apiece, plus one in the chamber, 37 rounds total carry." He fussed a little with the straps until he was satisfied and she could draw the weapon quickly and freely, then she put her vest back on.

"Okay, try the draw now." She did so. "Okay, now drop the magazine and insert a new one." She fumbled for a few moments getting the feel of how to grab the end of the magazine from the plastic spring clip holder, then fished one out smoothly and inserted it in the weapon. "You're a natural at this kid."

"Thanks uncle Tom... mind if I call you that?"

Tom laughed, "not at all."

"I just hope and pray we don't need these things. I hate to say it though, but it does make me feel a little better. Not quite so exposed and defenseless"

"Good, that's what it's for. Come on, let's get back upstairs."

They went out into the shop area just as Steve was coming down the stairs. "Hey you guys, check out this suit, it even fits."

Eileen went over and hugged him, he noticed the extra bulge and raised his eyebrows. "Your new wife is one hell of a pistolera, did you know that?" said Tom.

"Oh really? I did not know that. I guess I'd better watch my step eh?"

"As always buddy," Eileen said grinning. "Say, Uncle Tom, what's with all these old presses?"

"Ah..." Tom replied, "just a hobby, I like to design and make fantasy coins for make-believe places, or obscure events from history... that sort of thing." Steve and Eileen looked at each other with a "takes all kinds" expression. They filed back up the wooden stairs and met Peg coming in from outside.

"Eileen, come on, let's get you ready. Why don't you guys go on over and meet the guests. Looks like you're all dressed. It's just some of our local friends and some other folks who stopped at the restaurant and want to stay." Peg and Eileen disappeared up the stairs, Eileen gave Steve a wink as she went by. Peg handed a ring to Tom in passing. He nodded and put it in his pocket.

"Well young feller, I guess it's time to go over and meet the public. There's not much time for a bachelor party, but we may be able to raise a bit of a hoot."

"I'm following you," answered Steve. They went out the door, across the fifteen meters or so of plowed space and into the kitchen of Peg's Pancake Palace through the back door. The bright light over the door was shining brilliantly on the fresh white snow. There were two young men and an older woman busily working in the kitchen. A layer cake formed of crepes laminated together with alternating layers of a creamy filling and preserves was quickly taking shape. With murmurs of anticipation brightening the faces of the cooks, Steve and Tom passed through into the main room.

A roaring fire was shining forth from the big fireplace, and gathered at that end were a couple of dozen people. Two of them had taken guitars down off the wall and were engaged in a rendition of a complicated fingerstyle guitar classic that Steve recognized from radio play, but could not name. Tom tapped one man on the shoulder who turned around and smiled. "Steve Sanders, I'd like you to meet Pizza Bob, he'll be performing the ceremony for us." Bob stuck out his hand. He wore thick round glasses, had a long nose, and shoulder length gray hair. Steve grasped the hand and shook it.

"Hi Steve," he said, "you won't regret it I'm sure."

"Really? Do you know Eileen too?"

"Nah, I just always say that. So tell me, what kind of ceremony you want? I do 'em all you know."

"Well, to tell the truth, it should be pretty basic, we need to hit the road right afterwards and make some distance before dark."

"Ah, the 'breakneck special', no problemo mi amigo. I understand, short and sweet. I also understand this is a spur of the moment thing so there are no parents available. That simplifies things immensely, believe me. Is there a ring?"

"Ah yeah, I've got it." Said Tom.

"You sure? You wouldn't believe how many times I've done this and it turns out the ring's been laid down someplace or some damned thing."

"Nope, right here." Tom took the ring out of his pocket and showed it. It was a thin golden ring adorned with a tiny smooth heart-shaped stone of a deep blood-red color, set with three prongs. Tom instantly recognized it as one of Peg's favorites, 'the datolite heart ring' she called it.

"Very nice," said Pizza Bob, "Now make sure you know where it is and can produce it when asked for."

"Gotcha."

"Okay Steve, you know what to do?"

"No."

"Good, then just do what I tell ya. Right now I want ya to stick this name tag on, and go mingle around and meet people. As soon as we get the signal I'll cue the musicians to start the wedding march. You'll stand over here, Eileen will walk down from over there, and we'll hitch ya up."

Steve was drawn to the music, which was very good. An intense older man with a name tag that said "Marty K." was glibly fingerpicking a complex theme, while another old timer whose name tag simply said "J.B." flat-picked around it in a counterpoint that often seemed on the verge of careening off into nowhere, then returned to the center with emphasis. Behind him he heard a flute enter the melody, it was Tom playing. He had taken down one of the flutes from the wall. Evidently they were not simply ornamental, as he played it beautifully. Steve recalled Tom's comments about his gold Haynes flute and realized that he probably knew what he was talking about. Steve closed his eyes and drifted with the music, seeing visions of the churning waters of a big lake, the swaying of trees in the wind, and hearing the crashing of storm driven waves on a cold and rocky shore.

He was wakened from his reverie by a change in the music. The Wedding March! He turned around, and there she was. He had never seen her in a long dress before. She stood at the end of the room in a floor length traditional formal wedding gown of the sort you only see in movies anymore. He struggled to keep his mouth shut, then noticed a movement out of the corner of his eye. Pizza Bob was frantically motioning him to move to the center, near the fireplace.

As the music played Eileen walked slowly down the length of the room until she stood at his side, facing the fire, and Bob, who held out his hands and took theirs, putting them together and holding them. Then he spoke solemnly.

"Steve and Eileen, you have each chosen the other to be lifelong companions, is this true?"

"Yes." They both answered.

"Okay, then repeat after me.... Love is the greatest of all spirit realities.... If we have love, then we can lack for nothing.... I will love and cherish you, for you are part of me...." Steve and Eileen repeated the lines after him.

"Is there a ring?"

Tom stepped forward and laid the datolite heart ring in Bob's hand, then hesitated a moment, took one off of his own right hand and laid it next to the first.

Bob turned to the couple, handing Steve the datolite ring. Okay, put this on her finger and repeat after me. "Let this be a token of my undying love." After Steve had done so, Bob handed Eileen the other ring. "Okay, you do the same thing." She put the ring on Steve's finger and spoke the words. "Okay then," said Bob loudly, "all ya gotta do is kiss and yer married."

Steve and Eileen embraced and kissed long and tenderly. Pizza Bob then raised his arms and spoke to the crowd. "Let it be known that at nine PM on this day, Steve and Eileen were here joined in wedded bliss." Then he lowered his arms and grinned. "And now... let the wild rumpus begin!" He shouted. Everybody cheered and the music started up again in some kind of frantic dance theme. Somebody started up a frenetic rhythm on a big hand-drum. A table was rolled out with the now-finished cake on it. Pizza Bob headed straight for it and cut out a ridiculously big hunk which he devoured with relish. After that it was pretty much a free-for-all. Tom elbowed his way into the melee and made it back with three pieces, one each for Steve, Eileen and himself.

"You can't be bashful around this crowd, I managed to get you each a piece before the poor thing was ripped to shreds by the feeding frenzy." They ate their "cake", which was like nothing either had ever tasted. Peg wound her way over.

"Oh, that was so beautiful!" Her eyes were a little red. She came over and gave a big hug to Eileen. "Don't mind me honey, I always cry at weddings."

"Um, Aunt Peg, I think we'd better go change." said Eileen gently.

"What? Already? Okay okay, it's just not every day I have a goddaughter drop in to be married you know."

The two couples left the party in full revelry and slipped through the kitchen and out the back door. Once in the house Steve and Eileen went upstairs to change. Tom went out and opened the shed to warm up the old Willys. It started right up, as always, he kicked the heater on full blast and backed it out into the yard near the door. It was a light gray in color, or had been at one time. The body was a plain squarish box, with two doors and flat panel windows, one of the simplest and most reliable vehicle designs ever manufactured. Most of Steve and Eileen's things were already stowed in back, along with a few extra blankets and some foodstuffs that Peg had added for them. Tom came back into the kitchen and stomped the snow off his boots. Peg was just pouring hot water into a thermos. The smell of peppermint rose from it before she put the cap on.

Steve and Eileen came downstairs, dressed in their old traveling clothes again, and carrying a couple of small bags. "Well, I guess.... um..." Eileen stammered.

"Come on, group hug!" said Tom. The four of them clustered together for a long embrace. When they broke apart, Tom spoke up. "The Willys is warming up outside now, just throw in the last things and you're ready. Peg's got a thermos of hot peppermint tea to keep you going for a while. There's a manual and tool box under the driver's seat in case of trouble, but she's running pretty good. You'll probably need to keep the heater running full blast as cold as it is, even with the sun out, but there are extra blankets. Third gear is just a little tricky, you gotta push the lever a little to the right and jiggle it sometimes. Sometimes the dimmer switch sticks on highbeams and you have to kick it a couple of times...."

"Tom," said Peg, "would you shut up a minute, I'm trying to say good-bye to my goddaughter."

"Hey, just trying to help, we never got to go over this stuff."

"I know. Eileen, let us know when things are okay. I want to call your mom, but I won't until we hear from you. Be careful."

"Okay, and thanks so much."

"Our pleasure," said Tom, "we haven't had this much fun in ages. And Steve, you take care of this young lady, alright? And get that flute out and play it sometimes, It'll get sad just sitting in that case."

"Okay uncle Tom, and thanks for everything." In reply Tom turned and opened the door, taking their bags and throwing them over the front seat into the back. Steve got in on the driver's side, Eileen on the other. Peg whispered one last thing in Eileen's ear before closing the door.

There was a grating of gears as Steve struggled with the unfamiliar manual transmission, then the little thing trudged slowly around the side of Peg's Pancake Palace. Eileen looked back and waved. Tom and Peg were standing in the snow under the light over the door, with arms raised in gesture of farewell, one arm around each other. The newlyweds drove slowly through the parking lot and then turned left, heading back out towards the highway. Steve did in fact have a little trouble getting into third gear, but he soon got used to the trick of it, and within a few minutes they turned north on the four lane divided highway that was U.S. 41. The snow was still falling pretty heavily. They drove into the wind; the view out the windshield seemed like they were piloting a spaceship through a galaxy of stars. A sign appeared, glowing out of the darkness, announcing that the city of Oshkosh lay 34 miles ahead.

"We're going to Oshkosh bygosh!" said Steve, jiggling the gearshift a little. The steady pulsing of the old motor and the slightly oily smell of the vehicle had an exhilarating effect. They both giggled and shared a cup of hot peppermint tea from the thermos.

CHAPTER 31

Frank Giacoletti pulled the hummer to the curb on Shelden Avenue, and parked in front of Jerry's Bar. As they got out of the vehicle he said to Jimmy, "Got the wire set?"

"Yeah, we'll get audio for sure, and some video of the whole interview." Jimmy fingered the video aperture which looked like a tie tack pinned to the collar tab of his shirt.

"Okay then, let's go talk to Jack." They walked into the dimly lit room. A television in one corner of the bar was showing a hockey game, but reception was not very good, even on the cable channel. They moved to the bar and took adjacent stools. Only one other person sat at the bar, an elderly man at the far end, who paid them no mind. As they sat down a somewhat heavyset man in his late fifties rose from a stool behind the bar and walked over to them.

"What can I get you fellas?" he asked in a friendly voice. Frank pulled a plastic card out of his pocket and handed it to the man, who looked at it and seemed to grow wary.

"Couple of root beers maybe," said Frank, taking back the ID card. When the barkeeper came back with two brown bottles and glasses Frank added, "we're looking for a couple fellas that were in here last night, Digger Puttonen and Arne Harjaala. By the way, I'm Frank, this is Jimmy, and you are...?"

"Jack... and you're not the only ones. You're new around here aren't you? I never seen you before."

"We came up from Marquette this morning."

"In that blizzard? You guys must be nuts! But listen, I was told not to talk to anybody, not even other FBI agents, so there's not much I can say."

"Listen, it's okay, we're working with the SIB, Lenny Howarth sent us."

"Oh I see. Well, there's not much to tell. I guess you know about the arrangement I had with Howarth. I fulfilled my end of it, but I guess he screwed up on his end."

"We understand, we're trying to figure out how they slipped away from our guys. Could you please tell us about last night?"

"Well, I don't know, I'm really only supposed to talk to Howarth himself."

Frank looked around the room. "Is he here? Listen, he's probably stuck in the snow some damn place. It would save a lot of time if you could just tell us what happened, we'll relay the information when he arrives."

Jack looked unsure, then shrugged his shoulders. "Okay, whatever happens it's been a good steady check. Well, Arne was here like usual, early yesterday afternoon. Digger comes in later and sits down next ta him, right here where you guys are. Now, this Howarth guy seems to think Arne knows something important, but he's so screwed up in the head he can hardly talk. So I'm supposed to like, listen in on him from time to time and try to catch anything interesting. In return this SIB outfit pays Arne's rent and beer tab. If Arne starts making sense I'm to call Howarth right away. It's a sweet deal as far as I'm concerned. In fact I'd..."

"So, did Arne say something interesting?"

"Oh yeah, well, I was refilling their glasses later in the evening, and I heard Arne saying something about the old Quincy mine and Digger seemed real interested in what he was saying."

"Yes, so?"

"So nobody's ever been interested in what Arne says. He's all wrong in the head or something. Beyond the topics of eating, sleeping, and drinking, he usually just doesn't make any sense. So, I hit a little button here see, down under the bar? Howarth's guys installed it a couple years ago. Arne always sits in the same place, so they installed a little video recorder over there in the wall." He pointed out the half inch lens aperture concealed in a pine knot, and the directional microphone that looked like a stuffed teddy bear, sitting directly opposite them.

"Interesting, is it on now?"

"Nah, I was only to turn it on if I thought something interesting was happening. So anyway I went in the back and switched on the monitor, and I could see these guys were really talking up a storm about something. So, I called the number Howarth gave me, got him right away. He told me to keep 'em drinking until somebody else called, and to try to clear the rest of the people out of the bar, that he'd be here as soon as possible. Well there wasn't hardly anybody here anyway, and after a while these other guys left, so it was just those two. My beeper goes off, and it's some guy from your local office."

"Samuels?"

"Yeah, that's the guy, he says that he's got a couple guys up the street waiting and can I get them out the door? For some reason they don't want to come in here. Anyway, it's like 11:30 or so, I go over and I'm kinda like cleaning stuff behind the bar, and I take down the clock real sneaky like, and go in back and change the time to 12:45, you know, last call. So then they're out the door, and that's all I know until Samuels comes in this morning and says they disappeared."

Frank and Jimmy looked at each other. Jimmy made a minuscule eye motion towards the concealed camera. Frank picked up on it immediately. "So, Jack, you still have the recording of Digger and Arne's conversation?"

"Yep, just waiting for agent Howarth to come pick it up."

"Could we see it for a moment?"

"Oh gee, I don't know, I think I'm bending the agreement a lot just talking to you guys."

"No really, we just want to see what kind of recording it is."

"It's like a little disk thing, he showed me how to do it."

"May we please see the equipment?" Frank smiled his most friendly smile.

"Yeah, well, I guess you're okay. Right back here." He led them around behind the bar to a stock room in the back. A small device sat on a shelf.

"And this is the disk?" Jimmy said, poking a button and retrieving a small plastic square about the size of a matchbook.

"Yeah, but please, don't do anything to it."

"Don't worry." said Jimmy, as he inserted it for a few moments into a small device he took from his pocket. "Yep, same kind we use, just checking for compatibility. All this new optical computer stuff you know, it's really much too complicated." He handed the disk back to a grateful Jack and started moving towards the door, Frank followed. Jack looked suspiciously at the markings and seemed satisfied that it was the same disk.

"So I don't know what else I can tell ya. Haven't heard from Howarth again since then, but I did get a call from a lady at his office who said he was on his way. You guys hear from him?"

"We really can't discuss an ongoing investigation." Said Frank as he and Jimmy put on their coats.

"Oh yeah, right, well, good luck. And really, Arne's a nice old guy. I don't know what he's done, but try not to be too rough on him, he's had a tough life. Digger I don't know so well, but he seems nice enough."

"Okay, thanks." Frank replied as they walked out the door into the blowing snow outside. "Did you get it?"

"Yes sir, lock stock and barrel."

"Okay, let's get back over to Hancock and meet with Samuels and go over this thing." They walked down the street to the hummer, got in a drove back across the bridge.

When they pulled up in front of the old Kaleva Cafe on Quincy street, Samuels was just walking down the sidewalk. He came over to the car and greeted them.

"Any luck?"

"Maybe," said Frank, "we think we got a copy of a surveillance disk the bartender made for Howarth. You?"

"A little more background on the Harjaala guy. Weird stuff though, seems impossible."

"Yeah, that was our impression of what we found so far." They noticed an increasing number of people of all ages, walking on the recently cleared sidewalk carrying signs. The placards bore slogans such as: "Superior, the 83rd State", "U.P. for Da Yoopers".

Jimmy looked on with interest, then turned to Samuels. "What's all this?"

"Oh, just those secessionists again. The movement seems to be heating up a bit. They're a pretty peaceful bunch though, we don't worry about 'em much. About all they do is block traffic sometimes. Listen, maybe we should just get some food to go and take it back over to the office."

Frank looked in the window of the Kaleva and saw that the place was pretty packed. "Yeah, I'd rather have a bit more privacy I think."

They went in and selected some fresh pasties to go, from the glass fronted case by the cash register. Frank paid cash for them. They left the hummer there and walked the few blocks back to Samuel's office. The three men went into the break room and shut the door. Frank unwrapped the food while Samuels poured coffee for everybody, and Jimmy set up the disk to play. They ate the traditional miner's lunch quietly and listened to the surveillance tape, glancing occasionally at the image of Digger and Arne in the video monitor on the wall. Jimmy had keyed a transcription program during the playback, and handed out hard-copy transcripts of the taped conversation, when it ended, automatically labeled "Voice 1" and "Voice 2".

Samuels touched an intercom button... "Could you please bring in the bio data on Puttonen and Harjaala?" Then turned to Frank and Jimmy. "You realize of course that this Howarth guy is going to be pretty pissed about you snatching his surveillance data."

Frank leaned forward, one elbow on the table, with his chin in his hand. "Yeah well, maybe we don't have to say anything about it, not right away anyhow, the bartender doesn't know we copied it." Samuels shrugged. Frank said, "So, what do you think about this whole mess?" He winked at Jimmy to hold back, but was looking at Samuels.

Samuels sighed. "This is the weirdest investigation I've ever been involved with. First of all, both guys are clean, we don't have any probable cause or anything. There's no criminal investigation at all here. Then this bio data..." The door opened and a young man came in, handing Samuels a thin sheaf of papers. "None of this makes any sense, what is this guy, a time traveler or something?"

"Exactly the question," said Jimmy.

"Oh come on, what is this, reality or science fiction? I don't buy any of that garbage. I figure it's got to be some elaborate hoax, maybe to bilk investors, like that guy who sold tickets to Mars on a UFO a few years ago."

"And they acted out this whole scene for the hidden surveillance equipment?" Jimmy retorted.

"It's possible, maybe they tumbled to the bug."

Frank looked thoughtful. "Yes, it's possible. We should keep that in mind. But just for the sake of argument, what if it wasn't an act? What if these guys are for real... what then?"

"Then there are two possibilities." Said Samuels after a short pause. "One: they're both psychotic and are suffering from paranoid delusions and hallucinations, possibly alcohol or drug induced. After all, we have to remember that one of the other guys, this Josh Freeman, we found him dead of a drug overdose last year. So there could be something like that happening. Two: something really strange is going on."

"Okay," Frank went on, "we also know that Leonard Howarth is interested in the situation. That pretty much cuts out the paranoid delusion theory, that wouldn't be his line."

"You know him?"

"Yeah, some, years back. I can imagine that he might be interested in some sort of hoax, especially if they're going after rich or influential clients, but then the question is why? And why these two? Puttonen is reportedly worth millions on his own, as partner in Midnight Mining. He doesn't need to pull any two-bit scam for dough. Harjaala is a pauper, a drunk on the skids. Why would Puttonen team up with him?"

"Unless," said Jimmy quietly, "it's for real. We know that Puttonen's company is doing some cutting edge technical research, but they got a new management team and stopped publishing updates about a year ago. Maybe Harjaala's experience somehow connects with their research. That would explain Puttonen's interest. Remember, according to Harjaala's story the events took place inside the Quincy mine, about a mile directly below where Midnight Mining company has it's research labs."

Samuels snorted. "You mean you think it's actually possible that this Harjaala character spent 38 years underground without aging a day?" He turned to Frank. "Surely you don't believe such nonsense?"

Jimmy raised his eyebrows, shrugged his shoulders, and turned his hands palm up with a smirk. Frank sat quietly without answering for a long time. Finally he stood up and started to put on his coat. "I don't know what to believe. I don't get it either, but I'm not about to make any snap judgments without more information. I think it's time we paid a visit to the offices at Midnight Mining Company and asked a few questions. Anybody coming along?" Both the others got up and put on their outdoor gear.

When they emerged from the building Samuels motioned them to his vehicle, another black hummer. They got in and he drove them east past the hardware store on Quincy, then steeply up Dunstan Street, turning right on Mason. The chainlink gate with the sign announcing the offices of Midnight Mining company lay ahead. They pulled in through the gate and parked. A young man emerged from a gatekeeper's cubicle.

"Sorry, no visitors today, you'll have to leave."

Frank flipped open his ID. "We're from the FBI, official investigation. We'd just like to ask a few questions."

After looking at the ID carefully and comparing the photo to Frank's face the man shrugged. "Go ahead then, but don't get your hopes up, nobody's saying much about anything lately."

Jimmy stepped up and smiled. "Really? What's going on?"

"I don't know, they don't tell me much, but it seems like they're trying to get rid of Digger and James."

"Hi, my name's Jimmy, you know Digger? He's the one we'd like to speak with, if possible."

"Nice to meets you Jimmy, I'm Aaron. Digger left yesterday, looked pretty bummed out. I heard them talking as they checked out through the gate."

"Digger and who, did you say?"

"James Dolittle, one of the other original partners. I just heard them for a second while the window was down. Digger was telling James he didn't care about the money, it was the company he cared about."

"And you haven't seen either one since then?"

"No, not really."

"Not really?"

"Well, a car came driving by slowly, just a few minutes ago, while I was talking to one of these new guys. The people were just kind of looking in the gate. One of them sorta looked like Digger, but I couldn't be sure, they were all so bundled up."

"What kind of car was it?"

"Oh it was real old and beat up looking, I don't know the model or year, back before the turn for sure though. It was kind of a maroon color two door with a roof rack and lots of rust."

A Superior State of Affairs

"Anything else?"

"Just that Digger's a good guy. If he's in trouble, it's not his fault. It's these new guys, this Grundwalder and them, they're not nice people. They want to put in an automatic gate and fire me. You watch your step if you mess with them."

"I sure will, I appreciate the tip. I think we'll go up to the office now if that's okay. Thanks Aaron."

The snow began to fall again as Aaron waved. The three walked through the big flakes towards the entrance. The road narrowed and ended at a double metal door set into the solid rock. Frank pulled on the handle and it opened into a short and well lit passage leading to a small vestibule. Another double glass door led further on, There was a security card reader next to the door. A thick window on the left showed a surprised receptionist looking at them. Both window and door were of very heavy materials and construction. To Frank's professional eye they looked as though they were probably bullet-proof. The receptionist pressed a button on her desk and a friendly voice was transmitted into the vestibule.

"I'm sorry, we're not taking visitors today. If you don't have an appointment...." She looked to be about thirty, darkly complected, and pretty, with wavy black hair and brown eyes. She also appeared to be somewhat frightened, despite the thick window that separated them.

Frank held up his ID to the window, she looked at it closely and brightened furtively. She motioned for the others to show theirs as well, which they did.

She held a finger to pursed lips and motioned them to come through the double door. A barely audible click indicated that she had remotely unlocked it. The interior office was paneled and brightly lit, it could have been anywhere, and did not give the impression of being carved out of solid basalt rock. Looking over her shoulder towards a closed door further on she whispered. "What took you guys so long? I've been on pins and needles for two days." She stared at their confused faces. "Didn't the Sheriff's office send you?"

Samuels spoke. "I'm Fred Samuels, Hancock station. No ma'am, we've heard nothing from the county, we're here looking for Digger Puttonen, we'd like to ask him a few questions."

She looked alarmed. "They didn't call you? But the deputy, he was here, he said it was your jurisdiction, he promised they'd call."

"About what?"

" I haven't been able to leave for three days. This guy, this big guy with a scar on his face, he had a key card. He just walked right in here on Wednesday, and threatened to... to hurt me if I didn't..."

The door across the room opened and three men walked in.

One was thin and smiling, dressed in business attire. The other two wore workman's clothes, but with incongruously shiny dress shoes. Frank thought they looked vaguely familiar, as if he'd seem them in a book of mug shots.

The thin man walked forward smiling. The other two flanked the door. "Miriam, you didn't tell me we had visitors. Did they have an appointment?"

"No sir, they're from the FBI, wanting to talk to Mister Puttonen." The other two men disappeared back though the door at the mention of FBI.

"Hello, I'm Farley Grundwalder, chief of operations here. I'm sorry to be the bearer of bad news, but you won't find Mr. Puttonen here, nor Mr. Dolittle for that matter."

Frank put on his best poker face. "Oh? Could you tell us please, when is he expected to return?"

"Never I'm afraid," said Farley smiling in an oily way. "You see, they have both sold out their shares in the company. They cleaned out their desks the day before yesterday and left, for good. For all I know they've jetted off to Cancun or Rio to enjoy their newfound wealth."

"Hardly, with all the airports closed."

Farley shrugged and glanced at his watch. "It's really not any of my business anymore. Now if you'll excuse me, we really have a lot to do to get ready for the new owners. Miriam, would you please show our guests out?" Farley folded his arms and made quite clear that this was the end of the discussion.

The three agents looked at each other and got up. Miriam motioned them towards the door. They were halfway through when Farley suddenly turned and left. Jimmy looked questioningly at Miriam. "Are you okay? You want to come with us?" She looked unsure, glanced over her shoulder towards the door where Farley had disappeared, then suddenly turned, grabbed her coat from a chair and snatched a purse, then followed them out the door.

They walked out through the iron door into a gray maelstrom of blowing snow. The deep notch in the side of Quincy Hill that led to the adit served to form swirls and eddies in the wind that blew in gusts from the northwest. Miriam got out some keys and started towards the parking lot. Jimmy nodded to Frank, who understood immediately. The two older men went straight to Samuel's Humvee. Jimmy followed Miriam to her little Pontiac Electra, helping her to sweep off the heavy accumulation of snow. It had quite evidently not been driven since the blizzard began. She accepted his presence without comment and let him in on the passenger side. "Would you mind stopping down at the office for some coffee, and maybe some talk?" he ventured. She nodded and the little electric car hummed immediately into life and scooted quietly across the lot. Jimmy mused that, while they may not have a lot of range, and the heaters tended to be ineffective, the little electric cars sure started up reliably in cold weather.

He pointed towards the disappearing Taurus and she followed the few blocks to the FBI office. As they passed through the gate, Jimmy smiled and waved to a frowning Aaron, who still sat in the gatehouse keeping an eye on things. When they arrived at the office, just behind the other car, Jimmy escorted Miriam to the door, habitually looking around to see if they were being followed or watched. He noticed nothing unusual and went on in.

The three men went into the break room again, trying to act relaxed. Miriam sat quietly at the table with her purse before her. Samuels started fixing a fresh pot of coffee, then opened a box of donuts and arranged them on a paper plate. He put it in the center of the table and gestured to Miriam to make it clear that she was welcome to have one, then helped himself. Frank and Jimmy, as the visitors, kept quiet. Finally, Fred Samuels placed a small recorder on the table and said, "I don't believe we've been formally introduced. My name is Fred Samuels. I'm the station chief for the Federation Bureau of Investigation here in the Houghton/Hancock area. These are my colleagues Frank Giacoletti, and Jimmy Canaris from the Marquette office. Do you mind if we ask you a few questions?"

"No."

"Could you tell us your full name and job title please?"

"Yes. I'm Miriam Lopez. I am... or, I was... the head secretary/receptionist at Midnight Mining Company."

"So miss Lopez, how long have you worked there?"

"Just over a year now, just since they finished work on the new front office."

"Now, when we met you at the office just a short time ago, you mentioned something about the Sheriff's department. Could you explain please?"

"Things have been rather strange for the last couple of weeks. We received an offer to purchase the company outright, which Digger and James, the two remaining original partners refused to consider."

"And are you accustomed to addressing the owners of the company by their first names?"

Miriam smiled. "Oh yes, they encourage it. They're very friendly and familiar with the staff."

"And then what happened?"

"Well, I overheard Digger and James arguing with Farley Grundwalder several times about it. Farley wanted them to sell. You see, as representative of the university's interest in the project, He stood to make a lot of money for MTU and possibly further his career."

"Yes I see..."

"But Digger and James said no, so apparently that was that. But then, just last Wednesday evening, just before closing time, this guy walks in. I mean, he just walks right in, right through the security door."

"So... he must have had a key card?"

"I guess so, though I'm supposed to know everybody who's issued one, and I'd never seen him before. He was quite tall, two meters probably, and had a huge ugly scar running across his face like this." She drew a line with her fingernail on the right side of her face from her upper lip to her temple. "He told me that he wanted to speak to Farley Grundwalder. I said I was sorry, but visitors must have an appointment. Then he leaned over and stared at me and said... he said he'd... no I can't say it!" She began sobbing slightly.

"It's alright Miriam, you're safe here. So this man, he threatened you with bodily harm?"

"Yes."

"And what did you do?"

"I called mister Grundwalder on the phone to come to the front office right away."

"And did he?"

"Yes."

"And then what happened?"

"Mr. Grundwalder came in, seeming rather upset that I had called him over orders that he be undisturbed. He looked shocked to see the man there, scared, but it was as though he recognized him. Then two more strange men appeared in the vestibule. After a word from the stranger, mister Grundwalder motioned to me to let them in. It was the same two guys who were with him today. They all went into the research complex. I opened the intercom and listened in for a while, I could hear them arguing, and then the guy loudly threatened mister Grundwalder. I was afraid something bad would happen. That was when I called the Sheriff's department."

"And how did they respond?"

"The Sheriff himself came right over. I buzzed him in and told him what happened. He had me describe the man with the scar carefully, and then he said not to worry about it, that he'd take care of it, that since the guy was from out-of-state it was a federation matter and that he would alert the proper people to take action. They haven't let me leave for two days. Then when you guys showed up, I assumed he'd called you."

"When you listened in on the argument between the men and mister Grundwalder, did you hear anything that might help us?"

"Not much, except that the name "Mister Sherman" was mentioned several times."

"Why did you decide to leave with us?"

"Because I was afraid. I mean, it's been a good job and all, but those new men, they just give me the creeps. Something's very wrong there now."

"Do you live alone?"

"Yes, I have an upstairs apartment over near Suomi College."

"If you don't mind, I don't think you should go back there yet, just in case. I'd like to find out more about this situation, to make sure it's safe. I'd like you to stay with one of our female agents, if that's okay... just for a day or two?"

She nodded resignedly as Samuels shut off the recorder and pressed an intercom button. "Trish, could you come in here please?" A few moments later a middle aged black woman walked in.

"Trisha Johnson, this is Miriam Lopez. She may be a material witness in a Federation case. We believe she may be in danger, and she needs a place to stay for a few days."

"No problem sir." Trisha smiled. "Come on Miriam, you need some things from home, you just tell me, we'll have somebody go over for you..." The two women left the room.

The three men were left alone again. Samuels spoke up. "So Frank, what do you think now?"

"I don't know. I just about shit when I heard her mention Sherman."

"You thinking George Sherman?"

"Yeah, that's what I'm afraid of. I've dealt with his crowd before, they tend to play pretty rough. I'm not sure yet why he'd care about a little high tech company way up here in the sticks. Assuming that he does though... what's this about the Sheriff? Do you think he's dirty?"

"I'm worried about that too. I've had some isolated reports of some shady deals that Sheriff Maki may have been involved with, nothing on this scale though. I guess I'll have to give him a call and see what I can get."

Frank looked over at his companion, who sat with brows furrowed thinking hard. "So Jimmy, what's your assessment?"

"I think we got problems sir, big big problems. That place up there is like a fortress. I don't think that's entirely by accident. Are there any back ways in?"

"I don't know," said Samuels, "but I can find out."

"Also the gatekeeper Aaron mentioned an old rusty maroon car that passed the gate earlier checking it out, he thought he saw Digger in the car. You have some guys staking out Digger's house right?"

"Yeah, good idea, Digger's car has been sitting up there covered with snow all day. I'll pass on that description, and see if a car like that has shown up."

Jimmy removed a small device from his pocket. "I think I got some shots of those two guys that came in with Grundwalder at the office, we can download the images and see if we can identify them. Got a data port handy?" Samuels pointed to a console concealed by a plastic dust cover. Jimmy removed the cover, then inserted a cord from the device in his hand and pressed a button. Then he sat silently and felt under his shirt, fingering the little deerskin pouch, as data flowed from his handheld recorder to the massively more powerful office computer. He pulled out a slip of paper with Jamey Yellowknife's phone number on it. Somehow it made him feel better to know that it was there.

CHAPTER 32

The Wisconsin state line lay some miles behind as Jason Desnick drove the Bronco into Bruce Crossing, Michigan. He stopped at a Holiday station to buy a newspaper. The snow was still falling hard, and most people in the area were still digging out of the major effects of the blizzard the night before. Jason knew that they were getting near enough to the open water of Lake Superior to be within the "lake effect" band, the area within 30 or 40 kilometers of the shoreline where moisture falls as snow again after evaporating directly from the open water of the lake itself. He pulled up to the station, left the Bronco running and jumped out, running inside to pay for a newspaper.

When he got back in the vehicle he dropped a copy of the Mining Gazette in Leonard Howarth's lap. "What's this for?" asked Leonard.

"Oh, I just like to get a feel for the local scoop anytime I'm going into an unfamiliar area, one of the best ways is the local paper. We had to get at least this close just to find one. I didn't get a chance to look at it. Anything interesting?"

Leonard flipped that paper open and looked over the front page. "Hmm... Astronomers turn their attention to the sun, say that it may be entering a period of unprecedented activity. They're predicting solar storms, disruption of broadcasts, and great auroras for tonight and tomorrow night."

Harry leaned forward from the back seat. "Auroras? Wow, I haven't seen a good northern lights for years!" Leonard fixed Harry with a dour glare. "We're not here to trip out on northern lights. This could cause us problems with our communications. As if things aren't bad enough."

Jason smiled. "Anything else?"

"Let's see... Soopers rally for secession across the U.P. Marches being organized in all the larger towns."

"How about weather?"

"Okay... Snow expected to decrease today and tomorrow, turning warmer but windy tonight under cloudy skies. Low tonight, minus twenty Celsius. Clearing and colder tomorrow night, decreasing winds. It's been a record 48 hour snowfall, the biggest one this century so far."

"Give it time, the century's young yet."

"Not much else interesting, pretty ordinary local news." They rode along in silence for some time. As they passed through Painesdale Jason spoke up again.

"Okay, we're approaching Houghton, should be there in fifteen or twenty minutes, so, what do you want to do first when we get there?"

Harry leaned forward from the back to get in on the planning session. Leonard thought a moment. "I still want to keep communications silence, but I need to talk to Samuels and Giacoletti. I think the surveillance data should come first though, let's stop at Jerry's Bar and talk to Jack for a minute and pick up the disk, then go over and look up the local bureau boys to see if they've picked up our guys. Swing across towards the college on Montezuma, then back in through town; Jerry's is right on the main drag, can't miss it."

"You got it boss." They passed the mall and the outlying suburbs to the south of town, then came into the second largest metropolitan area in the western half of Michigan's Upper Peninsula. Hancock could barely be glimpsed across the shipping canal through the blowing snow. The near side of the lift bridge stood out in stark relief against the white cottony background. They swung around town, then came down the one-way main drag of Shelden Avenue from the east. They pulled up in front of the blue neon sign proclaiming Jerry's Bar, and got the parking spot right in front of the door as another car pulled out. All three men got out and entered the bar, with Leonard in the lead.

"Mister Howarth!" Jack got up off his stool immediately and came around the bar. "Gosh, it sure took you a long time, thought you'd never get here."

"Hi Jack", replied Leonard. "This is Harry and Jason. I understand that there was an alert on the Harjaala case. Did you get it on surveillance?"

"You bet, soon as Arne started talking sense I hit the button, just like you said, and then I called you. What's it all about anyway? Those other guys were pretty keen about it all too."

"Other guys? What other guys?"

"You know, from the Marquette station, that guy... uh, Frank I think. They were here, said they were working with you, asking questions about Arne and Digger."

"Frank Giacoletti?"

"Yeah, well, maybe... uh... I don't think he gave a last name."

Leonard beetled his brows and looked upset. "You were supposed to talk only to me right? That was our arrangement."

"Yeah well, you weren't here, and he seemed to know all about it, said he was working with you, so I figured it was okay."

"He said he was working with me? He mentioned me by name?"

"Yeah, so I figured it was okay."

Leonard Howarth sighed deeply and rubbed his forehead with his left hand.

Harry knew the signs. Leonard was very upset but trying hard to control himself. Jason watched the scene and was slightly amused by the theatricality of the production. Leonard spoke very slowly and clearly. "Okay Jack, what did you tell them?"

"Oh you know, just about Digger and Arne and the surveillance camera...."

"Did you let them touch it?" Leonard asked with a tone of resignation.

"Well, they wanted to see it, to see if it was compatible with their equipment."

"But did they touch it?"

"No, I was the only one that touched the recorder."

Leonard breathed a sigh of relief. "Good".

"That other guy with Frank, he only touched the disk for a second, that was all."

"The disk? What do you mean he touched the disk, what did he do with it."

"He had a machine in his pocket, he stuck it in the machine for just a second, just to see if it was compatible, he didn't have time to listen to any of it."

"SHIT!" Leonard exploded. "Dammit! Don't you see? He copied it, he copied the whole damn disk. It only takes a second. All this time, all this effort, and now Frank Giacoletti has his hands on the data before I do. I can't believe this is happening to me!"

Jack looked a little confused. "Hey, you guys are all on the same team right? And hey, the disk is right here, safe and sound, I even checked it after they left... and like, I still get paid right? We still got our agreement, don't we?"

Leonard's face turned red, and the veins stood out throbbing in his temples. It was obvious to both Harry and Jason that Leonard was about to lay into the poor barkeeper with a fusillade of invective that would probably knock the poor fellow to the floor. Jason quickly moved between Leonard and Jack, with his back to Leonard. "So Jack, show me the set up, I'm new on this case. Ah, the old camera in the knot hole trick, yes, very clever." He walked with Jack into the back room to pick up the equipment and the disk.

Leonard and Harry stood together alone in front of the bar. Leonard slowly calmed down, Harry slapped him on the back in a friendly way. "Okay, so they've got a copy of the disk... so what? They don't know what the investigation is about.

They're in the dark. You're still in control sir, you're still the senior officer, don't forget that."

Leonard gathered himself up. "Okay, you're right. If it was anybody but Frank I wouldn't be so upset, but we've gone head to head before. And how the hell did he get my name? I made sure it wasn't on any of the communications. I'm telling you Harry, the man's dangerous... a menace, I don't want him anywhere near me. We were friends once, in the same branch office, before the Federation, but that's over, and I don't want him involved in this any more than necessary."

Jason came back with the recording device, camera, and microphone, in a pocket sized zippered pouch. Leonard nodded, it was highly unlikely they would need it here again, then he abruptly turned and walked out the door. Jason looked over at Harry, who shrugged. Jason turned again to Jack, stuck out his hand to shake. "Okay then Jack, thanks for your help. I guess you can probably figure on Arne's place being available soon, and the old arrangement, well, I think that's probably over with. We'll get back with you in the next few weeks okay?" Jack shrugged resignedly and nodded.

When Jason got back into the driver's seat Leonard was already impatiently motioning to get the car moving. "Come on, let's get across the bridge over to Samuel's office and see what kind of mess we're in."

Jason looked over at him as the Bronco grunted forward over the packed snow. "So, what's with you and this Frank guy? Is there a problem here? Something personal?"

"Damn right it's personal! The son-of-a-bitch damn killed my partner and damn near killed me!"

Jason let the silence hang before venturing, "Care to talk about it?"

"You want to hear about it? Okay then," Leonard answered with an irritated edge to his voice. "It was back in Detroit, winter of ought seven and eight. We were both detectives. He was working homicide, I was on vice. We ran into each other now and then, you know, the two often seem to go together." Harry leaned forward from the back seat listening, incredulous. He had spent three years with Leonard, and had never heard so much as a peep about any of this. "So, I'm on a stakeout, we had like four gang style hits in as many days, all in the same part of town, the same M.O. We had a couple of suspects, dope gang enforcers from some new Chicago outfit trying to grab some turf. We figured they were maybe connected to this Sherman outfit but we didn't have any proof and nobody inside. We figured a big shipment would be coming in any day, and they were making room for their distributors. A car and a van roll up to the place and these guys start unloading suitcases, lots of them. So just then, Frank and a couple of his people come blundering right into the middle of it. The suitcases open up, and they're full of weapons. It was a huge damn firefight. They had fucking everything imaginable... grenades, rifles, rocket launchers, even an M-60 with armor piercing ammo. When it was over, my partner and my other two guys were dead, and I was shot four times, bleeding like a stuck pig. Both the officers that came in with Frank were shot to pieces, one of them a woman. The perps all got away except one guy that was wounded and left behind. Only Frank walked away without a scratch."

The Bronco climbed the hill into Hancock, Leonard pointed the way towards the FBI office. Jason said, "Okay, it was a bust gone bad, happens sometimes. Is it fair to hold a grudge against Frank just because he didn't get hurt and you did?"

"Oh that's not all! The guy we captured, he sang an interesting tune... said he worked for a "Mister Sherman," and that Frank was on their payroll, and if we didn't believe it, to check out his account at First Federation Bank. We did, and there was a cool half million just sitting in there, in Frank's name."

"So you think Frank was on the take?"

"Damn right! What else was there to think?"

Jason pulled into the parking lot. "So why is he still in the bureau then? If what you're saying is true, a board of inquiry would have booted him out in five minutes."

"He swore he knew nothing about it, and since he hadn't drawn any of the money there was no proof. The BOI felt like it was possible that he was being set up. So they didn't wash him out, they just sent him up here."

"But why would somebody try to set him up?" Jason asked. "Was he sniffing too close to something? And what about Sherman? Is it the same Chicago outfit involved in this mess?"

The car came to a stop a few spaces from the front door Leonard kept talking as he disengaged himself from the seat belts and opened the door. "Look, who the hell knows, right? I happen to think he's just dirty, so just watch yourself alright? If we get into a firefight stay as far as possible away from the guy. He's bad news I tell ya." He looked around the lot and noticed a black hummer. "Don't these idiots see that those damned black Humvees are a dead giveaway? Geez, it would make a used cigar think 'Feds'... probably means Giacoletti is here, he was always a big one for those things."

They strode up the steps. Leonard politely held the door for two women who were just leaving. Upon entering, Leonard went straight to Samuel's office. Fred Samuels was there behind his desk, with Frank Giacoletti facing him. Leonard ignored Frank, then offered his hand and spoke directly to Samuels. "Wednesday morning, three A.M."

"What?" Samuels replied, fluxxomed.

Leonard sighed and his shoulders slumped. "The recognition code... I know you received my urgent coded email."

Samuels brightened. "Oh, you must be agent Howarth. Pleased to meet you, I'm Fred Samuels."

Leonard simply nodded. "Listen, I hear you made quite a mess of the simple pickup I asked you for. Anything new on the situation?"

"Well... it was not quite so simple as it turned out. Yeah, we've got quite a bit of news though, have a seat and we'll talk. By the way, this is Frank Giacoletti, from the Marquette office."

Leonard did not offer his hand to Frank. "Yeah, I know who he is. Listen Frank, I really don't appreciate you guys snagging my surveillance disk. That's pretty damned low, even for you."

The comment seemed to get Frank's temper up. "Oh really? And where have you been all this time? You couldn't call and tell us about your travel problems? We get this coded, high priority order to drive up here in the middle of a goddamn blizzard to pick up two guys for talking in a bar, two guys who apparently have a talent for disappearing into thin air. We get here... we don't hear jack squat from you... and now you're pissed because we try to find out what the hell is going on? Well if you'd get off your high and mighty fucking horse you might see that we've found out some things you may find very interesting."

"Leonard closed his eyes and sighed heavily. "Okay, I'm tired, let's call a truce for now okay? What have you got?"

Samuels took over the explanation, sensing the discord between Frank and Leonard. "Okay, we've done some checking up on these two, especially Arne Harjaala. His life history is too bizarre to be believed, so that must account for The SIB being interested." He looked at Leonard, got no denial, and went on. "This Digger Puttonen establishes a connection with him, then they both disappear. It turns out that Puttonen, and one of the other original partners in Midnight Mining Company, have been leveraged out of the company, locked out of the offices. At the same time, some heavies that we think are connected to George Sherman are throwing their weight around, apparently trying to gain physical control of the place."

"George Sherman? What makes you think he's involved?" asked Leonard.

"The secretary there says she was threatened by a man who mentioned Sherman's name in a conversation she eavesdropped in on."

"Damn! This thing is turning into a nightmare." He closed his eyes and thought, then opened them and looked at Frank. "Okay, let's say it's him. What interest does he have in a company like this? Why not just buy it outright like he usually does? He's got the glitter."

Frank turned to face Leonard and spoke. "Apparently he tried and they wouldn't sell. Sherman, for some reason that we have not figured out, apparently wants the company badly enough to risk taking it by force. Back in the old Federal days of course, we'd have come down on him like a ton of bricks. He knows we're weaker now, and we're afraid he's bought off the locals, the county probably, possibly even the city police as well, so we probably can't count on any backup from them."

"Well this wasn't at all what I thought we were coming up here to work on," said Leonard.

"Oh, and that's another thing Lenny. We've been out of touch for a number of years, you and I. We know you're head of the Special Investigations Branch, but aside from the fact that you pursue paranormal activities that may have political repercussions, we don't know what interest you have in these two subjects."

"That's supposed to be highly classified information, how the hell did you even find out that much?" Leonard followed Frank's gaze and saw Frank's partner Jimmy at the computer console, fingers blazing at the keyboard, and the screen flickering with images and text in lightning succession. "Okay, don't answer that. I can see you've kept your fingers in the pie." Leonard glowered and it was clear to all that he felt he'd been betrayed.

"Lenny, listen, I know you may not believe me, but that incident in Detroit was a set-up." Frank pulled up a chair and sat backwards in it, leaning forward to accentuate his words. "I thought I was about to bust Sherman's whole operation wide open. I had solid data on his contract killing of politicos who were trying to stop the Federation. He must have had somebody inside the department, he set me up for the fall and tried to take you down to make it look good. I swear, as God is my witness man, that I never took a bribe in my life, not even a fucking candy bar. When you pulled out of that coma, I gotta tell ya that was the happiest moment of my life. Then that lying Sherman stooge fingered me, and from the look in your face, I knew you believed him, you and most of the rest, all except the captain. Man, it took the heart right out of me that you thought I'd do such a thing. I took the censure without complaining, hell, it was supposed to be my bust and there were five people dead. I felt like dog-shit man, what do you think? They sent me up here to do my penance, and here I've sat. Now there's something brewing, here of all places. It looks like it might be big... you're here, and Sherman's in it too. For God's sake Leonard, let's get it straight between us and work together on this thing alright? If we don't, that son of a bitch is gonna cut us to pieces."

As Frank spoke, Jimmy had stopped typing, the room was completely quiet. A cloud seemed to pass from Leonard's brow. His face went through an odd series of contortions and looked at Frank. "You're not shitting me are you?" Frank shook his head. "I don't know why, but I believe you. All these years I've hated your guts for what I thought you did. Now all of a sudden it's like a clamp has been taken off my chest and I can breathe again."

Unnoticed in a chair by the door sat Jason Resnick. His breathing was slow and deep. Sweat ran from his forehead, as if he'd just completed some strenuous task that had required every measure of his strength. A smile crept across his face as he saw Frank and Leonard grasp each other in a big bear hug. He glanced across the room at Jimmy, who looked back, gave a quick smile and winked. Jason was only slightly surprised at this signal, but more surprised when Jimmy made a motion with two of his fingers... a signal learned only by participants in a certain secret summer camp in Canada. Jason reached out with his mind and was met immediately by the familiar flavor of an intellect which had been trained in the same way as his own.

"Six, six, oh, six here. Well done and well met compadre!"

"Four, two, nine, seven. Often, only when we stop looking, do we find that which we seek."

"Indeed!"

When the awkward emotional moment of reconciliation between Frank and Leonard was over, Jimmy spoke to Leonard. "Sir, here's a synoptic report of what we've found out so far." He pointed to the computer screen. "Perhaps it would serve, in the interest of time, for you to glance through this. It's got the key conversation between the two subjects in the bar, plus our observations and conversations a few hours ago when we visited the Midnight Mining Company office. Also...", and now Jimmy glanced around the include the others, "we have positive I.D. on the two unknown men seen at the office, Scott Downing and Jeff McGuire. They are both known Sherman Enterprises hirelings, both with long criminal records. I'm afraid that pretty much confirms the Sherman connection. If, after viewing this material, and if you feel comfortable with it, I suggest sir, that you take us fully into your confidence as to the scope and substance of the initial investigation."

A young woman poked her head in the door. "Sir?" she asked, getting Samuel's attention. "I just talked to the surveillance team in Paavola. A vehicle matching the description you gave me parked several doors north of the residence under surveillance about thirty minutes ago. What should I tell them?"

"Uh, do nothing yet, just keep it under observation."

"Yes sir. And I thought I should mention that reception is getting spotty."

She left and closed the door behind her. Samuels looked around at Leonard. "We had a possible I.D. on Digger Puttonen in this vehicle. It's now parked near his house. It could be our man. Do you want to try to pick him up?"

"It could be him, then again maybe not." Leonard answered, "Let's slow down a little and try not to spook him again. First of all, these psychic types seem to be able to tell when they're being watched. Avoid any mention of the names in open communications. I need a few minutes to play catch-up with this other material. Let's start getting whatever information we can find on activities down at Sherman Enterprises while we're at it. Maybe we can get some kind of lead that way. I've got one of the best new content analysis programs with me here on terra-cube. I bet we could sift through tons of stuff pretty quick that way."

Frank looked over at Jimmy. "Tell ya what, I'll stay here with Lenny while he goes through our data, wouldn't mind reviewing it myself either. I have the feeling we might need to bug out on a moment's notice. Could you please walk down and drive the hummer back up here from where we left it?" He tossed the keys over.

"Sure thing Captain."

"If you don't need me, maybe I'll go along," said Jason, standing up.

"I wouldn't mind going for a walk either," echoed Harry.

"Go on then." Leonard answered happily. "Don't be too long though, we might need to be ready to move within the hour." He bent to the computer screen, with Frank leaning over his shoulder pointing out things on the screen, and Samuels watching.

The three younger men put on their coats and walked outside. The snow was still falling heavily as they trudged creaking down Reservation Street towards Quincy.

"That was the weirdest thing I've ever seen!" said Harry when they were able to draw abreast.

"What was?" asked Jimmy.

"Back there... Leonard changing his mind like that. All the years I've worked for him I've never seen anything like it. He's a stubborn cuss, a grudge-holding, bitter, vengeful man. I almost couldn't believe it when he seemed to just turn around like that."

Jason smiled. "I notice you said 'almost'."

"Well, it's like an answer to my prayers you know, like it's too good to be true. I've often wished he could be happier, but never really believed it could happen. I don't know how to explain it."

Jason shrugged. "Hey, people change, it's happened before."

"It's happened before?" Harry thought for a moment about the incident at the diner in Rhinelander... Jason had said something strange to the waitress and she had run out crying. Leonard automatically assumed that Jason had said something crude to her, but at the time, Harry's first impression was that she had shed tears of joy rather than hurt or outrage. He tried to piece together in his mind what this might mean, when they suddenly walked around the corner and into a crowd of people carrying signs and shouting slogans. The question was driven from his mind.

Directly in front of the Kaleva Cafe, and completely surrounding the object of their quest, was a crowd of at least a thousand people, completely blocking the street. An elderly looking woman addressed them with a handheld megaphone from a flatbed trailer parked immediately in front of the hummer. People were crowded all around, some of them sitting on the vehicle.

"Citizens of God's country: Are we going to let those Lansing bureaucrats from down below tell us how to live our lives?"

The crowd chorused a hearty "NO!"

The Federation has diluted the resources of the central government. Some of the states are too large to look after the interests of all their citizens. Northern California seceded, and look at the economic boom in that state. Texas broke into three new states, and we all know how that has worked for them. Quebec broke away completely and has experienced an economic miracle. I say it's time, we all say it's time, for the great State of Superior to stand on its own, to become a sovereign member of the states and provinces represented in the congress at Mexico City! No longer shall we be just some forgotten backwater district in the halls of congress."

The crowd cheered with a gusto belying their modest numbers. Jimmy noticed a movement out of the corner of his eye, and directed Harry and Jason's attention to a Sheriff's department cruiser that had just pulled up, closely followed by a television crew. While two uniformed deputies effectively kept the TV crew from deploying their cameras, the third uniformed person turned on the siren for a few moments to get everyone's attention, then used the cruiser's public address system. His distorted voice squawked across the snowy street.

"Now hear this. You must disperse immediately, you are blocking traffic on this road. This is an illegal gathering. This is Sheriff Bud Maki. You must disperse immediately or I will begin arresting people."

The person on the stage started in again. "Did you hear that people? The powers-that-be want to maintain the status quo. They're afraid they might not be such big shots in a more independent State of Superior. To hell with just blocking the street! We can block off the whole Keweenaw Peninsula if we want to!"

As Jimmy, Jason, and Harry watched in fascination, the crowd turned and converged on the Sheriff's vehicle and the news crew. They first restrained the two deputies so that the cameramen could get their equipment working, then trapped the Sheriff in his car. Before long they had all three uniformed officers handcuffed in the back of their own patrol car, and the whole crowd was marching down towards the lift bridge.

As the crowd thinned, the three FBI men moved towards the hummer and got inside, quickly locking the doors. As Jimmy started the engine and let it warm up, he said, "Is it just me, or did something seem wrong with all that?"

Harry responded. "Yeah, I've seen crowds before, but that was just too perfect. That was no mob acting spontaneously... it's almost like it was a planned, choreographed event. Do you think they can really cut off the whole peninsula?"

"If they've got somebody who knows how to work the lift bridge, then yes, they sure as hell can. Even if they can't work the lift they could easily block the bridge off with some heavy vehicles. Then the only way across the canal would be by snowshoe, ski, or snowmobile. And did you notice how they carefully got the news crew operational first, before they surrounded the Sheriff's vehicle? It looked like a carefully coordinated action to me, designed to appear spontaneous for the media."

"Do you think this could be connected in some way with these other events?"

Jason stared up the street towards the disappearing crowd. "I don't know, but I think we'd better get back up to the office, how about you?"

Jimmy answered by pulling the big vehicle out into the street and roaring off towards the nearest side street in order to double back to the FBI office. The elderly woman on the back of the flatbed watched them go, then took out a cel phone, dialed a number and spoke into it for a few moments. When she flipped the phone closed she stretched catlike in a surprisingly flexible way and smiled.

CHAPTER 33

Julius Miller drove as fast as he reasonably could, north on Interstate 94 past Racine Wisconsin. The snow was still falling gently, but the plows had done their work. With the iron self-control of his profession he calmed himself, refusing to give in to anxiety. It was all too true that he had never been thwarted this badly, not in his entire career, but the game was not over yet. Just two hours earlier he had received word through his sources at the highway department that the vehicle he sought had passed this way heading north. The vehicle he sought carried the two traitors, the former key computing services people for Sherman Enterprises. Aside from having eluded their planned execution for file tampering, the pair had sabotaged the main computer, and worse, they had absconded with all the backups and with some extremely sensitive files. Those files included at least one that implicated Julius himself in murder. No, there would be no pardon or reprieve from the sentence which had been set upon Steve Sanders and Eileen Donovan.

As Julius drove he set his exceptionally advanced computer system to collecting and organizing all available information about the pair. Somehow he had to try to predict where they were going. The interstate highway system did not extend much further into Wisconsin, and with it, ended the automated surveillance system that had given him his most valuable clue. Two hours. They could have turned west of course, towards Madison, but Julius was too much of a bloodhound to be distracted by such a remote possibility. No, they had been wounded, psychologically at least. They knew they were being hunted, and they would run as fast as possible to the safest place they could think of, like an animal running for safety up into a tree. But where would that be?

Julius adjusted his glasses, the special ones that enabled him to watch his computer screen even as he drove his car. Such things were, of course, frowned upon by the authorities, but so many of Julius' activities would have been frowned upon by the authorities, had they known about them, that one more was scarcely worth mentioning. He tried a search again of all bank or credit-card transactions, but they had not used a card since the major withdrawal several hours earlier. He felt confident that they would not, these people were scared, but not stupid. He thought about checking with the automobile dealer's association to see whether they'd bought another vehicle. They certainly had enough cash on hand to do so, but Julius knew that cash transactions were seldom reported until the next day. He went ahead and tried it anyway, receiving the expected result... there were no records of a vehicle transaction in either of their names.

Julius then initiated a search of all land ownership records in both their names, without turning up anything within the area towards which they were heading. He expanded his search parameters, first guiding his computer to consider first order relations... sisters, brothers, parents, grandparents and so forth. Most of their relatives were off in the mid-south or California, nobody seemed to own land in the north country. Unperturbed, Julius expanded the search to include second order relations... cousins, aunts, and uncles, related by blood or by marriage. A search of land records in those names turned up just a single hit. One of Eileen's uncles owned a one acre parcel of lakeshore property with a small cabin near Eagle River Michigan, far up on the Keweenaw Peninsula. Yes! It made perfect sense, a remote northwoods cabin far from contact with people would be the perfect escape. They would have been very difficult to locate there... except of course for this handy bit of information that Julius had been able to ferret out. He smiled to himself with a deep sense of pleasure, he felt that the success of his mission was now assured. Julius was now fully confident that he knew, without any doubt, exactly where they were going. They would probably drive straight through he thought, and talk to no one between here and there. Julius let his foot off the accelerator and slowed to the speed limit. There was no point in hurrying now. He would let them arrive ahead of him, that would be best. He would scope out the situation calmly, then decide how best to approach the targets. Yes, there was plenty of time now, no need to rush things. He thought again about the plan of using poisoned darts made of ice, and nodded to himself, confirming the decision.

He took I-94 right into Milwaukee, turning off at an exit in what looked like a better part of town. He went directly to a convenience store, filling up on fuel, and the asking the clerk for directions to a good hardware store. As it happened, there was a True-Value just a couple of blocks away.

Julius drove to the hardware store and used cash to purchase a few seemingly innocuous items. He had an employee cut a five-foot length of half inch schedule 40 white plastic tubing for him, then he picked out a cheap propane torch, a spark lighter, a small air canister of the type used for filling flat tires, an air nozzle with valve, a roll of duct tape, one piece of 80 grit sandpaper, and a small styrofoam cooler. He stowed his purchases on the floor of the back seat, he then stopped at a large warehouse type grocery store that was located along his route back to the freeway. There he purchased three roast beef sandwiches, a box of crackers, a block of feta cheese, some grapes (white and of the seedless variety), a bottle of cranberry juice, a box of cotton balls, and five pounds of dry ice. Back at his car he put the food on the front seat, and the dry ice into the cooler on the floor in back.

He elected to take I-43 north through Green Bay so as to have as much Interstate driving as possible before he was forced onto the secondary roads. After about a half hour's driving north he noticed a sign for indicating a roadside rest stop and he pulled off. There was only one other vehicle in the lot, a large truck parked with its engine running. Julius got out and walked to the restroom building. He went in, used the facilities, consulted the map, then broke off eight small icicles from the edge of the roof on the way out. These he placed carefully, so as to avoid breakage, into the dry ice container, which he shifted to the trunk of his car, wrapping it in a spare blanket he kept there.

Julius Miller then drove cheerfully, legally, and even courteously northward, slipping through Green Bay and heading towards the Michigan border at Iron Mountain as the gray snowy world changed inexorably to black. Highway 141 was well taken care of however, and Julius had no troubles along the way. He ate the first of his sandwiches and treated himself to some of the gourmet crackers and feta cheese. He stopped in at the Holiday station in L'Anse, Michigan later in the evening to fill up again on fuel. There were no cars parked at the station, but a number of snowmobiles stood outside dusted with fresh snow. He got out his new red air tank filled it right to the redline, 125 p.s.i. As he entered through the double glass doors, there were a number of teenagers sitting in the booths giving him the eye. The plump man with the bright eyes behind the counter noticed the air tank.

"Afraid you might get a flat eh?"

"Never hurts to be prepared."

"So... noticed the Illinois plates, you at the college then?"

"Oh no, just visiting for a few days."

"Ah, relatives then?"

"Just visiting the area."

"Well, we had a big blizzard last night you know, biggest of the century so far."

"Yes, I heard about that."

"Well, lots of roads are still not plowed, so you'd better stay on the main way."

"Yes, okay, I'll remember that. Thanks."

"Ya sure, you take care now."

Julius paid the man as quickly as possible, and left with an uncomfortable feeling of being watched, he turned back as he got into his car and noticed several of the kids in the gas station watching him. "Well hell, they probably don't have much else to do out here." He thought to himself and shrugged it off. He drove on into Houghton without incident, stopped at the Downtowner motel and booked a room for the night using one of the credit cards he kept in various aliases.

As the car left the Holiday station Jamey Yellowknife walked up to the counter. "Hey Mister Dobbs, who was that guy?"

"I don't know, there was something about him though, really made me uncomfortable."

"Yeah, I know, I think I felt it too."

"You get his license number?"

"Yeah."

"You might want to hang onto it, just in case."

"Yeah Mister Dobbs, I think I will."

CHAPTER 34

Digger Puttonen sat on the couch and watched Arne scratching Oby's ears. The black lab had taken an immediate liking to Arne as soon as they'd entered Ruth's house. The sound of a teapot whistle rising to a shriek came from the kitchen, then quickly died. The house was small yet cozy, very much like Digger's own place four doors down the street. The little town of Paavola had seen good times and bad, but its restoration as part of the Copper Country Parks project had been good for it; it was now a desirable little suburb of the Houghton/Hancock metropolitan area. Still, a little Federation money and a parks project could not completely eradicate the economic despair of an entire region that had been spiraling downhill for decades. At least, Digger thought, global warming had been of some benefit here. There might be flooding and hurricanes elsewhere, but the local low temperatures never seemed to get down into the minus forties that the old timers talked about. The snowfall, however, had certainly increased over the records set in the 20th century, global warming had meant moister air and more precipitation generally.

Ruth came back into the room bearing a tray with the steaming teapot and four cups. She set it down on a side table and sat down in a bentwood rocker opposite Arne. She smiled broadly at the sight of the old man and her dog getting on so well. Joan had been sitting quietly on the couch next to Digger. As Ruth set down the tea service Joan took a deep breath and opened her eyes from meditation. She had a slightly worried expression on her face as she turned and looked at Digger. The look conveyed much... a bond deeper than either of them would have thought possible on so short an acquaintance, as well as a concern. Suddenly Digger felt the prickly needles of suspicion tingling his scalp. He looked quickly around the room, but the feeling came from outside, not within the house. Joan noticed immediately...

"Digger, what's wrong?" she asked. Both Ruth and Arne looked up.

"I'm not sure. I just got a bad feeling, like... like someone knows I'm here." He got up and peered out of a tiny hole in the curtain on the south window. The dark blue Cherokee was still parked there. He saw one of the men turn and peer back in the direction of Joan's Nova, then turn back and put a telephone to his ear. I think we've been made, we may need to move again soon."

"Are they staying in their car?" asked Ruth.

Digger looked out again. "Yeah, for now, but it looks like they're interested in the Nova."

"Well then you've still got time for tea." She poured the four cups and served them out. "Okay, take a sip, relax, and tell me what you want to do."

Joan leaned forward and spoke to her friend. "We don't really know why, but it's obvious that the FBI is trying to pick up Digger and Arne. We think it has something to do with a hostile takeover attempt at Midnight Mining Company. It's quite possible that these aren't really FBI agents at all, but are impostors possibly even killers. I could tell if I talked to them, but I'm afraid it's too dangerous. Someone has already killed one of Digger's partners. So you see, we're in a bit of a mess." Digger peeked out the window again. The two men were still sitting there.

Ruth looked at them. "Listen Joanie, anything you want, you got it, okay? You just tell me what you want to do, and I'll help any way I can."

Digger turned away from the window. "If we could somehow get to my house without them seeing us, we'd have a lot more options. I've got some things there that might help us. We could maybe cut south, cross country on skis, back towards town without anybody being able to follow. The tag alders are thick down that way, but I know a couple of ways through. If we could get into the office and talk to Miriam for a minute, maybe we could get to the bottom of all this. But I don't see how we could get there from here, not if those guys in that car are watching the place, and now I've got a feeling they're watching this place too."

Ruth nodded thoughtfully for a moment, then brightened, walking to the kitchen for a moment, then coming back. "Come here for a minute guys, and look at this."

Arne, Digger, and Joan walked to the kitchen and followed Ruth's gaze out the back window. Several children were out there, happily playing and shoveling snow. "The neighbor's kids have built a system of tunnels all though their back yards. They're out there half the time when there's no school. I went out there with them last week. I think one of the tunnels goes pretty near to your house. Can you get in through the back?"

Digger looked up. "Yeah, I'd have to break a window, but we could do it."

"Okay, so you go through the snow tunnel until you're out of sight from the street behind your house, then through the snow and in. Will that work?"

Digger looked at Joan questioningly, she nodded. "I think so." Then he looked at Arne, who seemed worried.

"Hey Digger, I don't know," Arne said. "I never learned to ski you know, I'm okay on snowshoes, but.... I'm just really tired, feeling a little shaky."

Digger sighed heavily, but smiled. "Arne, I don't think you need to go with us on this trip okay? If you could stay here with Ruth...." He looked inquiringly at Ruth, who nodded firmly. "If you can stay here, you might just be able to do us more good. I don't think you're in any danger from these people, it's me they want... I think." Digger turned back to Joan. "I don't think they're trying to kill me, not these guys anyway. I don't get that kind of feeling from them, but still, I just want to get away."

Arne relaxed back into the chair, Oby nuzzled his hand to be petted. Arne looked from Joan to Digger with understanding and pride. "You kids will be okay ya know? Take it from ol' Arne, it's gonna work out okay, I jus' know it will. I'd like ta go with ya, at least, part of me would, but I'm really tired and I'm gettin' too old for all this chasin' around and stuff."

Digger and Joan began putting on their coats and boots again. "Listen Arne, if they come here, just tell the truth as much as you have to okay? Tell them anything... EXCEPT where we're going. Tell them we're going to try to make it to James' house in Lake Linden if you have to say something. We know James is already gone, so that should be safe."

"Okay Digger. Hey, I gotta t'ank ya."

"Thank me... for what?"

"You know, waking me up, or whatever happened in my head. I feel like you were part of that happening, it wasn't just an accident, it was something about you being there. Today I got da craving for beer in my gut, feelin kind shaky, but in my head I know I don't want it no more. I jus' wanna t'ank you for dat."

"What?" Digger looked confused.

"It's possible Digger," said Joan quietly. "We don't know much about your talent yet, you may have some empathic faculty as well as the cognizant ability." Digger looked at her quizzically for a moment, then turned back to Arne.

"I don't know Arne, all I know is... hell, I love you man!" Digger went over and hugged Arne, who stood up with Oby jumping at his side. "I don't know what's gonna happen, but you're right, I think it's gonna be okay."

"Yeah, I know, you just go do what you gotta do okay? And Digger...." Arne motioned for Digger to come close so he could whisper something. "You take care of dat young lady eh? Once in a lifetime somebody like dat comes along, believe me, I know. Don't you let her go now, not for anything, you gettin' da drift?"

Digger smiled. "Yeah, I hear ya." Ruth was at the back door giving the neighbor kids some cookies.

"Okay kids, my friends Digger and Joan want to see the tunnels okay? Show them the way to where they want to go, and then come back and I'll have some hot chocolate and cookies for you okay? You can call your mom from here to tell her where you are if you want, okay?" She turned back to Joan and Arne as if to say something, when the phone rang. She picked it up from the wall of the kitchen, listened a while, then spoke into it. "Yeah? Ah! Okay, thanks."

Joan said, "Everything okay?"

"I think so, that was Marsha, she just got a crowd all hyped up to try to block off the bridge. Said there was three young guys there picking up a black hummer, Federational plates, but they didn't lift a finger when the crowd captured the Sheriff, two of his deputies, and their patrol car. She said they looked like Feds, but weren't any of the local guys, they took off uphill right after."

Joan thought a moment, "Okay, not sure what it might mean, but we'll add it to what we know." She looked at Digger. "Shall we?" Then she turned to Arne, "Hey Arne, a lot has happened since you came home with me las' night eh? You'll be okay with Ruth here. We'll see you in a day or two okay?"

She hugged him and gave him a big kiss on the cheek, then turned to follow Digger out the door. The sky was still gray, and snow was falling sparsely, but the wind had picked up again and it seemed very cold. Ruth said softly behind her, "You be careful now."

Joan Smiled back, "Okay." Even as she said it, she felt a wave of insecurity sweep over her. She looked at the back of Digger's coat as they climbed down the back stairs of Joan's house, out of sight from the street. She wondered what those two FBI agents in the street wanted. Were they really FBI agents? Or were they killers trying to get Digger out of the way. Without talking to them she could get no sense of them, her psychic ability was strong, but limited to close range interaction. Digger could apparently sense attitudes farther away, but with less detail. For better or worse she was with Digger now, whatever happened, they would be together. For better or worse? Sounded like a line from a marriage ceremony... suddenly her cheeks reddened and she shook her head to get her mind back on the present problem.

They followed two children through the deep snow to a dark hole in a snowbank a few meters from the door. The kids, a boy and a girl, didn't give their names, but were extremely excited and proud to show off the result of their efforts. They beckoned and disappeared into the hole. Digger motioned Joan to go ahead of him, took one last look back in the direction of the mystery watchers, confirmed that they could not be seen from that angle, and got down on hands and knees.

The first thing he noticed was that it seemed much warmer all of a sudden. There was no wind, and the air was less bitterly cold. Secondly, while the darkness within the snow tunnels at first seemed complete, within a few moments he noticed that a soft glow came from the upper portion of the tunnel. Apparently the roof was quite thin. The two kids and Joan scuttled on ahead and Digger hurried to keep up. Their voices were curiously muffled as they emerged into a larger space in which they could all sit up together. The passage branched here and went in two directions other than the way they had come. The young girl, maybe about ten years old, spoke up. "We call this the North Pavilion. This way here leads over towards our house, that way goes on down the row of houses. Where did you guys want to go?"

"My house is four down from Ruth's, does your tunnel go that far?"

"Yeah, that's near the south end. So, you're trying to sneak to your house without those guys in that car seeing you?"

"Who told you that?"

"Hey, you think we're stupid or somethin'? Why else would grownups want to crawl around in snow tunnels? We noticed those guys have been sitting out there all day."

"Okay smartypants. Yeah, we'd like to get in without being seen, you think we can do it this way?"

"Sure, no problem. Hey, this is really cool, are you guys like spies or something."

Joan spoke up now. "So, what's you're name?"

"I'm Krissa, that's Joey, my brother."

"Well Krissa, we sure appreciate you guys letting us use your tunnel. I can see you've done a lot of work here."

"Yeah, we been workin' on it since last Saturday."

"It's really important to us that you not talk to those men out there at all okay? We're not sure who they are, they may be very bad men. Do you understand?"

"Our dad has a gun," said Joey.

"That's nice, but I don't think he'll need it. Just stay completely away from them, and if they ask you about us, try not to say anything that will help them," answered Joan.

"Wow, this is so cool! Come on, follow me," said Krissa, and scooted quickly off down the left hand tunnel on hands and knees. The other three followed and for a while the only sound was the huffing of their breaths and the scrape of their nylon pants and boots against the packed snow floor.

Digger tried to keep track of their progress, estimating that they were now crossing, beneath the snow surface, across the flat open space between the houses. If he stood up he would break through the roof, and almost certainly he would be seen. In places where the roof was particularly thin and the light particularly bright he could hear the rustle of snow particles driven across the surface by the wind. Digger well knew that distances in tunnels can seem deceiving, but still it seemed that they'd gone at least twice too far when Krissa and Joey stopped at a junction of two smaller tunnels. Digger was curious about something. "What did you do with all the snow? It seems too far to have dragged it all the way to the entrances."

"Oh, that's our little trick, we make several smaller tunnels to the side, and use them to throw out snow, then seal them back up. This one here goes out pretty close to your house, there's a big mound of snow there where we threw it. Then we closed the tunnel up to keep it warmer in here. If we open up both ends it gets a wind going through and gets almost as cold as outside."

"So, this way then?"

"Yeah, just go down there to the end, and dig your way out, you should be pretty close to the house. Seal the hole back up, if you would please?"

Digger patted the kids on the shoulder as he crawled past. "Thanks."

Joan stopped a little longer. "Okay kids, remember to stay away from those men, alright? I bet Ruth's got that hot chocolate ready for you by now."

Their eyes brightened and they scooted back up the tunnel with a hurried "see ya!"

Digger made his way about ten feet down the tunnel until it was filled with snow. Cautiously he scraped snow from the ceiling as close to the end as possible until he'd made a hole big enough for his head and shoulders. He crawled forward and squatted, sticking his head out. Sure enough, they had come far enough that Digger's house, only about twelve meters away, blocked the view from the street. Digger climbed out and beckoned Joan to follow, then they scooped loose snow with their arms to seal the hole they'd made into the tunnel. Wading in the deep soft snow, Digger forced his way to the back of his house. There was a back door and stoop that had obviously not been used all winter, snow was piled deeply up onto it, but like most outer doors in this country, it opened inward. Digger made a fist with his gloved hand and gently broke the double paned glass of the door, then reached inside and opened the bolt. The door swung grudgingly inward, leaving a crisp wall of snow standing at the lower edge, a wall which was quickly shattered and spread onto the hardwood kitchen floor by their hurrying feet. After Joan came in Digger closed the door as quietly as he could.

"I knew I should have kept the key to that door on my keychain, never needed it before though."

"Should we block it up with something?", asked Joan.

"Okay, but first, don't turn on anything electric, they may be monitoring power usage." Joan nodded. Digger quickly cut a rectangle out of a large cardboard box with a sharp kitchen knife, covered it with a plastic grocery bag, and taped it over the opening with a roll of gray gaffer tape that was lying on the counter. He scooped up the broken glass and dumped it in a trash can under the sink. Then they brushed the snow off each other and their boots, unzipped their coats, and moved out of the kitchen into the living room. Digger went to a front window and peered out though a crack in the blinds without disturbing them. "Yep, still there, they look bored."

"Probably are." Joan looked around the room, her first glimpse of Digger's house. You could tell a lot about a person by how they lived.

"I think we made it, I don't think they have a clue anyone's here," said Digger. "As long as we don't jiggle any blinds, pick up a phone, or use any electrical appliances, I don't think they can detect us."

"This is an interesting room," said Joan as she looked around. The floor was covered in a deep navy blue shag carpet, severely worn in the primary traffic lane. A wide-screen television and stereo unit took up one whole corner of the room. A coffee table sat in the center, covered with books, magazines and newspapers. The one spot on the table not occupied by reading material held an empty coffee cup. A couch that looked as though it might have been picked up from someone's trash sat along one wall, the cushions worn completely through in some places, several throw pillows lying randomly about. A recliner sat opposite, the wall behind it covered floor to ceiling with bookshelves, packed to the gills. Joan paused to examine the titles. Three shelves were devoted to technical manuals and textbooks, there was one shelf that was just history, but the rest of the shelves, four short but wide shelves, were packed with paperback novels, almost all of which were of the science-fiction and fantasy genre. Next to the couch, a glass fronted display case held mineral specimens: native copper, silver crystals, calcite crystals, and a fine display of datolite nodules of various colors, halved and polished. Joan looked over at Digger, who was watching her examine the room.

"So, what do you think? What can you tell about me from my house, now that you've seen it?"

"Well, there's no pretense here, you don't much care what people think of you. You like to enjoy yourself, and make no apologies for that. You're multifaceted, with serious academic interests, yet you enjoy escapist fiction, indicating you have lofty dreams. You like comfort, but you don't spend money extravagantly. You're a collector, but not manic about it."

"Is that all?"

"Well, I haven't seen your whole house yet, that's just what I get from this room."

"I can't believe we're just talking like this with those guys out there. What if they check the back of the house and find the freshly disturbed snow by the door."

"Do you think they will?"

Digger peeked out through the front window again. "No, they have their engine running to keep warm. They'll probably just sit there."

"Well then, we could hardly have found a safer place." She paused and her cheeks reddened as a thought came to her. "Show me your room?"

"Sure, this way." Digger led up a narrow stairway to a second floor. There were two rooms, the one towards the back set up as an office with more bookshelves, a desk covered with papers, and a computer system. The bedroom, facing the street, was quite simple. The floor was covered with a warm beige textured carpet, heavily padded. A king sized bed dominated the center of the room, nicely made up with thick feather quilts and many pillows. A dresser and small mirror to one side. There was no closet, but a standing rack held a sparse selection of clothes. Joan looked through them. They were mostly rugged outdoorsy things, just one suitcoat was in evidence. Judging from the dust on the shoulders it had not been worn for quite some time. "So, what else can you tell about me?"

"Well, I'd say you're a rugged individualist, or at least, you'd like people to think so. But the excess of pillows on the bed suggests a soft side." She turned towards him and looked into his eyes from about two feet away. "I think you gave up looking for a woman to share your life after you were badly hurt. And right now you're wondering if I'd like to get in the bed with you, and the answer is yes."

Digger's face went red to the ears. "I, uh, I was just thinking about us."

"I know." Said Joan, as she pushed Digger's coat off his shoulders on to the floor. He continued to protest.

"Come on Joan, we have to get our equipment together and get ready to get out of here."

She started unbuttoning his flannel shirt. "Right now, this instant?"

"Well..."

"Wouldn't it be better to leave after dark? We'd have a better chance of slipping away undetected."

"Well, yeah, I guess."

Joan pushed his shirt off onto the floor. "Well, it will be about two and a half hours until dark. Surely it won't take that long to grab a few things."

There was a pronounced bulging as Joan began to unbuckle Digger's belt. Finally he took her face gently in his hands and kissed her tenderly. "But Joan, we're in such danger. Wouldn't it be foolish to make love at a time like this?"

"I noticed some Heinlein among your science fiction collection. Do you remember the one about the many lives of Lazarus Long?"

"You mean, 'TIME ENOUGH FOR LOVE'?"

"Exactly."

"But the risk..."

"You may find, my love, that sometimes the element of risk can make the moment even more delicious."

Digger smiled. "Joan I..." He didn't get the chance to finish the sentence. She sat quickly on the bed, and pulled him down next to her. Speedily they removed their boots and got in between the covers. Between murmurs and giggles an occasional piece of clothing was flung out upon the floor. Their lovemaking was urgent but tender, and when it was over they lay spent in each other's arms, drifting into sleep. Just before slumber overtook them, a familiar rushing whine announced the approach of a jet aircraft towards the nearby airport. Digger had a momentary sense of discomfort at the sound, which quickly passed. There was a fleeting recollection of something that he had heard over the radio... that the airport had been closed due to the storm, but he shrugged it off. Joan snuggled closer to him and he drifted off with the musky smell of her hair in his nostrils, and the warm feel of her arms upon his chest.

CHAPTER 35

The whine of the two powerful jet turbines dropped to a lower pitch as Nate Crowell eased back on the throttle. He glanced at George Sherman next to him, busy scanning readouts and peering into the screen of the landing sequence computer. Nate dropped the nose into the rather steep descent corridor Sherman had chosen. The landing beacon was registering sporadically, but there had been no voice contact for half an hour, just static. It was cool in the cockpit, but Nate felt the steamy clamminess of sweat soaking the brim of his pilot's cap. Sherman poked some buttons on the console, then shrugged.

"Well, looks like it might be a manual landing, can't get anything from the transponder, there seems to be some hellacious interference out there." The floor level of thick clouds grew steadily nearer.

Nate knew Sherman well enough not to suggest diverting to another airport. "We can use the beacon as a set point for guidance, there's a backup program just for this purpose."

"The problem is that the computer doesn't seem to be locking on to the beacon," Sherman answered. " We can try it, but you'll have to be ready to take over manual control instantly."

"What about the runway? Is it clear?"

"All two way communications seem to be disrupted by this interference, so we can't get confirmation. I've got a man on the ground who said a half hour ago that he was arranging it. Jameson is my most dependable person. If it can be done, he can do it."

Nate considered. "I'll need to know soon. If there's more than a meter of snow on the ground we'd be better off coming in gear up, even if we take some damage. If we land with it down, our landing gear will probably be torn off by the drag, and we'd be in even bigger trouble. Either way sir... this plane may never fly again."

"Son, like I said, I don't care about that right now. If this operation is a success we'll make enough money to buy a million of these planes. If it fails... well, that's not an option. Just get us on the ground with no bones broken and you've done your job."

Nate took a deep breath as the plane plunged into the grayness of the cloud cover. He turned on the landing lights, which simply illuminated a few meters of whipping shreds. He turned the handle extending the main wing flaps, accompanied by an audible roar and a sensation of braking. He keyed the code for the Houghton County airport, giving the computer the key data of elevation, runway orientation, and relation to the beacon, then tried several times to synchronize the system to the beacon before it finally engaged. A simulated digital scene appeared on the view screen, showing a simplified representation of the topography they were passing over, with the runway highlighted in blue.

Nate hated these blind landings, and he already hated this one more than any he'd ever made. If he lived through this, he thought, it might even be time to retire. Such thoughts were quickly shunted aside as irrelevant to the problems of the moment... how to get this plane onto the ground and still walk away from it. In the viewscreen the runway was swiftly approaching; Nate dropped the landing gear. Sherman picked up the intercom and said gruffly, "We're approaching the landing now, brace for a rough one." He looked over at Nate. "You okay?"

"I hope so sir. As long as we have the beacon I think we'll be alright, I still would like landing clearance and confirmation on the runway condition though."

"Sorry, I'd give it to ya if I could... not available. Just do the best you can."

Nate swallowed, hard. "Yes sir." Nothing could be seen through the windshield. They were less than a mile from the runway now, dropping steeply towards its leading edge. The viewscreen flickered for a moment, then went blank. Nate felt a surge of adrenaline stiffen his neck, though outwardly he remained composed.

"Hmm, looks like we lost the beacon signal there," said Sherman calmly.

"Try to re-synch... the green button," Nate replied.

"Right." Nothing happened, then the screen flickered back to life for the merest moment before going blank again. In that fractional second Nate saw that they'd drifted west and were now heading straight for the control tower. He banked hard right and then straightened back out, hoping the maneuver had been enough, and peered into the window. Suddenly he saw the tops of a row of tag alder trees about two hundred feet below, before him was still a blank view, blinded by the blizzarding snow. Then, as if a veil were temporarily lifted, he saw the white openness of the runway ahead, saw that they were a bit low, still too far left, and to his horror, that it had not been plowed. Rows of drifts threw pale shadows across his path. He simultaneously pulled up on the stick, gave a little right rudder, and raised the landing gear, then backed off on the throttle. They fell belly first onto the left edge of the runway with a heavy thud, then began sliding. The intermittent grating of metal on concrete could be heard dully through the airframe, mixed with the angry groaning of the displaced heavy snow. Nate threw the engines into full reverse with right full rudder, but they had already started yawing to the left. They plowed through a heavy drift with a jolt, suddenly killing the screaming engines with packed snow. Control totally gone now, the stricken plane careened off the runway, across a wide open space, and into the chain-link fence along it's left side. The tearing screech of the metal fencing now replaced the grinding concrete noise, as the plane continued to slide, now more or less sideways, directly towards the control tower and the small terminal building. Sherman sat, arms crossed, gripping the shoulder straps of his restraint device. Nate struggled vainly with the rudder control to try to guide the craft. They slid inexorably towards the buildings, barely visible through the windshield which was now almost completely plastered with snow. Nate gave up and curled himself into a ball, bracing for impact.

When they hit the building it was almost an anticlimax, they had lost so much speed that they struck it with a simple and gentle "crunch", and were finally stopped. Nate peered through the cracked windshield into the interior of the airport terminal waiting room. Lights came on, a woman with a mop in her hand came running around a corner, screeched to a halt staring dumbfounded at the nose of the plane sitting where a row of chairs had been, then went running off again. The door to the cabin burst open and a man's head poked in.

"Damage report," barked Sherman.

"A few bumps and bruises, everyone is in operational condition. Having a little trouble opening the outer door." The man's eyes opened wide as he looked through the windshield.

"Use the one in back, this ones probably blocked."

"Yes sir." He backed out, leaving the door ajar. The men in back were already moving calmly yet quickly to exit the aircraft.

"Nice work Crowell, big bonus in it for you."

"Sir?"

"You got us here alive in record time in some of the worst possible conditions."

"But sir, the plane..."

"Come on, let's get out of here." Sherman had unbuckled his belts and was levering his bulk out of the copilot's chair. "When we get outside I want you to go into the terminal and say whatever you have to say. The boys and I are going into town. Just say we were going to Calgary and had an emergency or something, make up something that sounds reasonable. Use your company card and assure them that we're completely insured for all damages. Oh, and by the way, the plane's yours...

what's left of it... if you want it. The signed title's in the navigational pouch over there. If you don't want it, that's okay."

They filed down the cabin and out of the plane at the end of the line of men. Once outside Nate found that it was only a few dozen feet to a doorway into the terminal. Six men were busily unloading heavy black cloth bags into a pile in the snow. He glanced at the rear section of the plane, and saw that real damage was slight. He followed Sherman into the building, but it was obvious that Sherman had forgotten about him completely, concentrating totally on the next phase of his operation. Sherman was standing with several of his men confronting the woman Nate had seen through the window. Their words were not audible, but when Sherman grimaced at her menacingly she cowered and produced a set of keys. Sherman threw them to one of the men, who dashed off in the other direction. Meanwhile, the unloaded bags were being brought in and loaded onto several skycap's carts.

A few minutes later the man who had gone off with the keys came up driving a dump truck with a plow blade on it. At Sherman's direction the bags and men were loaded into the back. In a few moments they were aboard and the dump truck backed up, turned, and headed towards the parking lot and the main road. Nate noticed with an uncomfortable feeling that several of the men at the back of the truck now seemed to be openly armed with automatic rifles. He walked through the door into the terminal building. The woman was banging angrily at a telephone which was evidently refusing to operate. When his feet crunched on the mixture of broken glass and snow strewn across the floor she turned towards him and began to speak rapidly. He knew this was going to be unpleasant, but pulled a Sherman Industries credit card from his billfold and began the uttering of soothing words. Whether they would be effective or not he did not know. Already his mind raced with the thought of getting out of Sherman's employ, with a plane of his own. If only the damage were light enough that he could afford the repairs...

Out at the main highway the dump truck turned left and started towards Hancock. George Sherman sat at the right hand door. His two most trusted men next to him, one driving the big vehicle expertly. "Tony," he said to the one sitting in the middle.

"Yes boss?"

"Get Jameson on the line, I want to find out what happened back there, why he wasn't here." The man nodded and punched some numbers into a cellular phone, then handed the phone to Sherman.

After one ring it was picked up. "Yeah?"

"Jameson, Sherman here. Where the hell are you?"

"Still in Hancock, been having trouble getting he vehicles you wanted. Where are you?"

A Superior State of Affairs

"We're on the ground, but the plane is a wreck. Why didn't you have the runway cleared for us?"

"What? Damn that son of a bitch, he swore he'd do it!"

"The caretaker's wife said nobody had called, she didn't know a thing about it."

"Don't worry about it sir, I'll take care of him later. You just sit tight and I'll be there soon with the vehicles."

"Forget it Jameson. We've got a truck and are heading your way now. Meet us at the company office."

"Yes sir."

"And by the way Jameson, I am not pleased. This is the first time you've ever screwed up. This is a bad time to start, this project is very important."

"Yes sir."

"See you in fifteen minutes. Wait for us before going in."

"Yes sir," replied Jameson. Sherman handed the phone back to Tony.

"Damn it all, what's happening here? We can't have any more screw-ups. This has got to go down smooth the first time." They rounded the gentle curve around the frozen flatness of Boston Pond and came into view of the big Quincy number two shaft house, intermittently visible on the distant skyline through the blowing snow. He consulted an electronic pocket organizer, punched a few buttons, then said, "Stop there at the big shaft house. We'll drop a sniper team to maintain control of that possible entry point. That's the only possible way anybody could come in behind us once we take the front door."

"Gotcha boss."

They climbed the gently sloping hill towards the local landmark. At the base of the shaft house a small sign proclaimed tours and a gift shop. The parking lot had not been plowed recently; Sherman's driver lowered the plow blade and pulled into the lot. Another sign hanging inside the door of the gift shop announced the fact that the shop was closed. So much the better. Sherman jumped down from the truck and ran around back. He shouted, "Two man sniper team, front and center." Two men jumped down from the back of the truck, their black parkas dusted with snow. Bags were tossed down by others. "Okay, I want you two to get into this building, keep the cover man on the ground near the shaft entrance, the shooter up near the top of the tower. Under no circumstances is anybody to be allowed into the shaft. Use your own judgment, but somebody may try to take this building in order to gain access to the mine below. Keep them as far away from the building as you can. Tony will contact you by secure channel every hour. Keep sharp."

The two men simply nodded, shouldered their heavy bags and trotted to the gift shop door, expertly forcing it in a matter of seconds. As soon as they had disappeared within, Sherman climbed back into the cab of the truck, and they roared back onto the highway. Only a few cars had passed them during the stop. The men in back had kept their heads down, and if anyone wondered why a county airport truck was stopped at the mine shaft, nobody bothered to stop and ask questions.

The driver shifted to a lower gear as they came over the crest past the scenic overlook and started steeply downhill into Hancock. At Sherman's direction the driver turned left at the flashing yellow traffic signal at White Street, and continued downhill. Just beyond the corner, in the small plowed area in front of a county water pump station, was a battered white '99 Jeep Cherokee, with the engine running. An older, gray haired man sat behind the wheel. Sherman saw him there, but did not recognize his trusted lieutenant without the prominent scar, nor did he recognize the vehicle, and therefore disregarded him as an insignificant citizen. The truck turned left across the hillside almost immediately on Shafter, then left again on Sampson Street, making the jog downhill on Dunstan before approaching the old mine entrance via Mason Street. The gate was open, they drove through and were met by a young man holding his hands up. Sherman opened the passenger door and jumped down.

"Sorry Sir, we're closed."

Sherman glowered at him. "Son, you do as you're told and you just might live to see another day. Aaron's jaw dropped as twenty heavily armed men jumped down from the truck and began running towards the mine entrance. He reached for the cellular phone at his belt, but stopped when he saw the muzzle of the large bore weapon that George Sherman had pointed at his stomach. Sherman nodded his head and two men forcefully guided Aaron back into his tiny guardhouse, where he was tied up and searched. One of the men took his coat, hat, and badge, and took up his usual position in the guardhouse, while Aaron glowered from where he sat on the floor. A magnetic key-card was passed to the second man, who ran with it to Sherman.

Sherman moved in behind his men, who were making quickly towards the mine entrance. They clustered around it, guns covering every direction. When he was satisfied, George Sherman opened the iron door and entered the vestibule with Tony, their guns hidden. They quickly ascertained that nobody was in the front office, opened the inner door with the key card, and entered, moving quickly and quietly to positions of cover within the office. Using hand signals, Sherman assigned four men to cover the entrance, two inside, and two out. With two men covering the double door leading further into the workings, he let his men doff their heavy outdoor coats, before they began sweating in the relative warmth within the Midnight Mining Company administrative and research facility. They had just finished doing so when one of the men covering the inner door waved frantically, indicating approaching footsteps. All sixteen men took cover as best they could, except Sherman who stood in the middle of the room. The door opened and Farley

Grundwalder walked in, flanked by two other men. His head was turned sharply to his right, was obviously in the middle of a continuing conversation.

"Yeah? Well, that may be, but he's not here, so I'm in charge, you understand? Just because you...." Farley had caught something in the face of the man he was speaking to. He turned and with a shock, saw George Sherman, standing in the center of the office, wearing black fatigues, an ammunition belt, and holding a compact automatic weapon in his right hand, pointed at the floor. "Oh!" Farley stammered. "Mister Sherman. I didn't expect to see you here sir, not so soon." Sherman made a hand motion and sixteen men rose from their hiding places in the room. Farley shuddered for a moment, tried to regain composure. "Sir, I...."

"Shut up Grundwalder, I've heard it all before." He pointed to one of the men with Farley. "Jeff, Scott, come here a minute." Sherman turned away from where Farley remained standing and spoke softly with the two men. Occasionally they would look at Farley as some comment was made. The other men in the room regarded him with a cold stare, their guns were not aimed at him... not quite anyway, but it was clear to him that he was not regarded as on the same team, he wondered why. Finally George Sherman turned around and faced him. He smiled, but it was not a smile that brought comfort to Farley's heart.

"So, you're still trying to get control for yourself, is that right?"

"Well, mister Sherman, I'm a businessman. A businessman has to watch out for his own interests, of course. Obviously you want to become the controlling partner in this company, I understand and respect that. It's a big pie, I'm just looking for a little piece of it."

Sherman thought for a while before answering. "As I recall, from our conversation on your visit to my offices, you promised you could deliver the company to me on a platter... not just a controlling interest, but the whole thing. What about that?"

"Oh, heh, um... well, I thought I could initially, but as it turned out, even with a generous offer the partners didn't want to sell. I had to become forceful, as you know. I was the one who arranged for one of them to die suddenly of a drug overdose, in order to facilitate the transfer. I felt that such sacrifice and initiative on my part deserved something in return."

"You arranged it? An interesting perception of events. I seem to recall that I had to send one of my own men for the job."

"Yes, well, it was my suggestion, Farley answered defensively. "I thought that it would scare off the others."

"But it didn't work, did it? Your reading of the situation turned out to be faulty."

"But I was ultimately successful you see. Only just yesterday I finally got them out of here, locked them out completely, they're gone, nothing in the way to us taking over completely."

"Us?"

"Well, I just assumed..."

"You promised those idiots sixty million apiece right?"

"Yes... but wasn't that your offer?"

"Six weeks ago, yes. But things have progressed too far now for that."

"Too far?"

"Look around Grundwalder. I'm not kidding around any more. As of this moment this company is mine, no pun intended." The men looking at Farley chuckled grimly at their boss' little joke.

Farley's brows furrowed. "Then... what about me?"

"That is exactly the question we have to answer. What about you? Should we keep you on, or let you go?" Sherman holstered his sidearm and looked thoughtful.

Farley was encouraged. "Sir, you'd be crazy to let me go. I know almost everything there is to know about this operation. I am indispensable."

"Really, and how many others have you told I wonder... who else knows about the tempiloscope for instance?"

Farley looked around from face to face, feeling trapped. He sensed no friendliness in any of the faces looking at him, least of all Scott and Jeff, who had been his close associates for over a week. "Look, I didn't say anything to those FBI guys who were here."

"FBI? Who were they?" Scott whispered something to Sherman as Farley started talking.

"I don't know, some guys from the local station, looking for Digger Puttonen, one of the original partners."

"What were their names?"

"I don't know... some uh... Frank... uh... Jack-o-lantern or something..."

"Giacolletti?"

"Could be, yeah, I think that was it."

"What did you tell him?"

"Nothing, like I said. I just told him the guys he was looking for were not here and were not coming back, and to leave."

"And did he?"

"Yeah, I guess."

"You guess?"

"I told Miriam to see them out."

"Miriam?"

"Yes, my head secretary and administrative assistant, Miriam Lopez."

"There was nobody up front when we came in."

"No? She should have been there. Are you sure?"

"How much does she know?"

"Not much, as I said, she's just my assistant, more of a secretary/receptionist, you know... typing, buzzing people through the door, that sort of thing."

"So now the FBI has her, and everything she knows."

"What? How do you figure that?" Farley looked into the hard eyes of George Sherman and felt the icy fingers of fear claw upward through his bowels and grip his heart. "Hey now, I've put a lot of effort into this company, I'm part of it. I know a lot and could be very valuable to you."

"So you said before. Okay then, why don't you take me on a tour. I know that tours are usually somebody else's responsibility, but since you're the only one here and you're going to be so valuable to me, why don't you show me around?"

Farley brightened a little, seeing an opportunity to ingratiate himself. "Uh, okay, right this way then." Sherman made a hand signal, four men came to his side, the others, with help from Scott and Jeff, began sorting through paper files and opening programs at the office computers.

Sherman stopped Farley with a hand on his shoulder, then spoke in an aside to a large man standing nearby. "Tony, find out what the hell has happened to Jameson will you? It's not like him to be late."

Farley led Sherman through the double doors into the main research facility, as other men fanned out behind them to establish defensive positions and secure equipment. Farley tried to keep his voice on a positive note. He ushered Sherman past the doors of several of the important research laboratories, rattling off the names of the particular avenues of research and the pieces of equipment. They stopped at each and looked briefly over the labs and facilities.

They walked further down the tunnel and finally came to URRP, the Underwater Resource Recovery Project. Smoothly humming machinery filled a room off the left side of the tunnel. Farley showed Sherman the room in which the underwater robots, the "grunts" were repaired and serviced by automatic equipment. He showed off the computerized map of the mine, incredibly detailed, along with ore recovery plans and cost estimates. A pallet load of high graded copper/silver nodules sat in the room, ready to be shipped to a smelter. This operation was already paying for itself due to high copper and silver prices, even though it was still ostensibly a research project. A display panel showed the number of grunts working in the mine at the time, along with their locations, tasking, fuel status, and load. Again, Sherman was impressed.

They left the grunt lab and continued down the tunnel. When they came to the unusually heavy, vault-like door of the Temporal research area, Sherman stopped and gestured at the unmarked entrance. "This is the one I'm particularly interested in," he said. Farley slipped a card through a reader and slowly opened the heavy steel door. Sherman demanded, and received, the card that Farley had used. They walked down a narrow passage with two angled turns to another door, even heavier than the first, this one requiring that a combination of passwords be entered on an alphanumeric keypad, which Farley demonstrated. Sherman committed the passwords to his infallible memory. They then entered a large chamber, hewn from the living rock, and dominated by an immense piece of equipment at the center. Sherman was impressed. No photos or schematics had been permitted outside the facility. "So, this is it?"

"Yes sir, the tempiloscope. As you can see, it has its own high capacity optical mainframe control system and..."

"Why the heavy doors, is security considered that much a problem?"

"Oh no sir, they were concerned about some sort of explosion or something, a possible danger to the rest of the lab. You see, the clear sphere in the center of these triaxial field generators? During operation you can actually see images of things back in time in that globe. The machine does not actually retrieve the objects, at least, not yet, but it does transmit light and radiation. We were concerned that if someone were to inadvertently focus the device on, say, the center of the sun for instance, it might cause a serious fire or explosion before the connection was broken. That's why this room is totally sealed from the rest of the facility, except via those doors."

"We? You keep saying we."

"Well sir, I had to approve the expense, which was large. I had them demonstrate and explain the device, and finally I agreed that there was a significant danger to the rest of the facility in case of an accident."

"And the range?"

"Unknown sir. It has not been tested on anything more than a few thousand miles away, though theoretically it is supposed to be unlimited. The difficulty lies in determining the exact coordinates to specify. That's what all the computational power is for, there are dozens of variables which must be simultaneously accounted for. At least... that's what they tell me."

Sherman smiled inwardly. Yes, this was what he wanted, this was what he'd risked everything for. A time/space viewer. Those idiotic academic fools! Didn't they realize the power of such a device? With this power in his hands, soon, the entire world would belong to him. Complete knowledge could quickly be converted into complete control. He could know all the moves being planned against him, every secret of his enemies, every hiding place, every weapon. He successfully hid his excitement as Farley led him back out through the passage. He purposely left the inner door ajar and zipped the key card for the outer door into his shirt pocket.

They walked out to the tunnel again, turned left, and walked a hundred more meters or so to the end of the tunnel. The passage here intersected the Quincy number two shaft, before them was simply empty space and darkness, their voices echoed in an uncanny and frightening way. Sherman walked to the edge of the shaft and looked down into pitch darkness. Some seventy meters below, he knew, lay the water surface, where it had risen to the level of Lake Superior. One hundred and twenty meters above was the surface, where two of his men guarded the passage. Sherman could see nothing in the gloom in either direction, the glowing bulbs on the ceiling of the tunnel cast but a weak glow into the black void of the shaft. It had been a working mine shaft as late as 1945, when a disastrous fire swept through it, burning out every scrap of timber, even destroying the anchors for the steel rails that guided the ore cars up and down the shaft. In its heyday it was the deepest mineshaft in the world, over three kilometers in depth, one hundred and twenty levels deep, so deep that the air at the bottom was hot due to proximity to the earth's molten core. Now it was just a big hole in the ground, filled nearly to the top with water, but still useful as a research facility, and, thought Sherman, it was a very lonely place. He turned and regarded Farley Grundwalder much as he would have regarded cattle in a feedlot.

"So Farley, we must decide whether to keep you on, or let you go."

Farley tried to sound cheerful. "Sir, let me stay on with you, I can help train your people about this equipment, help you decide which of the old staff to keep and which to let go. I could be a great asset to you here."

Sherman sighed and shook his head sadly. "Well, I don't know. You've tried very hard, I grant you that, but you failed me on a key assignment Farley. It was your failure that made it necessary for me to come here personally, and it seems that you tried to gain more control for yourself than our agreement specified." Sherman and his henchmen moved casually in a way that forced Farley closer to the edge of the chasm. He glanced behind him at the dark void and began to get frightened.

"Oh please, I know I can do much better next time sir... really. And listen, it's all yours, I'd just like a job with your company. Remember, it was me who contacted your office in the first place, about the potential of Midnight Mining Company. I always knew it would be something big. I knew that a man of your character and ability was the right sort of person to lead this company." Farley had his back to the edge now, just a meter away.

Sherman considered for several tense seconds. "Maybe you're right, maybe we should keep you on." He smiled broadly and stepped forward, reaching out his right hand. Farley relaxed, and began reaching his own hand out. Suddenly, Sherman lashed out with a front kick to Farley's groin, he doubled over in pain. Sherman said sadly, "then again, maybe we should let you go." With both hands Sherman pushed the hunched-over Farley gently on the shoulders. Farley

Grundwalder stumbled back slightly, then felt only air under his foot. He struggled for a moment to regain his balance, then toppled backward with a shriek. The shriek ended suddenly with a thud as he bounced off the sloping wall below the tunnel into the darkness below. There were some indistinct rustling noises for about four seconds, then an echoing "Splooooosh" which slowly faded.

    The three men waited a few moments, but when no further sounds were heard, they retreated back into the more traveled areas of the facility. Sherman strode with confidence, certain now that his play for power would be successful. All he had to do was to get some of his better technical people in here to learn the intricacies of the equipment. He sent two of his associates back to the front office with instructions to disable all keycards except the ones they carried for entry at the front door, then he let himself back into the temporal studies lab, shutting the door behind him. The tempiloscope stood there, beckoning. He sat alone at the console and gazed at the digital readout which showed seven separate ten digit numbers, each continually changing, though at different rates and according to no discernible pattern. He picked up a three-ring notebook from the desk and began to read.

CHAPTER 36

Chris Jameson watched the dump truck go past, guessing correctly that the back was full of Sherman's shock troops. He followed at a casual distance and saw the capture of Aaron, the gatekeeper. He continued driving down Vivian Street trying to figure out a plan of action. His relationship with Sherman was over, of that much he was certain. The change which had swept over him made him steadfastly determined never to do another man's dirty work as long as he lived. He also felt some urge to thwart Sherman's plans to the best of his ability. He toyed with the idea of personally confronting Sherman, but rejected the idea as both dangerous and ineffective. At the bottom of Vivian he turned right on Cooper and back into the business district of Hancock. He watched distractedly as a crowd of people waving signs marched down Reservation Street towards the lift bridge. In the other direction he saw a black Humvee turn into a small plowed parking area. Three young men got out and walked up some steps into a nondescript brick building. Chris stared in disbelief... one of the men was the one who had spoken to him in the parking lot of the Skylight Diner in Rhinelander, some twelve hours and twenty light years ago.

Chris shook his head for a moment, then stared at the building into which the men had disappeared. A small sign declared that it was the Houghton/Hancock office of the Federation Bureau of Investigation. He turned up Reservation Street and pulled into the lot next to the Humvee, shut off the engine and sat there for several minutes as the windows began to fog up. Chris could recall no decision in his entire life that seemed one tenth as difficult as the one he was struggling with at this moment. He thought of the personal shame that would fall upon him by betraying his friends. Friends? Well... associates anyway. He reached for the car keys... then suddenly his phone started to beep. He jumped reflexively and hit his head lightly on the worn headliner of the Jeep.

He picked up the phone. "Yeah?"

"Tony here, we're in. Where the hell are you? The big man wants to see you A.S.A.P."

"On my way." Chris broke the connection before the other man could say anything else.

"On my way." He said to himself again, aloud, his voice loud in the enclosed car. "On MY way.... On my WAY.......... ON... MY... WAY." Chris finalized the decision and with a sigh of relief he put the car keys in his pocket, got out of the Jeep, and walked through the snow to the door of the FBI office.

A young woman seated at a desk smiled and said, "May I help you?"

Chris looked around a little. He could see the three men he'd followed going into a glass windowed room across the office. "Yes ma'am, I'd like to speak to someone about Midnight Mining Company."

"Yes sir, have a seat please? She motioned for him to sit in a straight backed chair by her desk. She walked across the office and knocked at the door of the room. When the door opened, she spoke to an older man for a moment, they looked in Chris' direction once. Then she came back. "Sir, would you come with me please?" He followed her to the room, was shown in and met by a group of six men.

"Now then, I'm agent Samuels," said one of the older men as he stuck out his hand. Chris took it and met the hearty clasp with equal strength. "And you are?"

"My name is Chris Jameson."

"And what can we do for you Mister Jameson?" said Samuels.

"May I sit down?"

"Oh, I'm sorry, of course, and take your coat off if you like, it's warm in here." Chris hung up his coat and sat in a chair at the table. The others were seated already. He looked around the table and met the eyes of the young man who had spoken to him in Rhinelander. He received a smile and a wink in response.

Chris thought to himself, "Could he have recognized me?" It did not seem possible, not with the thoroughness of his disguise, but there seemed to be no other explanation. He made a mental note to try to talk to this young man in private at some point. The others looked at him expectantly.

"Do you know anything about George Sherman?" asked Chris.

Samuels answered. "The wealthy industrialist that owns Sherman Enterprises? Yes... some... why?"

"Chris looked at them evenly and replied. "He's here. He landed in a small jet at the county airport less than an hour ago with a plane load of mercenaries. I feel confident in saying that he has, as we speak, taken physical possession of the offices and research labs of the Midnight Mining Company just a few blocks away."

"What?" Samuels jumped up out of his chair. Frank Giacoletti waved him back down.

"Mister Jameson, my name is Frank Giacoletti. May I ask you how you come by this information?"

"Yes sir. Until just a few hours ago, I was employed by Mister Sherman."

"In what capacity?"

"I was a professional persuader."

"Persuader?"

"Yes sir. I caused people to make decisions that would benefit Mister Sherman."

"I see. Is Chris Jameson your real name?"

"Yes sir."

Frank spoke to the side. "Jimmy, see what you can find out about our friend here." Then he informed Chris of his so-called "Miranda Rights".

Leonard Howarth leaned towards Chris and spoke without introducing himself. "And why should we believe you?"

"Well, if you don't care about your health you might go on up there and see for yourself. I'd be very careful though, his men are heavily armed and tend to be pretty trigger-happy."

"Are you saying that you think he'd try to kill FBI agents?"

"Believe me sir, Mr. Sherman doesn't care who gets hurt as long as he gets what he wants. He'd kill his own mother if she stood in his way. Actually... I believe he did, as a matter of fact."

Jimmy pulled two sheets of flimsy from the laser printer and spoke up. "Sir?" He handed the sheets to Frank, who looked back and forth from the paper to Chris.

"This picture doesn't look like you."

"No sir, probably not. I'm wearing makeup to hide the scar, a hair piece..." He pulled up the edge to show the brown hair beneath. "...contact lenses, and some false warts."

Frank continued to look at the file. "Orphan... UN invasion of Cyprus, wounded, disability discharge. No record for two years, then a murder charge, in Illinois, dropped for lack of evidence, implicated in extortion, racketeering, and assassination plots, an outstanding warrant for negligent homicide with a motor vehicle. Quite a list, and yet you've managed to stay out of jail, pretty lucky I'd say."

"Luck has nothing to do with it sir. I'm good at what I do, and Mister Sherman is a very powerful man, able to help his friends and associates."

"And which are you?" asked Leonard suddenly.

"Chris' eyes flared for a moment, then he answered. "Neither, anymore... a former associate, but never really a friend, though at one time I thought perhaps I was."

Leonard spoke up again. "And now you want to make a clean breast of it all, is that it? Your sordid past of extortion and murder will be laid on the table and your soul will be cleansed.""

Chris swallowed, took a deep breath, and answered. "Yes sir, I hope so."

Leonard shook his head and spoke vehemently. "I just don't buy it. I know your kind, I've collared scum like you for years. Guys like you don't just turn good, just like that." Leonard snapped his fingers. He looked into Chris' eyes and was met by a cold glare which quickly subsided.

Chris felt a momentary rage well up in him. He had half expected a happy, fairy tale reception, and was somewhat disappointed to find himself misunderstood. But on second thought, he understood the trepidation these men felt at his story. Would he have believed the story if he were in their shoes? "No," he replied to himself silently. "Really," he thought, "it doesn't make sense... such things simply don't happen, not in the real world." He buried his face in his hands and thought hard, tears starting to well in his eyes for the second time in an eternity. He could think of nothing to say. In desperation he stammered out... "I... I can't explain it sir. Something happened to me earlier this morning, something inside. I don't have a name for it. I don't understand it, but I'm not the same person that I was." He looked up and met Jason's eyes and felt as though a warm fuzzy blanket was being wrapped over him, keeping out the cold. He began to sob gently.

Samuels was doing something with the phone. "The line seems to be dead to the airport."

Frank drummed his fingers on the table. "So it could be true then. Jimmy, could you drive up there to the labs and just take a peek? For Christ's sake don't challenge anybody and get yourself shot, but just see what it looks like okay?"

Leonard looked at Frank. "You're taking this seriously then?"

"If it's bogus, we waste what... thirty cents worth of gas? If it's real," he nodded towards Chris, "then our friend here could be the break we need. What have we got to lose?"

"That's what I'm wondering." He looked doubtfully at Chris, imagining him to be a skilled actor playing the part he was assigned. However, Leonard could see no point to the charade if it was false, and too... perhaps he was thinking of the sudden and dramatic change in his own feeling towards Frank. "Okay then, Harry, you go with Jimmy. Get back here as quick as you can with whatever you can find out."

The two younger men put on their coats and hurried out. Samuels walked out of the room, followed by Frank and Leonard, who shut the door behind him.

Chris Jameson sat alone at the table with Jason Desnick. "Welcome home my friend," said Jason. I didn't expect to see you so soon.

Chris looked up at him. "What did you do back there?"

"I'm going to share a secret with you okay? I know something about you that you'd rather keep quiet, and so I'm going to tell you something about me, something that will help you understand. You see, I have an FBI badge, but that's just a cover."

"A cover? You mean, you're an agent from somewhere else?"

"Exactly. I go where I'm needed most, and the FBI cover is a convenient way to do that." Chris looked confused and suspicious. "No! I'm no saboteur or secret agent from some foreign country. I'm here to heal the wounded. Yes, including you. You see, sometimes things happen in a person's life that hurts them so badly that they can no longer function normally. I'm talking about a hurt to the mind, the spirit of the person.

"I happen to have the ability to feel another person's psychic pain, I'm an empath Chris. When I ran into you in that parking lot back in Rhinelander, I could 'see' your inner wound, even more plainly than I could see the scar on your face. I felt your anguish at all the children who had died there in Cyprus, and I heard the slamming of the door that had closed inside your heart. All I did was pry the door back, just a crack, and let the light shine in just a little bit. You did the rest Chris; you reached out from the darkness, opened that door the rest of the way, and embraced that light. You did all the hard work, and you succeeded! Whatever happens now, you have fought the real battle alone, and you have been victorious."

"What is your name?"

"You can call me Jason, Jason Desnick."

"Are you with the U.N.?"

"Well, yeah, I guess you could say that, but just between us, that's just another cover for an assignment from higher up."

Chris' jaw dropped open slightly, "Higher up? What do you mean? Are you... are you?"

"Who, him?" Jason pointed towards the ceiling. "Nah, I'm just one of his field ops. He's a good guy though, worth getting to know. Oh, looks like the others are coming back. Mum's the word okay?" Jason winked again, and Chris dried the tears from his eyes.

Fred Samuels, Frank Giacoletti, and Leonard Howarth walked back into the room. "Well, we just spoke to O'Hare," said Frank. "The airport's closed, but it seems our friend George Sherman paid some majorly big bucks this morning to have a runway opened for his plane. He took off heading north in an executive jet with a full load of passengers, all men dressed in black with heavy baggage. So... I guess that kind of supports your story Mr. Jameson."

Chris nodded. "I have a lot more to tell you, when you're ready to listen."

There was a commotion in the outer office, the door burst open. Jimmy and Harry walked in hurriedly. "Looks bad sir," he said to Frank. "There were two guys at the guard house that stopped us. One was wearing the same badge number that the other fella, Aaron, had on earlier I could read it with the binoculars. Further on there were two more men standing near the door. They didn't show any guns, but their parkas were bulky enough to conceal some pretty heavy heat."

Frank looked grim. "Alright then, looks like we're up against it. Samuels, get hold of the National Guard down in Iron Mountain, the State Police, the city cops, and the County Sheriff. See how fast the Guard can get a company of men up here. Have them bring some armor and an explosives expert. Jameson, how many men do you think Sherman has?"

"He maintains a strike team of about thirty. The plane would have been rather heavily loaded if he brought them all, but certainly there are not less than twenty."

"Twenty or thirty professionals? Damn! We wouldn't stand a chance, not against a force of that size."

"No sir, you wouldn't," Chris agreed.

"Are there any other ways into the mine?" Frank asked the room.

Samuels covered the mouthpiece of the phone with his hand. "There's the shaft house on top of the hill, it's a hundred and twenty meters almost straight down to the tunnel that leads to the research labs."

"You can bet that he's already got a team covering that possibility," said Jameson. "Besides, who's got a hundred and twenty meter rope?"

"Um, I do," said Jimmy. "Just one of those things I threw in the back of the hummer when we came up. Actually, it's a hundred and fifty meters."

Samuels was talking on the phone, then hung up. "The guard's already called out because of the protests down in Escanaba, they can't possibly get anybody up here in force for at least a week they say."

"A week!" Leonard exploded. "This is a goddamned crisis we've got here. What about the local cops?"

"The state boys have been told by the governor not to get involved with anything until the political situation becomes clear, they're taking a wait-and-see approach. I can't get any answer at the Houghton or Hancock Police stations, or the Sheriff's office for that matter."

Leonard looked exasperated. "Okay, this is getting ridiculous, I'm calling Washington and Mexico City. I've got a few chips I can cash in, we should be able to get a military strike force here in a few hours. I'll make the call from your office okay?"

"Yeah, sure, go ahead," Samuels answered.

Harry spoke up. "Are there no other ways into the mine except the front door and the shaft? What about ventilation?"

"The ventilation shafts are massively protected with heavy steel grates and motion detection systems. We helped design the security system, no entrance that way. As for other ways, well, there were nine shafts in all that entered the Quincy mine," said Samuels. Harry's face brightened. "But they don't all connect at every level, in fact, down here at the south end, what with the mine flooded up to lake level, the old number two is the only connecting shaft."

"What about using SCUBA gear?" asked Harry, straining for options.

"No, I think it's too deep. I think somebody told me once you'd have to go down to the eleventh level or something like two hundred meters below the surface to make it across. That would require specialized gases and equipment, and there's just no time for that."

Everybody shook their heads in agreement, it was simply not feasible. The front door and the shaft were the only possible access points, and with thirty men, Sherman could hold out long enough to.... to do what?

"Hey wait a minute." Jimmy interjected. "What's the point of all this? What's he trying to do? Let's try to figure that out. It must be something he thinks he can pull off quickly, before we can muster the force to evict him. It's an incredible risk he's taking by boldly walking in here like this. What's he got to gain?"

Chris Jameson, who had been sitting quietly listening, spoke up softly. "If you guys are through making guesses I'd be happy to tell you exactly what he's doing." All eyes turned to him. "Like I said, until this morning I was one of his most trusted associates. Up to you though, I don't mind just sitting here. Wouldn't mind a cup of coffee though."

They all looked at him, only Jason smiled. He stood up. "I'll be back in a second, you like anything in it?"

"Just a little sugar please."

"You got it." Jason left the room, came back in with the styrofoam cup of coffee, set it before Chris, who put his face down over the cup and took a deep breath. Jimmy started a recorder.

"Sherman's game is monopoly. He tries to gain control, through intermediaries, of controlling interests of crucial industries. He has... or had, I should say... a crack computer team that identified target properties. He then tries to purchase them outright, on the open market for a reasonable price. If that doesn't work, he would send myself, or another like me, to... persuade... usually at a lesser price. Sometimes relatives of the principals would have terrible 'accidents' and then the company would be sold cheaply, though not so cheaply as to attract too much attention. The focus of his computer search strategy was to identify those companies that would be valuable in a year or two, so he could buy them before their value shot up."

"And that was why he targeted Midnight Mining Company?" asked Jason.

"Yes. It was something quite unprecedented. His computer people projected that within ten years, Midnight Mining Company would be able to dominate the world market in a number of strategic areas, areas in which Sherman was already deeply invested."

"Such as..." prompted Jason.

"Well, um, I recall them mentioning pollution control, undersea mining, ore recovery, that sort of thing."

"Domination within ten years? Isn't that just unheard of?" The others sat back and let Jason run the debriefing, he seemed to be doing alright.

"Precisely so. And yet, every way they figured it, because of the important patents and developments, that was how it came out. So Sherman figures that when the news leaks, this little outfit is going to be one hot property. Also, he seemed particularly interested in a new invention they're calling a "tempiloscope". He made an offer of about double what the company was worth on paper. They refused. He doubled it again, and again they turned him down."

"And when was all this please?"

"We're talking just a few weeks ago. Finally, last week, Sherman called me to his office and asked me to persuade the principal shareholders to sell out. I drove up and convinced the financial representative, a Mister Farley Grundwalder, that he would be better served by acting as an agent for Mister Sherman than on his own. He agreed to use his position as comptroller/liaison from the university to edge out the remaining two of the original partners."

"And how did you persuade this Mister Grundwalder?"

"I told him that if he did not do as I suggested, that I would squeeze him by the throat until I had crushed his windpipe, then gave a brief but nonlethal demonstration."

Frank and Samuels gave a start, Jason held up his hand to keep them from saying anything. He went on matter of factly. "And did he do as you requested?"

"He tried, but the principal shareholders were stubborn. He claimed to have arranged the death of one of the shareholders already. He then suggested to me that if the two remaining shareholders, a Digger Puttonen and James Dolittle, were to suddenly meet an untimely demise, the legal transfer of company title might be much simplified. As I had not received authorization to apply sanctions of that kind in this matter, I delayed action. Then I was called to a board meeting in Chicago."

"A board meeting? The you are a member of the board of directors of Sherman Industries?"

"I'm sorry, no, not in the usual sense of the word. Mister Sherman maintains sole and personal control of all aspects of the company. What we call a 'board meeting' there is really a meeting of Sherman's top hit men. The calling of a board meeting means that someone is to be eliminated, and the selection of the method and place is to be made. I was unable to attend due to car trouble related to the snowstorm, I was detained in Rhinelander overnight."

"Wait a minute!" Said Harry, snatching up the photo from Chris' file and staring at it. "We saw you there, at the diner."

"Could be."

Harry looked back and forth between Jason and Chris. "Jason, you said something to him in the parking lot." He looked back at Chris. "And you said that it was this morning that you had a change of heart?"

"Look, that's a very personal thing okay? Right now I'm giving you crucial information about your adversary, do you want to hear it or not?"

"Yeah yeah, sorry." But Harry looked curiously at Jason.

"So, I talked with Sherman on the phone, scrambled, and he told me that his computer team had sabotaged and crashed his mainframe computer, causing his entire headquarters operation to shut down. They had managed to escape with an unknown quantity of extremely sensitive data, some of it related to this acquisition. Another board member was assigned the task of sanctioning the two traitors and recovering the data."

"And who is that board member?"

"That would be Julius Miller. A Chicago native, you may not even have a file on him, but he's one of Sherman's slipperiest killers."

Jason rased a single eyebrow in Jimmy's direction. He got the hint and began a search for information related to the name. "So, Sherman was too preoccupied to consider your problems?"

"Oh no, in fact, he decided to drop everything and come up here to deal with the situation personally."

"And were you given an assignment?"

"No, not directly. With Mister Sherman coming up it was not necessary to give me further instructions. I understood that The Puttonen and Dolittle sanctions were assigned to me, but that they could wait until Sherman's arrival and personal direction."

"And then what did you do?"

"Well, it was shortly after that, when I had what I guess would be called a profound spiritual experience. It was like nothing I'd ever experienced before, so I have difficulty explaining it." He paused for some time. "Suddenly I simply KNEW that what I was doing was wrong. Before... before, I was able to keep what I did for a living in some separate compartment that I never looked into. All at once I knew I had to quit working for Sherman."

"So you drove back up here?"

"Yes, I traded in my car and put on a disguise. I thought that perhaps I could stop him, but I didn't know how... I still don't."

Leonard came back through the door, his face told the story, and the news was not good. "We'll get no help from the military. The former Upper Peninsula representative has placed a formal secession proclamation before congress. She has declared the State of Superior to be in existence as of midnight tonight. The Pentagon is afraid that any military movement could spark violence in the population, which they can't afford, not after San Francisco back in '11. So folks, it looks like we're on our own."

Jason continued talking with Chris. Leonard sat down and started listening. "So Chris, have you communicated with Sherman since that time?"

"Yes I have, once while he was in flight, again about an hour ago, just after they'd landed, and the last time just a few minutes ago, just before I came in the door."

"And what was the gist of these conversations?"

"I spoke with Tony Capito, his personal assistant. The first time Tony asked me to see to the plowing of the runway, and the provision of vehicles for the men and equipment. I agreed, though I had no intention of actually doing so. I thought it best to wait as long as possible before letting him know that I was no longer loyal to him. I hoped that the plane might be forced to turn around, or even crash if the runway was not plowed. Evidently that was too much to hope for. In the last conversation, just a few moments ago in the parking lot outside, Tony told me they were "in", which I took to mean that they had successfully infiltrated the labs. I told him that I was on my way. It sounded as though Sherman was already quite upset at my continued absence. I'm afraid the charade can't go on much longer. He may already suspect my loyalty."

"And do you know the whereabouts of the computer people who skipped out with his data?"

"No sir, presumably they're running for their lives with Miller on their tail."

Jimmy spoke up. "I've got some stuff on Julius Miller. Appears to be highly educated, he has a master's degree in Organic Chemistry from the University of Michigan, did graduate study in criminology at Ohio State, but was turned down for his doctorate because his dissertation was on some unsavory aspects of toxicology. He is said to be an expert with various weapons, but has an especial preference for a variety of synthetic and natural toxins and hallucinogens. He has been arrested several times on suspicion, but was always released due to lack of evidence. He has been seen in the company of known Sherman associates several times. Here's his photo." Jimmy passed the picture around.

"Is that him Chris?"

A Superior State of Affairs

Chris looked at the grainy telephoto image. "Yeah, that's the little weasel alright. I'm impressed, I didn't think you'd have gotten even that much on him."

"Assuming that we can apprehend him before he does harm to these two others, do you have any evidence we can use to convict him Chris?"

"Me? Nothing but my testimony, but if you find those computer kids before he does, they probably have enough to throw him, Sherman, me, and probably fifty other guys in the clink for good."

"Do you have the names of those two people?"

"Yes sir, Steven Sanders and Eileen Donovan."

Frank broke in for a moment. "Jimmy, see if you can get a dossier on those two."

"Yes sir."

Then speaking to Chris again, Jason continued. "You do realize that technically, we'll have to put you under arrest?"

Chris nodded. "Yes, but you're going to need my help."

"I know," said Jason. "We just want to be sure we know where to find you, at least, for now." He winked at Chris conspiratorially.

Samuels stood up. "Well Mister Jameson, is there anything else you'd like to tell us?"

"Wasn't that enough? I suppose there's lots more, concerning things that happened in the past. But that can wait until we see whether we're still alive twenty four hours from now."

The sky outside had turned dark while they'd been talking. Samuels rubbed his ample stomach. "Hey, what about ordering some subs delivered?"

"Is there nothing else we can do tonight?" asked Frank. "What about your surveillance team on Puttonen's house?"

"Justin and Stephen? They should be okay, they'd call if there was any movement."

"Has anyone checked in with them?" asked Jimmy. "They've been out there a pretty long time, haven't they?"

Samuels leaned out the door. "Monique, see if you can get Justin and Stephen on the radio please... Yeah, thanks." Then to Leonard he said, "You still want this Puttonen guy for questioning? Looks like we might need to put him in protective custody before Sherman's boys perforate him." He suddenly got an uncomfortable look on his face.

"Yeah, that's what I mean," said Frank. "I'm afraid for the safety of your men up there if Sherman's goons come looking for Puttonen, they may come with heavier muscle than your guys have any reason to expect."

Monique stuck her head in the door. "Sir, the radio's completely jammed, all channels filled with static. Broadcast stations and satellite communications are all down, worldwide apparently. All I can get are ground cable phone lines. The word from Cheryl over at the phone company is that there's a huge solar storm or something, causing the interference."

Samuels' jaw dropped. "Uh... okay, thanks Monique."

"Sorry sir." She ducked out quickly when she saw how upset he looked.

Samuels was worried, and made no show of trying to cover it up. "Well that cuts it, I think we need to go on up and check in with them in person. It kinda blows the surveillance, not that they're all that secret sitting out on a lonely road at night. But I think you're right. I'm going on up. Anybody else?"

Frank looked at Jimmy. "Yeah, we've got a few more hours in us before we fall over. You got the I.R. scope with us Jimmy?"

"Yes sir."

"Maybe we can get a sneak peek at that shaft house as we're driving past eh? See if anybody's really up there. If not we might have found our back door."

"You guys be careful okay?" said Chris. "If you get hurt, you won't be the first by a long shot."

Jason laughed, "I hope that wasn't supposed to be a pun." Everybody looked at him, dead-pan. "You know... sniper team... long shot... get it?" Nobody else thought it was the least bit amusing except for Jimmy, who emitted a short snort.

Frank, Jimmy, and Samuels started getting ready for their trip up the hill to Paavola. At Jimmy's suggestion they decided to put on the heaviest body armor available under their parkas, just in case. Jason helped them adjust the straps. The very action was considerably sobering. Samuels also took the step of briefing his office staff of the potentially dangerous situation, he locked both doors to the station and gave instructions that someone should be awake all night, nobody to be let in unless they were known, and everyone to be armed at all times.

"Even me?" asked Chris Jameson, sitting quietly in a chair by the office door.

Samuels looked at Frank and Leonard, nobody dissented. "Looks like we have to trust you Chris. We're short handed, up against what could be a pretty strong force. Can you handle a weapon?"

With a barely detectable shrug of his shoulder, a large bore autopistol appeared in Chris' hand. Samuels gulped. "I didn't know you had that," he said.

"You didn't ask," Chris replied.

"Okay then," added Frank. "You guys hold down the fort, we'll go check on our surveillance team. I think we can write off the county boys as well as the city cops, I'm afraid they've either been neutralized already or bought off."

Jimmy added thoughtfully, "I still just wish we knew what was so terribly urgent that Sherman made such a sudden move. Surely he must know that within a week or two at most, we could get the manpower and ordnance to blow his ass out of there."

"And I wish I knew where Digger and Arne were," said Leonard."

"Arne!" shouted Harry. "That's it! Remember we were trying to figure out Arne Harjaala's strange story. It was as if he'd time traveled." They all stood looking at him in surprise, he spoke so seldom. But Harry's mind was always working, even though his mouth was shut. "That's the connection then... that thing you called a tempiloscope! They must be working on some sort of time travel thing up there, that's why Digger is so interested in Arne. And now Sherman's got wind of it. I mean... think about it for a minute. With a time travel machine, it wouldn't matter when he moves in and takes the place, as long as he gets the machine."

"And... as long as he has time to figure out how to use it," added Jason. "It's bound to be pretty complex."

"Right," Harry went on, "but once he's got it, he probably figures he's got the world by the short and curlies."

Samuels nodded. "Could be, at least it's the only theory I've heard yet that makes any sense, even though it's hard to believe. But I've got an immediate communications problem. You guys chew on that idea for a while and we'll be back within an hour. If we're longer than two, you may be on your own." They opened the door and went out into the darkness. Snow swirled in the light of the lamp over the door.

Leonard opened a briefcase and took out a small black box and set it on the table. "This is a very sophisticated and dedicated computer. It's a sort of lie detector, but we don't do anything so crude as attaching electrodes to the person. It works by analyzing stress patterns in speech, variations in syntactic structure, speed, pronunciation and so forth. We call it content analysis.

Chris, I'm going to take the tape of the interview we just had, and run it though the analyzer if you don't mind. If you're telling the truth, then of course you have nothing to fear, and you will have earned our trust."

Chris shrugged. "Be my guest," he said.

Leonard connected the recording device to the analyzer, and played the tape. They all sat and listened to it. Much of it Leonard heard for the first time, as he had been out of the room during part of the time when the recording was made. At the end of the interview, Leonard disconnected the machines and manipulated some controls. When he was satisfied he plugged the unit into the printer on a side table. Immediately a sheet of paper squirted out into a tray. Leonard glanced at it, his eyebrows went up.

"Well Chris, looks like you are telling the truth, you scored a ninety seven point three overall. I think that's one of the highest I've ever seen. See here, you are identified as 'voice one'. Ah... this is interesting. We have another listing for 'voice two', the person doing the questioning. Aside from Leonard, both Harry and Chris could also see the paper. They all looked up at Jason sitting across the table.

"What? Why are you looking at me that way?" Jason asked. Leonard handed the paper across. Jason looked at the notations, scanned the transcript confirming that he was the one identified as "voice two", and saw his score... fifty three point one. "So? What does it mean?"

"It means, agent Jason Desnick... if... that is your real name... that you're hiding something. I hope you don't mind if I ask you a few questions." Leonard pushed a button on the recording device on the table.

Jason gulped. "Here we go," he thought to himself silently. "Not at all," he said aloud.

CHAPTER 37

When Digger awoke it was quite dark out. He sat up with a start. Checked the clock by the bed... it was 7:15 PM. Joan stirred and yawned. "Come on Joan, we'd better get moving. Remember, no lights." Digger jumped out and went naked to the window, peering through a tiny gap in the shades without disturbing them. The Cherokee was still out there. They quickly got dressed by the light of the street lamps filtering through the shades. Digger threw a few things into a cloth bag and walked across the hall to his little office. There he rummaged in the desk and dropped several items into a small zippered pouch until it was nearly full. Joan couldn't be quite sure, but they looked like computer data storage modules. Digger then led the way quickly downstairs. They went into the kitchen, then through a narrow door and down a flight of wooden steps into the basement, where it was totally pitch dark. Digger closed the door behind him, then switched on a flashlight and handed it to Joan. "It's okay here, no windows." He got another flashlight from a workbench and started going over equipment.

"Can I help?", asked Joan.

"Sure, see if there's a pair of skis here that might suit you. I usually use those brown Trolls, but there are three other pairs, two with cable bindings that you might be able to use. Will your boots work do you think, or do you need some shoes too?"

"No, these will work, I've worn them with skis before." She took down the right ski of each of the two pairs, kicked her boot into the bindings to see which might prove suitable. "Yeah, here we go." She chose a set of dark blue Myhr touring skis. "I think I can adjust these bindings to work, I just need to shorten the side pieces a few turns."

"Good," he said, smiling at her. I don't regret taking that little break, not at all, but I have a feeling we'd better get moving. While she was working on the skis, Digger went to and fro around the basement picking up things and stowing them into two medium sized backpacks.

"Too bad we don't have a snowmobile eh?" Joan commented.

"I do have one... left it in town yesterday, right above my office. I threw a tarp over it, so it's probably completely covered with snow."

Joan finished adjusting the ski bindings, then stood up from her work and regarded Digger. "So, where are we going?"

"I guess I though of trying to sneak down on the lab entrance from above, through the woods. Maybe then we can see what we're up against. If we can get inside without anybody stopping us, I think we could do a lot. In a pinch we could try slipping into the mine down a rope from the shaft house on the hill. I've done it twice before, just for fun. It's a little tricky, but doable. We keep a rope there for emergency use in a locker at the gift shop. You ever rappel before?"

"Uh, yeah, a few times up at Cliffs Drive, just messing around."

Digger laughed. "Well then you'd really enjoy this. Anyway, I don't think we're in any big hurry, Farley doesn't know how to use the equipment in the temporal lab, and James is already holed up out in the woods. Let's just mosey on down and see what we can see okay? Oh, and one other thing I forgot to tell you... I love you. "Digger and Joan shared a long tender kiss. "Here, can you carry this?" He handed her a gray cloth rucksack filled to bursting.

Joan laughed. "Oh, so I'm to a be a beast of burden, is that it?" Digger just shouldered a pack that was slightly larger, picked up his skis and poles and motioned her up the stairs. They turned off their flashlights and emerged into the kitchen. Digger slipped to the living room to look out through the blind one last time.

"Sure enough, they're still just sitting there. Persistent cusses, I'll hand them that. I bet they'd be mighty pissed if they knew we'd flanked them."

"Should we bring any food?" Joan asked. "If we're in the woods for a while we might get hungry or thirsty."

"Well, I've got some surprise treats for later, but as cold as it is, we'll be in trouble long before we get hungry if we don't find a warm place to hang out." Trying as hard as possible to move quietly, not easy when carrying ski equipment through a small house, they moved to the back door. Digger carefully opened it, had Joan hand him the skis and poles which he put in the snow, then he closed and locked the door. He stopped to glance at his watch before he pulled his mittens up over the cuffs of his parka sleeve. It was eight o'clock straight up.

The wind was bitter as it whipped around the northwest corner of the house and threw tiny hard flakes of snow in their faces. The darkness was lightened by the filtering light of the street lamps. There at the back of the house, Digger and Joan were in deep shadow. They lay their skis on the surface of the deep snow, climbed up onto them, and latched their bindings. After a few moments of adjusting the pack straps, gloves, and pole straps, Digger took off in the lead cutting across his back yard towards the next row of houses so as to keep the house between them and the watchers parked out front. There was a moment of concern when Digger's skis fell through the ceiling of one of the children's tunnels, but that passed that difficulty without much trouble, slipped between two houses, and climbed down the high snowbank into the next road in the little development. Joan came up next to Digger. He said in a quiet voice, "Let's cut down the road for a few hundred meters, then we'll jump the snowbank and head across the fields, okay?"

The road surface was smooth and hard packed, with about four inches of fresh powdery snow on top. On such a perfect surface for cross country skiing they made very quick time. The far snowbank loomed, about six feet tall and nearly vertical. The big county snow blowers were efficient at clearing the roadways, but the banks they created could prove to be a real barrier to those trying to cross them. Hastily, Digger and Joan unbuckled their ski bindings, threw the skis up onto the bank, and started to climb over the top. A low rumble and a flickering glow to their right signaled the approach of a vehicle along the road from the highway. "Come on, I don't want to be seen!" Digger said hurriedly. He dropped to one knee and let Joan step on his other knee and clamber over. The headlights were sweeping along the snowbank towards them as the vehicle came quickly along the gentle curve. Digger jammed a foot into the snow and tried to leap for the top, he got his chest up onto the top, but his foot slipped out of its hold. He groaned as he started slipping backwards. Joan grabbed him by the arms and pulled with all her strength. His scrabbling foot finally found purchase, and he was over the top, falling on top of her in the deep fresh powder on the other side of the snowbank. The headlights flashed along the points of snow along the crest. They lay still and listened to the rumble of the engine and the groaning of the snow as the car passed. When it was down the road a few meters and they were again enveloped in darkness they both looked out after it. There was no need to comment on the fact that it was a black hummer... they just started getting their skis back on.

Again, Digger took the lead, breaking trail in a southwesterly direction, through country that, in summertime, was a weed choked bog. The deep powdery snow made the going slow and difficult. Diggers ski tips could not even be seen at all, slipping completely beneath the pristine surface covered with tiny drifts and occasionally the tip of what must have been a giant among weeds. He broke trail with his shins, and it was only the nylon gaiters he wore over his low topped touring shoes that prevented the snow from invading his socks and freezing his feet. As it was, while his toes were a bit cold, he was quite toasty warm otherwise. In fact, before they had gone quite a half kilometer he stopped. Joan stepped off his track and came up alongside. Digger leaned on his poles and breathed heavily. "Whew! This is turning into a workout. How you doing?"

"Okay, thinking about opening my jacket a bit, I'm feeling a little steamy."

"Yeah, good idea, we don't want to overheat and get soaking wet here. How are your feet?"

"Doing good. I've got these high topped boots with my pants leg over them, not getting any snow in."

"Good, like a sip of water?"

"Yah, sure eh?" She smiled and accepted the plastic flask that Digger took out from within his coat. There were some soft popping noises in the distance behind them. They both turned back towards the diffuse glow that marked the little village of Paavola. "I wonder what....." Joan began to say, when there was a bright orange flash that lit the sky momentarily, followed about a second later by a sudden deep "BOOM" that was immediately swallowed up by the snow in the air.

"I don't like the sound of that?" Joan said softly.

"Or the look of it for that matter." Digger agreed seriously. "I hope Arne and Ruth are okay. Come on, we'd better get going."

"Let me break trail for a while, I'm pretty fresh, you've been doing all the work."

"Alright," Digger agreed, but let's switch off more often, we'll be able to keep up a better pace that way." He looked down the back trail. The blowing snow was filling their track... but not very fast, probably not fast enough to hide their trail from someone looking for it. He glanced off in the direction of Paavola again, a faintly flickering reddish glow could be seen, the popping noises continued sporadically. He turned forward again and hurried after Joan, who was already moving ahead briskly, keeping the blue-white glow that indicated the lights of village of Pewabic straight ahead. Digger left the front of his coat zipped open, and felt a thrill as he sensed the cold air sifting through his sweater beneath. At least it would keep him from sweating, and he would not get cold as long as they kept moving.

A dark mass loomed ahead, consisting of countless thin but stout tree stems, packed tightly together. Joan could see no way through. Digger came up along side of her. "Ah, the tag alders, yes, there's a big stand of them here. We'd have to go quite a way in either direction to get around them."

"So, what should we do?"

"Not to worry! I like skiing to work, so I came out here last summer with a chainsaw and made a path through the thicket to shorten the trip, we should be pretty close. Let's see, is it right or left? Wait here a minute." Digger dropped his pack in the snow and skied off to the left. He was back about two minutes later. "Must be the other way, come on." He picked up the pack and broke trail to the right." After about thirty meters he stopped. "Yeah, here it is!" A slim white path could be dimly seen in the pale gray light, entering the tangled mass of thin stems.

Digger led the way into the narrow winding path through the trees. About fifteen meters from the beginning the path opened into a tiny clearing, just enough for the two of them to stand side by side. The closely spaced alders formed an effective windbreak. Digger stepped to one side and Joan came up next to him.

"It's nice here!"

"Yeah, this is a special place. I like to come here, lay a tarp on the snow, and just sit sometimes. I'm glad you got to see it."

"Me too, though we don't have a lot of time do we?"

"No, I don't think so."

"What do you think happened back there?"

"Oh, probably somebody's water heater blew up."

Joan simply looked at Digger with a disappointed expression. "Come on Digger, you know I can tell when people are bending the truth, you don't believe that for one minute."

"No, you're right, I don't. I think that there was gunfire, and an explosion. Something to do with those guys in the street and that other vehicle probably. The explosion could have been a car, but judging from the size of the fireball, I'd guess it was a house, it looked more like the explosion of a propane tank than gasoline."

"Your house?"

He shrugged. "I don't know, maybe." She looked at him again with an odd expression. "Okay, you're right. It was probably my house."

"You're worried about Arne and Ruth." She said it as a statement of fact, not a question.

"Yes, what if it was her house, your car is still there, what if those guys went up there and...."

"Digger, slow down. You know Arne. Focus on him, feel for him. Do you get a sense of him?"

Digger took a deep breath and closed his eyes, facing back towards Paavola. "Yes."

"What's it like?"

"He's worried, concerned."

"Okay. So, maybe they saw your house explode, and they're worried about us, it's only natural."

Digger nodded and smiled. "Yeah." He leaned over and kissed her. Their lips were icy cold, but the touch was warming. They took another small sip from the water bottle, then headed on out of the thicket. The short rest helped, but still, the heavy snow made for slow going. Even though they changed lead several times, they did not reach the next road crossing until almost quarter after nine. It was the Arcadia road out of Pewabic, and stood directly across their path. The fall of snow began to grow lighter, and Digger became more concerned about being seen. They could clearly see the nearer houses in the village, standing only a couple of hundred meters to their right. Beyond them to the southwest the gray mass of the old Quincy number two shaft house dominated the horizon, topped by a blinking red light. He looked at it for a moment, and had a fleeting impression that the blinking light was an eye searching for him. He shrugged it off, but Joan noticed. "What is it?"

"I don't know, just had a weird feeling when I looked at the shaft house, kind of a metallic taste in my mouth almost, very uncomfortable."

Joan looked him in the face for a moment. "Then I don't think we should go anywhere near it."

Digger looked west again, tried to shrug off the feeling, but it persisted. He nodded in agreement. "I think you're right. Just thinking about going there right now gives me the creepies."

The snowbanks were particularly high at the point where they encountered the road. They were in a low area to the east of Quincy hill that received a lot of drifting in windy weather. Digger motioned for Joan to follow and led towards the left, further away from Pewabic and parallel to the road. A little way further there was a spot where the wind had scooped the snow down, and the banks were shallow. They crossed here and continued in a due southerly direction, keeping the brighter glow on the horizon that marked the city of Hancock somewhat to their right. Twenty minutes later they crossed another road, and slipped quietly between two houses, continuing straight south.

"This is not the most direct path," Digger told Joan when they switched lead shortly after the road crossing, "but it keeps us a little more away from where people are. We're heading towards the ski hill at Mount Ripley. From there we'll cut along the ridge back towards Hancock, and then take a trail I know about down through the woods. I don't think Grundwalder even knows about it." Joan nodded. While she rarely had been in the particular area they were traversing, she was well acquainted with the general topography of the area. They were swiftly approaching the steep hillslope that led down to the more thickly inhabited districts along the Portage Lake shipping canal. The canal connected one side of the Keweenaw Peninsula with the other, and was frequently used as a shortcut or as shelter by large ships during storms on Lake Superior. At present of course, it was frozen solid, and any boats venturing onto the big lake at this time of year would have to take the longer way around.

They began to go slightly downhill now, and the light was growing brighter as they drew nearer to town. In a short time they encountered a broad and well traveled trail skirting the rim of the steep hill before them. The chair lifts were quiet, but it was obvious that it had been a busy day at Mount Ripley. Fresh powder always drew a crowd of serious downhill enthusiasts, their lightly dusted tracks were everywhere. Digger and Joan took the trail heading west now. It was wide enough and sufficiently well packed that they were able to use the "skating" step, and move quite quickly along, their tracks mingling with countless others. The west wind was now in their faces, but grew quickly less intense, and the snow finally stopped falling altogether. The city of Houghton lay below them across the canal, lights blazing, the University buildings lit up and busy looking. It was still early in the evening. In the far west there was a strange flickering glow on the horizon, too indistinct to identify. The city of Hancock lay below them, mostly hidden by the folds of the hillside, but evident because of the great glow it cast onto the low clouds above. They traveled nearly a mile in this fashion in less than fifteen minutes. The old mine buildings on Quincy hill were now clearly visible to their right when Digger called a halt. A narrow track ran obliquely downhill to the left.

"This is the way down to the mine entrance. The labs are almost directly below our feet, about a hundred meters or so."

Joan pointed to the west. "What do you think of that?"

He followed her gaze, and squinted. A widening rim of darkness edged the clouds, broken only by indistinct flickerings and moving bands of pale light. As he watched, a single unmoving point of light shone out and remained steady. "Ah!", he exclaimed.

"The clouds are blowing away, the sky is clearing. You can see a star or a planet there, just below the rim of the clouds."

Joan understood. "Oh, then it's the northern lights?" They looked at each other. "Whoa, they're pretty intense!"

"I bet it's going to be one heck of a show tonight! I've seldom seen them that bright so close to the horizon." They watched for a while in silence, then Digger said, "Come on, let's go see what's happening at the office."

He pushed off the wide trail and started down the narrow track. The shape of the path and the fact that there was hard packed snow beneath the powder indicated that a snowmobile had been this way in the last day or two. It did not go too steeply down, yet they had to snowplow from time to time to keep from going too fast. "Watch this curve!" Digger yelled back, then cut hard to the right across the slope to a level stretch. Joan negotiated the tricky spot without falling. "Hey, pretty good. That one gets me pretty regularly, even when I know it's coming. It's easy on the snowmobile, but you get going just a little too fast on skis sometimes. Now we have to switch back towards the left. There's a steep run, then you go between those two big maples there, and then it levels off for a bit, it's a fun little run, but don't get off the path when you hit the trees or you WILL hit the trees." He pushed off and swept down the slope at a pretty good clip, Joan went a few seconds later. In the dim light a bump in the path threw her off balance and she fell on her backside. When she caught up with him on the flat part he noticed the snow on her jacket, but made no comment.

"You didn't say anything about that hump in the middle of the fast part." Joan chided him.

"Oh, yeah, kinda forgot about that, hard to see huh?"

"Yeah."

"Well, it gets slower down here, the hill is steeper so we have to switchback a bit more. The turns are wide, so you shouldn't have any trouble." Again he led off, and there were no further incidents as they made their way down towards the old adit entrance to Quincy Mine. Finally he stopped and motioned for quiet by putting his hand up palm outward, he motioned downward and Joan could see that below them was a deep cleft in the hillside, lit from below by an electric light. The path continued down, but Digger stepped off it and removed his skis with a minimum of noise. Joan did likewise, sticking them vertically in the snow alongside his. He waded a few feet through the knee deep white stuff to a low mound.

Digger squatted down and spoke quietly. "This is my snowmobile, it's kind of a custom model, got it from a guy who races the things. The key's in the ignition, gas tank over half full, it's probably got fifty miles worth or so. If anything happens to me down there, you can get away on it okay?"

Joan squatted down next to him and grabbed him the front of his jacket. "Hey buddy boy, you can't get rid of me that easy. I'm stuck on you like snot on a fingernail."

Digger chuckled. "Okay. But let's be careful okay? Right down here is a place we can look down on the entrance and the parking lot. We'll be behind some bushes and against these dark trees so we should be pretty inconspicuous, but the snow has stopped falling, and sound will carry well. Let's try to move slowly and quietly." Joan nodded. "Okay, you warm enough? We'd better zip up tight to stay warm, we might be sitting still for a while."

They dropped their packs next to the snowmobile, which they left hidden. Digger took an object that looked like a small pair of binoculars out of his pack and put it in one pocket, a pair of smaller objects in another. Then he pulled a rolled-up foam mat out and carried it under his arm. They waded through the knee deep snow a few dozen meters to their right, then Digger motioned, and Joan could see the area in front of the door to Midnight Mining Company, not more than twelve or fifteen meters away and almost directly below them. He rolled out the foam pad, laid it in the snow and sat down on it, sinking deeply in. Joan sat down and snuggled up next to him, it was really quite comfortable. A single mercury vapor lamp burned above the door throwing sparks of cold bluish light from the myriad of fresh snowflakes coating the ground. There were four cars in the lot, two of them deeply covered with snow, the other two had been recently swept clear. They could see the guard shack away to the right. A dump truck with a plow blade mounted on it sat right in the gate, facing outward, blocking access. There were no people visible, and no movement.

"Looks pretty quiet," Joan said.

Digger pulled something from his pocket, flicked a switch, and handed it to Joan. "Try this, just like binoculars."

She put her eyes to the oculars and looked through it. The magnification was low, barely more than with the unaided eye. She panned the view across the parking lot until she covered the area near the door. In one of the parked cars there was a reddish glow in the shape of a person's head and shoulders. "There's someone in the car," she said quietly.

"Just one? Are you sure?"

She scanned the other car that had been swept off. A pale diffuse glow could be seen there, not as distinct as the first. "Yes, I'm pretty certain. Where'd you get these?"

Digger whispered. "Prototype model, one of our newer patents. It's just a regular pair of low power binoculars with an active matrix Thermal IR grid inserted into the optical path. Can't believe nobody ever thought of it before. The Audubon society is endorsing them for birdwatching. We're gonna sell a million of 'em. May I?"

Digger took the glasses and played with the adjustments. "Yeah. I think you're right. Someone was sitting in that other car not too long ago, the residual heat is giving that diffuse signal." He scanned over to the guardhouse. "Oh ho! Two people in the guardhouse, wait, no... three! The tailpipe of the dump truck is still warm, it must have been used quite recently. One of the men in the guardhouse is facing me through the window. I can make out his face, but it's not anyone I've ever seen before. Here you try again."

"I see him, no, doesn't ring a bell for me either. I only see two though, how do you make three?

"Look at the wall, low down at the right."

"Yeah, there's a pinkish area there."

"I think someone is lying down against the wall."

"In there? Doesn't sound very comfortable."

"It's probably not, but they may not be doing it by choice."

"The regular guard you think?"

Digger shrugged his shoulders. "Maybe."

"I'm glad these aren't on the market yet, or those guys might have them too."

"There are plenty of IR sensors available, don't worry about that. If they have any and know how to use them, they'll see us clear as day. Looks like they're not too worried though, whoever they are. That guy in the car almost looks like he's falling asleep."

Joan looked again at the car. "I think you're right, his head jerks forward every once in a while."

"Look around, can you see anything else?"

Joan lifted the glasses and scanned the hillside opposite, up towards the spot where they'd left their skis, then she twisted to scan the hill to the side. "Oh, up there, something moving."

"What is it?"

"I'm not sure, too small for a person, a porcupine maybe?"

"The thermoculars are great for that sort of thing. You'd be amazed how many more animals you see in the woods than without it."

Joan looked back at the people who were apparently watching the entrance to the mine. "Who do you think they are?"

"Without more data I'd hesitate to speculate. If something doesn't happen pretty soon though, we'll have to go someplace warmer to rethink our options."

"I'm starting to get pretty cold. What time is it?"

Digger pulled the cuff of his heavy mitten down and looked at his watch. "Almost quarter after eleven. You want some hot chocolate?"

Joan sniggered. "Sure, you got some?"

Digger fished two small canisters out of his pocket. "Here, take your glove off and hold the can, then bend this tab back and hold it until it's as hot as you want it, then bend it back the other way to drink." He demonstrated and in a few moments was sipping piping hot cocoa.

Joan followed suit. "Where did you get these?"

"Samples I picked up at an inventor's congress, I met the guy who has the patent on it. I'm thinking he'll make out like a bandit if he doesn't get ripped off. Isn't it great?"

Joan nodded, for a few more minutes they sat in the snow and sipped their hot chocolate, but sitting still like that, the cold started creeping in again. When she finished hers she tried to work out some of the kinks from sitting still so long, and leaned back into the snow to stretch, then looked up. She caught her breath. "Digger, look!"

He followed her gaze and saw that the ragged edges of the cloud cover were being swept away high above them, revealing a crystal clear sky... and in that sky a display of the Aurora Borealis was in progress that made the laser light show at a Pink Floyd concert seem like a children's pop-up book. Coruscating bands and swirls of intense color leaped and danced in total silence. They lay in rapt fascination for several minutes when a grating sound drew their attention once more to the metal door leading within the mountain. They sat up again to watch.

The door opened and two men came out, standing beneath the violet blue glow of the single bulb. They were joined shortly by the man who had been sitting in the car.

"Okay, try it again," said a deep gruff voice.

The second man punched some buttons on what looked like a phone. "Sorry Mister Sherman, still nothing."

"Damn, I was hoping it was the rock interfering. Hey you! What were you doing in that car, I thought you were supposed to be standing guard."

"Yes sir, I am, but it's so cold, I was just sitting in there to stay warm, I can still see good."

"Yeh, but you can't hear worth a damn from there. You'll be relieved at midnight, until then you stand here by the door, keep your eyes open and your ears sharp, sound that air horn if you need help. We're missing one guy already, I don't know where he is, but it could be bad news, so be ready for anything."

"Yes sir."

"You got a round in the chamber of that thing?"

"No sir, not yet."

"Well jack one in there, now."

"Yes sir." The young man worked the charging lever of a large bore assault rifle and stood to attention.

George Sherman turned to the other man. "We've got to establish communication with our sniper team on the shaft house. This damned interference is a hell of a nuisance."

The guard with the rifle chanced to glance upwards and exclaimed. "Look at that!"

George Sherman and his companion looked up, but appeared unimpressed. "It's the northern lights, caused by the same solar storm that's screwing up our communications. Keep your wits about you soldier, and keep your eyes on the ground." He turned to the other man. "Send a relief team up to the shaft house, I want that area secure."

"Yes sir," he answered. Then the two of them disappeared back into the mountain, and the door closed with a metallic "Clang," followed by the audible engagement of a heavy bolt from within. The guard outside stood in his assigned position, stamped his feet and looked alert.

Digger whispered softly to Joan. "Do you know who that was?"

"No, except the guard called him Mister Sherman."

"Right, it could only be Mister George Sherman, the wealthy industrialist who's been badgering Farley to sell us out. I guess he's finally managed it. As long as he hasn't figured out how to use the tempiloscope, we still have a chance. That's the key though, if he manages to get the knack of it, we're sunk."

"What do you mean, we're sunk."

"I mean everything Joan, your dreams, mine, the world. In the hands of an unscrupulous person it is ultimate knowledge, and thus ultimate power. He must have found out something about it or he wouldn't be taking this risk. But only me and James really know that equipment. We have carefully kept all the other researchers in specialized compartments, each knows a piece, but none of them know it all. If there was just some way that we.... "

Digger stopped whispering as the guard turned his head and appeared to be searching the gloom in their direction. Digger and Joan tensed but sat stock still. After a while the man turned around and started stamping his feet and rubbing his hands, every once in a while he would tip his head back and look upwards. Joan leaned over and whispered in Digger's ear. "Don't you think we ought to get going?" He nodded. With the greatest of care, and with agonizingly slow movements they rose from their seats, leaving the foam mat behind, and began to walk back towards their skis. The powdery fresh snow helped to muffle their steps, the greatest danger was the rustling of their clothing. They had only gone a few steps when the door clanged open again. They stopped and stood still. Four men emerged, from their manner and talk they had evidently been ordered to drive up the mountain to relieve the team in the shaft house. They stopped for a moment to speak with the guard at the door.

It was at that moment that Digger remembered the hot chocolate cans. He and Joan had finished drinking, then set the cans down in the snow next to them. He looked back and saw only one can in the snow by the depression where they had been sitting. He looked down, and, to his horror, saw the other caught in a fold of his parka, snagged by a sharp corner of the pull tab on a single frayed thread dangling from his jacket. He slowly moved his hand to try to grasp it, when, seemingly in slow motion, he saw it fall to the snow with an audible "clunk," then skitter down the slope and strike the base of the bushes that were screening them from view.

"Up there!" The guard yelled. "I heard something." The beams of flashlights pierced the bushes.

There was no more point in stealth, both Digger and Joan began moving as fast as possible up the path they'd made towards their equipment. A bright light shone on them from below. "Look, it's two people! Quick, sound the alarm." Someone pulled out a compressed air horn and let out three loud blasts. One of the men from the guard house came running, the door clanged open again.

Digger and Joan struggled uphill through the heavy snow. It was like a nightmare, their will urging them to speed, their legs weighted down, dragging through molasses, any moment they expected the shot, the searing hot sting, the smell of warm blood in the snow. There still appeared to be some uncertainty below however. Finally a gruff voice shouted "Shoot you fools." And the air was filled with the sound of gunfire. Fortunately by that time they were behind a wall of brush, so the firing was not accurate, but some of the whizzing noises in the air indicated bullets that were uncomfortably close. "Go on, follow them! Move it!" came the voice again.

Digger and Joan could hear the labored grunting of someone struggling up the trail when they reached their packs and the rounded mound of snow. Occasional unaimed shots rang out, crackling as they hit the trunks and branches of trees above them. Digger reached under the snow, found what he was looking for, and pulled back a tarp to reveal a sleek black snow machine. He quickly put his pack on over his shoulders so it hung to the front, and hopped on. Joan needed no prompting to sling her pack on her back and grab hold of Digger as the machine roared into life and leapt out of the hole it had been left in. A man rose out of the snow just in front of them as Digger hit the gas and twisted the handle to the right. A single shot rang out, shattering the windshield, then the man disappeared in a cloud of snow. With every bit of power the custom snow machine could muster, Digger piloted them up the trail until a few minutes later they reached the top of the ridge where they had stood on skis just a couple of hours earlier.

He stopped the snowmobile but left the engine running and turned to Joan, "You okay?"

"Yeah, I guess so, you?"

"He blew out a deep breath, "Yeah, I guess, except my pants feel kind of wet."

"Oh no, you didn't... wait, what's that smell?" Joan asked.

Digger felt the pack on his chest and sniffed. "Damn!, I don't believe it!"

"What?"

"Now I'm really ticked off, those assholes just shot our last hot can of hot chocolate!"

With a moment to catch their breath they both looked up at the sky, and said in unison: "Wow!" It was a display of the northern lights such as had never been seen in the living memory of anyone on earth.

CHAPTER 38

George Sherman sat alone in the temporal research lab deep within Quincy mountain, and put down the binder from which he had been reading. The material on the tempiloscope was fragmentary and highly technical, but he was able to gather enough from it to glimpse the capabilities of the technology he was trying to acquire. Still... he could see already that without expert technical help he would be unable to use the tempiloscope in the way he wanted to, in the way he NEEDED to, in order to make this paramilitary foray worth the incredible risk he had taken.

He searched haphazardly through the computer connected to the equipment, but found nothing explanatory... no "readme" files... nothing obvious. Hacking into somebody else's computer was not his special talent, he had other people for that. Sherman was only able to get so far as to turn the system on, and view the control screen on the computer, but what the seven sets of changing numbers might mean, he had no idea. His confidence, however, was still undimmed. He had faced challenges before, and had always overcome them, one way or another.

He opened the locked vault-like door, then closed it behind himself. At the outer door he did likewise, after making sure he still had the key card in his pocket. He jogged the half kilometer down the rough hewn tunnel in the light of the bare hanging bulbs, passing the doors to the various research labs as he went. It had been a brilliant idea to use the mine as company headquarters, he had to admit that. The main tunnels had been driven over a hundred years earlier, in hard stable basalt rock. Further excavations had all been done for free by the university, used as practical experience by classes in mining engineering. It had only been necessary to explain to them the shapes, sizes and locations of the rooms desired. The students did all the work, and were happy to get the chance to play with the drills and explosives. George smiled grimly. "And now, it's mine," he said softly to himself.

When he arrived at the front office he wasn't even breathing hard. One of his men approached him. "Sir?"

"Yes, what is it?"

"Here are the personnel files you asked for, all pertinent data on MMC employees and principals." Sherman quickly scanned the printouts.

"Alright. These two... Puttonen and Dolittle. They are the only ones who can damage us. These others are of little consequence, we'll hire them back if they are willing. I want a team sent out immediately to contain these two." He held up the files describing the personal information on Digger Puttonen and James Dolittle.

"Contain sir?"

"Contain... I do not want them running around loose. If we can capture them alive, they may be a source of useful information. If not, they must be removed permanently. Do you understand?"

"Yes sir. Capture alive if possible, but do not relinquish."

"Correct. Leave the dump truck here, block the driveway with it on your way out. Take one of the company cars out front, look around for keys, hot-wire it if you have to. Take three other men, and take the rocket launcher with you just in case. You have their home addresses, look there first. If you don't find them there, ask the neighbors. Tell them you're from the office of emergency services or some such crap. Then search the place and torch it, we want to limit their scope of movement. Of particular interest are computers and data storage devices. Bring back everything you can find." Sherman unfolded a map. "Go to Puttonen's place first, it's not far away, then try Dolittle's place in Lake Linden. Okay, get moving." Sherman handed the map over, and raised his eyebrows as if asking why the man was still standing there.

"Yes sir. Uh, there are a couple other problems you should be aware of."

"Yes?"

"We have been unable to reestablish contact with Mister Jameson sir. He has not reported in, and there seems to be some sort of interference that has blanked out all our cellular and radio communications. Routine inquiries around town demonstrate that the local hardwired telephone network seems to be intact. When I asked, the operator reported rumors of a severe solar storm. We have not been able to contact our team on the hill above."

"Thank you, I'll deal with it. You get that team together and get moving, I want those two dealt with one way or another before first light."

"Yes sir." The man called out three names. Some other men ran up, and after some quickly issued orders, they were gathering weapons and putting on their winter coats. Within three minutes of Sherman's order the strike team was heading out the door. Sherman called to him two other men who were busy at the computers.

"You two, forget this routine administrative stuff, there's another computer in back that's more important." They raised their eyebrows with interest at what this might be about. Sherman led them through the double doors and jogged down the corridor with the two men at his heels. Their eyes grew wide at the massive size of the doors to the temporal research lab, and the fact that the doors swung inward, apparently designed to withstand force from within, though the locks were on the outside.

He showed them the massive piece of equipment, then the computer console attached to it. "They call it the tempiloscope. This is what we came here for. We have to learn what it does, how it works, and how to use it. There's a binder there giving some elementary directions, and the computer console is the control. Boys, and this is not, repeat NOT a joke... we think it's some sort of time machine." He pointed to one of the men. "You're in charge. You tell Tony what you need, and you'll have it. Find out how we can use this thing, and there will be a big cash bonus in your next pay envelope. I just sent out a team that will try to capture the inventors. If they are successful you may use any means necessary to gain the information you need. For now, I hope that we can figure it out from what's available here. I'll help for a while, but I have other urgent matters to attend to as well."

"Yes Sir, may I ask, why the heavy doors?"

"I hear that they were concerned about the possibility of an explosion of some sort, so be careful."

"Yes sir," the two men chorused, and got busy going over the material in the binder and investigating the computer files. George Sherman walked around the machine and sought to get the feel of it. It consisted of four lobes arranged in a regular tetrahedron. Rectangular stainless steel casings projected from a central focal area on three sides and angled downward away from the center, while a fourth identical module projected straight up, so that the top was almost ten meters above the floor. Heavy cables led from the ends of each of the four lobes to a massive power supply. Sherman examined the service box and was surprised to find a 480 volt supply with 1000 ampere breakers. The massive cable fed into the device from an array of fuel cells in casings against the back of the room. Hydrogen and Oxygen cylinders stood in rows, connected by high pressure manifolds to the devices. A large three pole manual knife switch was mounted on the fuel cell casing. Sherman followed the cable connections and determined that the power was currently coming from a cable that led through a hole drilled in the rock, but could be switched at will to the fuel cells, which convert hydrogen and oxygen to water and electricity.

At the exact center of the tempiloscope itself, at the focus of the four lobes, there sat a clear spherical globe, approximately one meter in diameter. From the four modules, there projected clear glass or crystal cylinders which appeared to be of a piece with the sphere. Except for a portion of the sphere that could be directly viewed from the control panel, the entire central globe appeared to be surrounded by instrumentation of various sorts. Sherman began to examine these. One was obviously a commercial spectral analyzer, at least, this was inscribed on the casing and Sherman had no reason to doubt it. He saw something that looked like a video camera focused at the center of the sphere, and more plates, apertures, and nozzles which he assumed were detectors of various kinds. He traced the cables leading from the various devices, and found that they all converged at a panel directly behind the computer, probably all incoming data was accessible through the software.

He considered the arrangement of elements. Something must take place within the sphere that was at the focus of all the attention. To his dismay he saw that there was no opening of any kind into the clear sphere, it was completely sealed and appeared to be a solid seamless piece. He clicked it with a fingernail and heard a high pitched "clink" response which indicated to him that it was not made of plastic, but something hard, possibly glass or crystal. It appeared to have a wall thickness of at least three centimeters.

The man he had put in charge was just making some systematic forays into the computer, while the other man was making notes on the various screens that were called up. "Look here," said Sherman. "There are detectors arranged around this thing, all cables feeding towards the computer, there should be a way to access some data from these."

"Yes sir, I think you're right. I've got a screen now that asks us whether we want to view data from a test."

"Say yes."

"Now it asks which test number, and offers a list of one through four hundred sixty two."

"Try number five."

A screen appeared with a pull down menu, from which one could choose data from any one of twenty three different instruments, including real time video. "Choose video." Sherman decided.

The screen blanked, then an image of the clear globe appeared. Along the side of it there was a superimposed image of two time strips, with the date, and time, to the tenths of seconds. First the sphere went entirely dark, opaque within. Then a surface appeared near the top and slowly moved down to the center of the globe. It appeared to be the surface of the ground... there was dirt, and a fist sized rock sat serenely at the center. The video ran for some twenty seconds, during which time the view jerkily panned a few meters right to a clump of grass, and then past some dead leaves back to the rock. The image became shaky and disappeared, resulting in a clear globe again.

At the end of the showing they had to choose whether to run the video again, or go back to the former screen. They chose the latter and were popped back to the individual test menu. Sherman pointed to the screen, and chose an entry called "notes". It was a simple text field which contained the words:

"First panned surface image. Spatial control, positive stabilization. Temporal control displays local stability with target accuracy still randomized +/- 33%. Suggest adjust field D plus another 3.5 sec. az."

Sherman shook his head and did not understand the notations, but gathered more from context than some others might. While he was not a technician, he recognized the sort of shorthand that technicians used when discussing their specialties. Sherman next chose "time, location" and read the date that the test had been conducted, and the date represented by the screen image. It was July 12, A.D. 1721, the location was given as 47 degrees, 8 minutes, 2.13 seconds North Latitude, 88 degrees, 33 minutes, 12.65 seconds West Longitude.

Sherman spoke to the men. "Okay guys, looks like we're onto it now. This is what we're looking for, observation of specified location and date. We're going to go through some more of those tests and figure out how to control this thing. I think we'll be able to use it to find out what our enemies are up to." For almost two hours, Sherman reviewed the tests that Digger and company had been conducting for months. He saw the first tests in which humans were observed, the first live images of native American's before the voyage of Christopher Columbus. He saw tests in which the scene never moved, but the time axis was altered, so that a million years of erosion on a rock could be observed in just a few minutes. He found out how to access the detector data, that electromagnetic information could be received including the full spectrum from x-ray to radio, and from the notations he learned that some of these could be used to make exotic inferences about chemistry and temperature which could not be directly measured. He realized the incredible potential the technology offered for pure research, but laughed derisively at the fools who would only have used it for that. George Sherman had much bigger plans... plans involving military secrets, stock and money market manipulation, blackmail, extortion... and if, as he suspected, actual objects or even living persons could be transported... well then... what could stop him?

Finally, it was almost eleven thirty, and Sherman felt they were ready to try to run a new test themselves. He chose "new test" from the main computer menu, and was confronted with a "Password Required, Enter Password Now." message.

"Damn!" He exploded, then calmed himself. "Alright, who's our best man at breaking passwords?" The second man raised his hand, the first nodded agreement. "Okay, you've got his printout, I'll send someone down with a more complete dossier. Try everything, forwards, backwards, combinations. You know the drill."

The two men looked at each other and shrugged, then got to work. This sort of thing could sometimes take a long time. They got out a small and highly illegal device designed especially for such 'breaking and entering' tasks. It could be programmed with any words and numbers known to be associated with a person, and combined them in all possible ways, automatically trying each one until entry was gained. Still, the possibilities were astronomically numerous, and the length of time required to try each of thousands or millions of possibilities could run easily into the tens of hours. It was entirely possible that they would be here all night. Ah well, at least Sherman paid his help well, on time, and in cash. There were few other real benefits to this line of work. The other man reached into his bag and brought out a jar of instant coffee.

Sherman hustled back down the hallway. When he reached the office he yelled, "Tony!"

"Yeah boss?" The heavyset man ran lightly up, moving surprisingly quickly.

"Try Jameson again. I need him." Tony tried.

"Sorry boss, still no luck, haven't heard from either the strike team or the sniper team either, not since we got here, nothing. You think somebody's jamming our com?"

"Let's go outside, maybe it's this rock that's interfering." The look on Tony's face made it obvious that he hadn't thought of that possibility.

The two put on their coats, and without bothering to zip up, passed outside into the bright pool of light under the lamp above the door. Once there, Sherman said to Tony: "Okay, try it again." He did.

"Sorry Mister Sherman, still nothing."

The man who had been guarding the outer door climbed out of a nearby parked car and approached them. Sherman angrily rebuked him for sitting in the car instead of standing out in the snow where he could see and hear better. The guard called Sherman's attention to the northern lights, just visible now as the clouds began to clear. The display was spectacular, but Sherman was unimpressed. At the moment, the event was simply a nuisance, something that prevented effective communication with, and coordination of his forces. He turned to go back inside, and spoke to Tony. "Send a relief team up to the shaft house, I want that area secure."

"Yes sir.", said Tony, as they went back in through the outer door to the office beyond. They bolted the door and left the guard standing dejectedly by the door.

Once inside, George took off his coat and spoke to his associate again. "Take a three man team up there this time. I want the shooter well protected."

It took a just a few minutes for Tony to assemble his team. All of Sherman's men had multiple training backgrounds... they were tough, versatile men who took orders unquestioningly and followed them through. He regretted now his decision to hire those two computer people, those unmentionable cretins who had betrayed him. He had wanted the best, and they had been recommended highly. He mused that sometimes professional brilliance must be sacrificed for loyalty. "Well, Julius will take care of that problem," he said to himself with a wicked smile.

When Tony had his team ready, Sherman said, "Go ahead and take the dump truck this time, that way they'll recognize you more easily. And get back here quick, I don't like having so many people out at one time."

"Yes sir." Tony said, and he led the way out the door for the other three men laden with heavy baggage.

Outside they met the guard, and just after the door closed the guard yelled. "Up there, I heard something!"

Tony looked up the slope to his right but saw nothing for a moment, then caught a glimpse of two shapes struggling through deep snow. "Look, it's two people, sound the alarm!" he yelled.

The guard pulled out his compressed air horn and sounded three blasts. One of the two men at the front gate came running, and then the door clanged open and George Sherman stepped out. The men were struggling to make out the figures in the dim light through the brush and trees to try for a good shot. Sherman yelled "Shoot you fools," and grabbing the guard's weapon, he began shooting roughly in the direction that the fugitives were located. The figures moved beyond a hummock of snow and could no longer be seen from where the men stood. "Go on, follow them!" Sherman yelled. His face was beet-red with rage and frustration as his men struggled with agonizing slowness through the deep snow, shooting wildly ahead of them. He heard the roar of a snowmobile engine, one final shot, then the whine of the snow machine being ridden away up the hill.

"Tony's down! " came a shout from above, followed by... "They left some skis, and poles."

Sherman climbed up the hillside, the going a little easier now that the trail was somewhat broken. The three members of his team were preparing to carry Tony back down the hill. He had a nasty compound fracture of the right femur from being run over by the snowmobile. Tony gritted his teeth but refused to cry out.

"Did you see them?" asked Sherman when he reached Tony's side.

"Yeah, two people, a man and woman. I shot the guy point blank, right in the chest. I got him sir."

"Okay son, take it easy." He motioned for the three to go ahead and carry Tony down. Sherman looked at the skis lying in the snow, then followed the side trail to a place where two people had been sitting comfortably on a foam mat, apparently for quite some time. He picked up a can from the snow, sniffed it, was evidently surprised, then put it in his pocket. The other two men came slowly up the trail. "Bring all this, and anything else you find," he said to them. They quickly gathered the items, even finding the second can, and then started back down. Sherman could still barely hear the snowmobile fighting its way up the hill above, the sound was now mingled with a police siren approaching from below. George Sherman began to shiver slightly, though with his face in darkness it could not be told whether he was simply cold because of his lack of a coat, or whether it was a seething rage that made his body shake. He stomped back down the trail towards the door leading to, deep, dark places, far underground.

CHAPTER 39

Agent Fred Samuels drove the black Humvee up Quincy hill with the two agents from Marquette riding along. Frank Giacoletti sat tensely in the front seat, while Jimmy Canaris rode in back with a black nylon bag and an exceptionally long fiberglass case. As they passed the old Quincy #2 shaft house at the top of the hill, Jimmy rolled down the window and peered upwards through a device that looked like a short, fat, telescope.

"Can you slow down a little," he said.

"Not too much without looking obvious," replied Samuels.

"Okay, whatever you can give me. I think I'm getting something, but I'm not sure."

They passed the shaft house and started down the long gentle slope on the north side. Jimmy turned around in his seat to try to look backward at the old mine building. The shaft house was over forty meters tall, tall enough to house the giant pulleys that guided the cables from the steam hoist located a hundred meters to the east. It had been restored somewhat for the benefit of the tourist trade, but of course, the cables currently in place didn't really do anything except look good. The shaft itself was not quite vertical, and was wide enough for two parallel elevators that rolled up and down the steep shaft on rails. In the old days, one full ore car would come up as an empty one went down, minimizing the effort required by the hoist. The full ones would rise up into the shaft house, then empty copper ore directly into a rail car that would pull in below. Once or twice a day the lift operators would replace the ore car with a bailer and pull a bucket of water out of the sump at the bottom of the shaft. A with a slowly sinking ship, water was always trying to get in, and usually found a way. The shaft house looked rather a lot like a square silo, except for the west side, which sloped down at an angle of fifty five degrees to the ground surface... the angle of the shaft itself. Through Jimmy's thermal infrared scope the shaft house appeared as a dark mass, as cold as the surrounding air. But in one of the upper windows, right near the top, there was just a hint of brightness. He looked again. Yes... definitely... there was a source of heat up near the top of the building. He put down the scope and looked around with a knowing eye. He concluded that the window commanded a wide view of the northern approach. Other windows on the upper level catwalk probably commanded similar areas in other directions.

"Yep, we got a target in the top of the building alright," he said aloud. "It's a damn good spot too. He could probably pick off anything up to two klicks away with a good rifle."

"Well," said Frank, "let's not give him the chance."

"What's all the steam?" Jimmy asked, looking at a billowing white cloud rising into the air near the road.

"That's one of the other old shafts." Samuels answered. "The number two is the only shaft house that's been restored. The shafts blow steam in winter because the air below is warm and moist. There's a natural air circulation between them underground. Some of them are downdrafts, you don't see those, others are updrafts, and form that cloud when the outside air is cold enough."

They drove to the first turnoff on the right leading to Paavola, drove the half mile or so to the little village, then turned left on the second side street. There were houses along the left hand side of the street, none on the right. "There's the Cherokee," Samuels said, "looks like Justin and Stephen are still in it."

"And a little further down is the older model maroon car which that guard Aaron mentioned," said Jimmy.

"Maybe. The description wasn't precise," Samuels replied. "What is that, an old Nova?"

"Yeah," Frank said. "I'm pretty sure it is. It's got that characteristic scooped back window."

They cruised past the Cherokee, made certain the men inside recognized their captain, then pulled in behind them, back to back, and shut down the engine and lights. Samuels got out first to talk to the men, who were parked two doors north of the house which was under surveillance. Frank and Jimmy got out of the hummer and walked up to the passenger's side of the Jeep four by four. The two young men got out of their vehicle, and introductions were made all around.

"We were pretty worried sir," said Justin to Samuels, after he'd shaken gloved hands with Frank and Jimmy. "When we couldn't get through to you, we were afraid something had happened down there, but when we tried the commercial radio and couldn't get anything there either, we assumed there was some sort of EM interference. Stephen had a copy of this morning's paper which mentioned something about a solar storm and possible transmission problems."

"Yeah," added Stephen. "Aside from this old Chevy Nova belonging to a Joan Niemi of Chassell," he indicated it with a thumb over his shoulder, "that pulled in about two or so, and a couple of obvious locals coming home from work, not a single car has come by, the only activity has been some local kids playing in the snow, digging tunnels. We weren't sure how long you wanted us to keep up this stakeout. Besides, we're pretty obvious sitting out here like this."

"Not to worry boys, we're here to call you off and fill you in," said Samuels. "You're right, there's some serious radio interference all over, but that's the least of our problems. The case has taken a more serious turn. We'll tell you all about it back at the office, but a team of mercenaries came in through the airport today, and took over Midnight Mining Company, possibly with as many as thirty men."

"What?" Justin and Stephen chorused in disbelief.

"I'm quite serious. They appear to have seized control of the offices, and now we're pretty sure they have a sniper up on the number two shaft house as well. We can't get any State or Federation help for at least a week. It probably has something to do with this guy Puttonen, but we can't afford to wait around and find out. So drive on back to the office, we'll follow you. Try not to draw attention to yourself as you pass the shaft house."

The five men had just gotten into the two vehicles when another car slowly turned the corner and approached toward the Jeep. It stopped directly in front of Digger Puttonen's house, about forty meters away, and shut off the headlights. The FBI men ducked down in their seats and delayed starting their vehicles while they looked at the car, a late model Ford Taurus. Four men emerged from it, all dressed in black fatigues and heavily armed. One of them propped his weapon up on the roof of his car, facing the house, while the other three went to the neighboring houses, first on the left, then the right. Both houses were unoccupied and showed no signs of shoveling or others disturbance of the heavy snow leading towards the front doors. They then regrouped and ran directly for the front door of Digger Puttonen's house bashing it in with a sledgehammer and entering almost without slowing down.

"What the hell?" said Samuels.

Frank answered, "I guess somebody else wants this guy even more than we do. Looks like it's time to lock and load." The three in the hummer drew and checked their weapons, then at a signal from Frank, they jumped out of three doors at once. Justin and Stephen took the cue and followed suit a moment later. They all aimed at the man covering the house from the car.

"FBI!" yelled Samuels. "Freeze."

Instead of obeying, the man's reaction was to turn and immediately begin firing his weapon in their direction. Frank stood his ground and returned rapid fire from his pistol. Jimmy dived over the snowbank and returned fire from a prone position. The other three took whatever cover they could find behind the Jeep

Cherokee and began shooting. The man dived behind the car for cover, so they had a brief respite.

Jimmy yelled, "The house!" Three men burst from the house and fired weapons as they ran towards their car. Frank was caught in the open on the driver's side of the hummer. After his last shot, the slide had locked back, indicating an empty clip. With no time to reload, he turned to dive for cover behind the Jeep, but a short burst from one of the assailants stitched him up his right leg and side. He fell in between the cars with a cry.

Jimmy's ears were ringing from the cacophony of gunfire and Frank's cry. The stench of powder burned in his nostrils as Jimmy reloaded his weapon and fired slowly with careful and deliberate aim. One of the assailants went down. Another brought a long tube out of the car and set it on his shoulder. The other two continued to fire sporadically. Glass shattered, the thunk of bullets hitting metal was all around them. "Rocket launcher!" yelled Jimmy as he realized what the long tube represented. As one person, the FBI men still on their feet dived into the snowbank. But the shooter turned the weapon away from them, towards the house, touched the contact, and there was a whooshing noise followed immediately by a tremendous explosion that sent a plume of fire up into the sky, lighting up the scene as with daylight for a moment. The three remaining assailants then jumped into their car and tried to make their escape. Justin and Samuels kept firing, Stephen was down but still moving. Two of the attackers were shooting wildly out the windows of the car while third apparently was reloading the rocket launcher. Jimmy dropped his empty pistol and jumped down from the snowbank. Samuels apparently hit the man with the rocket launcher through the shattered windshield as they started backwards to try to escape. The launcher dropped to the street. Jimmy jerked open the tailgate of the hummer, reached the fiberglass case, flipped the catches and quickly brought out the big Barrett .50 caliber bolt action rifle. He chose a cartridge that was almost as large as a small banana, with an orange painted tip. The car was almost to the corner now, nearly a hundred meters away, trying to turn around. Jimmy chambered the cartridge and propped the rifle on the roof of the Jeep. He thought briefly about the location of the gas tank on a Taurus, aimed carefully, and gently squeezed the trigger. Snow leapt off the surface of the vehicle from the shock wave that followed the firing of the weapon, and Jimmy was knocked backward into the hummer by the tremendous recoil. At the end of the street, the Ford Taurus exploded in a ball of fire and slowly rolled backward into the snowbank. Justin ran down the street with gun at the ready to check out the one man laying in the snow, and the fate of the others in the car. Jimmy left the Barrett on the roof of the Jeep and knelt down by Frank, who groaned.

"Hey cap'n, how you doing?" he asked gently.

"Oh, it's you."

"Yeah, can you tell me where it hurts?"

"Uh, my leg."

"Yep, doesn't look too bad though." Jimmy slit open Franks pants leg with his knife and looked at his wounds by the light of the blue-white street lamp and the flickering yellow light of Digger's house burning. He was dismayed at the pulsating flow of blood and the odd angle the leg was lying at. He kept his voice light. "Anyplace else?"

"Uh, my side." Frank began to shiver.

"Yeah, you'll have a couple of nice bruises. Good thing you had your vest on sir. Could have been a lot worse." He grabbed a blanket out of the back of the hummer to help keep Frank warm, then quickly pulled his own belt off, and cinched it as tight as he could around Frank's upper thigh balling up his glove under it to put pressure on the femoral artery. "I'll be back in a second sir. Don't go away now." He was relieved to hear Frank snort with amusement at the remark.

People were starting to step out onto their porches, but Jimmy ignored them. He ran around to the driver's side of the Jeep. Samuels was tending Stephen, who had been hit in the right arm and cheek. "How's he doing?"

"Not too bad, what about Frank?"

"His vest stopped two to the torso, but he's got three to the upper leg, I think one of them hit the femur and nicked the femoral artery. There's a lot of blood. I don't think we have time to get to the hospital." He ran back to Frank and kneeled down.

"May I help?" said a voice from behind him. He turned and saw a middle aged woman carrying a stretcher. "My name is Ruth, I'm an EMT. What happened?" Jimmy explained the situation quickly and showed her the wounds. She nodded. "We've got to get him inside, right away." She laid the stretcher on the ground. She ran around to where Samuels knelt by Stephen, and looked him over and agreed that his wounds were not life threatening. "Could you help us please?" she said to Samuels. Justin returned, laid the rocket launcher on the ground, and sat by Stephen, who was sitting up by then, as Samuels followed Ruth to the back of the hummer.

"Okay, lift together... careful with the leg. That's it. Alright, take him into my house, right there, with the light on. We'll call an ambulance from there." Samuels and Jimmy picked up the stretcher and started walking slowly towards the house. Ruth ran to check on the progress of Stephen and Justin, who were walking. Jimmy noticed, without really thinking about it, that the old maroon Chevrolet Nova sat parked in front of the house they were heading for.

As they entered the house they were met by a very excited black Labrador, Ruth led it by the collar into another room, then closed the door. The she went immediately to the kitchen and picked up the phone and dialed 9-1-1. "Yes, we need an ambulance immediately at number 45 Mineral Street in Paavola, two injured.... What do you mean you... Yes I know that the radios are not working....

Yes.... multiple gunshot wounds..... Yes, the police are here now, it's two of them that have been shot..... Yes we'd appreciate that very much.... yes that's the number."

She turned around and with a worried expression knelt down by Frank and examined the wound again. "What news?" asked Jimmy. He did not need to be told it was not good news, her expression and the audible part of the conversation conveyed that much quite clearly.

"Busy night I guess, both ambulances are already out, they can't contact them without radio, so they'll have to wait until one comes in, it will probably be at least an hour. And no, before you ask, I don't think we should try to take him in ourselves, too risky."

An elderly man bustled into the room with a pan of hot soapy water and some cloths. He stopped to turn the thermostat on the wall up several degrees. The soap made a bright purplish foam and smelled strongly of disinfectant. Without explanation he began gently but professionally washing blood away from the Frank's wounds so that Ruth could see them. She loosened the belt for a moment, then tightened it when blood began pulsing through one of the wounds. Frank began to shiver again, gritted his teeth and tried to bear the pain. Ruth tore open a package of sterile gauze pads, lay several on the entry and exit wounds, then carefully slipped a wide, stiff, nylon band under the leg, cinching it down tightly with velcro straps. "He'll be okay for a while," She said quietly to Samuels and Jimmy by the kitchen door. "He needs hospital care for that leg, probably some surgical reconstruction of the shattered bone, but the blood loss is at a minimum now."

"What about the tourniquet?", asked Jimmy.

"It's not too tight, don't worry, you did it just right. I guarantee he won't lose the leg." Samuels looked towards Stephen, sitting in a chair cradling his arm while Justin held a scarf to his cheek.

"What about this guy?", he asked.

"Looks like a nasty slice on the cheek, close call but not serious, and the arm is okay, no bone involved." The old man moved to Stephen and helped put clean dressings on his wounds.

Justin spoke to Samuels. "Sir, all the perps are accounted for."

"Okay, thanks." Samuels started to turn towards the door, then hesitated.

Ruth noticed. "Look, you guys do whatever you need to do, we'll take care of your friends until the ambulance comes, okay?"

Jimmy knelt down by Frank's side. "Captain?" Frank opened his eyes, they seemed to have difficulty focusing, the shivering had subsided as the room warmed up. "We have to leave now, you'll be okay. You're not hurt bad, but an ambulance is coming to get you fixed up. I'll come see you later to let you know what's happening." He patted Frank gently on the chest as he lay quietly on the stretcher, and felt something in his coat pocket. Jimmy unzipped the pocket and retrieved a small round pebble with a mottled blood-red color. He placed it in Frank's right hand. Frank gripped it tightly and seemed to relax a little.

"Go on, shoo. Go shoot somebody, or whatever it is you guys do." Ruth waved Frank, Jimmy, and Justin out the door.

They looked down the street to the car, still smoldering, The house, still burning brightly, and at the body still lying in the snow. When they got to the street they checked out their vehicles. The Jeep Cherokee had taken the brunt of the assault. Every window was broken, and numerous bullets had damaged critical engine components. Both the radiator and battery were dripping fluids into the snow. Three of the four wheels sat with the rims pressed into the packed snow on the street, the tires hopelessly torn by bullets. The hummer had survived somewhat better. The driver's side windows had been shattered, and there were multiple bullet holes in the body panels and upholstery, but only one tire was flat and there was no damage to the engine or running gear.

Justin got to work quickly to change the flat tire, while Samuels and Jimmy searched the body lying in the street for any identification. They found only a weapons belt and a wallet with eight different ID cards, proclaiming the man to be Carlos Ruiz, and variously a member of several different law enforcement and public safety organizations, including the Marquette branch of the FBI. They moved him out of the street onto the snowbank, then returned to the hummer, now ready to roll. The snowfall was beginning to pick up again as the two local men got in. As Samuels was getting into the driver's seat, Jimmy took the Barrett down from the roof of the wrecked Jeep and inserted a big clip bearing five rounds into the receiver. He operated the long bolt to eject the spent round and chamber a new one. He then lay the rifle down in its case in the back of the hummer without latching the case shut. He slammed the back door shut as Samuels started up the engine, and then Jimmy jumped into the back seat behind Justin. The hummer passed the still smoldering Taurus slowly, then speeded up, leaving the scene of destruction behind. Just after they turned left on the highway they pulled over to make way for a hook and ladder truck hurrying towards them with lights on and siren blaring. It turned towards the visible flickering glow.

Frank lay on the stretcher in Ruth's house, his mind fuzzy from loss of blood. He vaguely knew that he'd been injured, but was unable t recall at the moment just what had happened. He felt something in his right hand, opened it and saw the pebble that lay there. He heard a voice in his mind echoing softly... "and for you, this stone of wisdom. When the choice is hard and the way unclear, this will help you..." He clutched it tightly and felt the fuzziness in his mind seem to lessen.

An old man's face looked down into his. "Hey dere guy, you're gonna be okay. We got da best people right here. Ruth gonna take care of ya 'til da ambulance come." Frank looked into that friendly face, heard the voice and seemed to recognize it, though he knew it was nobody he'd ever met face to face.

"Who are you?"

"Me? I'm nobody, jus' an old man helpin' a young buck who's gone and got hisself shot in da leg. Doan worry, I done dis sorta ting lotsa times in da war. You'll be okay."

"No, I recognize you from somewhere. Your voice...." He reached out dreamily towards the face with his right hand, and dropped the pebble, which bounced off his coat onto the floor.

"What you got dere?" asked the old man, picking it up. "Ah, a piece o' datolite, that's what it is. Hey, nice one too. You better hang on to dat, bring you good luck." He put it into Frank's hand again, closed the hand about the stone, and winked in a friendly way. Suddenly Frank gave a start.

"You're Arne. Arne Harjaala. You were with Teddy Roosevelt at San Juan Hill, that's what you said."

Arne smiled. "Son, you figgered me out. Ya, I was da cook wit' Teddy, but I doctored too, dat's what cooks did in them days. So you jus' relax and let ol' Arne take care of it. Doan worry 'bout a t'ing now. Just hold tight to your pebble and t'ink about when you were a kid, playin' in the water on a hot day."

"We were trying to find you... and Digger. Something's happened.... Sherman...." Frank tried to sit up and grimaced with the pain.

"You just lie still now. You let Ruth and Arne worry about it."

Frank relaxed and closed his eyes; Arne exchanged a worried glance with Ruth. Stephen was resting comfortably. How long would it be before the ambulance came? That was the question that occupied the minds of both Ruth and Arne, though Arne wondered too, about this man, and what they wanted with him. Frank fell asleep clutching the datolite pebble to his chest.

CHAPTER 40

Leonard Howarth sat at the table in the Hancock Michigan FBI office and looked hard at Jason Desnick. The content analyzer which sat on the desk before him was a tiny device, but extremely sophisticated, determining shades of truth and falsehood in spoken testimony. It was still an experimental technique, but one which Leonard believed in wholeheartedly. "State your name please."

"My name is Jason Everett Desnick."

"Could you please tell us where and when you were born?"

"Yes sir. I was born in Rio De Janeiro, in what was then the nation of Brazil, in 1986."

"What is your relationship with the FBI?"

"I was recruited as a freshman psychology student in college at Northern Michigan University in Marquette... that would have been in 2003. I attended the academy for two years after college, then served at posts in Philly, Dallas, Little Rock, and Spokane, before being sent to the Twin Cities."

"Are you a loyal agent of the FBI Jason?"

"Yes sir."

"Are you a member of any other organizations?"

"Yes sir."

"Such as?"

"I belong to a book club, a trails advisory council, The National Geographic Society...."

"I'm sorry, I should have been more specific," Leonard interrupted. "Are you a member of any military, paramilitary or political organizations that could have prior claim on your loyalty, superseding that to the FBI?"

Jason hesitated a moment. "Yes sir." Leonard looked very self-satisfied.

"Would you please describe the organization?"

"Sir, I must inform you that I am not authorized to reveal this information. I can tell you that the organization in question is a legitimate entity, and that we work tirelessly for the good of all mankind."

"Don't give me that crap!" exploded Leonard. "Any member of any two-bit terrorist cell would spout the same nonsense. You'd better come clean mister, or you're going to be in chains before you can blink."

Jason started to speak, then stopped as if listening. After a moment he continued. "I have just been authorized to divulge this information to you, on the condition that you pledge secrecy. I will first make a generalized statement. If you refuse to accept confidentiality after that, I must cease my disclosure. Agreed?"

"Go on."

"Very well, I provisionally accept that as a tacit agreement. I am a member of UNEC, the United Nations Environmental Command. I was recruited to the organization as a child of five, an orphan. I was brought up to consider myself a citizen of the world, not merely any one territorial nation or confederacy of nations, neither do I owe allegiance to any racial or ethnic group. The existence of UNEC is a matter of some secrecy, however the Prime Minister of the Federation and her close advisors, including our esteemed director, have direct knowledge of UNEC, it's purposes, policies, and functions. The director has full knowledge of my position within the FBI, in which I performed my duties as a fully functional agent, while awaiting my more important assignment."

"And what was this 'important' assignment?"

"Why, sir... to accompany you, here... on this mission."

"Oh, really? And what is your specific function on this assignment?"

"Sir, I am instructed that I have now reached the limit of my revelatory authorization, without first receiving your solemn pledge of secrecy. If I divulge this information, you will henceforth consider yourself recruited to UNEC, as you recently recruited me to SIB."

"Son, I'm asking the questions, and I have no intention...."

Jason Interrupted him. "You may, of course, confirm the generalities with the director personally."

"You must be joking. It's impossible, and you know it, to speak directly with the director of the Federation Bureau of Investigation. There is an intervening bureaucracy that is virtually interminable, believe me, I've tried."

"Sir, you need only mention this week's code word "Agamemnon," and you will be connected directly."

"You? You have the code word?"

"I have never used it."

Leonard considered. "And what of these others?" He indicated Chris and Harry.

"I have already revealed myself to Chris, I have no fear on his part. Harry, in case you have never noticed, is fiercely loyal to you. If you agree, I can take it as given that he agrees as well. Will you keep the secret?"

"And I can call the director to confirm this?"

"Yes sir, any time until noon eastern standard time on Sunday, when the code word will be changed."

"Alright. Contingent on the fact that I do get confirmation of the truth of what you're telling me, I do so pledge. Please continue."

"Thank you sir. UNEC was founded in the mid 1990's when it became apparent to some that global warming, ozone depletion, and environmental degradation had become the greatest threats humanity had ever encountered, possibly eclipsing even the specter of nuclear war. Yet this threat was mostly ignored by the political power structures of virtually every nation due to the limited time scale on which planning was done, and due to their parochially local viewpoints. Therefore UNEC was set up as an entity which could take covert action anywhere in the world for the specific purpose of improving the human condition through environmental enhancement. A plan was devised whereby agents, acting as UN relief workers in trouble spots around the world, would pick the brightest orphaned street children, under six years of age, and adopt them into stable families. They would be carefully indoctrinated to a word viewpoint, without specific national loyalty. As a side benefit of this program, it turned out that this selection process tended also to select those with high psychic potential."

"What?" gasped Leonard. "You mean there's a psychic dimension to this? But that's what I've been...."

"Precisely, the director allowed the formation of the SIB on the direct request of UNEC's "first speaker" as an unwitting adjunct to UNEC activities within Federation territory. Your higher purpose was to serve as a lightning rod, if you will... to focus attention to areas which deserve it, for you must understand that our people are spread very thin indeed. For this reason I was assigned to accompany you, and I would have found a way to do this even if the storm had not providentially made it a simple matter. I was flattered that you came to like me on your own, and recruited me to the SIB, though I would have preferred to have kept my UNEC ties secret for a while yet."

"Then why didn't you lie?"

Jason paused before speaking. "Sir, you should begin to realize, after all the research that you've done. Psychic ability is both learned and natural, like, for instance, ability in mathematics. There are specialties within the discipline, and many gradations of ability. But as with most things, for every gain there is a corresponding loss. Telepathy is the ability to attune the mind to recognize extremely delicate currents of thought that, for most people, go completely unrecognized. Such attunement makes it virtually impossible for the adept to tell a deliberate falsehood. For a functional psychic, telling a lie would be akin to placing a dam across a smoothly flowing stream. The currents of thought would thereby be hopelessly disrupted. For a true adept, even the attempt to do so would be virtually suicidal on a mind level."

Leonard looked searchingly at Jason before responding. "So, you have placed a network of psychics around the world, loyal only to the UN, and dedicated to saving the environment?"

"Precisely so, and the effort has not been entirely unsuccessful. The achievement of population stability by 2010 was largely due to UNEC's efforts."

"What do you mean? It's common knowledge that this was the result of biomedical advances in fertility control."

"Yes of course, that was the method. But if you were to obtain confidential files of the people directly involved you might find that there are certain leaps of knowledge that are unexplained by their experimental method. And too, didn't it seem just a little unusual that the plan was accepted so easily, even by the fundamentalist religious regimes. A great deal of effort was quietly expended behind the scenes to facilitate this result. Do you understand?"

"Yes, I think so. But what about now, what are you doing here? What has our situation here today got to do with any of that?"

"Ah. I don't have all the details of course, but I can tell you that a detailed analysis was made which indicated that this Midnight Mining Company had made an unexpected, yet absolutely fundamental, technological breakthrough. Their work will undoubtedly prove to be as world changing as that of Thomas Edison, Marie Curie, Nikolai Tesla, or any of many others whom history has shown to be technologically pivotal. It has also been projected that, for the change to be of positive benefit, the company MUST remain free and independent, accessible to the open marketplace. If any corporate or nationalistic entity were to gain control of it, the effect would ultimately be environmental destruction on an epic scale. So you see. It is no small matter at all, that George Sherman has physically taken control of the company. We are quite literally fighting here for the fate of the world."

"And you alone were sent here to prevent that?"

"Oh no, I am not alone. I have never been alone, though please understand that I am not at liberty, even now, to reveal names. You do not have, as they say, a 'need to know' at the present time."

"I see. I'm curious though, how are the various psychic abilities of agents classified and managed?"

"A summer camp is arranged for the recruited children that I described. I, for instance, was picked up on the streets of Rio when I was five years old, and raised with a family in Ontario. At the age of 13 or 14 such children are sent to a special summer camp, whose location I cannot reveal, where they engage in a series of specialized "games". The function of these games is to evaluate the natural abilities of the children, and enable their foster parents to plan for future development. Abilities are rated from zero to one, with zero being no ability at all, and one being full conscious control. Telepathic, telekinetic, empathic, precognizant, and remote viewing abilities are evaluated, and the strongest abilities enhanced through training."

Leonard considered. "I noticed you included empathic ability in that group. I am familiar with the others of course, but empathy, of what possible use is that to the UN?"

"Much use indeed sir. It is the only one of the psychic abilities which impinges on the emotions. It can be very useful in a tense situation, to soothe anger or resentment. Adept empaths are able to sense intense emotion. As I'm sure you know, communication between people is difficult if one does not understand the feelings of the other. An empath understands, and can sometimes act, with words, or direct mental therapy, to heal emotional wounds. Most conflict results from on or both parties reacting to emotional stress. Such wounds may fester for decades without external assistance."

"Emotional wounds?"

"Of course, we all have them, to greater or lesser degrees."

"I see." Leonard seemed to relax and accept these statements matter-of-factly. "Jason, can you tell me what your abilities are rated? Do you know? Are you given access to your own assessment?"

"Yes sir. Precognizance point two, empathos point seven, telekinesis point four. Other abilities stand at point one or below."

"Empathos point seven?"

"Yes sir."

"Is that high?"

"It's considered very high for a male sir, most adept empaths are women."

"And have you used any of your special abilities on this assignment since we met?"

"Yes sir."

"Could you please tell me when?"

"The first time was with our new friend Chris Jameson. The specifics are quite personal, and are not for me to reveal. If Chris wishes to discuss them, that is his choice. We met in the parking lot of that diner in Rhinelander, I strongly sensed a deep inner pain, and I simply reached out and opened a closed door a tiny crack in order to release that pain. That, at least, that is how it seems to me, it is a difficult experience to describe."

"And did you know at that time that he had any connection with our business here?"

"No sir. That came as a complete surprise to me."

"You simply performed this function as a routine action?"

"I'm sorry, there is nothing routine about it. It is simply my ability, my training, it is what I'm for, if you will. Like a doctor reacts to an accident to heal the body, I react when I sense emotional pain. Yet sometimes, I myself wonder, in situations like this, if some other will is not involved."

"Yet because of your action Chris has come to us in the nick of time with crucial information?" Jason shrugged and turned to Chris.

Chris spoke up. "I can't explain it really. I was thinking about something, something that happened a long time ago, something that has haunted my dreams and even my waking mind. Perhaps I can tell you about it, later, not now, not yet. I was simply walking to my car, and this young man here smiled and said a few words to me. They must have been exactly the words I needed to hear. In an instant, the entire world changed for me. It took hours to work out what it all meant, but it led me here. So, I guess you might say.... well, you can say whatever you want. All I know is, here I am, and here is where I want to be, where I need to be right now."

Leonard nodded and looked tired, as if he finally understood something that he'd been battering his head over for ages. "And the girl in the diner, the waitress?" He sighed.

Jason looked a little embarrassed. "Yeah, that too. I couldn't help myself. I try not to get involved sometimes, but then there she was, and it only took a word or two. It's as if you saw someone walking along with a dislocated shoulder, in terrible pain, but simply accepting it as their lot. With a simple push you can resocket the joint. It takes little or nothing, but to the recipient it means everything. Sometimes people are so close to realizing something important, they just need the tiniest of nudges."

"I see, any others?"

"Just the one."

"The one?"

Harry spoke up. "You and agent Giacoletti sir. Remember when he first arrived, you were ready to throw him out the window? Then all of a sudden you're good buddies? After Chris came in, I started wondering about Jason. The coincidences seemed unbelievable. Then when you changed your attitude, I knew."

"I'm sorry sir... I...", Jason stammered.

"You tampered with my mind?" Leonard stood up, glaring angrily.

"No sir, not really, just your emotions. Think about it. You had wrapped your pain and anguish about the incident in Detroit around your image of Frank Giacoletti. He then represented all your pain to you, which was a convenient way to keep it in a discrete package and deal with it. It might have been easier to keep you apart for a while longer, but we HAD to have you get along sir, it was crucial to the mission. All I did was detach your pain from your concept of Frank in your emotional center, your mind did the rest, I promise. In your heart you really loved Frank, I just helped you to see that, though I would rather you never knew that I had anything to do with it. It really changes nothing though, your relationship is healed and can never be broken again. By the way, Harry is rather good at this, don't you think?"

Leonard had sat down again while Jason was talking and lay his head on his hands on the table. He looked up. "So, what are you now? FBI or UNEC?"

"Both sir, now and always."

"Who is in command?"

"You are sir, though I hope that you will seriously consider my advice when offered on matters of my, er... specialty."

"Do you have any suggestions as to our present action?"

"Don't you want to call the director before you ask that?"

"No son, I don't think I need to. My making up with Frank after all these years is all the proof I need."

Jason nodded in appreciation. "One more thing you should realize sir," he added. "These abilities are strengthened by the physical proximity of two or more psychic adepts. I think you were on the verge of realizing that in your research, but I can give you the equations to calculate the effect if you like. If we can link up with others, whether UNEC or not, we will have a lot more potential at our command. Remember also that it can sometimes be used for communication purposes, which may be especially useful with the solar storm. Unfortunately I am not as good at transmitting telepathically as I am at receiving, which is why my telepathy rating is very low."

Leonard looked at Harry. "All these years we've been running around looking, and these guys were there the whole time, playing us like marionettes on a string." Harry looked worried, as if he expected Leonard to explode in anger. But Leonard did not explode, instead he started chuckling, then guffawing. He was almost falling off his chair when he got up, slapped Jason on the back, and said, "Damn, that's just about the funniest thing I've ever heard of. Okay kid, we'll play it from here. Looks like we've got more muscle on our side of the court than I thought, glad to hear it. But I was asking what you, or UNEC , thought should be the next move. Got any ideas?"

"Not much. I feel we've got to dislodge Sherman before he gains complete control, or we won't be able to, he will be able to use blackmail at high levels to prevent any military moves. We also need desperately to connect with this Puttonen fellow. Your intuition was 100% right on that one, he is the key. He is certainly psychic to some degree, though untested and suspicious of our motives.

Also, our friend Chris here is crucial, though I'm not yet sure why. All I know with respect to him is that I see disaster looming if he is locked up now."

"But what choice do we have? He has confessed to committing murder. We can't just let him go, and we don't have the manpower to have somebody watch him all the time."

"All I know is what I see, sir, but isn't it just possible that we might just happen to be looking the other way, and that he might just happen to walk out the door. After all, if he's not back in a couple of days we can always put out an APB on him."

Leonard shook his head. "Son, I don't know why, but I believe you, come on, let's go get a cup of coffee, I have a feeling it's gonna be a long night."

Harry, Jason and Leonard got up and walked out of the room towards the break room where the coffee machine was. On the way out they each touched or patted Chris on the shoulder. He got an incredibly warm feeling from their touch, a feeling of true friendship, a feeling he had not had in ages it seemed. He noticed that there was nobody in the office for the moment, shrugged his shoulders and decided to take the hint. He put on his coat and simply walked out into the night. The snow was falling gently now, the stuff on the ground lay sparkling in the light from above the door. He got into his car and drove out of the parking lot, steering aimlessly for the center of town. Not knowing what else to do he headed for the lift bridge towards Houghton. As he passed over the canal he noticed the protesters still there, holding their signs. They had not blocked off the bridge, at least not yet, but they had established a presence there. He drove into Houghton, swung around on Montezuma and back down Shelden to the west. He saw nothing of interest downtown, so he decided to make the circuit again. On reaching the end of Montezuma, he headed east towards Michigan Tech, saw nothing there, and turned around in the parking lot at Coed Hall. He headed back downtown again, cruising slowly down Shelden Avenue, looking for something, he knew not what. As he neared the Copper Crown hotel, he decided to turn downhill towards the waterfront and cruise through the covered parking area the city had built there some years ago. He drove down into it, his tires touching dry pavement for the first time in days, and went up and down the rows of cars, looking at them idly. One license plate caught his eye, it was from Illinois, the number seemed somehow familiar. It was a rather inconspicuous car, a gray Toyota Millennium, model year between 2012 and 2015. His eyes narrowed. It was, in fact, conspicuously inconspicuous. That particular model had changed very little over several years and had sold well. Gray was the fashionable color these days. He stopped and got out, looking around to see if anyone was looking. He got out a flashlight and approached the car, being careful not to touch it in any way, many of these had alarm systems built into them. The car looked rather ordinary within, the remnants of a sandwich, crackers, grapes, and cheese on the floor, and an empty bottle of juice on the seat. On the floor of the back seat there was a styrofoam cooler, a piece of white plastic tubing, an air cylinder, and a plastic bag bearing the name of a hardware store in Milwaukee. He walked back to his Jeep and got in. Something about the car stirred a memory, but he couldn't quite place it. Wait! That was it! Two weeks earlier, the last time he'd been called to a 'board meeting' at Sherman's headquarters... he had parked in the executive lot, and that car had been there. He knew it for sure now... he could see it in his mind, the exact license number, TWP 1079. Whose could it be? He was not sure, but it seemed likely it was one of the other 'board' members. If this was so, they could only be up to no good. It was even possible... no he scarcely dared hope. But yet, it was just possible it could even be Miller. And if Miller were here, that could only mean.... He smiled grimly to himself, drove across the lot to a vacant spot from which he could just see the Toyota, and wrapped himself in a blanket. He was prepared to wait as long as necessary. Unfortunately, beneath the concrete roof, Chris could not see the incredible display that the aurora borealis gave that night after the clouds blew away. But he had other things on his mind.

Leonard sat at the table with Harry and Jason and finished their coffee. Jason got up and walked out into the office. Leonard called out after him, "Is he gone?"

Jason looked out into the parking lot. "Yeah."

"I hope you're right about him," said Leonard, "he's a dangerous man."

"Don't worry," Jason answered, staring out into the night. "He may be dangerous, but I don't think we're the ones that have anything to fear from him. Oh! here's the hummer!" Jason heard Harry and Leonard get up, but kept looking out the window. He had a bad feeling. "Driver's side windows are broken, and I don't like the looks on their faces... Frank's not with them. I think there's trouble," he said aloud. Jimmy hurried in the door, behind him came Samuels and Justin, stomping snow off their boots.

Leonard took one look at the three of them, noted the torn and soiled coats, minor facial scratches, and general bedraggled look. "What the hell happened to you? Where's Frank?"

Samuels clapped a hand on his shoulder. "We've just been in a bad firefight, four men came to Puttonen's house while we were there. They're all dead. Frank and Stephen were hurt."

"Hurt? How bad? Where are they?" asked Leonard.

"Relax, not too seriously. Frank got it worst, three hits to the upper leg, one pretty bad, probably hit the femur. With the radios the way they are we couldn't get an ambulance up there, and didn't want to risk transporting them ourselves. We left them in good care, with a local who's an EMT," Samuels answered.

"Who were the bad guys?"

"One guess. We got a wallet full of phony IDs. Oh... and we confirmed the presence of a presumed sniper in the shaft house."

Leonard shook his head. "Dammit man, we can't just leave Frank up there, I have to go see him, right away."

"Relax would you?" retorted Samuels. "He's okay. You can go up if you want, you might want to look over the scene anyway, but he's in good hands, I feel sure of that." Samuels looked around. "Hey, where's that other guy, Jameson?"

Leonard looked distracted. "Him? Oh, he escaped."

"What?"

"Look, don't worry about it, we sort of, well... let him go. He's on our side now, I'm sure of it. He's more of a problem for Sherman than for us. I just hope he doesn't get himself killed."

"I don't know, sounds like a loose cannon to me," said Samuels. "Wait... what's that? Listen." They heard approaching sirens, moving fast. Looking out the window they saw two city police cars skid around the corner of Quincy street and head up Dunstan their wheels spinning.

They looked at each other for a moment, then Samuels said to Jason and Harry, "Could you guys go see what they're up to, try not to get involved okay?" They quickly threw on their coats and got into the Bronco, noting in passing the damage the hummer had taken in the gunfight. With a roar of the engine they spun out of the parking lot in pursuit of the wailing sirens.

Leonard watched them go, turned to Samuels with a sigh and said. "Jesus, I hope Frank's okay. I'm getting too damned old for this."

"He's a tough old coot," said Jimmy. "He'll be alright. Oh, and by the way sir, you might be interested to hear that Arne Harjaala is with him."

CHAPTER 41

Steve Sanders and Eileen Donovan stayed on the bypass around Oshkosh Wisconsin, the gas tank of the old Willys still near full. Consulting a map they turned onto Highway 45 a few miles north. They moved steadily along, consumed in conversation about the future of their life together. They still basked in the glow of their spur-of-the moment marriage earlier that evening at Peg's Pancake Palace. For the moment their former life at Sherman Enterprises, and the specter of pursuing assassins was forgotten. They sipped hot peppermint tea from a plastic cup, and sang some of their favorite songs. After a while the snow stopped, and they were able to make better time. About midnight they pulled into Eagle River Wisconsin and found an all night Holiday gas station with a snack bar. They had some food, filled up on gas, and decided to try to just drive on through to Eileen's uncle's cabin at on the lake Superior shoreline at Eagle River Michigan. When they came outside Eileen looked up at the sky and pointed. The clouds were quickly being whisked away, revealing a sky scintillating with intense auroras. They told the clerk in the station, who came out to watch too, then got into the Willys and kept driving.

Eileen took a turn at the wheel now, with Steve navigating. By 2:30 AM they were pulling into the outskirts of Houghton. They decided it would be wisest to simply head for the cabin, even though they realized it might be difficult to get into it with all their stuff at this hour through the deep snow, as the cabin sat well back from the road. As they headed across the lift bridge into Hancock they were stopped by a group of people with signs. There was an initial sense of panic, Eileen reflexively felt for the reassuring bulge of the pistol beneath her vest. She rolled down the window.

"Hi folks," said a young man pleasantly. "I see you have Wisconsin plates. We're just letting everyone know that as of noon tomorrow, this bridge will be closed until Superior is granted full rights as a state of the federation."

"Oh?" said Eileen. "I hadn't heard anything about it."

"Here, we got some early copies of this morning's Mining Gazette. If you want to get off the Keweenaw anytime soon, do it before noon tomorrow alright?"

"Yes, we will, thanks."

"What the heck is that all about?" asked Steve.

"You tell me, sounds like some sort of political secession movement. Right now though, it doesn't bother me that they plan to close the bridge, at least, not once we get to the other side."

"I'll second that! We can read the paper later."

Not knowing about the White Street shortcut, they stayed right on Business 41, taking Quincy Street all the way through downtown to Lincoln Street, before hooking back around and heading up Quincy hill. The shaft house loomed darkly on their right as they passed it. About a mile later an ambulance with lights on pulled out of a side road on the right and headed back towards town. It was followed by a fire truck with its lights off. "I wonder what that's all about," Steve commented, but they did not investigate further. Eileen kept driving north on 41 through Calumet, then the smaller towns of Kearsarge, Ahmeek, and Mohawk, finally traveling along a very dark and lonely stretch of highway towards Phoenix. "Are you sure this is the right way?" she asked. "It seems so far from anything."

"Isn't that why we came here?"

"I guess so. I haven't been up here in winter before, it looks so different. Where do we go from here?"

"The next major left, towards Eagle River, then north along the shore until we find the place. I hope there's a number or a sign or something." They found the left turn, climbed uphill for a couple of miles, then started down a long slope towards the lake shore, visible in the distance. Eileen stopped the car just over the crest of the hill.

"What's the matter?" asked Steve, as Eileen got out, leaving the engine running. It was well after three in the morning, they had not seen another car on the road for the last ten miles.

"Nothing, I just want to take in the view." Steve got out too, and walked around to her side. It was still cold, but the wind had died down. It was truly a beautiful vista. Two miles below them lay the lakeshore. The surface was frozen out for about another mile, in the distance beyond lay open water, glistening with the shimmering colors of the aurora. If anything, the display had intensified during the night, and now, out here, far from any bright lights, it was startling in its transcendent glory. They could have stood there all night watching, but they were very tired and began to get cold standing still.

"Come on," Steve said. "Let's go find the place, then we can go out on the lakeshore and watch some more if we want."

"I know, but it's just so beautiful, I don't want to turn my back on it even for a minute."

Steve took the wheel now, and they drove down the hill into the tiny village of Eagle River. It was a much smaller place than the town of the same name in Wisconsin... just a cluster of clapboard houses, with a bar and a gas station, both closed at night, and a tourist gift shop only open in summer. They slipped through town and turned up the lakeshore road. Cottage signs appeared at irregular intervals as they drove along. Sometimes they could see through the trees on their left to the wide expanse of ice stretching out from the lakeshore itself. Eileen fumbled with a Copper Country map, and an old tattered piece of paper with written directions to the cottage that had been given her with the keys.

"Slow down, we should be pretty close. We're looking for a sign that says, 'Herman's Haven'. It was all the rage to give silly names to these places. Wait, stop for a minute." Steve stopped the Willys. Eileen got out and went to the side of the road. Part of a sign was sticking out of the snow, she brushed the clinging white stuff off the upper portion and could see the weathered letters forming the word "Herman's". She came to the driver's side window, which Steve rolled down. "Yeah, this is it. Looks like nobody's used the place for a while. We'll have to get a snow shovel and make a place to put the car. I hear the plow drivers around here have no sense of humor when it comes to such things."

"Okay, but let's check out the cabin first," said Steve. The snow was very deep, over chest high, so they got a couple of pairs of snowshoes out of the back. Tom had packed them. After strapping them to their boots they clambered over the snowbank and walked about one hundred and fifty meters through the woods to a charming little log cabin. Steve had brought the snow shovel, which they used to clear a space in front of the door. It took some effort to clear a space large enough for the screen door to swing open, the cabin usually had only summer occupancy. Then Eileen brought out the key and unlocked the heavy ironbound wooden door. It swung inward on creaking hinges, revealing a dark interior which their small flashlights did little to illuminate. There was no electricity, but Eileen quickly located an oil lamp on a table, and lit it with a kitchen match from a box there. The warm yellow flame cast a cheerful glow on the rustic furniture, but failed to dispel any of the biting cold, which seemed somehow more intense here indoors than out.

"Steve, tell you what. If you'll go try to make some kind of parking space for the car, I'll get this place warmed up. There's a woodbox there by the stove, that should be enough until tomorrow, then we can look around for some more." Steve looked at his watch, it was almost four in the morning. He sighed wearily but there was still work that simply had to be done before they could relax. It wasn't exactly what he'd had in mind when he imagined his wedding night. He went back outside, put on the snowshoes, took the shovel, and started cutting a space in the side of the road for the Willys to be out of the way of the plow. Fortunately the snow was relatively light, and 20 minutes of strenuous effort was all that was required. He shouldered some bags of necessaries, and trudged back to the cabin. Along the way he spent a little more time looking around, and noticed another cabin, about 300 meters further up the shoreline to the north. A dim light shone out of the window, and a thin plume of smoke was curling from the chimney. When he arrived at the door of Herman's Haven, a pleasant sight greeted him. There were several more lamps burning now, and a roaring fire could be heard crackling in the woodstove, casting flickering yellow beams upon the wooden floor. It was still cold, but warming fast. Eileen stood by the stove rubbing her hands over it.

"Hey you, sailor boy. Come on over here and warm yourself by the fire." He smiled and joined her. The stove was really cooking, he thought that she must have found some very dry wood. After a while they warmed up considerably. "Look over there," she said. "I found a cedar chest full of blankets and quilts." Steve saw a deep wooden four post bed, thickly piled with warm looking covers.

"Ah, that looks good."

"You want to check out the northern lights again before we go to bed?"

"Yeah sure, probably never see it like that again in a lifetime." They zipped up their coats again and went out, putting on their snowshoes and walking the short way down to the lakeshore, out from under the trees. There seemed to be a spiraling circle of light off to the south, with flames of every color shooting down to the horizon. They knew that it couldn't possibly be making any noise, but could have sworn that the flames made a crackling sound.

They stood, arm in arm, gazing at the display. "Can you imagine Steve, what the Native Americans must have thought of this? I mean, we know that these are electrons from a solar storm being trapped in the magnetic field of the earth and exciting molecules in the upper atmosphere, but it must have been an intense religious experience for primitive people."

Steve agreed. "Yeah, I think I would have decided the world was about to end." He looked up and down the beach for a minute, then noticed a pair of figures a short way up the shoreline near the other cabin. He nudged Eileen. "Look, some other people up there." She followed his gaze. The people apparently noticed their attention and waved, starting to move towards them. The peculiar motion of their arms and legs showed that they were on skis.

Eileen spoke quietly to Steve. "I'm not sure I want to meet anybody here, I thought we were supposed to be hiding."

"Come on, let's not be conspicuous, we have no choice now. We'll be friendly but not offer information. Here they come..."

It was clearly a man and a woman approaching. "Hi there," said the man. "Have you ever seen an aurora like this? It's just incredible!"

The woman nudged him with an elbow. "You forget your manners. Hi, I'm Barbara, this is my husband James. We were just out admiring the northern lights and saw you down here. You just get in?"

"Yeah, I'm Eileen and this is... my husband Steve. I'm not used to this yet, we were just married today."

"Oh really? This is your honeymoon then!" said Barbara. "Well, congratulations! Gosh, Herman's place must be freezing!"

"Yeah well, we got a fire going, and we've got lots of blankets. I guess Uncle Herman never came up much this winter."

"No, said James, we'd see him most every summer though." The two couples stood for a while and just watched the lights. An occasional 'oooh' or 'ahhh' escaping someone's lips when there was a particularly spectacular flashing curtain of light, or intense burst of color.

After a politely long period of time had passed, Eileen said. "Lovely to meet you, but I'm so tired I'm about to fall asleep right here in the snow, no matter how bright these lights are."

"Of course, will you be staying long?" asked Barbara.

"At least a few days." Steve answered noncommittally.

"Oh good, then we'll have a chance to see you again. Perhaps we could have you over for dinner?"

"That would be lovely," answered Eileen in her most politely unpressing tones.

"Well, good night then, and congratulations, it is your wedding night, after all." The couple moved off up the shoreline in the ski tracks they had made coming down.

Steve held Eileen and kissed her nose. "You ready to turn in?"

"Turn into what?" Eileen giggled. Steve put his arm around her and they trudged back into the cabin, in lock step to avoid stepping on each other's snowshoes. The place was equipped only with an outhouse and chamberpot for plumbing, but fortunately they'd had the foresight to bring some bottled water with them for washing and drinking. Eileen used the sink first while Steve added some fuel to the woodstove. Then it was his turn, and when he came back into the main room he heard a shriek.

"What's wrong?"

"It's freezing in here!" She was shivering in the bed.

"Come on, hurry up!" Steve stripped off his clothes and slipped between the covers. They were still icy cold. "Come here you!" She pulled him to her body. They embraced fiercely then, finding the warmth of each other. Finally the covers started to warm up a little. Eileen snuggled her face into Steve's chest.

"You tired?" he asked.

"Tired? I'm exhausted. I can't ever remember having a day like this in my entire life." She looked at his face, barely visible in the glow from the woodstove. "Why do you ask?"

"Oh, no reason, just, you know, wondering... "

"Oh that... well..." she moved a hand sensuously across his chest and down to his thigh, "we have to think of some way to keep warm you know. I mean, we could freeze to death even."

"Oh, really?"

"Oh yes, I've heard of it. There's only one thing to do."

"Oh, and what is that?" But Steve received no answer to his question, at least, not a verbal one. But then, it has been said before that actions speak louder than words.

CHAPTER 42

The sound of the snowmobile was just fading into the distance as George Sherman came down through the deep snow to the main entrance to Midnight Mining Company. The police sirens had stopped their irritating ululation, but the blue lights were still flashing near the entrance, blocked by the dump truck and two of Sherman's men. He ducked in through the iron door in the solid rock of the mountain and checked on Tony, who had been strapped to a stretcher and fitted with an inflatable splint to support the broken leg. Sherman grabbed his coat and directed three men to move Tony into the corridor beyond the office, and to keep quiet. He walked outside in time to meet two officers of the Hancock Police Department, walking towards him, arguing loudly with two of his men.

"May I help you?" said George Sherman, in his most conciliatory voice.

"We have a citizen's complaint of gunfire coming from here, and these men are trying to prevent us from checking it out," said one. "Who are you?"

"My name is George Sherman, I'm the new owner of Midnight Mining Company. These are my employees. Unfortunately they seem to have forgotten their manners." He turned to his two men and spoke loudly and gruffly. "What do you think you're doing, harassing these public servants, get back to your posts this instant!" The men meekly withdrew, yet there was perhaps a hint of a grim smile on their faces as they did so. They realized fully that the rebuke was strictly for show. Sherman turned back to the officers. "Now, how can I help you?"

"Like I said, we're investigating reports of gunfire and a general disturbance. Some residents down the street called just a few minutes ago. These men would tell us nothing."

"Ah, well, we did have something of an incident just now, some criminals, probably youths out having fun, tried to break in and steal some things. Apparently they did not expect the place to be guarded. My men fired a few shots in the air to scare them off. They disappeared on a snowmobile. No harm done, and I don't intend to press charges, like I said, I think it was probably just some kids out having a little fun."

"Well, we don't have much of that kind of thing around here. And our residents don't care for gunfire, whether into the air or otherwise. I'm going to have to see the licenses for the weapons fired and file a report about it."

"Do you really think it's necessary officer? As you can see, there's been no harm done. We do appreciate your concern though, and I'm glad to have met you... officer...?"

"Lincoln"

"Officer Lincoln. A fine name. Thanks so much for coming out. Sherman extended his gloveless hand. Officer Lincoln took off his right glove and did the same, though reluctantly; he had the feeling he was being dismissed. When he took Sherman's hand he felt something besides flesh there, and as he withdrew it he recognized the feel of the thin plastic film that represented money these days. He glanced quickly at his palm and saw a folded wad of ten crisp, new, $500 Federation notes. He quickly pocketed them and put his gloves back on.

"Well Mister Sherman, I can see that you have things well under control here, I think we can record the incident as a simple misunderstanding."

The other, younger officer looked confused. "But Lieutenant, I thought you said..."

"Shut up Maki, we'll talk about it later." Then to Sherman again, "Sorry to have been of any trouble sir."

"No trouble at all. And by the way, be sure to catch the aurora tonight, it's tremendous."

"Yes it certainly is, thanks. Well, good night."

"Good night."

The police officers walked to their cars, turned off the flashing lights, and drove away. Sherman spoke to the three men who were to be the relief team for the Shaft house sniper post. "You three, get someone to drive you, get up there and relieve the other two. I want two people on the ground covering against anyone sneaking in. Who's the shooter? Okay, our communications are down, so you may have to make a decision on your own. I want to keep fighting to a minimum, don't just go shooting at cars on the road, even if they are police cars. But if you sense that the shaft has become a focus of attention and they're trying to get in, take them out. Be especially on the lookout for people on snowmobiles, especially two together on a snowmobile with a broken windshield. We don't want anybody coming in that through the shaft. Once inside, we'd have too difficult a time keeping track of them. Alright?"

The team nodded as one man. Two of them started hauling bags to the dump truck, while the third dashed inside for a few seconds, returning quickly with another man still putting on his coat. They jumped into the dump truck and drove off.

Sherman went back into the office. He surveyed the work in progress. Out of his original 30 men he still had 14 with him here in the office. Plus the two who had stayed here for the last week. He hesitated a moment, unsure of dividing his forces too much, but then called Scott and Jeff to him.

"Boys, you've been here the longest, you know your way around town better than we do. We need a couple of snowmobiles, fast ones, and we need them now. Do whatever it takes, beg borrow or steal them, but I want you two out after whoever it was that was snooping on us outside. The snowfall has stopped now, so if you get on it quickly, then I hope you can track them."

"I think I know were we can get the scooters," said Scott, "but we'll need money. There's a dealer down the street. If we offer cash I'm sure he won't mind waking up in the middle of the night."

"Okay." Sherman opened a bag on the table and pulled out a thick wad of cash. He took a small stack and laid it in Scott's hand. "Here's fifty gees. I expect some change."

"Yes sir!"

"You boys armed?" They showed pistols in leather shoulder holsters. "Okay, if you catch them, I want to find out what they know. Capture them if possible, kill them if not, but in no circumstances are they to be permitted to escape. Got it?"

"Yes sir!" The two grabbed coats and headed out the door.

Sherman walked about the office, checking the progress of his people, who were still busily investigating the computer stations, setting up defensive positions, and generally making themselves at home. He walked through the double doors to where Tony lay on his stretcher, his big meaty hands laying on top of a blanket. "Tony, Tony, what have they done to you?"

"Just my leg boss, it's been broke before, good as new in a few weeks. One of the guys already pulled it straight,"

"You comfortable here?"

"Yeah, okay, but I feel kinda useless. Isn't there something I can do?"

"Don't worry about it."

"I did get him didn't I? Nobody ever said for sure."

"Well the snowmobile drove away, there were no bodies on the ground."

"I was sure, I shot him pointblank, right through that little windshield, it must have hit him."

"Maybe he was wearing armor."

"Yeah, I suppose. Sorry sir, security was my responsibility. It never occurred to me someone would come down on us from above."

"Well, I don't think I would have anticipated it either."

"One thing bothers me though."

"Yes?"

"What if somebody does manage to come in through the shaft?"

"We've got a team up there to prevent that."

"Sure, but our communications are down, Maybe the air force comes in and blows their way in, how will we know?"

"Possible. What have you got in mind?"

"Look sir, all I can do with this leg is lay here, but I still got eyes and I still got hands. Put me back there where the shaft connects, give me a direct cable phone to you here. I still have my pistol; I can be your guard dog. At least, then I'd feel like I was doing something."

Sherman nodded. "Good thinking, I didn't want to waste anyone there, but your idea makes sense." Sherman patted him on the shoulder, then gave orders to four men to carry him on the stretcher down to the end of the tunnel.

Tony was a big man, but for four strong troopers it took little effort. One of them attached a spool of telephone cable to his belt and let it pay out as they went. Soon they were near the place where the dark shaft loomed at the end of the tunnel. Tony looked around a little, then had the men place him in a spot where he could see any activity at the mouth of the shaft, yet still be somewhat out of sight himself. Once the wiring connections were made he picked up the phone, and was relieved to hear it immediately answered. The four men trotted back up the tunnel towards the offices. The last light bulb of the tunnel lay almost 50 meters behind, the phone and gun lay on his chest. He propped his head up with a bag of his clothing he'd asked to bring along, and waited as his eyes grew accustomed to the dim light. He checked the glowing face of the stainless Rolex on his left wrist. It was quite late, almost one in the morning.

Never before in his busy life in the streets and businesses of Chicago had Tony ever been in such a place of utter silence. After minutes of listening intently, he could faintly hear the distant sound of water dripping. The sound echoed around in the shaft and tunnel until it lost all distinction of individual drops, becoming simply a faint but shimmering 'essence' of watery white noise. There he lay, the pain in his leg washing over him in waves from time to time, accompanied only by the echoing silence. In exhaustion he fell asleep.

CHAPTER 43

Digger Puttonen and Joan Niemi sat astride the idling snowmobile at the top of the hill. They had just come up the trail from their ill-fated fact finding mission to the Midnight Mining Company office below. To both the east and west this more well traveled trail ran. A hundred years earlier it had been the bed of the Quincy and Torch Lake Railway; well oiled iron steam locomotives had belched smoke and clinkers as they crawled along it, pulling heavily laden cars loaded with the fabulously rich copper ore from the Quincy mine towards the stamp mills a few miles away on Torch Lake. The trains were long gone, but the carefully graded bed of the tracks had proved, decades later, to be an ideal trail for skiers and snowmobilers in winter, and for hikers and bikers in summer. For the moment, Digger and Joan sat and watched the northern lights. Neither had ever seen them displayed so spectacularly, despite having lived in this country all their lives.

"Where should we go, we can't stay here," said Digger, breaking the spell.

"You're right, but I'm not sure. Do you know anybody in town who could help?"

"Maybe, but, well... I'm worried about Arne."

"Me too, and Ruth," Joan answered.

"Should we risk going back there? It may not be safe."

"Is anyplace? What else can we do?"

"Other than trying to get inside the labs, there's not much that would be useful. We know they have people in the shaft house now, probably with sniper rifles and IR scopes, so there's no way I want to get near there."

"Do you want to risk going back to Paavola then?" asked Joan.

"I feel like I need to check out the scene there, but it's not necessary for you to... not if you feel..."

Joan whacked Digger on the shoulder. "Damn you, don't be so patronizing. We just escaped through a hail of bullets together and now you want me to go sit by a fire while you play the hero? Nothing doing bozo! I told you I'm sticking with you, and for better for worse, that's how it is."

"Okay okay, geez I'm sorry. I just, you know..."

"I know, it's okay. Come on, put this thing in gear and let's head back to Paavola, I think we've found out all we can here. By the way, did you get hurt?"

Digger felt around in his pack, pulled out the smashed can of hot chocolate, still dripping, then felt further and pulled out a thick spiral bound notebook. Embedded in it was a flattened mushroom shaped lead slug with a flayed aluminum jacket. Digger pried the slug out of the notebook and looked at it. "Looks like it expanded when it hit the can, then didn't have enough energy left to penetrate the notebook. The sweater behind it absorbed the force. Good thing they were using softpoints, a solid jacket bullet would have zipped right on through. Pretty lucky huh?"

Joan gave hum a hug from behind. "Yeah. Let's be more careful okay?"

Digger gunned up the motor and turned east again, back towards Ripley, in order to stay far away from the shaft house dominating the horizon. They stayed on the main trail for about two miles, until they hit the road heading north towards Arcadia from Dollar Bay. They took this and were able to scoot along at good speed for a while, taking a couple of turns and ending up at Arcadian Hill, about a mile east of Paavola. Here they took to the fields again, avoiding the tag alder stands and approaching Paavola slowly through the deep snow with their lights off. Digger stopped the machine about 200 meters from the nearest house, but where they had a clear view of his neighborhood in the distance across the flats. A hook and ladder truck stood in front of the place where Digger's house had been, its blue and red lights flashing. He took out the binoculars and adjusted them, then examined the scene carefully.

"Here, you look." He handed the device to Joan. "It was my house alright, looks like a total loss."

"Oh Digger, I'm so sorry!"

"Not your fault."

"I know, but I can be sorry. I liked your house. I liked your bed. I was looking forward to spending a lot more time there."

"Yeah, me too," said Digger. They hugged.

Joan wiped some tears off of Digger's face with her glove. "It'll be okay, you'll see. You'll get the company back, and then you'll be able to buy new stuff."

"But I liked my old stuff."

"I know, but look at this." She handed him back the binoculars. "Nobody seems to be paying any attention to Ruth's house. They're probably just fine, but worried about what happened to us. They still don't know whether we were in there or not."

He looked. "You're right, we have to go over there. What if we circle around to the north, and park this thing off the road behind those trees. We could walk down the next road over, cut between the houses where those kids live, work our way through the snow tunnels and come to Ruth's back door without anybody seeing us."

"I think that might work." answered Joan. "Let's do it."

Fumbling around in the tunnels in the dark was a little awkward, but within about five minutes they stood on Ruth's back porch and knocked quietly.

It took a few moments, but a very surprised looking Ruth opened the door excitedly. She embraced Joan. "Oh, you're okay. God we were so worried! Did you see what happened?"

"No," answered Joan, as Digger closed the door behind him. We were halfway to Pewabic on skis when we heard the explosion and saw the bright flash."

"It was unbelievable. There was a gunfight on the street, right here in Paavola. It was like watching a movie or something. The four bad guys, whoever they were, started the shooting and blew up your house with some kind of rocket thing. The other guys who were sitting in the car out front, they were from the FBI, they shot back, and in about a minute it was over. The four bad guys were shot or blown up, and two of the FBI guys were hurt, one of them pretty bad."

Digger stomped the snow off his boots. "How do you know they were FBI?"

Ruth raised her eyebrows. "Two of them are here."

"What?" Digger asked in a harsh whisper. "Here? Now?"

"Yes, the two wounded men. The ambulance still hasn't arrived... I offered to take them in because of my EMT training. Arne's helping out wonderfully."

"Where are they?" asked Joan.

Ruth motioned with a thumb over her shoulder. "Right there in the living room."

Joan and Digger took off their coats, brushed the snow off their pants and took off their boots on polished wood kitchen floor. Digger went into the living room first, glancing at the wall clock on the way through the door. It was about quarter after one. Joan and Ruth stayed in the kitchen for a while, talking quietly. Digger saw Arne kneeling down next to a chair and adjusting a sling on a young man's arm. The man looked at him, pain clearly expressed in the one eye showing. The other eye was covered by a blood-soaked bandage that covered his left cheek. Arne turned around for a moment. "Hi dere, heard you come in da kitchen a minute ago. Good ta see ya."

"Good to see you too. These fellas hurt bad?"

"Nah, I seen lots worse, believe me. Dis is our friend Stephen. He's got a cut cheek here, prob'ly flying glass, and a flesh wound to da upper arm. It'll heal clean." Arne finished adjusting the bandages and Stephen relaxed back into the cushions with a sigh.

"What about over here?" Digger looked at the older man lying on a stretcher, apparently asleep.

"A little worse, three bullets in da upper leg. One is pretty bad, looks like it hit da bone. Back in my day it would ha' been hit or miss whedder da leg could be saved at all. I hear dey do wonderful t'ings now though. He's a bit sleepy, lost quite a bit o' blood. His name's Frank. He's been talkin' in his sleep some." Arne leaned close and whispered in Digger's ear. "Ya know, I t'ink dese guys are okay. He's been lookin' for us, but jus' wants to find out stuff. Dose udder guys layin' out dere in da street, dey come on 'em and jus' started shootin' like crazy, but dese guys gave back better dan dey got." Digger nodded.

He went back in the kitchen and put his arm around Joan, who hugged him back. Ruth looked at them and broke a smile. "What do you think?"

"I don't know, they seem like okay people."

"Yeah." Ruth answered. "I kinda like that guy Frank. He was babbling a bit a little while ago, when he recognized Arne. Said something about how you guys were in danger..."

"Yeah, we know that now." Digger said sardonically.

"Now yeah, but... I don't know. I just get the feeling these guys are on the level."

"You mean, you think we should talk to them?" Digger looked at Joan, who shrugged. "What about you Joan? You think we can trust 'em?"

"When he wakes up I'll talk to him, I'll be able to tell if he's trying to hide something."

"Listen, you kids tired or hungry or anything? Joan told me about what happened."

Digger thought for a moment. "What I'd really like to do is just sit down someplace warm and relax for a minute."

Ruth put on another pot of water to boil, while Digger and Joan went into the living room and lounged on the couch. The two injured men were both dozing, and even Arne had nodded off sitting in an overstuffed chair. Digger and Joan pulled their stocking feet up on the couch cushions and cuddled up as comfortably as they could. Within minutes they were asleep. When Ruth came in a while later with a fresh pot of herb tea, she looked at them and smiled. A plaid woolen blanket lay folded across the top of the couch back. She took it and spread it over them, the only response a comfortable murmur. She knelt down to check on Frank, taking the wrist that lay on top of the covers in her hand to check his pulse. Seeming satisfied, she went into the kitchen and sat at the kitchen table. It may have been a few years since she had done a stint in ER, but she considered herself "on duty" while patients lay in her living room. And it was not only those whose bodies were injured that she considered patients. She well knew the psychological disruption that attended the loss of one's home and belongings.

About quarter to two she heard a voice in the living room, and went to investigate. Frank had woken up and seemed disoriented. He saw her approach and kneel down by him.

"Where am I?" he asked. "Who are you?"

She smiled. "Hi Frank, I'm Ruth, I'm taking care of you until the ambulance comes." Digger, Joan, and Arne were waking up and listening.

"What happened?"

"You were in a gunfight, took a couple of hits to the right leg. You'll be okay, but you lost some blood, that's why you feel a little light headed." Frank got a horrified expression on his face. Ruth read it correctly. "No, don't worry about them. All your other friends are okay. Please relax. There, that's better."

"What about those other guys?"

"The ones who were shooting at you?" Frank nodded.

Ruth's voice turned grim. "They're still lying out there in the snow. A fire truck is there, but no other police cars have shown up, or ambulances for that matter. The radios don't work you know."

Frank sighed deeply. "Okay, I think I remember some. Where'd Jimmy go?"

"He's one of your friends?"

"Yeah, my partner, we came up together from Marquette."

"I guess they went back to tell somebody about what happened. Seemed like they had things they needed to take care of."

"But he doesn't know about Arne." said Frank.

Thus far, Frank's head had been turned away from the couch, speaking to Ruth. Digger spoke up from the couch. "What about Arne?"

Frank turned to face him. "You? You're here too."

"Yes, what did you want to tell your friend about Arne?"

"Look, mister Puttonen, you're in great danger. We've been trying to get in touch with you for days."

"Yeah I know. You sent agents to spy on me, chasing us around town... now my house is burned to the ground, I've been shot at, and they've stolen my company. What else do you want to do for me?" Joan elbowed Digger in the ribs and frowned at him.

"No," answered Frank, "you don't understand. Things have changed. We never meant you any harm."

"I think you'd better explain a little better."

"Listen, we were ordered to pick you and Arne up for questioning, that's all. A branch of the FBI called Special Investigations concentrates on people with psychic abilities. They had been watching you for years."

"Why?"

"I'm not sure, probably to try to recruit you eventually, or at least make sure you weren't working against them. They were also watching Arne, because of his strange experience, which we still don't quite understand. Some sort of time travel or something... Then when you two got together they figured something important was happening. They asked us to try to pick you up, to find out what it was all about."

"Who is 'they' Frank?"

"The leader of the SIB, Leonard Howarth, he's here in town. The local agency wouldn't have been involved at all, except that there was the storm, and Howarth was delayed getting here. Then you gave us the slip somehow."

"Why all the guns?"

"That's why we've got to warn you. George Sherman has taken over your company. We had no idea about any of that until just a few hours ago. We're guessing he feels he has inside information about your research project, maybe something he can use to blackmail the government. Otherwise, he must know that in a few weeks time we could get the military in here with enough force to blow him out of there."

"What research project?"

"We don't know for sure, we're guessing from Arne's presence that it's some sort of time thing... that's why we needed to find you. This thing has blown completely out of control in a matter of a few hours."

"So why do you think those guys came up here?"

Frank grimaced in pain for a moment. "Son, it doesn't take a genius. They want you, alive or dead. As long as you're loose there's the chance you'll team up with us. I think those guys were sent up here to try to capture or kill you. They probably would prefer to take you alive so they can force you to help them."

Digger sighed deeply, then motioned to Joan to follow him. They went into the kitchen Ruth and Arne followed. Digger asked Joan, "So what do you think, is he telling the truth?"

She nodded. "Without a doubt... every word."

"What do you think Arne? Can we trust these guys?" Digger asked. Arne nodded solemnly. "How 'bout you Ruth, you get a feeling?" She nodded also.

"Okay, I thought so too, but sometimes I feel I'm too trusting, I wanted to see what you guys thought. "If we're agreed, then we throw in with these guys." There were gestures of assent all around; they went back into the living room. "We've decided we believe you," he said to Frank. "We're willing to help you, if you'll help us."

Frank smiled. "Thanks. You know, you live your life being suspicious, it's nice to be trusted sometimes." Frank reached his right hand out weakly to shake with Digger, hesitated, put the pebble he clutched on top of the blanket and shook hands, smiling.

Digger noticed the pebble. "Do you mind?" he asked as he reached to pick it up.

"No, not at all. Do you know anything about it. Arne said something about it, I forget what..."

"It's datolite Frank. Where'd you get it?" Digger turned the tumbled and polished nodule over in his hands curiously.

"On the way up, we met some Ojibways down in L'Anse. One of them gave it to me. He told me it was a stone of wisdom. I don't know about that, but I felt comfortable holding it. Seemed to help me relax."

Digger handed him back the nodule. "Well, you just go right on holding it then. And by the way, you're within about a mile of where that nodule was found."

"Really? How do you know?"

"I'm something of a collector of datolite. I recognize the color and pattern. That came from the old Mesnard mine, also known as the Quincy number eight, not too far away. So in a sense, you're bringing it back home." Frank took a closer look at it, with new appreciation. "Oh, and I'd like you to meet Joan, she's good people." Joan winked and patted Frank's hand.

There was a rumbling noise outside; Digger looked out through the blinds. The fire truck was still there. Firemen were taking the bodies of three men out of the burned car and laying them in the snow, wrapping them in plastic sheets. He was surprised to see a beat-up Ford Bronco pull up in front of the house. "We have visitors!" he announced. "Anybody recognize them?"

Ruth took his place, looking out as four men emerged from the car. Three she did not recognize, but one was the young man she'd met earlier, Frank's partner. "Yeah, one of them's Jimmy, don't know about the other three."

"Jimmy's here?" said Frank, and smiled. "He's a good kid. Describe the others, will you?" Ruth described them quickly as they made their way up the shoveled walk. "Sounds like the SIB guy, Leonard, and the two guys he came up with. They're okay". A few moments later there came a knock on the door; Ruth opened the door and let them in.

Jimmy nodded in recognition to Ruth, then went directly in and knelt down next to Frank. "Hey Captain, how're you doing?"

Before Frank could answer, Leonard was there too. He squatted down and smiled at Frank. "Hey buddy, it's my turn now eh? Sitting at your bedside? What the hell did you think you were doing, getting yourself all shot up anyway?"

"Hi Lenny, sorry, I guess I messed things up again, but I have a surprise for you." He looked around, but Digger, Arne, and Joan were nowhere to be seen. "Well, I thought I did."

"What do you mean?" Leonard stood up as Digger and Arne walked into the room from the kitchen. Joan stood leaning against the doorway.

Digger stretched out his hand to Leonard. "Digger Puttonen," he said, "and this is my friend Arne Harjaala. I understand you'd like to talk to us."

Leonard accepted the handshake. "Leonard Howarth. Yes, very much. We have a serious problem on our hands, and I think you may be able to help us." Leonard was introduced to Joan and Ruth, then he proceeded to present his associates in turn. Jason, Harry and Jimmy were introduced as FBI agents. Stephen, sitting in the chair covered with bandages, just waved his good hand in recognition.

Ruth slipped into the kitchen, put a couple of leaves into the table, and got out some crackers and cheese. Frank was getting tired again after all the attention, and she suggested that the group move to the kitchen table to continue discussions. Frank insisted on being part of it though, and was carried to the kitchen and the stretcher laid across a couple of chairs where he could see everybody.

As they filed through the door, Arne spoke up. "You kids go ahead, whatever you decide is fine wit' me. I'm gonna stay here wit' my buddy Stephen." He indicated the injured man. "At least 'til da ambulance comes." Arne opened the door of another room and the black Lab named Oby came out, sniffed everybody, and then lay on the floor in the living room next to Arne.

Digger and Joan sat at one side of the table, with Leonard across from them. Harry, Jason, Jimmy, and Ruth pulled chairs up wherever they could.

"Frank filled us in on some of what you guys have been up to," said Joan. "What we need to figure out is... where to go from here."

Digger spoke up... "Frank suggested you thought Sherman might be trying to use some of our research material to blackmail the government."

"Yes, that was one guess. Is there anything you're working on that could be used that way?" asked Leonard.

"Yes, I'm afraid there is. We call it the 'tempiloscope', it's a device which allows us to observe any time/space location that can be described using a special seven-variable coordinate system."

"Observe? In what way?"

"Direct observation, specifically, detection of full spectrum electromagnetics."

"And what is so special about this?"

"Like I said, all you have to do is specify the coordinates, including both location AND time, and you can observe it."

"You must be joking, you can see backwards and forwards in time?"

"No, not forwards, only backwards or sideways. There are certain limitations you see..."

"Anyplace? Like... inside a locked vault, or a sealed room?"

"Of course."

"Oh my God!"

"Exactly. We've been keeping the whole project as secret as possible until we develop the ability to control it. It turns out to be exceedingly difficult to specify the correct coordinates for some place and time you wish to look. The coordinates are not directly related to the intuitive sense of space and time that we have."

"But if Sherman learns to use it..."

"It would be a wonderful research tool of course," Digger went on. "Historians, archaeologists, paleontologists, all such would be clamoring to use the thing for scientific research. But of course, it could also be used to spy on an enemy, discover secret plans, all the usual cloak and dagger type stuff. Observation satellites would become almost obsolete. You could sit right here at a desk and observe the launch console at a missile silo buried beneath the earth ten thousand miles away. If, that is... you know exactly where, and when, you want to look."

Leonard looked worried. "So that's it then. Sherman thinks he'll be able to use the thing to discover some kind of information he can use to blackmail the world. Do you think he can do it?"

"I don't know. Our research program is not yet completed, we've been working on the problem for weeks, but a simple intuitive way to aim the device has still proved elusive. We need a good decryption programmer for that. It's rather awkward to use the way it is, but not impossible. There is sufficient calibrated test data there... if he's got somebody even halfway good, he may figure out how to blunder around with it, given time."

"How much time?"

"Hard to say. It would depend on who he's got."

"Assume he's got the best, how much time before he could use the thing against us?"

"I don't know. They'd have to break a password... uh... if they got lucky, twelve to twenty four hours maybe."

Leonard looked pained. "Is that all? We don't have much time then. Is there any connection to the outside? Can we shut down the power supply?"

"You could, but they could just activate the backup. The temporal lab has its own fuel cell based power supply and is sealed from the rest of the facility by two large vault doors."

Leonard frowned. "Why? A security precaution?"

"No, there was concern that we could inadvertently specify the coordinates of the interior of the sun for instance, which might result in an explosion." Digger laughed softly. "The doors were put in to protect the rest of the facility from such a disaster, but of course, it's all a sham."

"Oh? Why is that?"

"If we ever really did make such an egregious error, the amount of energy that would flow through the portal before the equipment was destroyed would be enough to melt the whole mountain down to slag, it would be almost like a nuclear explosion."

"Oh my God! We've got to get in there."

Harry spoke up from the end of the table. "We think Sherman's bought off the local cops as well as the Sheriff's department. An awful lot of crisp new $500 bills seem to be floating around town in the hands of some influential people. We were able to trace their origin to a Chicago bank. It's not going to be easy to move against him, we may not be able to count on much help in town."

"Okay," said Leonard to Digger. "What are the options? He's got a lot of guys, we estimate thirty."

"Twenty six." Jimmy said softly.

"Yes, minus four is twenty six. Still it's a lot more than we have, and we have no time to bring in more."

Joan spoke. "The front door is guarded by three outside, and locked from within. Two are at the front gate, and one at the door itself." She put a piece of cheese on a cracker and chewed it thoughtfully. "They're going to be doubly watchful now."

"Oh?" asked Harry. "Did you have something to do with the little fracas a while ago?"

"Yeh, we slipped down from above on skis and heard Sherman order a relief sniper team up to the shaft house, then they heard us and started shooting, but we got away on Digger's snowmobile."

"So that confirms it, there is a sniper up there," said Harry.

"Yeah, better assume so," Joan replied.

Jimmy said, "We heard him tell the local cops that they were shooting in the air to scare off some kids." Digger showed them the notebook and flattened bullet. Jimmy looked at it and shook his head incredulously. "You're one lucky guy my friend!"

Digger shrugged, but laid the damaged notebook open on the table. It contained detailed sketches of the interior layout of Midnight Mining Company. "Aside from the front door and the number two, there are only the other eight shafts." He pulled out and unfolded a cross section map of the mine. "These are the main workings. Of course, they're flooded now up to the eleventh level. The tunnel from the old Vivian street adit, on the seventh level where all the research labs are, connects to the rest of the mine in only two places. The tunnel runs straight into the number two shaft, and just ends there, about sixty meters above the water."

"We thought of that, would it be difficult to negotiate?" Jimmy asked.

"No, not with a long rope, but as soon as you drop your rope, someone watching the passage would know you're coming. Besides, they're guarding the shaft house."

"Assume that's taken care of, consider just the problem of getting down to the tunnel."

"If someone was watching for you at the bottom, it would be suicide."

"Okay, what else?"

"When we started the ore recovery project, we cut a new access way for the grunts to the ore processing and repair station."

"Grunts?"

"Sorry, we call 'em that because of the noise their sensors make. They're little robot mining submarines that roam around the mine below the water level, refining the mapping of ore bodies, and recovering minerals the miners missed in the old days."

"Can we use that tunnel?"

"It's very deep, connects to the workings near the old number one shaft well below the water line."

"What about scuba gear?"

"Sorry, too deep for that, it's over a hundred meters under water."

Leonard considered for a while. "Let me ask you this. Which of these ways in do you think Sherman and his guys know about?"

Digger considered. "Well aside from the front door, they obviously know about the number two shaft, or they wouldn't be guarding it. The ventilation shafts are sealed with heavy steel grates and are too close to the office. They may know about the service entrance for the grunts, but my guess is that they probably don't take it seriously because of the practical difficulties I mentioned."

"Well if it's that deep it won't help us. We've been inside the front office," Jimmy said. "I'm afraid two well equipped guys could cut us to pieces. We're going to have to try something else."

"There's no point in challenging the manned entrances without more people," added Leonard, "which we do not have. We don't have time to wait for help, and yet we must get in there and somehow stop Sherman before he learns to operate the, uh... "

"The tempiloscope."

"Yes. So, we must decide."

"What exactly are we deciding?" asked Joan.

Leonard answered, as if it should be perfectly plain to everyone. "Why, how to destroy this tempiloscope of course, before Sherman learns how to use it."

"Destroy?" Digger jumped up from his chair. "You don't understand, this instrument is unique. If it is destroyed it might take years, decades even, to build another. We must capture it and use it."

"Use it? How?"

"We could demonstrate its usefulness to the world by exposing Sherman's crimes, catching him in the act, then he would be out of business forever."

"But you said you needed precise coordinates, how would you obtain these?"

"I'm not sure. I can do some, certainly locations within the mine. But James was the expert on targeting."

"Who?"

"James Dolittle, my partner. He went with his wife and children to a cabin on the lakeshore when things started getting heavy. He's got a cellular phone, but other than that he's incommunicado. Of course, the cellulars are useless with this interference."

"So you're saying we need him?"

"Not until we get to the machine, which seems to be our central problem at the moment. I just want to make sure that we all understand, the tempiloscope is not to be damaged."

"If it can be helped, Digger. Can the vault doors be locked from inside?"

"Yes, they can."

"So, we must reach them by stealth, before Sherman has a chance to lock the doors."

"Yes"

Leonard thought for a long time and sighed. "It's impossible. He's won. There's no way we can challenge the front door without more people and some heavy duty explosives. It's too dangerous to try the shaft house because of the snipers guarding it. Even if we took the shaft house, they'd chop us to pieces coming down the shaft, and we can't dive deep enough to use any of the other shafts, even if we had SCUBA gear, which we don't."

"There's one other thing I haven't told you about yet."

"What's that?"

"The grunts, one of them is fitted, experimentally, for deep sea rescue work. We've only carried dummies on it so far, but it may be possible to use the thing to enter the mine, it can dive deep enough."

"But how could you get to it?"

"I have a device, a remote control. Before I left the lab I programmed that one grunt for near surface mapping work in the area of the number six shaft."

"How many people can it hold?"

"Just one."

"No that's not enough."

"If one person could get in, they could make sure the area by the shaft was secure and allow the rest to come safely down."

"If the shaft house is cleared, and if there's some way to communicate..." Leonard protested.

"Got any better ideas?" Digger replied.

"No"

"Okay then, I'll try the grunt. If I make it in, we'll need some way to communicate."

"Would this work?" Digger heard the voice directly in his mind rather than through his ears. He looked around. Jimmy and Jason were smiling.

"Did you just do that?" It all had to be explained for those who had not heard. Jason and Jimmy had combined their psychic talents and were able to transmit to Digger. Joan heard it too.

"Okay then," Leonard was getting excited as he saw the idea might just work. "Digger uses his little submersible to enter the lab from below. How long do you estimate that might take?"

Digger looked at the map, traced a route on it, and calculated roughly in his head. "Four hours minimum, maybe five. They can dive deep and they're very reliable but they don't move very fast."

"Okay, in the meantime," Leonard went on, "someone needs to try to find your partner James."

"I'll go, said Ruth. I want to help, but I don't want to be around any gunplay. I know the roads around there, but somebody needs to tell me how to find the cabin."

"Good. If we get Samuels and Justin to keep watch on the front door, the rest of us will try to take the shaft house."

"Jimmy's quite a shot with the big fifty," said Frank from his stretcher. "Get him a clear line and he'll take out the sniper."

"There's a rope in the cabinet under the cash register at the gift shop, it's long enough to reach the seventh level." Digger said. There's also some webbing, descenders, carabiners and all that, whatever you need.

"We've got a long rope too," said Jimmy. Using both ropes we can get people down two at a time."

"What about me?" asked Frank.

"Wounded in action, old son," said Leonard. "You have a date with a hospital ward, whenever the damned ambulance gets here. Until then, you can mind the phone, we'll use this number as a connecting place."

"I don't like it!" Joan announced to Digger. "I told you I was sticking with you, and I don't want to be separated now."

"Look, there's no choice, there's only room for one in the grunt. You can go with Ruth. Don't worry, I'll be okay."

"You're just as stubborn as an old mule."

"I know," said Digger, as he accepted an automatic pistol and shoulder holster from Harry.

"You know how to use that?" asked Leonard.

"Yeah, well enough I guess."

"Here, you might need this too." Harry handed Digger a metal egg. "It's a concussion grenade. Press this button down all the way til it clicks, you'll have five seconds to get rid of it. Cover your ears and open your mouth, especially underground."

"Okay."

Digger put on his coat, picked up his pack, shifted some things into it from the pack Joan had carried, and started heading for the front door. Joan put her coat on as well. "I'll walk with you to the snowmobile," she said. He shook hands with the others, and they went out the door, walking up the street towards the snowmobile. "I can't believe you're doing this." Joan said to him, holding his hand as he tried to climb the snowbank to the snowmobile.

Digger said, "I know Joan, you can drive me to the mine shaft, it's just a couple klicks, then you can bring the scooter back. I won't be coming back out the same way and it would be best not to leave the thing sitting around there." She sighed heavily and shook her head in frustration, but not refusal. They climbed the snowbank up to the snowmobile. This time Joan took the controls. Digger's heavy pack was on his back, a dark hot chocolate stain below a small round hole that had not been there two hours earlier. He turned at a sound. In the distance he could hear a snowmobile engine, idling slowly. He peered into the darkness, but could see nothing. Joan started the motor, suddenly a light came on some way behind them and the other engine speeded up. Digger frantically motioned for Joan to get moving, she turned and saw the light bouncing across the snow towards them, then she gunned it and turned onto the street. Another headlight switched on at the end of the street. Now there were two other snowmobiles, one behind and one in front, closing fast. She took the first opportunity to get off the road, cutting through the spot someone had dug for their car. Digger looked over his shoulder and saw several figures standing on the back porch of Ruth's house, gesturing frantically, then they hit a hard bump and he had to turn his head back forward to keep it from being flung off.

One of the pursuers was still behind them, the other, could not be seen. Joan took off through the field heading west, then turned south and opened the throttle all the way. Digger shouted in her ear. "The road!"

Joan shouted back. "Hang on!"

"Oh my God!", thought Digger. "She's going to try to jump it!" He screamed "NO!" as they hit the snowbank and became airborne. It seemed as though they were flying for countless seconds. In the road below them Digger saw, for an instant, the astonished face of a man with a gun. He did not get off a shot until they had landed on the far side of the road and kept going. Behind them the other snowmobile did not attempt the jump. They were already fifty meters past the road when there was a volley of shots behind.

Digger let out a whoop of delight. "Wow, I never knew you could do that with a snowmobile!" He pointed over Joan's shoulder the direction he wanted her to go, slightly to the west of the track they'd taken on skis. They had not gone more than a kilometer when he turned and saw the headlight bouncing along their trail behind. They soon hit a snowmobile track heading west, and turned onto it in order to make better time. Soon they could both see the highway looming before them. Joan eased off on the throttle and got the machine down onto the snow covered pavement, then opened it up heading south. Digger pointed out a billowing cloud of steam a few meters off the road to the left. Suddenly the two unknown snowmobiles emerged into the road, one ahead of them and the other behind. Digger motioned to the left and Joan jumped the machine over the bank and slid right to the edge of the shaft.

"Come on," Digger shouted at her. "You'll never get away now, you have to come with me." A car had stopped and armed men were getting out. A couple of snap shots whizzed through the air near them. Digger stepped up onto the wet iron railroad rails that had been welded in a grid over the gaping hole in the earth. He pulled a section of chain-link wire back, then got down on his knees at a certain spot and pulled out a crowbar, which he used to lever one of the rails out of position. "You first," he motioned frantically. Joan wiggled into the hole. "Step over there, on that flat spot." He handed the pack down and pulled out the gun, he heard voices, people were beginning to appear just a few meters away. He snapped off two random shots in that direction, holstered the weapon, then let himself quickly down through the rails. He levered the loose rail back into position, laid the crowbar down and then guided Joan through the darkness to one side. Below them the blackness was utter and complete; a pair of steel rails disappeared quickly in the dim light. Above them the northern lights still played their silly games in the sky, seen through the rails above they looked like the dancing lights of freedom beyond the bars of a prison cell. A tiny flashlight appeared in Digger's hand. "Down eleven ties, count them," he said, and helped her jump quickly down the giant steps between the rotted wooden crossties. Then from behind her he guided Joan along a narrow ledge to the right, away from the opening above. On their right was a wall of wet muddy rock. On the left was a steep fall into nothingness.

They worked their way slowly along for about ten meters. Digger asked Joan to stay still for a moment, then he crept back to look up. There were black figures now, standing on the rails above, debating. Every now and then the beam of a flashlight pierced through the steamy darkness and shone down. He saw four of them there, their harsh weaponed forms stood out in stark silhouette against the scintillating beauty of the aurora borealis in full regalia. Digger and Joan were surrounded by the faint echoes of water dripping in the vast places beneath the earth.

CHAPTER 44

Julius Miller wakened at precisely three AM, as he did every day. In his line of work it often proved to be advantageous to be active at a time of day when most others are unconscious or groggy. He went into the bathroom and looked at himself in the mirror. His face reflected his fifty some odd years, smooth yet sagging, bland, somewhat round and babyish in appearance. People had said that he looked like a grocer, which satisfied him immensely. He was going bald on top, his hair had been a dark brown once, now it was speckled with emerging gray. He was one of the few professional corporate assassins of his caliber who steadfastly refused any efforts at disguise. His true face, open, trustworthy, benign... was his best asset.

He took his time getting ready for the day. One of the advantages of getting up very early included the lack of necessity for hurry, and if there was anything Julius Miller hated, it was the need to hurry. He brushed and flossed his teeth after taking a long hot shower. He found the water saving needle spray in the hotel bathroom irritating, but compensated by turning the water so hot he could barely stand it. Finally he dressed and went down to the lobby. He nodded to the sleepy looking night clerk in passing, shaking his head in amusement at the fellow's lack of self-discipline. Julius mused that his job was so ridiculously easy most of the time. People's awareness of their surroundings was so low, he wondered how the species had survived so long. He thought with unrepentant immodesty that it was because of people like himself.

Julius stepped out into the cold morning. The snow had stopped falling, and the sky shimmered with the aurora, so intense that he could see it clearly even here, on the city street beneath bright lights. The last time he'd been in this town it was to do a job, that Freeman kid. It had been so ridiculously easy to make it look like a simple drug overdose. He looked forward to getting out into the woods to the north where the northern lights could be seen better. He pulled his collar up, slipped on his gloves, and walked across the street and down the stairs to the covered parking area. On reaching his car, he tapped the six digit code on the door keypad that disarmed the alarm system and unlocked the door. From the back seat he gathered the items he had brought with him and returned to the hotel room. His attention was so focused upon his plans that he did not notice an old Jeep Cherokee with fogged windows across the lot.

He opened the styrofoam cooler and looked inside. To his satisfaction, there was still quite a bit of dry ice left, he would not have to make a special trip to buy more. The icicles he had left there were cold and hard. He took one out in his gloved hand and examined it. A cold fog fell from it towards the floor in the warm air, but the ice was clear and unfractured, bearing only a few small air bubbles. Julius laid the piece of coarse sandpaper on the edge of the bathroom counter and carefully sanded the wide base of the icicle until it was smooth and round. Then he chucked it into the cordless drill, set the drill for a low speed, and began slowly turning it against the sandpaper, thinning and smoothing it into a symmetrical needle of ice about ten centimeters long and about five millimeters in diameter, with a delicate and sharp point. As soon as the shape was satisfactory, he replaced it in the dry ice to keep it from melting and continued with the others. After an hour's deliberate effort he had produced six satisfactory projectiles. Two of the original eight icicles that he had brought had been flawed and were rejected as unusable... these were now melting in the sink.

He opened the box of cotton balls and took one out, carefully pulling it apart and fluffing it. He assembled and lit the propane torch, then held the base of one of the ice needles over the flame until it looked wet. He delicately wrapped a wad of cotton over the blunt base of the needle and allowed it to freeze in place before preening and adjusting the fluff to an even diameter. He smiled in satisfaction at the perfectly formed blowgun dart he had made. He continued until all six darts were similarly fletched. He made a bed of cotton balls in the cooler of dry ice, to keep the delicate projectiles from jostling and breaking. When completely satisfied in all details, he proceeded to the final step. He took from his case an aspirin bottle, turned it upside down and unscrewed a false bottom. A tiny vial of a heavy dark brown liquid was secreted there. Then Julius, with infinite care and finesse, took the cap off the vial and carefully dipped the tip of each needle, one by one, into the liquid. He watched with fascination as the organic molecules in the thin film of liquid crystallized on the surface of each delicate point. When he had the tips of all six projectiles coated with their lethal payload, he closed the vial, nestled each dart into its place in the nest and replaced the top on the cooler.

Julius worked on the piece of plastic pipe with the sandpaper, smoothing the ends, and paying especial attention to the inside. He blew crumpled wads of tissue paper through the tube until he was satisfied there were no projections or rough places that would cause problems. Finally, he fitted the connector at the base of the air gun to the hose on his pressurized air tank. He wrapped the nozzle of the air gun with duct tape until it could be thrust tightly into the end of the piece of plastic tubing. Again he tested it by blowing a piece of tissue through the tube with the compressed air.

When finally satisfied that his apparatus would work as planned, he gathered his things, checked out, and went to his car. The time was a little before five in the morning. It was still quite dark out as Julius left the parking area and drove back up Shelden Avenue. When he crossed the bridge into Hancock he knew approximately where he was going. Some people gathered on the bridge tried to stop him, but he gunned his motor and almost ran them down. "Street people and beggars!" he sneered to himself. "Why don't they get a job?" He did not recognize the faces of prominent community business people and University professors.

Julius was already halfway across the bridge before the engine of another car in the same parking area coughed into life. The faded white Jeep Cherokee eased out onto Shelden and began shadowing the gray Toyota Millennium. Chris Jameson had no fear of losing his quarry. A tiny plastic transmitter, carefully attached to one of the Millennium's fenders sent out a signal that could ordinarily be followed with ease. Even now, with electromagnetic interference from the solar storm as fierce as it was, an occasional pulse would get through, and that was all Chris needed. The hunter had become the hunted. Chris stopped on the bridge and rolled down his window.

"Evening sir." Said an elderly man bundled up against the cold. "We'll be closing the bridge at noon tomorrow in support of statehood for Superior. If you need to get off the peninsula anytime soon, you might plan to be below the bridge by then. They'll be closing the Mackinac as well, of course. Here's a pamphlet, and I have a free copy of the morning Gazette if you'd like to know more about it."

"Yes, thanks. And good luck to you!" Chris accepted the proffered items and smiled broadly at the activists as he accelerated again and continued on his way, staying at least three kilometers behind Julius Miller.

Julius followed highway 41 up onto Quincy hill, past the shaft house on his right. Two snowmobiles and several other vehicles were clustered there near the gift shop. Julius thought he saw movement as he passed. He was curious, as always, about what other people do in the early morning hours. At this stage of the hunt however, his mind was totally focused on the task at hand, and he never found out any more about it.

Julius continued on up through Calumet, into the desolate northwoods. At the lonely community of Phoenix he stopped to consult his computer map program for directions. Following its directions he turned left towards Eagle River and soon met a snowplow coming the opposite direction. With the road clear he was able to divert some of his attention to make sense of the rather arcane Township and Range map location for the cabin that he sought. The scale of the map he had was not ideal for selecting an individual cabin. Passing through the little village, he turned north up the lakeshore road, and started looking carefully. Most of the cabins looked as though they had been left closed up for the winter, only a few were occupied. He found two right next to each other that seemed to be in about the right place. Both had cars parked out front, and both had smoke streaming from the chimneys. He checked the map again, but it was impossible to tell which of the two cabins was the one he sought. He cruised slowly past, drove about two hundred meters around a bend and parked.

Julius put on his heaviest winter boots and extra clothing, and now prepared to ambush his prey. He decided to use one dart to test fire the simple air gun he'd made. He chose the least symmetrical of the poison tipped ice needles, inserted it point first into the tube, then shoved the tape wrapped nozzle of the air gun in tightly. He aimed at a point about four inches below a branch on a pine tree about ten meters away across the road, and squeezed the valve. With a quiet 'whoosh' the dart sped to the tree and shattered on impact. Julius walked over and examined the tree. A tiny dot of ice showed that the point had penetrated significantly, bits of cotton fluff clung to the rough bark. Against a softer target, like a human body, it might well have disappeared entirely. He was satisfied and proceeded to walk back down the road carrying the air tank and the plastic tube. One dart lay within the tube, the air gun jammed in place and ready. In his front jacket pocket were gently placed the other four remaining darts. The air tank was not absolutely necessary. He could, of course, also shoot the darts by blowing on the tube with his mouth, but not with anywhere near the speed or power the air tank provided.

There would be no chance for error, he had examined dozens of photographs of each of the targets, and knew their habits intimately. He had decided that there was now no point in keeping either of them alive. They had not, he felt, had time to relay any damaging information. Once they had been hit, the poison would begin working quickly, producing paralysis and death within minutes. The dart would then melt, and there would be no evidence to link him to the scene. The bits of cotton fluff would be a mystery, but he had been careful to handle them only with latex gloves, no DNA traces of any kind would be found on them. Blood tests done on the victims would merely reveal heavy dosages of opiates, and it was unlikely that an autopsy team would search for the much more subtle traces of the real killer once they had found such an obvious cause of death. He would then search their car and cabin to retrieve the computer data... plant some drug paraphernalia... mission complete. He felt a momentary sadness that it would be so easy, he had rather looked forward to more of a challenge. Ah well, best to simply get it done and be gone.

Julius walked slowly southward around the curve in the road and saw the two cabins before him. There were two cars parked at the furthest cabin, an old faded Willys sat in a recently dug spot, just off the roadway, plowed snow piled against it. Just behind the Willys was an older model Chevy Nova parked in the road, a rusted maroon in color. The Nova had obviously pulled in after the snow plow had passed. Closer at hand at the nearer cabin was a car parked off the road, so covered with snow that its make and model were indistinguishable. None of the cars was the Chevy S-10 that he had been keyed to search for, but that fooled him not in the least. Even a fool would have tried to switch vehicles if pursuit was known. It seemed to him that, at the earliest, they could not have arrived in time for their car to become as snow-covered as the nearest one. Therefore, he determined it was most likely they were in the second cabin. The presence of two cars in front of that cabin was somewhat disturbing. It meant that there might be others there as well. Dim light, as if from candles or oil lamps shone in the windows of both cabins.

The excitement began to build in him as he looked forward with anticipation to the hit... the shocked look on the victim's face, the horror as they realized their throat would not function, clutching at their chest wondering why they were drawing no breath. Julius looked up at the sky in wonder. No more beautiful morning could he have chosen for a kill. He had never beheld such beauty in nature. He stepped around the Nova and followed a roughly trodden snowshoe path to the door of the cabin, there would be time later for searching the vehicles. His boots sank to the knee in the deep snow, and his going was slow. He realized that he would have to dispose the boots as he was leaving clear prints. He rehearsed in his mind what he would say at the door. He would plead a car breakdown, a flat tire... could you help me please? Yes, of course. A piteous plea for assistance was almost always effective at getting people off their guard, especially when it came from such a frail and mousy looking little man. Yes, that would do nicely. He smiled with anticipation.

He held the air tank and tube in his left hand, the middle finger poised over the air valve. His right hand was free to offer in friendly greeting, or to quickly reload the tube with a fresh dart from his breast pocket where they lay nestled, points down in cotton balls, the tufts of their fletching just protruding from the pocket. He stepped onto the porch, making no effort at stealth, stomped the snow off his boots and knocked loudly. In his single minded pursuit of his goal Julius failed to notice a dark shape, silently treading is his steps behind him.

CHAPTER 45

Ruth drove Joan's old Chevy Nova north towards Eagle River. She had waited until everyone except Arne had left before taking off on this mission. She had been terribly frightened when she had seen Digger and Joan chased by the snowmobiles, and heard more shots fired. Jason and Jimmy however, assured her that the pair had escaped unharmed, impossible though it seemed. How could they possibly be so sure? There was some kind of "telepathic rapport", they had told her. Ruth had always known that Joan was a special person, but she had not suspected anything of this kind. She tried to relax, thinking that surely she had left the violence behind. But then... she had thought that once before, when she came here after years of ER work around Minneapolis and Milwaukee.

It was after five in the morning when she passed through Eagle River and turned up the lakeshore road. About a mile further along she met the oncoming snowplow, moving slowly, forcing the deep fresh snow into a bank along the side of the road. Around a bend she came to the place Digger had described. The road came near the lake and there were several cabins quite near each other. He had said there would be only one that was occupied, but Ruth saw two that had wisps of smoke emerging into the sky. She looked up. The sky shimmered with the aurora as if it were alive. But which cabin was it? Both had vehicles parked off the road, the first was an old Willys, the second was indeterminate due to a mantle of snow. Had Digger said what kind of car to look for? She didn't think so. Ruth hesitated, then pulled in behind the Willys. It just seemed like the sort of vehicle a friend of Digger's would drive. The snowplow had pushed so much snow up against it that she could not see the license plate.

She shut off the motor, confused at first when the engine dieseled for a few moments, the put it in gear and engaged the clutch, stopping it. Why didn't Joan get something newer? What a beast... to have to drive this old hulk! She got out a pair of snowshoes and stomped towards the cabin through the deep snow, trying to step in the same holes as those who had walked this way earlier. She stepped up onto the porch, recently swept off, and knocked. The cabin was completely dark within. There was only silence. She knocked again.

"Who is it?" came a male voice.

"My name is Ruth. I need to speak with James right away, it's an emergency."

"James?" The voice spoke through the door, muffled and indistinct.

"James Dolittle, please, it's very important."

The inner door opened. Ruth could see a disheveled looking young man wrapped in a blanket. "I'm sorry, there's nobody here named James. You must have the wrong place."

"He told me you might be afraid, he said to tell you that there's 'fire in the hole'. Please, I must speak with him."

"Who told you?"

"Digger, you know, your partner Digger Puttonen."

"Seriously ma'am, there's no James here, but the fellow at the next cabin is named James. I'm sorry, I don't know his last name, we just met last night."

"Oh, this really must be the wrong place then. I'm so sorry to have wakened you. Thank you very much." Ruth walked back to the road, and rather than drive the few meters, she left the Nova where it was kept the snowshoes on, and walked to the next cabin. Again she knocked on the door.

Again the voice came from within, "Who is it?"

"It's an emergency, I have a message for James Dolittle from Digger."

A rustling noise followed by the sound of feet hitting a wooden floor came from within. "From who?"

"Digger Puttonen, he said to tell you there's 'fire in the hole'. My name is Ruth."

A flashlight flicked on, scanning Ruth's face for a moment. The door opened and a man dressed in sweatshirt, sweatpants and slippers said. "Come in please." Ruth did so. She stomped the snow off her boots on a mat, and moved gratefully to the side of a roaring woodstove, while James lit an oil lantern.

A woman's voice, sounding sleepy, came from a loft above the kitchen. "James, what is it?"

"I don't know yet honey, an emergency message from Digger."

James' wife Barbara put on a dressing gown and came down from the loft. She put a kettle on the woodstove. Ruth had opened her coat and taken her gloves off, reveling in the heat. The heater is Joan's car was ineffective against the massive air leaks coming through the rusted holes in the body and floor.

"Alright Ruth, can you tell us what it's all about?" James said. Ruth sat down in a chair by the stove and told them everything... at least... everything she knew.

After Ruth had left the first cabin, Steve Sanders closed the door and walked back to the bed. Eileen flicked the safety back down on the nine millimeter pistol and set it on the night table. "What was that?" she asked.

"Some lady, said she needed to speak with James Dolittle right away. Message from Digger Puttonen." Steve's brows were furrowed in thought. Eileen could sense it, even in the darkness.

"Digger Puttonen? That's what she said? Are you sure?"

"Yes. I'm sure," answered Steve.

"But isn't that one of the guys...?"

"Yeah, I think so. It can't be a very common name." Steve shuffled to the north window, pushing back the heavy blinds and looking towards the neighboring cabin. "It's dark there, no wait... I see a light... Yes, they're letting her in."

Eileen got up hurriedly and got dressed. While she did that, Steve checked the wood stove and lit the oil lamp on the small kitchen table. Eileen opened a bag and took out her notebook computer, it booted immediately when she opened it. She shuffled through the bag of computer disks they had filched from their offices at Sherman Enterprises world headquarters the morning before. Steve was still getting dressed when she found the one she wanted, a copy of the briefing disk Steve had brought to George Sherman on the Midnight Mining Company situation. He was still putting his socks on, hopping on one foot towards the table when she brought up the appropriate screen.

"Look at this." She pointed. The names Digger Puttonen and James Dolittle were clearly listed as the two primary partners of the company, the two people who must be influenced if Sherman was to take over the company. Dolittle's address was given in Laurium. There was no mention of Eagle River.

Steve looked over her shoulder. "Is it possible?" he asked.

"Possible? Yes. Probable?... I don't think so."

"But if it's true, then we could help them, we have all the data." Steve said.

"But what if it's a trap?" Eileen was suspicious.

"How could anyone have traced us here so quickly? It's got to be for real. Besides, if they're in trouble, it's partly our fault. Who knows what Sherman's been up to since we took off?"

"Have we still got that newspaper?" Eileen asked.

"Yeah, I think it's in the bag with the food."

"Let's take a look at it." They spread the paper out on the table. The big headline was about the application of the Upper Peninsula to secede from Michigan and form it's own state as a member of the federation, complete with two senators and the usual complement of congressmen. The article went on to describe the demonstrations taking place across the UP, the closure of the bridges, and some of the legal and economic ramifications of secession. They turned to page two to finish the article, Steve scanned the page and pointed to a small item under the heading "business notes" ... "Midnight Mining Company Purchased by Sherman Enterprises."

Eileen thought hard. "What kind of feeling did you get from James and Barbara?"

"The neighbors? I guess I felt like they were the sort of people we could be friends with under better circumstances... I mean, if we weren't trying to keep a low profile. I liked them."

"That's what I thought too. What if we went over there, now, to talk."

Steve nodded, "Yeah, I think that's a good idea. They're obviously up and awake. Let's do it." They left the table and proceeded to finish getting dressed. Steve put on the Vorpal knife and harness, Eileen shrugged on the shoulder holster and extra magazines. The handgun still lay on the side table. There were footsteps on the porch, a loud knock came at the door. "Oh, it must be them," said Steve. He opened the door without challenging the visitor. He was surprised to see a small, middle-aged man with an air canister standing on the porch.

"Hello, I saw your light on so I hope I didn't wake you. I've had a flat tire just up the road here, wondering if you have an air compressor. My tank is empty I'm afraid."

Julius could not believe his luck, the door opened and they were both there, he recognized them immediately from their dossiers. His eyes quickly scanned the room without seeming to, and he saw the computer and the pile of disks lying out on the table. He did not want to shoot through the screen door, afraid that the dart might shatter and dissipate before finding its target. The bold approach... he reached for the handle and pulled. "You don't mind if I step in do you?" he began. His mind went into overdrive as he entered the tactical phase. Yes, the woman first, she was the threat, that's what the psych report said. She was also further away. When she is hit the man will turn to help her, they always do. That would give Julius the second or so needed to reload. He smiled warmly and nonchalantly swung the tube towards Eileen. Suddenly he felt a crushing blow to his left arm, his finger twitched involuntarily, there was a "whoosh" and the dart shattered harmlessly against the side of the woodstove, adhering fragments of the ice emitted a snakelike hiss. The tank and plastic tube clattered to the threshold of the door, his left arm broken and useless. Julius grabbed with his right hand for the remaining darts in his pocket. He managed to snatch two of them and whirled around lashing out at the face of the figure who loomed behind him. A hand blocked the blow, accompanied by a stifled cry of pain, a foot lashed out into Julius' chest with a crunching sound. Julius staggered backward through the door into the room, his mouth hanging open in exaggerated anguish. He reached to his waistband with his right hand, drawing a tiny derringer. Julius raised the weapon to aim at the figure kneeling across the threshold, clutching an arm. There was the loud report of a firearm being discharged in a small space. The derringer fell from Julius' lifeless hand as he collapsed in convulsions upon the floor, his tongue hanging out, eyes bulging.

Steve looked around to see Eileen, sitting on the bed, the pistol in her hand, a shocked expression on her face. "Are you alright?" he asked.

She nodded. "My ears are ringing is all."

He went to the other man, kneeling on the threshold in agony, holding his arm. "A tourniquet," the man gasped through clenched teeth, "quickly."

Eileen ran to the kitchen and hastened back with a piece of surgical rubber tubing her uncle used for siphoning water. Chris Jameson grabbed the tubing in his left hand, clenched one end between his teeth, and quickly wrapped it, tightly, around his upper right arm, just below the shoulder. "Okay, he gasped, now tighten it, tight as you can. Stick something in there and twist it."

Eileen found a wooden spoon and started to comply. Steve looked worried. "But why?" he asked. "There's no blood."

Chris snatched the glove off his right hand, there were two deep puncture wounds in his palm, a brown pustulent froth dripped from them. "Poison!" he gasped. "Forget the arm, it's gone. Just... get the.... tourniquet.... tight." Try as he might, Chris could not restrain a cry of pain. His hand felt like it had been dipped in molten lead, fire crept up his veins towards his shoulder.

Eileen twisted the tourniquet as tight as she could, the hand was turning blue. Suddenly Ruth was there. "What happened?" She asked in a calm but firm voice. Eileen tried to explain. James and Barbara were there a moment later. They helped to carry Chris to the bed. Ruth slit the sleeve off of Chris' right arm, looked at the black streaks creeping up beyond his elbow, sniffed at the wounds on his hand. She checked the tightness of the tourniquet, seemed content with it, then went to examine Julius, kneeling down beside him. The body still trembled slightly, the eyes wide open and glaring. She turned to Eileen. "You say this man was shot?"

"Yes, in the back."

Ruth shook her head. "He doesn't look like a man who's been shot. The opened the front of the coat and shirt. There was a tiny wound, wet with both water and blood, right above the heart just below where the breast pocket had been. Black streaks radiated from it across the chest. She shook her head. "This one's gone." She found the remnants of one of the darts in Julius' jacket pocket and placed it carefully in a plastic bag.

Ruth looked from Steve to Eileen, to Chris lying on the bed, and Julius, dead on the floor. "What in God's name is going on here?"

"It's Sherman." Chris croaked. "He wants you dead, all of you."

"Who are you?" asked Ruth.

"Chris... Jameson."

"Jameson?" said Steve, "But i know that name... you're..."

"NO! Not any more." Chris stammered out through clenched teeth. "I used to work for him, yes. This hand..." He looked at his right hand, which was already lifeless and turning pale blue. "This hand has done more bad things than I can bear to think of, probably more than you could imagine. But no more, it's dead now. He sent Miller after you, after you left. I've never heard him so angry. Something happened to me though, I changed, I decided to stop him, I tried my best, really I did." Chris started sobbing.

Ruth grasped it all in a flash of insight. "But you did Chris, you did stop him."

"NO, you don't understand. He's here, he came, with more men, too many. Those idiots don't have a chance! You don't know him, he's evil I tell you!"

"Shhhh, relax Chris. You have to relax, we don't want this poison to get past the tourniquet. It'll be okay, we'll go now, you saved them Chris, you did it." Ruth stroked Chris' forehead, for a few moments. As if a fever had broken he lay back and relaxed.

James looked from Steve to Eileen. "You mean.. you two are involved in this Sherman mess too?"

Eileen nodded. "Yeah, pretty deeply. We were his main programmers at headquarters. He decided we were too dangerous and was planning to have us killed. If this guy here is Julius Miller, which I believe he is, he was the one who was going to do the job. Steve broke one of their encryptions and we found out about it. Then we took off. I can't imagine how he could have tracked us here so quickly."

James looked more than interested. "Are you saying you're computer programmers? Decryption programmers?"

Steve answered, "Yeah, well, it's sort of a hobby."

"I can't believe this. Come on, we've got to get down there to the mine. Wait... have you got your programs with you?"

"Of course, right here." Steve indicated the pile of disks on the table, each capable of storing 64 terrabytes of data.

"Chris needs to get to a hospital, he'll need an amputation." said Ruth.

"How soon?" asked Eileen.

"Right away, there's no time to lose."

James went to his wife. "Barb, I have to do this, you understand. You'll stay with the kids?" She nodded.

Ruth spoke up. "The rendezvous is at my house in Paavola, just four doors north of Digger's. Once there we can find out what's happened so far. Arne is there waiting."

Eileen asked, "Arne? Who's Arne."

"Uh, a friend of ours, you'll meet him." Chris was squirming, struggling with something. "What is it Chris? Can I help you?" Ruth asked.

"My keys, get the Cherokee, it's just around the bend to the south."

She helped fish the keys out of his pocket, held them thoughtfully. "Are you sure?"

He glared at her in agony, tinged with amusement. "Would you get going! There's no time to drive that old Nova! If Sherman figures out how to use the equipment in that mine before we stop him. It's over, for all of us."

James grabbed the keys and dashed out the door to bring the Cherokee closer. Steve, Ruth, and Eileen grabbed a few necessary items quickly, then slung bags over their shoulders.

Ruth looked at Chris critically. "He shouldn't walk. We'll use that folding cot as a stretcher. Come on now, all hands." They helped the protesting Chris Jameson onto the stretcher and carried him out the door, down the trail through the snow, and into the back of the Cherokee. Ruth took the wheel, with James beside her. Steve and Eileen clambered into the Willys, fired it up and powered out of the deep snow the plow had pushed against them.

James rolled down the window of the Jeep and spoke to his wife. "Take care now, I'll be back in a while. Love ya." He kissed her quickly and then they were gone, the two vehicles making all speed back towards the 'big' city, and whatever fate waited for them there. Barbara stood alone on the dark road, thought of her two little girls, still asleep in the cabin, and started walking back. She turned just as the Jeep's tail lights disappeared around the bend. "Good luck." she said quietly. Shimmering curtains of light waved in an invisible magnetic breeze miles overhead as she trudged alone, through the snow to the cabin.

CHAPTER 46

Digger Puttonen stood watching and listening about ten meters below the collar of the Quincy number 6 shaft, where the shaft opened out into the top of the huge stopes and workings of the old Quincy mine. Around the edge of the rock protruding above him, he could see the shapes of men silhouetted against the glittering sky, and barred by the dark lines of the rails that had been welded over the opening to prevent anyone from blundering into the pit. He could hear the tones of their voices, but could not make out their words, the consonants were drowned in the echoing background noise of endlessly dripping water. He faintly heard the grating scrape of heavy steel, and realized that they had located the loose rail. He hurried back along a narrow ledge to where Joan was waiting. The ledge ran to the north, along the steep footwall of the stope. above their heads just a few meters was the arching ceiling of the stope. To their left was an inky black void plunging into darkness, the hanging wall of the stope nearly ten meters away.

"Well, I guess you're coming with me after all," Digger said resignedly. He pulled a headband lantern out of is pack and put it on her head, then put another on himself. "I think they're going to try to follow us. Let's try not to make it too easy for them." He led the way along the ledge for some distance until they reached a place where the ledge narrowed to only about five centimeters.

From the little he could see of her face, Joan did not seem too concerned, but her voice revealed her trepidation at their situation. "Uh, Digger. I don't like this. I'm afraid I'm going to slip."

Digger encouraged her. "You're doing great. Just a little further, then we reach the handrail." As promised, just before the most difficult point they found a rope strung along the wall. It was tied stoutly to a galvanized steel ring anchored into the rock, and affixed to spaced masonry bolts placed in the wall about every two meters. This they used as a handhold to help them along this tricky section. The rope was a stout 11mm braided nylon line and seemed to be in good condition.

In fact, Digger had installed it here less than two years previously. They moved cautiously along, trying to use as much of the ledge as possible and trying not to put their weight on the rope any more than necessary. Still, at one point Joan's foot slipped off the ledge, and the handhold proved itself to be essential. After about twenty meters of slow progress in this fashion the ledge became wider again, and they found the far end of the rope securely tied to its metal ring embedded in the rock.

Digger looked back towards the entrance and saw the beams of flashlights stabbing through the darkness. "Turn off your light!" He whispered hoarsely to Joan, as he did the same. At that moment a screeching shot echoed through the vast emptiness, and they heard the whine and ping of a projectile pass close by and strike the rock a few meters further on. Digger felt the heat of anger rise in his abdomen. Until this point he had been simply reacting to circumstances and had not had the time to find an emotional response to their predicament. Now however, he was acutely aware that people were actively trying to kill him, and his love. The anger rose in him as he drew the pistol from the holster beneath his jacket, braced his arm against the rock wall and pointed it back towards the slowly bobbing lights as the pursuers struggled along the dangerous path. He could not aim accurately because of the darkness, and the distance was something over one hundred meters. His temples throbbed with anger as he struggled to control the shaking of the weapon.

"Digger?" Joan's voice came softly. He felt her hand touch his back. He calmed down. "Think about what you're doing."

Digger's shoulders slumped. "What do you want me to do? They're trying to kill us." Digger half turned to face her in the utter darkness.

"I know," she said. "It's just... I'm afraid of what it would do to you, to kill a person like that, without warning."

Digger thought for a moment, then holstered the gun and felt for the knotted end of the rope again. He worked at the knot for a few seconds before realizing it was far too tight to be loosened, then pulled a slim stainless steel knife from a plastic sheath dangling from his neck on a chain. He sawed at the rope next to the knot until he had cut almost all the way through the rope at the ring, leaving just a few tiny strands of the sheathing still holding it together. He glanced back along the ledge, and could see by the bobbing of the beams of light that their pursuers were busy worrying about their own footing.

They switched their headlamps on and continued scuttling quickly down the wider ledge. At the moment Joan was too busy watching where she put her feet to marvel at the scenery around her, but Digger was well familiar with it. He was taking Joan along one of the paths he had made, to one of his favorite places. They had dropped into the Quincy number six shaft. Bare and plain on the surface now, it had once been the pride of the mine, indeed, it had been possibly the most profitable copper mine in history. When the miners reached the ore zone in this area back in the 1880s, they had encountered ore of a richness never seen before or since... entire car loads of it sometimes assaying at 60% copper by weight. The ore was so fantastically rich that, in their greed, the mine owners had skimped on the usual practice of leaving pillars of ore to hold up the roof. They had ordered men to go into the stopes to remove the pillars as well, replacing them with wooden posts. After a few years the posts had rotted and fallen into the yawning blackness below. This was not considered important, as by that time there were no miners anywhere nearby. The active portions of the mine were now far away and many levels below, so the possibility of a collapse was deemed inconsequential. The great open stope was a steeply angled room following the planar copper ore body, with a roof about one kilometer square, and with hardly a pillar to hold it up.

Nobody knew exactly where the copper had come from, that was the great geological mystery of the Lake Superior mineral district, but the rocks that bore the copper were relatively well understood. The story had been pieced together by legions and generations of geologists, each gathering a bit of information here, another clue there. Because of the potential wealth of mineral riches, a great deal of geological expertise was lavished here, and the picture of past events eventually became pretty clear.

About a billion years ago, in a period of the late Precambrian known as the Keweenawan, there had been a great rift in the earth's crust. In those days the crust was much thinner and the moon was much closer, resulting in intense periodic tidal flexing of the crust. In the area that would later become the Lake Superior district, the giant rift periodically disgorged floods of molten basalt rock in response to this tidal flexing. Basalt is a dark heavy rock, composed chiefly of mafic minerals and devoid of quartz. This mineralogy gives basalt a very low viscosity while molten, so that the floods of lava flowed many kilometers before they finally froze beneath the oxygenless skies of early earth. Like many other lavas, basalts contain some dissolved gases, and upon their release from the restraining pressures of the deep earth, these gases bubbled out of the lava and formed a froth at the top, which quickly hardened and froze in the cool air. Layer upon layer of basalt lava poured forth over hundreds of thousands of years, forming a layer cake thousands of meters thick. Some layers were as much as twenty meters thick. Every layer had it's frothy top, it's "amygdaloid" of gas filled voids. Eventually the great rift welded itself shut with this outpouring of molten rocks, and the great basin that had been periodically filled with molten lava, became filled with water. Sands and pebbles from surrounding volcanic mountains were washed by the action of rain and streams into the basin on top of the basalts. Inexorable forces of compression pressed inward from the sides of the basin, the center was pressed downward while the sides were folded upward into a great syncline. Somewhere far below, too deeply buried to be detected by ordinary geophysical methods, there must have been a copper rich intrusion. Hot acidic waters deep in the earth dissolved the copper and seeped towards the surface through the path of least resistance... the frothy amygdaloid zones of the buried flood basalts. As these mineral laden waters surged towards the surface, the pressure decreased, and with it the solubility of copper. Pure copper metal was precipitated out in the amygdules, the fissures, the cracks, in any weakness that could be found in the rocks. It was deposited in crystals, plates and masses, sometimes weighing several tons. The great stopes of the Quincy number six had been just such a place. An exceptionally thick lava flow with a thick and highly mineralized amygdaloid zone intersected the surface of the earth an angle of fifty five degrees on top of Quincy Hill. The basalts were more resistant to erosion than the sandstones and conglomerates, so they tended to stand out as ridges on the earth's surface. One basaltic arm of the great syncline eventually became Michigan's Keweenaw peninsula, the other arm was represented by Isle Royale, far out in Lake Superior.

Miners eventually came to the region to dig the copper ore, and, as miners do, they named the things they found. The great lode of the Quincy mine was called the "Pewabic". The miners drilled and blasted, mucked and hauled, frequently exploited terribly by the mine bosses from back east who cared more for tonnages and profits than for the safety or well-being of their workers.

There were many other minerals that characterized the deposits of the Lake Superior district besides native copper. Silver was often associated with the copper, as were calcite, epidote, analcite, prehnite, natrolite, thompsonite, datolite, and laumontite. The Quincy mine geologists well knew that several meters stratigraphically above the Pewabic in the hanging wall, there lurked a layer of laumontite. Laumontite is a zeolite mineral that tends to form in veins and masses of unconsolidated small crystals. It has very little tensile strength, and was known to the miners as the "widowmaker" because of it's weakness.

Then came the great Quincy Mine disaster of 1906. At about the time the surface waves from the great San Francisco earthquake reached the Keweenaw, the laumontite layer in the hanging wall of the giant stope in the Quincy #6 let loose. A seven meter thick slab fell from the whole one square kilometer area of the roof all at one time, the rubble falling nearly five hundred meters to the bottom of the stope. The immense rockfall displaced so much air downwards that it created an air blast thousands of meters below. Nobody was hurt by the rockfall itself, nobody was within a mile of the site, but over seventy men were killed by the incredible blasts of air that swept down the shafts and tunnels, tearing rails off the floors and smearing men on the walls like ripe tomatoes.

It was across the top of this very stope that Digger led Joan, the incredible void was the product not only of men digging into the earth for copper, but also the great collapse. The yawning immensity was beyond staggerment, virtually impossible to describe to someone who has not been there. They heard the echoing voices in the darkness, and felt an inky fear seeping upwards out of the gloom, clawing at their heels.

Digger reached a small alcove in the wall, a comfortable spot some two hundred meters north of the shaft. Beyond this they would have to go around a buttress, an irregularity in the footwall, and their lights would be easily visible to any who were trying to follow. Digger pulled Joan into the alcove, and made sure she had found a stable position, then he reached up and turned off her light, followed by his own. For a few moments the lovers caught their breath and let their eyes get used to the darkness, then they peered out and looked back towards the entrance. A pale gray gleam could dimly be seen drifting down from the shaft in the distance. The flickering beams of four flashlights punctuated the gloom, showing clearly in the thick moist air. They shone randomly about, then focused on the narrow part of the ledge.

A voice shouted out of the gloom, magnified and echoing eerily. "Hey, we just want to talk to you."

Digger whispered to Joan. "It's warm in here. We'd better take off our coats here, If we end up coming back out this way, we'll pick them up." They helped each other in the confined space of the alcove. Digger climbed up a few feet and jammed the coats into a crack in the rock, where the followers would be unlikely to find them.

The voice shouted again. "We know you're in here. Come on out and talk. I swear we won't hurt you."

He squatted down next to Joan. Every once in a while a light dimly flashed on a nearby point of rock. Digger cupped his hands to his mouth and shouted. "Go back! Go back or you will die here." Then he turned to Joan and spoke softly. "I'm hoping they'll give up. If not, we may have trouble. Just around this buttress the ledge ends, we have to go down to another ledge about ten meters lower. There's another rope there to help us, but we'll be exposed during part of that descent."

"Where are we going?" Joan asked.

"To the north and down, until we reach the water level." Digger answered. "This is the path I made to get to one of my datolite pockets. I come here sometimes to chisel out new pieces. The ledges were here, but I cleaned off the gravel and mud, and I put in the masonry bolts and the rope handhold for the tricky parts. Hopefully, with that rope behind us cut, it will prove a little trickier for them than it was for us."

The voice came again, echoing in the darkness. "We know you're in here. There's no way out. You may as well talk to us."

Digger peered around the corner. He spoke softly to Joan. "Two of them are on the rope." He held his breath, had he cut it through deeply enough? Suddenly he jumped up, switched on his light and yelled. "Hey there, what do you want to talk about?" The lead man crossing the roped section looked up, startled, one foot slipped. He put his weight on the rope and without warning it snapped. He toppled backward, holding the line, he buckled his knees to stay close to the wall, but slipped down the steep slope holding the line. When it came taut the line was too thin and wet to hold on. He slid with an agonized screech along it, until the bitter end slipped through his hands. He bounced once and sailed out into the open space, his flashlight spinning crazily, his scream cut off abruptly. The noise of his fall included not only the occasional thud of the body, but also the chattering of small stones that accompanied him. The echoes lasted nearly twenty seconds, and ended with a deep throaty sploosh as the body hit the water some two hundred meters below. Digger and Joan looked up to see the other man that had been on the rope, still struggling to hang on. This one had been closer to one of the anchor bolts when the line had snapped, and was able to hang on to the rope. He made it back to the ledge with some difficulty. Digger saw that their chance to move had come now that the three remaining men were obviously concerned with their own problems for the moment. Digger motioned to Joan to follow him. "Keep your light shining away from them at all times. If you turn back to look, turn the light off first okay?" She nodded.

  He led the way, twenty more meters along the ledge out around a bulge. A thick knotted rope hung there, attached to two bolts set in the rock. Digger turned his lamp off for a moment, then looked back at the men still struggling to cope with the narrow ledge. They were trying to rethread and tie the safety rope as they went along. They had almost certainly discovered by now that the rope had been cut. "Now's our chance Joan. keep your head turned away and they may not see us. He grabbed the knotted rope, and putting his feet against the steep basalt wall, started walking backward using the knots on the rope as handholds and small irregularities in the rock for footholds. He quickly reached another ledge some ten meters below, motioned for Joan to follow, and switched off his lamp. She took the rope with some concern, but found the process to be not as difficult as she feared. Still, she was nearly to the lower ledge when someone yelled. "There they are!" A shot rang out, the sound reverberating ominously. Joan heard the bullet strike the rock a foot above her hand, and felt the sting of rock chips pelting her face. It took all of her willpower to stay focused on the difficult climbing and not panic into a mistake. The very last bit was vertical, down onto the wide ledge where Digger stood. Joan felt Diggers hands helping her as she reached it, then pressing her against the rock. They stood on a flat shelf about a meter wide. If they remained flat against the rock, the bulge above prevented them from being seen.

  Digger spoke quietly. "Go on down this ledge until you reach the end of it, a couple hundred meters, I'll be right behind you." Joan moved slowly along the ledge, keeping her balance by using her right hand on the wall, and carefully placing her feet to guard against a slip. Digger reached up as high as he could with his knife and again cut the rope nearly all the way through, two knots above the bottom. That would make it very awkward for any followers to reach the ledge. He hurried along and found her waiting, holding a hanging rope. Five meters away the ledge continued, but the space between was smooth and void of hand or footholds, a trickling stream of water ran down through the middle of it. A rope hung down from above with a fixed loop in the end.

"Here's the pendulum." He said. "I fixed the anchor away up there about twenty meters, you sit in this loop and run across until you reach the ledge on the other side. Turn off your light for a second." When both their lights were off he looked back towards the pursuers. The men could not be seen, but their lights occasionally played out into the darkness. "Okay now look up for a minute." Joan looked and it seemed there was a tiny postage stamp of dim light above.

"What is that?"

"We're crossing below old the number five shaft. This is where the rails used to run."

"You mean, that's the sky? It looks so bright!"

"Compared to this, it is." Digger looked back. "Okay, those guys are getting too close for comfort, we need to cross the shaft now. I'll go first if you want. Just slip this loop over your head, and sit in it. See? It's strong enough, I promise. Now like this... run across the wall... over to... unnh... this side." He slipped out of the loop. "Okay here it comes, catch."

Digger threw the rope to Joan, who caught it and repeated the procedure. Once Joan joined him across the pendulum Digger looped the rope around a projecting rock, to deny the convenience to their pursuers. "This won't stop them, they'll still be able to climb up to get the rope, but it will slow them down. Besides, they may not be as trusting of my ropes after that first incident." He said nothing about notching the second one.

"So, you think that guy is dead?" asked Joan.

"The one that fell?" She nodded. "Yes, I'm afraid so. Not many people could survive a fall of a hundred and fifty meters bouncing down steep slope into water. Come on, let's keep going." Joan looked down, she couldn't see anything more than a few meters down. Maybe it was better that way.

"What about the second rope, the one coming down the slope?" asked Joan.

Digger hesitated. "They could have some trouble on that one too."

Joan decided the answer told her enough and decided not to press the issue. They continued along the narrow ledge, which now began angling downward perceptibly, leaving the sounds of their pursuers further and further behind. Ahead in the gloom there loomed a tremendous pillar of rock connecting the footwall with the hanging wall, the first they had seen. As they stepped onto it, Digger let out a sigh of relief. "Okay, we're past the worst part."

A terrified shriek punctuated the gloom echoing from the distance behind them. The sounds echoed and reverberated around them with a frightening quality. They dimly heard a thumping, followed by another distant splash. Joan shivered, but not from cold. "What was that?" she asked, though she already knew the probable answer.

"I would guess that somebody had trouble negotiating the climb down the knotted rope. I uh, shortened it a little," he said. He walked out onto the massive pillar, at least ten meters thick, to look back. In the distance, some three or four hundred meters away, he could see the pinpoint flicker of flashlights still coming in their direction. He took a spare flashlight out of his pack and set it on the pillar, aiming it back towards their pursuers. He walked casually back to where Joan sat, out of the direct line of sight.

"Go... back!" he yelled loudly, spacing the words so that they might be understood. The only answer was the reverberating report of firearms being discharged. They heard the smacking of lead bullets hitting the rock near the flashlight and turned their faces away to avoid injury by flying pieces. "Help me now," Digger said to Joan, as he started pushing a heavy rock towards the edge. "As soon as it falls, scream bloody murder, like you're falling." With her help the large boulder tumbled into the void with a loud rumble, taking some smaller rubble with it. As Joan burst forth with a horrified scream, Digger tossed a fist sized rock and knocked the flashlight off the edge, tumbling it into the darkness as well. His yell joined hers for a moment, then he stopped suddenly and put his hand over her mouth. The noise of the rockfall reverberated in the darkness, their echoing screams dying out slowly. He sat down with her in the rubble. "If we're lucky they'll think they've got us and go away," he said quietly. They sat there a few minutes, then Digger crept carefully out without light to look back. He could still see two flashlight beams, but they were pointed the opposite direction, and were growing more distant. He sighed with satisfaction. "Good! They've given up. Let's rest a while before we go on. That will make sure they believe they've killed us." He leaned back against the rock wall and got comfortable.

Joan said quietly. "I really had no idea."

"About what?"

"The mine, how big it was in here."

"Oh yeah, it's amazing isn't it?" he answered.

"I mean... on the surface, all you see are the buildings, sometimes you look down the shaft. I knew they were big inside. But, I never imagined..."

"Yeah, I know what you mean. In the movies whenever somebody goes into a mine, there's a tunnel, and some wooden timbers."

"And there's always a rumble before a collapse."

"Right! Well, welcome to reality. You are now in one of the largest mines in the world. The amount of rock taken out of this hole could build the Great Pyramid at Giza six times. The deepest shaft, the number two, went down a hundred and twenty levels, over three thousand meters. There were five hundred kilometers of tunnels, complete underground machine shops, and thousands of workers."

"And you know your way around it?"

"Only with a map."

"You have one with you... can I see it?" asked Joan.

"Sure." Digger clamped a tiny light in his teeth and fished around in his pack. He pulled out a crumpled photocopy of a map of the Quincy mine. "See? Here are the shafts. Here's where we came in, and here's where we are now."

"Just that far?"

"Like I said, it's a big place."

"Where are we going?"

"See this line I've drawn here? That's the current water level. We're going to go down this way to the water, then I hope my remote control will let me call the grunt."

"But what about me? You said there was only room for one."

"I know, it'll be tight, but we'll both fit. We'll have to, we don't have much choice."

"What if you can't get the grunt to come?"

Digger sighed. "One problem at a time please."

"Okay, okay. Do you think it's safe to move yet?"

Digger peered out once again. He could see no sign of the men that had been chasing them. "Yeah, I think so. You'd better give me a kiss though to make sure."

"A kiss? What difference will that make?"

"None, I just had to think of some way to get you to kiss me."

"You idiot! All you have to do is ask."

Joan pulled Digger to her, kissing him passionately. Here in the bowels of the earth, in Stygian darkness with the sounds of death still echoing in their ears, two lovers find solace in each other. They forget, just for a moment, the terrible fear that pursues them, or the daunting prospects of what lies ahead.

After a long while Digger leaned back to catch his breath, and turned on his headlamp. "Wow, I never kissed anyone like that... not here anyway."

"You!" Joan playfully slapped him on the shoulder.

Digger took one last careful look back in the direction from which they had come, but there was no longer any sign of pursuit. He gave Joan a hand up, put on his pack, and started trudging down a steep slope of rubble. He explained, "We've reached an area where some pillars were left to keep the entire thing from collapsing. They didn't want to leave them of course, the pillars are made of copper ore, see?" He thumped a projection with the heel of his hand, it rang dully. "Solid copper, they left it behind. We can walk almost all the way down to the water from here. The fall rock snags on the pillars you see, gives us a slope to walk down."

For a while they slithered among the stones, trying to stay as close as possible to avoid sending rocks tumbling onto each other. Finally they reached a drop off. Digger picked up a rock and threw it, about ten meters below there was a kerplunk.

Joan could see ripples radiating out from the spot. The water had been absolutely still, and clear as glass; she could have stepped right into it without seeing it at all. Joan was awed. "It's beautiful!" she whispered. She saw below them a shelf of rock, right at the water's edge. Suddenly she looked up curiously. "Digger, why do you come here?"

He thought a moment. "Well, I come looking for mineral specimens. In fact, I have datolite pocket not too far away that I've been working on for a couple of years."

"No, that's not enough, there's more than just that."

He hesitated. "I don't know, I just... I like it I guess. I like the quiet and the echoes, I like the smell, there's a stark beauty here that just calls to me."

"What about the danger?"

"The danger? Yeah, it's here. I don't go out of my way looking for it, but yeah, I suppose there's a sense of power in confronting a potentially dangerous environment and persevering. I don't ever feel I've conquered it though, I never lose respect for the hazards."

Joan nodded. "I think I can understand a little now. I always thought that guys who went in for dangerous pastimes were just self destructive, but that's not it at all."

Digger nodded, "Come on, one more drop to the bus stop, then we find out whether or not we have a ride." He reached behind a boulder and withdrew a coiled ladder of steel cable with aluminum rungs. He clipped it to a masonry bolt anchored in the rock, and proceeded to climb down. "Try to keep you weight close to the ladder." He called up. "Put one foot on each side." He demonstrated, climbing down the edge of the ladder. He held the ladder taut at the bottom as Joan came down. They stood now at the surface of the water, about level with the surface of Lake Superior, and at least two hundred meters beneath the top of Quincy hill above. Digger took off his pack and opened it, taking out a crudely scrapped together plastic box with a switch and light. He tied a piece of cord through a hole in one flange, then looped the other end around a rock. Joan watched curiously as he flicked on the switch, and let the device dangle in the water. The tiny red light made the water glow slightly. Then he sat down.

"Now what?" asked Joan as she sat beside him.

"Now we wait. According to James, this little bugger puts out the proper signal to call the nearest grunt to it. Before I left the lab I set one to patrol this area. It should respond... if."

"If?"

"If the grunt has not been reprogrammed, if it's close enough to detect this, if this thing works.... just... if."

They sat quietly together for about thirty minutes, leaning against each other and holding hands. Finally Joan thought she heard something, she looked up. Digger had cocked his head to one side. The she heard it again, louder, it was a strange sound, almost like a pig, like a... grunt."

Digger stood up and sighed with relief. "Looks like we get a ride after all." Joan saw something looming below the surface, it approached slowly and then gently breached the surface right in front of them. It was a long cylinder of stainless steel and bronze, some five meters long and two in diameter. It sat there vertically, the rounded end sticking out of the water. Digger threw a loop of rope over the end and pulled it close, then flipped open a small coverplate and punched some buttons. The hatchway opened with a hiss of compressed air, the number G-27 was painted on it. He took the remote device out of the water, switched it off, and clipped it to the bottom rung of the wire ladder.

Digger stood up and turned to Joan, bowing formally. "Madam, your captain requests that you climb aboard."

Joan curtsied. "Thank you sir." She slipped feet first through the hatchway. The grunt settled momentarily deeper in the water, then with a hiss it compensated and rose again. Her voice came muffled from within. "Uh, you're right, I think it's going to be a little tight."

"Oh? spouting poetry at me now? Here take this." He handed down his pack. "Make way!" Digger carefully lowered himself through the hatch, he stood nose to nose with Joan in a tiny space. He kicked his pack to make more room for his feet. "Let's see. turn this way, yeah. Hmmm, I guess I'll have to reach the controls over your shoulder. Can you scrunch over a little... yeah... Okay." Digger activated a keypad on one wall and the hatch closed above them. With a hiss of air and a barely perceived sense of motion, the grunt sank slowly into the water. The mine above reverted to the darkness and silence to which it was accustomed.

CHAPTER 47

The secret New York offices of the United Nations Environmental Command (UNEC) were a veritable beehive of concentrated activity. In her corner office overlooking the city, Anna Sorensen stared into the video monitor before her with some frustration. Staring back at her was the face of Carmelita Hernandez, the current Director of the continent-wide Federation Bureau of Investigation. Anna spoke fervently. "But Senora Director, you must understand, this is absolutely a UNEC operation. We cannot possibly give you complete control."

"My dear Miss Sorensen, you may be First Speaker of UNEC, but you do not tell the director of the FBI what to do. You have not yet usurped the continental sovereignty of North America. We have allowed your agents to use our service as a cover, we have indulged you so far as to allow this ridiculous Special Investigations group to have 'branch' status. I have never believed, nor do I now believe, in any of your fairy tales of agents with psychic powers. I find it amazing that you have gotten as much cooperation from the other continental agencies as you have."

"Senora please, do not shut the door on me. We must cooperate. The current UNEC operation in the place called Superior is absolutely critical."

"I agree that the situation is critical, I do not agree as to why that is so, neither do I agree with you as to what should be done about it. What we have there is nothing more than a group of disgruntled citizens who are unsatisfied with their government and wish to change it. This situation has occurred countless times in the past, and will doubtless occur many more times in the future. I, quite frankly, do not care if they have their little State of Superior. Whether they do this or not is absolutely insignificant in the larger scheme of things. The fundamental fact remains that my government, the Federation government of all of North America, the government of the ground upon which you now stand First Speaker... my government, by the agency of the Prime Minister in person, has directed me to obtain control of the strategic intellectual and technological assets located within our territory. Specifically I refer, as you are well aware, to the Midnight Mining Company. By tomorrow afternoon a convoy of continental guard units comprising one full armored division will be arriving on site to physically claim that control. When they arrive I will have no more control of the situation, Madame Powers is commader-in-chief of that force. Do you still cling to your ridiculous notions?"

First Speaker Sorensen was inwardly almost in tears, though outwardly she was the very picture of calm control. "Mrs. Hernandez," she appealed. "You have children, whom you love, is that not true?"

The director's eyes narrowed. "Do you dare to threaten my family?"

"No director, not at all. I merely ask you this to find if there is not something, someone, that you love more than yourself."

The director's eyes softened and she smiled. "Of course, I love my children dearly, I would do anything for them."

"And your Federation?"

"But of course, my loyalty has never been in question."

"Consider my position then Senora. I am charged, not merely with safeguarding the welfare of North America, nor even just the Western Hemisphere. I have all the world to worry about. In my heart I dearly love each and every one of the silly people that we share this little planet with, including your children and my own, yet to be borne. I tell you now, in complete and open honesty, that the situation we face is unique in the history of the world. If the North American Federation gains unilateral control of these strategic assets, the other continents will soon hear of it you can be sure, and will be compelled to strike before you can use them. The result, according to every computer simulation we have run, would be inevitable global nuclear war. We have eyes and ears in many places, and I can assure you in complete confidence that this is true."

"But my dear naive child," said Mrs. Hernandez, "what would you have me do? Are we to sit idly by while a predatory multinational corporation usurps this revolutionary technology, making it for sale to the highest bidder? If I were to allow this, I assure you that I would be replaced as director within a matter of just a few hours."

"No Madam, I would not suggest such a course."

"You are resolved then to this idiotic plan? You would send two of your agents, with their supposed psychic powers, along with a mere handful of my men from a backwater post... alone against this industrialist and all his resources?"

"They are not alone Madam, and they are good people. Superior must be given the option of self government. The technological and political aspects of the problem are inextricably linked. According to our projections it is the only way. There is no time for anything else, nor would any other plan be effective. It is imperative that the time manipulation technology be secured by the United

Nations, reserved for the use of all nations... every government must have access to this, or none. This is our only chance."

"You must be insane! The world balance of power would be completely upset. The entire world would change overnight!"

"Your statements are not all exactly true Madam Director. The world would change, very much so, that is true. But the balance of power would not be upset, not if all nations had access to the device. Rather, it would be balanced, much more perfectly balanced than ever before."

"But there would be no more secrets!"

"Exactly! Only in this way will everyone know precisely the assets and liabilities of everyone else. The present world political situation is based on fear, and fear results from the lack of knowledge. Only when the continental powers truly know each other can we build a lasting peace based on trust. And real trust comes only with the ability to independently confirm that the other party is telling the truth. Surely this must make sense to you!"

Madame Director Carmelita Hernandez looked thoughtful. "You are persuasive my dear, and I wish I could help. I am afraid however, that the matter is completely out of my control. I cannot recall the troops. They will arrive tomorrow afternoon, my powers last only until their arrival."

"But you must recall them, or influence the Prime Minister to do so. Global war will surely be the inevitable result if you do not. Do you wish to see your children incinerated in nuclear holocaust because of an action you failed to take?"

"No First Speaker," the director said solemnly, "I most certainly do not, but it is a risk I must take. But hear this now... Anna." The director spoke uncharacteristically, using the First Speaker's familiar name. "Those troops will move in, sometime after noon tomorrow... IF... the situation is not otherwise resolved. Do you understand?"

"Yes Madam, you are saying that we have until noon tomorrow."

"I cannot be specific, but I think you understand."

"And you will support any moves we make until then?"

"Indirectly of course, but I will do what I can. And good luck my dear, for all our sakes I hope... no... I pray... that you are right." The screen went blank.

Anna got up from her chair and hurried out of the office. The adjoining room was large and dimly lit. There were rows of comfortable cubicles provided with computer consoles of an unusual design, men and women sat there, lost in concentration. Several of them appeared to be deep in a trance-like state. A young man hurried to her side. "Ma'am, look at this." He showed her a complex chart. "The indices have soared in the last two hours. Clearly our agents must have linked up, but even that would not explain so large a jump."

"Yes, thank you Andre', this is exactly what I needed to know." She spoke up loudly. "People, listen please!" Each and every person in the room looked up immediately as Anna projected a state of alarm."

"People," she stated plainly, using voice speech as well as directed mindal projection. "Today we face our greatest crisis, perhaps the crisis our organization was created and designed to handle. Within just a few hours the Federation government of North America will launch a military assault to secure the new temporal technology located in the Superior region of what is now Michigan. If they succeed, global war will certainly result." There were murmurs of dismay in the room. "If the industrialist George Sherman prevails, he who now controls the facility where this technology is located, global war will also be the certain result."

"But First Speaker, are there no other alternatives?" asked a young black woman.

"Yes, just one. We have two agents on the scene, Jason Desnick #4297, and Jimmy Canaris #6606. We believe they have linked up and that there are also others with the ability present. Every possible adept must focus all available energy into this area," she pointed to a world map, "to the Keweenaw Peninsula on the south shore of Lake Superior. Attune earth grid immediately, enter location matrix, zone focus one half of one degree, centered on forty seven degrees, nine minutes North latitude by eighty eight degrees thirty three minutes West longitude. Begin immediately."

Slowly, as people settled down and became comfortable, all physical activity stopped. There were no footsteps, no clicking of computer keys, no chit chat or clatter of coffee cups. And Anna Sorensen herself, the First Speaker of the world's most powerful clandestine organization, sat silently on the floor with her legs crossed, sending every gram, every iota of her energy, her love if you will, to this one tiny area on the surface of the globe. In this capacity she was simply one among many... her love, together with that of many others, formed a soft yet irresistible wave of goodwill that washed across the landscape. And if it should happen that Anna Sorensen, the woman, sent just a bit of her love more specifically to one person within that area, to a certain someone with whom she had once fallen in love, a certain young man named Jimmy Canaris who was now in the center of the swirling storm... well, there was nobody in the entire world who would blame her.

CHAPTER 48

Ruth closed the back door of her house after watching Digger and Joan disappear into the night with two other snowmobiles hot on their tail. There were worried expressions all around. "What are we going to do?" she asked, looking to Leonard for an answer.

Leonard looked grim. "What else but to go ahead with the plan."

"But what about Digger and Joan? If they're caught or killed, then there's no chance..." Ruth began.

"Whatever happens to them, we've got to try to get in there."

Jason said, "I think it's time for a few phone calls sir. With radio traffic cut off, we can assume Sherman must be using the ground cable phone system, let's try to get a tap on them. Next, I think you should call the director to see what help she can offer us, then be sure Samuels knows what's going on."

Leonard nodded and went to the telephone on the wall. Jason looked at Ruth. "You've got good enough directions from Digger to find James Dolittle?" She nodded but looked upset. "Will you be okay on your own?" he asked. "I know you were planning to have Joan go with you, but... she seems to have some other problems on her mind at the moment."

"Yes, I can find it, don't worry about me, I'm concerned about you guys. I mean... I know you can take care of yourselves," she gestured with her head, indicating the situation in the street outside, "but thirty armed men in prepared positions and expecting trouble is very different from four guys in a car expecting to jump somebody unawares. And now, after this... they may have been seen coming out of this house. Another group may already be on their way here now."

Jason reassured her. "I don't think so. They're stretched pretty thin too, and have a lot of problems to worry about."

Harry spoke up. "Isn't there anybody around here we can count on, a local militia or something."

Ruth snorted, "Are you kidding? I know some of those idiots... armchair warriors and gunshop commandos one and all. Probably couldn't shoot their way out of a paper bag, besides, their politics tend towards radical anarchism."

"Just what we don't need right now," agreed Harry.

Jason was looking at Jimmy, who held a scrap of a paper napkin in his hand. "I have a phone number," said Jimmy. "It was given to me by the son of an Ojibway councilman while we were on our way up here, he said to call it if there were matters that would affect the tribe. Later his dad said they'd help if they were needed."

Jason looked interested. "You think it's on the level?"

Ruth spoke. "They've lived here a lot longer than we have. I'm somewhat familiar with their situation, the state government has literally forgotten them, and since federation the Bureau of Indian Affairs has gone from a turd to a absolute crock. They are isolated and feel frustrated. Offer them a district seat or two in the Superior State assembly... give them a significant piece of the action and you might be surprised. They are some amazing people."

Leonard hung up the phone. "Samuels is having the Midnight Mining Company phones tapped. Information will be sent to this number as available."

"Did you talk to the director?" asked Jason.

"Yes I did, she said there was not one, but two agents of UNEC here." Jimmy raised his hand. "You?" Leonard exclaimed. Jimmy nodded.

"UNEC? What's that? asked Frank. Ruth also wanted to know about it, so Jason asked them to keep the information confidential and gave them the one minute explanation. They wanted to know more, but were ready to let Leonard continue. Frank lay back on his cot and gave Jimmy a curious look from beneath knotted eyebrows.

"As you said, Jason, the code word got me immediate access to the director. When I spoke with her she seemed extremely agitated. She said that the Federation government has given us only until noon tomorrow to resolve the situation, then an armored division of the continental guard will move in to take over."

"But, isn't that good?" asked Harry. "Then we'd have the muscle we need."

"No," replied Leonard. "That means that the government will crush the secession movement and take over the equipment we've heard about. The director was extremely concerned that if the technology fell into their hands..."

"It would mean intercontinental war," said Jason.

"Exactly," replied Leonard with a start, surprised that Jason knew so much. "She has given us just until noon tomorrow to secure those assets in the name of the United Nations. If we fail, the troops move in."

"But... that's only a few hours," complained Harry, "It's not enough time."

"You're right, it's almost no time at all."

Jimmy stood up. "We have no choice then, I'm going to try this phone number, I hope it's not a cellular," he said. He punched in the number and waited.

He heard, "Hello, you've reached the offices of the Ojibway tribal council. Please leave a brief message and a number where we can contact you after the tone. Thank you. BEEEP."

Jimmy hesitated a moment... "Emergency message for Jamey and Joshua and Joe... the time is," he checked his watch, "three AM, Friday the twentieth. This is Jimmy Canaris, the slayer of the spike buck. Tell Chokes Horses he was right, a time of danger is indeed upon us. A gang of mercenaries has taken over the Quincy Mine. They are well armed and many, perhaps as many as thirty. We hope to take the shaft house and root them out by morning. If we fail, the Federation military will move in by tomorrow noon. If that happens, there will be no State of Superior and the tribal council will probably lose any power it ever had. If we succeed, the State will be born, and the tribe will gain at least two seats in the new assembly. We may possibly even be able to establish an independant republic. If you can help, come many, armed, and as soon as possible, to the village of Paavola. The command post will be four doors north of a house that burned last night. There will be a UN blue flag flying out front. Beware of the Quincy mine shaft house, it is occupied and they have snipers. My friends, if you can come, come soon, the destroyer is upon us."

"What was that all about?" asked Leonard.

"Hard to explain," Jimmy said. "I got a machine at the tribal office and left a message. If they get it in time, there's a chance we could get some help from there."

Jason nodded. "Okay then, what are our assets?"

Harry added them up. "We have the four of us still in good shape. Jimmy's got the big gun, we have a rocket launcher with one rocket, and we each have our personal weapons."

"What about Digger and Joan? Do you think they're okay?" asked Ruth.

Jason and Jimmy looked at each other for a moment, closed their eyes and concentrated. Jason said, "I get a sense of excitement, combined with an air of confidence. I think they're hard pressed but okay."

"If they've made it into the mine then they're going ahead with the plan. We've got to be there for them when they get inside." said Leonard. He looked at his watch. "If Digger's time estimate is correct, it will be almost dawn before they're inside the labs. We've got a lot to do between now and then."

Jimmy spoke again. "We know Sherman has one up in the shaft house. He'll be able to see a long ways, as bright as it is out tonight. We must also assume he's got IR capability. If we try any sort of sneaking around in the snow we'll just get picked off. It's almost certain they have at least one person, maybe more, on the ground, in the building or in nearby buildings covering the approaches. We need to get in about the time Digger's ready, I feel that Joan's staying with him now, which is what she wanted to do and that will increase their combined psychic index. If Jason and I are together, we can coordinate and communicate with them. I suggest we go up towards the shaft house, stay out of range of the sniper and keep a careful watch on the place. Maybe we can spot where the guards are placed. Then, when it's time, we move in. We may be able to do something with the rocket launcher. Once the shaft is secure we'll have to leave at least one person to guard our backs while the rest go in."

Harry pointed out, "That leaves only three for the inside assault team."

"Plus Digger and Joan, yeah."

Harry sighed and shook his head. "It's not enough, not against professionals. This is insane!"

Leonard smiled. "You're right. Come on, insane or not, let's go check it out."

The four FBI men helped carry Frank back into the living room. Frank grabbed Jimmy's arm before he stood up. "Jimmy, what's this UNEC stuff, why didn't you tell me?"

"Sorry sir, I was in deep cover. If there had ever been a need for you to know, I would have told you."

"So," Frank smiled. "I thought it was strange how your 'hunches' and wild guesses would always come off. There was more to it than just luck eh?"

"Didn't hurt my usefulness as an FBI agent did it?"

"No, you were always one of the best." Frank squeezed Jimmy hand hard. "You take care now okay? By the way, where's the rest of the body armor? I'd be stone cold dead tonight without it."

"Right out in the Bronco sir."

Frank's voice took on the gruff tone of command. "You just get your little butt out there and bring those back in and put them on. I don't want anybody heading out there without it, understand?"

Jimmy smiled, "Yes sir!" and saluted smartly. He trotted out to the Bronco and brought back a bag filled with personal body armor. They spent a few minutes putting them on the people that weren't wearing them already, and adjusting the straps and loops for a good fit, then put their jackets back on.

Ruth looked at them and shook her head. "You boys be careful now, you understand?" They assured her they would, then trooped out and got into the Bronco, roaring off into the night. Ruth looked at Arne, who shrugged. A few minutes later an ambulance pulled up to the door and, with advice from Ruth, the two silent and hurried medics picked up Frank and Stephen for transport to the county hospital in Hancock. "Don't worry Frank, I just have a feeling, everything will turn out okay." He squeezed her hand and nodded. The door of the ambulance closed and it drove quietly away.

Ruth went back inside. "You'll answer the phone Arne?"

"Ya sure, you can count on me, we'll be here." Arne scratched Oby behind the ears, the old dog looked up at him adoringly.

Ruth got her coat on, found the keys Joan had left on the coffee table, and went out the door. She stopped to hang up the blue flag that Jason had dug out of a pocket and handed her, then went to the street and started up the old Chevy Nova. The UN blue looked strange, flapping in the wind there in front of her door, but she liked it. She spent a few moments admiring the incredible display of the aurora, then gingerly forced the old Chevy into gear and headed north up the peninsula to look for Digger's partner, James Dolittle, in a cabin somewhere near Eagle River.

CHAPTER 49

The temporal lab was dimly lit. The giant piece of equipment sat in the center, with the walls of the room invisible in the gloom. George Sherman's face was lit by the gray-green glow of a computer monitor as he peered over the shoulder of an employee who was furiously pounding at a keyboard. The door to the room was not locked, and Sherman turned quickly when the door opened and his underlings Scott and Jeff came in. The looks on their faces did not give him the sense that their mission had gone well. Sherman stood erect and spoke to the men at the computer console. "You two, continue trying to crack these passwords, I will be back." Then he spoke curtly to the new arrivals. "Follow me!" They walked out into the rough hewn corridor; Sherman locked the doors behind them and headed at a brisk walk back towards the offices. "Report!" he barked.

"Sir, we followed the snowmobile tracks from here to the village of Paavola, where we engaged the pair of saboteurs."

"Yes... and?"

"They managed to jump the roadway sir, eluding us for a short time. I followed their trail while Jeff went around by road to try to head them off. We suspected they were heading for the highway. As expected, they came out onto the road, and we had them cornered, that's when the car came up with two more men." Scott paused in his narrative and Sherman grew noticeably agitated.

"So... what? You killed them?" he snarled.

"Not yet, 'they jumped the bank, fired a few shots at us, and then disappeared into a mine shaft sir, they were cornered, there was nowhere else they could go. We couldn't afford to leave somebody there to keep watch, so we followed of course. Scott and I stayed back and allowed the other two to go ahead. The path was very dangerous sir, the narrowest possible ledge above a huge drop, it was almost unbelievable."

"I don't give a damn about your aesthetic impressions you moron, just tell me what happened!"

"In two separate difficult spots, the other two men... I never got their names... fell, and are presumed dead. Jeff and I continued following, and finally we got a shot at the sappers, we cut loose with everything we had toward their lights and heard them fall, screaming."

"But you didn't actually see them die?"

"Sir, it was absolutely dark in this huge space, you can hardly imagine it. We saw their light, started shooting, and then we saw a flashlight pitching off into the pit, just like when our guy fell. We heard the screams and the crunching of their bodies on the way down. I would stake my life on the fact that they are now dead, but it would be almost impossible to get all the way down there to confirm it."

"So, you eliminated the sappers, but you did not find out who they were, and you lost two of my men in the process. Is that what you're trying to tell me?"

"Yes sir, but we have their snowmobile, perhaps we could trace the registration numbers?"

"Get on it right away." Sherman said resignedly and shook his head. "And you'd damn well better be willing to stake your life that you're right son, because if they show up again, I'll shoot you myself. Do you have anything else to report?"

Scott and Jeff looked back and forth to each other. Neither wanted to be the bearer of bad news. Scott bit the bullet... "Sir, a fire truck was there in Paavola when we arrived, a house was burned to the ground, and there was also a burned out Ford Taurus sitting in the street. It looked like it may have been the one our boys took from the lot."

"Casualties?"

"We saw four body bags in the snow, couldn't get close enough to identify them, but I suspect they were our guys. There was also a blue Jeep Cherokee, looked like it had been shot up pretty bad, so maybe our boys gave as good as they got." The trio arrived at the office and burst through the double doors.

George Sherman tried his best, but his legendary temper got the best of him. "DAMN!!!" he exploded at the top of his lungs. Every face in the office looked up to see what was the matter. He looked around at his crew. One injured and six dead or presumed dead already... and they had not acquired any of the information they desperately needed. "Listen up people." Sherman's deep voice resonated loudly in the room. "There are not going to be any more screw-ups around here. Is that understood?" Everybody looked around at each other and nodded. "I said... IS THAT UNDERSTOOD!?!"

"Yes sir!" they chorused.

"We have been engaged by the enemy, and have taken casualties of one injured and six dead. Enemy losses are unknown, probably negligent. We must assume that an assault could come at any moment. We've done all we can with these computers, the stuff we really want is in back. From now on security is the number one priority. I want a three man team in here constantly on the machine gun, plus two near the door on high alert, check in with the gate at two minute intervals on the hard wire intercom. Make sure your gas masks are handy, in this enclosed space they might try something of that nature. Do not open the door to anyone without hearing the proper password. As of this moment the new password is "Ambrosia". You three... relieve the two at the front gate, give them the new password and tell them to bring that guard in here, I want to question him. You two... relieve the man at the front door, from now on I want two men out there at all times, and keep your eyes and ears open. You four... I want a patrol roaming the corridor outside, down to Tony's station down at the end by the shaft, then back to here. Repeat until relieved. You four... get up to the shaft house to increase the force available there, I want an outer perimeter established. See if you can find a telephone up there that's on a ground cable, I want communications. Coordinate with the three men up there. Don't let anybody else in, nobody, understand? You others, stay here, man the phones. Support anybody who needs it. Line two is the guard house out front. Line six is a direct line to Tony watching the shaft. If he calls, scramble a strike team and get down there. I'll be in the temporal lab, if anything important comes up, send someone down to get me. Otherwise, deal with it. Keep that guard in here 'til I come back."

Sherman stomped off through the double doors and down the corridor as his men scrambled to fulfill their assigned tasks. He marched down to the temporal lab and walked in after unlocking the vault-like doors. "You guys getting anywhere?" he asked curtly. The two men jumped at the sudden and loud voice in the quiet room. "Sorry sir, still working on the password." He indicated a small device hooked through a cable to the computer. "It's checking about sixty possibilities per second. If he's like most people, he'll choose a password that is easy to remember, and uses some combination of simple names or numbers he's associated with."

"Anything else?"

"Yes, we're looking through this test data, thought you might find this one interesting." He consulted a clipboard, typed a few lines, and brought up data from test number 347. The video monitor clearly showed the face and desk of Teresa Powers, the Prime Minister of the North American Federal Union. She was bent to a task, writing a memo by hand, which she handed to an aide. The video crackled and ended. "And look at this sir, the time of test and time of observation are identical." He brought up 'notes' relative to the test. A few words were written... "PM looking well today, sell pix to Newsweek? ha ha."

"So it's true, it can be used for real time surveillance. Good, take down those coordinates, we may need them later."

"Yes sir."

"Carry on then, I want that password broken as quickly as possible. I'll send someone down who can run a message back to me if necessary. By the way, there will be a patrol coming by every once in a while, we're tightening security, things aren't going so well topside. Looks like we won't have anyone for you to interrogate after all."

George stomped out of the room and back down the corridor to the front office. The two men in the temporal lab glanced towards the door after Sherman had gone, then at each other. They had known Sherman too long to make any open comments for fear of listening devices, but their looks said all that was necessary.

Sherman passed the armed patrol going the other direction; he was pleased at their alert bearing and the way they would duck into the offices and labs they passed to check them. He began to feel more secure and comfortable in the knowledge that he was protected on all sides.

He walked into the office, spotted a man not doing anything. "You... go down to the temporal lab, towards the end on the left, sign's on the door. Keep your eyes and ears open, help them out with whatever they need. If they break the password, run down here at once and get me."

George Sherman then turned his attention to the little man tied to a chair. "So my friend..." he consulted a clipboard offered to him by one of the men, "...Aaron, you've worked here how long?"

"You're not my friend. If you were my friend you wouldn't be mean to me."

Sherman got the idea that the man was of a simple intellectual nature. He checked the personnel file on the clipboard again, confirming the assessment. He instantly changed tactics. "Oh my goodness, I'm so sorry, what have these fools done to you. Here, you scoundrel, take these ropes off our friend at once! Have you no manners you buffoon!" The ropes were instantly cut away. "There, is that better?"

Aaron rubbed his wrists and looked darkly around. "Yes, thank you."

"So now, how long did you say you've worked here?"

"Two years."

"Ah, and were you always outside in the guard shack or did you sometimes come in here."

"Oh, I often came inside, we had lunch here sometimes. They would give me milk and cookies." Sherman snapped his fingers, one of the men hustled off.

"That's nice. Did you ever go into the back, to the research labs?"

"Sure, once I went with a public tour, but another time Digger took me, and we went different places."

"Was it fun Aaron?"

"Oh yeah, lots of neat things. I really liked the grunts and the place where they come up on a chain. It's almost looked like the roller coaster rides at the carnival. They had a carnival once in Lake Linden."

"Yes, that's fun isn't it. Did you ever go into a room with a great big machine that shows pictures in a round ball?"

"Oh, yeah, that was really cool! Digger showed me once. I really liked that... But he said nobody was supposed to know about it. How come you know about it?"

"Oh well... Digger and I are very good friends. Tell me Aaron, what did you see when you looked in the ball."

"I saw an Indian, beating on a piece of copper with a stone hammer. Digger told me it wasn't an actor like in the movies, he said it was a real person, but hundreds of years ago."

"That's very interesting Aaron. Now tell me, in your job, do you have to remember a lot of things?"

"Oh sure, I'm a good rememberer. I remember people, and when they come in and when they leave. I remember how many cookies are left in the package, and how many jellybeans are in the jar in the break room. I remember lots of thing, I'm good at remembering things... But I don't remember you. I never seen you before, or these other guys who were mean to me."

"I'm sorry about that Aaron, it won't happen again, I promise. You'll be seeing us a lot more in the future. You see, I paid some money and bought this place from Digger, so it's mine now. But there's one thing my good friend Digger forgot to tell me Aaron, and now he's out of town and I can't seem to get hold of him. See if you can remember... how did Digger get the big machine to start? Did you ever see him do it, or did he tell you anything about it?"

Aaron closed his eyes and thought. "No, he was turned away from me, so I couldn't see what he was doing. He made some clicking noises on the computer thing like this..." Aaron reached out and randomly clicked keys on the computer terminal sitting beside him. "... and then the machine came on."

George looked at the black screen with white nonsense letters strewn across it in a line. He hit the down-arrow key to move the cursor down a line. "Aaron, could you do that again, please, I didn't quite see.."

"Sure, it sounded like this." He tapped on the keys again. The result was a completely different set of characters, but the row was of the same length... exactly 40 keystrokes in length. Sherman groaned inwardly, but tried to stay positive in front of Aaron.

"And did he say anything else, anything at all?"

"Well, he said you have to treat a machine like you'd treat a lady. You have to be gentle and kind, and be very polite, and sometimes, if she wants to, she'll do what you ask her to." George mused to himself for a moment that this was not exactly the manner in which he was used to treating ladies, and yet he still got what he wanted.

A man walked up with a container of milk and part of a bag of cookies. George looked at them a moment, fatigue and disappointment wearing on him. He spoke to the man. "Would you please take our friend to the break room and give him his milk and cookies? Then make sure he's comfortable there." Sherman made a motion as of a key in a lock with his hand. The man nodded. "Thank you very much for your help Aaron. This man here will give you some milk and cookies, and give you a comfortable place to rest out of the cold." They walked away and left Sherman sitting in the chair.

He got up and jogged down to the temporal lab again. "Any luck?" he said as he burst in?

"No sir, still working on it."

"I've got a strong suspicion that the password may be forty keystrokes in length."

"Forty sir? My God, the number of possibilities would be astronomical! What makes you think that might be it?"

"The security guard, something of an idiot savant with tremendous memory, he was here one day, heard it tapped out, then recreated the sound for me, twice. Forty strokes each time."

The man became excited. "Ahh, what about checking with common quotations then, finding ones of that length. It might be something of that nature."

"Yes do that!"

"Was there anything else sir, anything else he said?"

"Just some silly thing about treating a machine like a lady."

"Excuse me sir? Could you please repeat what he said, word for word, it might be a useful clue."

Sherman did so, surprised to find himself embarrassed at the words coming from his mouth, but even more surprised to see the look on the computer man's face. "That's it sir!" He pulled the plug on the automatic device running through every combination of words and numbers in Digger's personnel file. Instead he typed into the keyboard a few phrases, counting keystrokes as he went, backspacing, and then trying again.

"What the hell do you think you're doing?"

"Wait sir." He tapped at the keys. "I think he was giving a clue to the password sir... about being polite to a lady." With a sudden cry he shouted, "I think I've got it, watch this."

At the password prompt he typed: "pretty please with cream and sugar on it"

"Access granted, program test?" answered the computer screen.

A Superior State of Affairs

"Ha. The fool didn't even use any capital letters or numerals to confuse the issue. Be polite sir, that's what he said."

George Sherman was elated. He reached out to touch the "Y" key, offering them an entirely new screen with parameters that could be adjusted.

"Good work son. Alright, let's try to see if we can target this thing where we want it. See if you can give me the prime minister's office, start with the coordinates of that test we saw. Let's see if we can't get some information that will get those stuffed shirts by the short hairs. Start the video recorder the moment you get something." Then George Sherman sat back in his chair and laughed as he envisioned the awkward situation he would put them all in. They would have to let him into the circle of power then, he would have too much knowledge to deny him, no matter what the simpering fools thought of him personally. Then, slowly, he would begin to eliminate his rivals, until only he, George Sherman, stood at the top of the heap. The sound of his laughter made the two three men in the room with him very uncomfortable indeed.

CHAPTER 50

Digger Puttonen and Joan Niemi stood face to face in a very confined area, a cylindrical space barely taller than Digger, and only about one meter in diameter. The "grunt", an semi-automated utility submersible, was slowly sinking below the surface of the water deep inside the Quincy mine, two hundred meters below the snow covered landscape above. The only light in the tiny space was the yellowish glow of the control panel keypad on which Digger punched buttons.

"Okay, get ready..." he said.

"For what?" Joan asked, apprehensively.

"We've tested this thing with human occupants out in the lake, but never underground, so this should be rather interesting, what with the walls of the mine so close by." He punched two more buttons. As he touched the last one he said "Now!" The soft plastic walls all around them suddenly began to glow faintly, a pale greenish color. The grunting sound could be heard as an almost constant yet barely perceptible moan. Within a few moments images began to form in the green glow of the wall panels. With a sharp intake of breath, Joan realized that she was looking out through the walls of the submersible, seeing the surrounding rock of the mine. As the system warmed up the images became sharper, until she could almost have sworn that she was staring through a transparent skin, looking at the underwater part of the mine which was being lit up by a pale green lantern.

"It's amazing," she said. "What are we looking at?"

"You're looking at what is directly outside. If it's calibrated correctly, the rock surfaces are represented at actual scale and distance."

"It's incredible!"

"Well, our feeling at Midnight Mining Company is that most technology is too complex for ordinary people to use. We force humans to adapt to the machines instead of the other way around. People interacting with technology have been forced to limit their scope of perception and simply cope with the artificial complexity, or reject it. Our philosophy is that technology should be more intuitive, we want to make the devices do the work and let the humans figure out what it's good for. With this system you don't have to peer out of some tiny little porthole, or try to figure out how reality correlates with the display on an arbitrarily oriented video screen. We've lined the entire interior of the cabin with soft vinyl holographic display plates. You can buy the stuff in rolls now, some guys in Saskatchewan are making it. The computer senses what is outside using an array of special high resolution sonar sweeping modules. We display the result so that... you just look out, and there you are. You can pilot this baby entirely by feel, intuitively. We hope to market them as rescue vehicles that anybody can pilot with simple instructions. This is an experimental model of course, the commercial ones will probably be larger and much easier to operate, but you can get the idea." As they descended, the grunt approached the footwall rather closely. Digger stuck his hand into a slot and the grunt pitched forward slightly, to an angle of about sixty degrees, approximately matching that of the mine. He was now leaning somewhat on top of Joan.

"Sorry about that, we'd have bounced off the footwall if we'd kept going as we were. These things are pretty much self piloting in ordinary circumstances, but I've taken manual control. We'll just have to hope nobody's watching at the control panel in the lab, it would show a status change. We could leave it on automatic, but our progress would be very slow, they're programmed for extremely conservative piloting."

They continued to drop down along the footwall. "Digger, do you know where we're going?" Joan asked quietly.

"Sure. First we go straight down to get out of this maze of pillars, then we'll cut across the stope until we reach the fissure, that will be the tricky part. To get past the fissure we'll have to pilot through a narrow tunnel with a rather awkward current. Most of the way will be through wide open spaces like this."

"Aren't you worried about rockfall?"

"Well, things happen of course, there's always the odd chance of a loose rock shifting above us, but we really don't have to worry about any major collapse."

"Why not?"

"Well, the mine was started back in the eighteen hundreds. When they stopped bailing water in the nineteen forties it started filling up. It took fifty years before the water level in the mine finally equalized with the level of Lake Superior. The weight of all that water pushing on the rock has relieved a lot of the pressure differential that was causing the tendency for the rock to fail mechanically. So now the mine, at least the part below water level, is much more stable than it ever was in the past. That's one reason that the grunts make so much sense, we can send them into an area that would be far too dangerous to work if the mine was dry...

plus draining a mine like this would be incredibly time consuming and expensive. For our purposes though, we prefer a flooded mine, gives the robots a medium to work in."

She was stunned. "I had heard about the mining robots, I guess I thought they were tiny things, bringing up one little chunk of rock at a time."

"Some of the first ones were like that, but we needed to make them big enough to haul some ore, yet small enough to maneuver around in the old workings."

They continued to descend slowly. Joan looked around at the few visible controls. "How does it work?" she asked.

"Basically, it's like any other compact submersible, with a few improvements. We have air and ballast tanks all around us, fitted with pumps so that we almost never have to blow air to our surroundings. Our energy is supplied by rather special high capacity fuel cells and electric batteries. The main thing is the computer, a pretty big one, powerwise, though it takes up a very small space. There are two separate and independent modules running the same process. Each is a backup for the other in case of malfunction. It would never have been possible without the development of optical processors a few years ago. Just this holographic display alone takes some ungodly number of terabytes per second of processing power. It was just a matter of taking some components that were available on the open market, adding a few touches of our own, and putting them together into something that will accomplish a needed task." He looked at a depth gauge. "Okay, looks like we're at fifty meters." He made an adjustment and they stopped falling.

"Digger, what about air, I've done some diving before... aren't we going to have problems with decompression when we go back up?"

"Glad you're thinking! But no, it's all automatic. All we need to do is monitor the system and make sure it's working properly. The scrubber is already removing carbon dioxide from the air we're breathing, and as we increase in depth the computer will start to monitor cabin pressure. The hull can take at least thirty atmospheres easily, so for this run..." He tapped some keys and displayed a chart. "...no, we won't need any decompression time."

"What about the air though, will there be enough, I mean, for both of us?"

"I think so. We've only tested this with one person, and that was only in open water, and never to its limits. Well, we always try to overengineer, so I think we'll be okay if we try to not waste too much time and just get on with it."

Joan looked out at their surroundings, they weren't moving. "Okay, so, where do we go now."

"Well, we need to go south, thataway," he nodded his head. "And to do that we need to lay her down horizontal. The question is... do you want to be on the bottom or the top? There's not enough room to lie side by side and still operate the controls."

"Hmmm, I have a choice?"

"Yeah, I think it'll work either way, and we can switch later if it's too uncomfortable."

"I guess I'll try bottom first."

"Okay then, here we go." The entire submersible began to pitch slowly with the barely audible sound of hissing air and small pumps working, until it lay horizontal with Digger lying on top of Joan. Her back was against part of the holographic panels, which were soft, flexible, and thinly padded. Digger pushed his hands into two slots above her shoulders that served as guidance controls, supporting his weight on his elbows. With a gentle whirring sound from the screws, they moved off to the north at a speed that would be equivalent to a fast walking pace, maybe five or six kilometers per hour. Joan lay back and stared around her... at the glowing green scenery of the great canyon that they traveled through... and Digger's face, tense and focused in concentration, piloting the little vehicle.

After a while Digger whispered. "You okay? I hope I'm not too heavy on you."

"No, it's alright. You might think about making one of these a little bigger though."

"Maybe for open water use we could do that, this is about the limit for mining though. I hope you don't have claustrophobia."

"I think I'd know it by now if I did."

"I've never had the problem myself, but we're hoping that these holographic panels will help alleviate it in people who do, by giving the impression, if not the reality, of space. It looks like we're seeing right through the wall, but of course, these are solid walls, half a meter thick and stuffed with ballast tanks, piping and all that. It's an illusion obviously, but an effective one. Ah, here we are at last."

They had spent almost an hour negotiating the horizontal run to the north. Joan, lying on her back, turned her neck to the right and saw a pair of railroad rails leading from above and heading directly downward. In the greenish glow of the holographic display, the mine did not look particularly dark and terrifying, it was actually a little comforting. She thought that perhaps it was the greenish color that made her think of woods and fields in the springtime, even though she gazed upon lifeless, black, blasted rock deep within the earth. "Now what?" she asked.

"We have to go down again. Up ahead, between the number two and number six shafts, there was a major fissure, a very large crack in the rock. The ore in that region was low grade anyway, and the rock is very fractured and loose, so the miners didn't connect through it in very many places. There was a tunnel at about the eighth level at one time. That would have been convenient, but we've tried it before, and it's so choked with fallen rock that we can't use it, and we haven't bothered clearing it out. For now, we'll have to drop down to the sixteenth level to slip through a surviving connection I know of."

He pulled the nose of the grunt up almost to vertical again, and they proceeded once more to descend in elevator fashion. Joan breathed deeply when his weight was off her. "You sure you're okay?" he asked.

"Yeah, maybe I'll take tops next time."

"Alright. What we need to do now is descend along these rails until we see two big pillars, one on each side, then we go horizontal again."

Joan said to him, "I thought you said you'd never been here. You talk like you do this all the time."

"Sorry madam, just trying to exude confidence to keep the passengers happy."

"No, I'm serious."

Digger sighed through the concentration of piloting. "You're right, I have personally never been here before, but I have piloted grunts in this area by remote control, so I'm fairly familiar with the layout. They're fully capable of performing a routine task command and returning to base, but they will accept direct control signals as well. There are acoustic cables strung throughout the mine so that they're never out of range. We're constantly working on the mine map, adding detail. I've seen this holographic display, projected remotely in the lab above from a grunt that was down here. So yes, in a way I've explored this area. On the other hand, doing this in a simulator and actually being here are two very different things."

They fell slowly and silently through the depths. Digger's eyes were constantly on the depth gauge or looking around for obstacles which they might inadvertently strike. Joan was trying to see what Digger's hands were doing. "How are you controlling this thing? All I see is a couple of slots."

"Ah, the controls... that's something else we've been working on. Again, it's trying to make things intuitive so that anybody could do it. You stick your hands in here, sort of a glove-like affair, and then, you just push the direction you want to go. I've never flown a jet fighter, but we borrowed some of the control circuitry from them. Want to try it?"

Joan looked around. They were descending slowly through a rather narrow chasm, there were projections of rock, twisted metal, and other obstacles to look out for, Digger was constantly guiding around them. "Uh, no, maybe some other time when we're not in so much of a hurry."

"Oh yeah, sometimes I forget." They fell for a long while. Occasionally there were creaks and groan as the metal hull adjusted to the pressure increase, but Digger did not seem worried, so Joan relaxed. She looked down below their feet, and slowly they two immense pillars of rock emerged from the gloom, joining the hanging wall and footwall of the chasm. The two rails that once guided the ore cars on their journeys up and down the number six shaft continued between the pillars to their unseen end in the depths below. It was easy for Joan to forget that they were encased inside a thick canister of stainless steel and bronze, and to imagine that they slipped through the void in a flimsy transparent envelope, so realistic was the three dimensional holographic display. Digger stopped their descent just above the twin pillars and checked the depth gauge. "Okay, three hundred meters, we're here. You want to be on top this time?"

Joan nodded and said "Yeah, okay."

"Okay, push over there a minute, let me turn around..." Digger squirmed and managed to turn himself away from Joan. "Okay, now skootch around this way..." They moved together until he was facing the controls. "Alrighty then, here we go."

Digger laid the grunt over horizontally again and immediately accelerated forward. Joan lay on top of him, supporting herself on her arms. She had the feeling she was riding double on a sled as they zoomed along at a goodly clip. In about twenty minutes a pillar appeared below them, then a solid wall above, Digger slowed down and adjusted the angle of the grunt to slip through a gap between them. Again they were in a large open space. Digger played with the control panel again, and one part of the viewscreen became a separate window, showing a detailed map of the mine, with a glowing red dot showing their position.

"See, here is where we are, we've just slipped through this gap, and now we need to head for this tunnel here. It's not the only one, but it's the widest passage that's within easy reach and it's clear of fall rock, or at least it was last time I checked it." He tipped the grunt at an upward angle and continued along for a while, until a wall of rock loomed ahead. It looked more shattered and angular than the walls they'd been passing thus far.

Digger spoke softly in the confines of the tiny space. "This is it, we're in the neighborhood of the fissure now. Somewhere nearby in this wall is the tunnel that connects through to the other side. He stopped dead in the water and manipulated the sensor controls. Suddenly the rock walls lost their density, turned milky, and they could see somewhat into the rock."

"What did you just do?", asked Joan.

"Changed the frequency sweep to allow solid target penetration, we're looking for a tunnel, and sometimes it helps to see into the rock some. See? look up there, that shadow..." He made the craft slightly more buoyant and it rose slowly, until before them a tunnel mouth opened. The craft shuddered slightly and moved backward. He readjusted the sensors so that the rock walls solidified. "You see? We can look into the rock for a little ways, even from here. The technique makes it easy to chart out the locations of nearby masses of copper, even when they're still concealed within the rock. We'd get even better clarity if we put the sensors in direct contact with the rock, but we don't have time for that now. You probably noticed that we encountered a current here. The mine is so deep that geothermal heat is significant in the lower reaches. On the far side of this tunnel is the deepest shaft, the number two. The heat at the bottom causes a convection current in the water. Since there are so few connecting tunnels in this part of the mine, there's quite a pressure difference and the current can get pretty fierce."

Digger pushed his hands forward into the control slots, and the grunt jumped forward, bucking slightly against the current. Even at maximum speed however, the little craft moved slowly into the tunnel. The grunt shuddered slightly as turbulence in the current buffeted them about. The tunnel was not particularly long, only about one hundred meters or so, but their progress was slow, and they occasionally bumped slightly against the walls of the tunnel when they came too close. Digger struggled to keep them centered in the passage. After almost thirty minutes of tense effort, they suddenly burst out into the open again, Digger withdrew his hands to slow down. "Okay then, we're through, we're across the big divide." He showed her on the mine map. "Now we have to go back up again, and then make our way to the chainway." He slowly pivoted the grunt upright again, and they began rising slowly along the wall above the tunnel.

"What's the chainway?" asked Joan.

"That's how we get the grunts back into the lab. A couple years ago we cut our own narrow shaft down into the water from the lab, and installed a sort of chain railway. When a grunt is full of ore, or needs servicing, it noses into the bottom entrance near the number one shaft, hooks into an endless chain loop, and gets hauled up into the lab. Mostly it's an automated process. I'm hoping those guys up there will just leave it alone as they concentrate on the tempiloscope and maintaining security. I'm counting on the fact that they probably have no idea that it's possible for us to come in this way."

"What if they do, and are watching the chainway entrance."

"In that case my dear... well... I guess we're just screwed."

"Sorry I asked."

"WOW!" Digger exclaimed.

"What?" Joan was suddenly apprehensive.

"Look at that!" As they rose alongside the wall of rock they could make out some detail. There was a cavity about a meter across with a strange texture within... it looked somewhat like cauliflower, or the surface of a brain. There were some looses pieces lying there. "Datolite pocket"! Digger breathed, "big one too."

"Uh, Digger, do we have time to be messing around with rockhounding? I think we're in something of a hurry." Joan said this as the grunt stopped it's upward motion and pulled slowly in towards the rock wall.

Digger spoke through intense concentration. "Won't take a second Joan. The fissures are always where you find the datolite. I have never been able to explore this part of the mine, you don't get this kind of detailed visuals from the remote control hookup. WOW! Look at the size of that thing!" Digger manipulated some controls, and an arm reached out from the side of the grunt and deftly grabbed a large, loose, cauliflower mass about the size of a soccer ball. The arm withdrew and disappeared from the screen. Digger marked the spot on the electronic map with a blue dot, then urged the grunt to continue its rise. "The arm will put that in a little cargo hold down below. Usually the cabin, where we are now, is fitted as a cargo hold, open to the outside, and the mining robots fill the space with high graded ore to the limit of buoyancy. This model just has a small hold available to the outside. James and I packed some memory crystals in it before we sent this one out. I had more of an idea we'd just retrieve the crystals than that we'd use the grunt to get inside." Digger was rambling, speaking his thoughts aloud. He looked at Joan, who was eying him curiously. "Sorry about the sidetrip, couldn't help myself..." He looked up above them, and she followed his gaze. "Right now our problem is the ceiling above us, we have to find the old ore chute that will let us through. Once we make it though there then it should be a pretty straight shot to the chainway." As they rose, the walls seemed to close in, the stope was narrower than the ones on the other side of the divide, this one had not collapsed back in the 1906 disaster. Looking up, in the distance they could both see the old ore chute Digger was making for. It seemed to be very narrow, just barely big enough to fit the grunt through.

"Digger, isn't there another way, that looks too small."

"I hope not. We've mapped this area pretty thoroughly, but, um, well... we've never actually taken a grunt through the chute before."

Joan looked, and sounded, a little worried. "Then why are we going this way now?"

"Because the other path is long and complicated and would take too much time, way too much time... like so much that we'd run out of air before we got through. This way would be a straight shot home... if we can make it." Digger looked up and gauged the opening. "It may be a little tight. though." He slowly nudged the grunt up into the bottom of the ore chute. In the old days ore would have been shoved into this hole and funneled into waiting train cars on the level below. They heard a loud scraping on the sides of the grunt as they began to move through. On the upper side there were a lot of pieces of loose rubble sitting precariously near the edge. About half of the grunt had emerged from the upper end of the vertical chute, when they barely touched one of the loose rocks, one about a meter long. It pivoted and shifted position, falling against the side of the grunt, wedging it against the side of the chute, pinning it. They could see the rock easily, just a half meter away. The grunt settled with a groan at a slight angle against the side of the chute and hung there. Digger manipulated the power controls, they felt a shudder as he gave it full forward, then full reverse, but they did not move more than a centimeter or two. Digger sighed wearily, his shoulders slumped.

"Is that it then?" asked Joan calmly. "Are we stuck here?"

"I don't know. The regular mining grunts have all kinds of rock breaking attachments, chisels, power hammers, sonic disintegrators, pry bars, the works. If we had those tools we'd have no problem. We never thought they'd be needed with a rescue/research vehicle, so we used the extra space for the cabin interior and air tanks. All we've got on the outside now are the sensors and the grab arm."

"Can't you move the rock with the arm?" Joan asked calmly.

Digger sighed. I can try, but it's just not very strong. That's probably a hundred kilo rock, at least."

"Well come on... think of something! This is not where I imagined spending my honeymoon."

Digger smiled, turned his head and she kissed him on the cheek. "Okay okay, let me think." He actuated the grab arm, wiggled it a little and got it free. "Well, at least it wasn't pinned," he said. Digger used it to explore around the boulder that was wedging them. He strained with the arm, in several directions, but could not move the rock. He used the arm to pull smaller rocks away from the big one, clearing some space around it so that more rocks would not pin them if they moved the big one. Still, the large rock simply would not budge. After fifteen minutes of effort Digger pulled his arms from the control slots and slumped his shoulders. "I don't know Joan... it doesn't look good."

Joan drew on the deep well that was within her. She got her arms around his shoulders and rubbed the tense muscles. "It's okay, just relax and think. There's got to be a way... something else we can try. Digger closed his eyes and rolled his neck in response to Joan's massage.

"If only..." he began.

"If only what?" Joan asked, continuing to soothe his neck.

"Tools, if we only had some tools," he muttered. The suddenly he tensed. put his hands into the slots again. "Maybe there's another rock, something flat and thin we can use to get some leverage against this one," he said. Joan nodded enthusiastically, though she was doubtful. most of the chunks of basalt rock were pretty random and blocky. Digger adjusted the sensors again to see deeply into the solid rock.

The view changed, and they could see into the pile of rubble, or 'muck' as the miners called it. The blocks of basalt looked like pieces of clear glass. Chunks and strings of native copper could be viewed inside the walls, or mixed into the loose material. In one spot there was an object that shone brightly, like metal, yet was perfectly straight and a couple of meters long. "Well, whaddaya know," Digger said excitedly. "What incredible luck! Looky here, looks like somebody lost a big iron pry bar here under some rocks a long long time ago. If we can just..." He used the arm to move some smaller rocks over it, revealing one end of the bar. He worked for nearly twenty minutes trying to extricate it but finally was successful.

When the pry-bar pulled loose from the rock pile, the grab arm recoiled and the bar hit the grunt on top of the hatch with a resounding 'thunk'. "Oops," Digger said, "I just hit us on the head. Glad we're wearing a helmet." He started to manipulate the bar under the most exposed and available edge of the stone. He carefully got it into position, positioned another rock nearby as a fulcrum, and then pushed with the grab arm on the end of the bar. The boulder shifted slightly, the grunt moved a few centimeters. "Joan. I have to hold this bar down. I can't do this and pilot at the same time. You're going to have to help me. You stick your hand in this control slot... right here over my right shoulder. Got it?"

"Yes, it feels like a glove."

"That's right, now, using your fingers, just push up, the direction we want to go." She did so, the grunt made a slight effort but was still hung up. "Feel it respond? Push harder, hard as you can!"

Digger pushed down on the bar as Joan pushed the control, and suddenly with a loud scrape they shot out of the ore chute and straight up. Digger dropped the grab arm controls and pulled Joan's hand down out of the control slot. He smiled... "Didn't want us smashing into something at that speed," he said as the grunt slowed to a stop quickly. Below them they could see the rock, the bar, and some other smaller rocks disappearing silently into the ore chute and fading quickly from sight. Digger, facing away from Joan, twisted his head to try to look at her. "Good job girl, you okay?"

"Yeah, I'm fine. Let's try not to do that again okay?"

Digger smiled. "You got it lady, that was a little bit dicier than I was hoping for. We should have pretty smooth sailing from here on in though". Digger angled the grunt so that they were rising at about a twenty degree angle, and piloted the little craft upwards and southwards through the stopes surrounding the number two shaft. As they rose into shallower water, the outside pressure dropped, but the only noticeable change was in the gauge readings.

As they passed through the wider open area that marked the number two shaft, they saw that there was an object slowly sinking through the water towards them. Digger slowed the vehicle to a stop to investigate. It was not a rock, for it settled much too slowly. Digger allowed the grunt to rise to meet it. At last the details could be made out. It was a human body, slowly sinking along the footwall, tumbling over and over as it fell.

With a sharp intake of breath Joan recognized what it was, she clutched Digger's shoulders convulsively. With a final rolling motion the face swept past them, and Digger recognized the face. "It's Farley," he said, without emotion.

"Who?"

"Farley Grundwalder, the guy who kicked me out of the office. Looks like he fell into the shaft. That's strange though... he would never have willingly gone anywhere near it."

"Maybe he didn't fall."

"Yeah," Digger said thoughtfully. "Maybe we should be careful." They watched as the body continued falling into the depths, and then accelerated again towards the end of their journey. No further surprises were encountered, and about a half hour later Digger slowed the little craft and nosed towards a solid wall of rock. The digital depth gauge showed one hundred meters. There was just one small opening in the solid basalt wall, perfectly round. Above it and below it, tiny lights blinked. "Here it is." said Digger. "All we do is guide the nose between those lights and the chain hooks on and carries us up into the lab. You ready for this?"

"I don't know, what do you expect to find?"

"Hopefully, an empty lab. We get out of the grunt and into some fresh air... and then... well, I guess we see what we can see. We can't stay in here forever." He worked his hands down to his shirt pocket and handed a folded piece of paper over his shoulder to Joan. "Here's a map of the labs, just like the one we looked at back at Ruth's house, just in case we get separated. The grunt lab's about in the middle, the temporal lab's almost at the very end. The thing is... we don't know what we're up against. I have the pistol Harry gave me, with a couple of extra clips, and one small concussion grenades, but that's it. We can't just go in guns blazing like in the movies. This is real life. Those guys are playing for keeps." The grunt nosed into the opening and suddenly was grabbed by the automatic mechanism which started hauling it quickly up the tube at about a forty five degree angle. Digger took his hands off the controls and shut down the guidance systems.

Joan cleared her throat a little. "Uh, Digger... I didn't mention anything about it before, but, uh... Ruth gave me a little something before we left, said she thought I might need it more than she would."

"What?" asked Digger, confused.

"It's a little .38 revolver. Just five shots and no extra ammunition, but it's something."

"Good," he nodded, "keep it handy. Okay, here we go. It will pull us out onto a horizontal rack. We'll still be able to see a little, though dimly, the sonar doesn't work well out of the water, and since sound travels more slowly in air than water, the images will be exaggerated in size, and appear closer to us than they really are. At least we'll get a look around before opening up. See if you can snag that pack with your foot and push it up here."

Between them they managed to work the pack up between them to head height. Joan laughed and said, "So Digger, is this what people mean when they say they're in a tight spot?"

"I guess so," he laughed. "Look now, we're coming out of the water." They passed through the water/air boundary, and it seemed as though the walls of the tube closed in on them, though as Digger had explained, the effect was merely an artifact of the imaging system. Joan tucked the map of the labs into her shirt pocket. Digger fiddled in the pack until he found the pistol that Harry had given him. It was a small nine millimeter with an eight shot clip. The markings looked like it might have been from one of the old European Soviet satellite states. A real antique, but at least it had fired the few times Digger had pulled the trigger.

With a lurch the grunt pulled through an opening into a larger space, was dragged along a track, and finally came to rest lying on a cradle in a work station. Joan could see racks of tools and implements, presumably for repair and maintenance purposes. Digger peered around carefully. "Looks like there's nobody around. We should wait a minute though in case someone heard the noise and is coming to see what it's about. It happens all the time of course, during a normal day three or four grunts will come in. This is the custom job though, so it got put on this rack, the others go over there for recharging, unloading, systems check, and then they're returned to work. They're only put over here if they need repairs."

They waited a few more minutes, then Digger reached to open the hatch. Joan hissed... "Digger, look!" Two men had entered the room, crouching, weapons in hand. Digger froze. Looking out through the apparently clear side of the grunt it was hard to remember that they could not be seen. The bodies of the men looked frighteningly swollen and distorted by the imaging system, like some sort of monsters from a movie. The men's voices sounded distant to Digger and Joan, having to pass through all the machinery that surrounded them. They approached, looked at the floor, apparently noticing the dripping water. One man leaned close and peered at the submersible, his face horribly inflated. Suddenly the chain way started up again. The two men reacted by leaping for cover and training their weapons on the source of the sound. One of the standard grunts shuttled out of the charging bay into the chainway, was hooked onto the lift and began to descend to the water. The men looked at each other, seemed to understand the automation of the system, then went out the door, closing it behind them and turning out the lights.

"Looks like we lucked out, again. Come on, let's get out of here. I mean, it's been a cozy little trip and all, but I'm ready to stretch a little." Digger tapped a keypad and the hatch hissed quietly open. The only light was the glow of the control panels in the grunt and in the room. Joan, being on top, went out first with the pack, then Digger powered down the grunt and tumbled out. He closed the hatch again to make it look normal, then trotted over to the room control panel. Sure enough, there were a dozen grunts on patrol in the mine, but only G-27 was listed as under manual control. He switched it back to automatic to cover their trail.

He handed the IR glasses to Joan. She hung them around her neck, tucked into the open top of her flannel shirt. "These might be helpful, you can see quite a bit even in the dark sometimes, if there's a temperature difference between the air and the walls for instance."

"What about you?"

A Superior State of Affairs

He pulled an odd looking device out of his pack that he strapped on his head. It looked like a jeweler's loupe, a large pair of goggles that fitted down over the eyes but could be easily pivoted up out of the way. "Not to worry, I've got these." He went to the door, lowered the eyepiece, then placed a sort of double ended stethoscope device against it, nodded, and moved quietly to open it.

"Wait!" Joan whispered. "Digger, shouldn't we try to communicate, you know, like we tried before?"

"You mean with those guys up top?"

"Yeah, they should know we made it in safely."

"Okay, lets try." They closed their eyes and tried to blank out any conscious thought except their friends. Somehow, being together, it seemed easier.

"We made it in!" they tried to 'say' mentally together. "We're okay." They repeated it several times.

There was a pause, then they 'heard' quite clearly. "Congratulations! Things not going so well here. Plan still in effect. Try again in thirty minutes."

"Did you get that?" asked Joan.

"Yeah, what do you think it means about things not going so well?"

"I don't know." She motioned towards the door and squeezed his hand. "Shall we?" The corridor was lit by widely spaced bare incandescent bulbs. Digger and Joan slowly pushed the door open, checked both directions, and crept into the passage. They turned left and headed for the temporal lab.

CHAPTER 51

Steve was driving the Willys south on Highway 41 with Eileen beside him. He was doing all he could to keep the speeding Jeep Cherokee ahead from getting completely out of sight. The trip down from Eagle River had been uneventful except for the breakneck speed at which it was conducted. Ruth seemed to know or suspect something about the poison which had necrotized Chris' arm, and she was moving with all possible speed to get him to an emergency room. The crescent moon rode high in the eastern sky, presaging the approaching dawn. Ruth was about a half mile ahead now, approaching the outskirts of Calumet, the red tail lights barely visible. The Jeep slowed down a little coming into town, and they were able to catch up to it. Suddenly it pulled to the side and stopped. James jumped out and the Jeep roared off at high speed.

James waved to the Willys which stopped for him, he opened the door and dived into the back. "Chris was going into shock. Rather than take the extra time to drop me at her house she wanted to head straight for the hospital." He motioned to Steve to get going. "I know where to go, let's get down there and see what we can do to help." James leaned forward between the front seats, staring out the windshield, urging the old vehicle onward. There was little conversation as they sped southward, fishtailing on the curves, with the northern lights still blazing in the sky. The shape of the display seemed to change, almost as if it were solidifying out of thin air. A circular swirling patch of deep red color was visible high in the sky directly ahead of them; green and yellow streamers leapt from the horizon, pointing towards the central patch like Las Vegas casino lights. They stared in wonderment, too amazed to comment.

They drove past the airport entrance, found the road to Paavola, and turned left to approach the little village. James guided Steve through a right turn, and they stopped before a small house flying a blue UN flag. Steve shut the engine down and they all got out. James pointed out, with a shock, the smoking embers in the place where his friend Digger's house had once stood. If anything, the northern lights had become even more intense, seeming to swirl in the air directly above where the Quincy mine stood. The three of them walked up the to the front door of the house; James knocked. They heard the sound of barking, then an old man opened the door and invited them right in.

"Hi, I'm Arne Harjaala. Come on in outa da snow. You must be da ones Ruth went after den eh?" A big black Labrador bounced around excitedly and sniffed everyone thoroughly.

"Yeah," answered James. "She said this was where we could meet everybody and find out what's going on."

"Ya, well, I aint seen nobody in a while. Dey all went off to reconnoiter some time back. Da phone company called and said somebody's usin' da phone line at da gift shop on top o' da hill. Dis here's Ruth's dog, Oby."

"Hi Oby. What about Digger?" asked James.

"He an' Joanie went in da mine I guess."

"In the mine? Where?"

"Not sure, not da shaft house though. One of da udder ones we're thinking."

"That means he's using the grunt we fixed up, I hope it works. Oh! Arne, this is Steve and Eileen. We were very fortunate to find them, they're from Chicago and know a lot about what this Sherman guy is up to. We're hoping they can help us with a programming problem if we get inside."

"Hey, pleased ta meet ya," said Arne. "You guys need something hot? Tea? Coffee?..."

"No thanks Arne, we just want to find out what the situation is. Ruth was very upset about the whole thing."

"Well, Da FBI guys, four of 'em, went ta take a look see at da shaft house. Dey're still thinkin' dat might be da best way in. Hopefully somebody will come back here and tell us what's da deal. Where's Ruth?"

"We had a bit of weirdness ourselves. A hit man apparently tried to take out our friends here, when another fellow stopped him. It's a complicated story apparently. The hit man is dead, mostly by his own poison it seems, but helped along by a bullet. Ruth is taking the injured man to the hospital emergency room."

Arne nodded. "Well, she's good, so if she tinks it's serious, I'd go wit dat. I'm ta tell ya ta stay here til somebody comes, no sense everbody runnin' off and gettin' all shot up for notting. I'm puttin' da kettle on. Sit down a minute and relax. It's gonna be a long night, an' you gotta save your strength."

Steve and Eileen sat on the couch, James in the easy chair. Arne came back in the room. "So Arne," James said, "Ruth told us about some of what happened earlier. There was a gunfight on the street here?"

"Ya, four of da bad guys got shot dead right in da street. Two FBI guys were injured. Bad news da whole damn t'ing. We're thinkin' dey wanted ta get rid of Digger, but met up wit da FBI guys unexpected."

"I can't believe he moved this fast!" Steve said quietly.

"I can't believe we worked for him all those years and never saw what he was doing!" added Eileen.

"Well guys," said James, "I'm just glad you're with us, now, when it counts."

There was a noise outside, Arne went to peek out. "Ah, looks like somebody's come," he said.

The door burst open, Leonard hurried in and Harry came right behind, shutting the door behind him. Leonard started talking to Arne. "We saw Ruth fly past like a bat out of hell heading towards town. Who are you?" he looked at Eileen, Steve, and James.

"James Dolittle, Digger's partner." Said James, getting up and shaking Leonard's hand.

"Oh yeah, we were expecting you, glad you were able to make it to our little party. What about these two?"

"Steve Sanders sir. You're FBI?"

"That's right, Special Investigations Branch."

"Until yesterday morning, we worked for George Sherman at his Chicago headquarters, computer programmers and general information flunkeys. This is my wife Eileen. The quick story is that he was about to have us killed, so we walked out with a lot of his files, loads and loads of incriminating evidence."

"Tons!" added Eileen.

"Yeah, then he sent a hit man to take us out, but this guy Chris Jameson hit the guy from behind and saved us."

Leonard's jaw dropped open in surprise. "Chris Jameson? Oh my God, you must be the..."

Harry jumped in excitedly. "You're the two he was talking about! I can't believe this! We figured you were a thousand miles from here by now, with that Julius Miller guy on your tail."

"You know Chris?" asked Eileen.

"He walked into the downtown office a few hours ago, while we were trying to figure out what was going on. He just sat down and told us all kinds of stuff about Sherman's plan and operations. Then... it seemed like he had something he needed to do, so we let him go. He must have trailed this Miller guy somehow."

"Julius Miller is dead. Ruth is taking Chris Jameson to the hospital for an emergency arm amputation... some kind of nasty poison... Miller got a taste of his own medicine it seemed."

"So then, you guys have a bunch of Sherman's business data?"

"Yeah, all kinds of stuff, including dates and times of executions carried out, who the hit men were, and how much they were paid."

James spoke up excitedly. "Yeah, not only that but these guys also are into high level encryption algorithms, just what we need to finish programming the scope."

Leonard looked at the bag Steve carried. "Is that your computer and data storage?"

"Yeah."

"Can you upload some of that incriminating evidence against Sherman from here?"

"Yeah, at least the ones that are decrypted anyway. There's only a few, but they're pretty bad stuff... murder, extortion, that sort of thing."

"Okay. We should get that material to a safe place, those disks are still vulnerable as long as you have the only copy. Here's the phone number for the FBI central computer data bank, see if you can't upload a bunch of that as a backup, and so that nobody up at the bureau has any question about who and what we're dealing with out here. We've been wanting to nail Sherman for a long time, and I have something of a personal score to settle with him myself."

Steve and Eileen got out the computer and began hooking it up to the phone line. Once it was set up, the actual data transfer took only a few seconds.

"So," Harry said, "when we get into the lab complex, you three want to go directly to the temporal lab, right?"

"Right," answered James. "We'll try to rig a video feed from the scope and go public as soon as we have something useful."

"How can we get a video feed out of the lab?" asked Leonard.

"Depends on the situation. If the place is cleared of bad guys, we just hook up to an outgoing fiberoptic cable and badda-bing. If we have to try to get a feed out the back way while containing Sherman at the front, we'll have to string a cable down the shaft."

"Can we do that? Do we have the stuff?"

"Sure, I think there's a coil in the shed behind the gift shop."

"Well, I think we should get down there and get together with Jimmy and Jason. By the way are you guys armed?" asked Leonard. James shook his head, Steve showed the knife and Eileen opened her jacket to display the butt of the nine millimeter. "Well, there's at least one sniper up in the top window of the shaft house. He hasn't fired any shots yet, but we've had a look at him through the IR scope. Jimmy thinks he can take that one out with his Barrett. That's a bolt action sniper rifle that fires the fifty caliber machine gun cartridge, very accurate and with an incredibly long range. We've spotted six more bogeys on the ground at various places around the shaft house. Four are standing still and two are moving around. We're virtually certain that they are there specifically to keep anyone out of the shaft house, and prevent exactly the kind of backdoor assault that we wish to make. We're going to have to be careful as well as lucky to pull this off, but the breakdown in communications will help us, as long as they haven't been able to string a cable down the shaft. There's no two ways about it though, it's going to get rough. Take any computer stuff you'll need with you. Here is some body armor I'd like you to put on. If we had helmets I'd give you those too. Jason and Jimmy have established a position on the Pewabic road, within view of the shaft house but staying off the highway. We'll go coordinate with them and get this show on the road."

Harry finished helping them adjust the straps of their body armor. Then asked Arne, "Did the phone company call?"

"Yeah, I took it down, There was a call from da gift shop phone to da office. I wrote it down on dat paper."

Harry read the transcript:

voice one	"Perimeter established sir."
voice two	"Any sign of enemy activity?"
voice one	"We have a couple pairs of bogeys, staying out of range to north and east."
voice two	"If they come in range, take them out."
voice one	"Yes sir."
voice two	"Stay sharp."

"I don't like the sound of that," said Leonard. "Sounds like they've been spotted, we'll have to be extra careful."

"What should we do then sir?" asked Harry.

"We'll go and coordinate with Jimmy and Jason, they should know they've been compromised. Come on."

When Ruth arrived at the Emergency room entrance at the Houghton County Hospital on Michigan Street she was extremely concerned. Chris was in shock, undergoing some sort of systemic toxic reaction. She skidded to a stop in front of the ER door and honked her horn three times, then got out and ran inside. The doctor on call was striding towards the door and recognized her.

"Ruth, what's up?"

"Male caucasian, severe poisoning, some sort of organic." The doctor waved for assistance, an orderly came running up with a gurney. They went out the door into the cold wind. Ruth opened the tailgate of the Jeep. "It was a murder attempt, the poison was delivered to the right hand. We've got it isolated with a tourniquet, but I think some must be getting through to his system. The arm went necrotic in minutes."

Jerry took a quick look before helping to load Chris onto the gurney, then spoke to Ruth as they followed the orderly who hustled it back through the door. "You know this guy?"

"Not very well."

"How about a sample of the poison?"

She dug into her jacket pocket and took out a sealed plastic bag. There were a few brownish drops of water inside. "It was delivered on the end of a dart made of ice." Jerry made a face. "Yeah, pretty nasty. The ice has melted, but I think some of the agent is still there."

As they passed the nurse's station Jerry called out. "Prep OR, get somebody in the lab for an emergency poison analysis. I need blood workup stat. See if we have what he needs for a complete transfusion." The nurse immediately picked up a phone and started talking. Ruth walked alongside the gurney holding Chris' good hand. He was rambling and mumbling incoherently, trembling uncontrollably.

"Jerry, one thing you ought to know about, he seemed to know something about the poison. Before he passed out he said to forget the arm, like he knew what the stuff was and what it could do."

Jerry nodded. He was washing up, a nurse slipped on his rubber gloves. Behind him emergency preparations were under way in the operating room. A technician had retrieved the sample of the poison from the plastic bag using a pipette and was scanning it under a special toxicological spectrograph. Blood was being drawn and analyzed. An oxygen mask was being placed over Chris' face, while an intravenous anesthetic was prepared and implemented.

"I'll get back to you as quick as we know something, alright?" Jerry said.

He walked backwards through the door, leaving Ruth in the washroom. As the door closed Ruth heard the technician who had been analyzing the poison exclaim: "Whoa, Doc, would you look at that! Never seen it outside a textbook!" It did nothing good for Ruth's peace of mind that the toxic agent involved was a rare one. She walked back out to the waiting room. The nurse flagged her down to assist with the paperwork.

Ruth picked up the clipboard and started filling out whatever information she could. "How's Frank Giacoletti doing?" She asked the duty nurse.

"Who?"

"Frank Giacoletti, multiple gunshot wounds to the upper right leg, should have come in by ambulance about two hours or so ago."

"I'm sorry ma'am, we've had no admissions of that kind at all tonight. One of our ambulances is still out though, it's way overdue. We haven't been able to contact it because of the radio interference."

A cold chill ran up Ruth's spine as she dropped the clipboard from nerveless fingers and bolted out the door to the Jeep.

Jimmy and Jason were not surprised to hear confirmation that they had been spotted. The cars were parked on the Pewabic road, about a thousand meters from the shaft house. It was clearly visible, dominating the skyline at the top of the hill directly to their west. The moon had risen almost directly overhead, its glow failing to dissipate the intense northern lights, which seemed to focus their activity directly above the shaft house. A small circular area about the size of a full moon lay at the center of the swirling, spiraling pattern of color. It was the only part of the sky which was not glowing intensely.

Introductions were made for the people who had not yet met, and the IR scope was passed around so that everyone could see the faint outline of the suspected sniper looking out of the small square window near the top of the shaft house. Only one of the others was visible, standing in a darkened doorway of the old brick hoist building just east of the shaft house, but they had confirmed the presence of others. They discussed the various plans and strategies whereby they might dispatch the watchers and gain entrance to the shaft. They stood and debated for over an hour as the aurora swirled and shifted angrily, like storm tossed seas above the shaft house, and the moon passed its zenith. At least six defenders guarded the facility, heavily armed and in carefully chosen and distributed positions. The small group wishing to enter the mine was relatively lightly armed, mostly with handguns. The planned assault seemed a hopeless enterprise. Even Leonard, an experienced agent who had been involved in numerous bloody encounters, could see little reason for optimism. As they stood by the cars on the plowed road in Pewabic, Jason and Jimmy suddenly stiffened. They looked at each other, then at Leonard.

"Message from Digger and Joan sir," said Jason. "They report that they have successfully entered the lab complex in good condition. What can I tell them?"

Leonard sighed heavily. "Tell them we're trying our best to go ahead with the plan. Try again in a half hour, we should know something by then."

Neither Jason nor Jimmy alone had the ability to transmit telepathic messages clearly. It was one of the techniques they'd been taught in those UNEC summer camps long ago, to coordinate their minds to work together. Their abilities did not so much add together, as multiply. As soon as the message was delivered Jimmy said. "Sir, I suggest that we declare two primary goals at the outset. One is the gift shop, securing the rope and cable we'll need as well as the communications. Second is the man up top. He is the major threat at long range. The others we only have to worry about when we get close. Jason and I need to stay together in order to communicate with Digger and Joan. What if we pick a spot on the north or west side from which we can try to take out the sniper, and any others we can reach? The rest of you take the road to the south, and move towards the gift shop. If we're lucky, they'll expose themselves to one of us while worrying about the others. If we can put enough pressure on them, they may try to group together, then Harry can use the rocket."

Leonard looked around. "Any comments?" There were none. "Well, I don't like it, and I don't like taking armed civilians into a firefight, but it's all we've got." He looked at James, Steve, and Eileen. "You guys are to stay out of it as much as possible. Your part will come when we get inside. We can't afford to lose you now." They nodded He looked at Jason and Jimmy. "Where you going?"

"Jimmy pointed to an old crumpled copy of the USGS Hancock quadrangle topographic map. I thought we'd drive back towards Paavola the back way, while you slip through the other way. It'll keep them busy trying to track us both. Then we'll come right down through Franklin Mine across the highway to the west, and try to find some cover amongst the old buildings."

"Okay then, let's go!" said Leonard. The group split and got into two separate cars. Jason and Jimmy took the Bronco and followed their plan. They worked their way through the streets of Franklin Mine to within three hundred meters of the shaft house when they saw the flash of gunfire in the night and their radiator exploded. Jimmy already had the Barrett in hand as they dived out the doors, taking whatever cover they could against the snowbanks. Bullets thwocked into their vehicle and the snow nearby, followed by the report of rifle fire from the shaft house. Jimmy chambered an explosive round in the big gun and tried to set it up on the snowbank to aim, but the incoming fire was too intense. Jason fired a few shots over the snowbank to give him a chance. But the sniper apparently saw the big weapon being aimed and moved back from the window. Jimmy set it up on the snowbank, but now had no target. Flashes came from another window, lower down, and they had to get down again, bullet impacts showered their faces with snow. They could hear other weapons fire off in the distance beyond the shaft house. Jimmy closed his eyes for a moment, and reached inside his coat to grasp the little totem bag he was given... so long ago it seemed.

The five others had proceeded cautiously in the hummer towards the shaft house from the east, but as they approached, a burst of fire came from the window of one of the old brick buildings surrounding it. Windows shattered as they bailed from the damaged vehicle and took cover. They too were quickly pinned down against the snowbanks, taking sporadic fire from two buildings, including the one containing the gift shop.

They lay against the snowbanks, Jason and Jimmy west of the shaft house, Leonard, Harry, James, Steve, and Eileen to the east. Their occasional attempts at returning fire did little but pinpoint their positions for the well positioned defenders. Leonard lay back and groaned. "I knew I didn't like the plan. Damn!" He stared upward at the sky, the patterns in the northern lights grew more and more intense as he stared at them. The tiny circle of blackness above the shaft house slowly grew. The others in the group grew worried on sensing their leader's despondence. "What the hell is with the sky! Look at this!"

The others looked up in wonderment. James seemed to understand something. "Yeah look at it. It's... it's like some sort of vortex above the shaft house. The aurora is caused by electrons trapped in the geomagnetic field. Fluctuations in the field are usually seen as waving lines and curtains. But this is different, there's some sort of distortion of the magnetic field here. Oh my God!" he exclaimed, suddenly realizing something. "It's the scope, they've must have broken the password and turned on the tempiloscope. Leonard, there's no time to lose, we HAVE to get in there! Now!"

Occasional bullets ripped through the top of the snowbank, showering them with white powder. Leonard shook his head, tears coming to his eyes. "Do you think I don't know that? We're outgunned and outmaneuvered. We don't have a snowball's chance in flaming hell right now, it would take a miracle to just get us out of here alive, much less getting us in there now, a miracle! There's just....."

Eileen broke in, "Shhhh, quiet... listen... what's that?" Slowly a droning sound could be heard, seeming to come from all around. It sounded like a hive of giant bees, or a thousand lumberjacks with chain saws. The sound approached closer and seemed familiar, yet.... "What is it?" asked Eileen, the city girl from Chicago.

James laughed. "Sounds like snowmobiles, lots of 'em." The noise of the engines grew suddenly louder and a group of about two dozen snowmobiles came roaring up the road behind them. Rifle fire cracked from the buildings again, aimed now at the newcomers, and Leonard, Harry, James, and even Eileen took the opportunity to return the fire. One of the snowmobiles veered and plowed into the snowbank, the rider falling off and squirming in agony on the road. Half of the group of snowmobiles jumped the bank and headed for the buildings, while two stopped with their fallen comrade, and the rest roared past flanking the building. A dozen men armed with hunting rifles jumped off their snowmobiles and burst into the building. The firing suddenly stopped.

Two men with their hands on their heads were marched out into the snow, surrounded by the newcomers. They approached the road and were met by Leonard and the others, brushing the snow off themselves. A spokesman came forward and pulled back his hood.

Leonard strode forward and shook his mittened hand. "It's a miracle," he said. "Who are you?"

"I'm Joe Running Bear, Ojibway tribal council. We got a call you guys needed help?"

"Leonard Howarth, FBI. Oh man, am I ever glad to see you! What do you have here, about twenty, twenty five?"

"Over two hundred, we're just the group that came down this way. The rest split up to surround the place. What do you need?"

"This is incredible! How did you find us so fast?"

"Look at the sky." A young woman came running up to Joe and spoke quickly. He answered. "Okay, pick somebody to help you, get him on a sled and get him down to the hospital."

Leonard looked up for a moment, then shook his head to clear it. He liked to move slowly and carefully, giving himself time to completely understand every situation before taking action. He did not like the off-balanced feeling of events taking control. Still, he dealt with it well and explained the situation to Joe as quickly as he could. Joe Running Bear spoke to two of his men, who jumped onto their snow machines and roared off. "I sent them coordinate a mass assault. If you're ready, hop on and let's go take this shaft house." The members of the party each got on the back of a snowmobile, and they roared off towards the shaft house.

Jimmy and Joshua were still crouched behind the snowbank when they heard the droning of the snowmobile engines. They looked at each other quizzically for a moment. Then they heard gunshots and saw flashes from a window in the shaft house. The sniper was shooting at targets somewhere to the north, Jimmy could see only the muzzle of the sniper's weapon protruding from the window. He quickly ejected the explosive round from the chamber of the Barrett and replaced it with a black tipped armor piercing round. He tried to visualize the posture of the sniper in the building, then chose a point on the surface of the galvanized steel sheathing and fired. Apparently he missed because after a momentary pause, the sniper fired again. Jimmy chambered the explosive round again and aimed just below the small hole he'd punched in the building. When he fired again there was a bright flash as the round struck the building, making a large hole and scattering shrapnel within. The sniper's rifle fell out of the window to the ground.

Jason and Jimmy rose from their position and were amazed to see dozens of snowmobiles roar towards the shaft house from every direction. A group came up the road behind them and came to a stop. Hunting weapons were raised to the sky with loud whoops as hoods were thrown back, and Jimmy recognized a face among the many excited teenagers. "Jamey! Jamey Yellowknife! My God, it's good to see you. We'd almost given up hope."

"Thank the Great Spirit for that my friend. He guided us here. What do you need?"

"We've got to get inside that building."

"I know, hop on." The snowmobiles converged on the shaft house and firing ceased. Jimmy, Jason, and the group of younger Ojibways hurried across the highway as three men were led out with hands on heads... two more were dragged out, limp, and laid in the snow in front of the gift shop, just south of the shaft house.

Jamey Yellowknife looked over the bodies. "Good shot." he said to Jimmy. "That one was about to make some holes in some of my friends. I guess one of our guys got the other one, he was on the ground."

Just then another group of snowmobiles approached and stopped in the parking lot. Leonard jumped off the back of one and ran up to Jimmy and Jason. "You guys okay? Man, can you believe this? He looked at the group of captives and the two dead. "Seven in all, I think that's the lot of them." Several men took charge of the silent captives, tying them up and leading them into the gift shop. Leonard turned to the assembled crowd and spoke loudly. "Listen up. We will need to rappel down the shaft a hundred and twenty meters to the fourth level where the labs are. How many are experienced at this kind of ropework and can come with us?" Four of the men stepped forward. "Good. We also need a strong presence here to hold this position against any counterattack, maybe forty men. The main force should proceed to the main entrance on the hillside below." He turned to Harry. "You go with them, take the rocket launcher, it might be able to blow in that door." Then to Joe Running Bear he said, "Be careful down there, they have guards outside and a hardened position, maybe even some heavier weapons or explosives. What we mostly need, rather than an assault in force, is something to keep these guys busy while we come in the back way. Joe nodded, got on his snowmobile, and roared off down the highway with a strong force at his back, Harry rode on the back of Joe's snowmobile with the rocket launcher slung across his back.

One of the other Ojibways took charge of deploying men in a defensive perimeter around the shaft house, while the small team who would be descending into the mine gathered around Leonard. "We have not much time, and only two ropes, a hundred and twenty meters is a long way, but we'll need to drop down as quickly as we can. Jimmy, Jason, can you get a message to Digger and Joan? Tell them we've captured the shaft house and are about to descend." The two closed their eyes and engaged in telepathic conversation. "They understand sir, and advise to proceed with caution.

"Alright then. We'll tie the ropes up here on these girders, get that lock off of there. Let's move!"

One rope and associated equipment was brought from the hummer, the other was found in the gift shop where Digger had said it would be. They entered the shaft building and opened the trap door into the shaft itself with a key that James had found in the cash register. It took two men to lift the heavy steel trap door, which fell back with a loud "Clang!" The inky blackness from the shaft seemed to flow out onto the floor of the building, even as the approaching dawn lightened the sky to the east. Directly overhead the swirl the northern lights deepened and intensified, seeming reluctant to give up the sky to the approaching sun. The ropes were lowered through the opening. James and Leonard would go first, the others would follow as soon as the rope went slack.

Just as they were gearing up for the descent, Chris' white Jeep Cherokee roared up and Ruth rushed into the building. "Thought you'd want to know. The ambulance that was supposed to bring Frank and Stephen to the hospital... it never showed up, and has not been seen."

"What?" said Leonard incredulously.

"I don't know what it means either, but I thought you'd want to know. Chris is in the operating room now, he's in rough shape, but the doc's a friend, he'll do everything possible." Leonard nodded with a deep sigh, then looked at the opening in the floor, and the rope trailing into it from his rappelling device. Ruth nodded. "Good luck," she said quietly, and turned away.

James and Leonard carefully backed side by side through the opening, keeping themselves from hitting the lip of the door by using their feet on the rock below. Jimmy placed a piece of carpet he'd brought from the gift shop under the ropes to keep them from being cut on the sharp iron edge of the trapdoor frame. As soon as they had passed through the door, they were in another world: one where the only light is that which you bring with you, where the only colors are black and gray, where the only connection to the outside world is the thin strand of nylon rope from which you hang, where the air is moist with the smell of rock and clay, and the endlessly echoing sound of water, trickling and dripping, fills the heavy air. They flicked on their flashlights and, reminded by the echoes to take more than ordinary care to be quiet, descended swiftly into the darkness below, with only the tuneless humming of the rope through their braking devices disturbing the long and jealous slumber of the mine.

CHAPTER 52

Digger and Joan moved cautiously into the passageway from the grunt lab and headed north, moving as quickly and quietly as possible. Using the infrared binoculars Joan was able to determine that the patrol that had checked out the grunt lab a few minutes earlier had moved in the other direction, their warm footprints were barely detectable, glowing dull red on the cold poured concrete floor. The light from the bare bulbs hanging at thirty meter intervals on the ceiling gave a harsh light, casting thick shadows that somehow seemed welcome. The dark basalt seemed to absorb any light that fell on it. In the shadows where the direct light from the bulb did not fall, the darkness seemed impenetrable. The tunnel was neither straight nor smooth sided, though the floor was quite level and unobstructed. Back at the turn of the 19th and 20th centuries, this tunnel had served as a way for miners to come to work at the beginning of their shift. The tunnel entrance, called an adit, that emerged almost in the middle of the town of Hancock, had been the place they would report for work and clock in. If they were lucky they'd catch a ride on a low train car. If they missed the train they'd simply walk along this tunnel to the number two shaft, where they would board the big open mancar for transportation to the workings far below. The tunnel weaved back and forth in a slightly serpentine fashion, rather than being arrow straight. It was said that they tunneled in this fashion so that the bright headlights of a distant train would not blind people walking in the passage from far away. For Digger and Joan, the significant fact in all this was that they could not see very far at all, not much further than the next light bulb. They stopped and listened often, seeking shelter in the deeper shadows between the lights, and growing more nervous when they had to pass one of the glowing bulbs. They had passed about ten lights when they heard the quickly approaching sound of footsteps from in front of them. Fortunately there was a deep depression in the wall where they were, almost halfway between two of the lights. Digger pressed Joan into it, where they squatted on the floor, hiding their faces and making themselves as small as possible. A few seconds later, a man came jogging around the bend, heading towards the offices, he did not slow down, and apparently did not notice the two crouched in the shadows as he passed. Once he was out of sight and earshot they stood back up. Digger whispered. "We were lucky. Good thing he wasn't really looking. We've got to get out of this passage."

"How much further?"

"There's a storage area just ahead, then the temporal lab, maybe another hundred meters or so." Digger hurried ahead now, less worried about noise and more concerned about getting out of sight. They came to a locked steel frame door on the left. Digger took out a keycard, then hesitated. "There are some things in here we could use," he said, "but if I use this card to open the door, it will show on the screen in the lab security computer up front." He shook his head. "We have to assume they're monitoring that system, so we'd better not chance it."

Digger looked around the passage, the computer data conduit ran along the ceiling. Tampering with it would certainly set off an alarm. He spotted something else, on the floor. "Hello, what have we here?" He picked up a telephone cable lying against the far wall. This wasn't here two days ago. Looks like they have at least one line strung in here."

"Should we cut it?" asked Joan.

"Not yet. Come on, let's see what the situation is at the temporal lab, the cable may lead there." They hurried along the passage until they reached the heavy door leading to the temporal lab. To Digger's surprise, the telephone cable on the floor did not go through the door, but snaked on past. The heavy vault door, opening inwards, was ajar. Digger cautiously peered around it, drawing the nine millimeter auto-pistol out of his belt, and holding it nervously. Joan took out the little stainless steel .38 snubby Ruth had given her. They crept past the first big door, along the short zig zag passage, and to the next. There were voices within. Digger peeked carefully around the corner. Two men were at the tempiloscope control panel, talking excitedly. They appeared to be armed only with holstered handguns. A third man stood behind them leaning on the backs of their chairs, a light automatic rifle slung over his shoulder. To his dismay, Digger saw that they had managed to get past his password and had started the machine. There were images flashing erratically in the globe.

Digger motioned to Joan to stay where she was and give him cover, then he walked out into the room. The men heard him approach, but did not turn. "Look here sir," said the standing guard, "we're getting images inside the presidential palace."

"But you haven't engaged the stabilizer." said Digger. All three turned at the sound of his voice, staring down the barrel of his weapon in wide-eyed amazement. They seemed to weigh the odds, three against one, considering whether to chance it. Digger moved to his left, out of Joan's line of fire and they saw her there by the door, her weapon rock steady. Digger did not seem to them to be a threatening person, beyond the fact that he held a weapon. The cold light they saw in Joan's eyes as she protected her lover was something else entirely.

"Okay, one at a time. You first. Lay your weapons down over there, then lay face down with your hands behind your head.... Now you..... and you. Good." Digger ran to the outer door and closed it, locking it from within. Digger then came back and used some twelve gauge braided copper electrical wire to tie their hands behind their necks and thence to their belts at the back. He then lashed their feet tightly together and sat them all upright, back to back. When he had lashed all their hands together to a vertical metal pole, they were virtually immobile.

Joan finally entered the room, keeping an eye on the three men, who had thus far been silent. Digger flicked some controls on the tempiloscope, and the flashing globe went dark. "My name is Digger Puttonen, this is my machine you're playing with, and I don't appreciate it. Now I'm going to ask some questions, and I expect some answers. First, why is there a telephone cable strung in the passageway outside?" The men looked at each other, but remained silent. "It's a detonation cord for a bomb isn't it?"

"No!" one of the men shook his head. "No, there's no bomb." Joan nodded to indicate that he was telling the truth.

"So there's a guard stationed down the tunnel, by the shaft then?" Digger asked.

"No! There was going to be, but there's not one yet." Joan shook her head silently.

"I don't appreciate lies. Your boss is going down, do you understand? Your only hope is to come clean and deal with us. Now, we don't want to have to hurt anybody, but we will if we have to. So, tell me again about the guard down at the shaft?"

"There's just one guy..."

"Shut up! Sherman will skin us alive!" said the man who had been carrying the rifle. Digger got out a roll of duct tape and covered his mouth, leaving the other two able to talk.

"Yes, you were saying?"

"Look, we're just hired monkeys making a few bucks the hard way, I got no beef with you."

"Nor I with you. Now what about this fellow you were telling me about?"

"One of Sherman's right hand men, he got his leg broken a few hours ago, run over by a snowmobile. He's laying down there on a stretcher with a phone and a gun."

"And his name?"

"Tony."

"Thanks, now you guys just sit here for a while. I'm going to go have a talk with Tony. You stay out of trouble and I may be able to keep this she-devil from doing anything nasty to you. "Joan, you stay here and watch these guys okay? If you have to shoot, try for the kneecaps." The captured men reacted squeamishly to overhearing this comment. "We'll keep the inner door open for now, and the outer door locked. If you turn this, it will not respond to a keycard from outside. Don't open for anyone but me. Here put these on." Digger took the odd looking pair of goggles off his head. "We call this the 'speleoscope', works on the same principle as the imaging system we had in the grunt. You put this against the wall, rock is better than metal..."

She did so, and gasped. "I can see right through it!"

"Yes, into it and through it, all based on simulsample sweep frequency sound processing. You'll be able to see people walking past, though maybe not their faces. Try tweaking these two knobs for focus and clarity. Yeah, that's it. Okay, I'm going out there, when I come back, I'll put my hands on the door, like this, that will tell you it's me. Okay?"

"Okay, but you be careful, remember, they said he has a gun."

Digger picked up a pair of side cutters from a workbench. "I remember. Let me have the binocs." Joan handed them to him. "Oh, and if you hear from them up above... tell them to proceed, with caution." Digger opened the big door, checked the way carefully, then blew Joan a kiss and closed it behind him. He crossed the corridor and quickly cut the phone line lying there with his little knife. He trotted quickly to the left, towards the old number two shaft, wondering just what could have happened to cause Farley to end up in the water there. He imagined what it must have been like... He slowed as he approached the end of the tunnel, passed the last light and stepped forward softly into the deepening darkness. He thought he knew where they would have laid Tony's stretcher, glancing at the phone line, his guess was confirmed. Off to the right, with a view of both the shaft and the tunnel, the man would by lying. In the deep silence the man would surely have heard his approach.

Digger stayed in the deepest shadows and called out. "Hey Tony! You okay?"

"Who's that?" came a voice out of the darkness.

"My name's Digger." He heard the telephone being picked up, the keypad manipulated. "Sorry Tony, the line's cut. You'll have to talk to me."

"What about?"

"What do you think? I want you to throw out your gun."

"Sorry mister, no can do. You want my gun, you'll have to come get it."

"Listen Tony. Do you realize what Sherman is doing here? He's making a play to dominate the world by force and fear. It won't work. Even if he succeeds in this little project, he will ultimately fail."

"Talk 'til you're blue in the face mister, it'll do no good. Mister Sherman's been like a father to me. You can't change my mind."

"Okay Tony, listen, I want you to know I forgive you for shooting me in the chest, I know it was what you felt you had to do."

"What are you talking about?"

"You know, last night... and sorry about the leg, I was kinda scared and gunned the motor a little harder than necessary maybe..."

"YOU!!"

Digger could sense the anguish and confusion in Tony's voice. "Yeah, listen, it's no big deal, the bullet was stopped by some stuff in my pack, all you did was spill some hot chocolate on my pants."

"Aaaaagh!"

"No really, don't worry about it. Well, if you want I can take a rain check on the hot chocolate you owe me, or... you could just throw out your gun."

"Never!"

"Listen Tony, I've got some concussion grenades here. They're about the size of a duck's egg, painted, uh... kinda dark gray. There are some words painted on here, let's see... um... 'grenade, concussion, type D dash 5S'. You ever seen anything like that before?"

"Yeah," said Tony softly after a pause.

"Well listen, I've got plenty of reasons for being mad with you, but I'm tired and I've seen too many people die today. I can't seem to get angry, but I am in a hurry. Do you understand?"

"Keep talking."

Look Tony, I've never used one of these, but they tell me that all I have to do is press this button and count to five and it goes boom. I could just press the button and toss it over there if you want a closer look, but I'd rather not, you understand? I have no hard feelings against you, and I'm just not into that kind of thing for fun." There was a long pause.

"So, if I throw you my gun, then what?"

"Well, assuming you're playing straight with me, we get you to a hospital as soon as possible. I can't carry you by myself, so for now I guess you'll have to stay here. In a while some more people will be here, and we'll move you to a more comfortable spot. Is it a deal?"

"So, who are you? Are you FBI or something?"

"No, nothing like that, though we're expecting a visit from them soon. No, my name is Digger Puttonnen, I'm one of the principal partners of Midnight Mining Company. This is my place Sherman's trying to grab, and I want it back is all."

"How'd you get in here?"

"Sorry, maybe I can tell you that later."

"So if you cut the phone line, why do you want me out, If you know my name, then you know I can't move."

"Yeah well, some more friends are coming... lots of 'em."

"Down the shaft?"

"Yep, pretty soon now too."

"They'll never make it, there's guys all over the place up there."

"Not any more Tony. Don't you get it? It's as good as over. Sherman's got no chance anymore, if he ever did."

"What about mister Sherman?"

"What about him?"

"He left here just a few minutes ago, you didn't do anything to him?"

"Nope, he ran right past, we didn't touch him."

"We?"

"Hey, you don't think I'd try to break in here alone do you?"

Tony was silent for a long time. "If I give up, will you promise not to hurt him?"

"Gosh Tony, that's a tough one. It depends a lot on what he decides doesn't it? For my part, I promise not to hurt him unless I have to, to protect my life, or that of one of my friends. I'll be honest with you though, I can't guarantee what he will do when he finds out he's lost... you know Sherman better than I do. Will he give up without a fight do you think?" There was a long pause.

"Okay mister Digger..."

"Just Digger."

"Okay Digger, I don't know why, but I believe you." A Glock nine millimeter pistol skittered across the floor to near where Digger stood against the wall.

"Is that it then? No other weapons?"

"Just a pocket knife, you want that too?"

Digger walked out into the chamber, picked up the Glock made sure it was safe, then tucked it into his belt along with the other. "Nah, hang onto that, you might need it." He knelt down next to Tony. "You know, this is a neat spot, I come here sometimes myself, to just sit and listen."

"Listen... to what? There's just water dripping."

"No! Are you kidding? You mean you didn't hear them?"

"What? Hear what?"

"The voices. Don't you hear them? It's like there's voices way off in the distance. You can never quite hear what they're saying, but they're always there. Sometimes it's music instead of voices."

"Are you kidding?" said Tony earnestly. "Jesus man, I thought I was going nuts. You mean, you hear 'em too?"

"Yeah sure, always. Listen, there they are now..........."

George Sherman jogged down the tunnel towards the offices of the former Midnight Mining Company. He had stopped to see Tony after leaving the temporal lab, then used the phone to check with the office. He hurried now after learning that Scott and Jeff had hijacked an ambulance heading towards town from Paavola, and that the injured FBI man that had been on board had finally regained consciousness. He passed his roving patrol on their way back to the office and arrived in the canteen and found Frank Giacoletti strapped onto a stretcher, tipped upward at an angle on the table. Another injured man sat nearby, arm in a sling and his face bandaged. Two surly paramedics with tape over their mouths glared at him. Aaron, the former guard, sat at the table staring gloomily at a plate of cookies.

Two of his men stood by, one of them slapping a piece of rusted steel pipe in his hand. Sherman looked at the wallet one of the men handed to him. "Ah, Frank Giacoletti! I don't believe we've ever met face to face but I do remember the name. Detroit, about, oh... 2010 wasn't it?"

"Fuck you!" said Frank vehemently.

"Gosh Frank, I didn't know you felt that way about me," said Sherman with a sneer. "It was nothing personal you understand, just business. You were getting too close to my revenue stream, I had to do something."

"So you set me up to look like I was bought."

"Well, I was hoping you'd go ahead and take the cash and come over to my side, but since you didn't take the hint... and that was just when I was getting my assets off the streets and into legitimate industrials too. You could have been a great help to me Frank. By the way, how is Leonard these days? I haven't heard about him for a while."

"How should I know? The poor son-of-a-bitch thinks I tried to have him killed. He hates my guts."

"Yes, well... these things happen in your line of work, don't they?"

"You're not a very nice person mister Sherman," said Aaron. You talk nice sometimes, but you're all mean and rotten inside."

Sherman spoke brusquely to one of his men. "Shut him up!" They grabbed Aaron, put duct tape over his mouth and strapped him into a chair. "Now, Frank, let's put old times aside. I want to know all about it... what you're doing here, what you know, the whole thing."

Frank was in obvious pain. "Look, like I told these two," he nodded towards Sherman's goons, "we were called up on what we thought was to be a simple investigation."

"We?"

"Yeah, me and my partner, Stephen here." Stephen nodded. "We were to meet the local station chief and pick up some guy for questioning."

"And who would that be?"

"Michael Anthony Puttonen, of Paavola."

Sherman pursed his lips pensively and pinched his chin. "And what did you want to talk to him about?"

"I don't know, I wasn't told. Some guy was coming in from Washington to talk to him."

"I see, you were simply to pick him up and hold him... and did you do so?"

"No, we had a stakeout on his house, but he never showed. Then some guys came up with guns and a rocket launcher, I guess now that they must have been your boys. There was a fight and that's that. I got shot up. Maybe you can tell me why..."

Sherman interrupted Frank with an upraised hand. "I ask the questions. Who fixed you up with that tourniquet? It wasn't these fellows... I trust they'd have been a bit more professional about it."

"No, it was somebody from one of the houses, just a citizen that helped us out after the firefight."

"I see. So, where are the rest of your guys now?"

"I don't know, I passed out and didn't hear of any plans, but I think they may be back at the office. They were plenty mad after the attack. They were talking about going to pick up some explosives and then blow their way in here."

"And what made you think anybody was here?"

"One of your men talked."

"Oh? And who would that be?"

"Give up now Sherman, we have the scoop on you. They're going to blow that door off the side of the mountain and cut you to pieces."

"Sorry Frank, I think you're lying." Sherman sniggered paced back and forth a bit, then chuckled, and finally laughed out loud. "You? The high and mighty FBI are going to blow me out of here? HA! Ever since Federation my boy, your teeth have been pulled. You long for the old days when the U.S was running the show don't you? Janet Reno? Eh? Ruby Ridge? You've got four half-baked agents in the field and you think you can bluff me into thinking there's an attack on the front door? They don't even allow you to stock explosives, you know it and I know it so quit fucking around with me. If your men have the guts and stupidity to try anything at all, it will be the back door. But don't worry, if they do that, they'll find a nasty surprise waiting for them." George stood up, shook his head sadly, and spoke to his henchmen. "This is a waste of time, tape this one's mouth shut too. And get the uniforms off those two paramedics, the ambulance may yet prove to be useful.

Frank saw there was little left to lose, so he tried a desperate gamble. "Give up now George, and I'll see to it that you receive a fair trial."

"Ha ha ha, a fair trial? That's a laugh, in a few hours I'll be giving orders to the Prime Minister herself and the heads of all the other continental councils. You're playing out of your depth my friend. Gag this idiot!"

"No wait! Did you know George, that Chris Jameson turned state's witness this morning?" Sherman turned and stared at Frank. He put up a hand to stop the man about to duct tape Frank's mouth. "He came in of his own accord a few hours ago and gave us reams of evidence, tons... enough to send you and a hundred of your cronies to the slammer forever."

"What? What do you know about Chris Jameson?"

"Just what I said. He was your chief enforcer, 'persuader' I think was the term he used. The information he gave has already been uploaded to the central computers. It's over George, that's what I'm trying to tell you. It's all over but the shouting"

"No, you're lying! Jameson would never betray me."

"Why? Because you picked him up on the street and saved him from a murder rap? He told us about that George. But then you made him do... what? Fifty? Sixty more brutal murders? Innocent people? How far do you expect his gratitude to extend?"

"NO! You're lying!"

"I'm not lying, think about it! Give up now befo...."

"SHUT UP!" George Sherman whirled and hit Frank so hard in the face that he passed out. Sherman spoke to the unconscious form. "All over but the shouting? Well you're about to hear some real shouting." Sherman stormed angrily out of the room and down the corridor to the front office. He picked up the phone and buzzed line two to get the guard house out front. The phone rang three times before it was picked up. "Yes sir." said a voice.

"What the hell are you doing out there? I thought I made it clear I wanted the phone answered on the first ring."

"Sorry sir, just taking a leak... won't happen again." Sherman had trouble placing a face with the voice, though he knew his men pretty well as a rule.

"Well it had better not. Who is this? What's your number?"

"Uh, sixteen," answered the voice.

The blood drained from Sherman's face as he realized that his guards out front had been compromised. The assignment numbers for his men started at fifty. How had they managed it? How many were there? Had Frank been telling the truth? Had Jameson really gone over? He quickly rallied his thoughts. "Okay sixteen, everything alright out there?"

"Yes sir, all Ay Okay."

"Stay sharp, call if there's any problem." George Sherman went back into the office and nervously began fumbling at the catches of a heavy metal suitcase that had previously remained untouched. The men in the room looked at one another and their faces went pale.

Harry had gone south with Joe Running Bear and the larger Ojibway force. Most of the men had left their snow machines several blocks away in town, put on light snowshoes, and moved quietly to surround the main entrance to Midnight Mining Company. The sun was just starting to glisten on the tops of the trees when a hundred Native American men with high powered hunting rifles simultaneously rushed through the snow and took the guards at the entrance completely by surprise before they could sound an alarm. They were handcuffed, disarmed, and removed to a holding cell at the FBI office down the street, the entire operation pulled off without a shot being fired. Most of the force then hid in the woods, a few taking the places of the guards. Harry readied the rocket launcher, found a suitable stance leaning on a car by the guard house, and waited for a signal of some kind. The unexplained city ambulance that was found in the lot was moved outside the gates, the keys had been left in it. When the phone rang in the guard house Joe took it, answered as best he could.

"Do you think they bought it?" asked Harry when Joe hung up the phone.

Joe shook his head doubtfully. "I don't know."

Digger sat in the dark with Tony and they listened to the sounds echoing in the mine, sounding like voices. Then the voices grew louder and clearer, and two cautious lights appeared in the shaft. Digger called out, then went over and welcomed the two men who rappelled into the tunnel and quickly detached from the ropes. Both had submachine guns strapped over their shoulders. "James!" Digger called out. Man am I glad to see you."

James grabbed Digger in a bear hug. "We were worried about you old buddy! I was afraid what sort of reception we might find. Hey, I guess that grunt worked eh?"

"Perfectly. And welcome to Midnight Mining Company Captain Howarth. Over there is our friend Tony. He was working for Sherman until a little while ago, he was planning a reception of a different sort, but we've come to a sort of an understanding; I told him we'd get him to a doctor for the broken leg. Are there any others coming down?"

"Yes, six more, including two computer programmers James enlisted to help you."

"Fabulous!. Could you stay here and coordinate with them? When they get here, we're the first door on the right, you can't miss it. Just knock. This corridor is unsecured, so you'd better set up some sentries beyond the lab as soon as you have the people. I think Sherman has a patrol in the corridor, at least two people so watch out." Then he turned to James. "Come on, a lot has happened!" They walked cautiously south down the corridor towards the temporal lab, weapons at the ready, but no hostile presence was detected. Joan opened the door when she saw Digger's outline through the speleoscope. Digger came in with James, locking the door again behind them. "Joan Niemi, I'd like you to meet my business partner James Dolittle. Joan and I are... uh... you know... uh..."

"What are you trying to say Digger?... that you're lovers?" asked James.

"Ah, yeah, I guess so." Digger turned red to the ears. Joan smiled.

James reached out to shake Joan's hand. "Glad to meet the woman who can tame this wild man. It's about time, I must say."

"Thanks," said Joan, "and here are the guys who have been playing with your toys." She gestured to the three men tied up and sitting on the floor.

James turned to look at the speleoscope. "How far did they get?"

Digger answered, "Looks like they were struggling with the targeting, but they had some flickering images of the PM's office."

James looked at them appreciatively. "In a matter of a few hours?.. Not bad, when this is over, you think you guys might be looking for a job?"

"Y... you mean... you're going to let us live?"

"Sure, as long as you behave yourselves. What kind of an outfit do you think this is?"

"Count me in," said one of the men.

"Me too," said the other. The third man just glared at them angrily with his mouth taped shut.

"Well," continued James, "I'm sure you realize that in the present circumstances we can't untie you, but just keep quiet and watch what we're doing and you might learn something." James and Digger sat together at the control panel, leaving Joan to monitor the door, and began to discuss their options. Digger told James about Arne's story, and about his discovery of another possible set of solutions to the time equations. James told Digger about Steve and Eileen, Sherman's former computer whiz kids who were bringing their world class top decryption program with them. They would also be dragging a fiberoptic cable with them as they came down the shaft, in order to send out any useful video or data signal they could get. They fired up the scope and painstakingly worked to focus it in on the front office of the Midnight Mining Company, just a few hundred meters away; the scene flashed and flickered. Digger engaged the field stabilizer, and a view of George Sherman's face filled the screen, so suffused with rage and malevolent determination that they involuntarily recoiled from it before reducing the magnification to include the entire room.

CHAPTER 53

Steve and Eileen waited their turn at the ropes nervously. The lines had gone slack about three minutes after James and Leonard had dropped through the opening. Two of the Ojibway men had just entered the mine and their lights were rapidly disappearing below. Neither Steve nor Eileen had ever been interested in mountain climbing or spelunking or anything of that sort, and so they had no experience. One of the Ojibway men who would be going into the mine with them, a man who simply called himself Jayjay, took it upon himself to help them out. He showed them how to rig the diaper sling so as to support their weight on the thighs as well as the waist, how to double the carabiners with gates opposed for safety, and how to thread the rope through the braking device that would keep their descent to a reasonable speed. They practiced a little with a piece of rope hung from a girder, then suddenly the ropes went slack and it was their turn. They stood side by side facing away from the opening as others checked their rigging and gave them the thumbs up. Someone had found hard hats and electric miner's lamps in the back room of the gift shop, and these were fitted to Steve and Eileen as they prepared for the descent. The bag with the computer and data disks was slung at Steve's back. They had been assured of the strength of the lines, relatively new eleven millimeter nylon climbing ropes, with low stretch and a breaking strength of almost fifteen hundred kilograms. Still... they seemed so thin... such a narrow cord to trust an entire life to!

Eileen's fear of the descent was simply the ordinary and natural reluctance of putting the body in a position which it instinctively knows is dangerous. The rational mind may logically comprehend the strength of the line, the engineering of the braking devices, and the foolproof doubly backed up rigging. It is the animal mind, ever lurking just below human consciousness which screams out in protest, knowing only the potential drop below. For Steve, the situation was much different. It can perhaps be argued that no one making their first rappel ever faced a greater challenge than Steve Sanders did on that day. As a child he had suffered from an extreme fear of darkness. His older brother had constantly made fun of him about it. Once, his brother had locked him in a closet to tease him, then forgotten about him. Steve had screamed until he was hoarse, laid there in stark terror until finally his mother had come, hours later, looking for him. In later years he had slowly built up his tolerance to darkness, his ability to suppress the panic, but still it lurked there, threatening to ooze out through the cracks of the toybox in which he had supposedly locked it away. The terror welled up in his chest, threatening to choke him as he looked down into the pit. His legs began an uncontrollable tremble, the 'sewing machine' it was called in rock climbing terminology. Jayjay saw his discomfort and spoke encouragingly to him.

"Steve... Steve! Yeah, look at me. Here, let's flip your lights on. Okay, Steve, I want you to keep your eyes on a level. Look where you're putting your feet, look at your wife if you want to. You'll know it when you get where you're going. Keep your body leaned back, your feet flat against the rock. If you try to stand up straight your feet will slip and you'll hit your face."

Eileen stood next to him and Steve said quietly, "I don't think I can do this."

"Come on, just a few minutes and it'll be over," she said. Eileen took the initiative and stepped through the opening first, dangling below the steel trap door looking up. The dark well looked less fearsome with Eileen's smiling face looking up at him.

Jayjay spoke to Steve again. "Okay, ease it back, look at your feet, keep them flat. Step on through, feel the rock? Hold the rope a little more loosely, let it slip through your hand. Look at me! Yeah, there you go. We'll be following you in a few minutes, see you there."

Steve looked out of the corner of his eye at Eileen. He'd been warned not to stare directly at someone's face underground while wearing a miner's cap because of the blinding effect of shining the light in someone's eyes. The sight of his lover calmed him. "Hey babe, you want to go on down?" He had to force his mouth to form the words, as if there were some force inside him trying to hold them in. The words echoed in an uncanny way.

"Okay, you ready?" Eileen answered.

"I guess so." The hundred and fifty meters of rope in his right hand was heavy, he let loose his death grip a bit and began to slide, the rope making a humming sound as it slipped through the braking bar. He leaned back as he'd been told and found it not at all uncomfortable. He quickly got the feel of how hard to hold the rope to control the speed of descent. He tried to watch his feet, concentrating on careful placement to keep from slipping on the wet surface. They walked quickly backward, as Jayjay suggested, rather than bouncing as they always show in the movies.

About thirty meters below the shaft collar the walls at the sides simply disappeared, receding into the impenetrable distance. He felt like he was shrinking, as if he'd become the size of an ant in the immense pressing darkness of the chasm. He looked over at Eileen. Her face was set in concentration as she carefully but quickly placed her feet in descent. He smiled, he loved the way she could focus her entire being on a problem, it was something he had trouble with himself, he was always getting distracted. The nylon webbing under his thighs was beginning to become uncomfortable, but there was no way to shift it now. He felt his legs start to tingle a little with the reduced circulation, and tried to shake them back into life, it helped a little. Steve was peripherally aware of the echoing sounds of dripping and trickling water mingling with the scraping of their feet, but he was too intent on the task at hand to really pay it any attention. They had left the ordinary world of horizontal things behind far above. Here, there was only the shaft, nothing else mattered, nothing else even existed it seemed. As they continued to slide down the gossamer thin strand, the shaft began to seem normal, the idea of flat ground seemed to recede in his memory to something he had perhaps read about in a book, until Steve actually began to feel a strange comfort with the vertical environment. If only it was not so blasted dark! In his growing familiarity he lost some of his caution and looked up. He saw a tiny rectangle of dim light already far away in the distance above, seen through an immensity of... He felt that familiar horror rising again to strangle him, a sense of the darkness closing in about him. He felt that he would have to let go of the rope, his hand trembled and cramped where he gripped the rope that controlled his plunge. But then he quickly looked over at Eileen, who caught the motion of his cap lantern and looked back. Her smile seemed to wash away the choking fear. She was counting on him to be there for her, his wife!... Steve had barely begun to think about what that might mean. He looked at his feet again, then at the rope humming through the loops of the braking device. Steve saw a glint of light on the jagged points of the dark rock that did not seem to come from his lamp, nor from Eileen's. He chanced a look downward, and saw that some distance below them a light was shining up, checking on their progress. "We're almost there!" he croaked out. They passed a cavern on the left, a place they could have stopped to rest, but neither wanted to prolong the ordeal. Their feet were getting soaked in the gathering rivulet of water that took advantage of the shaft to find its way to the water table below. Steve looked again, it was only another twenty meters or so to go.

A voice called out from below. It sounded like Leonard, but it was distorted oddly by the echoing chasm. "Looking good guys, work your way to the left a little." In a few moments waiting hands were pulling them to safety in the yawning tunnel mouth. There was blessed light here, not only three other flashlights but the distant gleam of a real light bulb as well. Steve collapsed to the floor and pulled the rope through his gear to relieve the tension that seemed to be pulling him back towards the shaft.

"Relax, let me get that," said Leonard. He disengaged their rigging from the ropes and let the dangling weight of the lines snake back into the shaft again. More people would be coming down soon. Steve and Eileen sat on the floor and caught their breath for a moment. They held hands and kissed each other urgently. "First time?" Leonard asked.

"Uh no," said Steve, failing to understand Leonard's meaning. "We've been together a couple years."

"No, not that." Leonard smiled. "I mean the shaft, rappelling on a rope like that."

"Oh, yeah... first time."

"Well you did great. I've done it hundreds of times and that first step still gives me a weird feeling in the pit of my stomach every time. What about the cable, weren't you going to bring it down?"

"Sorry," Steve said, "we were having enough problems getting just ourselves down, the next guys will drag it with them. We thought it would be better if it wasn't in the way. Jason and Jimmy are working on getting the other end hooked up to an outgoing line topside."

"Oh I see, yeah that's okay. You guys want to go see the lab now?"

Steve looked at Eileen. "That's what we came here for," she said.

He looked back at Leonard. "Yeah, let's go." They got up and followed Leonard into main passageway. They passed one of the other Ojibway men who was talking to a man on a stretcher that they didn't recognize.

"Two more coming down in a few minutes Zeb," said Leonard. They'll be bringing the cable. Make sure you bring it to the lab as soon as they get here, then support Jack guarding the tunnel. He's alone out there and we can expect unfriendly visitors anytime."

"Okay!" said Zeb. Leonard led the way down the passage. Steve and Eileen switched off their cap lights when they got into the lighted area. They approached a cut on the right and saw the massive vault door fitted there. A man lurked in the shadows, but Leonard greeted him in a friendly fashion. He was holding one of the submachine guns that had been taken from Sherman's men in the capture of the shaft house, and also had a Winchester .30-30 lever action rifle slung across his back. He waved at them as they passed; Steve recognized him as Jack, one of the men who'd rappelled down the shaft just before he and Eileen went. Leonard walked up to the door and knocked, the sound was dull through the heavy steel plate. Immediately there was the sound of heavy bolts being drawn, and the door swung silently inward. A friendly female face greeted them in the rough hewn zig zag passage.

"Hi Leonard. Hi, I'm Joan, you must be Eileen and Steve? We've been expecting you." Joan shook hands with them as they came through the door "Go on in, the boys are playing with their toys in there," she said.

Leonard stopped and headed back out. "You guys go ahead, see what you can get going. I'm worried about the situation out in the passage." Joan shut the door behind him and locked it, then took up her station again, monitoring the passage outside through the speleoscope. She could see the shadowy indistinct forms of Leonard and Jack out there.

Steve and Eileen entered the chamber through a second heavy door and were amazed by the giant machine humming away in the center of the room. James turned and saw them. "Oh, here you are! Fantastic! Digger, this is Steve and Eileen. I'm hoping they can help solve some of our targeting problems."

Quickly Digger explained the situation. "This machine we call the tempiloscope, because it allows us to view, in the chamber there, locations specified in both space and time."

Steve and Eileen looked in the chamber. An image flickered there of George Sherman doing something with a suitcase. They recognized him immediately. "What are we looking at here?" asked Eileen.

"We've got real time in the front office. Looks like Sherman and what... seven guys?"

"What's he doing?" asked Steve.

"I don't know, something with that suitcase."

"Can you get a closer look?"

"I'll try." The magnification increased, giving them an excellent view of a desk stapler, then the scene flickered and went dark, there was a flash of light, then nothing. "Damn! Lost it again. see? there's the problem... for reasons which we still don't understand, it takes a seven variable coordinate system to specify any particular time and place you want to view. The numbers change in ways which seem to be chaotic, we have not been able to deduce the pattern. Therefore we have had to simply stab in the dark if you will, with varying levels of success. The method is awkward, time consuming, and inelegant. We've tried using canned pattern recognition and decoding programs to use as an interface, but haven't found anything that works fast enough yet. The problem seems to be that the interrelationships between the variables seem to vary continuously."

"A constantly varying encryption algorithm... fantastic!" said Steve. Eileen had opened the satchel on his back and was removing the little computer and a packet of optical data storage disks. Steve looked over the control panel in rapt fascination. "You mean... you guys are controlling this by adjusting each of the seven variables independently and actually getting results?"

"Well yeah, like I said, it's a pain in the ass," answered Digger, "but we haven't found any other way to do it."

"What about a joystick?"

"What? You mean like a video game?"

"Exactly!"

"But there are seven variables not including magnification, joystick controllers give you continuous coverage of only two, not to mention the interrelationships."

"Do they?" Steve handed James a 72 pin parallel cable. "Can you give me parallel link up to your CPU?" James dived into the maze of cable under the control panel. Steve went on, while Eileen shuffled through the disks and inserted one into the reader. "I'm something of a gaming freak. High level game controllers have lots more variables than just two. Here's one I rigged up myself for flight simulation... eight variables. Five on the stick and three on the pedals."

Digger looked over the crude looking handmade device. He started to see the possibilities. "So you're saying, if you can decode the interrelated functions that connect the variables, run the entire loop past the decoding module, and control them intuitively with this, then...."

"Exactly, you'll be able to fly the thing like a helicopter, any direction you want to go, up down, right left, forwards backwards, plus moving in time to the future and past. Will that solve the problems?"

"Fabulous, how long will it take to set up?"

"I don't know, we hooked in yet?"

Steve crawled out from under the control panel. "Should be all set."

"Okay, give me the seven variable signal to decode" said Steve. "Let's keep it simple, current location, present time."

Digger tapped at his keyboard for a moment. "Here it comes."

Eileen looked over Steve's shoulder as he scanned the incoming seven columns of data. She had loaded the pattern recognition module from disk. It was a massive program they'd worked on for years, written to take advantage of the optical processor's speed, trinary core structure, and parallel processing capacity. Pattern recognition was the core of any decoding concept. The upper part of the screen continued to display the seven incoming data streams. The lower part began to display pattern recognition symbology. "Look here" said Steve. Its got a logarithmic polar transformation that relates these two. Look, it's shifting already. Ah, now a sinusoidal relationship between these other two." The pattern recognition program found mathematical correlations, sometimes extremely complex and obscure, between discrete pairs of all seven of the sets of number. The pattern recognition criteria and transformations were then fed to a real-time decryption module for active seven dimensional matrix manipulation. Changes in the interrelationships would be actively monitored and adjusted during use. Finally Steve hooked up his juiced-up joystick and foot controls to modulate the filtering through the decryption module. Barely less than thirty minutes had passed between the time Steve and Eileen walked into the room and the point at which Steve stood up and offered the pilot's seat to Digger.

"So what does what?" he asked.

"I've got it rigged so that you can control angle of view and direction of motion with the joystick. The right foot pedal is magnification, the left one is the time axis. Go ahead, get the feel of it."

Digger looked around the room. He had been so intent on the tempiloscope that he had not noticed two of the Ojibway men arrive with Tony on a stretcher. Someone had brought the fiberoptic data cable, and Steve had already begun hooking it up to the sensor array surrounding the globe. Everyone was looking at Digger expectantly. He sat down and placed his hands and feet on the controls. An image appeared in the globe of Digger sitting at the controls, as if by closed circuit television. He moved his left foot. The scene remained stable but looked like a video run backwards. He ran it forwards again until it hit the present, where it stopped. He already knew that it would not and could not show the future, but he'd had to try. Then he tried the magnification, moved his right foot until the entire room was visible, then slowly began to manipulate the joystick. The viewpoint raced through the darkness of solid rock until he found the passage outside again. Everyone in the room was transfixed. He guided the viewer down the passage through the closed doors and into the office, there, Sherman was stringing wires around the doorway while his men were hurriedly packing things into satchels.

"It's a bomb!" shouted Tony. "He's got thirty kilos of plastique. He's rigging it up to blow if the door is opened." Digger had no time to be amazed or intrigued with how well and intuitively the new targeting system worked. He moved the viewer outside. A hundred Ojibway men were spread out around the entrance, and there was Harry with the rocket launcher trained on the doorway.

"Damn!" said Leonard, "They're too close, If that bomb explodes it would take off the whole front of the mountain, half those people would be killed."

"James, take over for me." James jumped into the pilot's chair. "Joan, we have to get a message to them above, right now." They tried hard to get Jimmy and Jason's attention concentrating on the message: "Pull everyone back from the front door. It is mined with a large bomb, will explode if it is opened. Get back at least 200 meters, evacuate the neighborhood," they sent.

"Understood, moving now. Video feed ready," came the hurried reply.

James pulled back from the view of the door. They saw Sherman and his men preparing to withdraw from the office into the corridor, and stringing a wire along with them. "They're coming this way!" he said. He backed the viewer to follow them and inadvertently veered through the side wall of the passage into the canteen. In stunned silence the little group around the tempiloscope saw the five bound and gagged people there, including Frank.

Leonard let out a short gasp. "My God, they'll be killed too if that thing goes off. We've got to do something!"

"Like what?" said Digger.

"Didn't you say that you might be able to use this thing to actually move objects?"

"Well yeah, but that just a theory, we haven't tried it yet. It would take weeks or months of testing before we'd be ready to try it."

"You've got just a few minutes before they get here."

"But there's no way!" protested Digger. "There's no time!"

"Digger" said James. "Listen to what you just said." He moved the joystick and left pedal. The image in the globe showed Digger saying, "There's no time!" His voice clearly came out of the speakers on the computer. Steve and Eileen were still busy on the sensor array, one had been rigged to monitor molecular vibration within the target globe and turn it into an acoustic signal... sound.

"Wait, maybe you're right!" said Digger excitedly. "Okay, run those alternate solutions through and see if we need any hardware adjustments."

James did so. "Looks like we'd need an enhanced field stabilization matrix on the number four generator."

"What would that take?" asked Digger.

"Oh, a dense cryptocrystalline mass of about five kilograms, density about... oh, three probably, and with a dispersed matrix of microfine conductive particles would do it."

Leonard groaned. "Where would we find something like that? We don't have time to order special refractory materials made!"

Digger squeezed his eyes shut in thought, then suddenly, as if he'd been hit by an electric shock he jumped. "Datolite!" he cried. It would be perfect.

James looked up. You know, I think you're right, but even so, that's a huge piece, I've never seen one that large outside of the Smithsonian or Seaman's."

"I have. We picked one up today, near the main fissure. It was lying there loose, I just picked it up with the arm as we went by."

"Are you kidding?" asked James excitedly. "My God, we could pull this off. Where is it?"

"It's in the hold-all of G-27, back in the grunt lab."

"Uh oh, not good! Look at this!" In the globe they could see Sherman and his men moving slowly up the corridor, past the canteen, heading in their direction. They appeared to be proceeding with extreme caution, weapons at the ready.

Digger looked up at Leonard's anxious face. "We've got to have that piece of datolite if we want to try to move any objects. But we may not be able to get there before Sherman does."

"We'll see about that." Digger stared into the globe. "Prepare to mark time... now." He whispered something into James' ear, then stood up. "Who's coming with me? We have to get that datolite nodule!" Leonard, Joan, Jayjay, and Zeb volunteered. They drew weapons, opened the door, and jogged quickly to the right, south in the passageway towards the grunt lab.

CHAPTER 54

Frank felt a gentle hand on his forehead as he regained consciousness, he awoke looking into the concerned face of Aaron. Nearby, the two paramedics who had been stripped of their uniform coveralls, were busy untying each other and the other wounded FBI man, Stephen.

"Hey mister, you okay?" asked Aaron. "That guy hit you pretty hard, you been asleep for a while." One of the paramedics came over and looked at him. His mouth was bleeding where his lip had been cut over his lower teeth, and the hinges of his jaw throbbed painfully. The ache in his leg was intense, and he had lost feeling in his right foot. They laid the stretcher back down flat again, and spoke together in concerned tones.

"You're Frank, right?" said one of them. Frank nodded. "Listen Frank, I'm not going to kid you, we need to get you to the hospital without delay or you could end up losing that leg."

"What happened?" asked Frank, "how did we end up here?"

"Yeah, you were out for a while after that guy socked you. Some guys blocked the road with a car, then forced their way into the ambulance at gunpoint. We've been sitting here for hours. Fortunately our friend here," he nodded towards Aaron, "managed to get his hands free. The question is... what do we do now? Those guys could be back any minute."

Aaron stood up. "I'll go look. They think I'm stupid, so they won't feel afraid of me. I'll be back." Before anyone could offer advice or caution, Aaron had slipped out the door into the hallway, closing it gently behind himself. Moments later he was back. "Come on! They're all gone. They just left some packages and wires by the door."

The two paramedics picked Frank up and carried him out of the canteen, down the passage, and through the double doors into the offices. As Aaron had said, the place was deserted, but two phone lines were now leading down the passage along the floor, and one of them led to a complex system of wires and plastic wrapped packages by the door. "Holy mother of God, it's a bomb!" said Frank as he looked at it. "Get me closer!" The paramedics carried him through the inner doors, which had been propped open, and laid down the stretcher. He gulped as he looked at it. Six packages, each with five kilos of high explosive, were distributed against the outside wall around the door. A black plastic box had been duct taped to the door itself, with a taut wire tied to the door frame. The phone cable connected to the box as well. From here, wires led to each of the parcels of explosive. "I need help here!"

"Yes sir mister Frank," answered Aaron.

"Son, do exactly as I tell you, alright?"

"I'm good at that, just tell me what to do."

"I'm afraid to cut any of the wires, this looks like one of those rigs that will blow if any of the circuits go down. Aaron, I want you to come over here. See this package here? It's kinda like modeling clay. The wire going into it has a little tube on the end, that's called a blasting cap, sorta like a firecracker. You need to pull the wire with its tube out of the clay. Be very careful not to break the wire okay? Then you'll need to go around and do the same with each of the others."

Aaron started to work on the first one. The wire had been tied around the parcel, so he had to manipulate the entire block to get it off. As soon as he had that one loose, Frank said, "Okay, now hand that package to this guy, and start on the next one. You, what's your name?"

"Tommy," answered the paramedic, standing in stocking feet and long underwear.

"Tommy, take that package of explosive and put it as far from here as possible, maybe back in the canteen, inside a cabinet, just in case." Tommy gulped and did as he was asked, not willing to ask the question that came immediately to mind.

Slowly, and with guidance from Frank, who lay on the stretcher, Aaron pulled the detonators from all six parcels of explosive, which were moved away. The six thumb-sized blasting caps dangled on their wires, just a few feet from Frank's face. Even these, barely larger than a firecracker, could throw deadly metal shrapnel at that range. "We need a stout metal box... a filing cabinet or something," said Frank.

"How about this?" Tommy held up the metal suitcase that had held the plastique.

"Yeah, perfect, bring it over here. Now, get all the blasting caps inside, and close the lid, but don't latch it, we don't want to cut any of the wires. Okay, let's get back out there into the office." Frank was carried the few meters into the office, behind a desk. "Okay, now somebody cut the cable." It took a minute to find something to cut it with, then Aaron located a pair of scissors in one of the secretary's desks. He hunched down and used both hands on the scissors to sever the thick cable snaking across the floor. At the instant the scissors cut through, there was a loud 'BANG' and the suitcase in the alcove jumped off the floor and blew open as all six blasting caps simultaneously detonated. "Alright then, let's get out of here before somebody comes back. We'd better wave a white flag in case somebody's covering the door."

Aaron taped a sheet of paper to a ruler, pulled the heavy bolt back on the steel outer door, and stuck the flag outside, slowly opening the door. The bright light of the sunny morning spilled in through the opening. He walked out and looked around. "There's nobody here!" he said. He led the way out into the snow. The two paramedics in stocking feet carried the stretcher with Frank, followed by the bandaged Stephen.

Two hundred meters away, from the upper floor window of an evacuated house, Harry sat with Fred Samuels and his younger agent Justin, watching the mine entrance through binoculars. He saw the door open and the waving of the white flag. Every pair of binoculars and every rifle scope was trained on the door in moments. They did not recognize Aaron or the two men in skivvies, but Harry reacted instantly when he saw Frank carried out into the open. "Hold fire, it's our guys. Help them out." Harry yelled to Jimmy and Jason waiting in the street below. Jimmy sprinted into the parking lot to Frank's side, followed by a small crowd of others. Somebody jumped into the driver's seat of the ambulance and backed it quickly into the lot. Frank briefly explained to Jimmy the situation as he knew it, including the location of the defused bomb material and the unknown whereabouts of Sherman and what was left of his mercenary force. Tommy and the other paramedic located spare coveralls and boots for themselves inside the ambulance, then strapped down their injured charges for the trip to the hospital. Ruth rode in the back with them this time.

The motley mixture of FBI agents: Jason Desnick, Jimmy Canaris, Harry Halbrook, Fred Samuels, and Justin, stood outside the open iron door with Joe Running Bear and a dozen of his men, debating what to do. The fact that the door had been booby trapped caused them to be concerned that other booby traps might be encountered further into the mine. Yet the fact that this bomb had been so large suggested that Sherman had possibly put all of his eggs, so to speak, into one basket.

"The big problem is," said Harry, "that we don't know our way around in there, we don't know where they're going."

"I do," said Aaron." Everybody looked at him. "Everybody keeps asking about the tempiloscope, so that's probably where they are."

"Do you know the way? Would you come with us?"

"Yeah, sure, people think I'm stupid, but I'm not." answered Aaron. It was finally decided that only six people would enter deeply into the mine... any more than that would just get in each other's way. Another dozen would come in part of the way, to occupy the office and canteen. Flashlights were located and distributed to the six who would be penetrating deeply. Most of Joe Running Bear's warriors outside resumed their former stations closer to the door. The sun had just risen high enough in the sky to peep down into the little dell in which the mine entrance lay, as the six men crept quietly into the passageway leading towards the heart of the mountain.

George Sherman tried to call Tony on line six, and found that the line was dead. There could be a simple explanation, but he preferred a cautious approach at this point in the game. It could mean that they'd been infiltrated. As Sherman retreated up the passageway from the office uncoiling a reel of wire, the seven remaining men glanced about nervously. They had seldom ever seen their boss quite so edgy. The typical arrogant self confidence that had previously defined the character of George Sherman seemed to have vanished, replaced by a puerile willfulness. He suddenly seemed to them like a child who had been discovered with his hand in the cookie jar, and who responded by unrepentantly stuffing his mouth. Several of the men had expressed varying levels of concern about the wisdom of mining the door with the huge bomb. "But sir," said one, "how will we get out of here if we collapse the whole front of the mountain?"

Sherman's answer was, "Let me worry about that!" Sherman himself felt far more confidence than he allowed to show. He had struck upon a plan that seemed to him an utter stroke of brilliance, one that demonstrated to him yet again his utter superiority over commonplace humanity, one which even his esteemed ancestor William Tecumseh Sherman would be certain to approve of.

George Frederick Sherman's mind, while self-centered in a fashion that few psychiatrists would find plausible, was exceptionally quick and adept, able to synthesize disparate data into a meaningful whole. Indeed, it was Sherman's mind which was the tool he used to control his vast industrial empire. True, his physical strength was slightly above average, but the force he exerted on the lever of commerce that shifted the flow of finances to his control was the naked forcefulness of his mind. He had read more into the internal reports on the progress of the tempiloscope research than even Digger or James had intended, further perhaps, than they themselves had seen or even imagined at the time. He saw there the inevitability of using the device as a true time machine. Immediately he struck upon the plan of using it to transport himself out of his present situation, and into the past, where his knowledge of future events would enable him to dominate the economic world. It was true that matters had apparently gotten out of hand in the current situation, but to Sherman it was simply the hand of fate, giving him his natural due on a platter. Here it was, the ultimate coup! He would disappear without a trace, and destroy any possibility of anyone ever following him. The data in the office would be destroyed by the bomb, the time machine and the associated equipment and computers... and the people... would meet the same fate in the laboratory, but only after he had gone. The matter of what would happen to these idiots who served him was inconsequential. They were tools, to be used and discarded when their usefulness was at an end. And their usefulness, in Sherman's estimation, was rapidly nearing its end. He would have thought, perhaps, of taking Tony with him, but Tony had joined the long list of minions who had failed him. It was too bad, but that's how it was.

Urging them to vigilance in case of infiltration, Sherman and his men moved cautiously north up the passage. Unbeknownst to any of the others, Sherman had another five kilograms of explosive in a blue satchel, attached to a simple but tamperproof timer. Once actuated it could not be shut off. They passed by the acoustics lab after stopping to check it thoroughly, then moved on towards the grunt lab ahead. Sherman had the two men dressed in the stolen paramedic's coveralls stay several meters ahead of the main group, and keep their weapons hidden.

Digger led the small group moving cautiously south down the tunnel. Every once in a while he brought the IR binoculars to his eyes, but detected nothing of interest. It was desperately important that they retrieve the datolite nodule from the grunt lab in order to modify the tempiloscope. The modification would, according to calculations, enable the machine to move objects in time and space as well as simply to observe them. Digger hoped that they could then temporally displace the bomb Sherman had rigged. There had also been mentioned the possibility of using the technique to move a mass of rock to block a passage. They kept their lights off and moved from side to side in the winding passageway in order to see as far as possible ahead of them. Finally, they approached the cut in the wall that marked the location of the door to the grunt lab. Digger felt a prickly sensation, like toothpicks prodding in the skin on the back of his scalp. It was unusual and very definitely uncomfortable. He suppressed his unease, squeezed Joan's hand confidently and then moved forward. The door was exactly as they had left it about an hour earlier. Digger motioned to Leonard and the others to watch the passage while he and Joan entered the lab. Both of them had weapons in hand.

"Come on," he whispered to her as he slipped through the doorway. The large chamber was dark except for the pale greenish light which came from the control panel. A deep thrumming came from the charging rack as energy was fed to one of the waiting robotic mining submersibles. A conveyor belt clanked noisily as it moved high graded copper ore from a freshly surfaced grunt still dripping with water, to a wooden crate sitting on the skids of an idle forklift. If they wanted to speak, they would need to shout above the noise, but there were no words necessary for the task at hand. The automatic machinery, of course, cared nothing for noise levels, and needed no light to carry out its programmed tasks. Digger scanned the room with the IR glasses, but saw no unusual heat sources that might indicate a lurking human presence. He moved quickly to the dormant hulk of G-27 where it lay on the maintenance rack. At the lower end of the craft, on the left near the main screws there was a small hatchway, some fifty centimeters square. Digger pulled out a small flashlight to penetrate the dim light and find the controls to open the hatch. Joan stood several meters away near the main control panel, trying to watch both Digger and the doorway. From where she stood she could not see Leonard and the other two men outside through the narrow crack of the barely open door.

Digger flipped open a tiny access panel, pressed a button, and the hatchway unlocked. He pulled the stainless steel door open and reached inside with both hands, retrieving a large cauliflower shaped nodule of stone that filled both his hands. He gasped in wonder as he looked at it in the tiny beam of the flashlight he held between his teeth Datolite! Digger had sought the rare mineral all his life, since the very first tiny nodule he had found at the age of six on the waste rock dumps of the Delaware mine. In all the world, this colored porcelainous gem material was found only here, in the copper country of the Lake Superior district... and the best of the best had always come from the Quincy mine. Far more scarce than diamonds, the material was so rare that most collectors outside the region were completely unaware of its existence. It had a hardness and texture similar to turquoise, but with a range of colors that varied from pink to blood red, and from green to lemon yellow. Pure mineralogical datolite itself was colorless or white, a simple hydrated silicate of calcium and boron. The color of the higher gem quality grades was imparted by finely divided particles of native copper or copper oxides distributed in the matrix. The best material was deeply translucent, and the rarest and most elusive color of all was yellow. Most nodules averaged the size of a fingernail. A fist sized one of good quality was considered a monster. Digger mused on the strangeness of the twist of fate that determined that the material they needed for the final tuning of the tempiloscope had exactly the characteristics of this natural material, formed in the bowels of the earth nearly a billion years ago, right here and nowhere else on earth. His tiny light played over the surface of the nodule, that light glowed back yellowly from the deeply translucent surface. He had never seen such a piece, though he knew every specimen in both the Smithsonian and the Seaman's mineral museums by heart. He tore his eyes away with effort, placing the mass gently into the otherwise empty pack he carried. He slung it on his back and stood up to rejoin Joan and head back to the other lab.

Joan looked over at him and smiled, relaxing her tense stance. Then suddenly Digger felt an overwhelming sense of wrongness sweep over him, the prickling at the back of his neck felt more like cold daggers of steel than toothpicks. Joan immediately sensed his change in mood, she involuntarily ducked and threw herself in his direction. A shot rang out, striking the grunt control panel immediately behind where she had stood. With a sizzling noise it emitted a few dull sparks and went dark; it had been struck in the power supply transformer. All the noisy machinery in the room went suddenly quiet as the brain which controlled it all was suddenly severed from its precious supply of electrical current. There was a commotion near the doorway. Joan scrambled across the floor and huddled in the darkness next to Digger. They scuttled behind some machinery connected to the maintenance rack. Suddenly the lights in the room went on, nearly blinding them. They could hear cautious footsteps on the floor. Digger peered out between two steel bars and saw Leonard and the other two men being held as human shields, their arms pinned behind them. He saw five others besides the ones holding the captives. They all wore black fatigues, except for two that wore the orange coveralls of paramedics. He made a hand signal to Joan... five fingers, then three. She nodded in understanding.

"Who's in here?" came a voice, coarse and threatening. Digger and Joan stayed as quiet as possible, scarcely breathing. Two men moved slowly into the room with weapons shouldered, taking cover wherever possible, searching the room methodically. "You may as well come out now, or do you want me to execute one of your friends?"

Digger and Joan were unsure what to do. It was incomprehensible to them that this man could be serious. It must be a bluff... it HAD to be a bluff, nobody in their right mind would.... Still, the terrible stabbing pain in Digger's neck would not go away.

George Sherman looked back at his three captives. It had been so ridiculously easy. The two men dressed as paramedics had gone forward first. When challenged by these three morons they had said they were responding to reports of injured people. All it took was the moment's confusion caused by this lie to get the drop on all three of them without a shot being fired. The noise level in the lab had prevented these others from hearing the disturbance. But now Sherman was in a hurry, with no more time to waste. He knew there were people in here, but neither who nor how many they were. With three of his men holding the captives, two at the door, and two covering the room, he felt comfortable enough to turn to the prisoners for information. He looked them over. Their hands were tied tightly together with wire behind their backs, and a second loop had been put around their necks, just tightly enough to be uncomfortable. Two had the ruddy complexion and eye shape of nearly full blooded native Americans. They were dressed roughly, and they glared at him proudly, he knew the type and thought they would be hard to bully. The third was of a different kind, the sort he knew how to deal with. Their weapons had been removed earlier, but he searched now for identification, found it in the inside jacket pocket, an FBI badge. He looked at it and smiled warmly with surprise.

"Ah," he shouted out gleefully, "my old friend Leonard Howarth. How are you?"

"Eat shit Sherman."

"No time. How did you get in here?" Sherman dropped all pretense.

"How do you think? Down the shaft of course."

"What about the men I had there?"

"Two dead, five captured." Sherman shook his head in mock sadness.

"How many of you came down."

"Fifty, with two hundred more coming."

Sherman laughed derisively, then with a sudden movement drove his fist into Leonard's solar plexus. Leonard jerked as if to bend forward, but was restrained by the wire around his neck. He groaned in pain. "You always were a lousy liar Leonard. How many?"

"Fuck off." Leonard gasped between his teeth.

Sherman drew his pistol and in one smooth motion, shot Leonard Howarth in the center of the chest. The man behind released his grip and Leonard fell heavily to the floor, lying on his face with his hands still tied behind him. A pool of blood slowly spread from his mouth and nose. Sherman moved to the next man in line, who looked at him without fear. "How about you? We'll try a different question. Tell me who else is in this room." Sherman slowly raised his gun to point at the man's chest. There was a long tense moment as the man closed his eyes.

"STOP!" yelled Digger. He stood up from behind the maintenance rack and stepped forward. "Who are you and what do you want?"

Sherman whirled. The two men ran towards Digger, He raised his hands in the traditional posture of surrender. One ran past Digger and pointed his weapon at Joan, who got up and strode forward angrily by his side. Their guns were quickly taken away, along with Digger's binoculars and his backpack. They were prodded towards Sherman by the two silent men. "So, who have we here?"

"I asked you first, and besides, it is customary for..."

"SHUT UP! If you want to live you will answer my questions, quickly, completely, and truthfully. Who are you?"

"I'm Digger Puttonen, this is Joan Niemi. You are trespassing in my laboratory, and I'd like you to leave."

"Oh I'll leave, in my own time and manner, mister Puttonen. Interesting, you're just the man I've been looking for. What have you got there in your pack?"

"Just a piece of rock."

"Really? You just saw what happens to people who lie to me. I expect the full truth from you." Sherman motioned for one of his men to open the bag and raised his weapon to point at Digger.

"He's right boss," said the man. "It's a piece of rock."

"What do you need with a piece of rock?" asked Sherman.

"It's not just any rock. It's a piece of datolite, it's needed to stabilize the number four field generator on the tempiloscope."

"Oh really?"

"Yes."

"And why do you need to do that?"

"In order to enable the scope to move objects in time as well as simply view them... we saw you rigging your bomb. We plan to translate it out of there before you can set it off."

"Well, I guess you'll have to alter your little plans then," said Sherman. He turned to one of the men by the door. "You... bring me that coil of wire and the detonator, hook it up, quick." Sherman turned back to face Digger and Joan. "Thank you for being truthful with me, but I'm afraid the plans have changed. You won't be translating my little bomb anywhere. I like it just where it is."

A man ran in with from the passage with the wire and began stripping the ends and connecting them to a black box. He jiggled with it for a few moments. "Sir, we've lost connectivity. I'm not getting the ready light."

"Shit! Oh it's probably just the bulb filament, broke from being knocked around or something. Give me the damn thing!"

Digger smiled openly. "You see, it's already gone, we've moved it where you can't use it."

"Oh really? Then what do you think of this!" Sherman pushed the detonation button on the box. There was no response. He pushed again and again.

"You see, I told you." Digger said calmly.

"I thought you said you needed this rock to do that."

"We do, or one more or less like it at any rate. But we don't need to do it now, this minute. I could move that bomb next week, or next year for that matter, whenever I get around to it, the result would be the same. You see? That's the beauty of the technology The fact that the bomb is not there, proves that you don't win."

"Or... that I chose to move it somewhere else." Sherman emphasized the "I" when he said this, getting a faraway look in his eyes.

"Oh well, if you're going to play that game..."

Sherman saw it all now. He saw how the hand of fate had given him everything he needed now. It was just a matter of bending others to his will, of continuing with the course until the ordeal was over, just as his famous ancestor had done. "Tie their hands, come on, get them moving, we're taking them with us. These others don't matter, shoot them."

"Wait!" shouted Digger. "Leave them alive and I'll cooperate with you."

Sherman shrugged and changed his order. "Tie them up, but be quick, not that it will matter in the end... Okay son, I did what you wanted, but you'd better tell me what I want to know. How many people do you have in the Temporal lab?"

"There were only five others, besides us here."

"You'd better be telling the truth, or something bad might happen to your little sweetie here."

"Leave her alone Sherman, I'm doing what you want." Digger looked thoughtful for a moment, as his hands were tied behind him. "But tell me, what do you want?"

"Later... get moving." He prodded them to the door. The two Ojibway men were securely lashed to the frame of the maintenance rack, their mouths taped. Leonard lay where he had fallen, face down on the floor. The little group moved up the passageway, the two phony paramedics in front as before, followed by Digger and Joan, the five other mercenaries, and George Sherman striding along in the rear, brimming again with unashamed self-confidence.

CHAPTER 55

Six people carefully picked their way across the deserted front office of Midnight Mining Company and proceeded into the dimly lit passage heading north, back towards the laboratories. Five of them were agents of the Federation Bureau of Investigation, two of whom were also undercover representatives of the United Nations Environmental Command. Aaron, the Midnight Mining Company security guard, led the way with confidence. Jimmy Canaris and Jason Desnick trailed just behind him, moving slowly and as quietly as possible, stopping often to listen. They had passed the canteen and proceeded onwards, when Jason and Jimmy looked at each other and suddenly stopped. Harry had seen the phenomenon before. "What?" he asked. "You hear from Digger?"

"Yes, bad news I'm afraid," said Jimmy. "Sherman is just ahead of us in the grunt lab, with six men. Two are dressed as paramedics. They've captured Digger, Joan, Leonard, and two others. Leonard's been shot in the chest."

"WHAT?!" whispered Harry hoarsely. "Shot?"

"Yes. We told him about dismantling the bomb, and that we're coming behind. He asks us to hang back, but be ready for anything."

"How far away is the grunt lab?" asked Harry.

"Not far." answered Aaron, "less than five minutes walk."

"What are we waiting for? We have to help Leonard!"

Jimmy shook his head. "No, not yet. It's too dangerous to try to engage them now, wait... They're preparing to leave..." Both Jimmy and Jason stood still with a far-off look in their eyes for several minutes, then both roused to action.

"Okay, they're leaving, come on!" The group started walking quickly but quietly up the passageway. Less than two minutes after Sherman had led his captives up the tunnel, the group came to the door to the grunt lab.

The door stood slightly ajar, Harry jerked it open and gave a cry of despair as he saw Leonard laying face down on the floor, blood pooling under his face.

Samuels and Justin worked to free Jayjay and Zeb, who quickly filled them in on recent events. Harry untied the wire from Leonard's hands and rolled him over; his face was smeared with blood coming from his nose and mouth, but there was no blood in the chest area! He then placed his hand against Leonard's carotid artery and found a weak pulse. Harry found the hole in Leonard's sweatshirt, and probed with his finger, finding the large caliber bullet lodged in the protective vest Leonard had been wearing under his clothes. "Sir? Leonard? Can you hear me?" he pleaded.

There was a groan, a fluttering of eyelids. "Harry? Is that you? Am I dead?"

Harry smiled. "Not yet sir, you're alive, your vest stopped the bullet. It just knocked you out for a while."

"It hurts... a lot... my face..." He spluttered in the blood streaming from his nose.

"You've probably got a broken rib or two, and I think you fell on your face, you might need a little dental work but you'll be okay."

Leonard groaned again as he recalled recent events. "Harry, Sherman... he's got Digger and Joan."

"Shhh, we know. You just rest."

"No!" Leonard struggled to get up, then groaned with the pain in his chest. "Help me!"

"Sir, you should really just relax and..."

"Help me damn you!" Harry gave Leonard support and he stood up, gritting his teeth with the pain.

"Sir," said Jimmy. We have been in contact with Digger and Joan. The group is moving up the passage towards the temporal lab. Digger is still asking us to hang back, I think he has a plan."

"A plan? What sort of plan?"

"I don't know yet, he was too busy to tell us."

"But we can't just sit here!"

"We don't have to, we can follow along behind, staying out of earshot. That way we can be ready to respond if they call."

"Damn, I hate these tunnels," said Leonard. I feel so vulnerable, there's no cover."

Jayjay spoke up. "We could bring some cover with us."

Harry looked over at him. "What do you mean?"

Jayjay jogged over to the heavy duty forklift. With a low moan the electric motor spun up, and he pulled it towards the group, who involuntarily backed away. The crate on the skids was nearly full of copper ore, chunks of native copper ranging from golf ball to softball size. "Prop those doors open and hop on, let's ride in style!" Leonard stood on the running board next to Jayjay, one hand to his chest breathing shallowly, while Zeb stood on the opposite side. Jimmy and Jason took positions on the forks, just behind the wooden crate of copper ore. Samuels stood on the hitch at the very back, while Harry, Aaron, and Justin jogged along behind. Jayjay piloted the vehicle expertly through the doors and then up the tunnel. It ran smoothly and quietly, nearly filling the entire passageway.

Digger and Joan marched along the passage behind the two men dressed as paramedics. George Sherman walked next to them, pistol held casually pointed in their direction. "So Mister Sherman, will you tell me what you want to do?" asked Digger. It seems obvious that you're not going to get away with just taking over the place."

George looked at him and considered. "Alright, I'll tell you. You are going to transport something for me, back in time. All you have to do is send it back and your worries are over."

Digger paused and looked around. None of the other men could hear them, the conversation was between he and Sherman alone, only Joan could overhear. "I see. How far back do you want it to go?"

"I'm thinking the mid 1960s."

"Do you realize how much power it would take to transport just one person back that far? The temporal energy displacement would be huge."

"What makes you think I'm talking about a person?"

"What else could possibly be of interest? You want to go back in time, thinking that you can change history. It won't work, since history shows that you didn't do it, then you don't do it."

"I'm not interested in your sniveling theories of time travel paradoxes. I have seen the equations myself, and I tell you that it can be done. The energy problem can be solved by bringing something else forward in time, using it as a counterbalance for the energy requirements."

Digger was impressed. "I had not thought of that! You may be right... but what would we bring forward?"

"I don't care, anything, a rock... it doesn't matter."

"And them?" Digger whispered, motioning with his head to indicate Sherman's men.

"They stay, I go alone."

"And what do I do with them?"

"I don't give a damn. You can turn them in, turn them loose, shoot them if you want to, I don't care."

"And that's all you want? If we go in there, you won't hurt anybody, like you did with Leonard back there?"

"I was in a hurry, that was a regrettably unavoidable incident, which gained me your cooperation. Besides, if we don't get into the lab, I will be forced to engage in another unavoidable incident, probably involving this charming young lady who you seem to be so fond of."

Digger and Joan did their very best to look horrified, to try to suppress the soaring hope that sprang into their hearts as Sherman talked of his ambitions. They reiterated to Jimmy and Jason, riding on the forklift just two hundred meters behind, "Hang back, do not engage." they said.

The answer came immediately. "Understood."

James sat at the tempiloscope and worked the joystick and pedals as if he was playing an arcade videogame. The difference was... the globe he stared at showed reality, not some computer generated fantasy world. He regretted for a moment the situation which necessitated that he use this incredible resource simply to track the progress of his friends within the mine. He could be witnessing the original crossing of the Bering land bridge some eighty thousand years ago, the landings of the Vikings in North America, or be listening to the actual words of Jesus of Nazareth in the garden at Gethsemane. This tool would revolutionize historical and anthropological research. Academics would pay exorbitant hourly rates to find out the truth of their particular field of study. It was almost obscene to use it in this way, yet here he was, using it merely as a spy scope to observe a real-time drama... still, that drama was approaching the outer door of the lab, and quickly... he dared not forget that fact. James looked over at Steve and Eileen. The live multichannel video feed was active, Eileen was busily making the final adjustments on the second camera covering the room. Steve had managed to drill a small hole through the flange of the outer door, to enable them to pass the fiberoptic cable through it and still lock the heavy door. Everything was going out on the cable, up the shaft, and was being piped through ground telephone connections directly to the studios of Global News, located in Montreal, Quebec. What was happening there, they did not yet know, but they hoped the live drama was interesting enough to gain some attention. There were two video monitors on the top of the console, one showing the room and everyone in it, the other showing the temporal view globe, and a portion of the control console.

All eyes in the room were glued on the monitor showing the globe. They all saw the dismantling of the bomb, the shooting of Leonard Howarth, the capture of the grunt lab, and now... they listened to the supposedly private conversation between Digger Puttonen and George Sherman. The captured men tied up on the floor reacted violently and angrily to Sherman's ostensibly secret betrayal of their loyalties. Tony, lying on the stretcher, sighed deeply and looked away. The group in the passageway was approaching.

James turned to the group of captives. "So guys, what do you think of Sherman now? He plans to escape and let us shoot you for all he cares." Tony said nothing, but the two men who had been working to try to operated the tempiloscope offered their services. James looked at the third man in the room when they arrived. "And what about you?" He stripped the duct tape from the man's mouth. "Where do you stand with Sherman now?"

"Yeah, let me loose, I'll help." James looked at Steve and Eileen, who shrugged.

"I'm going to leave you guys tied, like you're our prisoners. We're going to let Sherman in, and appear to do what he wants. He'll untie you guys, then when he's distracted by the preparations for sending him back in time, you guys get the drop on him okay?"

They agreed, then there was a knock on the door. In the globe they could all see Digger and Joan, with the others behind them, weapons at the ready. James pointed to the video camera covering the room. Steve hastily draped an old tarp over the camera so that the lens projected through a hole, concealing its presence. Eileen was at the door. "Who's there?" she called out.

"It's me, Digger, quick, open up." James reached up and switched off both monitors above the console, then switched off sound and shifted the point of view to the scene in front of the main door again. Eileen withdrew the heavy bolts, and the door swung silently inward. Digger stepped across the threshold, followed immediately by the two men that appeared to be paramedics. They grabbed Eileen who shrieked in protest, and shoved her ahead of them. Sherman stepped into the room after them, dragging Joan roughly by the arm. Sherman directed one of his men to bolt the door and another to untie the prisoners. Everyone was talking at once.

"Quiet! I am in control now," said Sherman, waving his pistol around threateningly, "You will all do precisely as I say. You! Get them all over there, except that one. Search them for weapons but don't bother tying them up, this won't take long."

Digger, singled out and kept near Sherman said, "I need James to help program this, he's better at it than I am."

"Okay, get busy, you know what I want."

"What's he talking about?" asked James.

"We're to send him back to 1967."

"But the energy..."

"We bring something forward at the same time, to balance it."

James considered for a moment. "You know, I think that might work. We'll have to open two windows at once... Ah, well, you'd better get that piece of datolite centered in the field collimator." Digger requested the pack from the man who had carried it, and under close observation, removed the giant nodule of the precious mineral and climbed up on an access ladder to the middle of the tall vertical field generator towering above them. He carefully removed a cover plate, and clamped the nodule into position with four winged screws. James had him move it and adjust the position several times, then announced it adequately balanced.

Sherman delivered himself of a speech. "Men, we are embarking on an adventure the likes of which has never been experienced on earth before. We are about to step fifty years into the past, with all of our knowledge and our tools. I have with me an advanced computer, more powerful than anything in the world of that time. We have a current encyclopedia of historical events, data on the last fifty years of stock prices, entire libraries of information stored on a few computer disks. With this information we, you and I, will forge a new and more powerful Sherman Industries, dominating the economy of the entire world."

Steve spoke out earnestly. "Sir, you can't do that. You'll change history, what will happen to those of us who remain?"

"That is not my concern, but I imagine that you'll find, when you walk outside, that Sherman Industries is the real and only power in the world. Now, you two," he pointed to the two men he'd had working on the tempiloscope. "Have you been watching what these guys are doing? Can you operate this equipment?"

"Yes sir, though it's not easy, they've made a number of modifications since you were here last."

"I want your hands on the controls."

"Sorry sir, I just don't have the touch. I... I'm afraid I'd do something wrong."

"Alright then, but you watch this guy carefully."

"Yes sir."

"I want to be sent back to 1967"

"Where do you want to retemporalize?" asked James.

"Chicago."

James shook is head. "Not precise enough, I need exact coordinates, and it should be someplace that there's not likely to be anybody. For one thing you don't want to retemporalize in the same spot as someone else. We don't know what might happen, but it would not be pretty. Also, you probably don't want anybody watching."

"How about here then."

"Well, this chamber did not exist in 1967, I could drop you in the passageway out there though, I know those coordinates precisely. The mine was shut down in those days, but the front the door was unlocked."

"Fine, get on with it."

James explained to Sherman's man, with Sherman listening. "You see, I set the rough coordinates first, then tune in the scope, to double check and refine the last three decimal places. You see?" In the globe there was a view of a dark mine tunnel, viewed by scanning the deep infrared band. "We can check to be sure what level we're on by dropping downward to check for the water level, which is two levels below us. The view dropped two levels to water, then back up. Okay, we're looking at it, the date stripe is over here, looks like... June 14, 1967. Does it matter the exact date?"

"No, that's fine. Now what do I do?"

"Mister Sherman! Be careful, they're going to try to jump you!" One of the men yelled out. "These two are traitors!"

Sherman jumped back and forced the two back with the others. "Thank you son, what's your name and number again?"

"Dawson sir, number fifty six."

"Good work Dawson. As a reward, you'll get to go next, right after me." Dawson beamed with pride and sneered at the others.

"Don't listen to him Dawson, you heard him, he plans to leave us all behind!" said one of the men.

Sherman drew his pistol and fired across the room, hitting the man in the left shoulder. "Let's have no more of that!" be bellowed. There was a grumbling among the men. "Alright alright, I admit it, I had planned to go alone. Digger was supposed to make some excuse as to why he couldn't send you after me."

"Not even me sir?" asked Tony.

"Sorry son, you need a doctor, running around in a time machine would be too hard for you right now. Dawson and you others can come, if you want."

"Watch out for him too sir, they're all in this against you, they made a deal with these guys, everybody but me."

"Et tu Tony?" Tony turned his face away. Sherman shook his head sadly and raised his weapon.

"Stop!" shouted Digger. "You said no more shooting if I cooperated." Something was welling up within Digger, an angry resentment that flushed his face red.

"These are my employees, we were talking about your friends." answered Sherman.

"It doesn't matter, let's get this over with, but no more shooting."

Sherman looked at Digger, lowering his handgun. " Have it your way then, if you can stomach traitors. Just watch your own back. By the way, I hope you don't mind if I request an inanimate test run, some of my baggage perhaps?"

"Not at all."

"Where do you want it?"

"Right there, in the middle of the floor is fine." James said.

Sherman made a pile of some weapons and a bag of civilian clothes and backed away. James keyed a control and a shimmering deep blue veil appeared in the air, humming softly. Through it they could see the floor of the mine tunnel, as it was seen in the globe. The veil bulged like the film of a bubble wafted by a gentle breeze, ripples were visible, dancing across its surface. It swept across the weapons and baggage which glittered with a yellow light, and then vanished with a pop. There was nothing on the floor.

"Now, show them to me." Sherman said. James pointed to the view in the globe. In the mine tunnel the weapons lay in a pile in exactly the same way they had lain on the floor. The time strip still indicated the same date in 1967.

"Alright, my turn, and don't jigger those controls, I'm watching."

"By the way," said Digger, "what makes you so sure we won't send somebody after you, to stop you."

Sherman smiled knowingly. "You won't have the chance, the Federation military is moving in a matter of hours. I did a little eavesdropping on the Prime Minister's office before you folks dropped in, they have decided to confiscate all this. So have fun, while you still have your toys to play with." Sherman stood where the pile of weapons had disappeared. He was wearing one of the miner's cap lamps that he had appropriated in the room. He also bore two satchels, a black one over his shoulder, and a blue one in his hands. He looked inside the blue satchel, reached in as if checking the contents, then zipped it up. He handed it to Dawson. "Here, follow me at ten minute intervals, I'll move out of the way. These are important computer data files that we'll need when we get there," he patted the satchel gently. "It's vitally important that you keep these with you at all times. Got it?"

Dawson stood proudly and saluted. "Yes sir!" Sherman stood there, gun in hand, watching the control panel as James arranged the temporal shift. Dawson looked from face to face in the room, his shoulders slumped as he suddenly seemed to make a decision. The blue veil appeared behind Sherman and swept forward, everyone in the room froze. Abruptly, Dawson made a quick motion; he tossed the blue satchel to Sherman just as the blue veil swept over him with a shimmering yellow glow. "Sorry sir," he said. "I changed my mind, I'm staying." George Sherman caught the bag reflexively with his left hand, a look of surprise on his face, and then he was gone. The blue veil disappeared with a loud pop. All eyes turned to the globe. George Sherman appeared in the mine tunnel, holding the blue satchel in his hand with a stupefied expression on his face, one which changed quickly to abject terror. He threw the bag in one direction and started running in the other, but got no more than a few paces when the globe filled instantly with light and roiling flame. The people watching involuntarily recoiled. James reached up and turned the sound on again. A booming echo rolled down the mine passage. He scrolled the viewer frantically in the direction that Sherman had run, but found only a burned and twisted hulk that had once been the living body of George Frederick Sherman.

There was a stunned silence in the room. None was more stunned than Dawson. "It was a bomb." He said simply after a long silence. "He wasn't going to bring me with him... he was going to kill us all... I... I didn't know." He sank to the floor, sitting with his feet curled up under him and started rocking back and forth, moaning softly.

"You saved us." said Digger softly to Dawson. "You saved us all!" There was no reaction. Four of Sherman's men maintained some sense of military discipline and retreated from the room, with weapons shouldered and ready, to the outer door. They opened it and fled down the tunnel south, towards the outside, where they ran straight into the forklift blocking the passage. Two of the men fired their weapons reflexively at the obstruction, but were felled instantly by returned fire from the FBI men. The other two surrendered immediately.

When the group in the passage reunited with those in the chamber, the room was filled with laughter and rejoicing such as had never been heard in this place throughout all previous time. Even the former employees of Sherman's were caught up in the swirl of relief that their ordeal had ended. At least a few of them had jobs to look forward to with Midnight Mining Company when the technicalities and legalities of the situation had been resolved. Leonard was on the verge of collapse when he was loaded, along with Tony, Dawson, and the other man Sherman had wounded, onto a pallet the fork lift for a ride back to the outside world and medical attention. Harry accompanied Leonard, while Jayjay, Zeb, and the two other Ojibways also walked out with the former Sherman people, to sort things out in the open.

Everyone seemed relieved that it was finally over. Those heading toward the outside disappeared out the wide door, leaving it ajar. Their voices faded in the distance, leaving seven people in the room with the tempiloscope. James was left sitting at the controls of the big machine. Digger and Joan stood behind him, arms around each other. Jason and Jimmy stood next to them, admiring the tempiloscope for the first time, while Steve and Eileen stood by to one side. James reached up and switched on the video monitors again, he looked back at Jimmy. "We've got all that on disk, but is that stuff going anywhere?" he nodded to the cable running across the floor. Sherman had not noticed it.

"Yeah, it's going to Global in Montreal. I only hope that they are doing something with it."

"Can we find out?" asked James.

"Yeah, we can try. Let's see, we need a voice side channel to talk to someone there. hmmm..." He started working on the wiring to set up another channel on the optical cable.

"By the way James, what did you move in order to balance sending Sherman back?" asked Digger.

"I really don't know, I didn't have time to choose, I just grabbed without looking."

"Can we tell?"

"I suppose, let's see... looks like... hmm... that's strange. I thought I was grabbing something from 1967 and bringing it forward, but it looks like it moved from 1906 and came it forward... uh... to 1944. Wow, that's weird!"

Digger's voice became tinged with excitement. "Show me!"

James went on. "Well, you probably noticed that I keyed to the level by choosing two levels above the water."

"Yeah, I did." Digger laughed.

"Well of course, Sherman didn't realize that in 1967 the water level was about fifty levels lower, at the fifty sixth. So even without the bomb he probably would never have gotten out of the mine alive."

"Pretty slick James old boy, I knew I picked the right guy to partner this thing with."

"Well..." James struggled to find the right time and location. "Here we are fifty fourth level... between the number two and number six, 9:34 AM, May 16, 1944. Whatever it is was dropped here." They stared into the globe, saw the veil of blue light appear, and leave behind... a man, a young man, thin, wearing an antique miner's carbide lamp and with blood-soaked rags tied on an injured leg.

"My God!" breathed Digger.... he was struck speechless.

"It's Arne!" said Joan. "Arne Harjaala. That's how Arne got there. You just did it now."

Steve and Eileen both looked confused. "Arne Harjaala?" asked Eileen. "We met him at Ruth's house right?" Joan tried to explain, but was having difficulty. She turned to Digger for help.

Digger sighed heavily and sat in one of the operator's chairs holding his face in both hands. "Can we do explanations later? I am so tired, I think I could sleep a week. What time is it anyway?" The chronometer on the computer screen declared that it was 11:22 AM EST, Friday the 19th, 2017.

CHAPTER 56

"No time for sleep yet Digger," said James with a tone of heightened concern. "Look at this!" James had moved the viewer to check on the situation outside the mine. A camouflaged hummer had pulled into the parking lot. Two helmeted men in the uniform of the Federation Unified Command Services (FUCS) were arguing with Joe Running Bear.

Digger chuckled. "The Federation gave us until noon right? It's 11:30, we made it, George Sherman is history... quite literally! Those guys aren't going to bother us."

"Well then what was Sherman talking about?" James asked. "He seemed to be awfully confident we weren't going to be able to do anything to stop him."

"The bomb of course," Digger answered. "He thought we were going to be blown up."

Joan spoke up. "No, I don't think so. I didn't get the sense of deception from him. I felt he was telling the truth, but simply not all of it." They all turned to the two FBI representatives still in the room. Jimmy Canaris was just standing up from hooking up an audio side channel to the fiberoptic cable going up the shaft.

Jason Desnick looked back at them thoughtfully. "You think the Prime Minister and her cronies might try a double cross?" Before they could answer he held up a finger to indicate that Jimmy was about to test his connection. They would not be able to decide what to do until they'd found out about the state of the video feed to Montreal.

Jimmy flipped one switch on the connection box and suddenly there was a voice in the room. "Hello? Hello? Anyone there? Hello? This is Jacques Thibodeau at Global News, please respond. Can you hear me?"

"We hear you! Monsieur Thibodeau, we hear you!"

"Praise Mary, holy mother of God! I finally got you! I've been trying for the last half hour. Who am I speaking to please?"

"I am Digger Puttonen, are you receiving our video signals."

"Yes, yes, but what is it? we don't understand. Where is your camera?"

"It's a remote viewer, totally new technology. I'm sorry, it's hard to explain in just a few seconds. We can see anywhere in the world, and at any time in the past or present, all from right here. Are you recording?"

"Mais oui... yes of course, and sending out on cable to our member stations, but we don't understand what we are showing, your camera seems to fly through the air."

"You have two video channels, correct?"

"Yes, one is the room, where I see you talking."

"Good, the other is this camera," Digger pointed to the videocamera which was focused on the globe. "The view within this globe is selected by a complex process involving a powerful computer and this apparatus." Digger gestured to include the huge field generation coils and power supply transformers. "The operator sits here, and using these controls can move the camera point of view in both space AND time. It is very important that you understand this. The time strip in the corner of your screen shows observer time and view time. Only if they are the same is the viewer looking at the present in the manner of an ordinary camera."

The news correspondent was incredulous. "Is this some sort of joke? You can't be serious! This is impossible! With this, you could see anywhere, there would be no secrets!"

"Precisely! This is why the Federation does not want the signal to be transmitted."

"I'm very sorry my friend, but I cannot believe this, it is too much. Can you prove it to me?"

"Yes, tell me where you are, exactly." Jacques gave street directions to the studio. On one monitor Digger brought up an almanac program, pinpointing the location on a world map. James pulled the viewer up into the sky above Hancock Michigan, then reduced the magnification until they could see all of Lake Superior. He then guided the viewer to the east, zooming back in upon the city of Montreal. Guided by the street map in the world atlas program, he found the building Jacques was talking from, zoomed inside it, and found Jacques himself, staring at the monitor, seeing his own image transmitted from hundreds of kilometers away. His mouth was open in astonishment.

"Now watch this! James, roll back the T-axis a bit." James moved his left foot and Jacques was seen moving awkwardly, like a film in fast reverse, then forward again, saying "Hello? Hello? Anyone there? Hello? This is Jacques Thibodeau at Global News.... " The two time strips had disengaged at the bottom of the monitor.

A Superior State of Affairs

Jacques looked around the room, trying to find the camera, but could not. "Yes, yes I believe you. My God, what a newsman could not do with this! Do you realize...."

"Yes, yes we do! Please listen carefully. It is vitally important that this signal be seen by as many people as possible. Someone will probably try to shut it down, but this is live news coverage of actual events."

"Yes of course, but please, this is why I needed to speak with you. The office of the Prime Minister has called and has demanded that we stop the broadcast of this signal. They say it is lies and propaganda."

"Jacques, you know and I know that a camera does not lie, it sees what is real. You see yourself exactly as you know yourself to be. These are not actors playing parts, these are real events captured by our remote viewer. This is the greatest news story of the century, possibly of the millennium. We're giving it to you."

"Yes, yes, of course, anything you want."

"Tell me, is the solar storm still blocking the airwaves?"

"Yes, it is terrible no? We try the satellites every thirty seconds. At times we get a moment of connection, then it is gone. We are switching to the ground cables. Some of the cables have not been used in years, we are having to find their connections. Every technician is working twenty four hours...."

"Please Jacques listen. Try to get this onto every cable available. Send direct to every government office worldwide if you can. We make history today my friend. If they shut you down, make recordings, make backups of the recordings and hide them in a vault. We will send you signal as long as we can. If this line is cut we will find another way. Transmit as long as you can. Will you do this?"

"Yes of course. The Prime Minister may go hang herself before I would give up a story like this! We will go live worldwide!"

"Someone here will be available to talk to you, for now I must go, we have much to do!"

Jacques waved off and began running excitedly about his studio shouting orders. James brought the viewer back to the Keweenaw peninsula and zoomed back in towards the Houghton / Hancock area. Digger pointed to an area on the screen, and when James had zoomed in on it they saw a large military convoy of trucks, tanks and support vehicles, miles long, winding through Painesdale and heading towards Houghton. "Here they come," said Digger. "What do you think they'll do?"

"Let's check the bridge." said Jason suddenly. James moved the viewer again. He was getting the feel of the controls and could now move it quickly and accurately, using the zoom and location controls in concert to cover ground quickly and zoom in on any area they wanted to examine. On the bridge stood a number of the statehood activists, the Soopers they called themselves, holding signs and stopping traffic. Several had gotten into the control booth at the top of the north pier and were preparing to lift the bridge in order to block it off from traffic. A soldier in the uniform of the FUCS was gesticulating wildly and arguing with a distinguished looking older woman. "Okay, now back to the front door again," said Jason. Joe Running Bear's men were now clustered in front of the door, looking defensive, denying entrance to the four men in uniform, one of whom gestured angrily. The door opened and the fork lift emerged into the sunlight. Suddenly everyone crowded around it.

"You want sound?" asked James.

"Not yet, let's check the shaft house," answered Jason. They were surprised to see another camo hummer there, and again, Jamey and the forty Ojibways with him were stubbornly refusing access to the shaft house by the khaki clad FUCS. "What do you think?" Jason asked the room. "Ever since the Federation combined the armed forces into a single chain of command, they've been more like the Prime Minister's personal army than anything else."

"We don't know what their orders are," said Jimmy.

"We could get close and listen," replied James

"We've got a world audience here, let's give Global something that will make the evening news." said Digger. "Let's try to get the Prime Minister again."

James guided the viewer quickly to the predetermined coordinates of the austere office of Federation Prime Minister, Madame Theresa Powers in Mexico City. James adjusted the magnification so that they could see the entire room. The PM sat behind her polished oaken desk and faced three standing men. "Do it!" she snapped in perfect North-Am English.

"But Madame, what will the other continents say?" said a man dressed in a dark blue suit.

"Let me worry about that. I have spoken with the leaders already."

"And the convoy?" said another, dressed in an ostentatious military dress uniform festooned with medals.

"That is your decision, you may order them to withdraw if you can move them fast enough. Now get out."

The men turned to leave as a door opened and a small man entered, gesturing excitedly. Madame, please, it is happening again!" She turned and flipped on a video monitor. On the screen appeared the view of herself, the view that James, Digger, Eileen, Steve, Jason and Jimmy stood silently and watched. Madame Hernandez turned and tried to find the point in space where the camera lens must be, and though she could not see it, she spoke towards it. She smiled sweetly and in the manner of a teacher addressing a class of favored pupils. It was not by chance that she had risen to her present position of power.

"Peoples of the world, you have been witnessing the indiscriminate use of a dangerous new technology. The North American Federal Union wishes to apologize for our oversight in allowing this to have occurred on our territory. A tiny and backward district of an insignificant province of the former United States thinks it can blackmail us into allowing it to secede and gain extra seats in congress. Such is not the case.

"We have seen that a predatory multinational corporation has tried to forcefully take this technology, and we have seen the unprecedented and dangerous power that these criminals have wielded to defend themselves. This abomination is far more dangerous than anything which the amoral proponents of supposed "science" have ever developed. In fact, it has come to our attention that there is a significant possibility that the device could accidentally self destruct at any time in a huge explosion.

"For this reason I have consulted with leaders of the other continental councils, and we have agreed that this device must be destroyed to preserve the safety and security of the world. We do not intend to allow this insult to our continental sovereignty to stand unanswered. Therefore, I have ordered a full armored division to ruthlessly crush the armed insurrection by the terrorist groups of Michigan's Upper Peninsula, and to destroy the laboratories of the terrorist group known as Midnight Mining Company.

"The United Nations will undoubtedly dispute our decision. But remember Cyprus! The UN is an ineffectual waste of time and resources. Only the continental councils have the will and the means to improve the living conditions of their peoples.

"Pay no attention to the lies and propaganda these terrorists broadcast. Their transmission will shortly cease. Good day." The PM sat down in her chair and became silent, patiently waiting.

The people in the lab looked at each other. Steve finally said, "What the hell is she doing? What terrorists?"

Joan shook her head. "It's all bullshit Steve. Our move to secession has been peaceful and legal every step of the way. She's marginalizing us."

Digger had an idea. "James, scroll back, let's see what she was talking about just before we came in." James took the T-axis back ten minutes.

Jimmy called out. "Our feed is down!" The light had gone off on the connection box, their link to Global News in Montreal had been severed. "Keep recording, I'll try to fix it." Jimmy took off at a sprint down the passageway towards the outside, Jason right behind him. Steve and Eileen checked the connections at the box and found nothing wrong.

"How'd they do that?" asked James.

"I don't know." said Digger, "but the timing was perfect. She used it to make her speech, and then whacked us. That was no accident!"

"I suppose they could have cut it anywhere in the phone system," Steve said. "They'd just need to find the signal and we'd be screwed."

"Well, let's hope those guys can get it going again," said James, "but at least we can see what we're up against, even if nobody else can. They turned to the globe of the tempiloscope and gave it all their attention, looking at events that had occurred just a few minutes previously. James turned up the sound.

Federation Prime Minister Theresa Powers was in her office with the three men. "Did you see what they did? They sent that man back in time. We can't allow it. We don't have much time, they could aim that thing at us here again at any time, no walls can stop it. The UN has warned us secretly that if we openly try to take the technology, they have information that we will be attacked by the other continental forces. I want options. I want to try to get that technology, but in complete secrecy, so that everyone thinks it's been destroyed. If that is not possible, then I want it destroyed completely and utterly so that nobody else gets it either. It would completely upset the entire structure of political and military power if everyone knew what everyone else was doing. You saw the report, if someone accidentally aimed that thing at the center of the sun, it would be a disaster, a huge explosion. If we have to do it, I want it to look like those idiots did it themselves, by accident. I want the biggest bomb we've got. Now, what do you have to offer me?"

The military man looked sheepish and spoke up. "A missile would be too obvious. We do have a few aircraft H-bombs, old ones, left over from the cold war."

Madame Powers looked at him with narrowed eyes. "I thought those were all supposed to have been dismantled."

"Yes, well, we had a few that somehow were never on the reports. There is a twenty five megaton gravity bomb at the base in Minneapolis. I took the liberty of having it prepared and mounted in an aircraft, in case you decided on this option." He looked uncomfortable.

"So what's the problem?"

"It's a suicide mission madam. In order to get close enough to drop the bomb right down the mine shaft, as we would need to in order for the crater to support the contention that the explosion came from within, we need a low level drop, and with a bomb of this size, there won't be sufficient time for the aircraft to escape."

"Isn't that what aircrews are trained for General?"

"Yes madam, but there is also the matter of my armored division of some ten thousand men and women, not to mention the thirty five thousand civilian inhabitants of the region."

"General, you don't seem to realize what's at stake here. I would gladly sacrifice the entire state of Michigan, plus two or three more states or provinces of your choice, in order to destroy the threat that this technology represents to our way of life."

"Yes madam.. but... can you be so sure?"

"Do it!" she snapped... The watchers recognized the line as the very one they had heard delivered in real time a few minutes earlier.

James looked at Digger and shook his head. "We're in deep shit buddy! We're playing in a game that's way out of our league. They're going to nuke us!"

Digger put his arm around Joan and held her tight. "Doesn't look good babe."

She looked up at him with a strange expression. "What are you talking about? What's a lousy twenty five megaton hydrogen bomb and a full armored combat division against the combined intellectual power of a half dozen Yoopers! Ha! I snap my fingers at their puny bomb."

"Joan, think for a second..."

"I am thinking, are you? Are you so ready to give up?" Suddenly the lights went out, replaced by the pale yellow gleam of the emergency battery backups. The globe and control panel of the tempiloscope flickered and died.

"The power, they've cut our power!" cried James.

"I'm only surprised it took this long," replied Digger as he jumped up and ran to the back of the room. "I'll get the fuel cells going, you guys get those doors closed, we'd better lock down!" Joan smiled as she saw Digger spring into action. He was the sort that could do anything, as long as there was something to do. He turned the valves on the bank of hydrogen and oxygen cylinders in the back of the room. The bank of fuel cells hissed for a moment, he switched on the monitoring panel, powered by battery, and saw needles climb slowly from the red zone into the green. Finally he reached out and pulled down the handle of a large manual three conductor switch, like something from a campy monster movie, separating the lab completely from the outside power grid and engaging the internal power. "Okay!" he shouted. James rebooted the computers and restarted the tempiloscope.

Steve and Eileen came over to inspect the system. "They burn hydrogen and oxygen to make electricity?" asked Eileen.

"Yeah, the idea was to have the system ready to go during any critical usage, so it'll switch over automatically in case of any accidental outage. I guess in all the excitement we forgot to get it on line."

"How long will it last?" asked Steve.

Digger thought. "We can go about four hours full bore with this. No more."

Joan stepped back into the room and closed the inner vault door. They felt their ears pop slightly as it sealed. Massive bolts slid into place. James was still working at getting the tempiloscope back in viewing mode again, working his way through the passwords and option menus. The box connected to the outgoing video line still showed that there was no live connection.

"What's going on outside?" asked Digger. James guided the viewer to the front door, where they saw Jason and Jimmy emerge from the mine and run to talk to Samuels, who still stood arguing with the uniformed man wearing colonel's bars. "Can you get us sound? With an adjustment the magnification closed in and they could hear the conversation.... Digger and Joan stood close and tried to communicate what they'd seen with Jimmy and Jason.

"Agent Samuels, a word please?" said Jason.

"Yes of course. Would you excuse me for a moment colonel?"

"I really don't see how..." the colonel answered, but Samuels had turned away, talking with Jason and Jimmy in private.

"Sir," said Jason. "We've lost video feed."

Samuels replied. "Not only that son, they've cut the power line."

"They have an internal power source that will last for a while," Jason said, "but without video feed we can't get the truth to the world. We're going up top to see if we can get it reconnected."

"Agent Samuels," broke in the colonel. He sported a handlebar mustache, and a holstered stainless steel revolver with pearl grips. "I really must insist. I am under strict orders, direct from Prime Minister Powers herself, to secure this area. I have a full armored division that should be arriving within minutes. I demand that you withdraw this ragtag group of terrorists and give me access to this facility before I have you all clapped in irons, FBI or not."

"And I've been trying to tell you that the area is already secure. Oh, and Colonel Akron-Ahfez, please forgive my manners, allow me to introduce you to my associates Jason Desnick and Jimmy Canaris."

"Pleased I'm sure," said the colonel testily. "Now, will you withdraw or won't you? When my column arrives I could destroy you all within a matter of seconds."

"If your column arrives you mean." Samuels looked at his watch, it was high noon. He then raised his eyes over the colonel's head and looked due south. The great span of the lift bridge was slowly rising to the top of the support towers, cutting off the peninsula from vehicular traffic. He pointed and handing over his binoculars, directed the colonel's attention to the opposite side of the shipping canal. Less than two miles away through the bare trees, the armored column could be seen winding its way down the hill towards the bridge.

With a shriek of anger the colonel whirled and called to his men, who jumped into their garishly camouflaged hummer and roared out of the lot. Samuels turned to Jimmy. "What can I do to help?" he asked. Jimmy looked past him, following the hummer out of the lot, past a TV new crew van. On the roof was an uplink antenna. He pointed and started running, followed by Jason. Two men from the van were trying to get past a cordon of Ojibways. One had a mobile camera, the other a microphone, he spoke into the camera.

"... and here at the offices of the Midnight Mining Company armed men surround the entrance to the old Quincy mine, saying nothing. What is going on

A Superior State of Affairs

here? That is the question we want answered. Does it have anything to do with the mysterious military convoy approaching from the south?"

Jimmy ran up next to the reporter, looked at the van and said, "Does that transmitter work?"

The reporter was flustered. "We haven't tried in the last few hours because of the interference, but yeah, it should. We're just recording now."

"Get in the van and get us up to the top of the hill, I'll answer questions on the way. Keep the camera rolling, this is the biggest story of the century, I guarantee it, and you'll be right on the scene. We'll get you live video feed from inside the mountain, where the action is."

The reporter looked at him incredulously. His salt and pepper hair and creased brown face told of the years he'd spent out in the weather on news remotes. He'd seen every bait and switch, every dodge and con game used to get rid of him. His suspicious nature was mollified by the open sincerity in Jimmy's young face. He made the snap decision that this was for real, hoping desperately that he was right. "Okay, let's roll out, keep the camera going." He motioned to the driver as they piled into the van. He sat at the front with Jimmy and Jason, while the cameraman got in back and kept the camera and lights on them.

"Good afternoon, I'm Jerome Washington with KCPR tee vee nine, News of the Copper Country. We just met this young man, who's offered to tell us about the situation here at the Midnight Mining Company offices in Hancock today."

"I am agent Canaris of the Marquette office, FBI. This is my friend and associate, agent Desnick. In conjunction with other FBI agents, a large contingent of volunteers from the Ojibway tribe, the partners of Midnight Mining Company, and several private citizens, we have just repulsed a brutal attack by mercenaries under the command of billionaire multinational industrialist George Frederick Sherman. He made the attempt to take by force a new technology which was developed here in Superior. This attempt failed, George Sherman is dead.

"This new technology is like nothing the world has ever seen. It is a camera of sorts, which the inventors call the tempiloscope. With it we can look into the past, to see places and events that have occurred. We can also use it to see the what is happening in the present in distant places. We have been transmitting live views obtained from this device this morning."

"Then that live feed from Global..."

"...Came from within Quincy hill. The Federation government feels threatened by the technology, and has taken steps to prevent our transmission. The convoy of troops which is now stalled at the lift bridge was sent to seize the tempiloscope for the benefit of the Federation military and government cronies. By contrast, the United Nations is seeking to obtain the rights to this incredible research tool and to make it available to every government and legitimate research enterprise on earth."

"But agent Canaris, if you are yourself a citizen of the Federation, how can you presume to tell us..."

"I consider myself a citizen of the planet Earth. My Federal citizenship lies one level below my global citizenship. I am a member of the United Nations Environmental Command. Serial number 6606, acting under direct authorization from the First Speaker, and I reveal this fact publicly, here and now, under specific clauses of the crisis contingency plan."

Jerome was speechless for a moment, one of the few times in his life he had ever lacked a quick comeback on a surprising news story. In the back of his mind he doubted the possibility that it could be true, but decided to play it for all it was worth, it would make an amusing crackpot story at any rate. "So agent Canaris, what is the crisis that makes it necessary for you to come forward and reveal yourself now?"

"Federation Prime Minister, Theresa Powers, acting alone and of her own will, has ordered that a nuclear bomb be dropped into the mine shaft on top of Quincy hill, if the effort by the military to capture the technology is not successful."

"But surely, no sane person...."

"The aircraft is already in the air, it will arrive in less than twenty minutes. The selected device is a twenty-five megaton hydrogen bomb, constructed in 1965, and which has been stored outside of Minneapolis, off ordinary military records. It has been secretly maintained with upgraded nuclear materials three times over the years. It is one of the most powerful bombs ever constructed, radius of the fireball is expected to be five kilometers, the zone of total destruction is projected to be a radius of ten kilometers, deadly even to people inside special bomb shelters. All living things outside of specially constructed shelters will be killed to a radius of some twenty kilometers, unprotected humans to a radius of fifty kilometers. The fact that it is winter will help reduce the radius of total fire destruction to only forty kilometers. Estimated loss of life is placed at thirty five thousand within the first hour. The Federation will declare that the blast was due to negligent use of dangerous equipment by the owners of Midnight Mining Company. Prime Minister Powers will express her regrets and condolences over the loss of life, and will then continue with business as usual. Are you beginning to understand what is about to happen here?"

"My God!" said Jerome, as the reality sank in. "We're just recording, we've got to get this out!"

"Precisely why we're going to the top of Quincy Hill," said Jimmy. "The tempiloscope creates a magnetic distortion directly overhead, We think it may provide a hole through the interference; we can use that to get your transmission up to the satellite."

"But what about getting it back down?"

"We can try to go simultaneous on as many channels as possible, add the signals together and try to filter out the interference noise that way."

"But what if it doesn't work?"

"Then nobody will ever know the true story." Jimmy smiled. "But if ya gotta go, I hear ground zero's about as quick as it gets."

The van raced to the top of Quincy hill, where the tight cordon of armed Ojibway men that Jamey Yellowknife had organized around the shaft house was effectively preventing the carload of FUCS soldiers from entering, and without resorting to the use of deadly force. "We have a fiberoptic cable coming up here from inside the labs below. We had it hooked into the phone lines, with a connection to Global News in Montreal, but somehow they cut us off, we need another way to transmit."

"Did you hear all that Dink?" Jerome shouted to the driver and uplink technician.

Dink looked around at them. His long black hair tied in a ponytail hung down over the back of the seat nearly to the floor. "Yeah. Hey, I saw that hole in the northern lights, yeah, I know what you're talking about. We'll just need to go about a klick north to shoot back through it to the satellite. There's a reel of cable, in the back, you guys grab the end, jump out, tie it off to something stout and connect it up, I'll get the uplink going. Don't worry about a thing man, the Dink is on the case!"

Jason and Jimmy squirmed past the cameraman, who swiveled to follow them, got a hank of cable in hand, and jumped out. "Soon as you get an uplink you start playing what you've got, keep a camera on the shaft house and the sky above it, we should have two more cameras from inside coming to you."

With a wave the van roared off to the north, seeking the elusive spot on the ground from which they could get a satellite link. Jason tied off the cable to a road sign so it couldn't be pulled away in case the reel snagged. Jamey came forward to meet them. He clasped Jimmy in a bear hug. "Hey Deerslayer, what news?"

"Hi Jamey. We've lost the cable connection from inside, we have to get it reestablished. We're going to try for a satellite uplink."

Jamey raised his eyebrows. "If you think you can do it." They hurriedly found the end of the cable from below and used a splice box to connect it to the one from the news van. Once that was done, there was nothing they could do but pray... so they did.

When the tempiloscope came back on line after the power outage, James used to see what was going on at the lift bridge. Two carloads of soldiers on the Hancock side were trying to yell at the rest of their division located on the Houghton side. The Soopers had retreated up into the control cabins on top of the lifting span. Soldiers were beginning to climb up the ladders.

"What abut this plane with the bomb... can we do anything about it?" asked Eileen.

"We can try." answered James. He reduced the magnification and scanned the path between Minneapolis and Hancock. They couldn't see anything, the magnification was too low. He zoomed in to a smaller area, looking down from above, but still it was too difficult to see anything moving against the clutter on the ground. James rubbed his eyes, he was getting tired and frustrated. None of them even noticed when the light turned from black to red on the video connection box.

"Can I try? asked Steve.

"Sure, give it a shot."

Steve zoomed back in on the shaft house, then rotated the viewpoint to look horizontally, and flew the scope like an aircraft heading southwest towards Minneapolis. He flew low and kept looking upward, hoping to see it. With all eyes on the globe they finally caught a glimpse of a speeding swept wing bomber heading their way. Steve aimed towards it, matched speed, and swooped in close, increasing the magnification until they were inside the plane with the crew. The pilot checked a clock and nodded to the navigator, "Don, time," handing him a gold plated key.

The navigator unbuckled his straps and made his way through a hatchway back into the bomb bay. A single massive payload hung there, gently swinging against its restraints. It was about four meters long, and nearly two in diameter. One end was rounded, the other fitted with heavy metal fins. The dark gray paint did not completely hide the welded seams on its casing. Their width indicated that the case must have been at least ten centimeters thickness of solid heat-treated steel, even thicker at the nose. White letters stenciled on the surface said "Bomb-practice dummy, H-25, Mark 16" He moved to the side of it, and using a special tool, removed an access panel. A light began blinking, which turned off after he inserted the key and turned it. He looked back towards the hatchway. Of the three men aboard this aircraft, he was the only one who knew that this bomb was no dummy, that beyond this panel there was more than an empty shell, and that this mission was most decidedly not a training exercise. Don had waited half a lifetime for this, and the excitement of finally getting to really set one of these babies off completely overshadowed his full knowledge that he had no chance of surviving the detonation. He turned a handle retracting four precisely machined bolts, then pulled out the tightly fitted metal plug. He looked into a cavity, the bowels of the weapon, within which he could see the gleaming and well made parts of a nuclear weapon detonation system. He reached inside and carefully withdrew four metal strips, each five centimeters by twenty, by pulling on their polished gold plated handles. They were cadmium neutron absorbers. If left in place, the bomb could not explode, no matter what was done to it. Once removed the bomb could not fail to explode. Redundant systems within the weapon had been designed by highly paid and extremely competent engineers to make absolutely, doubly, and triply certain that the necessary complex mechanical sequence of events would take place. The sequence would lead first to the detonation of a chemical high explosive, compressing the pit, a hollow sphere of plutonium, into a small enough volume that a nuclear fission reaction would take place. The intense heat, the flood of high energy neutrons, and the shock wave from the fission detonation would in turn compress and heat a tank of liquid deuterium and tritium by simple inertia until fusion temperatures were reached. The hydrogen isotopes would fuse to helium, giving up a tiny fraction of their mass in the process. At that point the power of the sun would be released, the few grams of matter converted to pure energy by Einstein's famous formula. From the sending of the electrical signal that triggered the multiple detonators of the chemical explosive, to the completion of the fusion reaction the entire sequence of events would take less than one hundred milliseconds. After that it was only a matter of the dispersion of all that energy into the surrounding environment. Don mused over the technological wonder of such a device. He took a few seconds to gaze at the interior before he switched its internal systems on and closed it back up. He had seldom seen such workmanship in anything made by the hand of man. Perhaps in the finest watches one might see such attention to detail. Every mechanical pivot sat on a jeweled bearing. Every electrical contact was plated with gold. Truly he thought, it was a thing of beauty, and the glorious flowering cloud that it would create, the energy of the sun brought to earth, that would be a glorious thing too, and though he would never live to see that cloud, he would become a part of it.

He closed up the panel and worked his way back to the cockpit. "What took so long?" asked the pilot.

"Hadda take a leak." answered Don.

"Next time, do that before we get into the target zone. Okay, strap down, we're getting ready for our target run. We're gonna drop this egg right down that mine shaft." The aircraft took a wide turn over L'Anse and Keweenaw Bay, and came towards Hancock at an altitude of about five hundred meters, three hundred meters above lake level. They had been ordered to drop their weapon so that it would fall directly through the roof of the Quincy number two shaft house, crashing through the floor plate and into the shaft. Their speed and altitude were chosen so that the bomb would enter the shaft at the precise fifty five degree angle that would send it straight down without undue disturbance. The pilot had been insulated from news programs, had been told that this was all part of an elaborate military exercise, and to expect to see an armored division on the ground. The pilot looked down at the frozen lake, the woods, and the houses, shining under a heavy blanket of pure white snow in the noonday sun. "Damn," he said, "Its sure is pretty up here. "I'm really glad this thing is just a dummy."

"Yeah, me too," answered Don, as he worked with the computer, setting fuse time and proximity detector. He estimated that the payload would be traveling at approximately 1,000 meters per second when it struck the shaft house. He would give it a delay of 300 milliseconds after inertial impact to let it penetrate to about the depth of the laboratories before detonation. He keyed in all settings, loaded them to the bomb, and said, "Weapons control to you Captain." Then Don sat back, his part finished, he had only to wait for the end. He smiled and wondered what it would be like.

"What can we do!" asked Joan. "Can't you grab that bomb or something?"

"I can try, but what do you want me to do with it?" asked Steve.

James spoke up. "If we try to throw it far enough into the past that there wouldn't be anybody around, it would take so much energy we'd melt the busbars, even using the push/pull approach."

"What about moving it in space, not time," asked Digger.

"Hey man, this isn't Star Trek! Our precision for that kind of translation is rotten, we couldn't get within a thousand kilometers of a target location, and even so, where on earth would we put it?" said James.

Eileen spoke up quietly. "Then don't put it on earth, send it out into space, send it a hundred thousand kilometers if you have to, or a million, whatever it takes."

James and Digger looked at each other, then started working frantically, there was not much time left.

Jerome Washington stood in front of the camera in a carefully arranged shot. Next to him, in the background, the Quincy number two shaft house stood proudly in the sunlight. People could be seen on the ground all around it. Dink had managed to find the hole above the shaft house, and had shot his tight uplink beam directly through it to Global's comsat. He used a multiband approach to try to get the downlink to the studios in Montreal. It had taken their computers and technicians about forty seconds to recognize and grab the signal. They were back on line, live to the world. Dink immediately gave them the interview with Jimmy Canaris that they'd recorded on the trip up the hill by high speed upload. They were sending two cameras live from inside the mine, and one more here, outside the van. Jerome took a deep breath. This was the big story, this could catapult him into the big time, maybe even an anchor position, if he lived through it.

"Ladies and gentlemen, this is Jerome Washington, just outside Hancock Superior, in the area formerly known as Upper Peninsula Michigan. Behind me is the Quincy number two shaft house. Members of the Ojibway tribe of Native Americans have encircled it and are now protecting the security of our video feed from deep within the mine. The inhabitants of this snow shrouded and proud region have been wanting to secede from the state of Michigan for many years.

Finally, yesterday afternoon, the official declaration of intent is made in congress, and within hours an armored division of the FUCS is attempting to gain control of the region and the assets of a tiny company investing in high technology. We have transmitted to you, candid coverage of the Prime Minister, in which she has given clear orders to drop a nuclear bomb on the building just behind me. If this plan succeeds, then in a short time everything, every person, every bird in the sky that you see here, will be reduced to vapor and ash. It is enough for me, for us, to know that our deaths will not be in vain if we are able to expose the criminal acts of our supposed leaders."

Dink made a groaning noise and pointed to the east. Jerome turned, and looked at it. The cameraman shifted, got a perfect profile of Jerome against the sky, the shaft house next to him, and the aircraft approaching, low and slow. "Ladies and gentlemen an aircraft is approaching. It looks like a light bomber, with Federation markings. Look, something's opening in the bottom, is it landing gear? No! It looks like a bomb bay door. Oh God! I think this is it! The plane is pulling up, I see something coming out of the plane. It's dark, falling... goodbye."

Over Jerome's head, just above the shaft house, there appeared a deep blue glowing ring, visible even against the bright sky. Within the ring was only darkness. Jerome didn't see it as his eyes were glued to the falling bomb, but the cameraman, and the camera, did. The pilot had done his job well, the finned gray-black cylinder fell directly towards the roof of the shaft house, through the blue ring, and vanished in a flash of yellow. With a loud rolling "pop" the ring vanished as well.

In years to come this piece of video would be one of the most famous news clips of this or any other century. Jerome Washington, his eyes closed, his face turned towards the sky, standing, trembling, the microphone held to his lips but with no words to say, a single tear rolling down his cheek, sparkling in the sun. For fully ten seconds he stood there, waiting for the end to come. There arose a joyous shout behind him, people there seemed to realize something wonderful had happened. Jerome turned to the camera. "We're alive! I don't know why, I don't know how, but we're here and we're still alive. We're ALIVE!" Never before had any television audience seen the naked emotional release of a reprieve from certain death that they saw in the face of Jerome Washington on that day. His future in journalism was assured from that moment. He would have offers and counteroffers to increase his current salary to obscene figures. But in this moment, there was only the joy of NOW.

Jimmy and Jason came running over from the shaft house. "Did you see that? Did you get it on camera?" The cameraman gave a big smile and thumbs up sign.

Jerome latched onto them. "Can you tell our viewers, what just happened here?"

Jimmy answered. "Yes, the Federation hierarchy has attempted to destroy the technology of the tempiloscope by destroying the entire region. What you saw falling through the sky was a hydrogen bomb with an energy yield approximately equal to twenty five million tons of tri-nitro toluene. If it had been permitted to detonate, almost everyone within fifty kilometers of this spot would be dead or dying, over thirty five thousand people."

"Then you're saying that the Federation decided not to detonate the bomb?"

"No, not at all. I'm saying that the people within the laboratories some hundreds of meters below us, using the new technology I spoke of, were able to take that bomb and move it instantly far away from here, tens of thousands of kilometers out into space, where it detonated harmlessly. But Jerome, you need to speak to them, not me. Can you interview my friend Digger Puttonen, who is currently down in the laboratories?"

Dink turned a monitor so that Jerome could see it, looking at Digger and the others standing by the tempiloscope. Jimmy and Jason suddenly received a powerful telepathic message. It was from First Speaker Anna Sorensen at UNEC headquarters. "4297, 6606, well done. One critical phase remains. We must assure that the rights of this technology are preserved for all peoples, under the aegis of the United Nations. Access must be available to all, for research as well as military purposes. More devices must be constructed. Determine how this may be accomplished. And, number 6606, when your mission is over, please wait for me, I will come to see you." Jason smiled at Jimmy and raised his eyebrows.

Digger was explaining to Jerome about the tempiloscope. "And so you see, there are reasons, due to the flow focusing of gravity waves below this region of the earth's crust, and the electrical conductivity due to the presence of copper in the crust, that this is the only region in the world where this machine could possibly work. We could build it on the surface, or in any other place, and it would do nothing. It depends on gravity waves for operation, and only here are they focused in the proper way to produce useful images.

Digger paused for a moment, then held a hastily written piece of paper in his hand and read from it, live to the world. "As representative of the hereafter named firm, I hereby propose that the Midnight Mining Company give and bequeath all rights to the tempiloscope, including the physical site which it occupies, in perpetuity, to the United Nations, to be administered by the United Nations Environmental Command with the following restrictions:

1. "A council of seven leading scientists from different continents, nominated by, and voted on by the world scientific community, will be authorized to allocate time on the equipment to researchers based on scientific merit. All data thus acquired to become public record, part of a free and open data base that may be accessed and downloaded by any interested party, academic or not.

2. "At least one half of the total available operational time will be thus made available to the academic and scientific community for bonafide research. Hardware and software modifications will be made such that current-time viewing and mass translations can be restricted as deemed necessary by the scientific council.

3. "A second council of seventeen military personnel, nominated by their respective governments, representing all the continents, and chosen by lot from among the nominees, will allocate time for surveillance and security purposes, based on merits of true security concerns. All data so acquired will immediately become public knowledge, part of a free and open data base that may be downloaded by any interested party, military or not. Mass translations will be closely controlled, and authorized only in cases of extreme duress, and as defensive measures only.

4. "That the Republic of Superior shall henceforth be fully recognized as an independent sovereign state, self-governing and strictly neutral with respect to continental powers, but within and subject to the supersovereignty of the United Nations alone.

5. "That the city of Calumet, Superior, as the geographical center of the Copper Country, shall be granted status as a United Nations host city. With provisions made for international visitors coming here to make use of the tempiloscope facilities.

"These five demands are the conditions for transfer of the material and intellectual property comprising what we call the tempiloscope. Midnight Mining Company retains the rights to all other patents, properties, and devices not specifically defined above. We forecast that other area mines will be reworked for installation of tempiloscopic facilities in the near future, and that we will help inasmuch as possible. If and when these terms are agreed to, I will turn over the facilities to accredited UNEC representatives." Digger folded his arms and stopped speaking.

"You heard it here first folks. This is Jerome Washington in the soon to be independent Republic of Superior. We are now waiting for some word from the United Nations. Just a moment, let me return you to Jacques Thibodeau standing by in Montreal."

"Good afternoon, this is Jacques Thibodeau. We have heard from Mexico City, the Prime Minister of the North American Federal Union is under arrest, along with a large fraction of her cabinet. She faces charges of treason and betrayal of public trust. We now have live coverage from New York, an emergency press conference has just been called at the United Nations building..." Another voice speaks...

"We're standing by in the press room at the UN waiting for a statement. Wait, here comes someone. I don't recognize her. She's speaking now..."

"My dear people of the world. My name is Anna Sorensen, and I represent the United Nations Environmental Command. I apologize for the fact that most of you have never heard of us. We have worked tirelessly for the last twenty years to assure that the world we leave to our children, to your children, is one which is reflective of our love and respect. Something truly wonderful has happened today. A new technology has arrived upon the face of the earth, and because of the courage and integrity of a few people, it will not be used to make war, or to gain advantage over our fellows, but to learn, to discover, to find truth. To the list of demands that has been put forth by Mister Digger Puttonen of the Midnight Mining Company, the United Nations Environmental Command agrees completely and without reservation. We see this as the opportunity for a new and closer bond between the continents and nations and peoples of the earth. I will personally travel to the new Republic of Superior to congratulate the inhabitants on their independence, and also to accept title to the tempiloscope. People of the world, rejoice with me, for today is the first day of the new age of light and life, when love shall prevail over fear, and reason over blindness. Rejoice and be glad!" She raised her hands above her head and smiled. The camera came in close, and the look on Anna's face... was so much like the look on Jerome's face at the moment when he realized he would live, that tears sprang into the eyes of millions of people worldwide who chanced to be watching at the time, and the billions more who watched countless replays of the events in documentaries for years to come.

CHAPTER 57

--Epilogue--

When dawn broke on Saturday morning, January 21, 2017, the sky was of the purest crystal blue and the crescent moon was riding high in the eastern sky as the first direct rays of the sun burst forth over the horizon and made the bare branches of the trees glow with a golden light. A gentle breeze blew from the south, the cold air seemed to hold a promise of spring to come.

At the hospital in Hancock, Michigan, Ruth awoke from a light dozing sleep on a vinyl covered couch in the third floor waiting room. The smell of fresh coffee made her nostrils flare. She opened her eyes dreamily and saw a phantom styrofoam cup floating there. She looked up, rubbing her eyes. A smiling male nurse held the cup for her. She sat up, yawned, and tried to work out the crick in her neck, accepting the cup gratefully. "They're awake, in case you'd like to see them," he said. She stood up and walked down the hall to a ward with six beds. She leaned against the door and looked in. The sun shone in the windows and made bright rectangles on the opposite wall. A nurse was checking the bandages on the stump Chris Jameson's right arm, she looked up, smiled at Ruth and left the room.

"How you guys doing?" she asked them. The words they answered with were all different, but the messages were the same... they were all doing great. There was a wide screen television in the room. They'd been permitted to watch the evening news the night before, and had heard the whole story finally revealed. At one end of the room, two of the beds had traction units. Both Tony and Frank looked uncomfortable, their legs raised in the devices, but neither complained, and they seemed to be talking amiably. Frank rubbed a red stone between his fingers, a nasty bruise was on his left cheek. Leonard's chest was wrapped up tightly, he had a bandage on his forehead, and his lips were badly swollen, but otherwise he was itching to get out of the place. Harry sat next to him in a chair, constantly encouraging him to just relax and take it easy. Everything was being taken care of. Harry had spent most of the preceding afternoon taking care of various details, including the disposal of bodies, the care of prisoners, the disposition of leftover explosives and weapons, and the gathering of various vehicles left in awkward places during the previous hectic day. Stephen and Elwood, the man Sherman had shot in the lab, lay near each other and talked, it turned out they had attended college together at Michigan Tech. Chris sat quietly at the end of the row. Ruth went and sat next to him.

"You gonna be okay?"

"What, because of this?" he asked, nodding towards the lost right arm. "I won't miss it. I regret a lot of things I did with that arm. Maybe it will make it easier to forgive myself now that it's gone."

"Chris, You know that there will probably be some charges brought... because of some of those things, now that all the Sherman files have been found."

Chris nodded. "I know, I'll pay whatever price I have to... to get that behind me. Whatever they want, I'll do it."

"I know you will. I just thought... well... maybe you'd consider some training in counseling. After seeing what you did for Dawson last night, bringing him out of that catatonia, I think you might have a gift for it. Wherever you end up, there may be people there who need you." Chris looked up at her, and hope welled in his eyes.

When the military light bomber returned from it's "training" flight to the Keweenaw Peninsula and landed in Minneapolis, the pilot and copilot climbed down the ladder, joking lightheartedly. Only the navigator, Don, remained behind, unsure what to do with himself, or why he was still alive. He slowly dragged himself out of his chair to the door. A pair of Military Police officers stood waiting for him at the bottom of the ladder.

In the special Independence Day issue of the Mining Gazette, besides feature stories about Superior's independent statehood and events relating to the crisis at Midnight Mining Company, there were two astronomy reports. The largest, on page 1, detailed the effects of the unprecedented solar storm that had disrupted communications worldwide for almost twenty four hours, and included photographs of some spectacular aurora. The second was a tiny one column item on page two, reporting a strange flash of light that was seen in the night sky over the eastern hemisphere. Triangulation of sightings put the distance at over two hundred thousand kilometers, or over halfway to the moon. Unconfirmed speculation based on amateur spectroscopy of the fireball suggested that it could have been a nuclear explosion in the 20 to 30 megaton yield range.

A raft of ten sleek blue helicopters with United Nations markings flew in precision formation, floating through the clear sky and settling on the barricaded highway near the Quincy number two shaft house. Jerome Washington stood in the backwash of their slowing blades as he waited for the UNEC First Speaker and her entourage to emerge. Dink the cameraman scuttled about, seeking the perfect angle for his shot. The doors opened and Anna Sorensen stepped out into the snow, followed by dozens of unarmed and smartly uniformed men and women wearing blue UNEC caps openly for the first time. She stepped up to Jerome and smiled warmly, shaking his hand. "So glad to meet you Mister Washington."

"The pleasure is mine First Speaker," he replied. "Welcome to Superior!"

"Thank you!" She looked at the camera, the shaft house in the background. "I have come to make formal acceptance of yesterday's offer by the Midnight Mining Company, and to establish the physical presence of a United Nations administrative group that will protect and manage the tempiloscopic facilities in the interests of all the member states of the world community."

Off to one side stood a young man, beaming with pride and pleasure at seeing her face. As the interview with Jerome ended and her people were being guided towards a group of buses for the trip to the mine entrance down the hill, Jimmy Canaris caught her eye. "Love is," he heard clearly in his mind. A phrase filled with warmth and promise.

"Love is," he replied the same way. Her smile told him all he needed to know. Those standing by heard nothing, saw only the two looking at each other for a few moments. But when they got onto the buses, Jimmy and Anna sat together and their hands clasped.

A hundred and twenty meters below, five people slowly wakened in the temporal lab, having slept uncomfortably on foam mats with only their jackets for warmth in the cool mine air. Their mouths were dry and they were hungry. Dimly though the double doors, a knocking could be heard. James guided the viewer to check the passage. Jimmy and Jason stood there, along with Jerome Washington, the newsman they had seen on TV the day before, a cameraman, and four others they did not recognize. There were no weapons in evidence. Joan opened the doors and let them in. The cameraman immediately scanned the room and found a spot to set up, with the tempiloscope looming in the background.

Anna Sorensen recognized Digger and walked up to him, extending her hand. "Mister Puttonen, I am here to formally accept your offer of this technology. From this time forward it will never be left unattended or used maliciously. Please accept my personal pledge that it will be used for the good of all mankind."

"Thank you First Speaker. On behalf of myself and my surviving partner, I turn over to you the passwords and operations manuals for the tempiloscope." They turned and smiled for the camera. The cameraman then turned to focus on Jerome, who gave his account of the news. In the background, Digger said to Anna privately, "Of course, it will take a little time to train your people. But right now, I haven't seen the sun in two days. I'm starving, and I'd just like to get out of here if you don't mind."

"Of course, I was about to suggest the same." Three of the UN people were left with the tempiloscope, while the rest of them walked down the tunnel to the front door. When they emerged into the sunlight, the madhouse scene was like nothing Digger had ever seen or imagined, outside of a hockey arena after a championship game. Hundreds of people crowded the tiny parking lot and burst into cheers at the sight of them. James' wife Barbara rushed up to him, with two little girls in tow, and embraced him fiercely, showering him with kisses.

An older couple ran out of the crowd and up to Steve and Eileen. "Aunt Peg, Uncle Tom!" cried Eileen. "How did you get here?"

"We saw you on the news last night of course, drove up right away." That group moved to one side and talked together excitedly.

An older man came forward and smiled at Digger and Joan. "Arne!" cried Digger. Arne hugged Digger, and then Joan.

"Hey, you kids been having too much fun eh?"

"Are you kidding? What I wouldn't give right now for a plate of your pancakes with bacon and toast."

"Did somebody say pancakes?" said Eileen. She introduced Tom and Peg to Digger, Joan, and Arne. Peg and Arne began discussing the finer points of pancake batter while the others quickly engaged heatedly in the more controversial matter of toppings.

Guided by Jimmy, Anna approached Joe Running Bear. "Sir," she said. "I want to thank you for everything you and your people have done this day. Without you, none of this would have been possible. I wonder if I could ask you a great favor though, to do just one thing more?"

Joe was entranced. "Name it and it's yours," he said graciously.

"The Soopers have some documents prepared, a constitution and so forth for Superior, but it will take a few weeks before special elections can take place. I wonder if you might be willing to act as President pro-tem until then?"

"Miss Sorensen, I..."

"Please say yes."

"Yes, of course!"

"Thank you. Just a suggestion, but you might consider working on establishing a new metallic currency sooner rather than later. I have a feeling the old dollar is not going to be too strong here shortly. If I'm not mistaken we've got a coin-maker here." She looked at Tom, whose ears had perked up at the mention of metallic currency. He began to envision a coin, with an image of a younger Arne Harjaala as a miner with a pick on the front.... and the inscription "Republic of Superior" around the top. Joe and Tom went off to the side to discuss the idea.

"Oh, and Agent Samuels!" Anna said.

"Yes Ma'am?"

"It is my understanding that the FBI no longer has any authority in Superior, is that not correct?"

"Why... yes, that's true." Samuels looked concerned.

"If you still wish to leave the area, you are free to go of course, subject to new FBI assignments, but if you are willing, I would like you to consider quitting the FBI to head up the effort to form a new Superior Public Safety Force. We will not need a military presence as such, but I wish to avoid a vacuum of police presence in the interim period. You can coordinate with President pro-tem Running Bear as to how you want to organize things."

"I'd be happy to assist, though the honor should really go to Frank Giacoletti."

"As you wish, but please take care of things yourself until he's up and about would you?"

"Yes ma'am, I'll do my best."

Anna turned to Jimmy. "Now, what else is there?" He guided her to the group earnestly discussing pancakes. "Steve Sanders and Eileen Donovan?" Conversation stopped as their attention was held by Anna. Her small stature and slight build did not in the least detract from the air of gracious authority that seemed to fill the air about her. "In consultation with Federation officials... NOT the Prime Minister by the way... we have debated the disposition of the collection of corporate and industrial interests known as Sherman Enterprises. It is our opinion that the greatest good for the greatest number may be achieved by keeping the corporation intact rather than breaking it up. We'd like it renamed Superior Enterprises, and in recognition of your experience, your abilities and your service in a time of crisis, we'd like you two to act, jointly, as Chief Executive Officers." Steve and Eileen were absolutely dumbfounded, finding nothing to say. Anna continued, "We feel there may be a possibility for a viable working partnership involving the manufacturing and marketing resources of Superior Enterprises and the intellectual properties and engineering capabilities of Midnight Mining Company." Digger, James, Steve, and Eileen looked back and forth to each other, all nodding vigorously.

"Joan Niemi," said Anna. "It has come to my attention that it is largely through your efforts that the political moves were made that enabled this secession to take place so smoothly and peacefully. Would you be willing to act as the Rebublic of Superior's delegate to the United Nations for the time being... at least until more permanent arrangements can be made?"

"I'd be delighted First Speaker," said Joan, flabbergasted.

"Arne Harjaala, I don't have any position to offer you, but you have suffered more from the events of yesterday than any other. The entire course of your life was disrupted, your family shattered, all by accident. Nothing I can offer would be adequate to recompense you for these difficulties. But simply ask of me whatever you will, and if it is in my power, it will be granted."

"Gosh Miss Anna, ya don't need ta do nothin' fer me. All I need is a little place ta stay outa da snow. I'm happiest when I'm cookin see, den I don't t'ink about dose t'ings so much."

"You wish is granted then," said Anna smiling. "We'll convert one of these buildings here to an apartment and restaurant where you may live the rest of your life as you see fit. If you wish to cook, I'm sure there will be many researchers flocking to use the tempiloscope facilities in the months and years to come."

"Ya mean... here? Where I can be wit my friends?"

"Yes, or wherever else you wish."

"Oh, here would be perfect. T'anks so much." Arne started sobbing, leaning on Joan who put her arms around him.

"Is that it then?" Anna Sorensen asked Jimmy. "Can we take these people out for something to eat? I think they deserve it."

"Yes," said Jimmy, looking around him, "except for one thing. I wanted you to meet Jason Desnick, you know... number 4297. He was right in the middle of this whole affair."

"Oh yes! He played a pivotal role didn't he? Where is he?"

Jimmy looked this way and that. "Now, where'd he get off to, I don't see him." Jimmy closed his eyes. A look of confusion came over his face. "That's odd, I don't feel him here either."

Jason Desnick smiled to himself as he walked across the Houghton/Hancock lift bridge. The Soopers had brought it back down again as soon as the announcement of Superior's independence had been made; the military convoy had already turned around and headed back towards its base. He had left his gun and his FBI badge in the glove compartment of the Bronco, along with the title, filled out in Harry's name. He had managed to keep his face out of the camera shots, but his FBI cover was now hopelessly blown. Everywhere around him people were shouting and car horns were honking in celebration of the newly independent Republic of Superior; he waved at the cars as they passed. The voice in his mind was as clear as if he was speaking to his supervisor face to face in a quiet room, much clearer than the telepathic communications between UNEC agents.

"Well done my son," said the voice.

"Thank you sir," Jason answered. "It was a narrow thing though."

"The greatest accomplishments usually are."

"I almost blew my cover. If Leonard had pushed his questions just a little harder while I was exposed to that content analyzer..."

"But he didn't. You achieved the objective with the absolute minimum of direct intervention. We like that you know, your actions have received excellent reviews at every level."

"Thank you sir. Do you have a new assignment for me?"

"As a matter of fact we do. There is a problematic situation developing in a region called Arkansas. We'd like you to apply your special talents there."

"Very well, how am I to get there?"

"Stick your thumb out."

Jason immediately turned around facing the traffic and stuck out his thumb in the traditional and time honored hitch hiker's salute. A rattling old white Dodge pickup truck fitted with clattering tire chains pulled to a stop. The young man driving leaned over and opened the passenger side door. He had conservatively long brown hair tied back in a ponytail and wore a faded blue plaid flannel shirt over his jeans. "Where ya headed?" the young man asked.

"Arkansas," answered Jason with a grin as he climbed in and slammed the door.

The young man just laughed and stepped on the accelerator. "Well Dang! Don't that beat all. Boy, you done come to the right place 'cause thet's where I'm aheaded!"

"Pleased to meet you, my name is Jason."

"Mine's Chester," said the young man, grinning and offering his hand to shake. "I figger we'll take old Highway 41 so's we don't get caught up in that there military convoy dealy wompus. That suit you?"

Jason smiled and reached to put on his seat belt. "Just fine," he said. "Just fine."

(appendix)

Glossary of terms used in SSOA

Mining terms:
adit	a horizontal entrance to a mine
amygdaloid	the frothy top of a basalt lava flow
crosscut	a horizontal tunnel cutting across the stratigraphy
datolite	a rare mineral, $HCaBSiO_5$, with unusual properties
dip	the angle at which a rock unit plunges downslope
drift	a horizontal tunnel parallel to the stratigraphy
foot wall	in mining, the angled "floor" regardless of steepness
hanging wall	in mining, the angled "ceiling" regardless of steepness
mancar	a mine train car designed to carry people
muck	gravel and rubble, resulting from excavations
ore chute	a narrow vertical excavation for the purpose of collecting ore
pillar	a piece of ore rock left in place to support the hanging wall
shaft	a vertical or steeply angled excavation to access ore at depth
shaft collar	the foundation left at the top of an abandoned mine shaft
shaft house	the structure at the top of a shaft for managing lifts and ore
stope	an area in which ore has been removed
stratigraphy	the arrangement of rock layers (generally younger above older)
sump	the very bottom of the shaft, where water collects

Other terms:

Yooper	a native resident of the U.P.
Sooper	political activist for Superior independence
tempiloscope	a device for remote viewing in present or past
speleoscope	a device for seeing into solid masses, such as rock

Acronyms: --- may be used with or without separating periods ---

U.P.	"Upper Peninsula" of Michigan
N.A.F.U.	"North American Federal Union"
S.I.B.	"Special Investigations Branch" (of the FBI)
F.B.I.	"Federation Bureau of Investigations"
U.N.E.C.	"United Nations Environmental Command"
F.U.C.S.	"Federation Unified Command Services"
G.Q.	"General Questioning" a temporary arrest warrant

S.C.U.B.A.	"Self Contained Underwater Breathing Apparatus"
O.R.	"Operating Room"
U.S.G.S.	"United States Geological Survey"
P.M.	"Prime Minister"
U.N.	"United Nations"

About The Author

Like one of the main characters in this book ,Tom Maringer graduated with a degree in Geology from Michigan Technological University and spent many days rockhounding and exploring the many abandoned mines in the Copper Country region of Michigan's Upper Peninsula. He has pursued careers as a pizza cook, knifemaker, cartographer, coinmaker, and teacher. His interests include solar energy, teaching natural science, geomorphology, sustainable living, exploring caves and mines, philately, numismatics and early coining technologies. He currently resides in Northwest Arkansas with his wife of many years and their youngest daughter where he works part-time as a natural science field instructor for a 5th grade program, and part-time as sole proprietor of Shire Post Mint, making fantasy coins.

LaVergne, TN USA
16 December 2009
167202LV00003B/2/A